Michael Dibdin

Dead Lagoon

Michael Dibdin is the author of nine other novels, including *Ratking*, which won the Crime Writers Association Gold Dagger Award, and, most recently, *Dark Specter*. He lives in Seattle, Washington.

BOOKS BY Michael Dibdin

DEAD LAGOON

❧

Michael Dibdin

DEAD LAGOON

An Aurelio Zen Mystery

VINTAGE CRIME/BLACK LIZARD
Vintage Books
A Division of Random House, Inc.
New York

First Vintage Crime/Black Lizard Edition, January 1996

The Library of Congress has cataloged the Pantheon edition as follows:
Dibdin, Michael
Dead Lagoon/Michael Dibdin.
p. cm.
ISBN: 0-679-43349-X
1. Zen, Aurelio (Fictitious character)—Fiction. 2. Police—Italy—Venice—
Fiction. 3. Venice (Italy)—Fiction. I. Title.
PR6054.I26D43 1995
823'.914—dc20 94-27271
Vintage ISBN: 0-679-75311-7

Manufactured in the United States of America
79B8

To my daughter, Emma

Venice: The Lagoon

0   miles   5

N

LAGUNA MORTA

MESTRE

Tessera

Torcello   Sant´ Ariano

Burano

San Francesco del Deserto

Treporti

Porto Marghera

Murano   Sant´ Erasmo

San Michele

VENICE   San Nicolò

San Giorgio

Porto di Lido

San Clemente   LIDO

San Lazzaro

Malamocco

Ottagono

Alberoni

Porto di Malamocco

LAGUNA MORTA

Fondi dei Sette Morti

Pellestrina

I Murazzi

Adriatic Sea

Chioggia

San Michele

Venice

0   yards   1000

N

FONDAMENTA NOVE

Ospedale
Civile

Campo
olomeo S M Formosa

Campo
San Lorenzo

ARSENALE

● San Pietro

The
Piazza

Campo
San Zaccaria

RIVA DEGLI SCHIAVONI

unta della
Dogana

Giardini
Pubblici

San Giorgio

Sant'Elena

DEAD LAGOON

❧

A ragged line of geese passed overhead, silhouetted against the caul of high cirrus, heading out towards the open sea. Over towards Marghera, a bloated sun subsided into a dense bank of smog, dwarfing the striped stacks of the refineries. Giacomo noted the rippled layers of cloud spreading across the sky like wash from a motorboat. The weather was changing. Tomorrow would be squally and cold, a bitter north-easterly *bora* raising choppy seas on the lagoon.

But tomorrow was another day. For now the air was still, the water smooth as oil, the creak of the oars against the thole and the gentle plashing of the blades the only sound. People thought Giacomo a bit odd, sculling out to tend his nets in this day and age. No one rowed any more except the yuppy oarsmen from the city's boating clubs. But Giacomo had no interest in reviving the picturesque traditions of the past. If he preferred oars to outboards, he had his reasons. On an evening such as this, the noise of a motor carried for miles across the water, and Giacomo did not want any inquisitive ears tracking his progress through the shoals and along the winding creeks to his destination.

His eyes alertly scanned the water ahead. The channel he was following was unmarked and the tide was ebbing fast. It would have been better to come at another time, but Giacomo simply carried out the orders he received by telephone. Tomorrow, the voice had said, so tomorrow it must be. He would be well enough paid for his pains. Meanwhile, he needed all his skill. The flat-bottomed skiff drew only a few centimetres, but it was always easy to run aground in these treacherous backwaters.

He raised his head, locating the long low ridge, exuberantly green, towards which he was making such slow progess along the tortuous windings of the tideway. To the east, the desolate swamps and salt-flats of the *laguna morta* – the dead marshlands, unrefreshed by tidal currents – merged seamlessly into the gathering dusk. The school-teacher on Burano said that there had once been a splendid city here, with fine palaces and churches and paved streets, all swallowed up hundreds of years ago by the shifting topography of the lagoon.

Standing in the stern of the boat, Giacomo paused to light a cigarette. The teacher was a good soul, and would pay well over the odds for crabs and mussels, but she'd had the misfortune to be born on the mainland, and it was well known that mainlanders would believe anything. Giacomo breathed out a lungful of smoke, which drifted indolently away across the water towards the drooping heads of the wild grasses on a nearby mudbank. The dull roar of a plane taking off from the international airport at Tessera reminded him of his business. Dipping the crossed oars into the water once more, he leaned forward with his whole body, urging the *sandolo* across the shallow water.

The light was fading fast by the time Giacomo beached the skiff on the flats exposed by the ebbing tide. He stepped out, his waders sinking into the mud, and hauled the craft clear of the water. Before him rose a mass of creepers and brambles, overgrown bushes and stunted trees, spilling down over the low wall sealing off the island. At the centre, a set of steps led to a bricked-up gateway. Slinging a blue canvas bag over his shoulder, Giacomo squelched off across the quagmire towards a stretch of wall completely submerged beneath the burgeoning greenery.

Beneath the overhanging shrubbery it was already night. Giacomo took a rubber-covered torch from his pocket and shone it round. A rat jumped from a hollow in the wall into the shallow water at its base. The hollow had been formed by the removal of two of the flat ochre bricks of the three-hundred-year-old wall. Giacomo remembered the effort it had taken, hammering away with a mallet and a cold chisel for the best part of twenty minutes. They built to last in those days, even for such clients as these. Other bricks had been gouged out above, and using these holds Giacomo scaled the wall and perched on the top. All was still. Even in broad daylight, people gave this particular island a wide berth. Nothing would persuade anyone in their right mind to venture there once darkness had fallen.

The surface inside was much higher, almost level with the top of the wall. Giacomo stepped down and started to push his way through the undergrowth, following a series of almost imperceptible markers: the torn ligaments of a branch dangling from a bush, a patch of flattened grass, the sucker of a bramble bush, thick as a squid's tentacle, lopped off clean by a fisherman's gutting-knife. The ground crunched and slithered underfoot, as though he were walking on layers of broken crockery.

A sudden scuttling noise brought him to a halt, wielding his torch-beam like a staff. The island was infested with snakes, and Giacomo tried with limited success to convince himself that this was the only feature of the place which scared him. He lit another cigarette to calm his nerves and pushed on through the spiny undergrowth, across the grating, shifting surface, until he made out the final mark: a dessicated bough leaning across a briar patch as though it had fallen from the dead tree above. One contorted branch pointed towards him, marking the path back. Another, bifurcated like a petrified hand, stuck out at an angle to one side. Following it, Giacomo quickly located the mound of shards, white in the torchlight. At the same moment, he heard the scuttling sound again.

It was only when he unslung the bag from his shoulder that he realised he had forgotten to pack the small spade he usually brought. Well, he wasn't going back, that was for damn sure. Nor had he any intention of touching the things with his hands. Tossing away his cigarette, he snapped a length off the dead bough and started to prod and jab at the mound, freeing a long femur here, the smooth gleam of a scapula there, a rounded skull, a big hip and pelvis. At last the dull gleam of the oilcloth wrapping appeared.

The stick broke as he redoubled his efforts. He hastily tore another from the branch behind him, and when that broke too used his boot to free the package. Breathing hard, he unwound the oilcloth, revealing three blocks wrapped in silver foil and plastic shrink-wrapping. They were about the size and shape of a cork float, but much heavier – precisely one kilogram each, in fact. Giacomo carefully lifted them in turn and transferred them to the canvas bag. Then he added the oilcloth wrapping and fastened the bag before turning for home.

The torch beam wavered and probed the darkness all around, seeking the gnarled bough which pointed the route home. It was nowhere to be seen.

Giacomo searched the shrubbery in increasing desperation until he found the broken branch entangled in the thorns. It must have keeled over when he snapped part of it off to use as a spade. For a moment he almost gave way to panic. Then, with an effort, he got

3

a grip on himself and started to study the undergrowth all around. It must be that way, surely, to the right of that squat, lopsided shrub. Yes, that was it. He recognized it.

A few metres further on, the path, if that's what it had been, petered out in a mass of briars twice as high as a man. He must have been mistaken. He started back, but he was unable to find the clearing where the cache had been located. Then he saw what looked like one of the markers guiding him back to the boat and threw himself at it, plunging through the shrubbery like a speedboat through breaking waves, ripping and tearing the undergrowth apart until its spiky tendrils fouled his limbs and brought him up short in an impenetrable mass of brambles.

Instinctively he glanced up at the sky, but the nebulous wash of cloud drifting in from the east had swallowed the stars. The evil jungle, its roots fattened on hundreds of thousands of human skeletons, pressed in on every side, shutting out the world.

Giacomo muttered a fervent prayer, a thing he had last done when a vicious combination of wind and tide had caught him and Filippo on a lee shore just beyond the northern mole at the entrance to the Porto di Lido. It had worked then, but he was less sanguine that his patron saint would intercede for him this time. Fishing was one thing, his present business quite another. Still, reciting the prayer helped to calm his panic. Disentangling himself from the briars, he worked his way through the undergrowth, searching for one of the signs which marked the path, trying not to think about what he was grinding and crushing under his boots.

When the man in white appeared, blocking his path, Giacomo felt a brief surge of relief at the thought that he was no longer alone. Then he remembered where he was, and terror rose in his throat like vomit. He forced himself to look again. The figure was still there, splayed across a mass of brambles, the panels of its jacket rippling and heaving as though in the wind. But there was no wind. Then he saw the face, what was left of it, and the rats running in and out of the sleeves. He took it in at one glance – a mass of half-eaten meat and tissue, the chest a bloody cage, the white suit ripped to shreds – and dropped the bag and fled, powered by an irresistible dread, a superstitious horror which sent him stumbling across that dune of human bones, tearing through the vegetation parasitic on that rich meal, running for his life and his reason from the isle of the dead.

*

4

On the way home from the bakery, she stops to buy some salad and fruit. The pale rain is still falling limply, covering the pavements in a greasy sheen and raising a rash of pockmarks on the surface of the water. Sebastiano and his son huddle over their produce under the green awning jury-rigged from the masts at either end of the barge.

'Eh, *contessa*! Take a look at this fennel! Fresh from Sant'Erasmo, the genuine stuff.'

Even though she knows he's trying to make a sale, Ada can't help feeling flattered at the way he calls her '*contessa*', without a trace of irony or obsequiousness, the way people did when titles were just a fact of life, a description like the colour of your hair or eyes. So she orders some of his overpriced fennel along with the salad leaves, apples and grapes. It is while Sebastiano is weighing out the fruit that Ada catches sight of the figure fixing her with his moronic leer from the other side of the canal, his cloak billowing about him.

'What's the matter?' says Sebastiano, looking up from the make-shift counter of slatted wooden boxes piled high with potatoes and lemons and tomatoes. Following her fixed gaze, he turns to look. The dead-end alley opposite is empty except for some scaffolding whose protective tarpaulin screen is flapping in the stiff easterly wind.

'Are you all right?' he asks, looking at her with barely veiled anxiety.

A wherry full of plastic sacks of sand and cement comes up the canal, its temporary foredeck of planks supporting a battered wheel-barrow and a cement mixer lying on its side. Going to the Pagan house, as Ada still thinks of it, even though Maria Pagan has been dead a year or more. Now some foreigner has bought the property and is paying a fortune to have it done up . . .

'Carry *la Contessa* Zulian's shopping home for her,' Sebastiano barks at his son, a gangling youth wearing a jacket inscribed *Washington Redskins*, a single gold earring and a baseball cap turned back to front. The boy scowls and mutters something under his breath to which Sebastiano responds with a guttural monosyllable. Father and son sway back and forth as their barge heaves at its moorings under the swell of the passing wherry, pinching the bald tyres which serve as fenders. Ada Zulian recalls seeing a motor vehicle, many years ago, when her parents took her to the Lido. Waving away the offers of help, she tells Sebastiano she'll pay him next week and trudges off, listing slightly to port, a bulging blue-and-white striped plastic bag in each hand.

On the stone pillar supporting the railing of the bridge perches a seagull with a bit of bloody liver in its beak. Ada carefully avoids looking it in the eye, lest she be beguiled. As she reaches the top step of the bridge, the gull tumbles sideways off the pillar, unfolding its wings and skimming the surface of the water before rising with a lazy flap to catch the wind which tosses it high above the houses like a scrap of paper.

'Ada!'

At first she is loathe to look round, in case there is no one there. But when the call is repeated she recognizes the voice of Daniele Trevisan. There he is, leaning out of his window on the other side of the canal.

'How's it going?' he asks.

Ada Zulian is suddenly overwhelmed by a giddy conviction that all this has happened before. Which it *has*, of course, years ago, before the war, before her marriage, when they were both young. Only then it was she at the window and Daniele below in the street, murmuring sweet nothings . . .

'Are you all right?' asks Daniele Trevisan, just as Sebastiano had earlier.

Ada grasps her bags and plods down the steps of the bridge, greasy from the rain. Everyone is always so worried about her! Ever since Rosetta suddenly reappeared, forcing Ada to go to ground among the lunatics on San Clemente, people have been overwhelmingly solicitious. She knows that she should be grateful for this show of concern, but in fact it rather gets on her nerves. In any case, what is she supposed to say? She knows all too well that it is impossible for her to discuss her real problems without all that solicitude dissolving in knowing looks and sniggers.

'The place is full of ghosts,' she mutters.

'What?'

'They should do something.'

Daniele regards her from his lofty perch with a gaze as unblinking as the gull's.

'Who should?'

Ada shrugs vaguely.

'The authorities. I'm thinking of calling them, making a complaint.'

Daniele Trevisan waves his hands and sighs.

'Come up a minute, Ada. Sit down and have a cup of coffee and a chat.'

She looks at him and shakes her head.

'I must be getting home.'

'Don't call the police!' he implores her. 'You don't want to start telling people you've been seeing ghosts again.'

'There was mud on the floor,' says Ada Zulian, but he doesn't hear.

'Keep the police out of it!' insists Daniele. 'If you need to talk to anyone, talk to me.'

Ada hefts her bags and goes on her way with a smile and a nod. Why is he so anxious that she should not phone the police? There is no doubt in Ada's mind that she is dealing with something real. The other time, with Rosetta, there had never been anything tangible. How she would have treasured it, if there had! But she had always known at heart that the little girl she had so desperately called home night after night, until some exasperated neighbour finally denounced her to the police, had never really been there in the first place. That frail and vulnerable figure lurking in the shadows at the edge of her mind had always been as insubstantial as thought, and Ada's frantic attempts to summon her nothing more than someone crying out in their sleep.

But this is different. She told Daniele two things, but as usual he only heard the one he wanted to hear, the one which fitted his idea of mad old Ada and her ghosts. He completely ignored what she said about the mud. But Ada has seen the mud. She has touched it and smelt it. She knows it's real, and she also knows that ghosts don't leave footprints behind them. So they can't be ghosts, the figures who haunt her house and scuttle along the margins of her life. What, then?

She shivers as she edges along the canal and turns into a narrow alley leading to the back door of Palazzo Zulian, formerly reserved for tradesmen and domestic staff. Everything has turned topsy-turvy now that people have forgotten the use of boats. No one comes and goes by water any more except the dead.

The first thing she notices is the chair, fallen forward across the dull marble pavement. It is of some wood as dark and heavy as pigiron, elaborately carved, centuries old, grotesque. It has stood there in the hall all Ada's life. She would gladly throw it in the canal, but that is impossible. Her duty is to preserve the family heritage intact. Besides, she couldn't lift the thing. It has moved, though, seemingly of its own accord. There have been many such incidents lately, objects seemingly coming to life in her absence like a flock of birds and settling back in a slightly different configuration. She has tried in vain to make out any pattern or purpose to the phenomenon. It is the very triviality of the whole thing which makes it so disturbing.

The staircase leading to the first floor is a shadowy tunnel burrowing upwards into the innards of the huge building. Ada clicks the switch uselessly. The bulb must have gone, like so many in the house. There are no servants now, of course, so she must get by as best she can until Nanni and Vincenzo call. At least her nephews have stuck by her, despite their frequent differences of opinion. Not that they're particularly warm or cordial, but at least they drive over from the mainland to see her every once in a while. That's something these days, when the young are worse than Turks. . .

She pauses at the top of the staircase, in the long hallway running the length of the building. Amplified by the bare vaulted expanse of the *andron* below, the lapping of wavelets against the disused watersteps fills the air, as though someone were swimming in the canal. For a moment it seems to Ada that she can hear something else, a whispering or rustling, somewhere nearby. Mice, no doubt. She has given up trying to keep them down since her cat died, and hasn't the heart to get another. There have been enough absences in her life as it is.

Leaving her bags on the landing, she opens the door into the first of the suite of rooms on the canal side of the building, the only one still in use. The great space is dark, the shutters tightly fastened. Surely she opened them before going out? Or was that yesterday? A noise behind her makes her start and look round, but it is only one of her plastic shopping bags subsiding. An apple tumbles over the collapsed rim and rolls away towards the edge of the top step. Just beyond, at the bottom of the long flight of stairs, its long bony arm upraised and pointing at her, stands a skeleton.

She runs inside the salon, slams the door shut and leans back against it, panting for breath. Which possibility is worse, that the skeleton is not real, or that it is? Nothing more happens. There is no

8

sound. It is a very long time before she can force herself to open the door, eyes tightly closed. When she opens them, the *portego*, the landing, the stairs and the hallway below are all empty.

Ada retrieves the errant apple, picks up the bags and carries them through the lounge to the kitchen. There is just enough light seeping in through the shutters to see her way. In the distance she can hear the shouts of the men working on the Pagan house. She leaves the shopping on the kitchen table and returns to the salon, reaching for the light switch. There is a searing flash and the skeleton stands before her, inside the room now, its claw-like paw outstretched towards her, the skull hidously grinning.

A hand grasps her shoulder. She whirls round. Facing her, at waist level, is a child with long blonde hair and a smooth, round alabaster face of utter purity and stillness, the very image of Rosetta. Moaning, weeping, Ada blunders across the room, bumping heavily into the skeletal form, scrabbling at the telephone.

The long convoy of carriages eased to a halt at the platform and the whirring of the locomotive died away. The driver clambered down from his cab and headed for the canteen, passing the rows of dark-ened trains drawn up at the other platforms in readiness for the early morning departures, still several hours away.

For a moment it seemed as though the train which had just arrived was also empty. Then a door opened, halfway along. A man stepped down to the platform and stood sniffing the air. He was tall and rather gaunt, with a pale, grave face dominated by an angular nose. He wore a long overcoat and a homburg hat, from beneath which emerged tufts of dark hair streaked here and there with silver.

The line of sleeping cars jolted slightly as a locomotive was coupled to the other end, ready to pull the train back across the long bridge to the mainland to continue its journey to Trieste. Reaching up to the floor of the carriage, the man lifted down a battered leather suitcase, slammed the door shut and set off along the platform. The station was deserted, the café and newsagent's closed. The man walked through the harsh glare of the foyer and out on to the broad steps where he paused again, scenting the air. Then, as though satis-fied, he started down the steps and turned left.

At the foot of the Scalzi bridge two youths were unloading bund-les of newspapers and magazines from a motorboat and stacking them beside a shuttered kiosk. The man spoke to them in dialect. One of the lads flourished a knife with which he slit open a pack of papers like gutting a fish. Money changed hands. The man turned away, scanning the headlines: MESTRE SMOG ALARM and GREEN LIGHT FOR THE LAGOON METRO.

He turned left again, off the broad thoroughfare and away from the shuttered shops, into an alley barely wide enough for him to carry the suitcase comfortably. His footsteps resounded like blows. A solitary cat fled at his approach, a half-eaten fish head hanging from its mouth. High in one wall, a single bleary window betrayed the presence of an insomniac or early riser. As the man passed under the lamp jutting out at first-floor level on its wrought-iron bracket, his shadow caught him up and sped ahead, looming ever larger across the rectangular paving stones. At the next corner he turned right, into another alley which gradually widened to form a wedge of open space with a rusty iron-capped well-head at its centre. Here, for the first time, his brisk steps faltered as the pavement went soggy beneath his feet, as though reverting to the marshy field it had once been. Memories crowded in on him like a gang of importunate child beggars.

The houses were built on three storeys: a ground-floor cellar with rectangular grilled openings, then the broad span of the main living area with its elegantly arched windows grouped in pairs, and finally the shallow square-windowed strip of bedrooms just below the roof. The uniformity of the façades was complicated by a horizontal and vertical grid of electric and phone cables, water and gas pipes, by metal strengthening bolts, exhaust vents, guttering, washing-lines, lamp standards and flowerpot holders. Some properties were smartly painted, ochre or russet, while elsewhere the plaster was flaking off like sunburned skin.

The man stopped in front of the most decrepit-looking house of all, facing the well. At ground level the plaster facing had virtually disappeared, revealing the pattern of red brickwork beneath. The shutters closing the first-floor windows were worn down to the bare wood, the scrolled and fluted stone sill was stained with brown streaks from the low metal railing. The doorframe was of the same white Istrian stone, with the number of the house stencilled on it in red paint in an oval frame. Beside the door was a bell-push shaped like an inverted breast. Above, a bowed strip of brass read ZEN.

The man took a key from his pocket and inserted it into the lock. The door creaked open. The passage inside was musty and cold. The light flickered yellowly to life, revealing a cramped vista of crumbling plaster, dull composite tiles, a set of stairs. Taking several rapid breaths, the man closed the door behind him and started up the steps. They twisted round to the left, doubling back on themselves to end at a small landing. A further flight continued up to the bedrooms. The man set down his suitcase and stood there gazing at the door, slightly ajar, in front of him. Then he abruptly pushed it open and barged in.

Emptied of its furnishings, the room looked spacious and serene, yet how much smaller than he remembered it! Whenever he had returned in his imagination – even a moment before, dithering on the landing – it had seemed a cavernous, epic space. He almost laughed, now, to see how insignificant it really was. But he did not laugh, for something in him died at that moment, and he knew that he had lost another and perhaps the most important of the few remaining threads which bound him to his childhood.

In the kitchen, a note had been left on the draining-board: *Dear Aurelio, I've done the best I can, the old place looks a bit shabby, what can you expect, at least it's clean and I've made the bed in your old room, we'll expect you for lunch, it'll be like the old days! Rosalba.* The man laid down the scrap of lined paper gently, as though it might break, and returned to the living room, where he set about opening windows, unbolting the heavy wooden shutters, pressing them back to lie flat against the wall and folding down the metal clips which held them in place. The cold night air flowed into the room, scouring out the lingering odours of absence and neglect. Leaving the windows open, the man returned to the door, picked up his suitcase and went upstairs.

On this floor, more of the original furniture remained, making the low-ceilinged bedroom feel cramped and stuffy. The mirror-fronted wardrobe which stretched the length of one wall created an illusory sense of spaciousness belied by the stale, confined air. The man laid his suitcase down on the bed and turned to survey himself in the wall of mirrors. His double looked back at him with a drawn, wary look and the air of someone stranded against his will in a remote and inhospitable hotel. Nothing suggested that of all rooms in the world this was the most familiar to him.

He opened this window too, breathing in the crisp, salty air. In the canal below, the murky water shifted and stirred. All else was still. The city might have been deserted. To someone accustomed to life in Rome, where the reverberant hum of traffic on the hollow *tufo* is a constant presence, night and day, such absolute, unqualified silence was troubling, as though some vital life function had ceased. The man turned back into the room, sat down on the bed and took his shoes off. Then, overcome by weariness, he lay down and closed his eyes against the sickly yellow light emitted by the lamp, a complex extravanganza of tinted Murano glass, all curlicues and convolutions . . .

A splashing roused him. He felt chilled to the bone, stiff, exhausted, confused. It took him a long time to realize where he was, and when he did the news was comfortless. It had all been a terrible mistake. He should never have come.

The noise which had awakened him was still there, steady, regular, reverberating in the confined space between the houses. He got up off the bed, swung his bare feet down to the chilly tiles the colour and sheen of parmesan and padded over to the window. There was still no sign of the dawn. The man glanced at his watch. It was just after five.

Further down the canal, by the bridge, a streetlamp partly illuminated a segment of the water. There was something moving there, a boat of some kind. As the man watched, it entered the patch of lighted water and was revealed in silhouette: a small dinghy being paddled by two bulky, shapeless figures. The craft rounded the corner and disappeared. Silence fell once more. Rubbing his eyes, Aurelio Zen closed the window and went back to bed.

When he awoke again the room was filled with an astringent brilliance which made him blink, an abrasive slapping of wavelets and the edgy scent which had surprised him the moment he stepped out of the train. He had forgotten even the most obvious things about the place, like the pervasive risky odour of the sea.

Since his mother had come to live with him in Rome, Zen had returned only rarely to his native city, brief fleeting visits to ensure that the house was still standing, or to wrestle some necessary piece of paper away from the *commune*. He had deliberately avoided examining the reasons for this voluntary exile too closely, pretending to himself and others that it was due to the demands of his career. There was something in that, but he sensed that there was much else besides; painful, murky matters which he kept filed away in an inaccessible portion of his mind under the vague heading 'Personal'.

Now, though, it was all gradually returning to him. The urgent plashing he could hear below, he realized, was the final ripples of wash from a vessel passing down the nearby Cannaregio canal. Last night there had been no such traffic, which is why the similar sound he had heard then had drawn him instinctively to the window. He recalled the dinghy, the muffled figures. The more he thought about the incident, the odder it seemed. What could anyone have been doing rowing around the back canals of the city at such an hour? Perhaps he had never woken at all. Perhaps it had all been a dream. No other solution seemed to make sense.

Outside, a skittish wind frisked about the courtyard, glancing off the stone walls, pouncing out from narrow alleys. The sun, barely veiled by haze, set up blocks of shadow seemingly more solid than the surfaces from which all substance had been leached by its slanting, diffuse light. Aurelio Zen slammed the front door behind him and set off towards the café on the quay of the Cannaregio. Rosalba had done wonders in getting the house habitable, but the cupboards and larder were bare. He should have remembered to bring a pack of coffee, at least.

When he reached the corner, his first thought was that he must have lost his bearings. Not only was there no sign of the café, but the barber's and ironmonger's next door had also vanished. Zen looked around him distractedly. Yes, there was the palazzo on the other side of the canal, and there the church. This *was* the corner, no doubt about it, but all that was to be seen was a stretch of grimy glass covered in faded posters protesting against the forcible evictions of sitting tenants. A workshop for carnival masks had taken over the shops next door.

A gaunt grizzled man came shuffling along the alley. He wore an ancient suit, a grubby pullover and tartan carpet slippers. Some distance behind him, a mangy dog trailed along dispiritedly at the end of a length of filthy rope.

'Excuse me!' Zen called. 'Do you know what's happened to Claudio's bar?'

The man's eyes widened in fright.

'Is it you, Anzolo? I never thought to see you again.'

Zen stared more closely at him.

'Daniele?' he breathed. 'I'm Aurelio. Angelo's son.'

The old man squinted back at him. His crumpled face was unshaven. A mass of red veins covered his nose. Three lone teeth remained in his bottom gum, sticking up like the money tabs in the huge silver cash register which used to lord it over Claudio's bar.

'Aurelio?' he muttered at last. 'The little hooligan who used to terrorize the whole neighbourhood and make his mother's life a misery? I can still hear her words. "For the love of God, Daniele, give him a damn good thrashing! I can't control him any more. At this age, it takes a man to keep them in line." '

He tugged his dog viciously away from a niffy patch of plaster it was investigating.

'How is Giustiniana, anyway?'

'My mother's fine, Daniele.'

'And what are you doing here?'

'I'm on business.'

'What sort of business?'

'I'm in the police.'

Daniele Trévisan drew back.

'The *police*?'

'What about it?'

14

'Nothing. It's just the way you were going . . .'

'Yes?' demanded Zen.

'Well, to be frank, I'd have expected you to end up on the other side of the law, if anything.'

Zen smiled thinly.

'And Claudio?' he asked.

'Who?'

The old man looked as bewildered as the victim of a practical joke. Zen waved at the locked door, the fly-posted window.

'Gone!' Daniele exclaimed. 'Claudio's moved down to the bridge, where the tourists are. You can't turn a profit round here any more. And what's the police business that has brought you here, if it's not an indiscreet question from an old family friend?'

But Zen had caught sight of the *vaporetto* approaching and hurried off, leaving Daniele Trevisan looking after him with a quizzical, slightly malicious smile.

At first it looked as though Zen would not be in time to catch the boat, but fortunately another ferry, bound for the station, arrived at the landing stage first, forcing its opposite number to throttle back and drift in mid-stream, awaiting its turn. The result was that Zen was able to saunter across the Tre Archi bridge and even light a cigarette before boarding.

As they passed the modernistic council houses on San Girolamo and emerged into the open waters of the lagoon, the full strength of the wind became clear for the first time. The boat banged and buffeted its way through the short, hard waves, swathes of spray drenching the decking and the windows of the helmsman's cabin. Zen's cigarette obliged him to stand outside, at the top of the stairs leading down to the saloon. It was rush hour, and the boat was packed with schoolchildren and commuters. They sat or stood impassively, reading papers, talking together or staring blankly out of the windows. Apart from the pitching and rolling, the crunch of the waves and the draughts of air laden with salt, not fumes, it might almost have been the bus which Zen took to work every morning in Rome. He eyed the children hunched under their satchels, chattering brightly or horsing about. They thought this was normal, he reflected, as he once had. They thought everywhere was like this. They thought that nothing would ever change.

At Fondamente Nove, Zen changed to avoid the detour to

Murano. It would have been quicker to get off at the next stop, by the hospital, and walk through the back streets to the Questura, but as he was in plenty of time he rode the *circolare destra* through the Arsenale shipyards and out into the sweeping vistas of the deep-water channel beyond. The wind's work was even clearer here, cutting up the water into staccato wavelets breaking white at the crest. They slapped and banged the hull, sending up a salty spindrift which acted as a screen for brief miniature rainbows and coated Zen's face like sweat.

When they reached the Riva degli Schiavoni he disembarked, crossed the broad promenade, bustling even at that hour, and plunged into the warren of dark, deserted alleys beyond. He was largely following his nose at this point, but it proved a good guide, bringing him out on a bridge leading over the San Lorenzo canal near the three-storey building which housed the police headquarters for the *Provincia di Venezia*. Zen held his identity card up to the camera above the bell and the door release hummed loudly. Since the years of terrorism, police stations had been defended like colonial outposts in enemy territory. The fact that the Questura and the *Squadra Mobile* headquarters next door were both traditional buildings typical of this unglamorous area of the city made such measures seem all the more bizarre.

The guard on duty behind a screen of armoured glass in the vestibule was sleepy and offhand. No one was in yet, he told Zen, a claim substantiated by the bank of video screens behind him, showing a selection of empty roooms, corridors and staircases. Zen walked upstairs to the first floor and opened a door at random. The scene which met his eyes inside was absolutely predictable to anyone who had worked in police offices anywhere in Italy from Aosta to Siracuse. The air was stale and stuffy, used up and warmed over. The bare walls were painted a shade of off-white reminiscent of milk left too long out of the fridge. A double neon tube housing, its cover missing, hung from the ceiling on frail chains. The available space was divided into three areas by screens of the thick frosted glass commonly associated with shower cubicles, set in gilt-anodized aluminium frames. At the centre of each squatted a large wooden desk.

Zen went over to one of the desks and looked through the contents of the three-tiered metal tray until he found what he was looking for:

a sheaf of computer printout stapled together at the upper left-hand corner. The top sheet bore the words NOTIZIE DI REATI DENUNCIATI ALLA POLIZIA GIUDIZIARIA and the dates of the previous week. The pages inside listed all the incidents which had been brought to the attention of the police during the period in question. Zen leafed through the pages, looking for something suitable.

It was a delicate business. He didn't want to attract unwanted attention by poaching a case which had already been assigned, or in which someone was taking a special interest for one reason or another. On the other hand, he couldn't just select some minor misdemeanour at random. There had to be something special about it to justify his being sent up all the way from the élite Criminalpol squad in Rome to take over the case. He was still puzzling over this problem when a familiar name leapt out at him.

He read the entry again, then dropped the document and lit a cigarette. The *contessa*! Christ almighty. For a time he was lost in memories. Then he looked at the page again. Two weeks earlier, Ada Zulian had reported intruders at her home, claiming that it was part of a campaign of systematic persecution which had been going on for over a month. She had renewed her complaints the previous week.

Zen looked up at the window. He nodded slowly to himself. That would do nicely. It was too trivial to have excited any interest from any of the resident staff, but the family connection would provide exactly the kind of illusory logic he needed to justify his involvement to anyone who asked. He noted down the date and case number in his diary and replaced the list in the metal tray.

When the Personnel office responded to the phone half an hour later, Zen went along and introduced himself. The clerk in charge dug out the chit which had been faxed up from Rome.

'Zen, Aurelio. Criminalpol. Temporary transfer regarding . . .'

He frowned at the form.

'That's odd. They've forgotten to fill that bit in.'

Zen shook his head.

'Typical! The people they're employing these days can't remember their own names half the time.'

He took out his notebook.

'It's to do with someone called Zulian. I've got the details here somewhere . . . Yes, here you go.'

He showed the reference number and date to the clerk, who copied them on to the chit.

'I'll need some office space,' Zen remarked. 'What have you got available?'

The clerk consulted a wall-chart.

'How long are you going to be here?'

Zen shrugged.

'Hard to say. A week or two at least.'

'There's a desk free in three one nine until the seventeenth. Gatti's on holiday until then.'

Room 319 was a small office at the front of the building, overlooking the canal. Zen was looking down at a refrigerated barge marked GELATI SANSON squeezing past the police launches moored outside the Questura when the door opened to admit Aldo Valentini, whose name figured alongside that of the absent Gatti on the door.

Valentini was a mild, scholarly-looking man with Armani glasses and a skimpy blond beard like grass which has been growing under a plank. He seemed pleased to have company, and suggested that he and Zen pop out to get some breakfast. As they emerged into the sunlight, bucking the incoming tide of staff hastening to sign themselves in so that they could slip out again, Valentini inquired about the reason for Zen's transfer.

'You must be joking!' he barked in the slightly nasal accent of his native Ferrara. 'Ada Zulian! A woman who doesn't even know the right time . . .'

Zen gestured impatiently.

'What does that matter, as long as she knows the right people?'

Aldo Valentini conceded the point with a shrug. He led the way to a bar at the end of the quay. A red neon sign over the door read *Bar dei Greci*, after the nearby Orthodox church. There was no sign of any Greeks inside, although the barman's accent suggested that he was from somewhere well to the south of Chioggia.

'All the same, *la Zulian!*' exclaimed Valentini when they had ordered coffee. 'God almighty, she's been in and out of the loony bin like a yo-yo for the last twenty years. This complaint of hers ended up on my desk, largely because no one else would touch it with a bargepole.'

He broke off to take one of the pastries from the plate on the bar.

'We searched the whole place from top to bottom,' he continued,

his moustache white with icing sugar from the pastry he had selected. 'Even put a man outside the front door. No one came or went,
yet the woman still claimed she was being persecuted. It's a clear
case of hysteria and attention-seeking.'

Zen took a bite of a flaky cream-filled croissant.

'I'm sure you're right. It's always the hopeless cases who want a
second opinion. I'll just go through the motions and then endorse
your conclusions. It's a total waste of time, but what do I care? There
are worse places to spend a few days.'

He washed the pastry down with a gulp of coffee.

'So, what's been happening round here?'

Valentini shrugged.

'Bugger all, as usual. Mestre and Marghera see a reasonable
amount of action, particularly in drugs, but we just don't have a big
enough slice of the mainland for it to add up to anything much. As
for the city itself, forget it. Criminals are like everyone else these
days. If you can't drive there, they don't want to know.'

Zen nodded slowly.

'What about that kidnapping that was all over the papers a few
months back? Some American.'

'You mean the Durridge business?'

Zen lit a cigarette.

'That must have livened things up a bit.'

'It might, if they'd let us near it,' Valentini retorted shortly.

'How do you mean?'

'The Carabinieri got there first, and when we applied for
reciprocity we were told the files had been returned under seal to
Rome.'

He shrugged.

'Christ knows what that was all about. Once upon a time we could
have pulled a few strings of our own and found out, but these
days . . .'

He pointed to the headline in the newspaper lying on the counter.
THE OLD FOX FIGHTS FOR HIS POLITICAL LIFE, it read, above a photograph of the politician in question. Zen picked the paper up and
scanned the article, which concerned alleged payments made by a
number of leading industrialists into a numbered Swiss bank
account allegedly used to fund the party in question. The paper's
cartoonist made play with the slogan adopted by the party at the last

election: 'A Fairer Alternative'. In a secondary article, a spokesman for the regionalist Northern Leagues hailed the development as 'a death blow to the clique of crooks who have bled this country dry for decades' and called for new electoral laws designed to radically redraw the political map of the country.

'It's total chaos,' remarked Valentini sourly. 'You can't get anything done any more. No one knows what the rules are.'

Feeling a touch on his arm, Zen looked round. A young woman with blonde hair, wearing a ski-jacket and jeans, stood staring at him, smiling inanely and stabbing one finger in the air. For a moment Zen thought she must be mad, or perhaps from some religious sect or other. Then he caught sight of the suspended rectangle of cardboard circling slowly in the draught above his head. The logo on each side showed a smouldering cigarette in a red circle with a broad slash across it.

'Don't tell me you can't even smoke any more!' he exclaimed incredulously to Valentini, who shrugged sheepishly.

'The city council passed a by-law making it compulsory to provide a no-smoking area. It's just for show, to keep the tourists happy. Normally no one pays any attention in a place like this, but every once in a while some arsehole insists on the letter of the law.'

He slipped some money to the cashier and they stepped outside. Already the sunshine was looser and more generous. Zen paused to look at a series of posters gummed to the wall. The design was identical to the ones he had seen earlier that morning, on the window of the closed café in Cannaregio, but these were much newer. At the top was a drawing of the lion of Saint Mark, rampant, its expression full of defiance. The huge black capitals beneath read NUOVA REPUBBLICA VENETA and the text announced a rally the following evening in Campo Santa Margherita.

'Total chaos,' Aldo Valentini repeated, leading the way back to the Questura. 'Every day it turns out that another big name, someone you would have sworn was absolutely untouchable, is under investigation on charges ranging from corruption to association with the Mafia. Result, no one dares to do a friend a favour any more. Nothing would please me more than to see this country turn into a paradise of moral probity, but how the hell are we supposed to get by in the meantime?'

Zen nodded. This was a conversation he had been having at least once a day for several months. By now he had the lines off by heart.

'It's just like in Russia,' he declared. 'The old system may have been terrible, but at least it functioned.'

'My brother-in-law's just moved into a new house near Rovigo,' Valentini continued. 'The telephone people tell him he'll have to wait six weeks to get a phone installed, so he gets on to the engineer and offers him a *bustarella*, you know. Nothing exorbitant, just the odd fifty thousand or so to move up to the top of the list.'

'The normal thing,' murmured Zen.

'The normal thing. You know what the guy tells him? "No way, *dottore*," he says. "It's more than my job's worth." Can you believe it? "It's more than my job's worth." '

'Disgusting.'

'How the hell are you supposed to get anything done with that sort of attitude? It's enough to make you sick.'

He tossed his cigarette into the canal, where a seagull made a half-hearted pass at it before landing on the gunwale of the outermost police launch.

Back in their office, a man stood framed in the sunlight streaming in through the window. He turned as Zen and Valentini entered.

'Aldo?'

He came forward, frowning at Zen.

'Who's this?' he asked suspiciously.

Valentini introduced them.

'Aurelio Zen, Enzo Gavagnin. Enzo's head of the Drugs Squad.'

Enzo Gavagnin had a large womanish face and the stocky, muscular body of a gondolier. He inspected Zen coolly.

'New posting?'

Zen shook his head.

'I'm with the Ministry,' he said. 'On temporary assignment.'

Enzo Gavagnin glanced at Valentini.

'An emissary from Rome, eh?' he murmured in a manner both humorous and pointed. 'I hope you haven't been giving away any of our secrets, Aldo.'

'I didn't know we had any,' Valentini replied lightly. 'Anyway, anyone who comes all this way to take the Ada Zulian case off my hands is a friend as far as I'm concerned.'

Gavagnin laughed loudly.

'Fair enough! Anyway, the reason I came was about that breaking-and-entering on Burano.'

'The Sfriso business?'

'If you want to reduce your work-load still further then you're in luck, because I've discovered that there's an angle which ties it in to a case we've been working on for some time . . .'

Valentini looked doubtful.

'I don't know, Enzo. If I shed two cases the same morning, people might start to ask questions.'

Gavagnin took Valentini's arm and led him away.

'It's just because of the possible conflict of interest. Naturally we don't want our on-going investigation compromised, so it's better all round if . . .'

The pair disappeared behind the glass panelling around Valentini's desk, becoming fuzzy, unfocused images of their former selves. Zen went into his own cubicle and dug the phone book out of the desk drawer. He looked up *Paulon, M* and dialled the number.

'Well?'

The reply was abrupt to the point of rudeness.

'Marco?'

'Who's this?'

'Aurelio.'

There was a brief pause.

'Aurelio! How's it going? I was reading about you in the paper just a while ago. That business in St Peter's. I used to go fishing with him, I thought, and here he is consorting with Archbishops and the like! Gave me quite a thrill. Are you here in town?'

'Yes. Can we meet?'

'Of course!'

'I need some advice, maybe some help.'

'Well I'm out delivering all morning, but . . . Do you know the *osteria* on the San Girolamo canal, just opposite the church?'

Enzo Gavagnin backed out of Valentini's cubicle, having concluded his business. He glanced shrewdly at Zen as he passed by.

'What's it called?' asked Zen.

'Damned if I know, tell you the truth! I've been going there after lunch every weekday for the last twenty years, but I've never bothered to ask about the name. Everyone calls it "The Hole in the

Wall". It's got red paint on the windows. Opposite the church. What's it about, anyway?'

'I'll explain later. Thanks, Marco.'

He stood up, buttoning his coat. The preliminaries were complete. It was time to go and pretend to do his job.

Her first thought, when the bell rings, is that it is just another trick, another in the succession of cruel practical jokes which seem designed to test her endurance, her fragile sanity. No one calls at Palazzo Zulian these days, except when her nephews drive over from Verona every weekend, as regular as the tides. But this is Tuesday, and Nanni and Vincenzo will be at work doing whatever it is they do . . .

The bell rings again, dispelling the lingering possibility that the whole thing had taken place in her mind. What happens twice is real, thinks Ada, sidling across the hallway to the room on the other side, overlooking the alley. An angled mirror fixed to a support just outside the window gives a view of the door, so that you can see who is calling without them seeing you, and decide whether to receive them. But immediately Ada whips her head back, for there in the glass is another face, looking straight back at her.

'*Contessa!*'

A strange voice. Not one of her tormentors, or a new one at least. She risks another look. The gaunt figure in a black hat and overcoat is still there, staring straight up at the tell-tale. It's no use hiding. If she can see him, he can see her. Stands to reason, Ada Zulian tells herself, reluctantly turning back towards the door and walking downstairs.

The stranger is tall and thin, with a hatchet face and clear grey eyes. His expression is stern, almost saturnine, yet his manner is courteous and respectful. He speaks the dialect with ease and precision, in the true Cannaregio accent – the purest in the city, Ada has always held. He hands her a plastic-covered card with writing and a photograph of himself. She frowns at the name typed in capital letters.

'Zen?' she says slowly.

She inspects him again, more critically this time.

'That's right, *contessa*,' the man nods. 'Angelo's boy.'

Ada sniffs loudly.

'Giustiniana's, you mean. Your father had only one thing to do with it, excuse me. Fancy going off to Russia and getting himself killed like that, leaving his wife here all alone! At least my Silvestro fell defending our territories in Dalmatia. What has Russia to do with us, for heaven's sake? Come in, come in, I'm feeling cold just thinking about it.'

While Ada locks and bolts the door again, her visitor stands looking about him in the bleary, uncertain light of the *andron*. The plaster feels clammy and cold and gives slightly to the touch like a laden sponge. A mysterious smile appears on the man's face as he absorbs the dank odours and the watery echoes seeping in from the canal at the other end of the hall.

'She used to bring you round here while she worked,' Ada continues, leading the way upstairs. 'And once she saw I didn't mind, she'd leave you here while she went off to do other jobs. Of course you won't remember, you were only a toddler.'

The man says nothing. Ada Zulian painfully attains the level expanse of the *portego* and waves him into the salon.

'What brings you here, anyway? Your mother never calls any more, not that anyone else does either. Not since that trouble I had with Rosetta. Anyone would think it was catching!'

'But I gather you've been having some more problems recently,' the man remarks cautiously.

Ada Zulian looks at him.

'Perhaps I have and perhaps I haven't,' she replies sharply. 'What business is that of yours, Aurelio Battista?'

'Well, since you informed the police . . .'

'The police? What have you to do with the police?'

'I work for them.'

Ada's laughter startles the silence. The man looks taken aback.

'What's so funny?' he demands.

'The police? But you were such a timid little fellow! So serious, so anxious, so easily scared! That's what gave me the idea in the first place.'

'What idea?'

'To dress you up as Rosetta! I still had all her dresses then, her little blouses and socks, everything. When I went to San Clemente, they took everything away and burnt it. But at that time I still thought she might come back one day. Really, I mean. Just walk in, as suddenly and inexplicably as she disappeared. I wanted to have everything ready for her, just in case. I wouldn't have asked any questions, you know. I would have taken her back and carried on as though nothing had ever happened . . .'

She looks away suddenly, as though she had seen something move in the nether recesses. Only one of the windows is unshuttered, and the dim expanses of the salon are further multiplied and complicated by a profusion of mirrors of every shape and size, all framed in the same gilded wood as the furniture.

'To tell you the truth,' Ada goes on at last, 'I think you helped keep her at bay. As long as you were there, running about in her dresses, Rosetta didn't dare show her face.'

She sits down on a low, hard sofa covered with worn dark pink silk.

'Either that, or it was the cause of the whole thing! Perhaps she resented the fact that I'd found someone to replace her, and decided to get her own back. It's hard to say. But you did look sweet, Aurelio! If only I'd thought to take some photographs.'

The man has been standing looking at her with an air of deferential attention. Now he claps his hands loudly and starts striding about the room with quite unnecessary vigour.

'Three weeks ago, *contessa*, you dialled the police emergency number and reported the presence of intruders in your house. A patrol boat was dispatched and the house searched from top to bottom. It proved to be empty. Subsequent investigations have failed to reveal a single fact to substantiate your allegations of trespass and persecution.'

He pauses impressively, looking down at the elderly woman perched on the antique settle.

'Well, of course!' she retorts. 'Do you think they're stupid?'

The man frowns.

'The police?'

She laughs.

'I know *they're* stupid! No, I'm talking about my visitors. They're far too sly to let themselves be caught by some flat-foot from Ferrara. Swamp-dwellers! They all have malaria, poor things. Runs in the family, rots their brains.'

'When was the last occurrence of this kind?' the man inquires in a decidedly supercilious tone.

'Last night,' Ada replies pertly. 'It was almost dawn by the time they finally left me in peace.'

'What happened?'

'The same as usual. It's the skeleton I'm most frightened of. It makes such sudden rushes at me.'

'How many of them are there?'

Ada shrugs, as if considering the matter.

'It's hard to tell. They come and go. Often I've thought they've gone, then suddenly another one pops out from somewhere.'

'Have they attacked you?'

She shakes her head.

'They just try and scare me, keep me awake all night, never knowing what's going to happen next.'

The man considers her for a long time.

'How do they get in?' he asks.

'Don't ask me! They just appear. In my bedroom it was last time. A light came on, I woke, and there they were.'

Despite herself, her voice shakes slightly as she remembers her terror.

'Was the front door locked?'

'Locked and bolted, as always. But nothing stops them.'

She pulls up the sleeve over her dress and displays a livid patch on her arm.

'There! That's what I got from bumping into one of them. There are others, too, not decent to be viewed. I showed the doctor, though.'

The man nods.

'I've read the file on your case,' he says. 'The medical evidence is apparently inconclusive. The contusions could have resulted from a collision with some household object. A chair or table, for example.'

'Do they think I go staggering about bumping into the furniture like some drunk?' Ada protests. 'Anyway, what about the mud?'

'The report mentioned some marks on the floor. There was no sign of shoe tread or other distinguishing features.'

He sighs deeply.

'You see the problem is, *contessa*, that after what happened before, people are disinclined to believe what you tell them.'

'I can't help that,' returns Ada flatly.

'On that occasion, you were convicted of causing a public nuisance by calling your deceased daughter Rosetta home every evening. You subsequently spent two years in a mental institution where you were diagnosed as suffering from persistent delusions. It is therefore only natural that without some concrete evidence that the phenomena you now describe have any reality outside your own imagination, it is going to be difficult if not impossible for me to take the matter further.'

'I didn't ask you to come,' Ada retorts.

Her visitor takes a notebook from his pocket and writes something on a page which he tears out and hands to her.

'That's my number,' he says. 'I'm only just round the corner, in the old house. If this happens again, give me a call, whatever the time, day or night.'

Ada looks at the number, then at his eyes. She nods.

Leaving the *palazzo*, Aurelio Zen turned left into an alley so narrow he had to walk sideways, like a crab. It seemed to come to a dead end at a small canal, but at the last moment a portico was revealed, leading to a bridge. The tide was out and the water had shrivelled to a gutter a few centimetres deep between fat expanses of black slime where tethered boats lolled like capsized beetles. A little further along the canal, the elegant façade of Palazzo Zulian stood out from its neighbours.

The air, walled off from the prevailing breezes, was heavy with the stench of mud. An assortment of débris was visible at the bottom of the water: the wheel of a pram, a punctured bucket, a boot. A large rat slithered across the mud and hopped into an open drain. In older buildings, people still kept a heavy stone on the toilet cover to stop the creatures from getting loose in the house.

The alley scuttled off between the houses on the other side, eventually joining a broader street with shops and a church. Zen made his way past doors whose numbers read like the dates of an impossible life: 1684–1679, 1635–1628. He crossed a bridge where a man was manoeuvring a handcart laden with cans of cooking oil up the ridged pavement on the wheels fitted to the leading edge. The house opposite was clad in scaffolding and sacking, with a large plastic chute to carry waste rubble to a barge moored alongside, now aground in the mud. A workman was shovelling sand out of another boat into a wheelbarrow which his mate was holding on the plank bridge they had rigged up.

Zen squinted at the frontage. Surely that was where the Pagan family lived? The two boys had been at school with him, although they were never part of the same set. Presumably they must have inherited by now and were having the place done up. He was surprised to feel a stab of envy. If only he could afford to have the Zen house turned into a proper home for all of them, with a separate flat for his mother and plenty of space for him and Tania . . .

He immediately dismissed the idea. It was absurd to think that he could make a life for himself here at this late stage. There was nothing here for him now. He had used the place up, converted it to experiences and memories that made up the person he was. To return would be to condemn himself to a form of spiritual incest. Nothing new could happen to him here, nothing real. Besides, Tania wouldn't want to move to a city which, despite its glamour, was essentially a provincial backwater. He walked on, frowning at the realization that this was the first time he had thought of Tania since his arrival.

Under the flat bland noonday light, the wedge-shaped *campo* looked like a small-scale replica of itself, a set of mocked-up frontages. How different it seemed in the eye of memory! Grand in stature, full of significance, peopled with a vast and various cast of every age and character, inexhaustible and yet coherent . . . Now it looked diminished, paltry and deserted. The city was dying. The paper Zen had bought earlier that morning had spelled out the grim rate of attrition. The preceding twenty-four hours had seen six births and twenty-one deaths. Twenty-one unique and irreplaceable repositories of local life and lore had been destroyed, while most of the six new citizens would be forced to emigrate in search of work and accommodation. In another fifty years, there would be no Venetians left at all.

Of all the houses in the neighbourhood, the Morosinis' had been the liveliest and most welcoming. It was identical in size and layout to the Zens', yet the two homes could hardly have been more different in every other way. The Cannaregio area was mid-way between the station and the slaughterhouse, and most local men worked for one or the other. Like Aurelio's father, Silvio Morosini was a railwayman, and he had taken full advantage of this once the war came. No heroics for Silvio, who had decidedly left-wing sympathies but also an uncanny sense of which way the wind was blowing and when to keep his head down.

Angelo Zen could also have claimed exemption – the railways were then the sinews of both the economy and the war effort – but he had preferred to volunteer and was sent off to serve in the ill-trained and worse-equipped token force which Mussolini dispatched to the Russian front in order to bolster his status with his German ally. There Angelo had disappeared, along with the tens of thousands of other Italians unaccounted-for and presumed dead. The growing certainty of that death, coupled with the lack of any proof which would permit its recognition, had infiltrated the Zen household like an icy draught from the frozen battlefields and prison camps where the *Armata Russa* had met its miserable and ignominious fate.

But where Zen's father was a dominating absence, celebrated at every turn by stilted sepia photographs of a figure whose third dimension increasingly seemed as hypothetical as the existence of an afterlife, Silvio Morosini was one of a crowd of unequivocally real presences jostling and clamouring for attention in the household of which he was the nominal head. In fact this position was filled by his wife Rosalba, who had been Giustiniana Zen's closest friend long before her marriage and was not about to desert her and the fatherless only child now that Rosalba's prediction that the union in question would come to no good had, God forbid, come true.

The result had been that Aurelio had grown up treating the Morosini house more or less as his own, and had often taken advantage of this freedom to escape from the intolerable spectacle of his mother weeping silently as she went about her work. The quarrels in Silvio's and Rosalba's home were frequent, open and vociferous, shows in which anyone present was expected to join, whether or not they were actually involved or indeed had any idea what the whole thing was supposed to be about. Everyone got their chance to yell and posture and strut about, and in the midst of these amateur dramatics the original cause of contention gradually frittered away, forgotten if not forgiven. The young Aurelio did not necessarily want to live permanently in such an atmosphere, but it certainly made a refreshing contrast to the stifling tensions of his own home, whose existence could not be admitted never mind assuaged.

Like the whole neighbourhood, and the city itself, the Morosini house was of course a quieter place these days. Rosalba had continued to keep in touch by letter and phone when Giustiniana moved to Rome to be with her son, and Zen had thus been kept informed of the children's marriages and of Silvio's death the previous year. It was nevertheless a shock to be confronted by the old woman who came to greet him at the head of the stairs. On the phone, Rosalba still sounded much the same as ever, and Zen had irrationally been expecting her to look the same. But the vigorous, bustling woman he remembered now bore an astonishing resemblance to his fading memories of Rosalba's grandmother, a legendary figure who had been born before Venice belatedly joined the newly unified Kingdom of Italy. All her features had drawn inwards towards each other, like a contracting universe, producing a compact, miniaturized version of the face he remembered.

'Welcome home, Aurelio!' she cried, embracing him repeatedly. 'I hope you found everything as you expected it. I did the best I could in the time, but it's no easy task to bring a house back from the dead when it's stood empty for so many years.'

Zen smiled warmly at her.

'You did wonders, Rosalba. A real miracle.'

Seeing her as she really was, he felt ashamed of having agreed to let her do the heavy work of preparing the house for his arrival, even though it had been her idea. He had merely phoned to let her know he was coming and to ask her to see if the house, to which she had a key, could be made habitable. He might have known that she would not trust anyone else to do the job properly.

'Let me take your coat,' Rosalba continued animatedly. 'I expect you find it cold here now you've got used to living down south.'

Zen sniffed the air appreciatively.

'Something smells good.'

'Oh, it's nothing much. A little *risoto de sepe col nero* followed by sole. Come in, come in!'

Installed in the large armchair in the living room, Zen sipped a glass of sparkling wine while Rosalba gave him a crash course in local news and gossip. The armchair had formerly been the throne from which Silvio Morosini had dispensed judgements and decrees and generally lorded it over his unruly clan. At that time, Zen would no more have dreamt of sitting in it than of touching the firm plump legs of Silvio's elder daughter Antonia, who was then causing him so much distress and bewilderment as the first member of the opposite sex he found himself unable to dismiss as 'just a girl'. Antonia, for her part, had regarded Zen as suitable football and playground fodder for her brothers, but of no conceivable personal interest to her whatsoever. And now she was a mother of four and an estate agent in Vicenza.

'. . . always flying off somewhere on the other side of the world. My grandchildren know Rio de Janeiro and Hong Kong better than they do our poor Venice. And when they do come, it's just to gawk like everyone else. Families are what we need, not tourists! But what can you do? There's no work, and the kind of rents they charge are just crazy, even though half the houses just stand empty . . .'

She broke off, perhaps remembering that the Zens' house had been unoccupied since Giustiniana's move to Rome.

'Some more wine?' she suggested, appearing in the doorway with the bottle. 'And then we can eat.'

They were joined for lunch by a young woman who was introduced to Zen as Cristiana Morosini. A late and unexpected addition to the family, Cristiana had been a mere toddler when Zen had joined the police and left the city for a series of postings on the mainland. She was now a good-looking woman in her early thirties, with a slow, sensual manner and a striking resemblance to Zen's memories of her elder sister. As she served the risotto, dark grey from the cuttlefish ink, Rosalba explained that Cristiana had left her husband, a local politician, after discovering that he was screwing one of his supporters.

'Mamma!'

'There's no need to be coy with an old family friend. He's seen you running around the house bare-arsed often enough, haven't you Aurelio?'

'Delicious,' murmured Zen, savouring the combination of nutty rice, chewy cuttlefish and unctuous sauce.

'I'm not being coy,' Cristiana protested. 'But *one* is a grotesque understatement.'

She held up three velvety white fingers.

'There was that rich bitch from the Zattere, for a start. Then there's Maria Luisa Squarcina, and don't forget the Populin woman. She denies it, but she would, wouldn't she? That's three, not counting various secretaries, journalists and assorted hangers-on. And those are only the ones everybody knows about. If you could fuck your way into office, Nando would be running the country by now.'

'And what brings you back home, Aurelio?' asked Rosalba. 'You said on the phone that it was work, but what kind of work exactly?'

Zen washed down a delicious salty mouthful with some more wine.

'Well of course it's strictly confidential . . .'

'You can count on us,' Rosalba assured him.

'We won't breathe a word,' seconded Cristiana.

Zen's mother used to say that there were two ways of making sure everyone in Venice knew something: you could either get every parish priest in the city to read it out after Mass, or you could tell Rosalba Morosini.

'The fact is,' said Zen, 'it's a bit of a fiddle. I've been feeling rather homesick, and I wanted to sort out one or two things to do with the house. The problem was that I didn't have any leave due, so I had to make it look like work.'

'You put in for a transfer.'

'Right. At the Ministry, where I work, we get reports from all over the country listing every crime reported and the action taken. Normally it all goes straight into the computer and gets pulped up into statistics, but I pulled out the reports for Venice and looked through them to find something suitable. Lo and behold, what do I see but the name of Ada Zulian . . .'

'*La contessa!*' cried Rosalba.

Zen nodded.

'Apparently she'd phoned in with a complaint about intruders in her house. So I pulled a few strings and had myself drafted up here on a temporary basis to investigate.'

The lie was as effortless and unpremeditated as the evasive clouds of ink emitted by the cuttlefish they were eating.

'Ada and her ghosts!' cried Rosalba, having served her guest another helping of risotto. 'It all started when her daughter disappeared. She never got over it. Lisa Rosteghin's sister was a nurse in the mental hospital on San Clemente, and the stories she tells about Ada . . . ! Apparently at one point a deputation of the other lunatics came to see the director to complain about her behaviour. "Excuse us, *dottore*," they said, "but you've got to do something – this woman's driving us crazy!"'

'I remember her sidling up to me in the street,' said Cristiana, wiping her lips with her napkin, 'and calling me by the dead girl's name in that creepy way she has. It put the fear of God into me, I can tell you.'

' "This woman's driving us crazy!" ' Rosalba repeated in a tone of hilarity. 'Mind you, she was always half-mad if you ask me. The Saoners used to rent a house from her at one time, and you know what? When she sent in her account, they found she had charged them for the paper and ink the bill was written with! Can you believe it?'

'What happened to her daughter?' asked Zen idly.

Rosalba's animation instantly evaporated. She shrugged.

'No one really knows. It was during the last years of the war. So many terrible things happened.'

She cleared the dishes and walked off to the kitchen. Zen looked up to find Cristiana's big liquid eyes fixed on him like a pair of sea anemones. He barely had time to register their soft, tenacious presence before her mother returned.

'Speaking of the Saoners, do you know what's become of Tommaso?' Zen asked as Rosalba served him a glistening leaf-shaped slab of sole.

'The younger brother? Well, that's the way I still think of him. He used to be your best friend, didn't he?'

A host of remembered images of his best friend rose briefly in Zen's mind like a flock of disturbed pigeons.

'We lost touch years ago. Is he married yet?'

It was Cristiana who replied.

'No, and he's given up his job to concentrate on politics. He's one of Nando's right-hand men.'

'I must look him up,' mused Zen. 'Does he still live in Calle del Magazen?'

'You're more likely to find him at party headquarters,' said Cristiana tartly. 'They're there most of the time these days, with the municipal elections coming up. Nando has inspired them to give their all to the movement – especially to the female supporters.'

'And how's Giustiniana?' asked Rosalba gaily. 'Have some more sole, for goodness sake. You're not eating!'

Aurelio Zen made his way slowly through the hushed and vacant spaces of the town in a daze brought on by the wine he had drunk at lunch, the grappa he had allowed Rosalba to talk him into having afterwards, and not least by his encounter with Cristiana Morosini, whose white flesh had somehow become inextricably confused in his memories with that of the fresh tender sole which had melted in his mouth. His mind was a jumble of contradictory thoughts and feelings, an inner landscape equivalent to the one all around him: blocks of every size and shape thrown together as though at random, like bricks tipped in a heap. Like so much else, this intimate disorder now seemed foreign to him, accustomed as he was to the planned vistas and grand boulevards of the capital. Everything was turning out very differently from what he had imagined.

He walked along the Fondamenta delle Cappucine in search of the wine-shop which Marco had mentioned. Up ahead, a canopy of evergreen shrubbery spilt out over a high wall, betraying the presence of one of the city's secret gardens, the original vegetable plots which had once lain at the centre of each of its hundred islands, providing produce for the inhabitants of the waterfront houses. As Zen passed beneath the tree, he saw that it was filled with feral cats, perched on every branch like a flock of birds.

The tide had turned, but it was still low enough to expose the mudbanks on either side of the San Girolamo canal. Two labourers were at work there, one pushing a wheelbarrow along a path of duckboards laid out from the quay, the other working with a spade in the canal bed itself, turning over slabs of slime as thick and black as tar. The fetid odour of the disturbed mud hung heavy in the air, a noxious miasma so strong it was almost tangible.

'Watch out!'

The cry came from above. Swivelling, Zen beheld an old woman staring down at him with what looked like indignation. He shrugged impatiently.

'What's the matter, *signora*?'

'The pipe!' she shouted back. 'You were going to trip.'

It was only then that Zen noticed the metal tubing stretched across his path, leading from a narrow lane at one side to a red barge, stranded by the tide, bearing the legend POZZI NERI and a phone number.

'Thank you!' he called shamefacedly to his saviour, who shrugged and ducked back into her house.

Zen stepped over the tubing and continued on his way. Living now in a city which had had mains drainage for over two thousand years, he had forgotten about the 'black wells', the septic tanks over which every Venetian house was built and into which flowed such effluvia as could not be discharged directly into the canals.

A little further along he saw first the church which Marco had mentioned, then the *osteria* itself. The trim was indeed red, or had been at some time within living memory. A faded sign over the door read 'Finest Wines of the Piave from our own Estate on Draught and in Bottle'. The interior was smoky and dark after the noontide glare outside, but even before Zen's eyes had adjusted he heard a familiar voice hail him with a long soft '*Ciao!*', rising and falling like a passing wave.

One of the card-players at the rear of the premises rose from the table and strode towards him, a calloused hand extended in greeting. Marco Paulon was a sturdy, muscular man whose hide looked as wrinkled and tanned as bacon. His face was a pudgy, shapeless mass in which his eyes twinkled, bright and shiny, like two metal buttons dropped into a bowl of polenta. He and Zen had not been especially close as children, but they had stayed in touch thanks to a mutually advantageous arrangement whereby Paulon kept an eye on the Zen property and undertook basic running repairs in return for the use of the ground floor as extra storage space for his haulage business.

He steered Zen to a vacant table by the window and shouted an order for two glasses of *fragolino*.

'What's all this about you and Ada Zulian?' he demanded cheerily.

Zen gawped. Surely not even Rosalba's grapevine could have disseminated his cover story so quickly. But it soon became clear that Marco had his information from the *contessa* herself.

'The old girl isn't up to carrying much these days, so I quite often pick up things she's ordered when I deliver to the shops, and then drop them off on my way back to Mestre. I went round just before lunch with a case of mineral water she'd ordered and she told me you'd been there. To be honest, I thought it was another of her hallucinations. Fat chance, I thought, the police sending Aurelio up from Rome on account of Ada Zulian!'

The proprietor brought two glasses of the sweetish foaming wine and the two friends drank each other's health. Then Zen leant forward and lowered his voice. 'Actually, I arranged it myself.'

Marco Paulon raised his eyebrows.

'Didn't anyone query it?'

Zen swirled his glass around, making the wine gyrate like a spinning coin. He closed one eye in an exaggerated wink.

'They probably would have, if I'd told them. So I put it about that I was being sent to look into the Durridge case. Do you remember? The American who disappeared here a couple of months ago. There was a big fuss about it in the press.'

Paulon smiled admiringly.

'You cunning bastard.'

Zen looked up at a calendar pinned to the wall beside Marco's head. Superimposed on the numbered squares for each date of the month was a wavy green line indicating the rise and fall of the tides in the lagoon. The trough was almost at the centre of the square for that day, indicating that low tide had been at noon.

'I don't suppose there's enough water to get about yet,' he said.

Marco frowned.

'Depends where you want to go. I've moored the boat up by Sant'Alvise. It never dries out there.'

He looked inquiringly at Zen, who sighed.

'The thing is, Marco, I need to make it look as though I know something about the Durridge case without actually wasting any time doing any real work on it. Know what I mean?'

Marco smiled again and shook his head.

'Still the same Aurelio! I remember you at school. You did less work than anyone in the class, yet you ended up with the best marks. I never understood how you did it. With the rest of us, it was what we didn't know that stood out, but you could take the two or three odd bits of stuff you remembered and make it look as though you knew more than the teacher! We *hated* you for it.'

Zen finished his wine.

'You're exaggerating,' he murmured.

37

'No I'm not!' Paulon returned aggressively. 'Look where it's got you. You have a cushy desk job in Rome while I'm humping crates of groceries around the city.'

Zen lit a cigarette and said nothing. After a moment, Marco Paulon smiled.

'But there you go! Whoever said life was fair?'

He took a cigarette from the pack which Zen had left lying on the table.

'So, Aurelio, what can I do for you? Don't worry about time. I can always make an extra run tomorrow if necessary.'

Zen lit Marco's cigarette.

'Ideally, I'd like to take a look at the island where this Durridge was living when he was kidnapped.'

'Where's that?'

'Quite a long way, I'm afraid. One of those old fortress islands out near the Porto di Malamocco.'

Marco Paulon smoked peacefully for a while.

'Police launch broken down, has it?' he murmured at length.

Zen signalled the proprietor to bring more wine.

'It's the crew I'm worried about,' he said. 'Some kids fresh off the farm who've taken a hurry-up course in boat handling at La Spezia. I can probably trust them not to drown me, as long as the fog holds off, but that's as far as it goes. What I need is an inside view from someone who knows the lagoon. Something to lard the report so that it looks like I've spent a lot of time on the case. Someone like you, in short.'

Marco Paulon nodded earnestly. He picked up the new glass of *fragolino* which had just arrived at the table.

'Welcome back, Aurelio. Welcome home!'

The two men downed their wine and bickered amicably over the bill, Zen gracefully giving way in the end. Outside, a warm wash of diffuse sunlight flattened every perspective, obliterating details and distinctions, calling everything into question. In a yard near the quay two house-painters were shaking and folding a dropsheet as big as a sail.

'It looks like Ada's complaint is catching,' Marco announced in a jocular tone. 'My cousin was telling me the other day about someone else who's cracked up and started seeing people who aren't there.'

They turned the corner into a broad swathe of shadow cast by the walls of an abandoned factory.

'Mind you,' added Marco, 'he's from Burano, and they're all half-wits out there. Especially my cousin.'

He leapt nimbly down into a broad-bottomed wherry moored alongside the quay. Zen followed more cautiously, stepping on to the rectangle of old carpet which protected the foredeck. The open hold was filled with an assortment of merchandise *en route* from the wholesaler's warehouse at Mestre to various retail outlets scattered around the city: shrink-wrapped tins of beans and tomatoes, plastic-covered demijohns of wine, huge cardboard boxes containing packs of soap powder, tampons and batteries.

Marco Paulon turned on the ignition and freed the tiller, then cast off the aft mooring line, secured to one of the wooden posts driven into the canal bed at regular intervals. He pointed to a marble plaque set in the wall of the former factory about a metre above the level of the quay. It bore an engraved line and the words *Marea alta 4.11.66.*

'They make so much fuss about the floods,' he remarked, 'but if you ask me the freak lows are even worse. You can't even get down the Cannaregio half the time, and as for the back canals, forget it! The whole city needs to be dredged urgently, but it's impossible to get any work done now the contractors have stopped taking bribes.'

There was a throaty roar as he started up the diesel engine, which then settled down to a steady hum much like a bus, but with a reverberant underwater growl.

'Let go forward,' he called.

It took Zen a moment or two to remember the significance of this phrase. Then he reached up and untied the remaining rope securing the *comacina* to its mooring, brought it inboard and coiled it neatly. A dark foliage of mud blossomed on the surface of the water as Marco put the motor in reverse with the rudder hard over to push the bow out from the quay. Then he engaged forward gear and they eased out into the canal.

'Guess who owns all that!' he shouted, pointing to the ruined factory. Zen made his way unsteadily past the cargo to join Paulon in the stern of the boat.

'Ada Zulian!' crowed Marco triumphantly.

'Really?'

'For years no one knew,' Marco went on. 'The *contessa* kept it quiet.'

39

Thought it was undignified for Zulian to be connected to anything as common as a cotton mill.'

He laughed explosively.

'The joke is, the place is worth more derelict than it ever was as a going concern. Here's Ada dependent on people like me doing her favours out of the kindness of our hearts, when she could make herself a billion any time she wanted just by selling that place!'

Zen ducked instinctively as they passed under a low bridge. Marco throttled back, then swung the tiller hard to the right, sounding the boat's siren as a warning to any craft which might be coming the other way around the blind corner.

'So what's the word about the Durridge business?' Zen asked.

Wedging the tiller under his expansive bottom, Marco produced a packet of cigarettes and offered one to Zen.

'How do you mean?'

'What have people been saying about it? What do they think happened?'

Marco throttled back to let a taxi pass by. The passenger, an adolescent girl in a wheelchair, gazed at them solemnly. Zen tried again.

'What sort of man was this Durridge? What did he do? Who did he see?'

Marco frowned and spat into the water. Zen's heart sank. His companion clearly knew nothing whatever of any interest about the vanished American, but no Venetian was ever going to admit to ignorance about anything.

'He was your typical rich foreigner,' Marco announced at length. 'Came and went all the time. Used the city as a hotel. Took no interest in *us*, the staff.'

He paused for inspiration.

'Used to give huge parties at his house. The watertaxi people made a fortune ferrying the guests to and fro. The caterers did well too . . .'

He broke off and pointed to a ponderous four-storey building which they were passing.

'Palazzo Zen, Aurelio!' he remarked jocularly. 'When are you moving back in?'

Zen smiled and dutifully surveyed the show-home constructed by his ancestors in those distant centuries when they had been one of the most illustrious and powerful families in the city. He was glad to allow Marco to change the subject and let them both off the hook.

Clearly there was going to be no easy way into the Durridge case. His information so far had been restricted to reading newspaper clippings, meagre snippets of information puffed out to several columns with speculations and repetitions and a photograph of Ivan Durridge in one of the white linen suits he habitually wore.

'I'll tell you one thing, though,' Marco continued with geater confidence. 'He was never kidnapped.'

'How do you mean?'

Paulon shrugged.

'If you ask me, it was like with Tonio.'

A double sheet of newspaper drifted slowly past. Looking at it, Zen recognized it as the same one which the barman had been reading when he had had coffee with Aldo Valentini that morning. As he scanned the headline – THE OLD FOX FIGHTS FOR HIS POLITICAL LIFE – he suddenly thought of a way to get access to the closed files on the Durridge case. But if the article was correct, he would have to move fast.

'Antonio Puppin,' Marco went on, answering the question Zen had ill-manneredly neglected to ask. 'Went hunting out on the saltmarshes one day and never came back. When his boat turned up adrift everyone feared the worst, although the body was never found. Anyway, a couple of years later he got caught by the Carabinieri at a roadblock near Grado – this was back in the terrorist years, and they were asking for everyone's papers . . .'

They swept under a high arched bridge and emerged with startling suddenness into the open lagoon just beside the busy ferry piers at Fondamente Nove.

'It turned out he'd done a bunk,' Marco shouted above the roar of the engine he'd just gunned up to full revs. 'He'd been working for the brother of an ex-girlfriend who ran a garage . . .'

Zen stopped listening. He'd lost track of Marco's story, let alone its bearing on the Durridge affair. That was how things were on the lagoon, where the hazy light and the pervasive instability of water defeated every attempt at clarity or precision, but also tempered the arrogance and aggression so prevalent on the mainland. This was what had formed him, he realized. This was the code he carried with him, the basic genetic circuits burned into his very being.

In the extreme distance, to the right of the cemetery of San Michele, the remote islands of Torcello and Burano were visible as smudges on the horizon, the latter distinguishable by its drunkenly inclined bell tower.

'What was that about someone seeing ghosts on Burano?' he murmured to Marco.

'Not *on* Burano. That's where the guy's from. Name's Giacomo Sfriso. He and his brother have a drift trawler they take out to sea, as well as a lot of tidal nets. Both in their mid-twenties, and doing very well for themselves by all accounts. Very well indeed.'

They rounded the mole of reclaimed land beyond the Arsenale, forming dry-docks and a sports field.

'Then one evening last month Giacomo went out in a *sandolo*,' Marco continued. 'No one paid any attention. Everyone knew the Sfriso boys worked round the clock. That's how they got so rich, people said. Darkness fell and he didn't come back, but still no one worried. Giacomo knew the lagoon like his own backyard.'

He swung the tiller over, dipping the gunwale in the water and sending the boat careening round towards the large white mass of San Pietro.

'Only when he finally got back to Burano, at five o'clock the next morning, still pitch dark out, he was babbling like a madman! No one could make out what the hell he was talking about. His brother Filippo called the doctor, who stuck a needle in him, but when he came around he was just as bad. Gibbering away about walking corpses and the like. Since when, according to my informants, that particular fish has been several centimetres short of its minimum landing length.'

The boat slid under the elaborate iron footbridge connecting the island of San Pietro to the Arsenale. These were the hinderparts of the city, a dense mass of brick tenements formerly inhabited by the army of manual labourers employed in the dockyards. Nowhere were there more dead ends and fewer through routes, nowhere were the houses darker and more crowded, nowhere was the dialect thicker and more impenetrable. It was not for nothing that the Cathedral of San Pietro, symbol of Rome's claims on the Republic, had been relegated to these inauspicious outskirts, while the Doges' private chapel lorded it over the great Piazza.

Marco brought the wherry alongside a quay opposite a slipway where a number of old *vaporetti* were drawn up awaiting repair or cannibalization. Securing a rope fore and aft to the stripped tree trunks sunk in the mud, he set about foraging among the packages in the hold.

'Give me a hand, will you?' he called to Zen.

Together they tugged the pile apart, separating crates and boxes until Marco at length dived in and emerged with a small cubical pack which, from the way he bent his knees to lift it, obviously weighed a lot.

'What's that?' asked Zen.

Marco heaved the pack on to the quay and wiped his brow. Leaping ashore, he tore open the pack and extracted a yellow leaflet which he handed to Zen.

'Back in a moment,' he said, and disappeared into an alley with the package, leaving Zen to peruse the leaflet. Like the poster he had seen earlier, it was headed NUOVA REPUBBLICA VENETA over the emblem of a lion couchant. The text concerned some complicated issue of city versus regional funding for improvements to the refuse disposal facility on Sacca San Biagio, and was clearly the latest instalment in a serial you needed to have been following from the beginning to understand. Zen had just reached the slogan in block capitals at the bottom – A VENETIAN SOLUTION TO VENETIAN PROBLEMS – when Marco jumped aboard again and cast off.

'Next stop your island,' he announced, revving the engine.

Zen waved the leaflet.

'What's all this?'

'Municipal elections the week after next.'

'But which party?'

Marco paused to yell a greeting at the skipper of a wherry proceeding in the other direction.

'Just a few local lads who think they can take on Rome and win.'

'And can they?'

Marco shrugged.

'I'd like to see someone do it. Everyone says it'll be a disaster, but what have the last forty years been for us? The city has turned into a geriatric hospital, there's no work, no houses, and all our taxes go to line the pockets of some Mafia fat cats down south. Christ knows if Dal Maschio will be any better, but he sure as hell can't be any worse, and if he makes those bastards in Rome shit in their beds then he gets my vote!'

Zen stared at him.

'Who did you say?'

'Dal Maschio.'

'Ferdinando Dal Maschio?'

'Do you know him?'

Zen shook his head.

'No, no.'

The boat slipped along the canal alongside the public gardens on the islet of Sant'Elena and then out, as if through a secret door, into the broad basin of San Marco. A big cargo vessel was gliding past, on its way from the docks to the breach in the littoral sandbar at Porto di Lido giving access to the open sea. A tug pulling two barges laden with rubbish ploughed past in the other direction, while ferries and fishing smacks crossed to and fro. Marco pointed the wherry's bows towards the distant island of San Clemente, where Ada Zulian had spent two years in the mental hospital. Out here in the open lagoon there were short sharp waves which slapped vigorously at the planking and splashed gobs of salt water into the men's faces. Marco throttled back to give way to a car ferry on its way to the Lido.

'I forgot to tell you the best bit about the guy from Burano,' he shouted as the waves slapped and hammered and the wherry wallowed in the swell. 'Guess where he claims to have seen this ghost?'

Zen shook his head.

'On Sant'Ariano!' cried Marco. 'The isle of the dead!'

His way clear again, he gunned up the engine and headed out of the shipping lane into the quiet backwaters behind San Giorgio.

'But it's no joke for Giacomo's family,' he concluded soberly. 'Seems he just hangs around the house all day, muttering to himself. He can't go to the toilet by himself, never mind handle a boat. His mother and brother have been driven nearly crazy themselves.'

The lagoon shimmered and shifted like fish scales in the sunshine. Aurelio Zen lay back, closed his eyes and tried determinedly to summon up an image of Tania Biacis, his . . . his what? Lover? Mistress? Partner? Part of the charm of their relationship was that it eluded definition. Despite this, it had always felt overwhelmingly real and solid, yet after only a few hours' exposure to the pervasive vapours of the lagoon Zen felt these certainties dissolving. He no longer had any vivid sense of Tania, no clear image of her presence, no aching void created by her absence. This was doubly ironic in that she was the reason he had agreed to Ellen's idea in the first place.

44

'The family are seriously unhappy about the way the investigation has bogged down, Aurelio,' Ellen had told him. 'Bill – that's my new guy, he's a lawyer – the firm he works for has the Durridge account, and I mentioned to him that I just happened to know this Italian policeman.'

The moment Ellen stopped speaking, even for an instant, the line went dead.

'I mean it's your town, Aurelio. You know the people, you speak the language. Anyway, when Bill put it to the Durridges' people they simply jumped at the idea.'

Despite the years since Ellen had left Zen and returned to her native America, her Italian had remained fluent, although her accent had deteriorated, the vowels flattened and denatured, whole phrases mumbled almost incomprehensibly, like an old man trying to eat without his dentures. It was chilling to recall that he had once found such mannerisms charming.

'The bottom line is – I'm quoting Bill here – they need a body. Dead or alive. Preferably the former, of course, but if the worst comes to the worst . . .'

She paused, and a dumb white silence intervened. It was as if one of them had hung up, as if the whole conversation had been taped and edited. Then she spoke again, and everything resumed as if there had been no pause, no lacuna, no doubt.

'Until then the whole estate is in turn-round. If you free up the cash flow, Bill says, you can name your fee. We're talking serious money here.'

'And a serious criminal offence,' Zen had returned dryly. 'It is strictly illegal for a state employee to engage in secondary paid employment . . .'

'Oh come on, Aurelio! You guys only work mornings anyway. Plus Bill can arrange for the money to be paid indirectly – into a numbered Swiss bank account if you like.'

It was tempting, but he would never have accepted if Tania had not just received a court order to vacate the apartment in Parione which Zen had found for her, and on which he had been paying the rent. Her position there had always been precarious – the landlord had been trying to evict her for over a year – but she and Zen had shied away from talking about the future. Whatever happened, painful and disturbing decisions would have to be taken, and they had

45

tacitly agreed to put them off as long as possible so as not to break the spell of a period of frivolous irresponsibility whose appeal lay partly in the knowledge that it could not possibly last.

The very fact that Tania had hinted that she might be prepared to live with Zen – and, inevitably, his mother – represented a major concession on her part. Only a few months earlier, he would have been overjoyed by this change of heart. Ever since Tania Biacis had broken up with her husband, Zen had been trying to persuade her to move in with him. Yet now the moment had arrived, he had immediately felt a stab of alarm, not least at the discovery that Tania and his mother got along. The two women had been introduced the previous month, and to Zen's amazement the effect had been one of mutual self-recognition. He had counted on being able to divide and rule. If his mother and his lover liked each other, where did that leave him?

He must have dozed off, for the next thing he was aware of was a mighty bump which sent him tumbling over sideways on the bilge boards. Looking up, he saw an enormous expanse of brick walling towering over the boat.

'Kidnapped!'

Marco made fast to a mooring ring set in the wall. He pointed disgustedly to the rickety metal ladder, slimy with weed, which scaled the face of the brick cliff.

'How are you going to get an unwilling victim down from there?' he demanded. 'Even if he was unconscious, you'd need a crane to get him in the boat.'

He bent over Zen, finger raised didactically.

'And on that particular afternoon you'd never have got the boat alongside in the first place. It was one of the lowest tides I can recall. The whole lagoon ground to a halt! You'd have thought someone had pulled the plug. Nothing but mud, as far as the eye could see.'

Marco Paulon lay back complacently on the after-decking.

'Take it from me, Aurelio. This American of yours has done a bunk! He'll turn up one day, safe and sound, just like Tonio Puppin. And who's to blame them? There are probably times you wouldn't mind dropping out of your own life for a while, hey?'

A miniature blizzard whirled up into the sunny air, momentarily enshrouding the figure of the man who stood talking into the pay telephone.

'Immediately, yes,' he insisted. 'Aurelio Zen. Z, E, N. Vice-Questore, Criminalpol.'

The scurrying breeze eased once more, and the tubular bars of expanded polystyrene packaging immediately fell back to the nearest surface. The man picked one up off the ledge of the telephone booth and toyed with it as he talked.

'Remind him of the Renato Favelloni case. Remind him that he told me if I ever needed anything I should get in touch. Tell him I'll call back in thirty minutes exactly. If I don't get a satisfactory response at that time, I shall have to reconsider my position.'

Once again the illusory snowstorm littered the air with flying white fragments caught up in the eddying wind currents at the corner of the square. Aurelio Zen snapped the one he had been playing with, replaced the receiver and plucked his phonecard from its slot.

There was no bar or café in this *campo*, which was dominated by the sprawling brickwork of a church as matter-of-fact as the abandoned factory belonging to the Zulian family. Zen turned down an alley tunnelling under the houses opposite. It crossed two low bridges over canals hardly wider than ditches. A torn plastic bag stamped with the name of a supermarket chain drifted slowly by on the incoming tide like a ragged jellyfish.

Zen turned in at a glazed door under a metal sign reading ENOTECA. In the small dark room inside, a few elderly men sat sipping wine and exchanging raucous remarks in slithering, sibilant dialect. Zen ordered a glass of red *raboso* wine and a roll smeared with the creamy white paste made from salt cod, garlic and olive oil. He settled back in a corner, glancing at his watch. He had given Palazzo Sisti thirty minutes, and five were gone already. It wouldn't do to be late. This was his one tenuous connection to the levers of power, the 'rooms with the buttons'. He had to handle it right. But there was no saying what *was* right, these days.

Some time earlier Zen had intervened in a murder investigation in Sardinia on behalf of one of the country's leading political parties. Although the outcome was quite different from the one which had been foreseen, it happened to serve the interests of the party in question just as well if not better. On his return to Rome, Zen had been summoned to a reception at party headquarters, located in Palazzo Sisti, where the elder statesman who was its leader had acknowledged his indebtedness with the words: 'If there's ever anything you need . . .'

At the time, this had seemed like a blank cheque. It could only be cashed once, so it was prudent to wait for exactly the right opportunity to present itself, but there was no hurry. A promise like this would remain valid for ever. Even the death of the politician himself would not affect the value of the undertaking he had given. The whole system within which he and everyone else operated depended on such unwritten contracts being honoured irrespective of the fate of individuals. If anything happened to *l'onorevole*, the promise he had made to Zen would simply devolve to his successors, along with countless others both owing and owed.

But now the unthinkable had occurred. Starting from an investigation into bribes allegedly paid to obtain construction contracts, investigating magistrates in Milan had gradually uncovered a network of kickbacks, slush funds, golden handshakes, graft, incentives, backhanders and hush money covering every aspect of business and government. Everyone had always known that such a network existed, of course. Indeed, everyone used it themselves in some minor respect at least, to speed up the bureaucratic mills or escape from some horrendous official maze. What no one had ever expected was that the extent of the corruption would ever be exposed, still less that those who had taken advantage of it at the very highest level would be arrested and brought to trial.

There had, after all, been countless such investigations before, and they had never got anywhere. It was precisely to avoid such a potentially embarrassing event that Palazzo Sisti had invited Zen to intervene in the Sardinian case, in which one of their fixers, a man named Renato Favelloni, was involved. On that occasion, as on so many in the past, they had been successful. But as the Milanese judges pur-

sued their investigations, naming ever more famous names and signing orders against the 'men beyond all suspicion', it gradually
became clear that something had changed. The labyrinth of power
was still there, but at its heart was an absence.

The minotaur was dead, and the choking currents of persuasion
and menace which had once stifled any attempt to map the workings
of its empire had fallen still. The judges continued implacably on
their course. Renato Favelloni was among those arrested, and true to
form had immediately done a deal with his accusers, betraying those
for whom he had worked in return for a potential reduction in his
own sentence. The result had been a flurry of judicial communi-
cations revealing the identities of those under investigation for
'irregular practices' and 'procedural abnormalities' – as though such
practices and procedures had not been both the rule and the norm
for the past half-century. The most eminent name on the list was that
of *l'onorevole* himself, whom the judges had requested should be
stripped of his parliamentary immunity so that they could proceed
against him.

This was something completely unprecedented, an almost unimaginable eventuality, but it was widely assumed that the matter
would go no further. Like all members of the Italian parliament,
l'onorevole enjoyed automatic immunity from judicial prosecution
which could only be lifted by a committee of his peers. The chances
of this happening seemed slim indeed. Politicans had always been
understandably reluctant to allow the judiciary to stick its noses
into their affairs. There was no reason to suppose that they would
voluntarily permit the prosecution of a man who had been a minister
in various governments for over fifteen years, one of the most
powerful and influential figures in the country, widely tipped as a
possible future president. If he went, which of them would be safe?

But those who reasoned thus had not yet grasped the full extent of
the changes which had taken place. This was not surprising. It was
humiliating to admit that the real reason why the judges in Milan
were able to succeed where so many of their colleagues had failed
had more to do with the collapse of the Soviet Union than anything
which had happened in their own country. Such an admission
involved recognizing that since 1945 Italian political life had been a
mere puppet-show reflecting the power struggle between East and
West. Now the strings had been cut, the show had closed and all bets

were off. Two days earlier, as reported in the newspaper which Zen had glimpsed floating in the canal, the parliamentary committee – 'motivated by a conviction since in the present climate justice should not just be done but be seen to, be done' – had voted to allow the judges in Milan to proceed against their eminent and esteemed colleague.

This was worse than death for *l'onorevole* and for all those associated with him. He would vanish for years into the Gulag Archipelago of the judicial process, awaiting a final verdict which was largely irrelevant. The damage had already been done. The parliamentary committee's decision was far more damaging than anything the judges could do, revealing as it did the extent to which *l'onorevole* was exposed, and the crucial fact that he had ceased to be an important political player.

Zen's only hope was that the favour he was actually going to inscribe on the blank cheque he had been treasuring all this while was so insignificant that *l'onorevole* would have no difficulty in meeting it, even in his present straitened circumstances. He glanced at his watch. In five minutes he would know. He finished the last morsel of the *bacalà mantecato*, washed it down with the final gulp of wine and went over to the counter to pay.

As he turned towards the door, he bumped into two men who had just come in. Intent on his purpose, he made to brush past, but one of the men seized his arm.

'My God, Aurelio, is it you?'

Zen looked round and gasped.

'Tommaso!'

The two confronted each other awkwardly while the other man looked on with a coolly appraising smile.

'I can't stop now,' Zen said hurriedly. 'Are you staying? I'll be back in ten minutes, less probably.'

Back in the windswept square, the strips of white plastic packaging were still frantically gyrating. As Zen made his way towards the pay phone, it suddenly started to ring in strident bursts. He stopped in his tracks, staring at it intently. Then he glanced at his watch. Exactly thirty minutes had elapsed since he had issued his ultimatum to Palazzo Sisti. Plunging into the fake snow flurries, he seized the receiver.

'Hello?'

The silence at the other end was deeply flawed, hollow, reverberant, mined with clicks and crackles.

'Hello? Hello?'

The response, when it finally came, was quiet and unhurried, as though rebuking Zen's panicky urgency.

'My advisers inform me that you uttered a threat against me. I trust this is just another of the innumerable mistakes and gross miscalculations of which they've been guilty.'

Christ, it was the man himself! Things must indeed have come to a pretty pass at Palazzo Sisti if *l'onorevole* was reduced to making his own phone calls.

'Nothing could be further from the truth!' Zen found himself saying in an obsequious tone. 'I wouldn't dream of presuming to . . .'

'Maybe not, but there are plenty who would. Men I've worked for and with this past quarter century! Now they deny they know me. Now they smite me on the cheek, spit in my face and hand me over, bound and gagged, to my enemies!'

'The only reason I am calling is . . .'

'They may think I'm dead and buried, but they'll see! When they least expect it I shall burst forth from the tomb and sit in judgement on those who have presumed to judge me.'

Having achieved this peroration, *l'onorevole* fell silent.

'Hello?' ventured Zen hesitantly.

'I'm still here. Despite everything.'

'When we met at Palazzo Sisti, *onorevole*, at the conclusion of the Burolo affair, you were kind enough to intimate that if I ever needed a favour then I should contact you. That is the only reason I have been bold enough to do so.'

The unctuous smarminess of his voice left Zen wanting to rinse his mouth out, but decades of servility could not be erased in a moment.

'What do you want?' *l'onorevole* demanded. 'There's a limit to what I can accomplish these days, but . . .'

Zen paused.

'I take it I may speak openly?'

'Oh, please! You take me for a fool? That's why I am calling *you*. Our tracer identified the number from which you rang earlier. I'm speaking from a secure line. But I haven't got all day, Zen. For the second time, what do you want?'

51

The square was still deserted, but Zen brought the receiver close to his mouth and lowered his voice.

'It's a question of access to a police file, *onorevole*.'

There was a brief silence.

'I'd have thought that was one of the few areas in which you were better qualified to act than I.'

'This particular file has been sealed.'

'Why?'

'That's one of the things I want to find out. It concerns the disappearance of an American called Ivan Durridge.'

There was a long silence. Zen eyed the circling flock of plastic flakes and said nothing.

'I seem to recall the affair vaguely,' *l'onorevole* said at last. 'What is your interest in it?'

Zen knew better than to try and conceal the truth from this man.

'Private enterprise,' he replied promptly. 'I've been retained by the family to look into it, but first of all I need to know why the case was closed. I can't afford to step on anyone's toes.'

There was a dry laugh at the other end.

'Neither can I.'

Another silence.

'I'll have to see what other interests are involved,' the voice replied at length. 'I'll ask around. Assuming I get a *nihil obstat* from my sources, how do you want the material delivered?'

Zen caught a glimpse of movement out of the corner of his eye. He looked round. A young man in overalls passed by carrying four wooden chairs, their legs interlocked, on his shoulders.

'I'll get in touch later today and leave details with your staff. Thank you very much for granting me this much of your valuable time, *onorevole*. I can't tell you how I appreciate it.'

At the other end there was nothing but the static-corroded silence, but it was some time before Zen replaced the receiver and turned away.

Back in the *osteria*, Tommaso was sitting alone at a table facing the door. He stood up and waved as Zen came in, then called to the barman to bring a flask of wine.

'I was beginning to think I'd imagined the whole thing,' he exclaimed, clasping Zen's shoulder and arm as though to prove that it was not in fact an apparition. 'How long has it been now? And then not even to let me know you're here! Honestly, Aurelio, I'm offended.'

'I only arrived this morning, Tommaso. And I was just about to contact you, as it happens.'

He pinched his friend's cheek and gave one of his rare unconstrained smiles. Tommaso Saoner looked exactly the same as he had for as long as Zen could remember: the perpetual dark stubble, the stolid, graceless features, the glasses with rectangular lenses and thick black rims through which he peered out at the world as though through a television set.

'Your health, Aurelio!' cried Tommaso, pouring their wine.

'And yours.'

They drained off their glasses.

'Where's your companion?' asked Zen.

Tommaso's expression grew serious.

'Ferdinando? He had to go.'

'Ferdinando Dal Maschio?'

Tommaso beamed in delight.

'You've heard of him? The movement is growing in numbers and importance every day, of course, but I had no idea that they were talking about us in Rome already!'

Zen produced his cigarettes, then looked round guiltily.

'Is it all right to smoke here?'

Tommaso frowned.

'Why ever not?'

'I was told this morning that the council had set aside non-smoking areas in all public places.'

Tommaso burst out laughing.

'Oh, for heaven's sake! That's just for the tourists. There's no such nonsense in genuine Venetian bars like this, where real Venetians go to drink good Veneto wine. Anyway, that bunch of crooks and incompetents on the council will be out on their collective ears in a couple of weeks, once the people get a chance to express their contempt for them. And as soon as we get in we'll repeal all their stupid by-laws.'

Zen offered his friend a cigarette.

' "We"?' he queried.

Tommaso declined the cigarette with a waggle of his finger.

53

'I mean the movement. *Nuova Repubblica Veneta*. What are they saying about us in Rome?'

Zen lit his cigarette, gazing at Saoner.

'I have no idea.'

'But you said . . .'

'I've heard about Dal Maschio, but not in Rome. It was here. From his wife, Cristiana Morosini. Her mother is a neighbour of ours.'

Tommaso's elation vanished as quickly as it had appeared.

'Don't take any notice of what she told you,' he retorted. 'It's all a load of scurrilous nonsense. Believe me, the things Ferdinando has had to put up from that whore, she's lucky he didn't leave long ago – and give her a damn good thrashing first!'

Zen considered his friend through a cloud of smoke.

'No doubt he deemed that such a course would have been politically inadvisable.'

Missing the irony in Zen's voice, Tommaso merely nodded earnestly.

'But she deserved it, believe you me. Most women would be proud to have a husband who has single-handedly transformed politics in the Veneto, broken the mould and offered a new and inspiring vision of a twenty-first century Venice, independent and revitalized!'

Tommaso's eyes were shining with enthusiasm. Zen poured them both more of the light, prickly wine.

'But not Cristiana,' Saoner went on bitterly. 'Instead, she did everything possible to undermine him, first ridiculing him to his face and in public, and then cuckolding him with a reporter from the mainland. Is it any wonder he sought solace in the arms of some of his admirers?'

He tossed off his wine and made a visible effort to change the subject.

'Anyway, that's enough politics. What happy wind brings you home, Aurelio?'

Zen emitted a self-pitying sigh.

'Mamma heard from Rosalba that Ada Zulian had been complaining about some sort of harassment. It's all in her head, of course, but to my mother Ada is still *la contessa* and nothing would do but I had to put in for a temporary transfer and come up to look into it personally.'

As he retailed this latest pack of lies, Zen marvelled at the way his cover story was changing and developing, growing ever more detailed and plausible with every telling. If he wasn't careful, he would start believing it himself pretty soon.

Tommaso nodded seriously.

'Funnily enough, we were discussing the Zulian family at a meeting just the other day. The *contessa* has been under a lot of pressure to sell that old factory they own, but like a true Venetian she's refused. *"Chi vende, scende."* The question we were discussing is what use to put such sites to when we come to power. Ferdinando used the Zulian case as an example. An international consortium has reportedly offered a fortune to turn the Sant'Alvise site into a hotel complex. That's out of the question, of course, but the problem we face is whether to develop such vacant land for housing or for light industry. Ferdinando's view is that . . .'

As Tommaso Saoner launched into a detailed analysis of the issue, Zen nodded and tried not to yawn. He hadn't much appetite for politics at the best of times, and none at all for the lunatic-fringe, single-issue variety. No wonder Cristiana had lost patience with her husband if this was the kind of thing she had to put up with at home. As the image of her plump, sensuous features floated into his mind, Zen found himself thinking over what Tommaso had said about her, and wondering idly just how much of a whore she really was. Shaking off these fantasies with a stab of guilt, he reminded himself to ring Tania.

' . . . within the context of a viable long-term development strategy,' concluded Saoner, eyeing Zen in a manner which suggested that a reply was expected.

'Absolutely!' said Zen. 'I totally agree.'

Tommaso frowned.

'You do?'

'In principle,' Zen added quickly.

'What principle? The only principle involved is whether Venice is to belong to us Venetians or to a bunch of foreigners who buy up property at inflated prices which our own people can't afford, so that our young folk have to emigrate to the mainland while half the houses in the city stand empty.'

Zen stubbed out his cigarette.

'I'm pretty much a foreigner myself these days, Tommaso. And my house is standing empty.'

Tommaso looked startled. He barked a rather aggressive laugh.

'Don't be silly, Aurelio! *You* don't have to account for your actions. You're one of us, a true Venetian born and bred. What you do with your property is no one's business but your own.'

He clasped Zen's hand and looked him in the eye.

'Why don't you join us? The movement needs men like you.'

Zen gave an embarrassed shrug.

'I don't know anything about it,' he said, withdrawing his hand.

'You know everything about it,' Tommaso replied fervently. 'You know it in your bones.'

He continued to scrutinize Zen with a child-like candour and intensity which made Zen feel acutely uncomfortable. He shrugged again.

'I've never joined a political party in my life.'

'We're a movement, not a party! And the people who're flocking to join us are precisely those who've never had anything to do with the established parties, who are fed up with the old corrupt gang and the empty slogans. You've had plenty of experience of that, I'll be bound. Why, I was hearing a year or two ago about the way you were used by those bastards propping up this rotten government! That murder in Sardinia. Palazzo Sisti were up to their necks in that, weren't they? But in the end the whole thing got blamed on some local girl who had very conveniently got herself killed. Typical! But things are changing, thanks to movements like ours.'

He clutched Zen's arm again.

'There's a rally tomorrow evening, Aurelio. Why don't you come along? Meet the people who are making things happen here and then make up your own mind!'

'I'll see,' said Zen vaguely. 'I think I may be doing something.'

All the exaltation drained from Tommaso's face. He stood up and threw some money on the table.

'Well, I mustn't keep you from your work any longer, Aurelio. What's bothering *la contessa* this time? Has she started seeing visions of her dead daughter again?'

'It's skeletons in the bedroom now,' Zen replied.

Tommaso laughed and shook his head.

'Poor old girl.'

They walked to the door together.

'Does anyone know what actually happened to Rosetta Zulian?' Zen asked as they stepped out into the covered alley.

'She disappeared,' Tommaso replied vaguely.

Zen nodded.

'But no one seems to know how or when.'

'Does it matter? It was all so long ago.'

'Not for Ada,' Zen insisted. 'I'm sure she's dreaming these ghostly intruders who are making her life a misery. But like all dreams, it must be a distortion of something real. The more I know about what actually happened, the easier it will be for me to sort out what's going on.'

'Sounds like a job for a psychiatrist, not a policeman,' Tommaso Saoner commented dismissively.

He was about to turn away down a side alley when he suddenly paused and looked back at Zen, his glasses glinting in the gloom.

'There's someone who probably does know what happened, if anyone does,' he said slowly.

'Who's that?' demanded Zen.

Tommaso Saoner smiled knowingly.

'Come along to the rally tomorrow night and I'll introduce you. Campo Santa Margherita, seven o'clock.'

He slapped Zen's shoulder jovially.

'It's wonderful to have you back in the city, Aurelio! Venice isn't Venice without her sons. Until tomorrow!'

Aurelio Zen walked slowly home through the darkening streets. The routes leading to the railway station and the car parks were already packed with the human tide of commuters, students and tourists which washed into and out of the city every day, temporarily boosting the population to what it had been fifty years before and creating an illusory air of vitality. But once evening came the ebb set in, draining away this transient throng and revealing the desolate reality.

The thought of this diurnal tide reminded Zen of what Marco Paulon had said about the Durridge case: if anyone wished to kidnap Ivan Durridge from his island home, they could not have chosen a worse time. Marco remembered the day in question all too well. The low tide that afternoon had been exceptional, draining the lagoon to over a metre below its average level and stranding Paulon on a mudbank halfway to Murano.

'I was stuck there for four hours in the pouring rain with a cargo of beans and salt cod. I'd been going that way for years, at all states of the tide, and never run aground. It rained so much I had to pump out the bilge three times, yet there wasn't enough water outside to drown a butterfly! So when I heard on the news next morning that this American had been kidnapped, I thought to myself, I'd like to have the boat they used. You couldn't have got within fifty metres of the island that afternoon!'

The memory of Marco's words sparked a fugitive idea in Zen's mind, something to do not with Durridge but with Ada Zulian. He tried in vain to corner it as it scurried about the fringes of his consciousness. And meanwhile he kept walking, veering to right and left without the slightest hesitation, unaware that a choice had even been made. It had all come back to him, that intimate, subconscious knowledge of the city built up over years of boyhood exploration, a whole decade of wandering through its intricately linked ramifications. Despite the span of time which had elapsed, virtually nothing of that urban fabric had changed. He thought of his conversation with *l'onorevole*, of the Burolo affair and the terrifying bleakness of the Sardinian landscape. There he had felt vulnerable, incompetent and exposed, totally out of his depth. This was just the opposite. He went on his way, secure and confident, enveloped by a city whose devious, introverted complexities were as familiar to him as the processes of his own mind.

Durridge, Zulian ... What *was* the connection? Intruders, perhaps? But Ada Zulian's poltergeists, if they had any existence outside her fears and fantasies, seemed completely gratuitous manifestations, devoid of any motive except mischievous mockery. Indeed, the great problem with believing in them at all, apart from Ada's history of mental disturbance, was that it was impossible to see why anyone should go to so much trouble for so little purpose. Why waste your time scaring a solitary old lady when with the same skills you could make a fortune burgling one of the city's more affluent residents?

But then why kidnap an American millionaire and fail to make a ransom demand? Perhaps Marco Paulon was right, and Durridge had simply staged a dramatic disappearance for reasons of his own. Certainly there was no indication that he had felt himself to be at risk. Although his home was quite literally a fortress, it could hardly have been less secure. The 'octagons', as they were known from their shape, were originally built to defend the three gaps in the sandbars which divide the lagoon from the open sea. Most were now in ruin, but one of those just inside the Porto di Malamocco had been bought in the fifties by an English eccentric who had completely renovated it.

Many rich people aspire to own islands, but an island in the Venetian lagoon, within sight and easy reach of the city, yet perfectly private, verdant and isolated, is a privilege reserved for very few. Ivan Durridge got his chance when the Englishwoman, old and ailing, sold her *ottagono* for a small fortune. Expecting some ostentatious pleasure pavilion, Zen had been surprised by what awaited him at the top of the metal ladder leading up the brick walling. The floor of the artificial island was now covered in trees, shrubs and plants artfully arranged to form a dense, seemingly natural garden.

In its midst stood the guardhouse, a long low structure of military severity which had been skilfully transformed into a residence retaining the essential characteristics of the original while suggesting something of the rustic pleasures of a country cottage. The only visible security precaution was a faded notice warning intruders to beware of the dog. Of the dog itself there was no sign, and judging by the condition of the notice it might well have departed along with the previous owner. Zen wandered idly about the property, inspired less by the sense that there was anything to be discovered than by the beauty of the spot and the need to spend some time there in order to justify putting Marco to the trouble of bringing him. He was standing on the lawn in front of the house, looking up at the ragged blue patch of sky visible through the encircling foliage, when a cry disturbed his reverie.

'Hey!'

Zen had grown so accustomed to the peace and quiet that he started violently. The thought that he might not be alone on the island had never occurred to him. He looked round. At the corner of the house stood an elderly man dressed in baggy dark overalls.

'What are you doing here?' he demanded gruffly.

Zen lit a cigarette with elaborate nonchalance.

'Well?' the man demanded, walking across the lawn towards him. 'This is private property.'

'Police.'

The man's expression of mute hostility did not change. His face was marked with a series of concentric wrinkles, like ripples on water.

'And you are . . . ?' barked Zen.

'Calderan, Franco.'

'What are you doing here?'

'Doing? I live here! I'm the gardener and caretaker. I worked for the English *signora*, then for the American.'

Zen sniffed sceptically, as though this were a transparent fiction.

'Where were you the day your employer disappeared?'

The man frowned.

'I've already made my statement.'

'So make it again!' snapped Zen. 'Or are you afraid the two accounts won't tally? Maybe you've forgotten whatever pack of lies you made up the first time?'

Franco Calderan stared down at the lawn, on whose flawlessly even surface were imprinted two parallel lines like skidmarks. He glared at Zen, as though he were responsible for this blemish.

'I told them the truth! It was Tuesday, my day off. I rowed over to Alberoni and caught the bus to go and see my sister and her family, same as every week. They can vouch for me!'

Zen's sneer indicated the value he ascribed to alibis which depended on the corroboration of the suspect's relations.

'Who knew that Tuesday was your day off?'

'Nobody! Everybody!'

'First you say one thing, then another! Why are you lying? Who are you trying to protect?'

Zen broke off, appalled at himself. Why the hell was he browbeating this old man? But he had been a policeman too long not to try and make Calderan sweat a little in return for his surly welcome.

'I'm not protecting anyone! Everyone knew that I went to see my sister on Tuesdays, and have done these thirty years!'

He took a step forward, confronting Zen openly.

'Anyway, what are you doing coming out here and raking all this over again? I've been through it all often enough already! Or haven't you bothered to read what I told your colleagues?'

Calderan's eyes narrowed as a new suspicion struck him.

'You say you're from the police? Let me see your identification.'

Zen had obliged, and after some further acrimonious exchanges he had been able to depart in a relatively dignified manner. But the experience had merely had the effect of making his private investigation of the Durridge affair seem even more of a mockery. The case had already been fully investigated, and at a time when clues and memories were still fresh. What hope had he of solving the mystery now, three months after the event?

While these thoughts occupied Zen's mind, his internal autopilot steered him through the viscera of San Polo and brought him out at a small wooden landing-stage on the sinuous waterway which dissected the city. The ferry which served it was at the other side, and Zen joined the young couple waiting on the pier. The man was gazing with glazed eyes at the water, a hiss like distant surf emanating from the personal stereo headphones inserted into his ears. His partner, who was heavily pregnant, was reading a copy of *Gente* magazine featuring an article on the home life of Umberto Bossi, 'the charismatic leader of the separatist *Leghe*'. Both were wearing dark glasses and energetically chewing gum.

As the ferry made its way towards them, Zen remembered that he must give Palazzo Sisti a fax number to which they could transmit the file on the Durridge case. No country had taken to the new electronic technology more avidly than Italy, where it had cut through the Gordian knot of the postal service at one stroke. For decades, people had debated ways and means for reforming *la posta*, with its endless rules and regulations, the surly arrogance of its superabundant staff, and above all its inability to get a letter to its destination in less than a week. Now the debate was over. Those who had access to one of the miraculous machines had leapt straight from the nineteenth to the twenty-first century, while the rest – including Zen, in this instance – remained bogged in the quagmire of the twentieth.

The Questura had a bank of fax machines, of course, but given the degree of irregularity involved in this transaction it would be too risky to have the incriminating file sent there. Whom did he know with a fax machine? Marco Paulon, perhaps, but he'd asked Marco enough favours for one day. Besides, he wouldn't be home. When he'd dropped Zen off in Campo San Stin, where he had a delivery to make, Marco had mentioned that he was going to visit his cousin on Burano and catch up on the latest stories of crazy fisherman and walking corpses.

The ferry bumped alongside and the passengers disembarked. Zen walked down the wooden steps, handed his five-hundred-lire coin to the boatman and stepped aboard. Tommaso Saoner would either have a fax machine or know someone who did, but Zen's encounter with his former friend had been such an unsettling experience that he didn't feel confident about enlisting his help in such a delicate matter. It was of course notoriously difficult to pick up the threads of a relationship which had once been so close – it is not only the houses of one's childhood which seem diminished when one goes back – but Zen had been almost shocked by the change in Tommaso. This political movement he had got himself involved with seemed to have affected him like a religious conversion.

The only thing like it he could remember was the playboy son of one of his colleagues at the Questura in Milan who had become a Maoist. One evening he walked into a dinner party in the family home and shot one of the guests, a leading judge, with his father's revolver. Almost more chilling than the act of violence itself had been the boy's unshakeable conviction that he had acted rightly, in the only manner either comprehensible or justifiable, and that anyone who did not do likewise was either a hypocrite or a cretin, and in either case condemned to the dustbin of history. But that was back in 1978. No one got excited by politics any more. How could Tommaso have fallen hook, line and sinker for some fringe party whose programme, from what Zen had heard of it, sounded like total lunacy? Christ, he'd probably be the only other person at this rally he'd promised to attend!

The ferry headed out into the crowded waters of the *canalazzo*. Zen and the young couple, standing amidships, swayed back and forth as the wash of passing vessels struck the hull. The ferrymen standing at bow and stern rowed steadily, pushing their oars into the water in short thrusts, as though turning over soil. Soon they nosed in at the pier on the other bank, where another cluster of passengers stood waiting to cross. Zen set off along the alley leading back from the water, walking on the boards which had been laid down to cover a trench for a new gas main.

When he neared the Ponte Guglie, he went into a grocer's shop which was still open. The shop was dim and vaulted, so densely crowded with goods that it was almost impossible to move. As Zen's eyes adjusted to the gloom, he made out the owner lurking at the counter like a spider in its web. He bought some coffee, mineral water and a packet of biscuits for breakfast. The grocer rang up his purchases on one of the huge state-of-the-art electronic registers required by the tax authorities, which looked as out of place in these troglodytic surroundings as a computer in a cave.

Hefting his green plastic bag of purchases, Zen continued along the Cannaregio canal, his feet aching at the unaccustomed exercise, and turned off into the alley which gradually widened into the triangular *campo* with the circular stone well-head, its carvings obliterated by time and touch. He noted the strip of whitened paving, caused by droppings from the birds which perched on the power and phone cables crossing the street at this point. How often had he come this way? How many times had he followed this route home? The thought inspired a sort of vertigo. He recoiled from contact with all those other selves, each of which had seemed so absolute at the time, but were now revealed as just another in a restless, flickering series of imposters. I'm getting as bad as Ada Zulian and that fisherman from Burano, he thought. I should never have come. I should have stayed in Rome, where you can drive everywhere and no one believes in ghosts.

The house felt cold and empty. As Zen opened the door to the living room, the telephone started to ring. He stood, staring at it but making no attempt to answer. It rang eleven times before cutting off with a brief peep. Eyeing the instrument warily, Zen set down his shopping and circled round the room to the window, and threw open the casements. The cool evening air flowed in over the sill, setting up currents and eddies in the whole room. He had the sensation that the floor was rocking gently back and forth, like a boat at its mooring. It was some time before he became aware that he was not the only one enjoying the dusk. From one of the bedrooms on the top floor of the house opposite, a young woman stood looking down at him.

Zen waved to her.

'Good evening.'

Cristiana Morosini smiled vaguely and nodded. She seemed to be about to say something when the phone in the room behind him began to ring again. With an impatient shrug, Zen turned away to answer it.

'Hello? Who? Tania! Oh, I was just going to call you! Did you ring a moment ago? No? I just got home and it was ringing as I came in, but I couldn't reach it in time. I thought it might have been you.'

He dug out his cigarettes.

'Oh, all right. It doesn't look as though there's much to be done, but I'll stretch it out as long as I can . . .'

He paused to light up.

'Of course I'm missing you, sweetheart, but it's a question of the money, isn't it? I mean that's why I'm here. The family are paying by the day, so the longer I take over it the better, no?'

He clasped the receiver to his ear for some time.

'Of course I appreciate your situation, Tania. I just hope you appreciate mine. It would be nice to get a little appreciation, once in a while. It's not that much fun camping out in this house like a squatter.'

Whorls of smoke from his cigarette drifted like weed about the room, delineating its tidal currents and stagnant pools.

'Because this is not my real work. That's what's different about it. I don't have to run errands for Americans. I'd be much happier to stay in Rome, go through the motions at the office and then come round and see you in the evening. But we've got to think about the future. We can't go on in the way we have been, and my apartment isn't large enough for all of us to share, so unless we get some money from somewhere . . .'

He broke off and listened, sighing.

'I'm *not* angry! But quite frankly I've got enough problems as it is without having you phoning me up to nag me because I don't sound sufficiently sorry about not being there. Understand? Under the circumstances, I think you could show a little more consideration.'

He held the receiver away from his ear. It continued to emit angry squawks. He set it down on the table and walked back to the window. Cristiana Morosini had disappeared. He walked back to the table and picked up the phone, but the vocal ostinato had been replaced by a steady electronic humming.

Replacing the receiver, he walked through to the kitchen and opened the window there. The increased flow of air immediately cancelled all the existing currents, scouring out a new deep channel from one window to the other. Zen leant on the windowsill and gazed morosely down at the darkly mobile surface of the water in the canal below. He had completely failed to strike the right note with Tania. She had wanted to be reassured, to be soothed and wooed, and he hadn't been able to do it. It was like a language he had once learned, but had forgotten.

Similar episodes had occurred before, but never when they were apart. Until now, separation had always brought out the best in them, and when they were together such failures were quickly forgotten. But now they were apart, a conversation such as the one they had just had became emblematic of more general shortcomings, problems and inadequacies in the relationship as a whole. Judging by Tania's manner, she felt that there was no shortage of these.

He let his spent cigarette drop into the canal. The tide was high again, just as it had been when he had looked out from the bedroom on the morning of his arrival. He closed the window and walked back to the living room, where he picked up the plastic shopping bag. He eyed the phone briefly. It wasn't too late to call Tania back and apologize, to talk the whole thing through and . . .

He turned away and carried the shopping through to the kitchen, where he arranged the items artistically on the bare shelves. It *was* too late. He felt divided from Tania by infinitely more than the actual distance between them. It was as if she were on the other side of the world, or even some other world.

He stood back, admiring his work. It might not be the home beautiful, but at least he could have a cup of coffee in the morning. As for the evening looming up before him, big, blank and empty, that was a much less alluring prospect. He would have to find somewhere to have dinner, for a start. The prospect of eating alone in some dreary, over-priced *trattoria* did not appeal. When he spoke to Tania, he had deliberately exploited the drawbacks of his situation for dramatic effect, but the fact remained that in many ways it was not enviable. Despite this, he hadn't the slightest desire to be anywhere else, least of all back in Rome.

As though in response to this thought, the phone began to ring again. For a moment he toyed with the idea of not answering. The last thing he wanted was to have to resume the laborious task of trying to communicate meaningfully with Tania. He had nothing whatever to say to her. But it would only make matters worse in the long run to hide there, pretending not to be home. Heaving a deep sigh, he walked through to the living room and picked up the receiver.

'Aurelio Battista, is that you?'

'Who's this?'

'Oh thank God you're there! I've rung twice already but there was no reply. I think I'd have gone mad if you hadn't answered this time!'

'*Contessa?*'

'They're here! It's worse than ever! They've got knives! For God's sake come quickly!'

By the time he turns up, of course, her shield and strength, her bold avenger, the intruders have cleared off. He searches every room in the *palazzo*, but there is no one there. As she told him earlier, they're not stupid. Neither is he, Giustiniana's son. He was always quick on the uptake, even as a child, she'll give him that. Ada recalls being astonished, sometimes, by the things he'd come out with, finding a connection between two things she'd quite forgotten about, or hadn't even noticed in the first place.

That's no comfort here, though. She herself has still got all her wits about her, whatever folk may say, and much good it's done her. Mere human intelligence is powerless against the adversaries she faces. The Church might have helped, but Ada turned her back on God after what He allowed to happen to Rosetta. She does not go so far as to deny His existence, but she'll be damned if she'll acknowledge it.

This time, though, she almost blurted out a prayer. It had never been so bad before. She had grown used to the continual harassment, the sudden scurries and scampering in the dark, the flashing and stabbing lights, the shouts and screams and mocking laughter. It was all horrible, but at least the ritual seemed to have rules which until tonight had never been broken. The most important, from her point of view, was that whatever the creatures might get up to in the way of noise and nuisance, they never actually laid hands on her.

She'd known for a long time that they *had* hands, because in her panic she had sometimes run up against them. They were sub-stantial all right, whatever people might say. But until now all physi-cal contact between them had been accidental, the result of her panic and their inability to get out of her way fast enough. That she could just about tolerate, but what had happened tonight was quite unspeakable, just too awful for words . . .

Which is precisely the problem, she finds, when she tries to explain. Whatever she says, however she phrases it, the whole thing sounds unreal, phantasmagoric, even to her. She doesn't even quite believe her own experience, so how can she expect anyone else to do so? She glances once again at Aurelio Battista, crouching beside her on the low hard settle. His tone is sympathetic enough, but she's already beginning to regret having phoned him.

'Does it hurt?' he asks, dampening the rag in the dilute vinegar she is using as an antiseptic.

Ada dabs the shallow cuts across the inside of her wrists.

'It's nothing.'

He shakes his head.

'I'll call an ambulance boat, *contessa*. We must get these injuries seen to.'

But that's precisely what she doesn't want. It's one thing having the police involved. Despite Daniele Trevisan's warnings, the policemen she's dealt with so far have been perfectly correct, for all their evident scepticism. But the doctors are another matter altogether. Ada will never forget what they did to her the last time, even though she cannot actually remember in any detail what they *did* do. Never again, that much is certain. She'd rather slit her wrists than go back to San Clemente!

As it is, she is not even being consulted. Giustiniana's boy is speaking into the telephone, giving orders in a peremptory way, referring to her as 'the patient', as though she were some sort of object. To get her own back, she blots him out in turn, replacing him with an earlier version dressed in a skirt and blouse, playing with one of Rosetta's dolls, all alone in this vast cold salon, dwarfed by the furniture . . .

'They'll be here shortly,' says the other Aurelio Battista. 'Now then, what became of the knife?'

She points to the other side of the salon, towards the enormous dining table reputedly made from the timbers of a captured Turkish galley. 'The dragon table', little Aurelio used to call it, crawling about its giant legs carved in the form of claws . . . As he is again now, down on his hands and knees to gather up the carving knife lying there on the floor.

'Is this yours, *contessa*?' he asks, carrying the knife towards her by the tip of the blade.

Ada nods dumbly.

'It's so blunt,' she murmurs.

He sets the knife down on a chair and stands looking down at her.

'One of them held my arm while the other cut me,' she explains. 'He had to press quite hard, the knife is so blunt. It hurt.'

But it's the fear rather than the pain she remembers most clearly. She knows now that they weren't trying to kill her, but at the time she had no such assurance, and her terror was so extreme that she had lost control of her bladder. She does not tell Zen that her principal concern had been to remove all trace of this before he arrived.

'Can you describe the intruders?' he asks, sitting down again.

Of course she can. But she is unwilling to do so. She knows only too well that the grotesque appearance of the figures, with their exaggerated features and fantastic costumes, sounds totally absurd, something from a nightmare. And sure enough, as she talks about the tall one with the huge hooked nose, sunken eyes and gaping rictus, his voluminous clothes chequered like a harlequin, a knowing look comes over her visitor's face.

'Do you go out much, *contessa*?' he asks casually.

She carefully disguises the fact that she cannot see the point of this question at all.

'Once or twice a week to the shops . . .'

'You never go to the Piazza, for example?'

She looks at him in bewilderment. The last time she went to the Piazza was before the war, when her husband was still alive. Who would she go with now? And why?

'Whatever for?' she demands.

The man shrugs.

'Some people just like to go and stroll about there, to see and be seen. At carnival, for example.'

Ada Zulian tosses her head.

'Carnival is for children. I have no children.'

They confront each other for a moment over this. Then the man nods, as though acknowledging what it cost her to say this.

'This is the second night that this has happened,' he says, moving to a less painful topic.

Ada nods.

'And before that?' he asks.

She thinks back, but before she can answer he comes back with another question.

'Is there any pattern to these . . . experiences?'

'How do you mean?' she replies warily.

'Do they occur at any particular time of day, or any particular day of the week?'

Ada spots the trap just in time. The doctors asked her just such a question the last time, about Rosetta's reappearances. That was before she was on her guard with the doctors, when she still trusted them, before she knew what they were capable of. So she told them the truth, that her daughter appeared each night at exactly six o'clock. Her inquisitors had seized on that with evil glee. Six o'clock, they pointed out, was precisely the time that the real Rosetta had been expected to return home on the day she vanished. The fact that the hallucinations conformed to such a regular pattern was incontrovertible proof that they were manifestations of an obsessional delusion.

Well, she learned her lesson the hard way, but learned it she did. She won't be caught that way again.

'No,' she replies firmly. 'They come at any time they please. There's no pattern at all.'

Aurelio Battista frowns.

'Are you sure?'

'I can prove it!' cries Ada triumphantly.

She gets up and marches over to the cabinet in which she keeps the set of leather-bound folio volumes which her father used to record the accounts of the family cotton business. It is in the ample acres of blank pages at the rear of these volumes that Ada enters every day, in a hand so minute as to be practically illegible, the credit and debit balance of her own life.

She pulls out the volume she is currently using and flips back through the pages to the point, just over a month earlier, when these manifestations began to occur. In a steady, even tone, showing no trace whatever of excitement or disturbance, she recites the date, time and duration of each intrusion to Aurelio Battista, who writes it all down solemnly in his notebook.

As Ada replaces the huge volume in the cabinet, vindicated by the facts, she hears the seesaw clamour of a siren outside and sees a flashing blue light infiltrating the shutters on the windows at the front of the house, above the canal. In an instant, all her hard-won serenity deserts her. Can Giustiniana's boy really be going to turn her over to the doctors?

'I'll need the key to the waterdoor,' he tells her, putting away his notebook.

A cunning idea suggests itself to her.

'The waterdoor? But that hasn't been used for years. I've no idea where the key is.'

The siren dies to a guttural groan beneath the house. Aurelio Battista walks over to the window and undoes the fastenings.

'Make fast to the mooring rings,' he calls down. 'We'll be down in a moment.'

He turns to Ada. The flashing blue lamp on the roof of the boat makes the whole room pulse.

'The key, *contessa*?'

Ada returns to the cabinet, opens a drawer and paws around among the keys of all shapes and sizes, some antiques, some modern copies, each labelled in her father's pedantically legible script.

'I've really no idea where it can be,' she says. 'Heaven knows when the thing was last opened.'

In fact she remembers all too well. It was when her father's condition became critical and he had to be moved to hospital.

But her visitor is not to be deterred from his purposes so easily.

'Then we'll walk round to the bridge,' he tells her. 'There are steps down to the water there.'

He fetches Ada's coat and leads her downstairs. But when they reach the *andron* he leaves her and walks over to the massive door at the end giving on to the canal. And there the key is, of course, attached to the wall by a nail. When the man lifts it off, a rusty silhouette remains behind on the plaster. The throbbing of the launch makes the whole entrance vibrate.

He inserts the key into the lock, which turns smoothly. The door swings open under its own weight without a sound. The tide is high enough for the ambulance to be roped in against the watersteps. One of the attendants jumps ashore while the other manoeuvres a gangplank on to the paving of the hallway. Aurelio Battista is shouting instructions to the other man, who nods earnestly. Something about what is to be done with her once they reach the hospital. With a sinking feeling, Ada acknowledges that matters are slipping out of her control. She has tried so hard, but now it is suddenly all too much. She starts to scream, to struggle, then subsides to the paving and lets them have their way with her. There is a flurry of movement,

71

a clink of instruments, a sting in her arm, and then everything tactfully recedes.

He almost didn't go home. If it hadn't been for the carving knife, which he'd wrapped in newspaper in a crude attempt to preserve any fingerprints, he would probably have wandered off looking for a suitable place to eat. As it was he went home first, and that changed everything.

Approaching the house up the long wedge of the *campo*, he noticed that the lights were on. He knew he hadn't left them on himself. His mother had lectured him too often as a child about the shameful waste of leaving lights burning in an empty room, as well as the danger of a fire if a burning electric bulb – it was impossible to explain to her that there was no actual flame – were left unattended.

For a moment, he thought twice about entering the house. What had happened to Ada Zulian had shocked him more than he had allowed himself to reveal. Even if her injuries were self-inflicted, and the balance of probability had to lie in that direction, this new development was very disturbing. A degree more pressure on the knife blade would have been sufficient to sever the artery. Such had been the implied message of those shallow cuts on Ada's wrist. For some reason Zen felt it to be directed at him, at his presence in the city, his intrusion into whatever was going on.

Putting aside these fancies, he opened the front door as quietly as possible and made his way upstairs. Long before he reached the landing, he could already hear noises from the living room. His only weapon was Ada's knife. Grasping the handle through the newspaper wrapping, he crept across the landing and stood listening by the door. There was no question that someone was moving about in there.

Footsteps approached the door on the other side. Zen stood there, clutching the knife. The knob turned and a woman appeared silhouetted in the doorway. Zen lowered the knife.

'Good evening,' he said, as though the whole situation were perfectly normal.

Cristiana Morosini gestured awkwardly.

'I thought you'd gone out to dinner,' she said. 'My mother's feather duster is missing. She thought she might have left it over here. I used the key you left with her to get in.'

Zen nodded and walked past her into the living room.

'Ada Zulian phoned,' he said.

He set the wrapped knife down on the table.

'How is she?'

'How is she?' Zen repeated, a hysterical edge creeping into his voice. 'Not so good. Not so good at all. She tried to kill herself, or make it look as though she had.'

Cristiana Morosini rolled her eyes.

'Not again!'

Zen glanced at her sharply.

'It's happened before?'

Cristiana nodded.

'A couple of years ago. She slashed her wrists with a kitchen knife. Fortunately one of her nephews found her in time, and they managed to patch her up. But Mamma's right, you know. This is a case for the doctors.'

Zen shrugged.

'Well, the doctors have got her now. I packed her off to the hospital.'

'Were her injuries that serious?'

He shook his head.

'It's just to keep her under observation, really. I want to make sure she's not left alone until I have a chance to think the whole thing over and decide what to do.'

This neutral topic exhausted, they stood awkwardly eyeing each other. Zen glanced at his watch.

'Would you like to have dinner with me?' he demanded abruptly.

Cristiana shrugged.

'I've already eaten. Mamma made *sopa de pesse*.'

'Come and keep me company anyway. As an old friend of the family. I'm lonely, Cristiana. This place gives me the creeps. I don't know why I've come. I don't know what I'm doing here. I need someone to talk to. I also need a fax machine. Do you have a fax machine, Cristiana? If so you could satisfy all my needs.'

They looked at each other in silence for a moment. Then Cristiana smiled and started to button up her coat.

'There's one at the office where I work. As for eating, the places round here aren't up to much, but there's a pizzeria which isn't bad. We could go there if you like.'

Zen luxuriated for a moment under her intense lambent gaze.

'I'm in your hands,' he said.

'Oh God, there's Gabriella Rosteghin,' exclaimed Cristiana with a gleeful laugh. 'That means this'll be all over the neighbourhood tomorrow morning.'

'What will?' murmured Zen.

'You and I, of course.'

Zen looked over at the giggling group of teenage girls casting glances in their direction from the other end of the pizzeria.

'We haven't done anything yet,' he said mildly.

'So much the better! Gabriella prefers it that way. It gives her more scope. She doesn't need to worry about fitting in with the facts.'

Zen sipped his beer.

'Tell me about this *Nuova Repubblica Veneta* business,' he said. 'What's it all about? How did it get started?'

Cristiana sighed and shook her head.

'About four years ago, Nando joined the *Lega Veneta*, which had just been formed. I told him at the time that he was making a mistake. Politics draws you in, little by little, until you forget everything else. Mind you, no one had any inkling how popular the League would prove to be. Even Bossi thought it would take at least a decade to convince people that there was a viable alternative to the traditional parties. In the event, of course, the thing was a runaway success from the start. Everyone began to scent the possibility of power. That's when the trouble started.'

The pizzas they had ordered arrived, Cristiana having decided that she could after all manage something, and for a while they turned their attention to eating.

'I saw Tommaso Saoner today,' Zen said, pausing to gulp some beer. 'I didn't recognize him at all. It might have been a different person, the way he was talking.'

Cristiana nodded vigorously.

'That's just what happened to Nando. He's changed completely, just as I predicted. He used to be easygoing, and such fun! But the moment he got involved in politics he turned into a total fanatic. It's a drug. It gets into your blood and you become a different person.'

They ate in silence for a while.

'That's what caused the split with Bossi,' Cristiana went on.

'Nando wanted the *Lega Veneta* to take its distance from the Northern Leagues, which he claimed were too dominated by Lombardy. Although the Dal Maschio family is Venetian, Nando was brought up in Pavia, and he's never forgotten how the people there made fun of his accent. Anyway, his proposals were turned down, so he promptly resigned along with Saoner and a few others and formed his own breakaway group.'

'And do they really want to resurrect the Venetian Republic?'

Cristiana nodded.

' "Our past is our future, our future is our past." That's one of Nando's slogans. It doesn't make any sense, does it? But he really believes it. He isn't a charlatan, like so many politicians. He believes everything he says.'

She pushed her half-eaten pizza away.

'Anyway, that's enough about him!'

She sized up Zen with her eyes for a moment.

'You're married too, aren't you?'

He shrugged.

'Legally, yes. But that's all in the past. And *my* past is certainly not my future. Not if I've got anything to do with it, anyway.'

Cristiana laughed.

'Children?' she asked.

Zen shook his head.

'Although I sometimes feel as though there's another me that's still married to Luisella and is probably a father by now.'

He looked at her.

'Do you ever feel that? That every time you come to a crossroads in your life, there's a ghostly double which splits off and goes the other way, the route you didn't take. I know exactly what he's like, my married version. I might as well be him. I could easily be. It just so happens that I'm not.'

He smiled wryly and got out his cigarettes.

'Listen to the pizzeria philosopher! Sorry, I'm talking nonsense.'

The bevy of teenage girls passed by their table on the way out.

'*Ciao*, Cristiana.'

'*Ciao*, Gabriella.'

Swathed in smirks and giggles, the group sallied forth into the night. With their departure, the room seemed to contract, becoming a smaller and more intimate space.

'Do you ever think about coming home?' asked Cristiana lightly.

'Home?'

'To live, I mean.'

When Zen did not reply, she added, 'But perhaps you have a reason for wanting to stay in Rome. Something, or someone.'

He shook his head slowly.

'Only my job.'

'But you could get a transfer here if you wanted.'

'Probably. But I haven't had a reason for coming back here. Not so far.'

He looked at her.

'It's your home,' said Cristiana. 'Isn't that reason enough?'

Zen shrugged.

'It's more often seemed a reason for staying away. Those ghostly doubles I was talking about are thicker on the ground here than anywhere else.'

There was a brief silence between them.

'Speaking of ghosts, Ada Zulian described one of her intruders to me this evening,' Zen murmured, as though to himself. 'She said it had a large hook nose, a fixed grin and gaping eyes and wore a loose-fitting costume in black and white check, like a harlequin. The other had pale flawless features, neither male nor female, and was dressed in a cloak of gold and scarlet.'

Cristiana sniffed dismissively.

'Sounds like carnival.'

Zen nodded.

'Exactly what occurred to me. But where could Ada have seen carnival costumes? She hardly ever leaves the house, and then only to go to the local shops. You don't see people dressed up like that in this area. She doesn't have a television and never reads the papers.'

'Perhaps she remembers it from when she was a child.'

Zen drained off the last of his beer and clicked his fingers to summon the waiter.

'When Ada was a child, the carnival didn't exist. The children got dressed up as bunnies or cowboys or pirates, and there was a dance for the parents if the weather was good, but that was all. The chichi spectacle they put on these days, with all the jet setters from Milan and Rome dolled up in fantastic costumes which cost the earth, that's all a recent invention. I'm willing to bet that Ada Zulian has never seen a "traditional" Venetian carnival outfit in her life.'

'She must have done,' retorted Cristiana, standing to put on her coat. 'Otherwise how could she describe it?'

Outside, a fine drizzle had started to fall. They walked home through the deserted streets and over the darkened waterways as though they owned them, as though the whole city were their private domain. The knowledge that they were a subject of gossip lent a nimbus of glamour to what in different circumstances might have seemed a fairly homely outing.

They also laughed a lot. Cristiana Morosini had a mordant, malicious sense of humour which Zen found refreshingly direct after months of feminist earnestness. In principle he agreed with Tania's views – or at least did not disagree with them enough to argue – but they were relentlessly correct and offered no scope for heartless humour. As Cristiana recounted a succession of decidedly unsisterly anecdotes about a mutual acquaintance, Zen found himself responding with a warmth and freedom he had not felt for a very long time.

When they reached their houses, they stopped, suddenly awkward.

'Well, good night,' said Zen. 'Thank you for coming along. I really enjoyed myself.'

'So did I.'

She took a card from her purse and handed it to him.

'This is where I work. The fax and phone numbers are on it. Give me a ring and I'll tell you whether anything has arrived.'

Zen watched her walk to her door and unlock it. She looked round and waved, and only then did he turn away.

By morning, a dense fog had settled on the city. When a combination of high tides and strong onshore winds flooded the streets with the dreaded *aqua alta*, the council posted maps showing the zones affected and the routes on higher ground which remained open, but the fog respected no limits. It ebbed and flowed according to its own laws, blossoming here, thinning there, blurring outlines, abolishing distinctions and making the familiar strange and unlikely.

'What the . . .!'

'For the love of . . .!'

'Watch where you're going!'

'You think you own the street?'

Catching sight of a dishevelled elderly man with a dog at his heels, Zen hastily slipped back into the enshrouding obscurity of the fog before he got entangled in another episode of Daniele Trevisan's vaporous reminiscences. But he had not gone much further before another collision occurred.

'Excuse me!'

'Oh!'

'Rosalba?'

'Ah, if it isn't Casanova himself!'

'I beg your pardon?'

' "I'm just going over to see Wanda," she tells me last night. That's Wanda Dal Maschio, Nando's sister, somehow they've remained on good terms despite what's happened. The next thing I know, Lisa Rosteghin's phoning me to ask who's the tall dark stranger Cristiana's been seen having a pizza with!'

Zen gave a feeble smile.

'I just wanted to catch up on the local gossip.'

'Of course!' returned Rosalba heartily. 'Once Cristiana got back and I found out it was you, I knew there was no question of any hanky-panky. Why, you're old enough to be her father!'

Zen's smile slowly faded. Rosalba picked up her shopping and slipped back into the fog, disappearing within moments.

'Thick as snot,' her voice called back. 'Mind how you go, Aurelio.'

On the Cannaregio, a slight breeze was at work, stirring the fog into currents of differing density. The palaces and churches fronting the canal came and went, the forms firming up and vagueing away like a print from an old photographic plate damaged by the ravages of time. A barge nosed through out from a side canal into the main channel, hooting mournfully. Similar sirens and signals, muffled by the moist air, resounded in the distance.

Zen was making slow progress towards the ferry stop when he was hurled headlong to the cobbles, banging his knee and shoulder painfully. Getting up again and looking round, he saw the line of tubing over which he had tripped, straight lengths of metal bolted together with blue concertina inserts in plastic to accommodate corners. Down at the quayside one of the ubiquitous red barges marked POZZI NERI would be moored ready to receive the contents of whichever septic tank was being drained that morning.

He picked up his briefcase, lit a cigarette and continued on his way across the bridge to the floating platform where a dozen people were already waiting. Spectral in the fog, the massive wooden pilings chained together to form a tripod securing the platform, their tops phallically rounded, looked like an idol dedicated to some god of the lagoon. From time to time invisible craft passed by, the wash making the landing stage shift restlessly at its moorings.

At length a muffled cone of light appeared in the fog, gradually brightening and widening until the boat itself became visible, one of the *motoscafi* with a rakishly high bow like a torpedo boat. The waiting crowd filed on board and the ferry continued cautiously on its way, creeping through the water, the engine barely turning over, the searchlight at the bow scanning back and forth. Once they cleared the mouth of the Cannaregio the water started to heave dully, making the boat yaw and wallow.

At Fondamente Nove, where he had to change, Zen stopped off in a bar for a *caffè corretto*. The barman had the radio on, and Zen caught the end of some local news item about a fisherman who had been found drowned somewhere in the northern lagoon. The police were said to be investigating. Zen tossed off the scalding coffee, heady with grappa, and wandered over to the window to look for his ferry. The steamer to Burano and Treporti was just casting off, but there was no activity at the pier where the number 5 stopped.

On the wall beside the window was another of the calendars which he had seen the previous day at the *osteria* where he had met Marco Paulon, with the fall and rise of the tides in the lagoon superimposed on the days of the month. Zen lifted it down from its hook and copied the information for the earlier part of the month into his notebook, glancing out of the window from time to time. There was still no sign of the *circolare destra*. After waiting five minutes, he decided to walk.

Away from the slight breezes of the open lagoon, the fog blocked the winding cuts and alleys, as thick as silt. Zen waded through it, narrowly avoiding a number of close encounters with walls, canals and other pedestrians, until he emerged at length in Campo San Lorenzo. A blue-and-white launch was just setting off from the Questura with the ear-splitting roar to which police drivers always aspired, whatever their vehicle. Zen climbed the stairs to the office he had been assigned on the second floor. Aldo Valentini was standing by the window, looking out at the swirling grey pall.

'Filthy stuff,' he said vehemently, catching sight of Zen's reflection in the glass. 'Coats your throat and lungs. Can't you taste it? All the pollution from Mestre and Marghera packaged for your convenience in easy-to-breathe aerosol form.'

Zen slumped behind his desk and phoned the Ospedale Civile. Putting on his most brutal tone, he cowed an unwilling functionary of that institution into briefing him on the condition of Ada Zulian. Eventually he was connected to a woman doctor who reported that the patient had made a complete recovery and was anxious to go home but was being kept at the hospital in accordance with the instructions which Zen had given the ambulance crew the night before. She had been visited by her nephews, who had strongly supported their aunt's right to be discharged if she so wished.

'And of course they're absolutely right,' the doctor concluded. 'Quite apart from the considerable pressure on our facilities here, it's no part of our business to keep patients confined when they're able and willing to leave.'

'I quite understand,' Zen murmured soothingly. 'Thank you so much for your forbearance. Unfortunately there's a bit of a demand for transport at present, but I'll come and pick up the *contessa* just as soon as a boat becomes available.'

He hung up before the doctor could reply. Opening his briefcase, he extracted a bundle wrapped in newspaper and folded back the wrapping to reveal a large carving knife.

'Where can I get this printed?' he asked Valentini.

'The lab's at the university. If you leave it with Renaldi in the basement he'll have it sent over. I'll take it down for you, if you like. I've got bugger all else to do after getting bumped off the Sfriso case.'

Being from Ferrara, Valentini pronounced it 'Sfrizo'. Zen looked up.

'Isn't that the break-in you were talking about yesterday?'

'It wás. Now it's a drowning. Out by Burano.'

Zen suddenly recalled what Marco Paulon had told him on the way to the *ottagono* the day before.

'Sfriso? Is he the same man who claimed to have seen the dead on Sant'Ariano walking around?'

Aldo Valentini nodded.

'And now he's joined them. One of the monks rowing back to San Francesco del Deserto fished him out of the water yesterday afternoon. I spent most of last night at Burano, trying to piece together what happened, only to get in this morning and find that Gavagnin has taken over the case. He's giving the brother a hard time downstairs even now.'

'Why did they take you off the case?'

Valentini scowled.

'Damned if I know. First of all Gavagnin tried to take the break-in away from me. Claimed it was linked to some drugs case he's working on. I couldn't see it. The Sfriso brothers were just a couple of typical Burano fishermen.'

'What was the break-in about?'

'It happened one Sunday while they were at Mass with their mother. The house was torn apart, but nothing was taken. A neighbour saw the intruders leaving and phoned one one three, but by the time we got a boat there they were long gone. The only strange thing about it was that the Sfrisos wouldn't co-operate. They didn't want to pursue the matter, they said. Wouldn't even file a complaint until I told them they had to.'

Zen nodded to show a polite interest.

'And now one of them's dead. Is there any suggestion of foul play?'

Valentini shrugged.

'I didn't see any, but it's out of my hands. Gavagnin must have pulled some strings upstairs this time. They didn't even bother to discuss it with me, just told me to hand over the file.'

He sighed.

'It's really pissed me off, I can tell you. First interesting thing happens in months and it gets pulled out from under my feet.'

He took the carving knife from Zen and wrapped it up again.

'What was this used to do?'

Zen briefly ran through the events of the previous night. Aldo Valentini yawned loudly.

'I'll bet you anything you like the prints on the handle are hers.'

Zen shrugged.

'Probably. Still, I'm going to have to put a man in the house. I don't want her dead next time.'

'It'd be better to get the old girl committed again. The chief isn't going to agree to tying up personnel indefinitely to keep someone with her psychiatric record from slitting her wrists. We're not running a nanny service, you know.'

Zen put his finger to his lips.

'If I do that, I'll be out of work too,' he said in a stage whisper. 'I only just got here, for God's sake. I want to spin it out for a week at least.'

Valentini smiled broadly.

'Oh well, put like that, of course, the case for ongoing police intervention becomes overwhelming. I'll take this downstairs, then go and grab some breakfast.'

He headed for the door, shaking his head.

'Bastards!'

Once Valentini had gone, Zen phoned the Questore's office. Francesco Bruno, the provincial police chief, was out of town, and the call was taken by his deputy. Zen outlined the history of his involvement with the case so far and explained why he wished to post a guard inside Palazzo Zulian. The Deputy Questore at first expressed considerable doubts about this, and an even greater amazement that a Criminalpol operative had been commissioned to investigate such a comparatively insignificant case.

'Exactly!' Zen retorted triumphantly. 'This woman clearly must have powerful connections to have me sent up here. It is therefore all the more essential that we do not leave ourselves open to any possible criticism. How's it going to look if we wash our hands of the affair and then she goes and kills herself?'

The Deputy Questore speedily acknowledged the force of this argument. Armed with this authorization from on high, Zen spent the next twenty minutes punishing the internal telephone system until he had made the necessary arrangements. He then typed up a confirmation, took it down to Personnel and extracted a receipt, thereby giving the staff an interest in seeing that his orders were actually carried out.

Back at his desk, he rang *Serenissmi Viaggi*, the travel agency where Cristiana Morosini worked. He had phoned Palazzo Sisti before leaving home to pass on the fax number, but the subordinate he had spoken to then had been unable or unwilling to reveal whether or not *l'onorevole* had been successful in obtaining the material Zen wished to consult. So his disappointment at not being able to speak to Cristiana herself, who had gone out on some errand, was mitigated by the news that a fax transmission in his name had indeed arrived and was awaiting collection.

Zen grabbed his hat and coat and hurried out. The light in the corridors and stairwell seemed slightly hazy, as though the drench all around had seeped through the walls to taint the air inside as well. Somewhere below a door slammed shut and a pair of metal-tipped shoes began running along an echoing passage. Zen continued down. As he reached the landing he met a tubby, choleric man dashing up the stairs two at a time.

'Aren't you Enzo Gavagnin?' said Zen.

'Well?' snapped the other, whirling round.

'Aurelio Zen, Vice-Questore. We met yesterday. I'm here on secondment from the Ministry.'

Enzo Gavagnin's eyes became smaller and more intense.

'Excuse me! I for one have no time to chat.'

'Oh quite,' Zen murmured languidly. 'Sounds like a big case you're working on. A drowned fisherman, eh? I've never heard the like! Did he slip on a squid or get his waders caught in the winch?'

Gavagnin glared at him.

'Go fuck yourself,' he growled in dialect.

Outside, the fog was thicker than ever. Buildings loomed up like ships, towering above the narrow lanes where featureless figures slipped in and out of the clammy banks of vapour. As Zen passed on the corner, he caught sight of Aldo Valentini drowning his sorrows with a sandwich and glass of wine. For a moment he was tempted to join him, but he kept going, stopping at a bakery to buy half a loaf of olive bread. He chewed contentedly as he walked along, savouring the warm pulp of the dough and the sweet black putrefaction of the olives.

Serenissimi Viaggi was in an alley just north of the Piazza, lined with shops selling carnival masks and costumes. A group of tourists passed by like soldiers on patrol in enemy territory, bunched for protection, cameras ready to shoot at the slightest opportunity. One of them looked at the posters in the window of the agency and frowned, momentarily disturbed by the idea that a city he thought of only as a holiday destination was offering holidays elsewhere.

Inside the small shop were two desks piled with brochures and timetables and computer equipment. One was unoccupied. An anorexically cadaverous woman with unnaturally white skin and black hair was seated behind the other. She did not look up as Zen entered.

'Good morning,' he said. 'I'm Cristiana's friend. I've come to pick up the fax which arrived for me.'

The woman sighed mightily. She stood up and walked over to the other desk. After rummaging through the papers scattered there for some time, she returned with a large envelope which she handed to Zen, still avoiding any eye contact but fixing the half-eaten loaf in his hand with a look full of disapproval.

'Thirty-eight thousand,' she said.

'I beg your pardon?'

The woman tapped the keys of a printing calculator.

'Fourteen pages fax reception at two thousand a page equals twenty-eight thousand, plus five thousand handling fee makes thirty-three, plus VAT at fifteen per cent four nine five oh say another five equals thirty-eight thousand in all. Do you want a receipt?'

Zen paid and shuffled out into the fog, clutching the envelope. He turned right, off the main street, away from the crowds, glancing at the shopfronts to either side. In Campo Santa Maria Formosa he found what he had been looking for: a small, cosy wine bar, almost empty at that hour. The walls were panelled with varnished laths, as though the hull of a boat had been flattened out like *pollo alla diavola*. The windows were screened by a lace curtain hanging on a rail. Brass lamps with bulbous glass shades cast patches of soft yellow light in the intimate gloom.

At the bar, a brown-flecked marble slab, three men stood discussing the merits of various models of outboard engine. Zen took a seat at a trestle table near the back of the room, facing the door. When the barman came over, he ordered some breaded crab claws and a quarter litre of white wine. He waited till the man had gone, then opened the envelope and spread the contents on the table.

The document faxed by Palazzo Sisti consisted of fourteen pages of double-spaced typing. There was no heading or other indication that the text formed part of an official report, the material having been retyped on to plain paper in order to conceal the source or to edit out any items which might have compromised friends or allies of *l'onorevole*.

Zen skimmed quickly through the report, then went back to the beginning and started again, reading more carefully and making marks and comments in the margin here and there. The first thing he learned was that the missing man's real name was not Durridge but Duric. He had been born in 1919 in Sarajevo, a city as notorious then, in the aftermath of the war which had been sparked off there, as it was again now that it had been abandoned to its fate by a world seemingly eager to demonstrate that it had learned nothing from the horrors of the intervening seventy-five years.

Zen casually placed the envelope over the fax sheets as the barman returned with his food and drink. He tore open one of the golden-breaded pincers, exposing the pink bone, and savoured the sweet flesh with sips of wine while he read on. When Ivan Durič was twenty, another European conflict engulfed his country, only this time he was able to take an active hand. Unfortunately he backed the wrong faction, and when Tito's Communist partisans took power of the new Yugoslavia the Durič family were forced to make a hasty exit. They slipped across the Adriatric to Italy and thence to the United States, where Ivan changed his surname and went on to make a fortune in the trucking business.

Zen finished the last of the crab. He poured himself more wine, lit a cigarette and went back to the report. Durridge had first come to the attention of the Italian authorities in March 1988, when he had bought the *ottagono* in the lagoon and applied to the local Questura for a residence permit. Since then, according to the records of the frontier police, he had come and gone between Venice and Chicago four or five times a year. There were only two other instances of his name in official files. The first was a complaint which Durridge had made towards the end of September the previous year about an alleged trespass. The other, just over a month later, was when Franco Calderan phoned the Carabinieri to report that his employer was missing.

' . . . weed fouled round the screw then . . .'
' . . . tilt the whole issue and clean it by hand . . .'
' . . . still swear by the little Fiat my father used . . .'

Zen blew an almost perfect smoke-ring towards the ceiling and called for more wine. Franco Calderan had returned from his day off on the Lido shortly after five o'clock that afternoon, the 11th. He used his own small dinghy for the crossing, and as soon as he approached the landing place he noticed that his master's boat was absent from its mooring.

This boat, a traditional broad-beamed *topa* fitted with a Volvo diesel engine instead of the traditional lugsail, had not been seen since. Durridge never used it without Calderan aboard, having learned the hard way about the hazards of navigation on the lagoon when he ran aground south of the *Fondi dei Sette Morti* and had to spend the night aboard in the open until a fishing vessel returning to Chioggia threw him a line. Since the boat was nevertheless missing, the investigators' assumption was that it had been taken by the same person or persons who had abducted Ivan Durridge.

As Marco Paulon had already indicated to Zen, the time frame for such a kidnapping was extremely tight. Durridge was known to have been on the island shortly after one o'clock that afternoon, since his sister had spoken to him on the phone from Florida. By two o'clock at the latest the tide would have been too low to permit embarkation or disembarkation from the *ottagono*. The possibility that the kidnappers had arrived by air was briefly considered, but ruled out because of the difficulty of landing a machine on the small patch of lawn which was the only open ground anywhere on the island, and entirely surrounded by mature trees – the Carabinieri themselves had had to come and go by boat throughout their investigation. One thing which no one questioned was that the American was a textbook target for a professional kidnapping: rich, solitary and living in isolation. All that was necesary to confirm this hypothesis was a ransom demand.

Thus far the report was quite clearly a more or less literal transcription of a file opened by the Carabinieri in Venice. The investigation was proceeding normally at local level, with no hint that the case had any further implications. Then, early in January, the Carabinieri suddenly received instructions from their superiors at the Ministry of Defence ordering them to suspend all activity relating to the Durridge case and forward any existing files and related material under seal to Rome for 'assessment'.

The final section of the transcript consisted of selections – this was where the editing had taken place – of an internal memorandum addressed to a figure referred to only as 'a senior official in the Defence Ministry'. It ran as follows:

> With respect to the case to which you refer, a parallel agency has recently revealed a previous interest in Ivan Durridge/Durić which might be prejudiced by inquiries at judicial level. These have therefore been suspended in the interests of state security while the agency in question conducts its own investigation, the results of which will be communicated to all relevant parties and institutions in due course.

Well that's that then, thought Zen, draining his glass of wine. 'Parallel agency' was a euphemism for the secret service organizations, in this case probably the Defence Ministry's own SISMI unit. Whether Durridge had been their agent or their target was of no more than academic interest. Anything involving the secret services was out of his league. The most he could hope for was to massage the evidence so as to keep his private investigation going a little longer in the interests of siphoning as much money as possible out of the Durridge family. But how?

He pored over the fax again. Almost every lead seemed to have been exhausted. Eventually he spotted two possible openings. The first concerned the earlier landing on the *ottagono*, back in the summer; the other the fate of Durridge's boat. Neither could remotely be described as promising, but by rapidly juggling them both he might manage to convey a mirage of solid progress and attainable goals to his employers, given their understandable desire to be deceived.

Back at the Questura, he set the wheels in motion. Durridge's complaint to the police following the landing on his island in September had been duly logged at the time, and while the Carabinieri had been forced to send all their records to Rome, the Questura had received no such request for the simple reason that they had never opened a file on the Durridge case in the first place. Zen simply phoned downstairs for the relevant documents and ten minutes later they were on his desk.

To his disappointment, they seemed to offer no possibilities for fruitful exploitation and development. Not only had the three trespassers been apprehended and identified, but they were all respectable local men. Giulio Bon was from Chioggia, where he ran a boatyard. His companions lived in the city itself. Massimo Bugno was a crewhand on ACTV's ferries and waterbuses, while Domenico Zuin owned a watertaxi.

As luck would have it, a police patrol boat had been in the area when Ivan Durridge's complaint had been received on the 113 emergency number, and it was able to intercept the intruders as they left in a boat belonging to the said Zuin. All three protested their innocence. They had not known that the island was inhabited, assuming it to be abandoned like so many others in the lagoon. They had meant no harm, intending only to share a bottle of wine and a game of cards.

Zen got up from his desk and walked to the window. Now the fog seemed to have penetrated not just the building but also his mind, woozy from the wine. He had grown soft after years in the south, where people cut their wine with Coke and only the rich kids thought it chic to get pissed on imported beer. Back home again, he had automatically slipped back into the northern tradition, drinking a grappa with his morning coffee and then keeping a slow burn going with glasses of wine all day, but his brain could no longer handle it.

He lit a cigarette, whose smoke rubbed up against the glass like a cat, as though seeking union with the fog outside. There was nothing in the trespassing incident that he could show the Durridges' lawyer. That left the boat. Returning to the desk, he called the office which kept records of all craft licensed to operate on waterways within the Province of Venice and asked them to send over details of any boats registered since the 1st of November previous.

Only then, having exhausted every pretext for further delay, did he go downstairs and order a launch to take him to the Ospedale Civile and the inevitable confrontation with Ada Zulian.

If Zen had been worried that his presence at the rally of the Venetian separatist movement that evening would be in any way conspicuous, he was reassured immediately on rounding the corner into Campo Santa Margherita. With the coming of night a fidgety, fickle wind had sprung up, thinning out the fog. It was evident at a glance that the huge irregular space was awash with people.

Normally a political gathering on this scale would have attracted a highly visible police presence, squads in riot gear massed in the streets all around, not so much in anticipation of any real trouble as to convey the none-too-subtle message that whatever the featured speakers might propose, neither they nor their supporters should forget that it was the State and its agents alone who disposed.

In this case, however, Zen himself was the only policeman present, as far as he could see. Perhaps after all the revelations of recent months the State was finally losing its nerve, or perhaps it had more dangerous opponents to impress with its shows of force. For the people who had come to hear Ferdinando Dal Maschio were no angry students or striking workers. Their advanced age and undemonstrative demeanour marked them out as ordinary, law-abiding residents of the Dorsoduro quarter, not given to breaches of the peace or violent excesses of any kind.

They were packed most densely at the far end, where a temporary podium had been erected. At the back of the stage, beneath a banner showing a lion rampant and the name of the party, four men sat listening to a fifth who stood haranguing the crowd through the loudspeakers mounted to either side. On the fringes of these core supporters a second crowd had gathered, less committed but hovering there, looking about them or moving aimlessly back and forth, sampling the speeches, not yet convinced but letting themselves be wooed.

It was here that Zen took his place, as of right, amongst the waverers and spectators. He had spent the first part of the afternoon trying to get Ada Zulian to accept the idea of having a police guard in her house during the hours of darkness. Zen had supposed that the old lady would have been comforted by such conspicuous protection, instead of which she had protested vehemently against this 'gross invasion of privacy'. Zen had not been helped in his efforts to soothe her by the rough-and-ready manners of Bettino Todesco, the policeman who would be on duty that night, or by the fact that he had to take Ada's fingerprints in order to compare them with those which might be found on the knife.

In the end, Ada had insisted on phoning her nephews. Nanni and Vincenzo Ardit had driven over from their home in Verona as soon as they heard that their aunt was in hospital and were spending the afternoon in the city, where they had the use of one of the family's properties not far from Palazzo Zulian. It was thus only a matter of moments before one of them turned up to lend his aunt moral support.

Vincenzo Ardit turned out to be a pleasant surprise from Zen's point of view. He was a fit, strong man in his early twenties, with the cropped hair and wary eyes of one who has recently concluded his military service. Quietly spoken and evidently used to dealing with Ada, he calmly explained to her the benefits of having an official presence in the house for a limited period 'to prove that you aren't simply imagining these terrible things'. Ada held up her bandaged wrists and demanded to know if this wasn't real enough, but this display of pique showed that she knew she had given way on the major issue.

Zen and her nephew spent a further hour soothing Ada's ruffled feelings before they could leave her alone with the uncouth Todesco, who was confined to a small room leading off the main landing, with strict orders to venture no further unless summoned. When Zen left, Ardit walked with him to the end of the alley, evidently with the purpose of being able to talk freely.

'My aunt is a very sick woman. What she needs is extended hospitalization and medical attention, but unfortunately her last experience was so horrific ... It was back in the dark ages of psychiatric treatment, in the early fifties. They shot her full of drugs and gave her electric shocks. The result is that she'll do anything to avoid going back.'

He sighed deeply.

'So far Nanni and I have gone along with her wishes. But if this suicide attempt is repeated, we'll have no choice but to insist on getting her the treatment she so desperately needs.'

Zen left Ardit to his family duties and made his way home, feeling totally exhausted. Having showered, he made the mistake of lying down on the bed for a moment. When he opened his eyes again the room was in darkness and the bells of San Giobbe were striking eight o'clock. As a result, the NRV rally was more than half over by the time Zen got there. The present speaker was holding forth on the need to encourage a revival of small shops and businesses by curbing 'bureaucratic busybodies' and relaxing the 'intolerable and unjust tax burdens' under which they presently laboured.

A glance at the faces all around revealed the expediency of adopting this political line. Almost without exception, the people attending the rally were the *piccola borghesia* incarnate. The wilder rhetoric of separatism might appeal to the romantics among them, but in the end it would be the bread-and-butter issues which would sway the majority. None of them liked having some politician in Rome tell them what they could or couldn't do, particularly now that Judge Antonio Di Pietro and his colleagues had confirmed their long-held suspicions that those very same politicians had themselves been doing exactly as they pleased all along.

The speaker was loudly cheered as he returned to his seat and one of the men seated at the back stood up. Even through the veil of mist, Zen recognized Tommaso Saoner as he stepped forward to introduce the evening's star speaker. After a lengthy pause, during which the clapping and shouting grew ever more intense and rhythmic, the leader of the *Nuova Repubblica Veneta* emerged dramatically from the crowd itself and leapt up on the platform.

Ferdinando Dal Maschio was only superficially the man whom Zen had glimpsed in the wine bar the previous day. The physical outline was the same – the wiry build, of medium height, with sharp, angular features and an unruly mop of light brown hair – but the overall effect was completely different. In the *osteria*, Dal Maschio had appeared an unremarkable individual with a slightly dopey air, someone you might go drinking or hunting with but whom you wouldn't trust to post an important letter. Now he was transformed. As he strode across the stage and grasped the microphone, he seemed to radiate authority, vitality and utter conviction.

Almost as soon as Dal Maschio started speaking, Zen realized that he was listening to one of life's natural orators. Part of the fascination was that his voice did not fit his boyish looks. Deep and gravelly, with an rasping edge he must have picked up during his childhood in Lombardy, it was the perfect vehicle for the savagely mocking assault on the 'elected Mafia' in Rome with which he started. There were roars of approval from the crowd as Dal Maschio excoriated the vices of the political class which had run the country since the war.

'We might forgive them their inefficiency if they weren't arrogant as well. We might be prepared to overlook their arrogance if they weren't also corrupt. And their corruption wouldn't stink quite so much if they hadn't spent the last fifty years preaching about the need for high moral standards and the rule of law. But inefficiency combined with arrogance plus corruption times hypocrisy? Heh! No, my friends, that's too much for them to try and shove up our arses!'

This sudden lapse into vulgarity brought a storm of cheers. Dal Maschio had won their minds, now he had conquered their hearts, revealing himself to be one of them, a plain man who used plain words. But he was also astute enough to know that attacking the easy targets in Rome, however popular it might be, was not enough. He had warmed up the crowd with his opening tirade. Now it was time to move closer to home, and to prepare his vision of an alternative future.

'Ecologists speak of a species "at risk". Much fuss has been made about the fate of whales and elephants, of rhinos, tigers and porpoises.'

He paused abruptly, giving his audience time to wonder what any of this had to do with their concerns.

'But there is a species far more important than those, and far closer to our hearts, which is equally endangered, and yet no one lifts a finger to save it. That species, my friends, is the Venetians!'

Dal Maschio stood back, allowing the storm of cheers to subside.

'Already it is late, very late!' he cried passionately. 'In the fifty years since the war, we have lost no less than half our entire population, and those that do remain have the highest average age of any European city. And do not let us forget that those official figures in no way reflect the real dimensions of the problem, since they include all the foreigners who have moved here and forced the price of property through the roof, outsiders who share nothing of our common heritage yet make it impossible for many of us to live in our own city!'

This brought more cheers.

'It's not just a question of numbers,' Dal Maschio went on, his face suddenly grave. 'Repopulating Venice is not the only issue at stake. Even more vital is the preservation of our distinctively Venetian culture, and for that the time is desperately short! We have literally only a few more years to repatriate the thousands of our citizens who have been forced to emigrate and for the older generation to pass on its skills, tradition and language to the young. After that the chain will be broken beyond any possibility of repair, and one and a half thousand years of Venetian history will be over. If the city survives at all, it will be as a theme park for rich tourists, as Veniceland, a wholly-owned Disney subsidiary with actors dressed up as the Doge and the Council of Ten and catering by McDonald's.'

Dal Maschio paused, giving his audience time to appreciate this dire prospect. When he spoke again, it was in a low, matter-of-fact tone in dramatic contrast to his previous delivery.

'But that need not happen. It will not happen. We shall not let it happen.'

He broke off, gazing blankly before him as though lost for words. When it finally came, his next phrase had the hushed intensity of a revelation, of a great truth communicated for the first time.

'We Venetians must take control of our own destiny.'

He nodded, as though working out the logic of this insight he had just been granted.

'For over a century we have let ourselves be beguiled by the chimera of nationalism. We freed ourselves from the shackles of the Austrian empire only to hand ourselves over to the hegemony of Rome. And now that regime has been exposed for the rotten sham it is, there are those who urge us to deliver ourselves meekly into the power of Milan!'

A surge of murmurs from the crowd greeted this reference to the rival Northern Leagues.

'That may make sense for others,' Dal Maschio went on, the aggressive edge returning to his voice, 'for those regions which have historically acknowledged the supremacy of the Lombards, or those who have insufficient resources to support pretensions to independence.'

A pause, then he switched back into his declamatory mode.

'But we are different! Venice has always been different! Istria and the Dalmatian coast have always been closer to us than Verona, Corfu and the Aegean more familiar than Milan, Constantinople no more foreign than Rome. Where others look inward, we have always looked outward. That difference is our heritage and our glory. The New Venetian Republic will revive both! We shall make the city a free port, renew our historic relationship with the newly emergent republics along the Dalmatian coast, and offer significant commercial and financial advantages to businesses, all with a view to making Venice once again the leading interface between the Eastern Mediterranean littoral and Northern Europe.'

Dal Maschio took a drink from the glass of water on the stand beside him. He smiled broadly, one of the boys again.

'But besides all that, we have one great advantage over other folk. It's also our great scourge. I'm talking about the tourists, of course.'

He nodded approvingly as a chorus of laughter went up from the crowd.

'As we know all too well, there is no one on this planet who wouldn't like to visit our city if they could, and no one who has done so who wouldn't like to return. Over twenty million such "guests" come to call on us every single year, and what do we see for it? Next to nothing! Most of them spend less than a day in the city, and the few who stay longer are serviced by international hotel chains whose profits end up in Paris or London or New York. Such tourism is like the *aqua alta*, flooding the whole city, making normal life impossible and leaving nothing but shit behind!'

A loud burst of applause greeted this sally. Dal Maschio raised his hand for silence.

'But if we dam that flood, my friends, it will generate enough hard cash to provide the basis of a vigorous and stable economy! Tourists pay an average of fifty dollars a head to visit the Disney theme park outside Paris. How much would they be willing to pay for the privilege of visiting the most famous and beautiful city in the world? At present they walk in free, as if they owned the place! Anyone intending to visit the New Venetian Republic would require a visa, for which we would charge . . . What shall we say? A hundred thousand lire? That would ensure the New Republic an immediate, guaranteed annual income of two thousand billion lire!'

There were gasps from the audience. Dal Maschio shrugged coyly.

'That's not bad, is it? In fact it's well in excess of the gross national product of several emergent nations. But for us it's only the beginning. Far from being an idle dream, independence is the only policy which can realize the unlimited potential of our unique city. But we must not fall into the trap of complacency, my friends. Do not waste your votes just because you believe – absolutely correctly, mind you – that our victory is a foregone conclusion. Let us not merely win these municipal elections, but win them massively, decisively, with an overwhelming landslide which sends a clear signal to the morally and economically bankrupt regime in Rome! Let's force them to call elections at a national level in the immediate future, so that we can liberate ourselves once and for all from the burdens which have weighed us down for so long, and begin at last to forge our own destiny in this unique and incomparable city state!'

Dal Maschio turned away. It seemed the speech was over, and scattered applause broke out. Then, as though struck by a sudden inspiration, he grasped the microphone again and continued with hoarse vehemence.

'Fifteen hundred years ago our forefathers gathered here, on the bleak mudbanks of the lagoon, seeking refuge from foreign domination, from oppression and servitude. They turned their back on the mainland and, over the centuries, made of this inhospitable and unpromising site a city which is one of the wonders of the world. They never bowed to emperor or pope but always held their own course, owing allegiance to no one but always seeking to further the interests of the Republic. Maybe they weren't always too particular about the methods they used or the people they allied themselves with, but for over a thousand years they made the name of Venice respected and feared. If we wish to be great again, if we simply wish to survive, we must follow their example – as Europeans, as Italians, but first and foremost as Venetians!'

The applause which followed was lengthy and enthusiastic. From the fringes of the crowd some wag yelled 'Self-rule for the Giudecca!' but this sarcasm was swamped by repeated ovations for Dal Maschio and his associates.

Zen was just wondering how he could attract Tommaso's attention when a pair of youths wearing NRV armbands appeared at his elbow and urged him to join up. One was short and chubby, his soft baby-face features contradicted by a small slot of a mouth and hard, shifty eyes set rather too close together. His companion was older and slighter, with a small moustache, long oily perfumed curls and wrap-around sunglasses tapering to a point at his ears. Zen declined their exhortations to 'stand up and be counted', and when they persisted he told them that he was there to meet Tommaso Saoner.

The elder of the two activists looked at him sharply.

'Are you called Zen by any chance?' he demanded.

'No, it was my father's name.'

The born-again Venetian did a double take, then shook his head to show that he had no time for jokes.

'Tommaso told us to look out for you,' he said curtly. 'Come this way.'

The pair moved off, shoving their way roughly through the crowd. The podium was now darkened, and volunteers were already beginning to dismantle the structure. Under one of the plane trees whose roots made the paving warp and buckle like choppy seas, Ferdinando Dal Maschio was meeting his public. He greeted them familiarly, as though each were already an old friend, a member of the family. It was an impressive performance, all the more so in that it looked entirely natural.

Stationed around Dal Maschio and unobtrusively controlling access to him stood a ring of his lieutenants, including Tommaso Saoner and a chubby man with watchful eyes whom Zen recognized with a shock as Enzo Gavagnin. The elder of the two youths went up to Saoner and spoke to him briefly. Tommaso looked over to where Zen was standing and waved him to approach.

'Well, Aurelio, what's your verdict?'

Saoner's face was flushed, his pupils enlarged, his movements jerky and his breath rapid. Zen recalled what Cristiana had said about politics being a drug. In different circumstances, he would have assumed that Tommaso was drunk.

'Good turnout,' Zen replied shortly.

But Tommaso was not so easily put off.

'And Dal Maschio?' he asked eagerly. 'What did you think of him?'

Zen shrugged.

'He's a natural politician.'

That got through.

'Stop beating about the bush, Aurelio! Are you with us or against us?'

Zen eyed him with mock alarm.

'Is there no other choice?'

'Not for someone like you, a Venetian born and bred! You heard what Dal Maschio said. We have only a few years left, a decade or two at most, to save the city and everything that makes us what we are!'

'I thought the speeches were over, Tommaso.'

Enzo Gavagnin wandered over to join them. He nodded curtly at Zen, then turned to Saoner.

'Friend of yours?'

Tommaso glanced at Zen.

'He used to be.'

Gavagnin detonated a bright yellow gob of spit on the pavement.

'And now?'

Tommaso Saoner shrugged suddenly and forced a smile.

'Oh, Aurelio's all right. He'll come round in the end. The logic of our arguments are inescapable. There is simply no other viable response to the problems we face.'

He took Zen's arm and steered him away from the menacing attention of Enzo Gavagnin.

'Come and meet Andrea.'

Tommaso led him out of the dispersing crowd, right across the *campo* and under a low portico leading under the houses. The caged lamp on the whitewashed ceiling cast the pattern of a gigantic spider-web on the ground. A small courtyard narrowed to a blind alley ending at a small canal. The tide was high again, the water lapping invisibly at the steps. Zen felt a surge of relief that Bettino Todesco was on duty at Palazzo Zulian. All might not yet be well, but at least the worst had been averted.

Eight houses faced each other across the yard, not counting the upper storeys built over the portico. Tommaso stopped at the last on the right-hand side. The plastic nameplate above the bell read DOLFIN.

'I don't know if he's home,' Tommaso murmured. 'He doesn't have a phone, so we'll have to take our chances.'

'What makes you think he knows anything about Rosetta Zulian?' asked Zen.

Tommaso shrugged and rang again.

'I recall my mother saying that his name had been linked to that affair. I don't really remember the details, but if anyone knows anything about it this long afterwards it'll be Andrea.'

A window high above their heads opened with a loud creak.

'Who's that?'

The voice was that of an elderly male, the tone peremptory to the point of rudeness.

'Tommaso Saoner. I've someone here who wants to meet you.'

'But do I want to meet him? Or is it a her? Have you turned pimp in more ways than one, Saoner? I've been trying to shut out the sound of your beastly speeches all evening.'

'It's got nothing to do with politics, Andrea. This is an old school friend of mine, Aurelio Zen.'

'Zen? You mean Stefano? No, he died. Guido? Biagio? Alberto?'

'Aurelio!' shouted Tommaso.

Zen could just make out the grizzled head leaning out of a window high above amid the swirling mist.

'There's no one by that name. I knew an Angelo Zen once, but he's dead.'

'I'm his son,' Zen called out.

'Angelo Giovanni,' the voice continued unheedingly. 'We were Young Fascists together, among the very first to join. But he had no children. I believe there had been a boy who was stillborn. And before he could make any more, Angelo went off to Russia and . . .'

'Are you going to keep us standing here all night?' demanded Tommaso.

'All right, all right! Don't be so impatient!'

A moment later there came the buzz of the door-release. Tommaso pushed the door ajar.

'I've got to get back,' he told Zen. 'There's a policy meeting I must attend. Maybe I'll catch you later, if Andrea hasn't managed to persuade you that you don't exist!'

He strode back through the portico and out into the lighted *campo*, humming with activity. Zen stepped inside and stood uncertainly in the hallway.

'Come up!' called a voice somewhere above.

Zen closed the door and started upstairs. When he reached the first-floor landing, he found himself confronted by a gaunt man in his eighties, wearing a voluminous dressing-gown of some thick red material and resting on a rubber-tipped cane. His face was heavy and jowly, as though all its youthful qualities had drained to the bottom.

'What was that about Tommaso being a pimp?' Zen asked him, feeling the need to take the initiative.

The old man cackled sourly.

'He's been trying to get me to join this political movement he's involved with, the ones who were shouting in the square just a moment ago.'

He ushered Zen through an open doorway.

'I've told him over and over again that I'm finished with all that. I got taken in once, but I was young and stupid, and at least Mussolini was the real thing! To be fooled again at my age, and with a cheap imitation like this Dal Maschio – no thank you!'

The room they entered was of about the same dimensions as its equivalent in Zen's house, but so crammed with possessions that it appeared much smaller. Every scrap of available wall space was covered by furniture or shelving, which in turn supported a vast array of objects of all kinds: a ship's bell, coins and medals, torn fragments of a flag, a fossilized fish, the six-pronged *ferro* from the prow of a gondola, stray bits of statuary, books in Arabic and Greek, instruments either medical or musical, a coiled whip, a girl's ivory hairband . . .

'Where on earth did all this come from?' asked Zen, looking round wonderingly.

'It's loot.'

'Beg pardon?'

Andrea Dolfin regarded him with a malicious eye.

'Don't you know your Venetian history? You should, with a name like Zen – if that *is* your name. Ours is a history of plunder and rapine. Next time you're passing through the Piazza, take a look around. Virtually everything you see was stolen. We extracted more booty from our fellow-Christians in Constantinople than the Turks ever did. And in my own small way I'm carrying on that tradition.'

He waved Zen towards a square leather chair with a high back and short legs.

'Sit down, please, and tell me what I can do for you.'

Zen lowered himself with difficulty into the chair, which seemed to have been made for a fat dwarf.

'I am a police official,' he said. 'I'm working on a case involving Contessa Zulian. Tommaso thought you might be able to tell me what happened to her daughter Rosetta.'

Andrea Dolfin stood staring down at him in silence for some time.

'Rosetta Zulian.'

He shuffled slowly, his bare feet encased in battered leather sandals.

'This is Tommaso's revenge,' he murmured in a low voice. 'I made mock of his zealous rantings, and in reprisal he has sent you here with a cargo of terrible memories.'

He turned, looking back at Zen from a shadowy recess at the rear of the room.

'Do you drink, at least?'

Zen made a gesture indicating that he had been known to take a drop from time to time. The old man opened a sideboard and produced a dark brown bottle and two none-too-clean glasses.

'Recioto di Valpolicella,' he announced as he hobbled back towards Zen. 'Made by my son, as a hobby. This is the 1983. The '81 was a dream but it's all gone. This could use a little more time, but it's not bad even now.'

He poured them both a glass. Zen sipped the rich ruby dessert wine. The flavour was almost overwhelmingly grapey, full of restrained sweetness, mellow yet intense.

'So you're from the police?' remarked Andrea Dolfin, subsiding in a grubby upholstered armchair and propping his feet up on a ebony *putto*, half of its head torn away to expose the jagged, splintered grain of the wood. 'Perhaps I shouldn't have made such a point of telling you about my loot.'

Zen gazed at him over the wineglass and said nothing.

'Not that the people I took it from made any objection,' Dolfin went on. 'They were above such things by then, you see, or below them. In a word, they were dead.'

He smiled a small, remote smile.

'There was nothing I could do for them, but in some cases I felt able to give some of their possessions a good home. Later, when the war was over, I meant to trace some of the relatives and try and give

101

the stuff back, but what with one thing and another I never got around to it.'

He looked at Zen.

'Shocking, eh? Are you going to take me in?'

Zen was silent a moment, as though considering the idea.

'Tell me about Rosetta Zulian,' he said at last.

A spasm contorted Dolfin's features for an instant. Then it vanished as though it had never been and a dreamy, vacant expression appeared on his face.

'What can I tell you? It all seems so long ago, so far away . . . Rosetta was a strange, solitary child. She never played with the other kids in the neighbourhood. She preferred to go her own way, making her friends where and as she found them. Her closest friend was a girl from – would you believe it? – the Ghetto. You can imagine how the *contessa*, with her ridiculous pretensions, felt about that!'

He leaned forward to pour them both more wine.

'The friend's name was Rosa, Rosa Coin. I lived in the area myself at the time, in Calle del Forno, just off the Ghetto Vecchio, and I often used to see them coming and going. The similarity of their names was not the only thing they had in common. Both had the same wavy brown hair, the same sallow skin and dark eyes, the same skinny, angular, hard little bodies. In a word, they were doubles. And not just physically. They shared a certain same intensity of manner, swinging from exaltation to despair in a moment. Even their interests were similar. Rosetta played the piano, Rosa the violin. They used to joke about forming a duo, once the war was over . . .'

The old man's expression became grim.

'It seemed so easy to say at the time. The war brought its hardships, of course, but for most of us life carried on much as before until Mussolini was overthrown. Then the Americans and British invaded from the south, and the Germans from the north, and for the next two years the country became a battlefield.'

He snatched a gulp of wine.

'Even then we got off pretty lightly here in Venice, apart from the Jews. Two hundred of them, including the Coin family, were deported to the death camps.'

'And Rosetta Zulian?' Zen put in a trifle pointedly.

Andrea Dolfin smiled and nodded.

'The old man is losing track of the subject, eh? It's true. When I start to think about those days, I sometimes get confused, and forget who was who and what really happened. It's not hard to do in the case of Rosetta Zulian, because what *did* happen was so incredible.'

He clicked the forefinger and thumb of his right hand.

'She vanished, just like that! In the spring of 1944, it was. She would have been about fifteen. One afternoon she left home, telling her mother she would be back by six. She was never seen again. No body was ever discovered. No trace of her, alive or dead, was ever found.'

Dolfin shook his head sadly.

'The *contessa* never got over it. Her husband had been killed just a couple of years before, and now this. She started making absurd accusations.'

He shot Zen a glance.

'That's why I had to move, to tell you the truth. She started putting it about that I'd done away with her daughter.'

Dolfin shrugged.

'Normally I'd just have laughed it off, but it was a difficult moment for me just after the war. There were people who had it in for me because I'd been in the party. As though I'd been the only Fascist in Venice!'

He laughed bitterly.

'She even made a formal complaint to the police! Nothing came of it, of course, but there were plenty of folk prepared to believe that there's no smoke without fire, enough to make life in the old house impossible for me. So I pulled up my roots and moved over here to Dorsoduro. The people round this way are quite different. They don't care what you may or may not have done fifty years ago, just as long as you leave them in peace now.'

He stood up painfully, wrapping the russet dressing-gown about his spare form.

'And then that fool Saoner expects me to sign up for his fantasies of an independent Venice! I might, on condition that we bulldoze the Cannaregio and make it into a car park. So many terrible things have happened here, so many crimes, so many horrors. Who wants to remember all that? We'd all end up like Ada Zulian, talking to people who aren't there and ignoring those who are.'

Recognizing that the interview was at an end, Zen stood up, buttoning his coat.

'Thank you for your hospitality,' he said. 'The wine was excellent.'

'It is not so bad,' Andrea conceded. 'I'm sorry I'm unable to tell you any more about Rosetta Zulian.'

He looked Zen in the eye.

'I fear it's just one of those episodes which will remain a mystery for ever.'

The next day dawned dull and cold. Aurelio Zen was up to watch as the light imperceptibly reclaimed the eastern sky. He had paid for his late afternoon nap with a broken, restless sleep from which even so early an awakening came as a relief. He had no idea how long he had slept. It might have been hours or minutes, but his abiding memory of the experience was of a continual tossing and turning which was the outward expression of his inner turmoil.

His visit to Andrea Dolfin the night before had merely served to confirm his sense that everything was slipping away from him. The old man's parting words had echoed his own realisation that the fate of Rosetta Zulian, like that of Ivan Durridge, and for that matter his own father, would quite likely never be known. The few facts he had gleaned stood out like objects scattered at random in a dark room, illuminated by a beam of light whose brilliance only serves to emphasize the impenetrable obscurity all around.

Anxious to dispel this paralysing sense of hopelessness, Zen dressed rapidly and set out for the Questura on foot without even pausing to broach the packet of coffee he had bought the day before. The day was established by now, but the light was still mean and grudging. The keen wind which had seen off the last of the fog blew the pigeons down the streets towards him like flying débris from an explosion.

When Zen reached his office, having stopped off in a bar to get his caffeine count up to par, he discovered that the province's maritime registration office had faxed over the details he had requested. The list was not extensive. Ivan Durridge's boat had been the broad-beamed *topa*, once a common sight on the lagoon but now largely superseded by more utilitarian models. Since the 1st of November of the previous year, only three such vessels had been registered. Of these, one was still powered only by the original lugsail and could thus be discounted. The remaining two had both been equipped with diesel engines, one a Volvo, the other a Fiat.

Zen consulted his watch. By now it was after seven, and Marco

Paulon would have made an early start to catch the tide. He looked up his number and dialled. The phone was answered by Signora Paulon, who informed Zen curtly that her husband could be reached on his mobile phone. Zen thanked her and dialled the number she supplied. A brief series of electronic beeps were followed by a gruff shout above the noise of a labouring marine engine.

'Well?'

'Good morning, Marco.'

'Aurelio?'

'Where are you?'

'On the way to San Lazzaro with a load of paper for the Armenians' printing press. What can I do for you?'

'I hear that that fisherman from Burano you were telling me about was found drowned.'

'Poor bastard. After whatever happened to him on Sant'Ariano, his brain must have snapped. Christ protect us all from such a fate.'

'A word of advice, Marco. How do I trace the serial number of the engine of a missing boat?'

For a while there was only the gurgling throb of Marco Paulon's boat bucking out across the lagoon.

'Probably the easiest way is to trace the boatyard which sold or serviced it,' Marco replied at length. 'They'll be bound to have those details on record.'

'Of course. Thanks, Marco.'

'Any time. Hey, what about coming to dinner one of these days? Fabia's telephone manner may stink, but she's also a lousy cook. On the other hand, how good do you need to be to cook fish?'

'Good enough to buy it fresh and not mess it about too much.'

'Give me a call when you're free. How about Sunday?'

'Sounds good to me.'

'We'll be expecting you.'

Zen dug out the office copy of the Venice Yellow Pages and looked up boatyards. Then he started a series of phone calls, identical in form and content.

'Good morning, this is the Questura of Venice. Can you tell me if you sold or serviced a converted *topa* belonging to Ivan Durridge, spelt D-U-R-R-I-D-G-E? You're sure? Thank you. Goodbye.'

There were about thirty-five yards altogether, and Zen had recited his formula over twenty times before he struck lucky. It seemed that

Durridge had had his boat overhauled every year by a small family firm on the Giudecca from whom he had bought it in the first place. They evidently remembered him with affection.

'Of course, the American. So kind! So friendly! He always brought a present for my little boy when he went away. We were shocked by what happened. What an appalling tragedy! Is there any fresh news?'

Zen said enough to impress on the boatyard owner the importance of the information he sought and then popped the question.

'The serial number? Yes, of course, I'll have it in the books somewhere. It was a Volvo, I remember that. Hold on just a minute.'

In the event it was more like five minutes. Meanwhile Zen went through the registration list again. The Volvo-engined *topa* was owned by one Sergio Scusat. Like all those in the city, the postal address supplied consisted of a number followed by the name of the *sestiere*, in this case San Polo. Zen was searching the desk drawers for a copy of the directory which converted these postal codes into street addresses when the receiver lying on the desk began to squeak. He picked it up and noted down the serial number of the motor fitted to Ivan Durridge's boat. It was the same.

He was just thanking the boatyard owner when Aldo Valentini walked in, yawning loudly.

'Are you here already?' he exclaimed. 'I thought you Romans lived in lotus land.'

Zen replaced the receiver with a bang.

'Where the hell do you keep the street directory?' he demanded.

'There's only one copy that I know of,' Valentini replied through another mighty yawn, 'and it's jealously guarded by Bonifacio down in Admin. He might let you consult it if you suck his cock nicely. On the other hand you might prefer to take a walk to the bar where we went the other day. They keep a copy under the counter. Come to think of it, I'll come with you.'

In front of the Questura a gleaming wooden launch was drawn up, its idling engine puking out water from time to time. A self-consciously good-looking man in a tweed suit and cashmere overcoat was just stepping ashore. He nodded minimally to Aldo Valentini as he walked past.

'The chief,' muttered the Ferrarese to Zen. 'Francesco Bruno, son of a teacher from Calabria. Currently spends most of his time sticking his bum out of the window trying to decide which way the wind is blowing. You and I may have our problems, not least trying to make ends meet on our salaries, but it's really tough at the top these days. How are you supposed to know whose orders to ignore?'

A black-headed gull swooped down as though to attack its reflection in the water. With a loud splash it seized a chunk of sodden bread and flew off, dropping a line of soggy bomblets along the canal.

The *Bar dei Greci* was empty apart from a child sitting on a table swinging his legs as he read a comic. The barman had been replaced by a stout woman wearing a flowery pinafore. Zen asked her for the directory and looked up Sergio Scusat's address while Valentini skimmed the local paper. The headline read POLICE QUESTION DROWNED MAN'S BROTHER.

'Enzo's gone out on a limb on this one,' Valentini remarked as they sipped their coffee. 'Under the new Code he's only got till six o'clock tonight to screw something out of Filippo Sfriso to justify having held him in the first place, and by all accounts he isn't going to get it.'

Zen inspected the photographs of the Sfriso brothers: blurred images evidently blown up from a family snapshot or identity card mugshot.

'What's the story?' Zen asked politely, not really wanting to know.

'In my humble opinion, it's a concatenation of absurdities,' Valentini pronounced with a theatrical gesture.

He paused, then repeated the phrase with evident pleasure.

'A concatenation of absurdities! I spent several hours interviewing the family before Gavagnin took over. The mother kept insisting that no son of hers would take his own life, but she couldn't suggest why anyone else would either. He was only a fisherman. Why would anyone bother killing him?'

'In that case, why is Gavagnin giving the brother such a hard time?'

Valentini shrugged.

'Because that's how he gets his kicks. But I don't think he'll get much change out of Filippo Sfriso. As for Enzo's drug angle, Sfriso told me that his brother had got involved with some girl in Mestre who's into hallucinogenics. Obviously Giacomo must have taken a trip that went wrong and started seeing corpses. That's all there is to it. What's Enzo want to do, bust some no-hope users trying to take a break from the grim realities of life in Mestre? Christ, I'd probably use the stuff myself if I had to live there.'

As they strolled back along the quay, Aldo Valentini repaid Zen's courtesy by asking how the Zulian case was coming along.

'Too well!' Zen returned. 'The way things are going, I'll have to come up with an excuse to stay on a few more days.'

'Aren't you missing the *dolce vita* down south?'

A fugitive smile appeared on Zen's lips.

'Perhaps I'll try and muscle in on the Sfriso case,' he murmured.

Aldo Valentini stared at him blankly a moment before bursting into laughter.

'You and your Roman humour!' he cried. 'You nearly took me in for a moment there!'

Back at the Questura, the two men shook hands and went their separate ways, Valentini to open a file on a case involving the hijacking of a barge conveying two removal lorries loaded with the entire possessions of a Dutch millionaire, Zen to engage one of the police launches with a view to calling on Sergio Scusat.

As though to give the lie to the sneering comments he had made earlier to Marco Paulon, the helmsman turned out to be an excellent and experienced seaman. Mino Martufò was from Palermo, and he had spent most of his time in boats from his earliest childhood. He handled the launch with a nonchalant panache which left Zen hovering between exhilaration and apprehension as they went careening round corners and under bridges, siren blaring and lamp flashing, totally ignoring the posted speed limits and leaving all other traffic wallowing queasily in their wake. But all to no avail: Sergio Scusat was not at home. His sister, who was looking after the children, told Zen that her brother might be found at a construction site on the Sacca San Biagio, one of three small islands at the western tip of the Giudecca.

The launch roared off again through the back canals of Dorsoduro, narrowly avoiding a collision with a taxi full of fat men with video cameras and skinny women in furs, past tiny intricate palaces and vast abandoned churches, under bridges so low they had to duck and through gaps so narrow they touched the fenders of the moored boats. Then at last, with a dramatic suddenness that took Zen's breath away, they emerged into the Giudecca channel, the deepest and broadest of all the waterways within the city.

The wind seemed much stronger here, chopping up the water into short, hard waves which shattered under the hull of the launch. The car ferry to Alexandria was steaming slowly down the channel, and Martufò sent the launch veering dangerously close under the towering bows of the huge vessel, keeling over with the force of the turn, the gunwales sunk in the surging torrent of white water. Then they were across the channel and into the sheltered canals separating the Giudecca from the *sacce*.

These small islands were some of the last areas in the city to be built on, remaining undeveloped until the 1960s. Zen could remember rowing across to them when they were still a green oasis of allotments and meadows. Now Sacca Fisola was covered in streets and squares, shops, schools, playgrounds and six-storey apartment blocks. Except for the eerie absence of traffic, it was all exactly identical to suburbs of the same period in any mainland city. But here there were no cars, no lorries, no motorbikes or scooters. The children played in the street, just as children everywhere had done a century earlier, but in a street flanked by the sort of brutalist architecture associated with chaotic parking, constant horns, revving two-strokes and blaring car radios. Here, the only sound was the lapping of the water at the shore. The overall effect was extremely unsettling, as though the whole thing were a hoax of some kind.

· The construction site where Sergio Scusat was working was on a small islet to the south of the Sacca Fisola, with a fine view of the garbage incinerator which occupied the eastmost island. Scusat was the foreman of a team of labourers repairing an apartment block. Access was by a concrete jetty jutting out into the water. As the tide was still high, they were able to come alongside. Zen stepped ashore and walked over to the other side of the jetty, where a broad-beamed boat with a curving prow was tied up. He climbed down into the stern and opened the engine housing.

'Where's the serial number on these things?'

Mino Martufò joined him and pointed to a series of numbers etched into a small plaque to the left of the block letters reading VOLVO.

'Hey! What do you think you're doing?'

The shout came from the scaffolding on the apartment block. Two men were slapping mortar on a section of external walling. A third stood staring down at the jetty.

'Scusat?' Zen called back.

'Well?'

'Police!'

The man slipped down through the scaffolding as nimbly as a monkey and walked over to where Zen was standing.

'What's all this about?' he demanded.

Sergio Scusat was a short, wiry man, his sallow face covered as though in make-up powder by plaster dust. His paper hat, folded from a newspaper page, had a party air at odds with his morose expression.

'Is this your boat?'

'Well?'

'How did you acquire her?'

Scusat looked at Zen and blinked.

'I bought her.'

'When?'

'Just before Christmas. I answered an advertisement in the *Nuova Venezia*.'

'Who was the vendor?'

'A boatyard. It was all legal and above-board. She'd been out of the water for years, but they'd overhauled her and put in a reconditioned engine. She's a good boat and the price was right. What's all this about, anyway?'

Zen regarded him for a moment.

'Have you got any proof of sale?'

'It was a cash deal. I handed over the money, they handed over the boat. What's the problem?'

'So you have no way of proving that you in fact acquired the vessel in the manner you have just described?'

'Why should I need to prove it?'

Zen glowered at him.

'The boat is stolen property.'

'I paid good money for that boat!' Sergio Scusat retorted truculently. 'There were no documents for her because she'd been laid up for so long. That was why they had to sell her cheap.'

Zen eyed the man sceptically.

'And who are "they"?'

'The boatyard I bought it from! Down at Chioggia.'

Zen eyed him.

111

'Would the owner's name be Giulio Bon, by any chance?'

'That's right! Why?'

'Ah!'

Zen closed his eyes for a moment, then looked back at Scusat.

'I must ask you to come with me to the Questura, *signore*.'

The man shot him a look of sullen fright.

'I've done nothing wrong!' he cried.

'No doubt, but I need to take a written statement of everything you have told me before I can proceed further.'

He pointed to the launch, gurgling quietly beside the concrete jetty.

'This way, please.'

Aurelio Zen strolled slowly through the east end of the city, the maze of former slums crushed in between the Pietà canal and the high fortress walls of the Arsenale. This was a secretive and impenetrable district, of no particular interest in itself and on the way to nowhere else. In Zen's childhood it had had a tough – even dangerous – reputation, and he had rarely ventured there. The rest of the city was etched into his mind like a map, but this one forgotten corner was a blank where he could still get lost.

And that was the idea: a sense of physical disorientation to match the one he felt inside. His initial spasm of elation at the breakthrough in the Durridge case was now just a fading memory. That had been young love, aware only of its own delight. Now it was time to get serious, to decide whether to make something of it, to settle down and found a family, or to break off the affair, walk away and try and forget the whole thing ever happened.

All this dangerous excitement was the more unwelcome in that Zen had anticipated nothing of the kind. His purpose in searching for Durridge's boat had been the search itself. He hadn't remotely expected to find anything of interest, only to be able to lay his labours before the family like a dog panting mightily before its owner in lieu of the stick it has failed to fetch. When he'd phoned Ellen the night before, after returning from the NRV rally, he had got the impression that some such gesture in return for the fee the Durridges were paying him – not that he had seen any of it yet – was desirable if not essential.

On the face of it, the reappearance of the missing *topa* was just what Zen needed to make the family feel that they were getting value for money, particularly in view of the link to Bon, one of the three men who had trespassed on Durridge's island home a month before the American disappeared.

But what was good news for the Durridge family was not necessarily good news for Zen himself. The material which had been made available to him through the good offices of Palazzo Sisti seemed to suggest that the Durridge case had been closed down because of its political sensitivity. If that was so, then any policeman or magistrate who sought to reopen it would be putting himself at risk to some extent. The question was how grave this risk was. Did it justify giving up the Durridges' money? The terms of Zen's private investigation were not only generous in themselves, but Ellen had passed on the news that the family had offered an additional lump sum of one hundred thousand dollars payable in the event of the discovery of the missing man, dead or alive, and the arrest of those responsible.

That was more than twice Zen's annual salary, which like that of all police officials had been frozen for the past five years as part of the government's drive to reduce public spending in a country where each newborn baby came into the world owing over half a million lire. Nevertheless, even a year earlier Zen would have had no real doubt as to which decision to take. Money might be very desirable in all sorts of ways, but it was no substitute for life and health and nights free from gnawing anxiety and bad dreams.

But things were changing fast in Italy. These days, the men who woke from nightmares between sweated sheets were the very ones who had inflicted the experience on Zen at the time of the Aldo Moro affair, and for many years after. Now *their* names were being spoken of in connection with that event, and with all the other horrors of post-war Italy – spoken not furtively, in corners, but in committees of the Senate and the Chamber of Deputies. In a world where a judge could go on record as saying that the Italian Mafia and the Italian government were one and the same, nothing and no one was sacred any longer.

In such a world, it was no longer possible to calculate the odds with any certainty. The hand which had closed the Durridge file might even now be in cuffs, unable to influence even its own fate, never mind that of others. Or, on the contrary, it might still be hovering over the buttons of power, all the more dangerous and unpredictable for the knowledge that its days were numbered. There was simply no way of knowing.

Zen stopped on a bridge, leaning over the railing. The walls of the canal, exposed by the tide, presented bands of colour ranging from brick red at the top through green and blue to a brown which turned slime grey underwater. He had no idea where he was. Time seemed to have stopped. The sky was overcast, an even grey. There was no breath of wind in the airless canyons of these back canals. The houses all around were shuttered, silent.

Zen looked down, staring at the pitted black metal of the railing. It was the French who had added these refinements when they put an end to the Republic's thousand-year independence. Until then the city's bridges had been mere arcs of stone, to all appearances as weightless and insubstantial as their reflections, across which the inhabitants went nimbly about their business. Not only were guardrails or balustrades unnecessary for a people who spent half their life in boats, but they were, as Silvio Morosini had once remarked, 'an insult to the water'.

Zen let go of the railing and straightened up. He crossed the bridge and turned right, then left, then right again, striding along with ever greater determination. He knew where he was now, and where he was going, and what he would do when he got there.

'Dating from *when*?'

'Nineteen forty-five or six.'

'If it still exists, it'll be in Central Archives.'

'Where's that?'

'On the Tronchetto. You have to send in a written request. The stuff is supposed to arrive next day, but don't hold your breath. Some sections are either missing or inaccessible. It's best to fax your requirements, mark it "extremely urgent", and then send a follow-up every hour or so until something happens. Number's in the directory.'

'Thanks.'

Zen replaced the receiver. Taking a sheet of headed notepaper from the drawer, he wrote *Denunzia fornita alla P.G. dalla parte di Zulian, Ada in re Dolfin, Andrea* in the wide, curling script he had been taught at the little school just opposite the Ghetto in the years immediately after the war. He remembered thinking of the Ghetto then as something from ancient history, like the doges and the Ten and the galleys, a prison island where the Jews had been shut up in the far-off days when such minorities had been persecuted. The fact that there were almost no Jews living there any longer had merely seemed to confirm its anachronistic nature.

He finished writing out his request for the archive file relating to the complaint which Ada Zulian had made about Andrea Dolfin at that time, now itself part of history, and was just about to take it downstairs to the fax machine when the phone rang.

'Yes?'

'Could I speak to Aurelio Zen, please?'

'Cristiana! What a pleasure to hear you.'

'How did you know it was me?'

Zen sat back in his chair and put his feet up on the desk.

'Your voice is very distinctive,' he said.

'No one else seems to think so.'

'Then they must be stupid.'

There was a gurgle of laughter at the other end.

'But then I was already thinking about you,' Zen added.

There was a pause while they waited to see who was going to make the next move, and what it would be.

'I went to see your husband speak last night,' Zen remarked.

'Did the earth move for you?'

Zen laughed.

'No, I had to fake it. But he certainly knows how to work a crowd.'

'You should see his way with women.'

Zen was about to add another line of banter when the roar of a motor outside made the windowpanes rattle.

'Just a moment,' he told Cristiana.

He got up and went over to the window. A police launch had just come alongside the quay below. In the cockpit, a muscular man wearing a pair of oil-stained overalls stood beside a uniformed patrolmen. Zen went back to the phone.

'I have to go, Cristiana. Something's come up suddenly. I'll call you back.'

'Don't bother with that. I'll see you later.'

'I don't know exactly when I'm going to be able to get home.'

'I'll be there,' said Cristiana, and hung up.

Zen replaced the phone slowly. The engine noise outside died away and was replaced by a babble of voices. He crossed back to the window. The launch had now moored. The man in overalls was standing on the quay beside his police escort, who was being harangued by another man. The patrolman shrugged largely several times and gestured towards the Questura. The other man turned round, looking straight up at the window where Zen was standing. It was Enzo Gavagnin.

Zen ran quickly to the door, threw it open and sprinted along the corridor and downstairs, two steps at a time. The group of men had reached the vestibule by the time Zen got there. Enzo Gavagnin marched straight up to him.

'What the hell's going on?'

Zen was so breathless he could not answer at once.

'Todesco tells me you authorized him to bring this man in,' Gavagnin went on aggressively.

'Have you some objection to that?' Zen gasped.

'Giulio is a friend of mine. I'm not letting him be persecuted by some arsehole from Rome who thinks he can come up here and throw his weight about as much as he likes!'

Zen turned to the patrolman, a hulking, pop-eyed individual with a face like an over-inflated balloon.

'Anything happen at Palazzo Zulian last night, Todesco?'

'Nossir.'

'No incidents of any kind?'

'Nossir.'

'Very good. Take Signor Bon up to my office.'

'Yessir.'

Enzo Gavagnin thrust himself in front of Zen, staring at him with an air of barely-contained fury.

'Let me see your warrant!'

Zen glanced at him.

'Signor Bon is not under arrest.'

'Then what the hell is he doing here?'

'I need to ask him a few questions.'

'With regard to what?' snapped Gavagnin.

'To a case I'm working on.'

'Valentini said you were working on the Ada Zulian case. Would you mind telling me what the fuck Giulio has to do with that?'

Zen shrugged.

'Everything connects in the end, Enzo,' he remarked archly. 'We're all part of the great web of life.'

Gavagnin scowled.

'And what were you doing at the rally last night?' he demanded. 'Is that connected to the case you're working on as well?'

'What were *you* doing there?' Zen shot back.

'I happen to be a founder member of the movement, just like Giulio,' Gavagnin replied stiffly. 'Unlike you, we're true Venetians, and proud of it!'

Zen nodded solemnly.

'But I hear your granny screws Albanians,' he murmured in dialect.

'*What?*'

Ignoring him, Zen turned away and followed the clattering boots of Bettino Todesco leading his charge upstairs.

Zen sat behind the desk, Bon in front of it. A female uniformed officer stood over a reel-to-reel tape recorder on a metal stand, threading the yellow leader through the slit in the empty reel. Outside, the sky lowered dull and flat over the furrowed red tiles and tall square chimneys of the houses opposite, on the other side of the canal.

The policewoman straightened up. 'Ready,' she told Zen, who nodded. The reels of the recorder started to revolve. Zen recited the date, the time, the place.

'Present are Vice-Questore Aurelio Zen and Sottotenente . . .'

He glanced inquiringly at the policewoman, a svelte but rather severe brunette who contrived to make her duty-issue uniform look as though it sported a designer label from one of the better houses.

'Nunziata, Pia,' she replied, having paused the tape.

' . . . and Sottotenente Pia Nunziata,' Zen continued. 'Also present is Signor Giulio Bon, resident at forty-three Via della Traversa, Chioggia, in the Province of Venice.'

He cleared his throat and turned to gaze at the subject of the interview.

'What is your occupation, Signor Bon?'

Giulio Bon had been staring at the floor between his feet. He shuffled uneasily, working the toe of his right shoe about on the fake marble, and mumbled something inaudible.

'Speak up, please!' Zen told him.

'I'm a marine engineer.'

The voice was hoarse and clipped, with the characteristic boneless accent of Chioggia.

'Meaning what?' Zen demanded.

Bon shrugged.

'I've got a diploma as a marine engineer.'

'I don't care if you've got a degree in Greek philosophy,' snapped Zen. 'I asked about your occupation, not your qualifications.'

Giulio Bon stared mutely at the floor for some time.

'I run a boatyard,' he said at last.

'You're the sole owner?'

'My brother-in-law has a financial interest, but I look after the work.'

'Alone?'

'I employ two men full-time, and there are others I can call on when it's busy.'

'Their names?'

Bon mumbled a series of names which Zen noted down.

'What sort of work does the yard handle?' he asked.

'Repairs, servicing, laying up.'

'Do you also sell boats?'

Bon became very still. Only his foot moved jerkily about on the glossy paving.

'From time to time,' he said.

'How many do you sell every year?'

'It varies.'

'Roughly?'

Bon shrugged.

'Perhaps half a dozen.'

Zen nodded. He lifted a paper from the desk.

'I am passing Signor Bon the extract from the Register of Vessels supplied by the Provincial authorities, reference number nine five nine oblique six oblique double D stroke four.'

Bon scanned the sheet of paper quickly. His expression did not change except for a minute tightening at the corner of the mouth.

'Do you recognize any of the boats listed?' Zen inquired.

'No.'

'I refer to the vessel identified as VZ 63923.'

'I can't be expected to remember the registration number of every boat that passes through the yard.'

'This was rather a special boat. A *topa*. Beautiful craft, but they're getting quite rare these days. Dying out, like so many of our traditions.'

Bon did not respond.

'And there's another reason why you might remember this particular boat,' Zen went on once Bon's failure to reply had registered. 'It was one of the very few which you sell each year. And you sold this one less than two months ago. On the fifteenth of December, to be precise.'

119

Bon sat absolutely still and silent. Zen let the tape run some more.

'Now do you remember?' he demanded.

His tone was as sharp as the crack of a whip. Bon flinched as though struck.

'It's possible,' he mumbled.

'Possible? It's not possible that you *don't* remember. You are on record as saying that selling boats is not your main business, just something you do from time to time, no more than half a dozen a year. How could you possibly forget selling a craft as rare as a *topa* just before Christmas?'

'Okay, all right! Maybe we did sell it!' shouted Bon, his restraint suddenly cracking. 'So what?'

'Where did you get it from?'

Bon closed his eyes, breathing deeply.

'I'd need to consult my records.'

Zen lit a cigarette. He leant back in his chair, staring coldly at Bon across the desk.

'According to a sworn statement made in this office this morning, you informed the purchaser that the vessel had been laid up for years prior to being overhauled and fitted with a reconditioned engine. The witness, Sergio Scusat, further deposed that the price had been substantially reduced owing to the fact that no documents were available for the boat. He said that you claimed this was because she had been out of the water for so long that no one could trace the previous owner and she would have to be re-registered. Is that true?'

Guilio Bon shifted in his chair but said nothing.

'Why are you being so evasive?' murmured Zen silkily.

'I'm not being evasive! I just can't remember. Is that against the law?'

Zen allowed the silence to frame this outburst before continuing tonelessly.

'The *Nuova Venezia* has confirmed that you placed an advertisement in the paper to run for the second week of December, offering a diesel-engined *topa* for sale. Sergio Scusat has testified that he bought the boat from you on the fifteenth. All I'm asking you to do is to confirm or deny the truth of the account you then gave him as to the vessel's provenance.'

Bon looked at his knees, at the wall, at the ceiling.

'Wait a minute,' he said. 'It's all coming back to me.'

Zen puffed a smoke ring which hovered in the air above the desk like a detached halo.

'Of course!' Bon continued. 'It was that old hulk we found round the back of the shed when we resurfaced the yard. God knows how many years it must have been sitting there. The hull was still sound, though. They built them to last in those days. All we needed to do was replace a few timbers here and there.'

'And install an engine,' Zen put in, apparently addressing the neon light fitting.

There was no reply. Zen lowered his head until his gaze met Bon's.

'Where did you get the engine?'

Bon waved one hand vaguely.

'There are various suppliers we use from time to time, depending on . . .'

'You told Scusat that the engine was reconditioned. There can't be many suppliers of reconditioned Volvo marine engines in this area.'

'"Reconditioned" is a relative term. It was probably some engine we had lying around the yard somewhere which we'd stripped down ourselves and reassembled.'

'But it would still have had a serial number,' Zen mused quietly. 'To sell a craft without papers is one thing, but no one's going to touch a motor whose serial number has been filed off. Besides, as you probably know, these days there are techniques for recovering, markings which are no longer visible to the naked eye.'

There was a knock at the door. Zen gestured to the policewoman, who paused the tape. The door opened to admit a burly man with a bushy beard and a mass of fine wavy hair. In his grey tweed suit and black cape, he looked like a bear got up for a circus act.

'Carlo Berengo Gorin,' he said, thrusting out an enormous hand. 'I represent Signor, er . . .'

He gestured impatiently at Giulio Bon, then swung round on Zen.

'Are you Valentini or Gatti?'

'Aurelio Zen.'

The *avvocato*'s eyebrows shot up.

'Zen? Weren't we at school together? Yes, of course! The basketball ace! The height, the grace, the movements which so bewitched the opposition that they stood like statues while you danced your way through them to notch up yet another point!'

Zen stared dumbly at the lawyer. Despite his height, he had never played basketball in his life. Gorin beamed reminiscently.

'Happy days!' he sighed. 'Now then, will you kindly inform me of my client's precise legal status?'

Zen felt his stomach tense up. The revised Code governing police procedure which had come into effect in 1988 had changed many aspects of its predecessor, especially regarding the rights of witnesses and suspects and the degree of latitude accorded the police. In many ways this had been a positive step, putting an end to practices which had led to so many abuses in the past, when they had been justified by the need to win the battle against political terrorists such as the Red Brigades. Nevertheless, the new approach suited neither Zen's habits nor his temperament.

This possibly explained why he could never remember the precise norms and procedures which the revised Code prescribed. Like all senior officials, he had had to attend a course on the new system, but his position with the élite Criminalpol squad meant that in practice he had been largely spared any need to change his working practices. Criminalpol officials intervened only in the most important cases, and were usually accorded a fairly free hand by the magistrates involved.

But this was very different. Not only was Zen not acting under the aegis of the Interior Ministry in the present instance, he was not even supposed to be investigating the Durridge case at all. He was on his own, and any initiatives he took would have to respect the letter of the new law if they were to pass the scrutiny of the Public Prosecutor's Office. He had known this all along, but he had been counting on the fact that a small-time boatyard owner like Giulio Bon probably wouldn't know his exact rights under the new system either, still less have access to a lawyer who could make them stick.

Zen looked at the intruder, who was waiting expectantly for an answer. It was odd that a man like Bon should be prepared to pay the kind of money Gorin must charge. It was still odder that Gorin apparently did not know his client's name.

'I have reason to suppose that this man possesses information relating to a case I am currently investigating,' he said carefully. 'I have therefore had him brought here to answer a few questions.'

'What is the case?' asked Gorin.

'It concerns the sale of a boat.'

Gorin frowned.

'Involving an infraction of which article of the Code?'

'That remains to be seen,' Zen replied stolidly.

'Have you informed the Public Prosecutor's Office?'

'Not yet.'

Gorin turned to Bon.

'Signor, er . . .'

'Bon, *dottò*. Giulio Bon.'

'Have you answered any of this official's questions?'

'Yes.'

'Since your legal representative was not present, whatever responses you may have given are inadmissible as evidence. Do you wish to answer the questions again in my presence?'

Bon looked up warily.

'Do I have to?'

Gorin turned to Zen.

'Do you intend to place Signor Bon in detention or under arrest?'

This was the crux. Zen had enough evidence against Bon to hold him for questioning, but under the new Code he would have to communicate this fact to the judiciary. That would mean officially revealing his involvement with the Durridge case, and his position was still too weak to risk that.

'Not at present,' he replied.

Gorin turned back to Bon.

'There is therefore no necessity for you to answer any questions, or indeed to remain here, unless you wish to do so.'

Bon stood up quickly.

'I've already told him everything I know!' he blurted out. 'I've got work to do! Why should I waste my time here if I don't have to?'

'Why indeed?' echoed Gorin.

Bon looked from Gorin to Zen and back again. With a snort of defiance he pushed past the policewoman and walked out. Gorin waggled a hairy finger at the tape recorder.

'Now then, what about that?' he asked.

'What about it?'

'Since the interview it records was conducted irregularly, the existence of the tape constitutes a violation of my client's civil rights. Under articles 596 and 724 of the Criminal Code, it is an offence to make recordings of speech acts and other discourse without the written consent of the parties involved. Did my client grant such consent?'

Zen shook his head.

'Then I must ask you to surrender the tape.'

Zen frowned.

'It is not the existence of the tape which is at issue, but that of the recording.'

Gorin smiled.

'A fine distinction, *dottore*. But since the recording subsists through the medium of the tape, for all practical purposes the two are one and the same. I must therefore ask you once again to hand over the offending article.'

Zen wagged his forefinger negatively.

'It is true that the recording cannot exist without the tape, *avvocato*, but the reverse is not the case.'

He turned to Sottotenente Pia Nunziata, who had been watching this exchange open-mouthed.

'Rewind the spool and erase the recording.'

'Yes, sir.'

Gorin stepped forward, waving his hands impatiently.

'No, no, I can't be expected to hang around here for however long it takes to erase this illegal recording.'

The policewoman fended him off with an icy look.

'Our equipment is fitted with a high-speed dubbing facility which makes it possible to erase a tape like this in a matter of minutes.'

To prove her point, she pressed a button and the tapes began spinning rapidly. Gorin stared at her for a moment, then stepped back and waved graciously, conceding the point.

'In that case, I need detain you no longer. Good day!'

With a debonair smile and a courteous nod, the lawyer swept out. As soon as his footsteps had receded, Pia Nunziata switched off the tape recorder.

'Shall I make a transcript, *dottore*?' she asked Zen.

Zen frowned at her.

'But that tape's blank now.'

The policewoman shook her head.

'I made that up. There's no high-speed facility. I just put it on fast forward.'

Zen smiled slowly.

'*Brava!* But now, if you please, erase it properly.'

He watched her rewind the tape once more, disconnect the microphone and press the red button. Then he got his coat and hat and walked out. The existence of any record of his interview with Giulio Bon was now a threat to Zen, since the questions he had asked contained numerous clues to the real reason for his presence in the city. That was why he had been so concerned to stop it falling into the hands of Carlo Berengo Gorin, especially if Zen's idea about how the lawyer had come to be summoned to the Questura proved to be correct. In that case the fighting was going to get very dirty indeed.

Zen walked quickly downstairs to the first floor, where he stopped to read the montage of typewritten announcements pinned to the staff noticeboard. Most concerned minor changes to rotas and shift schedules, and were of limited interest even to permanent staff, but Zen was apparently so absorbed by them that he did not even glance round when a door opened further along the corridor.

' . . . again, Carlo.'

'No problem.'

'See you on Saturday, then.'

'*Ciao*, Enzo.'

'*Ciao*.'

Footsteps started along the marble flooring. Zen moved his head towards a notice pinned at the extreme right-hand edge of the board. He glanced briefly along the corridor, then turned his back on the two men, closing his eyes to study the image they retained: Carlo Berengo Gorin striding towards him consulting his watch while Enzo Gavagnin rolled up his shirt sleeves and stepped back into his office.

Once the lawyer had started downstairs, humming quietly to himself, Zen walked along the corridor until he heard the unmistakable tones of Gavagnin's voice.

' . . . one more time, *Filippino mio*, just to make quite sure we understand each other. I wouldn't trust you to be able to find your own arsehole without a map, and I don't want there to be any mistake about this, know what I mean?'

Just then someone came out of an office further along the corridor. Zen turned and walked away, his lips contorted in a bitter smile.

The sickly light outside was quickly giving up the ghost, and it seemed to have got even colder. Zen turned left, past the separate building occupied by the Squadra Mobile. A pigeon came winging towards him as though intending to smash into his face, then banked aside at the last minute and came to rest on a wall tipped with broken fragments of green glass. Zen crossed the canal, passed a line of plane trees, their bark flaking like old paint, and entered the dingy bar on the corner opposite.

He ordered a coffee, fighting the temptation to ask for a shot of grappa, and sat down at a red plastic table with a view of the entrance to the Questura, where he studied his reflection in the darkening glass. There was no trace of the fury seething within. It was bad enough to have a hundred-thousand-lire-per-hour lawyer stick his nose into a case that had just been starting to show promising signs of getting somewhere. It was even worse to discover that the lawyer in question was ignorant of his client's name, and must therefore have been retained by someone else. But worst of all was the realization that this someone else was himself a policeman.

It was perfectly clear what must have happened. Enzo Gavagnin had witnessed Bon's arrival at the Questura, either by chance or because he had been tipped off by Bon. He had taken violent exception to his friend's detention, and when he failed to bully Zen into backtracking he had called in Carlo Berengo Gorin. That Zen was not prepared to swallow. Being obstructed and frustrated at every turn by politicians, judges, journalists and *mafiosi* was all part of the job, but when your own colleagues started to undermine your efforts that was something which had to be avenged. It remained to be seen just how much damage Zen could do in return, but at least he knew where to start. He glanced at his watch. Just after five. He had about an hour to wait.

By the time the lone figure finally emerged into the harsh brilliance of the security lights mounted above the entrance to the Questura, Zen had consumed three cups of coffee, five cigarettes and read the previous day's issue of *Il Gazzettino* from cover to cover. The man was wearing a brown padded jacket, jeans and leather workboots. Zen recognized him at once from the photograph he had seen in the local newspaper that morning. When he emerged on to the quay, the man was almost out of sight in the darkness, but by running along the canal to the next bridge he was able to catch up before they reached the busy streets around Campo Santa Zaccaria.

After that it was easy. The man walked steadily, without stopping or looking round, until they emerged from the network of alleys on to the broad promenade of the Riva degli Schiavoni. Here he crossed to one of the ACTV kiosks and bought a ferry ticket. Zen followed him down the walkway to the landing stage, where a crowd of passengers stood clutching bulging shopping bags, holding children or reading papers. He took up a position directly opposite the man he was following, making no attempt to conceal his presence. The man was in his early thirties, quite short and slight, with a shock of greying hair, protuberant ears and a perpetually surprised look. He moved with the fluid, restrained, vaguely simian gestures of the sailor, as though the ground might start to pitch and roll beneath his feet at any moment.

A waterbus bound for the railway station lurched alongside, but the man stayed put. He and Zen were one of only five people left after the number 8 set off towards the distant lights of San Giorgio, passing the incoming number 5, which they both boarded. The man took a seat in the bow section. Zen sat on the bench opposite. The man looked him over without interest. The *vaporetto* continued its circuit of the city, calling at the Arsenale, the gas works at Celestia and the hospital just beyond. The next stop was Fondamente Nove, where the man got off.

The quayside was packed with commuters on their way home. Zen stuck close to his quarry as he shouldered his way through the throng towards the lights of the bar. Here he consumed a ham roll and a glass of beer, while Zen had another coffee and a cigarette. Again their eyes crossed, and this time the man held Zen's gaze briefly. The television behind the bar showed puffs of smoke rising from a small town set in a wooded, mountainous landscape.

' . . . brought to fifty-five the number of deaths in the Muslim enclave during the recent fighting,' the newscaster announced. 'A spokesman for the Bosnian Serbs denied allegations that a new campaign of ethnic cleansing was underway . . .'

Outside, a ship's hooter sounded a long blast. The man finished his beer and made for the door. He barged through the crowds to the gangway marked 12 and boarded the white steamer moored there. He made his way to the forward saloon and sat staring straight ahead while the vessel shuddered off across the shallow strait towards Murano. As they cast off from the quay by the lighthouse, he got up and went out on deck.

In the far distance, a train moved slowly across the invisible bridge to the mainland like an enormous glow-worm. The man took out a packet of cigarettes, extracted one and put it between his lips. He was still fumbling in his pocket for his matches when a flame suddenly appeared in front of his face. He whirled round, his eyes full of terror.

'Who are you? What do you want?'

Aurelio Zen released the catch of his lighter, restoring the darkness.

'What did you tell them, *Filippino mio*?' he murmured.

'Nothing! I told them nothing!'

The words were spat out. Zen produced the flame again and scrutinized the man's face.

'Yes, but did they believe you?'

Filippo Sfriso laughed bitterly.

'The cops don't give a tinker's fuck what happened to Giacomo!'

Zen applied the flame to the tip of the man's cigarette.

'Then why pull you in, Filippo? Why hold you so long?'

Sfriso inhaled deeply.

'To make sure I got the message.'

'What message?'

This time Sfriso's laugh had an even more mordant edge.

'You should know!'

Zen lit one of his own cigarettes. The two men eyed each other in the brief interval of light.

'Don't play games with me, Filippo,' murmured Zen menacingly.

'Games? You're the one who's playing games! Pretending not to know what's going on when you're the ones pulling the strings!'

He broke off, gasping for breath.

'Enough, all right?' he went on dully. 'You've made your point. Do you think I wouldn't hand the stuff over if I knew where it was? What am I supposed to do with something like that? I don't know how to sell it or what to charge. What do you think I should charge? How much is my brother's life worth? What's the going rate?'

His voice rose again, a ragged yelp raw with pain and hatred.

'You bastards! You never believed him, did you? You thought he was playing games too. Bastards! Giacomo was my brother. I know

128

when he was lying, and this was no lie. What he said was true! He saw a dead man standing up as straight as you or I, with rats gnawing his chest and a mess of maggots in his eyesockets. He lost his nerve, just as you or I would have done if we'd seen something like that, in that place, at that time of night. He dropped the stuff and ran for his life, and neither of us have been able to find it again. That's the *truth*!'

He broke off again, near to tears. When at length he resumed, it was in a raucous whisper.

'But you didn't believe him. So you tortured him, holding him down in a tub of water for minutes at a time, until you overdid it and he drowned. And then you set your bent policemen on me to make sure I went along with your story that his death was an accident. Just fuck off, will you? Kill me too if you want, but while I'm still alive let me grieve in peace.'

He tossed his cigarette overboard and strode back to the lights and warmth of the saloon, leaving Zen alone in the seething dark studded with faint, misleading beacons.

It was late when Zen got back to the city. He walked home feeling tired, cold and dispirited. Despite his best efforts, everything kept going wrong. His encounter with Filippo Sfriso had merely served to emphasize the degree to which he was out of his depth. The idea had been to shake Sfriso till he rattled and see what tumbled out, in hopes of uncovering something he could use to get even with Enzo Gavagnin. But in the event it had been Zen who had been shaken to the core by what Sfriso had told him, and still more by what he had evidently assumed Zen already knew.

At best Zen had been hoping to come up with some information which, given the right presentation and packaging, would make Gavagnin look foolish or incompetent in the eyes of his superiors at the Questura. Valentini had remarked that Gavagnin had gone out on a limb over the Sfriso case; Zen's idea was to saw through the branch behind him. Gavagnin was already vulnerable to a charge of procedural irregularity in wresting the case away from a colleague and then detaining the brother of the drowned man for two days without any apparent evidence that foul play was involved. All that had been needed to complete his discomfiture were a few piquant details such as Filippo Sfriso should have been well placed – and amply motivated – to supply.

Instead of which the Buranese, assuming that Zen was one of the people 'pulling the strings', had turned the official version of the case inside out. Not only had Giacomo Sfriso been murdered, but Enzo Gavagnin was apparently acting on behalf of his killers. That was not at all what Zen had wanted. His intention had been to leave Gavagnin with egg on his face, not facing disciplinary proceedings which might result in a fifteen-year jail sentence. Besides, nothing could be proved. Even if Filippo Sfriso could be persuaded to make public his allegations, it would still come down to the word of a common fisherman against that of a senior police officer.

Zen entered a small square whose sealed well had been replaced by a standpipe. The tap was dribbling water into a red plastic bucket from which a mangy cat was drinking. The animal fled as Zen approached, cowering in the shadows to watch him pass. Suddenly a church clock started to strike the hour, nine clangorous blows which served to turn Zen's thoughts to the evening before him.

It offered little consolation. His arrangement with Cristiana had clearly fallen through. He had warned her that he might be late, but at the time he had had no idea just how much he would be delayed. There was nothing to eat or drink in the house, and by now the shops were all closed. Even the restaurants would be starting to shut their doors, except for the youth-oriented *pizzerie* such as the one he and Cristiana had visited the night before, and the prospect of going there without her seemed too grim to contemplate.

He unconsciously slowed his pace the closer he got to his destination, as though trying to delay the inevitable. But all too soon he found himself standing before his own front door. Having tried and failed to think of any alternative, he dug out his keys and went in. The air inside reeked of the damp seeping up through the stone flooring from the waterlogged soil beneath the houses. Zen checked the metal letterbox, which contained an advertising flyer and a dead leaf, and then stomped wearily upstairs. He had not felt so low since the night he arrived.

He opened the door to the living room and was about to switch on the light when he noticed that the darkness in the room was not quite complete. The woman sitting on the sofa laid down the book she had been reading and rose to her feet with a smile.

'Cristiana!' he cried.

He smiled with pleasure and amazement.

'You *are* late,' she said, in a tone devoid of reproach.

'I had no idea you were here or I'd have phoned,' he said, taking off his coat. 'But I thought you'd have gone home ages ago.'

'I don't really have a home.'

'At your mother's, I mean.'

She shrugged, walking towards him.

'Mamma is wonderful, but I feel like a child around her.'

'You're not a child.'

She nodded, holding his eyes.

'And while being an adult has its drawbacks, the great advantage is that you can do what you like.'

'Within reason.'

131

'Even without, sometimes.'

He stood staring at her, beaming like an idiot.

'It's wonderful to see you, Cristiana!'

Judging by the slightly severe suit and silk blouse she was wearing, she had come straight from work.

'Have you had dinner?' he asked.

She shook her head.

'You?'

'No. And there's nothing in the house.'

'I brought some stuff. Nothing fancy, but at least we won't starve.'

Embarrassed by his emotion, Zen walked over to the sofa and picked up the book which Cristiana had been reading, a thick volume entitled *The History of the Venetian Republic, 727–1797*. The title page was inscribed 'To my dear wife, this testimony of our glorious heritage, with love, Nando.'

Zen looked up at Cristiana.

'Gripping stuff?' he inquired ironically.

'It's not bad. Your family's mentioned quite a lot. One of them was a rabble-rousing reformer and another one a famous admiral.'

'And if I remember correctly, they both made a habit of winning all the battles and then losing the war. It must be a family trait. Living proof of that "glorious heritage" your husband makes so much of.'

Cristiana raised her eyebrows slightly.

'You really don't like Nando, do you?'

Zen shrugged.

'I don't like politicians in general.'

'But there's more to it than that.'

He nodded.

'Yes, there's you.'

She smiled and turned away. There seemed to be something about her which did not quite fit the crisply professional clothes, some hint of intimacy, some chink in her armour.

'I'm starving,' she said. 'I'll put the pasta water on.'

Zen followed her out to the kitchen. On the table stood a stoppered litre bottle of red wine, a packet of spaghetti, a fat clove of purple-skinned garlic, a small jar of oil which was the opaque green of bottle glass abraded by the sea, and a twist of paper containing three wrinkled chillis the colour of dried blood.

'*Aglio, olio e peperoncino*,' he said.

'I told you it was nothing fancy.'

As she set the heavy pan on the stove and tossed a hail-flurry of coarse salt into the water, Zen suddenly understood the rogue element in her appearance. Her breasts moved waywardly inside the sheath of silk, belying the brisk message of her formal clothing with their seditious whisper.

'Presumably all this overtime means that your work is going well,' she remarked casually. 'Or are you just trying to beef up your pay cheque?'

'I thought I was on to something today, but then someone stepped in and spiked it. Local politics.'

'Politics?'

'I mean interests, alliances,' he said, taking a broad-bladed knife out of a drawer. 'Mutual protection.'

'Nando says that's all politics is anyway.'

'And he ought to know.'

'I mean that's all he thinks it *should* be. He says the rest is just dogma and outdated ideology.'

Zen laid the blade of the knife on the clove of garlic and hit it sharply with the heel of his hand.

'Where did you learn that trick?' asked Cristiana in a tone of admiration.

Zen lifted the tissue-thin skin away and set about chopping up the clove.

'From my mother.'

'Nando can't even make coffee. "I fly planes, you look after the house," he always says. "Any time you want to swop, just let me know." '

'He's a pilot?'

'He flew ground-attack helicopters for the air force. He often says it was the high point of his life. That's why he went into politics, I think, in search of new thrills. He tried business, but it didn't have enough edge.'

'What did he do?'

'He's a partner in a firm called *Aeroservizi Veneti*. They cater to rich people needing to be taxied to and fro, businessmen wanting to charter a small jet to Budapest, that sort of thing.'

She laughed.

'I remember the day he proposed, he took me for a tour all over the lagoon in a helicopter, flying low. As we were hovering over the water in the middle of nowhere he suddenly got up from his seat, leant over me, kissed me and asked me to marry him. Later he told me that he'd put the helicopter on automatic, but I didn't know that at the time. I was terrified. So of course I said yes, just to get him back at the controls!'

Zen poured the olive oil into a small pan, set it on a low flame and added the chopped garlic.

'Quite the lad, eh?'

'Oh yes. And with *all* the girls.'

The lid of the pasta pan started to rattle. Cristiana tore the spaghetti packet open with her sharp white teeth. She emptied half the golden rods into her palm and lowered them into the pan, where they gradually unbent and began to move freely, like underwater weed. She looked up at Zen, who had been watching the swell and sway of her breasts. Their eyes held a moment, then he turned back to the counter and began to shred the chillis.

'Are these really hot?' he asked.

'I've no idea. Those small ones are often the worst.'

'How many shall I put in? Three? Four?'

'I can take it if you can.'

Dense with gluten, the pasta water gurgled like hot mud. Zen scattered the flakes of chilli over the slices of garlic, which had turned a pale gold in the warm oil. Cristiana laid a large bowl, two plates, glasses, forks and spoons on the kitchen table and unstoppered the wine. She fished a strand of spaghetti out of the water and tested it.

'What do you think?'

She passed the rest to Zen, who bit into the clammy filament.

'Still a bit chewy.'

'It should be. The oil will finish it.'

She drained the spaghetti and dumped the tangled mass into the bowl, where Zen anointed it with the scalding oil.

'Ready!'

They sat facing each other across the table, the steaming tub of pasta between them. While Cristiana served them each a plateful, Zen poured the wine.

'So what have local politics to do with Ada Zulian's ghosts?' Cristiana asked, winding spaghetti on to her fork.

'Ada? Nothing!'

He frowned suddenly, realizing his slip.

'No, that was . . . I was talking about a different case.'

'You're working on something else?'

'Sort of.'

'Is that what that fax was about?'

He nodded.

'It's all a bit confidential, actually.'

'I can keep a secret.'

He looked over at her and smiled, holding her eyes for a moment.

'It concerns that American who disappeared a few months ago from an island in the lagoon.'

Cristiana gasped.

'Swallowed a bit of chilli,' she explained.

'It was all over the papers for a while. Everyone assumed he had been kidnapped, but there was never a ransom demand.'

'I seem to remember reading something about it. Has something new come up?'

'Yes and no.'

She shot him a glance.

'Meaning you don't trust me.'

'It's not that,' he said quickly – too quickly.

Cristiana gave the facial equivalent of a shrug and went on eating.

'The American's boat disappeared at the same time he did,' Zen told her after a moment's hesitation. 'I think I've found it.'

She opened her eyes wide.

'Where?'

'Here in the city. The man who took it was probably supposed to scuttle it, but he was greedy. He sold it instead.'

He took a gulp of wine to cut the aromatic oil coating each strand of pasta.

'But where does politics come into all this?' asked Cristiana.

'The man in question has friends.'

'Who are they?'

'I don't know, but they had a lawyer there ten minutes after I'd started my questioning. And this was one of those lawyers you normally make appointments with a year ahead. Name of Gorin.'

'Carlo?'

'You know him?'

She frowned.

'We . . . Nando knows him, I think.'

She hoisted a last forkful of pasta to her mouth. A dribble of oil ran palely green down her chin. Zen reached over and wiped the oil away with his fingers, then licked them clean.

'Wonderful,' he said, setting his own plate aside. 'I haven't had that for ages. So simple, yet so good.'

Cristiana smiled and poured them both some more wine. Zen held up his packet of cigarettes.

'Do you mind?'

'I'll have one, if I may. I'm an occasional smoker.'

'I know the feeling. I'm an occasional non-smoker.'

They smoked in silence for some time.

'You miss your husband,' said Zen abruptly.

It was not a question.

'In a way,' replied Cristiana. 'It's not easy being a single woman in this place. It's like being a child again. Everything you do is subject to scrutiny and comment.'

'Does your mother know that you're here?'

Cristiana shrugged.

'I expect so. There's always someone watching.'

In the next room, the phone started ringing shrilly.

'Damn!' said Zen, getting up. 'Don't go away.'

Cristiana smiled ruefully.

'Where would I go?'

The moment Zen picked up the receiver, he knew it had been a mistake to answer the phone.

'Aurelio? Where the hell have you been? Why haven't you been in touch?'

'Hello, Tania.'

'I've been trying to get hold of you all day! We both have.'

'Both?'

'Your mother and me.'

'The old firm.'

'What?'

'How are things? Rome still there? I suppose it must be. Eternal city and all that.'

'Are you drunk?'

'I'm happy.'

'Happy? Why?'

'Why am I happy?'

Laughter pealed out from the kitchen.

'Who's that?' demanded Tania. 'Have you got someone there with you, Aurelio?'

'Of course not. It was someone in the street outside. The windows are open.'

'I see. Well, *you* may be happy, but I'm certainly not, and neither is your mother. Maybe you should think about that.'

'Maybe I should.'

'All you seem to care about is yourself. Out of sight is out of mind as far as you're concerned. I've been talking about you to your mother, Aurelio, and I have to say that I find what she's told me extremely disturbing. It confirms a lot of things I'd already suspected about you.'

'Like what?'

'Like the fact that you're deeply selfish. That you don't give a damn about other people. They're just a means to an end, as far as you're concerned.'

'That's what my mother told you?'

'Not in so many words, but the things she told me made it quite clear that you'd been ruthlessly self-centred and manipulative ever since you were a child.'

'It didn't occur to you that she might have an axe to grind herself, Tania?'

He was angry by now, and his tone showed it.

'What do you mean?'

'I mean that she's jealous of this woman who's threatening to alienate the affections of her darling son and do disgusting things to him in bed, so she's doing everything she can to frighten you off so that she can have me all to herself again.'

There was a brief silence.

'That is the most shocking thing I've ever heard anyone say about their mother. For God's sake, Aurelio! What kind of monster are you? Are you seriously suggesting that your mother is sexually jealous of me? That's just totally sick! It's the most disgusting thing I've ever . . .'

Zen quietly replaced the receiver on its rest and walked back to the kitchen. Cristiana raised her eyes to meet his.

'What was *that* all about?'

He shook his head wearily.

'Don't ask.'

He slumped down in his chair again. He had just lit another ciga-rette when the phone began to ring again. He sat staring tight-lipped at the table. The phone rang eleven times before stopping.

'Persistent,' commented Cristiana when the noise finally stopped.

As though in response, the phone started trilling again. This time it rang fifteen times.

'Not to say obstinate,' Cristiana added.

After a brief pause, shrill bursts of ringing jarred the silence once again. Cristiana stood up.

'May I?'

Zen breathed a long sigh. He waved at the open doorway. Cristi-ana marched into the living room and lifted the receiver.

'Yes? Who? No, there's no one here by that name.'

She slammed the phone down and unplugged the cord from the socket. When she straightened up again, Zen was standing behind her. He caught hold of her shoulders, turned her towards him and kissed her on the mouth. They measured each other with their eyes in a final brief interval of lucidity, then blindly collided again.

It was the strangeness that woke him, the presence of another body in that bed where he had always slept alone, and which was not quite wide enough for two. He closed his eyes and lay back on the pillow, smiling at some memory from the night before. The sheets were still damp with sweat, the whole bed perfumed with evocative scents.

Cristiana shifted slightly in her sleep, as though the memories which were keeping Zen awake had reached into her dreams too. And indeed it might all have been a dream, so unlikely did it seem in the chill darkness of – was it really only ten to six? He put his watch back on the bedside table and rolled over, seeking the precise position which would enable him to complete the jigsaw of sleep.

But whichever way he turned, images of Cristiana darted through his mind like silver fish. All the other women in his life had made him feel that however much they seemed to be enjoying themselves in bed, in the end they were only doing him a favour. With Cristiana, it had been abundantly clear from that very first kiss that everything she did was done for her own pleasure as well as his. She displayed an eager greed for caresses of all kinds, an inclusive sensuality which had brought a succession of climaxes in its wake and raised Zen to a state of exaltation he had never experienced before.

Shying away from the memory of some of the things he had said and done, he sat up in bed. Sleep was clearly out of the question. He had a momentary urge to grasp Cristiana's plump white shoulder, to turn her over and start feeding on her breasts and belly. Instead, he forced himself to turn back the covers and stand up. What had happened had happened, but to start acting like an adolescent in heat at his age, and at this time in the morning, would be ridiculous.

He walked quickly across the icy tiles to the bathroom. But even beneath the tepid spray of the shower, thoughts of Cristiana's languorous, compliant body gave him no peace. It occurred to him for the first time that he might be making a complete fool of himself. This prospect finally succeeded in calming the tumult in his loins. He had no precise idea what sort of humiliation might be in store for him, only a lurking sense that he was vulnerable in various ways.

He dressed and went downstairs to make coffee. By the brutal light of the bare bulb in the kitchen, love's sweet dream faded still further. What had they done? What were they going to do? Above all, what were they going to say to one another? The prospect of greeting Cristiana, of having to sit down and make small talk, filled Zen with limitless dread. The conversation of their bodies the night before had been as effortless and natural as the soft declension of surf on a beach, but to convert that exchange into the hard currency of language and everyday life seemed a daunting prospect.

The coffee gurgled and gushed. He poured himself a cup which fumed in the chill air and scribbled a note to Cristiana, explaining that he had had to go in to work early and would ring her later that morning. Deciding that this looked cold and bureaucratic, he tore it up and wrote another, attempting to explain the riot of emotions in his heart. That ended up in the bin too. The note he eventually left on the table owed more to the first draft than the second, but with several allusions to his feelings about what had happened the previous night.

Outside, the darkness was still untouched by signs of dawn. It was much colder than it had been the day before, a still, rigid cold. There was hardly a breath of wind. The only sounds were the lapping of water and the cries of gulls circling high above. Zen set off walking fast, burning off the energy surging through his body. Thinking about his youth, as he had often done in the past few days, it seemed like a film overlaid with grandiose gushing music which flooded every banal scene with emotion and made it seem transcendent and unique. Being older, he thought, meant living the same film without the music.

Now, though, the soundtrack was back in place. He felt strong and vigorous, invincible and serene. The doubts and difficulties which had beset him earlier now seemed trivial. A woman had offered herself to him and he had satisfied both her and himself. What could touch him? He kept up a cracking pace all the way to Santa Maria Formosa, his breath blossoming thickly in the frigid air. He passed a street-sweeper mending his broom, a convocation of feral cats, a somnambulant barman setting out his tables, a kid of eighteen folding back the tarpaulin over a moored boat. All seemed to eye him with admiration and envy, waving him past, wishing him well.

At that hour, the isolated *palazzo* on the San Lorenzo canal which housed the Questura di Venezia was to all appearances as deserted as the rest of the city. Zen walked upstairs to the first floor, and then along the passage to the door marked GAVAGNIN – RUZZA – CASTELLARO. Inside, a solitary fly buzzed in feeble bursts against the window whose glass was bleary with the first hints of dawn. Enzo Gavagnin's territory was immediately discernible by the extent of the damage surrounding it. The wastebin was dented, the ashtray overflowing, the scar and burn marks on the surface of the desk that much more numerous and profound, the litter of memos, notes and files on top of it that much messier and more impenetrable.

Zen turned over the papers one by one. He waded through reports of drug dealers, suppliers, users and informers. He searched through the desk drawers and the filing cabinet in the corner of the room, all without learning anything other than he had already guessed: that Enzo Gavagnin was a professionally respected officer with a heavy workload and a wide range of contacts in both the force and the local underworld. All this was to be expected. After half an hour, Zen had found nothing to justify his suspicions even to himself, let alone a cynical superior.

At any other time this might have discouraged him, but that morning he was invulnerable to setbacks. Lighting his first cigarette of the day, he thought it through again. He was pretty sure that the litter on the desk would yield nothing. It was too ephemeral, too heterogenous and too likely to be dispersed by a careless or over-zealous cleaner. A cleverer man than Gavagnin, calculating on precisely such an assumption, might have decided that this made it the perfect place to hide a sensitive document. But Gavagnin was not clever, at least not in that way. If he had something to hide, he would *hide* it, and not in plain view.

What would he be hiding? That was the key. If Zen knew what he was looking for, he would know where to look. If Filippo Sfriso's allegations were true, Gavagnin would need to be able to pass on news, to give and receive instructions. That meant a phone number, perhaps more than one. Where would such a man keep them?

Zen closed his eyes and concentrated, creating a mental hologram of Enzo Gavagnin, an image he could revolve slowly in his consciousness, seeking the answer to his problem. Who was Gavagnin? A swaggering, unscrupulous fixer, energetic and resouceful, but utterly devoid of any moral sense. Someone incapable of imagining that anything he did could be wrong, even though he knew it was illegal. Someone who would not be troubled by this contradiction. Someone above suspicion in his own eyes.

In short, a mamma's boy. Mothers fell in love with their sons when their husbands proved unfaithful, Zen believed. This explained his own predicament, his need to be confirmed by the women in his life, and his excessive response when – as last night – this occurred. For Signora Zen had never had the chance to grow disillusioned with her husband, who had disappeared in Russia, an immortal hero whom his son could never hope to supplant. Gavagnin, on the other hand, having been bathed in the river of maternal adoration, felt himself immune to the contingencies of everyday life. Like Achilles, however, he might be wrong about that.

Zen had already noticed the phone book on his first search, in the bottom drawer of Gavagnin's desk. It was two years out of date, lacked a cover and started midway through the names beginning with C. Zen picked it up and fingered the flimsy pages. There were various marginal marks and underscorings, but Zen was looking for something simpler, something gross and blatant, something *meant*. And towards the middle of the book he found it, in an advertising insert printed in colour on shiny paper, easy to find. Beneath a picture of a leather armchair, three numbers had been noted down in a jerky handwriting which Zen recognized from other documents written by Gavagnin.

The numbers made no sense in themselves, which merely strengthened Zen's conviction that he had found what he was looking for. They each consisted of nine digits, the first four written separately, as though they were area codes. Zen picked up the phone and dialled the first number, but got only a continuous tone indicating that no such connection existed. He tried the other two numbers with the same result.

Taking a blank sheet of paper from the top drawer, Zen copied out the three numbers and sat staring at them for some time. Then he picked up the phone and tried dialling the digits without the initial zero. That didn't work either, nor did dialling just the last five digits, ignoring the prefix. He lit another cigarette and pored over the sequence of numbers once more. After some time, he lifted the receiver and dialled once more, adding the final digit of the prefix to the five which followed. This time the number rang.

There was no answer. Zen depressed the receiver and tried the same method with the next series of digits. This time he was connected to an answering machine.

'*Leave your message after the tone,*' recited a recorded male voice with a strong Veneto accent.

Zen hung up and tried the last number. The response was immediate.

'Well?' demanded an irascible male voice.

Zen had been planning to say he'd got a wrong number, but he had a sudden, gleeful inspiration.

'This is Enzo,' he said in an approximation of Gavagnin's guttural tones.

'Why are you calling at this time in the morning, for fuck's sake?'

On any other day, Zen would have hung up at that point. He already had the confirmation he needed, and to proceed further might ruin everything, if the man the other end realized that he was not in fact Gavagnin. But he was feeling too good to stop. Besides, what could go wrong on such a morning? His luck was in. He was on a roll.

'Filippo has agreed to co-operate,' he murmured.

There was a long silence.

'That's not what you told us yesterday,' the man replied with a new edge.

'This happened last night. After I told him that his mother would be the next to have an accident.'

This time the silence seemed to last for ever.

'You exceeded your instructions,' said the voice. 'You should have consulted us.'

Zen said nothing.

'Do you have the goods?' the man asked.

'I know where they are,' replied Zen, and replaced the receiver.

He folded up the paper with numbers and put it in his pocket, then replaced the directory in the drawer. That should give Gavagnin something to think about, he thought as he walked upstairs with a mischievous smile.

His own office was as he had left it the day before, except that the

143

wire tray contained a buff memorandum from the Forensic laboratory with the results of the fingerprint tests on the knife used to attack Ada Zulian. As he had expected, the only prints on the knife – apart from a partial of Zen's thumb on the base of the handle – were identical to those taken from the *contessa* herself.

Zen dropped the memo into the file he had opened on the case. Although it told him nothing he did not already know, it was a timely reminder that he had better cover his tracks by devoting some time and energy to the investigation which was the notional reason for his presence in the city. He prowled about the office, trying to think of a way to force the issue.

A sudden racket drew him to the window. In a barge moored on the opposite bank of the canal, a man was stripping the bark off a tree trunk with a chain-saw. As Zen watched, he shaped the end to a rough point and then manoeuvred the stake into position with a rope before ramming it down into the mud with a pile-driver mounted in the bow of the barge. Within minutes, the mooring pole was in place. The whole city was constructed on a subterranean forest of such piles, Zen recalled, laid down centuries ago to stabilize the mudbanks of the lagoon and make them habitable.

For some reason the thought triggered a surge of panic, an intolerable sense of constriction, asphyxiation and dread. His earlier elation was abruptly banished as though it had never been. A moment before he had been thinking about walking to the *Bar dei Greci* for some well-earned breakfast, buoyed by the knowledge of a job well done and a rival elegantly dished. Now all that had been swept away by an overwhelming need to get out, to escape from this wasteland of water and stone, and feel solid ground beneath his feet again. Similar attacks of claustrophobia may well have been one of the factors which had driven earlier generations of Venetians to colonize substantial stretches of the Mediterranean coastline. Aurelio Zen's solution was less ambitious but just as effective.

In the early sixties, a relative of Silvio Morosini who worked in one of the glassworks on Murano had been sent to New York for two weeks as one of a group of Italian artisans demonstrating their traditional skills at a trade fair. On his return, the instant celebrity was fêted at a huge dinner party. Everyone was agog to hear from his lips what the fabled city of skyscrapers and millionaires was really like.

After a suitably impressive pause, the latter-day Marco Polo duly pronounced. 'New York,' he said with a dismissive shrug, 'is Mestre.'

Mestre certainly wasn't New York, but for therapeutic purposes it would do. Zen went downstairs and commandered a launch to take him 'as a matter of the greatest urgency' to the concrete and asphalt expanses of Piazzale Roma, from which a taxi sped him across the aptly named Ponte della Libertà to the mainland. As the diesel-engined Fiat traversed the freeways and flyovers of Marghera, where the pall of pollution was so bad that vehicles could only be driven on alternate days depending on whether their registration number was odd or even, Zen felt his crisis gradually easing. By the time he had paid off the taxi and walked down a street clogged with stalled and honking traffic and across a piazza filled with rows of parked cars wedged so tightly that it would have been easier to climb over them than to find a way through, he could no longer remember why he had come. To leave those quiet streets and that clean air, for *this*? The idea was palpably crazy.

He made his way on foot to the station buffet, where he breakfasted badly and expensively before catching a train back to the city. As Zen watched the slums and muddle of the mainland recede, he noticed an electronic sign attached to the tower-block offices of a local bank. Unlike similar displays elsewhere, this one showed not only the time and the date but also the state of the tide. A simple calculation yielded the information that high water that evening would be around nine o'clock. Which suited Zen nicely.

Back in the city, he made his way on foot to Palazzo Zulian. The sun was just showing through the thick haze, a white disc which might have been the source of the cold which gripped the air. Just before turning into the narrow passageway leading to the door, Zen inadvertently stepped in a large turd which the dog's owner had disguised with a sprinkling of sawdust. He cleaned up the mess as best he could, wiping his shoe along the wall and pavement, but he was not in the best possible humour as he approached Palazzo Zulian. Nor was his mood improved by a raucous shout from overhead.

'Go away! Get out of here!'

He looked up. Ada was not visible, but the voice was hers.

'Be off, I say!'

'Not until I've spoken to you, *contessa*,' Zen replied.

A head emerged from the carved window at first-floor level.

'Ah, good morning, Aurelio Battista! So you've finally decided to show your face around here. About time too!'

Zen gawked up at her.

'Thanks for the welcome,' he retorted sarcastically.

'I wasn't talking to you! I didn't even know you were there. I was shouting at that tomcat on the wall. I made the mistake of throwing him some scraps last week, and now he sits there all day staring at me like a beggar. Now stay put and I'll send your man down to open the door. Let me tell you, I'm going to give you a piece of my mind!'

Ada drew back into the house and closed the window. Zen looked round, and was reassured to see that the cat in question did in fact exist. Noticing his glance, it gave a self-pitying mew.

'Piss off,' said Zen.

The cat blinked and looked away disdainfully. Inside the house there was a clatter of boots on the stairs. A key turned in the lock and the door opened to reveal Bettino Todesco clutching a service revolver.

'Ah, it's you, chief,' he said, putting the weapon back in its holster.

'Who the hell did you think it was?' Zen snapped, pushing past.

'Well she said it was, but I don't take that much notice of what she says any more.'

He leaned forward and whispered confidentially to Zen.

'If I have to spend another night here I'll go round the bend myself.'

Zen frowned at him.

'Why, has anything happened?'

Todesco shook his head lugubriously.

'I wish something *would* happen. Anything would be better than having to listen to that woman maundering on. If she's not bitching about this, she's moaning about that, or talking to people who aren't there. Gives me the creeps, I can tell you.'

Zen nodded.

'All right, Todesco, go off home and get some rest. But be at the Questura by six o'clock this evening. I need you for an operation I have in mind.'

'Very good, chief.'

Zen made his way up the stairs leading through the mezzanine level to the hallway transecting the house from front to back. The diminutive figure of Ada Zulian stood silhouetted against the window at the far end.

'So you've dismissed your spy,' she remarked sourly, 'but I suppose he'll be back. A fat lot of use it was calling the police! I complain of intruders in my house, and all they do is force another one on me.'

She sniffed suspiciously. Zen shifted uneasily in his shoes. There was still a strong stink of dogshit. Some of the stuff must have got trapped in the crack between the sole and the uppers.

'I should have listened to Daniele Trevisan,' Ada Zulian went on. 'He told me to keep the police out of it.'

'Well then, you'll be glad to hear that we're about to get out of it,' Zen snapped.

Ada put her head on one side and stared up at him. Her face looked inexpressibly ancient, a palimpsest of all the faces it had ever been: baby, child, adolescent and the whole parabola of womanhood. It was all there, superimposed like layers of paint.

'What do you mean?' she inquired mildly.

'I mean you win, *contessa*! You want the police out of your hair and I want you and your bullyboys out of mine. Is it a deal?'

Ada Zulian peered at him.

'Are you feeling all right, Aurelio Battista? Come into the salon and I'll make some camomile tea to calm you down.'

'What will calm me down is you calling off your friends and relations!'

'I don't know what you're talking about.'

'Oh come on, *contessa*! You told people about the police guard on the house . . .'

'I mentioned it to my family . . .'

' . . . who mentioned it to their powerful contacts, who mentioned it to my superiors at the Questura, who have been making my life a misery ever since. Fair enough! I was only trying to protect you, because you were a family friend, and this is the thanks I get!'

He walked right up to her, emphasizing his points by stabbing one palm with two fingers of the other hand.

'That policeman who just left will not be coming back, *contessa*. Understand? Neither will his colleagues. Neither will I. You won't be bothered with any of us any more. And all I ask in return is that you get in touch with all the people you complained to about me and tell them to very kindly stop breaking my balls.'

Ada glared at him.

'There's no call to use that sort of language.'

'I don't care what sort of language you use, *contessa*, just as long as you get the message across.'

He turned on his heel and walked back to the stairs.

'And if the intruders return?' Ada called querulously after him. 'What will become of me then?'

Zen turned and stared back at her implacably.

'But they won't return, will they? They were never here in the first place. They never existed, except in your dreams. And I have enough real work to do without trying to police people's dreams.'

He nodded curtly.

'Good day, *contessa*. And goodbye.'

Zen paid for his broken sleep and early rising with a blurred mental focus which ensured that the rest of the day passed in a dopy haze punctuated by various isolated episodes which forced themselves on his attention, one being the moment when Enzo Gavagnin publicly accused him of being an undercover agent acting for the Ministry in Rome.

The encounter took place in the *Bar dei Greci*, where Zen had gone to try and blast away his mental fog with stiff draughts of *espresso doppio ristretto*. When Gavagnin appeared beside him at the bar, Zen was reading a newspaper report of a speech by Umberto Bossi, demanding immediate national elections to 'restore credibility to the government before the demands of local demagogues for regional autonomy lead to the break-up of Italy'. A leader commented that now Bossi saw a real chance of achieving power at national level, he was distancing himself from those such as Ferdinando Dal Maschio who were still pursuing the separatist goals which Bossi had once espoused.

'What the hell were you doing in my office this morning?' demanded Gavagnin aggressively.

'I don't know what you're talking about,' Zen replied.

Thanks to his dazed condition, this was literally true. He had temporarily forgotten that he had ever visited Gavagnin's office, let alone why, and thus had no trouble sounding innocently baffled. But Gavagnin's fury was not assuaged.

'Don't try and deny it!' he snapped. 'When I got in this morning I couldn't breathe for the stink of those camelshit *Nazionali*. You're the only one in the building who smokes them.'

Zen merely shrugged and went on reading the paper. Gavagnin snatched it from his hands.

'Admit it, you're a spy!' he shouted. 'A snooper from the Ministry. All that bullshit about being sent up here to look into some madwoman's stories about things going bump in the night! What a load of crap! It's us you're investigating, isn't it? You're checking us out on behalf of your masters in Rome. That's what you were doing in my office. Going through my papers to try and find something to use against me. And why? Because I'm with the *Nuova Repubblica Veneta*, and we've got the old regime shitting in its pants!'

He continued in this vein for some time, but Zen simply stared levelly at him and said nothing. As time went on, Gavagnin's tone became distracted rather than confrontational, his tone more pleading than threatening. In the end, he turned on his heel and stalked out.

Another of the landmarks punctuating Zen's prevailing mental fog had been the arrival of the documents relating to the complaint which Ada Zulian had made about her near-neighbour at the time, Andrea Dolfin. They were brought – with a speed and efficiency belying the warnings Zen had received – by a uniformed messenger attached to the Central Archives of the Province of Venice, recently re-sited in a custom-built concrete bunker beneath the car park on the artificial island of the Tronchetto.

The move from the Archives' former premises in a *palazzo* facing the Rialto had led to considerable disruption and, it was rumoured, the loss of several thousand documents. This still left a few million to shelve and classify, however, but by good luck the items which Zen had requested the previous day were evidently lodged in one of the sections that was up and running. Zen lit one of his despised domestic cigarettes and settled down to study the sheets of stiff parchment-like paper covered in heavy typewriting. The document, dated May 1946, consisted of the *denuncia* made to the authorities by Contessa Ada Zulian, resident in the eponymous palace, concerning the alleged activities of Andrea Dolfin, resident in Calle del Forno, followed by a report into the investigation subsequently carried out by a *commissario di polizia*.

The draft of Ada Zulian's statement ran to almost fifteen pages. Reading through them, Zen could not help smiling faintly at the increasing frustration of the police officer who had interviewed her, evident even in the bureaucratic language employed. 'The deponent was asked to address herself to the substance of the complaint . . .' 'A number of allegations concerning other residents of the Cannaregio district, being extraneous to the matter in hand, have been omitted . . .' 'The deponent was yet again urged to express herself with greater brevity and concision . . .'

There was nothing humorous about what the *contessa* had to say, however. Stripped of her characteristic longueurs and digressions, the essence of her accusation was that the said Andrea Dolfin had three years earlier kidnapped and murdered Rosa Coin, daughter of Daniele Coin, formerly resident in Campo di Ghetto Nuovo.

Although Ada's charges were unsubstantiated by any evidence, they were sufficiently grave to force the police to launch an investigation. The conclusions of the resulting report hinged on two key documents. The first was a photocopy of an extract from German records listing those Venetian Jews deported in 1943. The names of all seven members of the Coin family appeared, but the entry for Rosa Coin had been crossed out and the comment 'Found hanged' added in the margin.

This initially appeared to support Ada's allegations. Andrea Dolfin had been for a time a prominent member of the Fascist administration in Venice, and although he had lost his official status when Mussolini was overthrown, he remained a trusted figure enjoying good relations with the occupying German authorities. Given this fact, and the lack of any other evidence as to how Rosa Coin had met her death, Andrea Dolfin was regarded as a suspect by the police and was questioned on a number of occasions, but without result.

The investigation was dramatically terminated by the arrival of a letter from the supposed victim herself. So far from having died in 1943, it appeared that Rosa Coin was living in Palestine, the sole survivor of her family. A former neighbour in the Ghetto had written to her, revealing Ada Zulian's allegations, which Rosa proceeded to refute point by point. Her letter made it clear that she was not only alive, but that she owed her survival to none other than Andrea Dolfin, who had used his privileged position to shelter her during the final months of the war. Once Rosa's identity had been confirmed by the British authorities in Palestine, the case was immediately dropped.

Zen was reading the final lines of the report, which noted that Contessa Ada Zulian had been diagnosed as suffering from 'hysteria and delusional melancholia' since the disappearance of her daughter in mysterious circumstances, when the phone rang.

'Yes!' he barked gruffly.

'Hello, sweetie.'

A smile spread slowly across Zen's face.

'Well, hello there,' he breathed.

They shared an intimate moment of silence.

'How are things?' Cristiana asked at length.

'Things are fine. Things are great. Never have they been better.'

'Good.'

'How about your things?'

'They're not complaining either.'

Another long supple silence.

'When can we . . .?' Zen began, but Cristiana had started talking at the same moment.

'. . . make it tonight, unfortunately.'

'Oh.'

'Don't think I wouldn't love to, but I have to turn up with you-know-who for this press gala at the Danieli.'

The quality of the silence which ensued was rather different.

'I thought you were separated,' Zen said at last.

'Not publicly. Can you can imagine what the media would make of a story like that, especially just before the elections? Nando's made plenty of enemies who would just love to get their hands on some juicy scandal.'

'Why should you care?'

'For one thing, because I don't care to have my name dragged through the gutter. And for another, because I want to keep on the right side of Nando.'

'I see,' said Zen icily.

'No, you don't. You don't need to. But I've got to be realistic. Nando's already a very powerful man, and the way things are looking he stands a good chance of being elected mayor next month. There's nothing to be gained by making a sworn enemy of someone in that sort of position. They can do too much harm. By going along with public appearances when he asks me, I keep some leverage.'

She laughed deliberately, to lighten the mood.

'I don't want to end up like your ancestors, you know.'

'What?'

'Renier Zen and . . . what was the other one? You said last night they had a habit of winning all the battles but losing the war.'

'Oh. Yes. But listen . . .'

'Just a moment!'

There was a noise in the background and Cristiana greeted some-one who had come into the agency.

'The boss,' she explained in an undertone to Zen.

'Shall I call you back?'

'That's all right. Now you were enquiring about seat availability over the weekend period, I believe?'

Zen grinned broadly, his fit of pique forgotten.

'It wasn't so much *seats* I was thinking of . . .'

'That's simply the formula we use at booking stage,' Cristiana returned crisply. 'You would of course be upgraded automatically at check-in.'

'Sounds good. When are you free?'

'Let me just check the computer . . . The earliest slot would appear to be tomorrow afternoon.'

'What time?'

'The flight leaves at . . . Ah, we can drop the charade. *La signora* has gone to powder her butt. Where were we?'

'When are you free tomorrow?'

'I've promised to take Mamma shopping in the morning, and we're having people to lunch. Say between two and three?'

Zen sighed.

'That seems like a long way off.'

'It's the best I can do.'

He pulled himself together.

'Of course. I just can't wait to see you again.'

'Till tomorrow.'

She hung up. Zen relinquished the receiver more gradually, loath to slip back into the mental miasma he could already feel rising to claim him.

The next thing of which he was distinctly aware was the arrival of Aldo Valentini, a cigar betwen his lips and an air of infinite self-satisfaction on his glowing features.

'Ah, the pleasures of food!' the Ferrarese exclaimed enthusiasti-cally. 'What is sex compared to a great lunch? Am I glad Gavagnin took that Sfriso case away from me! What's up with our Enzo anyway? I just passed him on the stairs and he looked through me as though I were a ghost.'

'A well-fed ghost, evidently,' commented Zen, who had eaten nothing but a mass-produced pastry during his trip to the mainland.

'You have no idea, Aurelio! Those lads at the Gritti really know their stuff, I can tell you.'

Zen looked suitably envious.

'The Gritti Palace? Did you win the pools?'

Valentini smiled.

'In a manner of speaking.'

He flopped down in a chair and put his feet up on Zen's desk.

'I have just seen the new, clean, honest, dynamic Italy of the nineties, Aurelio, and it works! In fact it works just like the old one.'

He puffed on his cigar a moment.

'The only difference is that the payment's in kind these days. The way things are, no one can afford to leave a paper trail. Even cash is getting too risky now that the banks are starting to co-operate with the judges. You can't draw a thousand lire from your account without ending up on a database, but in a few hours the meal I just consumed will be just a glorious memory and another gob of sewage in some *pozzo nero*.'

'I see. Who was your host?'

'A local citizen who has an interest in the outcome, or the lack of it, of a case I'm presently working on.'

Zen frowned.

'You could have been seen together.'

'So what? In order to express the nature of his interest in greater detail, the citizen in question proposed that we meet for lunch. Nothing wrong with that, is there? Management are always going on about the need to forge closer links with the general public and thus promote a softer, more caring image of the force.'

Zen yawned.

'I think I'd better go home and get some sleep. I've got to work this evening.'

'How's the Zulian business coming along?' demanded Valentini, heading for his cubicle.

'Well, I haven't been offered any free lunches so far.'

Valentini laughed.

'On the other hand,' Zen continued as he headed for the door, 'I have a feeling that things might be about to get interesting in other ways.'

'Three tens.'

'King and queen beats that.'

'And ace wins.'

'Shit.'

The four figures sat huddled around a low table. The flame of a wax nightlight flickered in the tangled currents of their breath, thickly visible in the unheated air. The only sounds were the flutter of the cards being shuffled and dealt, and the soft patter of wavelets against the hull. Once more the players bent forward, trying to make out what kind of hands they were holding without tilting their cards too far towards the light and the eyes of the others.

'Chief?'

'I'll take two.'

'Discard.'

'Pass.'

'Oh shit!'

'There's a lady present, Martufò.'

'And the worst of it is she keeps winning.'

For a few minutes there was only the slap of cards on the table.

'I'm out,' called a man's voice.

'Dottore?'

'Me too.'

'Nunziata?'

'Three jacks.'

'Not again!'

'I always said it was a mistake letting women join the force,' commented a man with a strong Southern accent.

The speaker yawned loudly.

'Christ, but it's cold!' someone else remarked.

'Keep your voice down,' murmured the tallest figure, opening the curtain over the cabin window a crack and looking out.

'What time is it, anyway?' demanded the man on his left.

'Just gone ten,' said a woman's voice.

A pulsing orange light suddenly appeared in the corner of the confined space. The tall man reached over and threw a switch.

'Yes?'

'Contact,' said a tinny voice.

'How many?'

'Two.'

'Don't let them spot you.'

He switched off the radio and blew out the candle.

'Is it them, chief?' asked the man to his left.

'How the fuck do I know?' the tall man snapped back. 'Total silence from now on. If anyone screws this up, they'll be on foot patrol in Palermo next week.'

'Is that a promise?' muttered the man with the Southern accent.

'Shut up!'

The four sat perfectly still in the darkness, listening to the play of the water beneath them. Only after some time, and then very gradually, did another set of sounds become apparent, a different and more purposeful rhythm complicating the gentle ostinato to which they had grown so accustomed that they had almost ceased to be aware of it. The disturbance gradually approached and passed by. A moment later it ceased altogether. There was chink of metal, several thuds, a grunt. Then silence fell.

'Let's go!'

There was a flurry of movement in the darkness. Someone slipped outside, making the boat rock. Then they were mobile, gliding silently across the darkened water towards a wall towering over them like the face of a cliff. A distant streetlamp, hidden from where they had been moored, cast its pallid flickers on the scene. By its light they could make out Mino Martufò crouched on the foredeck, hauling in the sodden hempen rope which he had secured to a mooring post on the other bank of the canal on their arrival three hours earlier.

As the unmarked motor launch came alongside, its bow nudging the inflatable rubber dinghy tied up by the crumbling steps greasy with weed and mud, the Sicilian leapt ashore and made fast to a rusty ring-bolt in the wall. He then held the launch alongside the steps while Zen and Pia Nunziata disembarked. Bettino Todesco drew his service revolver and covered Zen as he mounted the steps and pushed open the massive waterdoor at the top.

'Wait here,' he whispered to the others.

Once inside, the darkness was complete. The few feeble glimmers which filtered in through the doorway were at once swallowed up by a resonant, cavernous reservoir of darkness. Zen stepped cautiously forward, following the wall with the tips of his fingers until he reached the stairs. He glanced back at Todesco and Nunziata, framed in the open doorway. Overcoming a strong sense of reluctance, Zen turned away and started up the stone staircase.

There was not a sound to be heard in the house. When Zen reached the hallway running the length of the first floor, he paused uncertainly. The light was better here, a dimness informed by faint reflections of a streetlight somewhere outside. He turned left and began to climb the next flight of stairs. This had been forbidden territory when he had visited the house as a child. An absolute distinction existed between the show spaces of the *piano nobile* and the private rooms on the floor above. The young Aurelio had had the run of the former, but the latter were taboo, and even now he had to overcome a sense of dread at venturing up the staircase mimicking the public one he had just climbed, but on a smaller, more intimate scale.

He had gone about halfway up when a sound in the yawning darkness above brought him to an abrupt halt. *Sounds*, rather: shifting, superimposed layers of keening edged at moments with shrill, grating shrieks. Zen felt his skin and scalp bristle all over. A shiver passed down his spine. Then a long, lingering scream split the night like lightning.

The sheer intensity of fear in it acted as a trigger, releasing Zen from his stupor and sending him dashing up the shallow steps, scrabbling for the rail to regain his balance, tumbling clumsily out on to the landing where the stairs ended. The cacophony was louder here, the strands more distinct: a continuous groaning and wailing punctuated by dull blows and panic-stricken howls of terror. Groping his way towards the source of these sounds, Zen blundered into something hard and hollow which resounded loudly from the contact.

The din inside at once faltered, then broke off altogether, dying away in a succession of grunts and heavy breathing. Then a panel opened in the darkness, a rectangle flickering and shimmering with a ghostly luminescence. Zen rushed forward and abruptly collided with a figure which appeared in the doorway. It gave a startled cry and tried to push past. When Zen held on, they both went tumbling to the floor.

A woman started screaming for help. Another figure burst out of the dimly lit room. It rushed at Zen, and a sharp blow struck his head. He twisted away, still grappling with the first assailant, and was gratified to feel the next kick cushioned by that body. He looked up at the figure standing over them, and gasped. Above him stood a skeleton, the skull grinning horribly, the bony structure glowing white in the darkness.

The sight momentarily paralysed him, and by the time he had recovered the figure with whom he had been grappling had wriggled away and sprung to its feet. It towered above him, lanky and loose-limbed in a flowing white Pierrot costume and an expressionless mask whose rounded features were as smooth as alabaster. Zen crawled backwards, trying to get to his feet, as the clown and the skelton closed in.

A shot rang out somewhere below, incredibly loud, precise and authoritative. There was an answering scream and a series of shouts, then two more shots. Leaping nimbly over Zen, the skeleton disappeared from view. Zen twisted round just in time to see the clown's foot lash out at him. He took the blow on his chest and hung on, wrenching the foot around, but it came off in his hand. He looked again, and found he was holding a Nike trainer.

The clown staggered away through the doorway. Zen struggled to his feet and followed, ignoring the shouts echoing up the stairwell. The door slammed shut in his face, but he barged it open again with his shoulder and stumbled into the room. He took in at a glance the elderly woman in bed, her face a mask of terror, and the figure running towards the open window on the other side of the room.

'Police!' he yelled. 'Freeze!'

The clown sprang on to a dressing-table and jumped out through the window. A moment later there came a loud splash, a succession of confused voices, then an incredibly brilliant light. Zen ran over to the window and looked out. The searchlight on the forward deck of the motor launch was trained down at the canal, pinpointing the flowing white costume spreading like a stain on the water. The figure had been trying to swim away, but now it turned, blinded by the light, and caught hold of the boathook which Mino Martufò was holding out from the stern of the launch.

Zen closed the window and turned round. Ada Zulian had sat up in bed, the covers clutched around her, staring indignantly at him as though *he* were the intruder.

'It's all right, *contessa*,' Zen told her. 'You're safe now. We've got the bastards.'

He hurried to the door and downstairs, turning on the lights as he went. When he reached the *portego* he almost tripped over someone lying sprawled on the marble paving. He stopped, gazing in horror at the blue police uniform, the long hair, the puddle of blood all around. Pia Nunziata opened her eyes and attempted a pallid smile.

'It isn't as bad as it looks,' she muttered.

Zen knelt down beside her.

'I had no idea they'd be armed,' he said helplessly.

'They weren't.'

'But . . .'

'It was Bettino.'

'*What?*'

The policewoman's attempted shrug turned into a wince and a groan.

'It was an accident. He didn't know I was following him. We heard the racket upstairs and came running. I happened to bump into him, and he must have thought . . .'

Zen shook his head wearily.

'Where are you hit?'

'My arm. The upper part, where it's soft. It's just a flesh wound. I don't think there's any danger.'

She glanced down at the fingers of her left hand, clutched tightly around the sleeve of her uniform jacket.

'It's starting to hurt, though.'

Zen straightened up.

'We'll get you to hospital right away.'

'The worst of it is, the bastard got away.'

'Todesco?'

'The man in the skeleton costume. Bettino was so concerned about me that he didn't even try and stop him. Martufò was looking after the canal side, but the man got out by the street door and ran off.'

Zen nodded.

'It's all right, I'd thought of that. Now then, can you walk or shall I get a stretcher?'

Grimacing with the pain, Pia Nunziata got to her feet. Zen took her elbow to help her up.

'Not that fucking arm!' she screamed.

She looked at him.

'Sir.'

Downstairs, the doors at either end of the *andron* had both been thrown open and a gentle current of air flowed through the echoey space, emptying out the odours of mould and decay. As Zen and Pia Nunziata made their way slowly down the staircase, two patrolmen in uniform entered through the street door, escorting a lanky figure in handcuffs dressed in a skintight black costume with the outline of a skeleton superimposed in white fluorescent paint.

'Sons of whores!' the young man shouted angrily. 'This is an outrage!'

'Load him into the boat,' Zen told the policemen.

'We've committed no crime!' the skeleton protested. 'We're members of the family!'

'Wait!' called Zen. 'On second thoughts, dump him over there in the corner for now. We've got to get our colleague to Emergency, and we can't hang about waiting for an ambulance.'

He pointed to a massive iron hook protruding from the stonework.

'If he gives you any trouble, suspend him by his cuffs from that for a while.'

'You'll regret this, you heap of shit!' shrieked the skeleton.

Taking no notice of this outburst, Aurelio Zen led the injured policewoman across the worn marble slabs and out of the waterdoor of Palazzo Zulian.

Gobs of slush fell in slanting lines through the air, tautening at moments to rain which drummed on umbrellas and slapped against skin, colder and harder than the sleet. The crowds in the narrow streets manoeuvred like craft in a crowded channel, tilting or raising their umbrellas to avoid fouling or collision. As if all this were not bad enough, hooligan gusts of wind played rough and tumble with anyone they caught, slitting open seams and sneaking in at cuff and collar until your clothes felt wetter in than out.

Despite the weather – to say nothing of a night both shorter and a good deal more stressful than the one he had spent with Cristiana – Aurelio Zen entered the Questura the next morning with the air of a conquering hero. Not only had he demonstrated in the teeth of professional and public scepticism that the case on which he was engaged existed independently of the workings of Ada Zulian's florid imagination. He had also solved it, and in the most dramatic and absolute fashion, capturing the persons responsible in the act and at the scene of the crime. It was a coup such as every official dreamed of, an unqualified success, secure from any of the stratagems by which judges and juries contrive to frustrate the police and deny them their rightful triumphs.

This euphoria lasted all of two minutes, such being the time it took Zen to climb the stairs to his office, where he was greeted by a familiar figure, beaming jovially and exuding an air of collusive bonhomie.

'Good morning, *dottore*. I wasn't hoping to see you again so soon. God, it's cold! There's snow on the way, if you ask me.'

Zen eyed Carlo Berengo Gorin with open hostility.

'What are you doing here?'

'Same as yesterday! I'd like to be more original, but I'm only a hireling, when all's said and done.'

Zen stared at the lawyer truculently. Then he turned and slammed the door shut behind him.

'Another visit? This must be costing Enzo Gavagnin a fortune.'

Gorin frowned.

'I think you must have . . .'

'How much do you charge to take on a case like this, *avvocato*?' Zen demanded, hanging his rain-spattered overcoat on the stand. 'Whatever it is, a type like Giulio Bon doesn't have that kind of money to throw around. He'd rather sweat it out for the duration and then tell me to fuck off when my time's up. He knows the rules. He'd no sooner hire a lawyer to spring him from a routine questioning than he'd hire a limousine to take him to the airport. And if by any chance he did, he'd go for the cut-price end of the market.'

He sneered at Gorin as he brushed past and sat down at his desk. Success in the Zulian case had made him confident.

'I worked out that much at the time,' he said, lighting his first cigarette of the day. 'And when I saw you leaving Gavagnin's office, and remembered how he'd carried on when Bon arrived, I knew that he must have summoned you. Nice gesture for an old friend, I thought. Shitty thing to do to a colleague, but nothing more to it than that.'

'Excuse me, but . . .'

'But then I realized that what's true for Bon is true for Gavagnin. If he'd called a lawyer, why the most expensive in the city? It's a routine case, after all.'

Zen gazed intently at Gorin.

'Or perhaps it isn't. And perhaps you have special rates for certain . . . friends.'

The lawyer stroked his beard, in which bright beads of water were nesting.

'I believe we're at cross-purposes, *dottore*,' he said with an embarrassed smile. 'When I said that the purpose of my visit was the same as yesterday, I was speaking generically.'

Zen shook a parcel of ash off his cigarette into the metal wastebin.

'Then perhaps you'd be good enough to get to the point, *avvocato*. I have work to do.'

'Perhaps not as much as you think, *dottore*.'

'Meaning what, *avvocato*?'

Gorin shrugged and heaved a long sigh.

'You're going to have to let them go, you know.'

Zen nodded lightly, as if this were something he had foreseen and which made perfect sense.

'Let them go,' he repeated.

'I'm afraid so.'

There was another pause.

'Who are we talking about?' Zen inquired urbanely.

Carlo Berengo Gorin looked taken aback for a moment.

'Why, the clients of mine you arrested last night! The Ardit brothers.'

Zen felt himself starting to hyperventilate. He drew largely on his cigarette.

'Ridiculous!' he snapped.

'What's ridiculous?'

Feeling the need to assert himself, Zen stood up and walked over to the window. In the canal below, a collapsed red umbrella edged past on the incoming tide. Zen turned to face Gorin.

'The men in question were arrested last night at Palazzo Zulian, which they had entered illicitly, in the act of carrying out an assault on the owner. The timely intervention of the police, led personally by myself, prevented their criminal designs and the pair were arrested *in flagrante delicto*. The entire matter has been communicated to the Public Prosecutor's Office, which is in the process of opening a dossier on the case. The matter is therefore in the hands of the judiciary, and I fail to see how I can be of any assistance to you.'

'Who's handling it?'

Zen consulted his noteboook.

'Dottore Marcello Mamoli.'

Gorin shook his head sadly.

'In that case, I doubt there's anything I can do for you. Marcello and I were at law school together. He was always a stickler for procedure.'

Zen scowled at him.

'I don't need you to do anything for me! Save that for your clients, *avvocato*. They're the ones who need help.'

'On the contrary, *dottore*. Why do you think I bothered coming here in the first place? I wanted to give you a chance to avoid getting covered in shit. You're one of us, after all.'

'What do you mean, one of us?' asked Zen.

Gorin looked at him but said nothing.

'And what do you mean by covered in shit?' shouted Zen angrily. 'It's your clients who're in it up to their necks!'

'What's the charge?' murmured Gorin.

Zen counted on his fingers.

'Breaking and entering. Resisting arrest with consequent injury to a police officer. Intimidation. Attempted extortion.'

'Breaking and entering is out. They had a key.'

'They *stole* a key.'

'They were given one by their aunt, the *contessa*.'

'A key to the street door, yes. But not to the waterdoor, which is how they came and went.' Gorin shrugged.

'If you give someone a key to your house, you are granting them access to the property. The fact that my clients chose to travel by water rather than on foot is of no legal significance whatsoever.'

He grinned maliciously.

'As for the injury to your officer, I have to say that I think it unwise of you to bring that up, since I gather that the individual in question was wounded by a gunshot inflicted by one of her colleagues. Certainly neither of my clients could have been responsible, since they were not armed. Why would they be? They were visiting their aunt.'

'They weren't visiting her!' Zen exploded. 'They were terrorizing her! They were trying to drive her mad, or rather trying to make everyone believe she *was* mad!'

Carlo Berengo Gorin looked pained.

'There is no evidence whatsoever to support such wild allegations.'

'No evidence! This has been going on for weeks, *avvocato*! What would they have had to do, in your view, for there to be evidence? Kill her?'

Gorin waggled his forefinger in the air.

'There is absolutely no proof that my clients were responsible for the earlier intrusions – or indeed that they ever took place at all.'

'But that must be the presumption.'

Gorin oscillated his hand in the air, fingers outstretched, as though turning a large doorknob back and forth.

'If it weren't for the testimony of the *contessa* herself, perhaps,' he murmured. 'But that alters the balance of probability quite dramatically.'

'What testimony?'

Carlo Berengo Gorin looked from side to side, sighing.

'I really shouldn't be cutting you in on the defence case, but, well, as one Venetian to another ... When she's summoned to appear before Mamoli, Ada Zulian will tell him that last night's episode, so far from being one in a long series, was quite different from anything she had experienced before. Her nephews' performance, it seems, was so crude that she guessed immediately that it was them. It lacked all the fluidity and "other-worldliness", to use her own term, of the previous manifestations.'

Zen violently hurled the butt of his cigarette, which had burned down to the filter, into the bin.

'That's absurd! The carnival costumes the accused were wearing corresponded exactly with the description the *contessa* gave me of the figures who have been tormenting her. No one's going to believe that it was sheer coincidence.'

'Of course not. But you're not the only person whose ear she bent about these ghostly apparitions of hers. The old girl's been going on about it to her nephews for weeks, and last night they played a little trick on her by dressing up in carnival gear and acting out her fantasies.'

Gorin shrugged.

'Many people may consider such a jape was in extremely question-able taste, to put it mildly. There is, however, nothing remotely illegal about it.'

He shook his head mournfully.

'I'm afraid you're going to have to let them go, *dottore*.'

Zen glanced at his watch, then at the slashing rain outside the window.

'There's another charge I omitted to mention,' he told Gorin sol-emnly. 'One of the brothers referred to my men as "sons of whores", while the other called me a "heap of shit".'

Gorin laughed a little uneasily.

'Oh come on Zen! You'll hear that kind of thing down at the bar any day.'

'That's different. If someone insults me when I'm off duty, that's a personal matter. I can choose to ignore him or to retaliate. But last night I was abused whilst carrying out my duties as a state function-ary. The offence was thus not only to me personally but to the office I hold. To let such a thing go unpunished would be to undermine the

165

authority of the legal process and inded the very fabric of an ordered, democratic society.'

Gorin gestured with his hands cupped together, appealing to sanity and common sense.

'Be reasonable, *dottore*! If you go round bursting into the homes of respectable citizens in the middle of the night, firing off guns in all directions, you can't expect a very warm welcome!'

'Your clients are in contravention of article 341 of the Criminal Code, which penalizes insults to the honour or prestige of a public official, made in his presence and during the execution of his duties. There is no question of their being released at the present time.'

Gorin gave him a long, measured look.

'All right,' he nodded, 'if that's the way you want to play it. But it isn't going to look good you clutching vindictively at 341 because your main charges have gone up in smoke. This is the second time in twenty-four hours that you've screwed up. If you're going to take such a hard line, I'll mention your irregular detention of Signor Bon to Mamoli. I don't think he's going to be very impressed. Nor do I think that he'll be taken in by this vindictive and spiteful attempt to harass my clients on a technicality. You may be able to get away with that sort of high-handed behaviour in Rome, but here in Venice we still have standards.'

He turned and strode across the office to the door. Zen stood quite still, staring fixedly at the space which the lawyer had just vacated. He was still in this trance when Aldo Valentini arrived.

'Our friend Enzo is deep in the shit!' cackled the Ferrarese gleefully. 'Having got back from bum-sniffing the politicos, the boss has summoned all the departmental heads to his office to hear the party line. Not only has Gavagnin not shown up, he hasn't even phoned in to apologize. And Francesco Bruno is a man who doesn't take kindly to being stood up.'

Zen nodded absent-mindedly. Valentini looked at him more closely.

'Is something wrong?'

Zen sighed.

'What's the biggest mistake you can make in this job?'

Valentini shrugged.

'There's so many to choose from. Accepting too small a bribe?

Making a pass at Bruno's wife? Failing to make a pass at Bruno's wife?'

He slapped his thigh loudly.

'I've got it! It's taking Bettino Todesco along on an operation without unloading his pistol first.'

Zen shot him a hurt glance.

'Nice one.'

'How is she, anyway?' asked Valentini with a smile to show he'd meant no harm.

'At home, recovering. A couple of days' leave and she'll be fine. But she was lucky. That fool Todesco could have killed her, firing blind like that.'

'What's going to happen to him?'

'An official reprimand, loss of accumulated promotion points and compulsory attendance at a firearms retraining course. But that's nothing compared to the unofficial hazing he'll have to put up with around here. It's tough enough being a policeman without having your own colleagues shooting at you.'

He collected his coat and hat and made for the door.

'See you later, Aldo.'

'Wait a minute!' the Ferrarese called after him. 'You haven't told me about the biggest mistake you can make in this job.'

Zen turned in the open doorway. He closed his eyes and squeezed the bridge of his nose between thumb and forefinger.

'To take it seriously,' he murmured. 'To think you have any hope of achieving anything. To imagine that anyone is going to support you.'

The quay outside the Questura glistened greasily under the steady drench. Mino Martufò, draped in a waterproof cape, was securing the mooring lines of one of the police launches.

'Are you doing anything?' Zen asked him.

'Where to, *dottò*?'

'Palazzo Zulian.'

He stepped aboard the launch. Freeing the mooring rope, Martufò followed, pushing off with his foot. He revved the motor, bringing the craft around, then engaged the throttle. The bow lifted and they surged off along the canal, riding a thick cushion of wash. Zen stood facing forward, eyes closed, gaunt and unsmiling, the raindrops dripped down his cheeks like tears. Mino Martufò looked at his superior with concern.

'We really fixed those bastards, sir, eh?'

Zen did not respond. Emerging into the crowded waters of the *bacino di San Marco*, the Sicilian dragged the launch into a slewing turn, narrowly missing an incoming ferry and a barge piled high with crates of artichokes.

'Take it easy,' Zen told him tonelessly. 'This is the new Italy. We've got to foster good relations with the public. We could be privatized at any moment.'

Martufò glanced twice at his superior before judging it safe to laugh heartily.

'After all the talk about botched jobs and cock-ups, it's really great to have taken part in an operation that was a total success from beginning to end,' he enthused. 'Okay, it was a shame about *la Nunziata*, but like I said when we were playing cards, they should never have let ladies join.'

'You think that your virile flesh would have resisted the bullet better?'

There was no further talk until they drew near Palazzo Zulian. Rain pocked the surface of the canal. There was not enough water to get the launch up to the water-steps, so Zen disembarked by the bridge and walked around to the street door.

It was opened by Contessa Ada Zulian in person. She inspected Zen suspiciously.

'Where are they?' she demanded.

'Where are who?'

'My poor nephews! I was told they would be at liberty again by now, but I've rung their house several times without . . .'

Zen brushed past her into the dank expanse of the lower hallway.

'*Do* by all means come in,' Ada commented with pointed irony. 'Make yourself at home. Perhaps you'd like a drink, or even a meal. Can I offer you anything?'

'You can offer me an explanation, *contessa*.'

Ada put her head on one side and stared at him with the impersonal acuity of a gull.

'But there is nothing whatever to explain.'

Zen marched up to her and stared her in the eye.

'I came all the way up here from Rome to take on your case, a case which no one else believed in, simply and solely out of the goodness of my heart, because you're an old acquaintance of my mother's. I

168

have been openly mocked by my colleagues at the Questura for insisting on taking your complaints seriously when everyone else had decided that you were out of your fucking head.'

'There's no call . . .'

'I've bent over backwards to help you in every way possible, even giving you my home telephone number so that you can call me at any hour of the day or night. Perhaps because I'm an outsider here now, to whom everything feels at once familiar and strange, I succeed in deciphering the pattern which no one had spotted – including you, *contessa* – and set a trap resulting in the arrest of the two people who have been tormenting you for so long. And what thanks do I get? You tell Gorin that you're prepared to lie in your teeth in order to get them off and make me look like the biggest idiot of all time!'

Ada gave a slight shrug. She turned away and started upstairs.

'But they're my nephews.'

'I don't care if they're the Patriarch's catamites!' Zen shouted as he started after her. 'Don't you understand what they were doing? Don't you understand what they *would* have done, sooner or later, if I hadn't intervened?'

Ada Zulian walked upstairs without replying. When she reached the gleaming gallery on the first floor, she turned to face him.

'You take everything so literally, Aurelio Battista. But then you always did. I remember once when Giustiniana left you here, you . . .'

Zen stopped on the last but one step, so that they were on a level.

'They would have killed you,' he said quietly.

Ada gave a little burble of laughter.

'What *are* you talking about? It was just a silly prank! Nanni's always had a taste for practical jokes, and Vincenzo will go along with anything his elder brother suggests.'

Taking her arm, Zen led her into the salon and pushed her down on the low sofa. He sat down beside her and leant close, his voice a mere whisper.

'At first, their plan was to have you declared mentally unfit. And they very nearly succeeded. All the people I spoke to when I arrived here were convinced that your story of ghostly intruders was proof that you had finally taken leave of your senses. With your previous history, your nephews would have had no difficulty in having you committed. They would then have applied to have control of the family affairs transferred to them, on the grounds that you were mentally unfit to manage the estate.'

Ada Zulian smiled vapidly at him. Her bright, shallow eyes twitched to and fro, refusing to engage his.

'After a suitable interval,' Zen continued, 'they would have entered into negotiations with interested parties over the sale of the old mill site on Sant'Alvise. A plot like that must be worth billions, but Nanni and Vincenzo wouldn't want the money going to their mad old aunt. Nor could they withdraw huge sums from your account without attracting comment, so they would probably have done a deal with the buyer. The sum named in the contract, and paid to you, would be a fraction of the real selling price. The difference would be paid into a numbered bank account which Nanni and Vincenzo could tap any time they needed a little spending money for another Porsche or a new wardrobe.'

Ada's smile was still there, fixed in place as if by glue.

'What an idea!' she murmured.

'But my arrival forced them to step up the pace. They had been counting on the fact that no one would bother to investigate your complaints very seriously. The police had a quick look around and put a man on the door to see whether anyone came or went. That didn't bother your nephews, of course, since they were moving around by water. Given the state of the back canal here, they could only operate for an hour or so each side of high tide, but it gave them the run of the house, unobserved by anyone – although I caught a glimpse of them rowing home the night I arrived.

'But once I took over the case Nanni and Vincenzo realized that they were going to have to change tactics. They attacked you physically for the first time, scratching your wrists with the carving knife. That's why I put a guard inside the house. If I hadn't, they would have returned the following night and repeated the attack, except this time the cuts would have been deeper. They might have used the evidence of your slashed wrists to demonstrate that you were once again suicidal, or they might have gone all the way and made sure that your next "suicide attempt" was successful.'

Shaking off Zen's grip, Ada Zulian got to her feet.

'This is preposterous and insulting nonsense! If you will not stop defaming my relations in this way, I must ask you to leave my house immediately.'

'How can you pretend that the earlier episodes had nothing to do with Nanni and Vincenzo? You *know* it was them. No other explanation makes any sense.'

Ada Zulian gave him a haughty look.

'My daughter walked out of this house fifty years ago and has never been seen again. Does that make sense?'

Zen slapped his forehead.

'For the love of God! If you imagined those other intrusions, how do you explain that each of them happened to coincide with the period when the canal giving on to the waterdoor happens to be navigable?'

Ada shrugged impatiently.

'Perhaps it's got something to do with the moon. That's what controls the tides, isn't it? I always feel a bit odd around full moon.'

'Why didn't you suffer from these hallucinations during the period when your nephews knew that there was a police guard in the house?'

Ada made a bored moue.

'I really neither know nor care, Aurelio Battista. And now – if you've quite finished – I have various tasks which require my attention.'

Zen stared at her, breathing hard, trying to control his fury.

'Don't patronize me, *contessa*!' he hissed. 'My mother may have scrubbed your floors and dusted your furniture, but that doesn't make me your drudge and factotum, to be dismissed when my usefulness is at an end.'

He was gratified to see fear in her eyes, but she said nothing more. Making one last effort, he cupped his hands together, imploring her understanding.

'If you don't back me in this, I shall have to let your nephews go.'

Ada sniffed.

'Do you expect me to perjure myself just to further your career?'

'I'm thinking of you, *contessa*, not me! Once your nephews are loose, you'll be in the same danger as before. Is that what you want? To live in terror of what they might decide to do next?'

A smile spread slowly across Ada Zulian's thin lips.

'Oh, I don't think I shall live in terror,' she replied calmly. 'You need have no fear about that, Aurelio Battista. On the contrary, I have every reason to suppose that my nephews are going to be very nice to me for the foreseeable future. Very nice indeed!'

He walked back to the Questura. It was colder than ever, and the rain had turned to a soft barrage of sleet which glistened briefly on clothes and hands before vanishing. Zen pulled down the brim of his hat and plodded along, contemplating the ruin of his hopes and plans. He had foreseen various ways in which the Ada Zulian case might collapse or backfire, but he had never expected to be outwitted by an old woman everyone agreed was crazy. I should be so crazy, he thought glumly.

He had been made use of in masterly fashion. Even if the *contessa* had not guessed earlier that her nephews were involved – which would suppose a superhuman degree of cunning and courage – she was clearly in no doubt about it now. That much was obvious from the complacent way she had dismissed Zen and his fears for her safety.

Of course she was in no danger from Nanni and Vincenzo! They knew only too well that the one thing standing between them and a stiff fine or prison sentence was Ada's statement that their 'silly prank' had been but a crude imitation of the experiences she had complained about earlier. Should she choose to withdraw this assurance at any time in the future, they would face immediate prosecution.

It was a perfect arrangement for everyone concerned. Ada had her nephews exactly where she wanted them, without the family being dragged through a public scandal. As for Nanni and Vincenzo, having to be 'very nice indeed' to their aunt was a small price to pay for being spared the consequences of their actions. The *contessa* was happy, and so were her nephews. The only loser was Zen, who had been totally outsmarted. And there was nothing whatever he could do about it.

This knowledge was hard enough to bear in itself, but the real blow was that with the collapse of the Zulian case he no longer had a valid motive for remaining in Venice. This meant an end to any hopes of solving the Durridge affair, but that was of secondary importance. His only interest in the fate of Ivan Durridge had been as a means of extracting money from the family which he could use to rent a larger house in Rome – large enough to share with his mother and Tania – and the charms of this living arrangement had abruptly faded. No, the real problem with leaving Venice was that it meant kissing goodbye not to the Durridge case but to Cristiana Morosini, with whom he belatedly realized that he was in love.

Emerging into a small *campo*, Zen paused for a moment to take his bearings. A series of posters on a billboard opposite showed a chic young couple setting out for a night on the town. Providing equal time for a less glamorous view of life, a clothes-line strung between two balconies overhead displayed an assortment of grey, baggy underpants and knickers. Zen continued on his way, carefully avoiding the stick of drips dropping from the washing to the pavement beneath.

The prospect of his appointment with Cristiana that afternoon now induced a kind of panic. And yet just a few days before, everything had seemed so easy. His desire for Cristiana had been pure and simple, uncontaminated by the murky complications of a sustainable relationship and unthreatening to his existing obligations and commitments in that regard. He had been in control then, the consumer selecting his pleasures, the tourist arranging his itinerary.

Now all that had changed. That infant eroticism, biddable and easily satisfied, had grown up into a moody, fractious adolescent, making demands, issuing statements, taking positions, unsure of its own identity and contemptuous of other people's. Whatever happened between him and Cristiana that afternoon, it would never have the serendipitous quality of that first encounter. From now on, whatever happened would be *meant*, something to be weighed and measured and taken responsibility for. He heaved a long sigh. The medical authorities were quite right: there was no such thing as safe sex.

It was Sunday tomorrow, so whatever happened he would have a day's grace in which to try and find out what Cristiana's feelings were. She had said she would be free between two and three. That gave him time to sign off at the Questura and have lunch somewhere before going home to wait. He strode along more rapidly. The sleet had eased and people were out and about, fitting in a last burst of activity before retiring home for a lunch of coma-inducing proportions.

He passed a carpenter's workshop stacked with lengths of wood of every size and shape, leaning at all angles in all directions, every piece covered with a layer of fine sawdust as thick as fallen snow. In the barber's next door, an unhappy boy of about eight was being shorn while his family looked on from a line of chairs arranged along the back wall. Zen was paying so much attention to these little scenes that he almost didn't see the jointed metal pipe snaking across the pavement until it was too late. In the event he was able to change pace just in time and avoid tripping.

He walked on, taking in the red tanker barge marked POZZI NERI tied up next to the bridge and the flotilla of smaller craft moored alongside, blocking the canal. A comprehensive array of emergency services was represented: the Carabinieri, the city police, the fire and ambulance brigades. Even as Zen watched, a uniformed figure emerged from a boat marked VIGILI URBANI, clambered over the intervening vessels to the quay and ran off along the alley from which the pipes led back to the sewage tanker.

Zen frowned. After a momentary hesitation, he turned into the alley where the *vigile* had disappeared. The line of tubing was longer than he had imagined, leading through a maze of narrow lanes and low porticos, all deserted. At length it emerged into a spacious courtyard surrounded on all sides by tall tenement houses from whose windows people were staring down at the scene below. About a dozen more, mostly men in uniform, were grouped loosely around a circular opening in the centre of the yard. A motorized winch mounted on a tripod had been erected over the manhole and a taut cable descended into the darkness beneath.

Zen only realized that the cable was moving when a head and shoulders appeared in the opening. Two men in orange waterproof gear stepped forward and helped a third clamber out on to the pavement of bricks laid in a herringbone pattern. He was wearing a black rubber wet suit and a breathing apparatus, and was covered from head to foot in umber slime. He detached the end of a white synthetic rope which had been tied to his belt and passed it to the others, who made it fast to the cable on which he had been standing. Then one of them set the winch in motion once more.

Zen went up to a man in the uniform of a Carabinieri major and asked what was going on.

'Body in the cesspit,' he replied shortly, barely glancing at Zen. 'This is the fourth time they've tried to bring it out. Keeps slipping off the rope.'

This explained the strain visible on the faces of the men working the winch. They didn't want to have to send their colleague back down to the subterranean cistern which received all the sewage of the surrounding tenements, much less replace him themselves in due course. Lovingly they coaxed the cable inch by inch on to the drum, taking up slack with leather-gloved hands to avoid any jerks or shudders which might precipitate its cargo back into those feculent depths.

'Maintenance people found it when they came to drain the tank this morning,' the Carabiniere muttered under his breath. 'Took the cover off and were just getting the tubing set up when one of them caught sight of this face looking up at them from the surface of the shit below. Poor bastard nearly fell in himself. And you are?'

Zen was spared having to reply by a loud gasp and stifled cries from the other spectators. Something had appeared in the hole at the centre of the courtyard, something as smooth, shapeless and sticky as a bar of softened chocolate. With evident reluctance, the three men clustered around the winch, laid hands on it and began to pull. But the object appeared unwilling to be hauled into the light of day. Again and again it jammed in the opening. The men shouted warnings and instructions to each other, desperate lest it escape them yet again.

At last they got its centre of gravity over the rim of the *pozzo nero*, and the six hands guided it clear of the hole and let it slump down on to the brick paving with a soft squelch. The racket of the winch died away. Under its sheath of slime, the object was only just recognizable as a human body. The men set about freeing the cradle of rope looped about its limbs. The Carabinieri officer pushed through the circle of onlookers.

'Can you clean it up a bit, lads?' he asked one of the men.

'Gino's just gone to fetch some water, sir.'

The corpse lay face down, the hands clasped behind the back. Close to, the stench of fermenting excrement was almost unbearable. Everyone stood in embarrassed silence. At length a clatter of boots announced the return of Gino, staggering under the weight of two pails of water. Standing as far from the corpse as possible, he poured the contents of one bucket over its back. It at once became clear that the hands were not clasped but tied together, the thumbs tightly bound with copper wire. Equally clearly, the victim had tried hard to break free: one of the thumbs was almost severed.

'Clumsy job,' said the Carabinieri major in a tone of professional disapproval. 'He'd have drowned anyway, and if they'd gone back and uncovered the manhole once he was dead they could have passed the whole thing off as an accident.'

'Perhaps they didn't want to pass it off as an accident,' murmured Zen.

'What do you mean?'

'Maybe they wanted to send a message. To keep the others in line.'

'What others?'

Zen shrugged. One of the men wearing gloves heaved the inert body on to its back. The viscous brown filth clung to it like mud, smoothing out the features and draining into the open mouth. Someone in the background started to retch. With obvious reluctance, Gino picked up the other pail and poured the water unceremoniously over the head and chest of the corpse.

'Jesus!' breathed Zen.

The Carabinieri officer glanced sharply at him.

'Do you know him?'

Zen nodded slowly.

'Then who is he? And who are you, for that matter? Do you know who killed him?'

Zen raised his head and gazed at the blank wall opposite.

'I did,' he said.

He turned and walked quickly away, then broke into a run. Behind him voices were calling to him to stop, but he couldn't stop. There was too much to do and to undo, too much to remember, too much to forget.

He ran almost all the way to Campo San Bartolomeo, pushing ruthlessly past anyone in his way, and up the steep steps of the Rialto bridge. Pausing briefly for breath at the top, he raced down the other side and out on to the wooden jetty where three watertaxis were moored. In the cabin of the first in line, five men sat chatting familiarly over plastic cups of coffee. Zen appeared in the companion-way and demanded to be taken to the San Tomà pier. One of the men looked up at Zen with an expression which mingled contempt and pity.

'San Tomà? That's just a few hundred metres along the canal. Two stops on the *vaporetto*.'

'I'm in a hurry!'

The man shrugged.

'It's not worth my while for a fare like that.'

Zen climbed down into the cabin and thrust his identity card into the man's face.

'If you don't get this tub under way in ten seconds, I'll have your licence revoked and you'll spend the rest of your life humping frozen fish and tinned tomatoes around town.'

Shocked by the violence in Zen's voice, and not realizing that it was directed not at them but at himself, the men sprang into action. Within moments the taxi was cutting its way through the turbid waters, its bow aimed at the *volta del canal* where the city's central waterway snakes back on itself, heading east towards the open sea.

From the pier at San Tomà it was only a short walk to the offices of the Procura. The entrance to this organ of the Italian State was an apt symbol of that institution as a whole: six large doors led into the building, but only one was open. Zen joined the crowd of people shoving their way in and out and made his way upstairs to the Deputy Public Prosecutors' department.

Marcello Mamoli was 'in a meeting', he was informed by a woman with a pinched and put-upon expression hunched over a typewriter in the reception area. For once the euphemism proved correct, as Zen discovered by opening a selection of doors further down the corridor. As though in deliberate contrast to the windowless glory-hole in which their secretary eked out her working life, the space inside was pointlessly vast. Six men were seated around a table which glistened like an ice-rink, and was only slightly smaller. All six looked round as the door opened. One of them got to his feet and stood staring furiously at Zen.

'What is the meaning of this intrusion?'

Zen strode over to the table.

'I must speak to Dottore Marcello Mamoli.'

'Must you, indeed?' retorted the other sarcastically. 'And who might you be?'

'My name is Aurelio Zen. I'm with Criminalpol, on temporary secondment to the Questura here in Venice.'

The magistrate smiled coldly.

'Extremely temporary, from what I hear.'

He straightened his shoulders and glared at Zen.

'I am Mamoli. What possible justification do you have to offer for bursting in on an important and confidential meeting in this way?'

Marcello Mamoli was a pale, fastidious-looking man of about forty whose small, sharp features were partially mitigated by a large pair of bifocal glasses.

'I apologize to you and your colleagues for the interruption,' Zen declared in grovelling tones, 'but this is a matter of the greatest possible urgency.'

Mamoli regarded him with disfavour.

'On the contrary, *dottore*, it has been a total waste of everyone's time! I am shocked and surprised that the Ministry thought it worthwhile troubling me with such a farce. My colleagues and I have had dealings with Criminalpol operatives many times before and I'm glad to say that we have generally been impressed by their level of professionalism. That makes it all the more unaccountable that you should have been taken in by something like the Zulian case, a transparent tissue of . . .'

'This has nothing to do with Ada Zulian.'

Marcello Mamoli was clearly not pleased to have been wrong-footed.

'Then what *is* it about?' he demanded icily.

Zen took a step forward.

'A colleague of mine has been killed. I think I know who did it, and why, and who else is in danger. But we must act at once. Every second is precious. That's why I came directly here instead of going through the usual procedures. Let me speak to you in private – or, if you're too busy, to one of your colleagues.'

Mamoli paused. Like the taxi drivers, he was impressed above all by the intensity of Zen's tone. The hint that he might lose an important case was also well timed. With an apologetic smile to the other magistrates, as though to say 'I'd better humour this maniac before he gets violent', he walked past Zen to the door.

'This way!'

Once in the corridor, he turned to stare levelly at Zen.

'I hope you know what you're doing.'

Zen nodded confidently.

'I know exactly what I'm doing.'

Mamoli led the way to an office at the end of the corridor and shut the door. He did not sit down, nor did he invite Zen to do so. Zen walked straight over to the desk, picked up the phone and dialled the Questura.

'Aurelio Zen speaking. Do we have a *commissariato* on Burano? No? Then give me the squad room.'

'Now listen,' Mamoli exclaimed, 'I've stood just about as much of this as . . .'

'Is Todesco there? Put him on.'

He turned to the furious Mamoli.

'Just one moment, please! This can't wait.'

He put the receiver to his ear once more.

'Todesco? Aurelio Zen. Now pay attention. You're to take a boat and get over to Burano immediately. No, not Murano, *Burano* – B as in Brescia. Go to the home of Filippo Sfriso. The address will be in Gavagnin's file on the case. Take two or three men with you. Put Sfriso himself under arrest. Don't worry about the warrant. I'll have one by the time you get back. He's to make no phone calls, speak to no one. Understood? If at all possible, bring his mother along too. If she won't budge, leave an armed guard on the house.'

There was a pause.

'Well you'll just have to find someone to cover for you,' Zen resumed with silky menace. 'And please try not to shoot any of your colleagues this time, Todesco. You almost killed someone last night. This is your chance to make amends before I write up my report.'

He hung up and turned to face Mamoli. The magistrate was by now bursting with indignation.

'What the devil do you think . . .'

Zen cut him off.

'I apologize for my apparent rudeness, *signor giudice*, but time is pressing. Less than an hour ago, the body of Inspector Enzo Gavagnin, head of the Drugs Squad at the Questura of Venice, was recovered from a cesspit in a courtyard by San Canciano. He had been murdered, thrown into the sewage with his hands tied and left to drown.'

Mamoli's indignation instantly evaporated.

'Go on.'

Zen paused, trying to marshal his thoughts, to remember what he could admit and what he must conceal, which facts he could present openly to Mamoli and those whose origin or significance he must disguise.

'Three days ago, a fisherman named Giacomo Sfriso, resident on Burano, was found drowned in the lagoon. There was no evidence of foul play, yet Enzo Gavagnin insisted on opening an investigation and brought the dead man's brother in for questioning.'

He broke off and gave an embarrassed smile.

'Enzo told me all this himself, off the record. He and I had struck it off from the moment I arrived here. Our parents used to be neighbours, and . . .'

Mamoli nodded impatiently.

'Quite, quite.'

'I asked him why he was taking such a hard line. He told me a story which frankly I found hard to believe at the time. He claimed to have received death threats from a powerful drug cartel he had been fighting for years. When I asked what this had to do with the Sfriso brothers, he said that he knew that they were involved with this organization, although he lacked sufficient proof to make a formal request to proceed. He claimed that Giacomo Sfriso had been murdered by the gang, and hoped that Filippo, shocked by his brother's death, would now agree to co-operate.'

'And did he?'

Zen shook his head.

'Not fully, although he apparently supplied some telephone numbers which Enzo hoped to exploit. But before he could do so, the threat to his life which he mentioned to me had been brutally substantiated. What I'm asking of you, *signor giudice*, is authorization to hunt down my friend's killers!'

Leaving this passionate declaration ringing in the air, Zen quickly reviewed this fiction to ensure that it covered all the essential points. Satisfied, he looked up at Marcello Mamoli, who was gazing at him with renewed interest.

'I need the following powers,' Zen went on quickly. 'First, interception of all telephonic traffic on the numbers Sfriso supplied to Gavagnin. Second, surveillance of the addresses corresponding to those numbers. Third, a warrant for the arrest of Filippo Sfriso on the grounds of reticence concerning the criminal activities already mentioned. Fourth, round-the-clock protection for Sfriso's mother, who might otherwise be at risk from the gang. And lastly, authorization in principle to follow up any leads which may arise in the course of these and related enquiries.'

Marcello Mamoli raised his eyebrows.

'In short, a free hand.'

Zen shrugged.

'In my experience, it's quite normal for Criminalpol operatives to be granted a relatively wide degree of latitude in their investigations.'

'And you would naturally check with me before taking any initiatives which might prove, ah, controversial.'

'Naturally.'

Marcello Mamoli walked over to the window. It had started to rain again, and fat drops slid slowly down the panes, leaving tracks like slugs. The magistrate consulted his watch.

'It's now almost four o'clock,' he said without looking round. 'You've got forty-eight hours to come up with something solid.'

It was only then that Zen remembered his appointment with Cristiana.

Filippo Sfriso's return to the Questura was in stark contrast to his unceremonious departure two days earlier. The police launch which had been dispatched to fetch him from Burano cut through the Arsenale, avoiding the more direct but constricted backwaters where it would have had to slow down. Although it was still light, the curtains in the cabin were tightly drawn. Next to the helmsman stood a patrolman in grey battledress cradling a machine-gun.

Emerging at the south end of the Arsenale canal, the launch turned hard to starboard, passing astern of a *vaporetto* landing-stage being towed away for installation or repair, and shot in under the Selpolcro bridge without any slackening of pace. It screeched past an orange-and-green garbage barge hoisting a street-sweeper's cart aboard and surged along the canal, creating a wash which had the tethered vessels heaving at their moorings like frightened horses, before revving loudly in reverse at the last moment to slide in alongside the Fondamenta di San Lorenzo.

While the helmsman jumped ashore and secured the mooring ropes, the armed patrolman took up a position on the quayside, glancing alternately to left and right. Then the door of the cabin opened and the burly figure of Bettino Todesco appeared in the cockpit. He surveyed the scene briefly, then disappeared back into the cabin. A moment later he emerged, handcuffed to a figure whose head and shoulders were swathed in a blanket. The pair stepped ashore and hurried across the quay and into the open doorway of the Questura.

Forty seconds later, Filippo Sfriso was sitting in an office on the second floor of the building. The shutters were closed and Todesco stood guard at the door. Sfriso looked as though he were in shock. His body was subject to uncontrollable spasms of trembling, his face was pale and expressionless, his gaze vacant. Neither man spoke. The door opened and Aurelio Zen walked in. Filippo Sfriso rose slowly to his feet. He stared at Zen, his eyes widening in terror.

'You!'

Before Zen could answer, Sfriso picked up his chair and threw it at him. Zen managed to raise one hand in time to fend it off, but one of the legs scraped his forehead painfully. Meanwhile Sfriso was off and running for the door. Bettino Todesco was taken by surprise, but managed to grab one of Sfriso's legs as the Buranese got the door open. They fell to the floor in the corridor, locked together in a violent struggle.

Sfriso started kicking his captor's head with his free leg, but Todesco hung on gamely until Zen came to his aid. Between the two of them they succeeded in subduing the prisoner, but Todesco was understandably keen to administer some punishment for the abuse he had suffered, and under the circumstances – the scrape on his forehead was quite painful – Zen was content to indulge him. Then they dragged Sfriso back into the office, where Zen dangled his police identity card in front of Sfriso's battered face.

'That was stupid, even by your standards. You're already under arrest for *reticenza*. Now I can add resisting arrest and assulting a police officer.'

'I thought you were . . .' Sfriso began.

'I know what you thought,' Zen interrupted hastily, before Sfriso revealed too much about Zen's irregular activities in front of Todesco. 'You thought I was another "bent policeman", like Enzo Gavagnin.'

He took out his pack of cigarettes and lit up.

'But you were wrong,' he went on. 'You said more than you should have done, the other evening, and you said it to the wrong man. That was stupid too. But you *are* stupid, Filippo, aren't you? You and your brother. Otherwise you would never have got mixed up in any of this.'

Sfriso hung his head and said nothing. Zen smoked quietly for a while, looking down at him.

'These men are killers,' he said at length. 'They kill indirectly, by peddling drugs to kids in Mestre and Marghera. But they also kill directly, as you know only too well.'

He walked over to Sfriso, sitting down next to him.

'You told me what they did to Giacomo,' he said. 'They seem to like drowning people.'

After what seemed like an age, Sfriso's head slowly came up. He stared blearily at Zen, who nodded.

'This time it was the turn of Enzo Gavagnin,' Zen murmured. 'They wired his thumbs together and threw him into a cesspool. Like with Giacomo, they did other things to him first. Do you want to see the photos? Clearly they didn't believe Gavagnin's protestations of ignorance any more than they did your brother's.'

He leaned close to Sfriso.

'What about you, Filippo?' he breathed. 'You're the only one left now. Do you think they'll believe you?'

He leaned his head quizzically on one side.

'I wouldn't rate your chances particularly high, myself. They didn't believe Giacomo. They didn't believe Gavagnin. Why should they believe you?'

He crushed out his cigarette underfoot.

'No, I think it's a pretty solid bet that they'll assume that you're holding out on them too. I wonder what they'll do to you. Leave you to drown slowly in a tank of shit like Gavagnin? Or will it be something even more original? What do you think they'll come up with? And *when*? How long will it be before your mother loses her other son?'

Sfriso's face crumpled and he began to weep.

'Stop tormenting me!'

Zen laughed harshly.

'No problem, Filippo! I'll leave that to them. Unless you agree to co-operate.'

'What is it you want?'

'Everything. Names, dates, places, people. The whole story from the beginning, up to and including your brother's death and your interrogation by Gavagnin.'

A sly glint came into Sfriso's eye.

'And in return I get a free pardon?'

This time Zen's laughter was openly contemptuous.

'Of course! Plus a state pension for life and a villa in Capri. No, Filippino, all I can undertake to do for you is to save your miserable skin. When you come to trial, the fact that you've co-operated will of course weigh in your favour, but I'm afraid you're still going to have to spend several years behind bars. Not an attractive prospect, I know, but it beats moving permanently to San Michele.'

Conflicting emotions chased each other across Filippo Sfriso's moist features.

'You're trying to trap me into confessing,' he blurted out.

Zen waved casually around at the office.

'Do you see anyone taking notes or making a tape recording? We're just having a chat, Filippo. If you agree to my proposition, I will summon the lawyer of your choice before starting the interview, which will be conducted in his presence and according to the usual rules.'

He broke off, glancing at Sfriso.

'Which lawyer would you nominate, incidentally?'

Sfriso barked out a laugh.

'Do I look like someone who has a lawyer on call? I'm just a poor fisherman.'

'Hardly poor, and not just a fisherman. Otherwise you wouldn't be needing a lawyer.'

Zen looked up at the ceiling.

'Let me suggest a few names. How about Carlo Berengo Gorin, for example? They say he's very good.'

He glanced back at Sfriso's face as he spoke Gorin's name. There was no flicker of recognition.

'Anyone you like,' muttered Sfriso. 'It's all the same to me.'

Zen smiled and nodded.

'*Bravo*. That was the right answer.'

He offered Sfriso a cigarette.

'I think we can do business,' he said languidly. 'Are you interested?'

Filippo Sfriso stared at the packet of *Nazionali* for a long time. Then he prised one loose and put it between his lips, nodding slowly.

At nine o'clock that night, Aurelio Zen called Marcello Mamoli at his home on the fashionable stretch of the Zattere, near the Santo Spirito church. Before doing so he tried Cristiana once again, but there was still no reply. Mamoli, on the other hand, answered almost immediately.

'Well?'

'This is Aurelio Zen phoning from the Questura, *signor giudice*. I have taken Filippo Sfriso's statement.'

In the distance he could hear the sounds of the meal from which the magistrate had been summoned by the *donna di servizio* who had answered the phone.

'Is this really so urgent that you must disturb me during dinner?' demanded Mamoli.

'I wouldn't have done so otherwise,' Zen retorted.

He himself had not yet had a chance to eat anything.

'A copy of the full statement will be with you tomorrow, *signor giudice*, but I'll summarize the main points and outline the action I propose to take.'

'Please be brief. My guests are waiting for me.'

Zen mouthed a silent obscenity at the phone.

'The Sfriso brothers were involved in a drug smuggling operation for a syndicate based in Mestre,' he said out loud. 'They would be given the name, description and ETA of the carrier, typically an oil tanker or a bulk freighter bound for Marghera. The drop took place at a prearranged point out at sea. The package was heaved over the side with a float on it, and the Sfrisos came up in their fishing boat and hauled it in. Some time later – it might be days or weeks – they were phoned with instructions about passing on the packages.'

Mamoli grunted.

'The Sfrisos acted as a cut-out for the gang. Thanks to them, there was no direct link between the smuggling and distribution ends of the operation, thus limiting any damage due to arrests or tip-offs. The ship was clean if it was searched on arrival, and the drugs were only handed over when they were needed for immediate sale. Naturally it depended on the syndicate being able to trust the Sfrisos with large amounts of pure heroin, but this wasn't a problem until . . .'

'So where do we go from here?' Mamoli cut in.

Zen took a deep breath.

'To Sant'Ariano.'

'Where?'

'The ossuary island up in the northern lagoon where the dead from all the church cemeteries were dumped when the land was needed for . . .'

'I am tolerably familiar with the history of the city,' Marcello Mamoli replied icily. 'What escapes me is the connection between Sant'Ariano and the affair we have been discussing.'

'Sant'Ariano is where the Sfrisos stored the packages of heroin between receiving and delivering them. The place has such a sinister reputation that hardly anyone ever goes there. They dug a cache somewhere on the island and went to pick up fresh supplies as and when they needed them. One day last month Giacomo went to collect the remaining three kilos of one consignment. When he got back he was babbling madly about meeting a walking corpse and there was no sign of the packages. Filippo has searched Sant'Ariano many times since then. He located the site of the cache easily enough, but it was empty. The island is covered with dense undergrowth and Giacomo apparently got lost and abandoned the heroin somewhere in the middle of it.'

'Just a minute,' Mamoli told him. Lowering the receiver, he called to someone in the house, 'Please start without me. I'll be there in a minute.'

'Hello?' said Zen tentatively.

'I'm here,' Mamoli snapped back. 'Please get to the point.'

Zen's tone hardened.

'The point? The point is that somewhere on Sant'Ariano there is a canvas bag containing three kilos of heroin. If we can recover it, we can set up a meeting, lure the gang into a trap and smash the whole operation. Sfriso has agreed to co-operate.'

Mamoli grunted.

'Why don't we just substitute another package? Or use a dummy?'

'Each package is sealed and bar-coded to reveal any tampering. The contact man would spot the fake package at once. We could arrest him, but the others would get away and the . . .'

'So what do you propose?'

'I would like to order an immediate search of Sant'Ariano.'

'Then do so, *dottore*.'

'I have your authorization to proceed?'

'Certainly. And now I must . . .'

'By whatever means seem to me most appropriate?'

'Of course. And now I really must get back to my guests. Good night, *dottore*.'

In the end, Zen decided to take the copy of Filippo Sfriso's statement to the Procura in person. It meant a long detour on his way home, but he had nothing better to do. In fact the walk was just what he needed to think through the problem facing him, to weigh up the options open to him and perhaps even come to a decision. It was a fine night for walking. An abrasive, icy wind had dried and polished the town, making the stonework sparkle, the metal gleam and burnishing the air till it shone darkly. The tide was high, and the cribbed water in the small canals shuffled fretfully about.

Although Mamoli had given him a free hand, Zen knew that he would have to take the responsibility if anything went wrong. This seemed all too possible. Not only did he have to locate a small canvas bag on an island several thousand square metres in extent and entirely covered with impenetrable brush and scrub, but he had to do so without the gang knowing that any search had been made. Both Giacomo and Filippo Sfriso had told them on many occasions how and where the missing heroin had been mislaid. The gang had no doubt tried more than once to recover it themselves. If they learned that the police had instituted a full-scale search of Sant'Ariano, they certainly wouldn't respond when Filippo Sfriso announced a few days later that Enzo Gavagnin's fate had jogged his memory, he had located the stuff and when would they like to drop by and pick it up?

As he cut through the maze of back alleys between Santa Maria Formosa and the Fenice, Zen found himself shying away from the thought of what had happened to Gavagnin. The pathologist's report had been faxed over from the hospital, and Zen was not likely to forget the details of the injuries inflicted on Gavagnin before he died, nor the phrase 'the presence of a considerable quantity of excrement in the lungs and stomach' under the heading *Cause of Death*.

That was true only in the sense that boats sank because of the presence of a considerable quantity of water in the hull. In reality, Enzo Gavagnin had been killed because of what Zen had said on the phone the other morning. He had been so eager to get even for Gavagnin's slights that he had made up some story on the spur of the moment without even considering what the consequences might be. He had been as irresponsible as Todesco. Zen too had fired blind, and with fatal results.

Buffeted by biting gusts of wind, he crossed Campo San Stefano and the high wooden bridge over the *canalazzo* before entering the sheltered passages and paths on the other bank. At the offices of the Procura, he watched the caretaker deposit the sealed envelope containing Filippo Sfriso's statement in the pigeonhole marked MAMOLI, returned to the cold comfort of the streets. As he passed the monstrous sprawl of the Frari, he caught a whiff of cooking borne past on a gust of wind from someone's supper and realized that he had eaten nothing since the morning. Until now the sheer press of events had sustained him, but as it receded he suddenly felt absolutely ravenous. It was by now almost ten o'clock, and the only places open would be those catering to the city's vestigial youth culture.

He walked down to the Rialto bridge and made his way to Campo San Luca, where the dwindling band of young Venetians hang out of an evening. The main throng had already departed, but a number of *locali* remained open to serve the hard core. Zen chose the one which seemed to be pandering least to the prevailing fashion for American-style food and drink, and ordered a pizza and a draught beer. While he waited to be served, he lit a cigarette to calm his hunger pains and tried to ignore the attention-seeking clientele and concentrate on his immediate problems.

Although he recognized his responsibility for Gavagnin's death, he didn't feel any exaggerated sense of remorse. That would have been pointless in any case. All he could do now was to try and bring the killers themselves to justice. They had murdered Gavagnin because they believed he knew where the cache of heroin was hidden. That proved that they had not managed to locate it themselves. If Zen could succeed where they had failed, he could consign the whole gang to the *pozzo nero* of the prison system and – in his own mind at least – be quits. But how to find Giacomo's missing bag in the first place?

Assuming that the required manpower was available, such searches were normally a relatively simple matter: you organized a line of men and walked them across the ground. Such methods were clearly impossible on the terrain in question. Zen had been to Sant'-Ariano once, forty years before, on a dare with Tommaso. They'd taken a small skiff belonging to the Saoner family and rowed all the way, up beyond Burano and Torcello, past abandoned farms and hunting lodges, on towards the fringes of the *laguna morta*. He had never forgotten the silence of those swampy wastelands, the sense of solitude and desolation.

The Germans had mounted an anti-aircraft battery on the island during the closing months of the war, so it was not quite as untouched as it would have been five years earlier, or as it would be now that the undergrowth had reclaimed the clearing and access road which had been made. Nevertheless, both he and Tommaso had been overwhelmed by the aura of the place. It was not only the thought of the unknown, uncountable dead whose remains had been tipped there like so much rubbish, thousands and thousands of bones and skulls, a whole hillock of them held in by a retaining wall. Almost as frightening as those reminders of mortality had been the evidence of life: a profusion of withered, gnarled, spiny plants and shrubs which sprouted from that sterile desert, and above all the host of rodents and reptiles which scuttled and slithered and nested amongst the bones.

The arrival of the waiter with Zen's order banished these memories. But as he wolfed down the pizza, scalding his tongue in the process, he realized that a conventional search of Sant'Ariano was out of the question. The only way it could be made to work would be by giving each man a machete and a chain-saw and felling every tree, shrub and bush on the island. They might find the heroin, but they wouldn't catch the gang. What he needed was a totally different approach, something quick, effective and unobtrusive. Unfortunately he had a gnawing suspicion that it didn't exist.

The pizza was a sad imitation of the real thing, but it filled his stomach. He was just lighting a cigarette to go with the rest of his beer when Cristiana Morosini walked in. She was with three other women, and did not notice Zen at his table in a corner at the back. He drew hard on his cigarette and tried to think what to do. Cristiana was bound to catch sight of him sooner or later, and if he hadn't greeted her by then she would be even more annoyed with him than she already was. That Zen really knows how to treat a woman: first he stands her up, then he cuts her dead.

In the event the dilemma was solved for him almost immediately. Cristiana and one of the other women got up and walked towards Zen's table, heading for the toilets at the back of the premises. When she saw him she hesitated an instant, then smiled coolly.

'*Ciao*, Aurelio.'

She turned to the other woman.

'Be with you in a minute, Wanda.'

Zen stood up, gesturing embarrassedly.

'I've been trying to phone you all afternoon . . .'

'I was out.'

'I'm dreadfully sorry about missing our appointment. Something unexpected came up suddenly, a dramatic development in the case I'm working on.'

Cristiana raised her eyebrows, whether in interest or scepticism it was hard to tell.

'Not to worry,' she replied. 'I was busy myself, as it happens. Nando insisted on flying me down to Pellestrina for another photo opportunity. He's confident of carrying the city itself so now he's concentrating on the islands.'

She looked at him speculatively.

'So has this dramatic development anything to do with the Durridge case?'

Zen shrugged awkwardly.

'It's not really something I can discuss in public.'

She met his look with one of her own.

'I can't just abandon my friends like that.'

'Of course not. But I'm planning to stay up late anyway. There are one or two things I need to think over. If you want to stop by for a nightcap later . . .'

At that moment the woman called Wanda – who must be Cristiana's sister-in-law, Zen realized – emerged from the toilets. Cristiana nodded lightly and turned away.

'We'll see,' she said.

Zen walked slowly home, puzzling over the significance of Cristiana's continuing intimacy with the Dal Maschio family. She might be separated from her husband, but she still evidently went out with his sister and came running when he snapped his fingers. Zen felt a scorch of indigestion in his gut, partly from eating too quickly and partly from jealousy. For a supposedly estranged wife, Cristiana seemed to be at her husband's beck and call to an astonishing degree. He didn't blame her for keeping on the right side of such a powerful man, but he did wonder where the limits of her compliance might lie.

Not that there was anything to complain about in this trip to Pellestrina, a bizarre community three kilometres long and a stone's throw wide, built on a sandbank in the shadow of the *murazzi*, the massive sea defences erected by the Republic three hundred years earlier. Zen smiled, imagining how Dal Maschio would have worked that into his speech. 'What these walls have been for three centuries, the *Nuova Repubblica Veneta* is today – a bulwark protecting our culture, our economy, our very homes, from being swept away by the storms of change and decay!'

In order to provide a suitable dramatic photo, Dal Maschio would no doubt have piloted his wife to Pellestrina in a helicopter owned by the company in which he was a partner. As a former air force ace, he would have been able to make a spectacular landing on some patch of grass or sand which looked too small to ...

And then, in a flash, he saw the solution to the problem which had been obsessing him all evening! The way to locate the missing three kilos of heroin on Sant'Ariano was to go in *vertically*, not hacking through the scrub but dipping from the sky! He was so pleased by this revelation that he would have walked right past his own front door if he had not almost bumped into someone coming in the opposite direction.

'Christ!' the man screamed.

Zen peered at the dingy figure dressed in a military greatcoat over what looked like a pair of pyjamas. The cord he was holding in one hand gradually went slack as a dog bearing a marked resemblance to a mobile doormat hobbled into the ambit of the streetlight.

'What on earth's the matter?' Zen demanded.

The man shook his head in confusion. His eyes were still dilated in terror.

'I thought it was . . .' he whispered hoarsely.

'Thought it was who?'

Daniele Trevisan swallowed hard.

'Someone else.'

Zen walked up to him.

'Do you mean my father?' he asked tonelessly.

Daniele Trevisan bit his lip and said nothing. As though in sympathy, his dog raised one leg and voided its bladder against the wall.

'You mistook me for him the day I arrived,' Zen reminded the old man gently.

Trevisan assumed a self-pitying expression.

'I'm getting old,' he whined. 'I get things confused.'

A barbed wind whipped through the *campo*, spraying a fine white dust of snow in their faces.

'Listen, Daniele,' Zen said weightily, 'my father is dead. Do you understand?'

To his amazement, the old man burst into peals of mocking laughter.

'Understand?' he cried. 'Oh yes! Yes, I understand all right!'

Zen stared menacingly at him. Daniele Trevisan's hilarity ended as abruptly as it had begun.

'Of course,' he muttered in a conciliatory tone. 'Dead. To be sure.'

And without another word he shuffled away, dragging his reluctant dog away from the patch of urine-soaked plaster.

At first it looked as though the clouds which had hidden the sun for most of the week had fallen to earth like a collapsed parachute, covering every surface with a billowy white mantle. The next moment, shivering at the bedroom window as he clipped back the internal shutters, Zen thought vaguely of the *aqua alta*. It was only when he became aware of the intense cold streaming in through the gap between window and frame that he realized that it was snow. A sprinkling of fat flakes was still tumbling down from the thick grey sky. Every aspect of roofs and gardens, pavements and bridges, had been rethought. Only the water, immune by its very nature to this form of inundation, remained untouched.

He glanced back towards the empty bed, its sheets and covers decorously unruffled. Although he had stayed up till well after midnight, Cristiana had not shown up. He tried to persuade himself that this was all for the best in the long run. By standing him up, she had evened the score and demonstrated that she was not someone to be trifled with. Next time they could meet as equals, with nothing to prove to each other. As long as there was a next time, of course.

He dressed hurriedly, dispensing with a shower, and made his way downstairs, stiff with cold. The primitive central heating system only operated on the first floor, and as it did not have a timer it had to be switched on manually each morning. If he had known it was going to freeze, he might have risked the wrath of his mother's parsimonious household gods and left the thing on all night. As it was, there was nothing to do but put on his overcoat and hold his fingers under the warm water from the tap to unjam the muscles.

Having assembled the coffee machine and put it on the flame, he returned to the living room and picked up the phone. Despite the day and the hour, or perhaps because of them, the Questura answered almost immediately. Zen identified himself and asked to be connected to the nearest airborne section. This turned out to be situated in the international airport at Tessera, on the shores of the lagoon just outside Mestre. Zen huddled miserably on the sofa while the necessary connections were made. He had never felt so cold in his life. He recalled that first flurry of snow during his encounter with Daniele Trevisan, and then the old man's bizarre behaviour, the way he had mistaken Zen for his father, and his father's disappearance in the icy wastes of Russia so many years ago. . .

It was several minutes before the duty officer at Tessera responded, and several more before Zen could impress on him the nature and urgency of the task before them. By then, the entire house was filled with a horrible stench compounded of burning coffee and melted rubber. Zen slammed the phone down and ran into the kitchen to find the *caffettiera* glowing red-hot at the base and emitting clouds of nauseating black smoke. Having warmed his hands under the running water, he had evidently forgotten to put any in the machine.

He threw the windows wide open to air the place out. Snowflakes melted dampy on his eyes and lips in frigid mockery of the caresses he had been denied the night before. He ran cold water on the coffee maker, but it had fused up solid and was evidently past repair. With a sigh of disgust he tossed it into the canal at the back of the house and returned to the living room, where he phoned Marco Paulon and made his excuses for not being able to come to lunch after all. Then he called the Questura again and arranged for a police launch to collect him from the Ponte Guglie in half an hour.

It must have been an illusion, but it seemed less cold outside the house than in. A solitary row of neat, closely spaced footprints was the only flaw on the glistening surface of the *campo*. They led back to a house two doors from the Morosinis. Signora Vivian, thought Zen automatically, a big raw-boned woman who ate like a horse, walked like a bird and had attended early Mass every Sunday since her first communion.

Zen set off down the alley to the Cannaregio, scuffing up heaps of downy snow with every step. The city was muffled and mute. Even the perpetual ostinato of water, the constant undercurrent of Venetian life, had ceased. Zen trudged on towards the Guglie bridge, where he found a café open. He ordered an espresso with a shot of grappa on the side, on account of the cold, and scanned the headlines in *La Stampa*. A leading industrialist had committed suicide rather than answer questions about alleged fiscal irregularities. A judge claimed that 'an unholy alliance' of the Mafia and the Secret Service was responsible for recent bomb attacks in Florence, Rome and Milan. Four children had been killed and eleven critically injured by a mortar attack on a school in Bosnia. Neo-Nazis had kicked a black teenager to death at a bus-stop in London. Milan were favourites for their local Derby with Juventus.

The snow had thickened by the time Zen left the bar. The police launch was already tied up by the water-steps at the foot of the bridge, the crew slapping their arms and stamping their feet in a vain attempt to keep warm. They didn't much like having to turn out on Sunday, especially one when the weather was providing a sharp reminder of just how close the lagoon was to the glacial peaks of Austria and the frozen plains of Hungary. The personnel of the airborne section weren't going to be that keen either, but that was just too bad. Time was of the essence. For Zen's plan to work, the drug syndicate had to believe that Filippo Sfriso had been so shocked by the murder of Gavagnin that he changed his mind about trying to cheat them. They would of course *want* to believe it, which made matters easier, but for the scenario to be credible Sfriso would have to be able to deliver as soon as the gang contacted him on his release from custody the following day.

The launch cut a swathe through the grey waters of the Cannaregio, passing an almost empty *vaporetto* heading in the other direction. Once they were clear of the canal the helmsman opened up the throttle and the boat surged forward, flanking the dingy northern flanks of the city before bearing round towards Murano and the dredged channel to the airport. Although the sky was overcast, the air was clear enough to reveal the snow-clad Dolomites over a hundred kilometres away to the north. With the wind chill it felt bitterly cold in the cockpit, but Zen stuck it out with the two crewmen as a matter of principle. By the time they rounded the bend leading up to the moorings outside the airport terminal his face felt as though it had turned to bone.

The police airborne unit was housed in a utilitarian block which had formed part of the original military airfield at Tessera, now being transformed to serve the needs of international tourism. As one of the specialized departments of the force, offering both glamour and higher pay, the airborne division attracted a different class of recruit from the general intake, and Zen was favourably impressed by the group of men to whom he was introduced by Leonardo

Castrucci, the commanding officer. Unlike police drivers, whose reputation for reckless aggression was notorious, the flight crews had a reserved and dependable air.

Knowing that the success or failure of the enterprise depended to a large extent on the degree of dedication these men brought to it, Zen went out of his way to get them on his side. He greeted them one by one, asking where they were from and how they felt about being posted to this part of the country. Within five minutes, the natural resentment they felt about being hauled out of bed at eight o'clock on a freezing Sunday morning for a spot of compulsory overtime was forgotten in a sense of shared enterprise and professional pride.

'Okay, lads,' Zen said, stepping back to address them as a group for the first time. 'We all know the frustrations of police work well enough. The jobs where the only people we can get our hands on are the poor bastards who never knew which end was up in the first place, while the ringleaders get off scot-free. The jobs left dangling because someone thought we didn't have quite enough evidence to proceed, or because the outcome might have inconvenienced somebody else's cousin's aunt's mother-in-law's stepson.'

There were smiles and a stifled laugh. Zen nodded soberly.

'Today, by contrast, we have a chance to achieve something real, solid and unequivocal.'

He pointed to the laminated map of the *Provincia di Venezia* which occupied most of the wall to his left.

'There's a gang of drug dealers operating in our territory, peddling heroin on the streets of our towns and cities. We can put each and every member of that gang behind bars for the next twenty years.'

He walked over to the map and pointed out an irregular sliver of white in the northern lagoon.

'This is the island of Sant'Ariano, just a few kilometres east of here.'

There was no visible reaction from the group. Zen had already ascertained that none of them was from Venice. They did not know about Sant'Ariano's sinister vocation, and he had no intention of enlightening them.

'Somewhere on that island is a canvas bag containing three kilos of pure heroin with an estimated street value of half a billion lire. But its value to us is far greater. We know the identity of the gang's courier, and he has agreed to deliver the drugs under our supervision. We can draw the gang into an ambush, put them under surveillance, identify their base and smash the whole operation once and for all.'

He held up a monitory finger.

'But time is pressing! We need to locate the drugs by this evening at the latest. The island is covered with dense scrub and shrubbery, and we have no idea whereabouts the bag is. To make matters worse, it will probably be at least partially covered by snow.'

Zen looked round at the four men, making eye contact with each in turn. He shrugged casually.

'In short, I'm asking you to do a job which would normally take several hundred men a week, to do it in a few hours, in total secrecy, and in the middle of a blizzard.'

Smiles gradually replaced the crews' initial look of apprehension. Zen held up his hands in a gesture of disclaimer.

'I'm not a pilot!' he exclaimed. 'I simply have no idea what's feasible and what's not. What I *do* know is that the only way of locating that package in the time available, given the nature of the terrain, is to go in from the air. If you can't do it, just say so. I won't try and argue with you. I'll just apologize for ruining your day off, go back to the city and tell my bosses that there's nothing to be done. You must decide. The fate of the investigation is in your hands.'

He sat down and lit a cigarette, pointedly ignoring the others. After a moment's silence, the pilots started to shuffle and glance uneasily at each other.

'We'd need two machines,' one of them said eventually.

'We could go in low to scatter the snow,' another put in.

'It's the vegetation that'll be the problem.'

'One man on a hoist with something to part the branches . . .'

'Or a metal sensor? There must be some metal on the bag, a zipper or something.'

There was a silence.

'It'll be damn tricky,' someone said.

'But we can do it,' Leonardo Castrucci concluded firmly. 'And you must do me the honour of riding in the lead machine with me, *dottore*.'

Zen opened his mouth in horror, but no sound emerged.

He sat gripping the metal frame of the seat with both hands as if his life depended on it. If only it had! Zen had never felt so frightened in his life, even on the rare occasions when he had had to face armed criminals. Even at its worst, that fear was natural. This experience was altogether different, a nebulous, visceral terror, triumphantly irrational. In vain he invoked statistics indicating that people who did this every day of their working lives were nevertheless in more danger driving to the airport than they ever were once aloft.

The only saving grace was that the violent juddering of the helicopter disguised his own trembling, just as the roar of the engine hid his involuntary moans and cries. He looked past the hunched figure of Leonardo Castrucci at the dark shape of the other helicopter, hovering stationary a hundred metres away to the south. Although the snow had thickened to a pointillist pall which made the operation yet more difficult and hazardous, it at least ensured that the search could be conducted in perfect secrecy. Potential spies on the few inhabited islands in this part of the lagoon might be able to hear the distant noise of the helicopters, but with visibility down to a few hundred metres there was no danger of them being seen.

For the searchers, the snow was just one more in a series of factors stacking the odds against them. The powerful searchlight attached to the bow of each machine was trained down, creating a cone of light in which the puffy flakes swam like microbes under a microscope. Above the open hatch in the floor of the helicopter, the co-pilot stood ready to raise or lower the metal cable wound around a hoist. At the other end, the third member of the crew dangled from a body harness among the shrubbery, searching the foliage with an alloy pole held in his gloved hands.

'Go!' said a voice in the headset clamped to Zen's ears.

Castrucci eased the machine forward.

'Stop!' said the voice.

And there they hung, rotors whirling, trapped in a mindless hell of noise and turbulence while the man on the hoist searched the next patch of ground. Zen glanced nervously at the man in the pilot's seat beside him. Not the least part of his torment was the sense that Leonardo Castrucci did not normally do this sort of thing any longer, but felt obligated to put on a show to impress his guest. It had been a matter of nods and winks, exchanged glances and unspoken words between the younger pilots. It would be just his luck to get himself killed by some superannuated ace trying to show off. Perhaps Cristiana would end up the same way, with Dal Maschio trying too hard to impress the crowd at some election rally somewhere. The thought seemed oddly comforting.

'Go! Stop!'

A large-scale chart of the island had been photocopied and ruled out in strips running north-south, which the two machines were sweeping alternately. Castrucci had calculated that the search would take about five hours, but it was becoming clear that it would require far longer than that. Indeed, it seemed increasingly unlikely that they would be able complete the operation before the darkness closed in and made it impossible.

'Go! Stop!'

For Aurelio Zen, every minute seemed an hour, each hour an eternity of living hell. He had always been afraid of flying, paralysed and stupefied by the sense of the emptiness beneath. So far in his professional life he had mostly managed to avoid travelling by air, but that morning he had totally failed to see the trap until it was too late. The men of the airborne section had naturally taken it for granted that Zen would wish to be present during the search he had instigated, and Zen had not dared to risk dissipating the *esprit de corps* he had so painstakingly created. As he was led to his doom, he had prayed that helicopters provided a different flying experience from other aircraft.

'Go! Stop!'

It was different all right. It was much, much worse than he had ever imagined possible. The lurches and jolts which filled him with panic on ordinary planes, the mysterious and alarming noises whose significance he pondered endlessly, were all intensified a hundred times, and without the slightest remission.

'Go! Stop!'

He looked out of the window, trying in vain to locate the other machine. Until now they had been moving at roughly the same rate along their notional strips of territory, but now the blue-and-white hull bearing the word POLIZIA and the identification number BN409 was nowhere to be seen. He was about to say something to Leonardo Castrucci when the intercom crackled into life. This time it was a different voice.

'We've found something.'

Castrucci banged the controls in frustration, tilting the whole machine violently to port. The co-pilot grabbed the hoist to prevent himself tumbling out of the open hatch, there was a shriek from the man on the cable below, and Zen found himself mumbling an urgent prayer to the Virgin. Having got the machine back on an even keel, Castrucci vented his anger at his subordinate.

'For Christ's sake, Satriani! How many times do I have to tell you to use the proper call-up procedure! You're not phoning your mistress, you know.'

After an icy silence, the intercom hissed again.

'Bologna Napoli four zero nine calling Cagliari Perugia five seven seven. Come in, please.'

'Receiving you, Bologna Napoli four zero nine.'

'We've found something.'

Zen switched on his microphone.

'Is it the bag?' he demanded eagerly.

There was a brief crackly silence.

'No, not the bag.'

'What then?' demanded Castrucci irritably.

'The man on the hoist reports . . .'

The voice broke off.

'Well?' snapped Castrucci.

'He says he's found a skeleton.'

Without even realizing it, Zen had tensed up with expectation. Now his whole frame slumped despondently.

'This island was used as a dumping ground for all the cemeteries of Venice,' he told the distant pilot. 'Nothing could be less surprising than to find a skeleton.'

'This one's wearing a suit.'

Zen stared straight ahead at the grey, wintry sky.

'A suit?' he breathed into the microphone.

'And it's standing upright.'

The discovery of the heroin came almost as an afterthought. The corpse had been removed by then, after being photographed from every conceivable angle. At first they tried to transfer it to a stretcher in one piece, but the moment they disturbed it the whole thing fell to the ground in a dismal heap. After that it was a question of trying to pick up all the pieces. Some of them still had portions of gristle and flesh attached to them, and the skull and scalp were more or less intact. Quite a lot of clothing was also recovered. They bundled the whole lot into a body bag and hoisted it into one of the helicopters to be flown back to the city.

Aurelio Zen went with it, and thus missed the moment when a scene-of-crime man doing a routine sweep of the area stumbled over the canvas bag a few metres away from the bramble bush across which the body had been lying. By the time the news reached him at the Questura, its significance had been overtaken by events to such an extent that his initial reaction was one of irritation. Another complication he would willingly have done without!

After a moment's thought he called the switchboard and asked to be put through to Aldo Valentini. The Ferrarese was not at home, but a woman who answered the phone volunteered the information that the family were lunching with their in-laws. Zen dialled the number which she gave him and waited in some trepidation for Valentini's reaction. It soon turned out that he need not have worried.

'Aurelio! *Ciao!* What's going on?'

'We've got a bit of a crisis I'm afraid. I'm sorry to disturb you, but it's urgent.'

Valentini's voice dropped to a whisper.

'You mean I get to get out of here?'

Zen laughed with genuine relief.

'I thought you would bite my head off for ruining your Sunday!'

'My Sunday is already comprehensively ruined, courtesy of my brother-in-law. If you can give me a cast-iron excuse for leaving, you've got a friend for life.'

'Where are you?'

'Rovigo. Where the relative in question resides.'

'I'll have a helicopter there in half an hour.'

'A *helicopter*?'

'Like I said, this is urgent. I'll call back later with details of the pick-up.'

He hung up and immediately dialled another number. There was a long pause before the connection was made, another before anyone answered, and when the reply came it made no sense to Zen.

'Is that you, Ellen?' he asked tentatively.

A burst of incomprehensible verbiage followed. He was just about to hang up when he heard a familiar voice speaking broken Italian.

'Aurelio? What's going on? Do you know what time it is?'

'This can't wait, Ellen.'

'Five in the goddamn morning! *Sunday* morning!'

'I think we've found him.'

As in their earlier conversation, every pause seemed disturbing because of the acoustic flatness caused by the satellite equipment switching the circuits to more profitable use. It was as if the line had gone dead, yet the moment he spoke again the connection instantly resumed. The quality of silence was evidently meaningless in electronic terms.

'I'm going to need his dental and medical records and anything else you can lay hands on which might assist in the identification of the remains,' Zen continued. 'Ideally a DNA profile, if one exists. Get on to this lawyer about it. What's his name? Bill?'

'That's who you just spoke to.'

'I'm so happy for you,' Zen replied nastily. 'He sounds a real fire-eater.'

He lowered his voice.

'But listen, *cara*. Tell him to keep this under wraps until further notice, all right? It looks as though there may be some powerful players involved, and my position is already extremely delicate.'

Ellen spoke distantly in English. A disgruntled but incisive male voice replied. Zen didn't understand a single word the man said, but he took an instant dislike to him.

'Do you have a fax number?' Ellen asked in Italian.

Zen consulted the internal directory and dictated the number to her.

'Bill wants to ask a few questions,' she told him.

There was a brief exchange in English off-stage before Ellen returned to translate.

'Is he dead?'

Zen tried to remember what Ellen looked like in bed. All he could call to mind were her nipples, large and dark and surprisingly insensitive, judging by how hard she liked them tweaked.

'The person we found is certainly dead. Very dead.'

Another off-stage buzz while this was translated for Bill's benefit.

'Where was the body found?' Ellen asked in Italian.

'On an island in the lagoon.'

More whispering, then Ellen's translation.

'Have you any idea what happened and who is responsible?'

Zen glanced at the window. It was no longer snowing, but the sagging sky looked ready to burst anew at any moment.

'Nothing worth discussing at this stage. But if the case is going to break, it'll do so in the next forty-eight hours. Until then I need a free hand. That means a press blackout and no interference from the family.'

Ellen duly translated. There was a pause, then a brief male response.

'Bill agrees,' said Ellen.

'Bravo for Bill.'

He grinned maliciously.

'Is he good news in other ways?'

'What's that supposed to mean, Aurelio?'

'If you don't know by now, it's too late to learn.'

'It's never too late,' Ellen retorted.

Zen laughed.

'I've discovered that too.'

'So I gather,' remarked Ellen primly. 'Tania, isn't it? Is *she* good news?'

Zen's smile abruptly disappeared.

'All the best, Ellen,' he said with finality.

'And to you, Aurelio.'

She breathed a long transatlantic sigh.

'I'd like to see you happy, but somehow . . .'

'Somehow what?'

This time the synthetic silence went on so long that he began to think that they really had been cut off.

'Somehow I just can't imagine it,' Ellen said at last.

Zen instinctively touched his genitals in the gesture traditionally used to ward off bad luck.

'Just make sure the material I requested gets here on time,' he told her coldly, and hung up.

Aldo Valentini arrived shortly before three o'clock, having been plucked from the bosom of his in-laws by helicopter and deposited at a landing pad in the hospital complex just north of the Questura. Despite these excitements, the Ferrarese looked poised and spruce in a Sunday leisure outfit which had evidently cost considerably more than the off-the-peg suits he wore to work so as not to upstage his boss Francesco Bruno, who prided himself on being a snappy dresser. Aurelio Zen was there to meet him, the soles of his shoes soaked from the melting slush all around, coat and tie flying in the mini-hurricane created by the rotors.

'Did everything go all right?' he asked as Valentini stepped out, ducking unnecessarily to avoid the spinning blades.

'I just wish someone would lay on something like this every time we have to go over there! It's only three or four times a year, but the prospect fills me with dread weeks before, and the memory lingers for months afterwards.'

'What's so awful about it?'

Zen couldn't have cared less – an only child, deprived of any close relations, he had always considered family life a sanctioned form of incest – but he needed to keep Valentini sweet.

'It's Virgilio,' Valentini explained as they walked back along Calle Capello. 'The guy's a librarian and he's envious of this glamorous and exciting lifestyle which he thinks I have. If I tell some anecdote about the job he accuses me of not being interested in *his* work, and if I suck up to him like he wants then he gets pissed off because he thinks I'm being patronizing. You can't win.'

Zen agreed that in-laws were notoriously a problem, and privately congratulated himself on not having any.

'Anyway, this helicopter transfer certainly did wonders for my prestige,' Valentini went on. 'They were dying to know what it was all about, but I made it clear that my lips were sealed.'

He glanced at Zen.

'What *is* it about, anyway?'

Zen kicked a mushy mound of snow out of his way and gave Valentini a rapid rundown on the progress of the Sfriso case. The wind had moderated and veered round to a mild sirocco with just enough easterly steel in it to keep off the rain. As a result, the city was filled with piles of snow like rotting garbage.

'That's a real coup!' Valentini exclaimed with a low whistle. 'Congratulations, Aurelio. But where do I come into it?'

'I want you to take over the case.'

Aldo Valentini stopped and stared at Zen.

'Why would you give something like that away?'

Zen clapped him on the arm.

'Because underneath this cynical exterior I'm a saint!'

He grinned at Valentini's expression.

'No, I didn't really think you'd buy that. The truth is simpler. The case is going to be taken away from me anyway. My remit here only covers the Zulian affair. No one's going to let me hijack a big breakthrough like this, and as long as it's got to go to someone else, why not you? It was yours originally, after all.'

Valentini sighed.

'Thanks, Aurelio. I really appreciate it. But it won't work.'

'Why not?'

'If drugs are involved, it'll go to Ruzza or Castellaro. It's their area of competence, after all.'

Zen shook his head decisively.

'Their area of incompetence, you mean. Their boss was working hand-in-glove with the gang. Gavagnin had been bought and sold, and who knows how many of his colleagues with him? There's no telling how far the rot may have spread, and it would only take one tip-off to ruin the whole operation. Bruno is going to give the follow-up to someone outside the Drugs Squad whether he wants to or not, just to cover his own back.'

A slow smile spread across Valentini's face as he acknowledged the truth of this. The stakes in a successful outcome to the Sfriso case could hardly have been higher. Even more than smashing the drug gang, it was a question of dishing the Carabinieri, who had lifted the Gavagnin killing from under the noses of the police. Their own colleague's death being investigated by their hated rivals and sworn enemies!

One of the many welcome innovations of the new Criminal Code had been provisions for greater co-operation between the various law enforcement agencies – five, if you counted the Border Guards, the Forestry Guards, and the enforcement arm of the Ministry of Finance – but this amounted to little more than fine words without any bearing on the realities of the situation they purported to describe. As long as the competing power bases at ministerial level were each allowed to maintain their own police forces, those forces were going to be in competition.

In this case, the *Polizia* had opened a file of their own on Gavagnin's death, but the military had all the relevant information and they were playing it very close to their chests, using every delaying tactic in the book. The result was a grudge match with huge amounts of ego and status at stake. Any police officer who succeeded in dishing the Flying Flames over this one would be guaranteed not just fast-track promotion but legendary status amongst his colleagues for the rest of his career.

Having unloaded the Sfriso case on to the willing shoulders of Aldo Valentini, Zen phoned Marcello Mamoli. The Deputy Public Prosecutor was a good deal less amenable about being disturbed at home on Sunday than Valentini had been.

'This continuing invasion of my private life is absolutely intolerable, Zen! I'm simply not prepared to go on living in a state of perpetual harassment.'

Zen assumed his most ingratiating tone.

'A hundred thousand apologies, *signor giudice*. I would not have presumed to disturb you at such a time if it were not that there has been a development which absolutely changes the scope and thrust of the investigation . . .'

'Get on with it!'

'The search of Sant'Ariano which you so wisely instructed me to undertake has been an overwhelming success. We have recovered not only the missing consignment of heroin, but also a corpse.'

Mamoli was silent a moment.

'Has the victim been identified?'

'Not yet, *signor giudice*. It was however recovered in close proximity to the bag containing the heroin, and the presumption must be that it was this body, viewed by torchlight in the dark, which convinced Giacomo Sfriso that he had seen a walking corpse.'

'But on Sant'Ariano!' exclaimed Mamoli. 'Why should anyone be killed there? Why should anyone be there in the first place, come to that?'

'These are the very questions to which I hope to have answers shortly, *signor giudice*. Filippo Sfriso has named three men whom he suspects of having a hand in his brother's death. They are Giulio Bon, of Chioggia, and Massimo Bugno and Domenico Zuin, both from Venice. I would like authorization to take all three into custody and question them separately about these events and related matters.'

He had retailed this lie with complete assurance, but now he held his breath. Everything depended on Mamoli's response. After a moment the magistrate sighed.

'Very well, Zen. Seeing as it's Sunday, I'll let you run with this for now. But tomorrow I'm going to want a full accounting of the measures you have taken, and God help you if it doesn't add up.'

It took Zen the best part of an hour to organize the paperwork and logistics of the next part of the operation. This was the part of his work he had always disliked, particularly in a strange town where the staff were just names, their characters and capabilities unknown to him. In the end he divided the task between three separate teams, each with its own boat. He took charge of the first, and chose two names at random from the duty sheet to lead the other two.

The three launches left just after half past four. The raids were synchronized to prevent any tip-offs, while the return to the Questura was staggered so that none of the detainees knew that the others were also being held for questioning. Giulio Bon and Domenico Zuin were both at home watching Milan play Juventus on television, while Massimo Bugno was picked up at a nearby bar where he had gone to play cards.

At the Questura, the three were taken to separate offices which Zen had commandeered on different floors of the building, where he visited them in the course of the early evening. Zuin and Bugno both seemed bewildered by what had happened. When Zen offered them the services of a court-appointed lawyer, Zuin shrugged as though it had nothing to do with him, while Bugno protested incoherently that there must have been some mistake.

'Too fucking right, son,' Zen told him in dialect. 'And you're the one who made it.'

Giulio Bon was an altogether stiffer proposition. The only statement he made was to demand the services of his lawyer. Zen nodded helpfully.

'What was his name, again?'

Bon frowned.

'The same as before!' he insisted. 'The plump one with the beard.'

'I've yet to meet an undernourished lawyer, and so many of them wear beards these days, particularly the ones who are losing the stuff on top. Unless you can recall the name of your legal representative, Signor Bon, I'll have to select one off the rota.'

Bon scowled but said nothing more. Leaving him in the charge of an armed guard, Zen returned to his office. He was in no hurry to proceed. The longer the three were left to soak in their own sense of anxiety, isolation and helplessness, the more likely one of them would be to crack when the time came. And one was all the leverage Zen needed to break the Durridge case wide open.

He sat down and lit a cigarette. Mamoli had made it clear that the state of grace which Zen currently enjoyed was exceptional and must end with the start of the next working week. The next stage would be to apply for arrest warrants and turn the three men over to Mamoli for formal interrogation, but before he did that he would need either a confession or some substantial piece of evidence. There was no certainty that he would be able to obtain either, particularly with his official position under threat now that the Ada Zulian investigation had folded. Not only had he no authorization from the Ministry to investigate the Durridge case, but officially speaking there was no such thing. He was a phantom chasing a chimera.

In short, it promised to be a stressful and exhausting twenty-four hours, and the first thing to do was to make sure that his emotional flanks were covered. He picked up the phone and dialled the Morosinis' number. It was Rosalba who answered, and before he could get in a single word Zen had to sit out several minutes of being told off for not coming to Sunday lunch. His protests that he had not known that he was invited merely made matters worse.

'What were you expecting, a piece of pasteboard with gold lettering? Do you think we would want to send an old family friend to eat Sunday lunch all alone in some miserable *trattoria*? Is that the kind of people you think we are?'

Quickly trying a new tack, Zen started to explain that he had had to turn down an earlier invitation from the Paulons.

'Fabia Paulon?' exclaimed Rosalba indignantly. 'That slut couldn't cook an egg without . . .'

'In any case, I've been at work all day.'

'On Sunday?' cried Rosalba, hardly pausing in her stride. 'What are they thinking of? Let them get some of the younger men to do it. There's no cause to drag an old man like you out of the house on his one day of . . .'

'Is Cristiana there?' Zen cut in.

'I'll call her. And listen, Aurelio, come to dinner tomorrow.'

'If I'm free.'

'Free? What is this, a prison? Make yourself free!'

Zen smiled minimally.

'I'm working on it.'

'What?'

'Just call your daughter, will you?'

'What's it about?' demanded Rosalba, suddenly suspicious.

'I need to have a word with her about her husband.'

Rosalba grunted and put the phone down. Zen stubbed out his cigarette and stared at the window. The winter dusk was gathering like a hostile mob. Footsteps crossed a distant floor and then a cherished voice caressed his senses.

'Aurelio.'

'Hello, darling.'

'I'm sorry I didn't make it last night, but I just couldn't get rid of the people I was with.'

'What about tonight?'

There was a pause.

'Mamma said you wanted to talk to me about Nando.'

'That was just to give me a reason for calling. I don't want to put you in an awkward position.'

'Or yourself,' Cristiana added tartly.

'That too. So, what about it?'

'Would about seven be okay? Or earlier?'

Zen's heart leapt.

'Earlier, earlier! Now.'

She laughed.

'I'm at the office now,' he said, 'but I'll come straight home. Will you be there?'

'Is this all to do with the dramatic development you mentioned last night?'

'Very much so. I'll tell you when I see you. Will you be there when I get back?'

There was a brief pause.

'Yes.'

Zen smiled secretly.

'Yes,' he echoed.

What a pleasure it is to walk out of an evening, a nephew at each elbow lest she slip on the snowy pavement! They're at her beck and call these days, dear Nanni and sweet little Vincenzo. She has only to suggest how nice it would be to take a walk and perhaps drop in on Daniele Trevisan for a chat and a cup of something warming, and before she knows it they'll be ringing her doorbell, eager to oblige.

Ada can remember a time, and not so long ago either, when things were very different. Weeks would go by without her seeing her nephews. Even worse, she was treated to midnight visits by mocking simulacra who borrowed Nanni's clipped, high-pitched voice and Vincenzo's stooping stance for their own malign purposes. They led her a merry dance for a while, these apparitions, but in the end she turned the tables on them – and with a vengeance!

Nothing's too much trouble for Nanni and Vincenzo nowadays. They call on her every day, run errands for her, do her shopping, bring presents and generally lavish attentions of all kinds on her. And if by any chance they happen to be forgetful or remiss she need only mention Aurelio Battista, son of her old friend Signora Giustiniana, whom she helped out with some cleaning work when her husband went off and got lost in Russia. 'Dispersed', they called it in the papers, but Ada knew what that meant. People used to vanish in those days. It was almost normal. A child here, a man there, a whole family . . .

For her part, Ada still thinks of Aurelio Battista as that effeminate, long-haired lad she used to dress up in Rosetta's clothes while his mother went the rounds of the neighbourhood, trying to make ends meet. But apparently for other people, Nanni and Vincenzo included, he is – she giggles at the thought – a Very Powerful and Important Official. Having cleaned the boy's bottom when he had an accident, Ada remains unimpressed by these trappings of authority, but Nanni and Vincenzo seem to be completely taken in. The happy result is that whenever she wishes to bring her nephews to heel, she has only to drop a passing reference to her friend's son – the merest casual comment, such as 'Dottore Zen called by yet again yesterday, but I pretended to be out' – and in an instant, as though by magic, the boys become completely tractable! It is a weapon all the more effective in that she hardly ever has occasion to use it.

This evening, though, had been one. Having been molly-coddled as children – Ada had warned her sister time and time again that central heating rots one's moral fibre, but would she listen? – Vincenzo and Nanni are reluctant to venture out in what they call cold weather. They should have seen the winter of '47, when the canals froze over and people walked across to the Giudecca! But as usual, all Ada had to do was mention quite casually, in passing, that her friend the policeman had dropped round again and tried to get her to implicate her nephews so that he could have them arrested and thrown into prison to await trial, and how after a while she had started to wonder if it might not be easier just to give him what he wanted and be rid of this new harassment, which was almost as bad as the previous one . . .

Speak of the devil! There *is* Aurelio Battista, picking his way towards them along the snow-encrusted alley. She knows by the way the grip on her elbows tightens that Nanni and Vincenzo have seen him too. A flurry of anxiety, the first for days, troubles the surface of her new-found serenity. She hopes there won't be a scene, just when everything has worked out so nicely.

The tall figure striding towards them glances up, taking in the trio ahead. He eyes them each briefly, his gaze lingering a moment on Ada, then passes by without the slightest glimmer of recognition. Vincenzo glances at Nanni, who lets go of his aunt's arm. Crouching down, he scoops up a double handful of the soft wet snow, moulds it firmly into a ball as hard as a rock and, before Ada can work out what he has in mind, hurls it. She watches bemusedly as it speeds through the darkening air, then Vincenzo yanks her round and marches her along the street towards Daniele's house.

Behind them, a cry rends the silence. Ada wriggles free of her nephew's grasp and looks round. Aurelio Battista stands rubbing the back of his head and staring at her. His hat lies capsized on the snow near by. Ada wonders what can have happened. Perhaps he's troubled by migraine, poor boy. She suffered from it herself at one time, before that role was usurped by other and greater torments, and she dimly recalls that just this sort of cold, wet weather often brought it on. Something has certainly made Giustiniana's boy very tense and snappy. Snatching up his hat, he strides towards her.

'Come along, Auntie,' croons Vincenzo softly.

They have almost reached their goal. Dear Daniele! How pleased he will be to see them. He used to be rather sweet on her at one time – well, besotted, actually. And under different circumstances she might easily have been tempted, because Daniele Trevisan was then one of the handsomest lads in the neighbourhood, and with very winning manners, considering his origins. But for a Zulian to ally herself with someone whose father was in trade was of course quite out of the question.

They have arrived. Nanni is already ringing Daniele's bell, while Vincenzo brushes a trace of fluff off the sleeve of her coat. What dear, thoughtful boys they are!

But what's this? Aurelio Battista suddenly shoves his way rudely between them, fixing her with his eyes, waving his finger in her face.

'Give them to me, Ada!' he spits out. 'Give them to me, and I'll tell you what really happened to Rosetta.'

At least, that's what he seems to say, but of course it's quite impossible that he could have spoken those words, or indeed anything remotely resembling them.

'Don't you want to know the truth, Ada, after all these years? Give me your nephews and I'll tell you!'

It is only now that she belatedly realizes that the figure before her is not Aurelio Battista at all, but some species of demon which has assumed his form. As always, the knowledge that she is not faced with anything real and irremediable is both disturbing and obscurely comforting. She is determined to retain the initiative, however. She is an old hand when it comes to dealing with this sort of thing.

'What do you know about it?' she demands with a sneer.

The creature before her leans closer.

'I know about Rosa Coin.'

It steps back, nods once, then turns and walks off, merging almost immediately into the massed shadows.

'Come on, Auntie dear,' urges Nanni.

Before her, in the open doorway, Daniele stands looking at her with the same smile as all those years ago, when he used to stand for hours beneath her window, waiting for her to show her face.

'You'll catch your death standing out there in the cold,' he tells her kindly.

But she is not standing. She is sliding, slipping to the icy pavement where she thrashes about like a landed fish, gasping for air, biting her tongue in a vain attempt to silence the endless screaming in her head.

By the time Zen reached home he had got the trembling under control, but his breath was still spastic and his heart clamoured for attention. It was only when he saw lights on in the house that he remembered that Cristiana was waiting for him.

Her presence, so ardently desired just a little while ago, now seemed an inconvenience he could well have done without. After what had just happened he needed time to unwind, to unclench his knotted psyche and become himself again, the self he recognized and was prepared to take responsibility for. The last thing he wanted at such a moment was to have to play sophisticated and ambiguous courtship games with the daughter of an old family friend.

Cristiana must have heard the front door open, for she was waiting for him at the top of the stairs. The tight-fitting red sweater and jeans she was wearing emphasized the contours of her figure. As Zen reached the landing, she stepped forward and laid her hand on his shoulder. She was bending forward, as if to kiss him, when saw the expression on his face and drew back.

'What's wrong?'

He shook his head.

'Nothing.'

He led her inside the living room and closed the door behind them, shutting out the world.

'I ran into Ada Zulian out walking with her nephews,' he said as he took off his coat and hat. 'One of them threw a snowball at me. It sounds childish, but it actually hurt quite badly. It hit me on the ear, and he'd squeezed it down to a ball of ice.'

'What did you do?'

Zen shrugged awkwardly.

'There were only one thing to do, really, and that was ignore it.'

'You could have thrown one back.'

'That would really have been stupid. Besides, it would have missed. I'm a hopeless shot.'

Cristiana disappeared into the kitchen.

'Isn't there a law against assaulting police officials?'

'Of course, but I can't invoke it. Everyone knows that I tried and failed to bring that pair to court. If I charged them with assaulting me with a snowball, I'd make myself a complete laughing-stock. Which is precisely what the little bastard was counting on.'

Cristiana reappeared with a bottle of spumante and two glasses. Zen forced a smile.

'What are we celebrating?'

'My freedom.'

As she untwisted the wire cage securing the cork, Zen had an involuntary mental image of Enzo Gavagnin's blue, partially severed thumbs.

'How do you mean?'

Cristiana popped the cork and filled their glasses.

'Finish telling me about Ada Zulian. What *did* you do in the end?'

'Oh, I was wonderful! I ignored the nephews and went for Ada herself.'

She handed him his drink.

'*Cincin!*'

They clinked glasses.

'What do you mean, you went for her?' asked Cristiana.

Zen sighed deeply.

'I've had quite a stressful few days, one way and another, and getting hit by that snowball was the last straw. I'm afraid I went completely over the top.'

'What did you do?'

'I . . .'

He broke off, biting his lip.

'Christ, it was unforgivable!'

Cristiana took his hand and drew him down to the sofa.

'I'll forgive you.'

He sat staring blankly at the worn patch of carpet which covered the centre of the floor.

'I told her that I knew what had happened to her little girl, the one who disappeared.'

He turned to meet Cristiana's eyes, then looked away again.

'I said I'd tell her if she agreed to testify against her nephews.'

Cristiana nodded briskly, as though all this was quite in order.

'And what did she say?'

Zen laughed harshly and gulped at his wine.

'She didn't say anything. She threw a fit. Collapsed in the snow, writhing around, foaming at the mouth, screaming her head off.'

'God!'

'It happened right in front of Daniele Trevisan's house. He and the nephews took her inside.'

He glanced at Cristiana.

'I'd like to know how she is. I don't suppose they'd talk to me, but . . .'

'Of course.'

She picked up the receiver and dialled.

'Mamma? I'm over at Wanda's. She says that Lisa Rosteghin heard from Gabriella that Ada Zulian has had some sort of fit in the street right outside Trevisan's place. Have you heard anything about it? No? Well, listen, could you phone Daniele and find out? We can't, you see, because he'd want to know how we found out and then it might come out about Gabriella and Beppo Raffin, the kid who lives across the street, whereas you could make out you heard from Signora Vian . . .'

She paused, gazing vaguely into indeterminate space.

'No, don't call us. We're . . . we're not actually at Wanda's. We went out. I'll phone back in a few minutes. Okay? *Ciao.*'

She turned back to Zen and sipped her wine.

'And your freedom?' he asked.

She laughed.

'That was just an excuse to open some bubbly. Do you know what my bastard husband has done? Flown to Rome with that bitch Populin! He's got a cover story – some televised debate on the break-up of Italy – but basically we're talking dirty weekend.'

She touched Zen's hand.

'Have you got a cigarette?'

He dug out his battered pack of *Nazionali*. It had a rumpled, collapsed look. Zen squeezed the sides experimentally.

'Precisely one,' he said, shaking the remaining cigarette free.

'Oh, I won't take it if it's your last.'

He removed the cigarette from the packet and placed the tip against her lips.

'Let's share,' he said.

'It wouldn't be so bad if I hadn't been trying so hard to act the good little wife for the benefit of the press,' Cristiana went on, inhaling deeply.

Zen squeezed her hand sympathetically.

'Quite apart from that,' he murmured, 'it might not be such a bad idea to keep a certain distance from Dal Maschio.'

Cristiana passed him the cigarette.

'You mean he's in some sort of trouble?'

He put the tip, damp from her saliva, into his mouth.

'Would that bother you?'

She glanced at her watch.

'I'd better see what Mamma has found out before she gets impatient, tries Wanda's number and discovers that she hasn't seen me since yesterday.'

Rosalba Morosini had evidently found out quite a lot, and proceeded to give her daughter a lengthy account which Cristiana subsequently passed on to Zen in abridged form.

'Ada's all right. They were about to call a doctor when she came out of it. The nephews tried to get her to lodge a complaint, but Daniele refused to testify against you.'

'Good for him.'

Cristiana stared at him.

'Do you really know what became of the little girl?'

Zen handed her back the cigarette.

'No more than I know what became of my father.'

She crushed out the cigarette and poured them more wine.

'And Nando?'

Zen tried to shrug it off.

'Oh, I expect I'm just jealous, that's all.'

She looked at him acutely.

'That's not all.'

He looked away.

'Not quite all, perhaps.'

She took his hand between hers and carried it to the upper slope of her breast. They looked at each other.

'This is strictly confidential, of course,' he began.

'Of course.'

Somewhere in the distance, a ship's hooter sounded a long, mournful note.

'There is no evidence against Dal Maschio himself,' Zen murmured, moving his hand slightly. 'But some of his associates appear to be implicated in a number of investigations currently proceeding . . .'

He broke off.

'I sound like a policeman,' he said.

'You *are* a policeman.'

'I don't want to be. Not now.'

'Have you got any more cigarettes?'

'Upstairs.'

She nodded slowly.

'Upstairs,' she said.

He was woken by a cry below the window.

'*Spazzino* PRONTI!!!'

Zen lay back in bed, listening to the other tenants tossing down their bags of rubbish for the street sweeper to add to the pile in his hand-cart. He felt clear-headed, relaxed and lucid. There was no doubt about it: Cristiana was good for him.

This time she had not been able to stay the night. Rosalba was expecting her home and would have phoned Wanda Dal Maschio if her daughter had not reappeared. It would have been perfect if she had still been there, a warm, sleepy presence, a token that what had happened the night before had indeed been real. Unlike the previous occasion, Zen now had no anxieties about facing Cristiana by the cold light of morning. On the contrary, he was already missing her. They had stayed up talking late the night before, and there had been no moment of awkwardness or strain. Everything had seemed perfectly easy and normal, as though they had known each other all their lives.

The house did not feel quite as cold as the day before, and when he threw open the window it was clear that a thaw had set in. All but the largest heaps of snow were already gone, leaving only a faint sheen of water which made the worn paving stones gleam like a fishmonger's slab. Diffuse sunlight lent a vernal suppleness to the bright, clean air. It was a day for assignations and excursions, a day to tear up your plans and arrangements and make things up as you went along, preferably in the company of a friend or lover.

As he set out in search of his morning coffee, Zen's heart sank at the very different prospect before him. It seemed absurd to spend such a day sitting in poky, neon-lit offices being lied to by the likes of Giulio Bon. He no longer cared one way or the other about the Durridge case. But there was no alternative. It would be as dangerous now to abandon the investigation as to pursue it – perhaps more so. The only way he could justify the measures he had already taken was by seeing the thing through to the end.

At the Questura, he surveyed the various options open to him and tried to decide how to proceed. Based on the way the men had reacted to being taken into custody the day before, Bugno seemed the weakest link in the chain, so Zen sent for him first. While he waited, he skimmed through the man's file. Born in 1946, married with three children, an employee of the muncipal transport company ACTV, Bugno had no previous convictions. The only black marks against him were a failure to vote in a recent general election and the complaint of trespass made the previous year by Ivan Durridge.

Massimo Bugno had a big bald head, a deeply-indented broken nose, a weak chin, bushily compensatory moustache and the general air of someone who fears that he has forgotten to turn off the bath water. He was evidently considerably less refreshed than Zen by the night he had spent in a cell in the windowless annexe behind the Questura. Zen invited him to sit down. He glanced at his watch.

'What shift are you on this week, Massimo? Your workmates will be starting to wonder what's become of you.'

'Why are you holding me here?' Bugno whined. 'What have I done?'

Zen lifted the file off the desk in front of him.

'On the 27th of September last year, you and two other men landed on a private *ottagono* near Malamocco. The owner called the police, and you were subsequently apprehended by a patrol boat.'

Bugno frowned.

'That's all over!' he protested. 'No charges were ever brought. It was all a fuss over nothing, anyway. We were . . .'

He hesitated.

'We were fishing. The motor packed up. We drifted on to the island. We left as soon as we could.'

Zen raised his eyebrows.

'Fishing? That's not what you told us at the time.'

Bugno dampened his lips rapidly with his tongue.

'Well, it was something like that. I don't exactly remember.'

Zen nodded.

'Let's see if your memory is any better when it comes to your next visit to the island.'

'You're mistaken. I've never been back there.'

Zen was surprised and dismayed in equal measure. For the first time, Massimo Bugno had spoken with a casual ease which carried complete conviction. Suddenly Zen had the horrible sensation that his whole theory about the Durridge kidnapping was totally and utterly wrong. His reaction was to lash out.

'Still feeling big and brave, are we?' he sneered at Bugno. 'Your wife isn't, I can tell you that much. She's been ringing every five minutes wanting to know what's going on and when she can expect you home. She's worried, the kids are terrified, the neighbours are gossiping, but what can I tell her? It all depends on you, Massimo.'

Bugno wrung his hands piteously.

'What do you want me to do? What do you want me to say?'

'The truth!' Zen shouted.

'But I've told you the truth!'

Zen swung his fist as though to strike him, then drew it aside at the last moment and drove it into his palm with a resounding smack.

'Stop messing me about, Bugno!'

Bugno looked abject.

'I'm sorry, *dottore*! I'm really sorry! I just don't know what you want me to say.'

'What were you doing on the eleventh of November last year?'

Massimo Bugno frowned.

'November?'

'November, yes! Are you deaf? Answer the question!'

Suddenly Bugno's face cleared.

'The eleventh? Ah, well, that weekend I would have been out of town.'

Zen laughed contemptuously.

'Had the alibi nice and pat, didn't you? Now I *know* you're guilty, Bugno, and so help me God I'll get a confession if I have to beat it out of you.'

'It's the truth! I was on the mainland, near Belluno, at my father-in-law's farm. I can prove it!'

'Oh I'm sure you can dig up a few relatives who are prepared to perjure themselves on your behalf.'

'It's my father-in-law's birthday!'

'The eleventh?'

'The eighth.'

'What's the eighth got to do with it? Don't try and confuse the issue!'

'You don't understand. His birthday is on the eighth, but the kids were in school and Lucia and I had to work. We drove up there at the weekend and stayed over till Sunday evening. I was nowhere near the city on the eleventh!'

Bugno stared fixedly at Zen, as though trying to hypnotize him into belief. There was no need for that. Zen had no doubt that Bugno was telling the truth. On the other hand, he couldn't afford to turn him loose until he had questioned the other two men.

'Have it your own way!' he snapped, and called the guard to have Bugno taken back to the cells.

Before dealing with Massimo Zuin, Zen phoned down to the local bar for a *cappuccino* and a pastry. A few minutes later Aldo Valentini breezed in, followed almost immediately by Pia Nunziata, her right arm in a sling, carrying a beige envelope in her left hand.

'What are you doing here?' Zen asked her indignantly. 'You're supposed to be taking the week off.'

The policewoman nodded.

'I was going to, but all my friends, relatives and neighbours kept popping in and ringing up every five minutes to ask how I was. In the end I decided I'd rather be at work.'

She handed him the envelope and walked out, almost colliding with the waiter carrying Zen's breakfast. Zen gave him a tip calculated to ensure an equally prompt response next time, then tore open the envelope and scanned the four sheets of flimsy paper inside, headed *Heyman, Croft, Kleinwort and Biggs, Attorneys at Law*. In the next cubicle, Aldo Valentini was typing frantically.

'How's it going, Aldo?' Zen called.

'Still waiting for the gang to call, Sfriso's at home with a tap on the line, I'm trying to organize a rapid response for any of the scenarios they might throw at us, enough to drive you round the bend, didn't sleep a wink all night.'

Zen dipped the last bite of pastry in his coffee, then stood up and put on his hat and coat. Domenico Zuin was going to have to wait.

Outside, a gentle drowsiness pervaded the air. Zen turned left, walking north towards the hospital complex behind the church dedicated to the hybrid San Zanipolo. A boy on a miniature bicycle was dashing about the square at high speed, ignoring the ritualistic cries of 'Come here!' from his mother, who was chatting expansively to a friend by the bridge. Zen walked along the quay lined with mooring posts painted in blue-and-white stripes like barbers' poles, and entered the imposing courtyard of the hospital.

The pathology department was located in a remote outbuilding on the other side of the huge ex-conventual complex. Zen made his way through groups of patients in dressing gowns and visitors clutching flowers and fruit and walked down a tree-lined alley to a green door marked HISTOPATHOLOGY. A dingy corridor inside led to a room packed with laboratory equipment. A young woman in a white coat directed Zen to a small room on the other side of the lab, where he donned a gown and rubber boots. Already the air was tainted with the cloying odour of formaldehyde.

Inside the post-mortem room there were six metal tables, three of them occupied. An assistant was sewing up a female corpse whose body cavity now contained a pair of rubber gloves, strips of blood-soaked muslin and a copy of the morning's *Corriere dello Sport*. At the next table, another assistant pulled the caul of cut scalp down over a male cadaver's face and set about sawing the skull open. Zen asked him where he could find the pathologist. The man waved vaguely with the bone-flecked saw at a glass-fronted office in the end wall where a florid man in a white plastic cape and rubber boots was talking loudly on the telephone.

' . . . and then once Anna and Patrizio finally turned up, nothing would do but we all had to sit through the whole thing again from the beginning! Do you believe it? And when Claudio tried gently to tell him that enough was enough, he got completely pissed off and started asking what kind of friends we were . . . It's absurd! He's only had the damn thing a month and already he thinks he's Visconti.'

He glanced up at Zen.

'Anyway, Marco, I must go. What? That's right, the corpses are getting restless, heh heh. Speak to you later.'

He put the phone down.

'Now then, what can I do for you?'

Zen introduced himself and inquired about the progress of the autopsy on cadaver 40763, such being the number assigned to the remains which had been found on Sant'Ariano.

'Done, finished, complete,' the pathologist remarked carelessly. 'I like to get the really putrid stuff out of the way early on, if at all possible.'

Zen handed him the sheets faxed over by the law firm representing the Durridge family.

'I believe this is medical information relating to a missing person,' he said. 'It's in English, but . . .'

'So's half the literature,' the pathologist retorted. 'You want to know if it's the same man?'

He glanced at the material, then walked over to the door, beckoning to Zen. The pathologist led the way to the far end of the post-mortem room. On an isolated table lay a long plastic bag with a zipper running from one end to the other. He opened the bag, releasing a stench which overpowered even the pervading odour of formaldehyde. Inside lay a partially reassembled skeleton and an assortment of bones, some of which had bits of flesh and gristle clinging to them. The pathologist removed the jawbone and compared the teeth to a sketch in the fax, then bent over the skull and repeated the process with the upper jaw.

'Looks like a perfect match,' he murmured. 'There's a couple of missing teeth, but they probably broke loose on impact.'

He pointed to a row of jars at the foot of the table, where various organs were floating in pink liquid.

'Tough organ, the heart. It survived even this degree of decomposition.'

He patted the skull lightly.

'Our subject suffered from coronary artery disease. According to these medical records, so did this American.'

'So it's the same man?' Zen asked eagerly.

The pathologist gestured a disclaimer.

'I can't issue an official identification without running some tests on the other data in here.'

'But off the record . . .' Zen insisted.

'Off the record, I'd say there's very little question that it's the same man.'

Zen released a long sigh.

'I suppose it's impossible to determine the cause of death with the body in this condition?'

'In most cases it would certainly have been very difficult,' the pathologist replied. 'But this one is perfectly straightforward.'

He pointed to the base of the skull.

'Observe this lesion. The cervical vertebrae have been driven straight up into the skull. And again here, the fracture dislocation of the hips and the multiple pelvic fractures.'

He looked at Zen.

'The evidence speaks for itself.'

'And what does it say?' Zen inquired dryly.

'The man fell to his death.'

Zen gaped at the pathologist.

'Fell?'

'Oh yes. And from quite a considerable height. At least the fourth floor, and probably higher.'

Zen laughed.

'That's impossible!'

'I beg your pardon?' the pathologist returned with a piqued expression.

'There are no buildings where this man was found! There are no structures of any kind, only bushes and shrubs.'

The pathologist zipped up the body bag.

'Perhaps he died elsewhere and the corpse was subsequently moved to the site where you found it. There is no way of telling once the flesh has gone. But I can assure you that injuries such as these can occur only in the way I have described.'

Zen nodded meekly.

'Of course, *dottore*. I didn't mean to . . .'

'There are minor variations, depending on the primary point of impact. I recall a case a few years back, an air force trainee whose parachute failed to open. He landed on his head, with the result that the vault of the skull was driven down over the spine. That presents very similar lesions to this one, but with cranial impact you also get extensive fracturing of the vault and the base of the skull. That is absent here, so he must have come down feet first. It's purely a matter of chance.'

He removed his rubber gloves and shook Zen's hand.

'Leave these medical details with me and I'll send over a full report in due course.'

Zen was so deep in thought as he left the hospital that he did not notice the funeral when he tried to push his way through the cortège and was indignantly repulsed. Only then did he become aware of the dirge-like bell strokes, and the blue motor launch bearing a coffin submerged in flowers and wreaths with sprays of lilies and palm leaves crossed with violet ribbons. He took off his hat respectfully as the hearse cast off for the short trip to San Michele, followed by a line of watertaxis bearing the mourners.

Once the crowd had dispersed, he began to walk slowly back to the Questura. But though his pace was deliberate, his mind was racing. The Durridge case had entered a phase of extreme delicacy, and Zen knew that he needed to decide exactly what he was going to do and not do before making his next moves. A mistake at this point would not only jeopardize any hope of bringing the investigation to a successful conclusion, but might well leave Zen himself at risk, professionally if not personally.

All the elements of the case were now before him. It was just a question of fitting them together in the right way, so that the overall picture could be deciphered. And the key to the puzzle, he felt sure, was the question of how Ivan Durridge had died. How could a man fall to his death when there was nowhere to fall from? As for the pathologist's idea that the corpse might have been moved subsequent to death, that was simply not credible, given the terrain. It would have been possible to transport the body to Sant'Ariano by boat, assuming you knew the lagoon well, but no one could have carried it across the island through that dense undergrowth. It would have had to be hoisted into place using a crane, or . . .

As he entered the Questura, the policeman on guard behind the armoured glass screen in the vestibule called to him.

'The Questore wants to see you in his office immediately, *dottore*. Top floor, first on the right.'

Francesco Bruno was sitting behind his desk initialling papers when Zen entered. Well dressed, carefully groomed and quietly spoken, there was nothing about him to suggest the policeman. He could equally well have been a senior manager in a multinational company, or indeed a political figure with a high public profile.

'Ah, at last!' he murmured as Zen came in. 'I was beginning to think you'd gone back to Rome already.'

'Sorry, sir. I just slipped out for a moment to look into one or two things . . .'

Bruno waved impatiently.

'I've got nothing against my officers popping out for the occasional coffee. Unfortunately the matter I have to raise with you is rather more serious.'

He picked up a copy of a newspaper lying on his desk, folded it carefully and handed it to Zen. The article was headed ELDERLY VENETIAN ARISTOCRAT THREATENED BY UNDERCOVER POLICEMAN. The text below describéd how Contessa Ada Zulian had been accosted in the street by an official working for the Ministry of the Interior, who had attempted to blackmail her into altering her testimony to allow the State to prosecute her nephews. When Contessa Zulian refused, the official - 'whose name is known to this paper' – made a number of cruel and gratuitous references to a personal tragedy suffered by the Zulian family. The *contessa*, whose health had long been extremely fragile, collapsed and had to be taken to a nearby house, where she made a slow recovery. The article went on to condemn this 'typical example of the arrogance and brutality of Rome', and invited readers to make their indignation clear by voting overwhelmingly for the *Nuova Repubblica Veneta* in the forthcoming municipal elections.

Zen glanced at the cover of the newspaper.

'This is a party journal,' he remarked, tossing it down on the desk. 'They're just playing politics.'

'Playing to win!' retorted Francesco Bruno. 'If the opinion polls are right, they're likely to be the biggest party on the city council after the local elections. Ferdinando Dal Maschio will be a person of immense power and influence in the capital of the province whose police chief I am.'

Bruno kept looking straight at Zen, but there was a strangely absent quality about his gaze, as though he weren't really seeing what he was looking at.

'Times have changed, *dottore*! It's just not good enough any longer for police officers to swagger about like a pack of licensed bully-boys. It's essential for all of us to realize that we are the servants of the public, not its masters. Accountability is the name of the game.'

He got to his feet, sighing loudly, and wandered over to the window.

'Here we are, trying to build a new Italy, with nothing but the old materials to hand! I appreciate that it's difficult for the older personnel such as yourself to change your ways overnight, but this incident involving the Contessa Zulian is completely unacceptable by any standards. There is simply no excuse for it.'

He turned to face Zen.

'I simply won't permit this sort of heavy-handed loutishness to wreck the carefully nurtured public relations which I and my staff have been at such pains to build up. You Criminalpol people come and go, but the rest of us have to live and work here. To do so successfully involves winning and retaining the respect and trust of the local population, and more especially their elected representatives.'

Francesco Bruno sat down and started initialling documents again.

'I've issued a press statement to the effect that your transfer here will cease as of midnight tonight,' he said without looking up.

Zen did not move. After some time, the Questore raised his head and nodded once at Zen.

'That's all.'

On the way back to his office, Zen met Pia Nunziata and asked her to come and have a coffee with him.

'You're supposed to be on sick leave and I've just been told to clear my desk,' he said when she looked doubtful. 'Technically speaking, we're not here in the first place.'

The *Bar dei Greci* was empty apart from two elderly men mumbling at each other over their glasses of wine. Pia Nunziata asked for a mineral water. Zen ordered himself a coffee and a grappa. He felt he deserved it.

'Why have they told you to leave?' the policewoman asked as they sat down.

'I was sent here to investigate the Zulian case, and there is no Zulian case.'

'But we caught them red-handed!'

Zen shot her a curious glance, then nodded.

'Ah, I forgot that you've been away. They wriggled out of it, I'm afraid. The *contessa* refused to testify against her nephews, and without that we can't proceed. So you got shot in vain, and I'm out of a job.'

He lit a cigarette, blowing the smoke upwards and making the *No Smoking* sign revolve lazily.

'Nevertheless, there is one small matter I'd like to clear up before I leave, and I was wondering if you would help me. I haven't time to do it myself, and I need the answer quite urgently.'

'I'll be glad to help,' Pia Nunziata replied simply.

'But without telling anyone what you're doing, understand? Now I've been given my marching orders, it might complicate things.'

The policewoman nodded.

'You can rely on me.'

Zen held her eye for a moment.

'I need some technical information relating to air traffic. I don't know where flights in this area are controlled from, but it's probably either the international airport at Tessera or the NATO airbase at

Treviso. What I want is a record of any low-altitude flights over the lagoon on the eleventh of November last year.'

He sipped his grappa while Pia Nunziata laboriously copied this into her notebook.

'Do you want me to write it for you?' asked Zen.

'It's all right, thanks. I'm getting used to writing with my other hand.'

'Get whatever information you can, in as complete a form as possible, and above all as soon as possible. By tomorrow, this will be history.'

'I'll do what I can, sir.'

The policewoman left to start her inquiries, while Zen finished his cigarette and grappa before returning to the Questura to interview Domenico Zuin, an encounter he regarded with considerable apprehension. Apart from Giulio Bon, there was no evidence that either of the men who had taken part in the first landing on the *ottagono* had also participated in the kidnapping of Ivan Durridge a month later. Bon was linked to this event through his sale of Durridge's boat, but any attempt to interrogate him directly would result in the intervention of Carlo Berengo Gorin. As for Massimo Bugno, it now appeared likely that he had no connection with the kidnapping.

That left Domenico Zuin as the key to the whole affair. If he could be persuaded to co-operate, Zen stood a real chance of achieving enough progress in the Durridge case to force Francesco Bruno to extend his transfer. But that was a very big if. Zuin was a much tougher proposition than Bugno, and the tactics which had proved successful in that case would not necessarily work in the other. Bugno was an employee, accustomed to following orders and obeying those in authority, while Zuin was an entrepreneur, a member of the privileged élite who formed the city's watertaxi monopoly. He couldn't be so easily cowed or browbeaten, as he proceeded to demonstrate the moment he was led into Zen's office.

'I want a lawyer.'

Domenico Zuin had a trim, muscular body and one of those faces Zen associated with Americans: hair like an inverted scrubbing-brush, skin that looked as if it had been shaved down to the dermis, excessively white teeth and slightly protuberant eyes.

'I'm saying nothing without a lawyer present,' he insisted.

Zen shrugged.

'I'm not asking you to say anything. I'll do the talking. I want to fill you in on the situation, so that when we bring a lawyer in and make everything official, you'll have a clear idea of how you want to play this one.'

He offered Zuin a cigarette, which was refused with an abrupt jerk of the head. Zen lit one himself and exhaled a cloud of smoke into the air between them, transected by a seam of dazed sunlight.

'Basically I'd say that you're looking at a minimum of two to four,' he continued conversationally. 'I can't see squeezing it below that, whatever we do. On the other hand, it could well be more. A *lot* more.'

He picked up Zuin's file and scanned the contents.

'Let's see, what have we got here? Two counts of bribery. One aggravated assault, charges dropped when witness withdrew. A few run-ins involving under-age rent-boys. Nothing that need concern us.'

He tossed the file back on the desk.

'I can see no reason why we shouldn't land you a nice two to four in that VIP facility near Parma where they're putting all these corrupt businessmen and politicians. You wouldn't object to sharing a cell with them, I suppose? You might even make a few useful contacts.'

He gazed over at Zuin, who was staring at the floor, visibly struggling to keep his resolution not to speak.

'That's assuming we can position Giulio Bon correctly, of course,' Zen went on. 'Ideally, we need the third man to come in with us. It would look much better that way.'

Zuin glanced up quickly and their eyes met for a moment.

'I can quite see why you decided not to take Bugno along the second time,' Zen murmured. 'Not a good man in a crisis.'

Zuin's eyes started to twitch from side to side, as though dazzled by every surface they landed on.

'I don't know what you're talking about,' he muttered.

Zen gave him a look, level and lingering.

'Yes, you do. What you don't know – what nobody knows yet – is that we've found the body.'

The skin over Zuin's cheekbones tightened.

'All that's left of it, that is,' added Zen, stubbing out his cigarette.

'But that's enough to tell us who it was and how he died. Which changes everything. It means we're talking about murder.'

There was a knock at the door. Zen got up, walked over and opened it. Pia Nunziata stood in the passageway, holding a folder which she passed to Zen.

'That *was* quick,' he commented.

'It was very straightforward,' the policewoman said. 'I phoned the airport, they looked out their records for that day and faxed them over.'

Zen thanked her and walked back to his desk, looking through the papers. Domenico Zuin sat staring at him with an expression of extreme anxiety. Zen suddenly had an idea.

'It looks like you've left it too late,' he murmured, shaking his head sadly. 'I had hoped to let you off lightly, Zuin. Make out you just went along in the boat, didn't have any idea what it was all about, that sort of thing. Bon is the one I had targeted. He was the one who screwed the whole thing up by selling Durridge's boat, after all. It seems only fair that he should take the rap.'

Zuin's shock was evident on his face.

'Didn't you know about that?' asked Zen. 'I suppose Bon claimed he'd scuttled the thing, but in the end his greed got the better of him. You can get quite a nice price for a *topa* these days, even without the proper papers.'

He sighed.

'Anyway, he's decided to go for a pre-emptive strike.'

He tapped the sheets of paper.

'One of my colleagues has been interviewing Bon downstairs. This is a draft of his statement. I'm afraid he's dropped you right in it. He claims he only went along to handle the boat and had no part in what followed. But what's really damaging is where he says . . .'

He pretended to pore over the page.

'Here we are. My colleague asked about how you left the *ottagono*. Bon replies, "I left in the same way we arrived, by boat." Question, "With Domenico Zuin." Witness, "No, he remained on the island." Question, "Then how did he get off again?" Witness, "The same way as Durridge, presumably." '

'He's lying!' Zuin burst out.

Zen shrugged.

'He's talking. And that's all that counts.'

233

He came round and sat on the edge of the desk, looking down at Zuin.

'You don't seem to understand. This American disappears. There's a brief flurry of interest and then the whole thing dies down. Now, suddenly, his body turns up. All hell's going to break loose!'

He spread his hands wide in appeal.

'Try to see it from my point of view, Zuin. I've got an illustrious corpse on my hands. I need someone I can take to the magistrates in the next few hours. I'd rather it was Giulio Bon than you, but if you clam up and he plays along there's nothing I can do. You're looking at a minimum of ten to fifteen, and if they believe Bon it'll be life. *Ergastolo*. Life meaning life. Meaning death.'

Domenico Zuin slammed his fists down on his thighs.

'You can't let him get away with this!'

Zen frowned.

'The only way around it I can see is to get the other man on our side. You must have taken someone else along, a replacement for Bugno. If he supports your version of events, we could still swing it.'

Zuin looked down at the floor.

'He's dead.'

'Pity. Anyone I know?'

'You should do,' Zuin replied caustically. 'He worked here.'

Zen gazed out through the window.

'Of course,' he murmured.

He got up, walked quickly round the desk and picked up the phone.

'Get me the Law Courts,' he told the switchboard operator.

He looked over at Domenico Zuin.

'I'm going to take a chance on you,' he declared. 'If we move fast, we might just be able to pip Bon at the post.'

He turned back to the phone.

'Hello? This is Vice-Questore Aurelio Zen phoning from the Questura. Please send a court-appointed lawyer over here immediately. I have a witness who wishes to make a statement.'

The bells of the city were all pealing midday as Zen left the Questura and crossed the small square on the other side of the canal. Trapped by the walls on every side, the sound ricocheted to and fro until the whole *campo* rang like a bell. Nevertheless, the chronology they represented was only one – and by no means the most important – of a number of distinct strands of whose progress he was aware.

Since Francesco Bruno had issued his ultimatum, time had become as real a player in the Durridge case as any of the people involved, and Zen knew that success or failure depended on how well he mastered its ebb and flow, its tricky, shifting tidal currents. The clock hardly came into it. Already he had accomplished more in a single morning than in most weeks of his professional life. What mattered was the sense of utter commitment to the case which had come to him as he stood before Francesco Bruno like a schoolchild before a master and heard himself being dismissed. As a result of that experience, Zen knew exactly what he was working for.

The ideal which inspired him was nothing as abstract as Justice or Truth. His dream was personal, and attainable. Having scored a great coup by solving the Durridge case where everyone else had failed, he would apply for a permanent transfer and return in triumph to his native city. He would bring his mother back from her exile in Rome, back to her friends and the way of life she had been forced to give up. Once the Durridge case came to court, Cristiana Morosini would have the perfect excuse for divorcing her disgraced husband. And a year or so later, she and Zen could marry without exciting any adverse comment. The Zen house would be a home again, once more to resound with laughter and life.

He checked his euphoria. Much remained to be done. The next hurdle to be surmounted was lunch with Tommaso Saoner.

'I'd be delighted, Aurelio,' Saoner had replied urbanely when Zen phoned to invite him, 'but unfortunately I've already got an engagement.'

'Break it.'

There was a pause before Saoner's laugh. He sounded embarrassed by his friend's peremptory tone.

'I'm afraid I can't, Aurelio.'

'I'm afraid you must.'

This time Saoner's laugh was drier.

'Don't play the policeman with me.'

'I'm playing the friend, Tommaso. But the policeman isn't far behind, and neither are the judges and the courts and the reporters and the television cameras. I'll be at *El S'ciopòn* at half past twelve.'

As he walked towards the restaurant, situated in an alley near the church of San Lio, he was was suddenly brought up short. The scene before him – a certain combination of bridge, canal, alley, courtyard and wall – was just one of an almost infinite repertoire of variants on that series which the city contained, and it took him a moment to work out why this particular example seemed so significant. Then he realized that this was where he had seen the moored boats of the emergency services and the jointed metal tubing which led to the septic tank in which Enzo Gavagnin had met his hideous death.

The Carabinieri were evidently still hard at work on the case, for there were two of their launches tied up alongside. As Zen crossed the bridge, a uniformed officer emerged from one of them. He glanced up at Zen, then looked again.

'Rodrigo! Pietro!'

Two Carabinieri rushed out on deck, brandishing machine-guns. The officer had already leapt ashore. Zen looked round, trying to spot the object of their attentions.

'Stop!' yelled the officer.

'Halt or I shoot!' cried a younger voice.

Zen stepped back to let them pass, and promptly tripped over a panic-stricken cat dashing past. Both went flying, but the cat recovered quickly and scampered off. Running boots clattered to a halt by Zen's ear. A rough hand grasped his collar and rolled him over to receive a gun barrel in the eye.

'Move and you're dead,' the man holding the gun informed him succinctly.

Zen did not move. He did not speak or even, to his knowledge, breathe. Slower footsteps neared on the cobbles.

'That's him all right! It's the old story of the murderer always returning to the scene of the crime. He's a cool one, though! He was standing right next to me when we pulled the body out of the cesspool. Even asked me what had happened! Then he turned to me and brazenly admitted that he'd killed him. Well, we've got him now.'

Zen gasped in pain as a pair of plastic handcuffs bit into his wrists. One of the patrolmen held a machine-gun to his forehead while the other searched him for concealed weapons.

'He's clean, boss.'

'Right, let's go!'

The two patrolmen hauled Zen to his feet.

'Have a look at my wallet,' Zen murmured to the Carabineri officer.

'Trying to bribe me, eh?' the man shouted. 'That's a very serious offence!'

'In my jacket pocket, left-hand side.'

The major looked at Zen sharply.

'Keep him covered, Rodrigo!' he barked. 'Pietro, search him!'

Knows how to delegate, this one, thought Zen.

'Here it is, sir,' said Pietro, flourishing Zen's black leather wallet.

'Check the identity card in the window,' Zen told him.

The Carabiniere's eyes flicked down.

'*Cazzo!*' he exclaimed.

'What is it?' the major demanded irritably. 'What's the matter?'

Pietro handed over the wallet to his superior.

'He's a fucking cop!'

Thanks to this delay, the restaurant was almost full by the time Zen got there. There was no sign of Tommaso, so Zen ordered some wine and water and munched at the breadsticks to stave off his hunger. After fifteen minutes he gave in to the waiter's pointed requests to take his order. The room was now packed and several people had been turned away. Zen ordered the set lunch – spaghetti with clams followed by grilled sardines and *radicchio di Treviso al forno* – and stuck his head in his newspaper.

The main stories concerned the latest episodes in the long-running saga of corruption in high places, and Zen dutifully ploughed his way through a leading article suggesting that while on the one hand the events currently unfolding were a political and social earthquake without parallel in the history of mankind, a cataclysmic upheaval compared to which the French and Russian revolutions were largely cosmetic rites of passage, it was perfectly clear to any sophisticated observer that nothing had really changed and that the whole affair was simply one more example of the national genius for adapting to circumstances, despite the earnest lucubrations of commentators from abroad who had as usual missed the point, bless their cotton socks.

The inside pages featured a gatefold spread showing the leader of the *Nuova Repubblica Veneta*, accompanied by his charming and attractive wife, being acclaimed by his enthusiastic supporters in

Pellestrina, Burano and Treporti. There were shots of Dal Maschio at the controls of the helicopter he had piloted to each of these outposts, shots of Dal Maschio striding purposefully about the streets greeting the inhabitants and kissing babies, shots of Dal Maschio addressing an election rally. 'Venice is the heart of the lagoon,' he had reportedly declared, 'and the NRV is the very heartbeat of Venice. Keep the lagoon alive! Keep Venice alive! Vote for the New Venetian Republic!' At his side Cristiana stood smiling vacuously, sensuously solid in a pink dress and a fur coat worn off the shoulder.

The first course arrrived, and Zen folded up his paper and started to eat. The clams were the genuine local article, *vongole veraci*, stewed in olive oil with garlic and parsley until the shells opened to reveal the tiny morsels of tender gristle inside. Zen slowly worked his way through them and the long strands of spaghetti soaked in the rich sauce. He was winding up a final coil of pasta when Tommaso finally arrived to claim the chair opposite.

'I couldn't get here any earlier. I had to change all my arrangements. What the hell is this about, Aurelio?'

The waiter loomed up. Tommaso took off his heavy glasses, which had steamed up, and said he'd skip the *primo* and have whatever was quickest to follow.

'What's going on?' he demanded as soon as the man had gone.

Zen wiped the oil off his lips with his napkin.

'I need some information.'

Tommaso Saoner replaced his glasses and regarded Zen coldly.

'I'm not an informer, Aurelio.'

Zen lit a cigarette.

'Supplying information to the police doesn't make you an informer, Tommaso. On the contrary, it's the duty of every good citizen.'

Saoner poured himself some wine and broke off a crust of bread.

'Information about what?'

About Ivan Durridge.'

Saoner glanced away, then quickly looked back at Zen.

'Who?'

Zen shook his head in genuine embarrassment. Tommaso Saoner had been his friend for years at a time when a minute lasted longer than a month did now. Where were they now, that Tommaso and that

Aurelio, so much more alive than the pallid impostors who had succeeded to their titles?

'You know who,' he said. 'Everyone knows.'

He puffed out a cloud of smoke.

'But you know more than everyone, Tommaso.'

Saoner frowned.

'I thought you did when I phoned you,' Zen went on, 'and now I'm sure. Don't try and lie to me, Tommaso. It won't work. I know you too well.'

'I don't know what you're talking about.'

A faint smile appeared on Zen's lips.

'It's a funny thing. All the people I've spoken to about the Dur-ridge case have said exactly the same thing. Domenico Zuin, Giulio Bon, and now you. Is it some formula you're taught when you join?'

The waiter brought the main course, and for a moment Saoner took refuge in the distraction offered by the task of filleting the sardines.

'Join what?' he asked eventually.

Zen sighed impatiently.

'Come on, Tommaso! You may not consider me a friend any longer, but please don't treat me as a fool.'

He stabbed a mouthful of the pink and purple chicory leaves, their delicate bitter flavour rounded and filled out by baking.

'Zuin and Bon are both members. So is Massimo Bugno, who went along on the reconnaissance but didn't measure up. So they replaced him with Enzo Gavagnin, who was not just a member but one of Dal Maschio's lieutenants. Like you.'

He stared across the table at Saoner, who had stopped fiddling with his fish.

'Gavagnin may have been braver than Bugno, but he wasn't very bright. It was he who tipped me off to the link between the *Nuova Repubblica Veneta* and the Durridge case in the first place. When I had Bon brought in for questioning, Gavagnin revealed that both Bon and he were members. And the next thing I know there's an expens-ive lawyer by the name of Carlo Berengo Gorin beating at my door.'

He observed Saoner flinch, and nodded.

'You know him, don't you? And I learned from . . .'

He paused. He had almost named Cristiana!

'... from a friend that Dal Maschio does too. I suppose he's the party lawyer.'

Tommaso Saoner feigned a bored shrug.

'What's all this got to do with me?'

Zen unhurriedly ate some grilled sardine before replying.

'Domenico Zuin has made a full confession of his part in the kidnapping of Ivan Durridge. It was made freely, in the presence of Zuin's legal representative, and I have it in my office now, ready for delivery to the Deputy Public Prosecutor.'

'I repeat, what's it got to do with me?'

Zen looked him in the eye.

'You were once my best friend, Tommaso. I'm giving you a chance to get out while there's still time.'

Saoner stared at him, his expression alternating between anxiety and anger.

'And what makes you think anyone will believe whatever pack of lies this man has trotted out?' he sneered.

Zen shrugged.

'I'm sure that Zuin has trimmed some of the details, and twisted others to cast himself in a good light. For example, he claims that he never left the boat, and that it was Gavagnin and Bon who took the foreigners ashore. That may well be a lie. I couldn't really care less.'

He stripped the bones of his last sardine, exposing the succulent flesh.

'What foreigners?' Saoner asked with deliberately casualness.

'He doesn't know who they were or where they were from. He didn't recognize the language they spoke, but it wasn't Italian. There were four of them, all young and tough-looking. Zuin picked them up from a hotel near the Fenice in his taxi, along with Bon and Gavagnin. Bon had told him that the men wanted to be landed on the island in the lagoon which he and Bon had explored earlier with Bugno.'

He pushed his plate aside and lit another cigarette. Saoner's food lay untouched.

'In the late morning, while the tide was still high enough, Zuin ferried them all over to the *ottagono*. He claims that the foreigners went ashore with Gavagnin and Bon while he returned to the city and got on with his work. Of course he subsequently heard about the disappearance of the American, like everyone else. But he'd been paid, and it was none of his business.'

'That's all?' Tommaso inquired ironically.

'It's enough.'

Saoner laughed contemptuously. Zen regarded him with a serious expression.

'Look at it this way, Tommaso. Zuin landed six men on the island. We know that Giulio Bon took Durridge's boat, just to confuse the issue, and as the tide was ebbing he must have left fairly soon afterwards. We also know that Durridge was still on the island shortly after one o'clock, when he spoke briefly to a relative on the telephone. By then it was too late to approach the island from the water. And yet when Franco Calderan returned at five o'clock from visiting his sister on the Lido he found the place deserted.'

He leaned forward.

'*So how did Durridge and the others get off the island?*'

Saoner shrugged impatiently.

'This is your life, eh, Aurelio? Picking over theories about what might or might not have happened, like a pack of grubby, dog-eared playing cards! Well I could play that game too, I suppose, only I'm too busy living.'

Zen looked at him and nodded.

'I'm glad you and your friends are having so much fun, Tommaso, but someone has to clean up after you.'

'Leave the party out of it!' Saoner snapped. 'You don't have a shred of evidence to implicate us. What if Zuin and his confederates happened to be members? So are thousands of ordinary, decent, hard-working Venetians! They are our strength and our pride! They guarantee the future of this city, Zen, while people like you can only grub around digging up dirty secrets from its past.'

He got to his feet.

'Nothing you've said amounts to any more than unsubstantiated, opportunistic slander. Now that we are close to getting our hands on the levers of power, our enemies will move heaven and earth to throw a spanner in the works.'

'The Sayings of Chairman Dal Maschio, page ninety-four,' retorted Zen.

Saoner flushed.

'I'm not just a parrot, you know.'

'You mean you thought up that cheap rhetoric yourself? That's even worse!'

Saonér stared down at him coldly.

'We were once friends, Zen, but that doesn't mean that I have to listen to your insults.'

He turned away. Leaving enough money on the table to cover their meal, Zen hastily rose and followed him out of the restaurant.

'Wait, Tommaso! I'm sorry if I offended you. It just worries me to see how you've fallen under the spell of these people. I'm sure you have nothing personally to do with Durridge's murder, but . . .'

Tommaso Saoner swung round on him.

'Murder?'

A couple entering the restaurant looked at them sharply. Zen took his friend's arm and steered him further along the alley.

'We found the body on that ossuary island we once visited together,' he murmured. 'It wasn't much more than a skeleton itself after the vermin and the birds had eaten their fill. But they don't eat bones. Durridge's were shattered, the spine rammed up into the skull.'

He gripped Saoner's arm, pulling him round and looking him in the eyes.

'How do you pluck a man off one island and drop him on another in such a way as to break every bone in his body? What do you think, Tommaso? Which of the greasy playing cards would you pick from the pack?'

They stared at each other for a long moment. Then Saoner twisted violently away.

'Leave me alone!' he shouted in a voice edged with desperation. 'I didn't ask you to confide in me! I don't know what sort of game you're playing, and I don't want to know! Just leave me alone! Leave me alone!'

He strode rapidly away down the alley. Zen started after him, then stopped, turned and set off slowly in the other direction.

The day might earlier have seemed an augury of spring, but by mid-afternoon the realities of February had asserted themselves. Once past their peak, both the warmth and the light faded fast. Darkness massed in the chilly evening air, silvering the window of Zen's office to form a mirror which perfectly reflected the decline of his hopes for the Durridge case.

Giulio Bon would not talk. For almost two hours, Zen had interrogated him in the presence of Carlo Berengo Gorin. Much to Zen's surprise, the lawyer had made no attempt to intervene. On the contrary, he had ostentatiously turned his back on the proceedings, dividing his attention equally between the arts supplement of *La Repubblica* and a large cigar which he extracted from its aluminium tube and fussed over for some considerable time before it was ignited to his entire satisfaction.

Zen had been prepared for Gorin to do everything in his power to obstruct the smooth progress of the interrogation, but with Domenico Zuin's statement already on its way to Marcello Mamoli he had felt confident of prevailing. Indeed, he had rather looked forward to being able to repay Gorin for the slights he had suffered the previous week. The case against Bon was overwhelming. However much Gorin might fuss and fidget, he would be forced to concede defeat in the end.

It took Zen only a few minutes to realize that the lawyer's air of apparent complacency was the very opposite of good news. If Carlo Berengo Gorin was not perched on the edge of his chair, ready to pounce at the slightest hint of a procedural inexactitude, it was not because he sensed that the game was lost but because he knew he had already won. Too late, Zen realized that he had made a fatal mistake in revealing the extent of his progress in the case to Tommaso Saoner.

Saoner must have passed on the information to his associates, who had contacted Gorin with an offer for Bon's silence. This might have taken the form of a simple cash injection or, more likely, of some similar offer combined with a promise of political pressure on the Appeal Court once the *Nuova Repubblica Veneta* 'got its hands on the levers of power'. This had then been communicated to Bon by Gorin during the initial consultation to which they were entitled under the provisions of the Criminal Code.

Once that deal had been struck, any business which Zen might have hoped to transact was dead in the water. If there had been any hope of an eventual breakthrough, he would have been happy to continue the interrogation through the night if necessary. As it was, after going through the motions of confronting Bon with the statement Zuin had made implicating him as the prime mover of the second landing on the *ottagono*, and failing to get any response, he abandoned the proceedings.

Zen still had one more card up his sleeve. Getting out the folder containing the information which Pia Nunziata had obtained from air traffic control at Tessera, he walked across the office to the wall-map of the Province of Venice. The extract from the records showed all the flights which had been logged on the day when Ivan Durridge had disappeared. Zen had already deleted most of the entries, which referred to arrivals and departures at the airport. There was also a certain amount of toing and froing around the city itself, most of it centering on the Naval college on Sant'Elena and the Coastguard headquarters on the Giudecca.

Once all this had been eliminated, there remained three flights whose course would have taken them near Sant'Ariano. One of these, a training flight out over the Adriatic from the USAF base at Treviso, could be discounted. The remaining two were civil flights, both involving helicopters. One originated at ten o'clock in the morning in Trieste and overflew the lagoon en route to Vicenza. The other commenced shortly before two in the afternoon from the San Nicolò airfield, calling at Alberoni, on the southern tip of the Lido, before continuing to Gorizia, a city in the extreme north-east of the Friuli region, straddling the border with what had until recently been Yugoslavia. The machine involved was registered to a company named *Aeroservizi Veneti*.

Zen ran his finger across the shiny surface of the map, locating the various places mentioned. There was San Nicolò at the northern tip of the Lido. There was Alberoni, a few kilometres from the *ottagono* where Ivan Durridge had made his home. At this scale, Gorizia would be somewhere on the ceiling, but it looked as though the route passed more or less directly over Sant'Ariano, marked with a cross on the map, and thence over the plains of the Piave and Tagliamento rivers.

The door at the other end of the office crashed open and Aldo Valentini came running in.

'It's on!' he cried.

He went rapidly through the drawers of his desk, snatching papers, a map of the city, a pistol and shoulder-holster.

'It's going to be a nightmare! The gang's obviously suspicious. Instead of the usual straightforward drop they've told Sfriso to take the heroin to a bar in Mestre and await instructions. They'll probably string him along for hours before they make their move.'

The phone started ringing. Valentini snatched it up.

'Yes? Yes? Who? What?'

He laid the receiver down on the desk.

'It's for you!'

Zen walked over and took the phone from him.

'Hello?'

'Hello, Aurelio.'

It was Cristiana.

'Well, hello there.'

Aldo Valentini dashed back to the door.

'Best of luck!' Zen called after him.

'For what?' asked Cristiana.

'Colleague of mine. He's got a difficult operation coming up. You came through on his line, for some reason.'

'I don't understand. When I asked for you, they said there was no one of that name in the building. What's going on, Aurelio?'

Zen smiled ruefully. Already he had become a non-person.

'I'll explain later,' he told Cristiana. 'When can I see you?'

She sounded embarrassed.

'Well, that depends when . . . when you're free.'

'About eight?'

'Oh that's too late!'

He frowned momentarily.

'Too late for what?'

'I mean . . . couldn't we make it earlier?'

'How early?'

245

'Would about six be all right?'

Her tone sounded oddly constrained. Zen took this to be a good sign, evidence that she was in the grip of the same turbulence that was disturbing his own emotional life, drawing them both away from the tried and familiar towards a new future together.

'Will that give you time to get home after work?' he asked.

There was a brief silence at the other end.

'That's not a problem,' she said at last.

She sounded so strange that Zen almost asked her if she was all right. But these were not things to discuss on the phone. In a few hours they could work it all out face to face.

'Then I'll see you at six,' he said.

There was a brief pause.

'Goodbye,' said Cristiana.

Zen hung up, wondering why she wanted to see him so urgently. Perhaps after what the switchboard had told her she was afraid that he was going to abandon her and take off back to Rome without any warning. He could see how plausible that might look from her point of view. His tour of duty in the city had come to an end, he'd had his bit of fun with her, now it was time to go home. Zen smiled. He'd soon set her mind at rest about *that*.

But first he had a less agreeable task to perform. Whatever the motivation for the dressing-down he had received at the hands of Francesco Bruno that morning, he could not deny that it had been richly deserved. He glanced at his watch. There was just time to call in at Palazzo Zulian and make his apologies before going home to keep his appointment with Cristiana. They might very well not be accepted, but under the circumstances it was the least he could do to try.

Yet instead of collecting his hat and coat and going out, Zen found himself picking up the phone again. Now that the sustaining momentum of the Durridge case had receded, he had lost his steerage-way and was drifting at the whim of every current. The thought of Ada Zulian reminded him of his mother, and he realized with a guilty start that he had not phoned her since leaving Rome a week before. Reluctantly, he dialled the familiar number.

'Hello? Mamma? Are you all right? You sound different.'

'It's me, Aurelio.'

'Sorry?'

'Me, Tania. Remember?'

For a moment he wondered if he'd dialled the wrong number.

'Tania!' he exclaimed over-effusively. 'How are you?'

'Your mother's out.'

'Out? Where?'

For a moment there was no reply.

'And you, Aurelio?'

'Sorry?'

A sigh.

'Where are *you*?'

'Still here in Venice, of course. Where do you think? I'm sorry I haven't been in touch, but I've been very busy.'

'Of course.'

'Is everything all right?'

'Everything's all wrong.'

'Sorry?'

'STOP SAYING SORRY!'

'Sorry. I mean . . .'

'You're *not* sorry, you don't give a damn!'

There was a shocked silence.

'You're a heartless bastard, Aurelio,' Tania said dully. 'God knows why I ever got involved with you.'

Zen held the receiver at arm's length a moment, then replaced it on its rest. He felt as though he had just had a bruising encounter with a rude, angry stranger in a language which neither of them spoke well. All that remained was a confused sense of bafflement, aggression and – above all – meaninglessness. For while the slightly bizarre tone of his conversation with Cristiana would be resolved the moment they met, his failure to communicate with Tania, both literally and figuratively, was caused by deep structural flaws in the relationship which could never be resolved. He felt absolutely certain of that now.

He gathered up his things and headed for the door. He was turning the handle when Valentini's phone rang again. Thinking it might be some urgent communication about the drug bust, Zen went back to answer it. At first there seemed to be no one there. Then he distinguished a low sound of sobbing.

'Aurelio, I'm sorry. Please forgive me. I've been so lonely, and it's been a terrible time. The landlord sent the bailiffs in. I got back from work to find the door barred and all my belongings piled up in the street. It would all have been looted if one of the priests from the College next door hadn't kept an eye on it.'

She paused, but he didn't speak.

'I moved to a hotel for a few days, but as soon as your mother heard what had happened she invited me over here. She's been wonderful, Aurelio. We're getting on really well.'

She sighed.

'I know I've been difficult, Aurelio, but you must try and understand it from my point of view. I married young and it went disastrously wrong. I didn't want to make another mistake I would live to regret. That's why I've been so cautious about the idea of us living together. But you've been right to insist. Relationships never stand still. If people don't grow closer together then they get further apart. For a while it was fine us being lovers and living separate lives, but not any more. That stage is over. We must move on.'

She paused. Again Zen said nothing.

'I want us all to live together,' Tania went on in a quiet, firm voice. 'I want us to be a real family, to have a home and children and be together all the time. Your mother needs that. She needs company, particularly with you being away so much of the time. That's why she's always going off to babysit for those friends of yours, the Nieddus. That's where she is now, by the way.'

Still Zen did not speak.

'We don't need to talk about this on the phone,' Tania said. 'I just wanted to let you know how I feel, and to know that you understand, and that you share that feeling. I've been so lonely, Aurelio, after that awful row we had last week. I don't know what all that was about, or who was right or wrong. I don't care. All I want to know is when you're coming home.'

'This is my home.'

There was a long silence.

'What did you say?' Tania asked at last.

He stared sightlessly at the desk, its surface wrinkled with the indentations of ball-point pens.

'Aurelio? Are you there?'

Zen gripped the receiver tightly.

'I said, this is my home.'

'But what does that mean, Aurelio? What does it mean?'

248

He sat quite still, saying nothing. After a time there was a click the other end, then an impersonal electronic tone.

It is some time during the long, sleepless night that it occurs to Ada that her persecution may not have ceased but simply taken on a new guise.

She has never slept well, even before there was a reason to stay awake, deciphering each creaking board and squeaking hinge, fighting off her drowsiness lest she wake to find the intruders already there, in full possession. She can barely recall what it means to sleep well. A sort of absence, wasn't it? A stillness like the lagoon on a hot summer night. From time to time, like a passing breeze, a dream would ruffle the otherwise invisible surface. Then the intimate, horizonless darkness closed in again, and the next thing you knew it was morning.

It's been years since she slept like that. Now she is no longer always sure when she's dreaming and when she's awake. Perhaps there is no essential difference. Nothing seemed more real than Rosetta, after all, and yet she vanished without the slightest trace or explanation, just like a dream. Had she only dreamt that she'd had a daughter? That would be both a comfort and a clarification, if she could bring herself to believe it. But she can't. Despite the years that have passed, she can still recall the silky fuzz on the child's arms, the milky smell of her breath, her oddly pedantic intonation, the tender shade of those hazel eyes . . .

Her dreams are not like that. They may be scary or confusing, devious and deranged, but they cannot make her weep. Perhaps that's why Ada prefers their company. At all events, she gets a lot of ideas as she lies there night after night, suspended between sleep and wakefulness. They are not pleasant or useful ideas. They are certainly not the sort of ideas she would choose to have, if she had a choice. It can't even be said that they are better than nothing – nothing would be infinitely preferable – but they are all she has to go on. Ada is used to mending and making do.

The idea she had in the night was especially unwelcome, so much so that she pushed it to one side and took refuge in the restless, exhausted prostration that passes for sleep with her. In fact it is not until she hears the bell, goes to the window and catches sight of the figure standing outside the door below that she even remembers what it was. Her tormentors have not relented, they have merely changed the form in which they present themselves. And with the diabolical cunning which typifies them, the vehicle they have chosen is the man who claimed to be protecting her from them – her shield and strength, her bold avenger.

It all makes sense! Aurelio Battista, Giustiniana's boy, that milksop dreamer, turn out a policeman? She'd known from the beginning that the thing was utterly absurd. Her new idea makes much better sense, but the sense it makes is so horrific in its implications that it takes Ada quite some time to master the trembling which has taken over her limbs at the knowledge that the man standing at her front door is no more the real Aurelio Zen than the cruelly mocking figures which had disrupted her life for so long were the real Nanni and Vincenzo.

The doorbell rings, long and insistently. Ada draws back hastily from the window before the figure glances up at the angled mirror and catches her looking at him. But of course it's no use hiding. They know she's there, and are merely going through the motions of requesting admittance. If she does not respond, the phantasm below will simply turn on its shadowless side and slip into the house through the joints in the stone like vapours from the canal. Better to face the threat boldly and try and fend it off with some invention of her own. After all, she is no slouch at fabrication herself.

The expression of mingled shock and suspicion on her caller's face when Ada opens the door and graciously bids him enter demonstrates that this was the right thing to do. Her opponents have been thrown off balance and for the moment she has regained the initiative.

'Come upstairs,' she says warmly 'and have ... have a glass of something.'

She was about to offer tea, but realized just in time that this would mean leaving the room and taking her eyes off the intruder. She knows better than that.

'I just came to apologize, *contessa*,' he mutters in a respectful tone as they walk upstairs.

Ada fixes her visitor – she decides to call him Zeno – with an untroubled eye.

'Apologize? Whatever for?'

The look he gives her is almost comic in its consternation.

'For what happened yesterday. I shouldn't have allowed myself to be provoked like that, but . . . Well, I'd had a difficult day at work. When your nephews started to taunt me, it was just the last straw.'

Ada laughs archly as they enter the salon.

'I admit I was a trifle taken aback by your comments.'

Her visitor looks suitably mortified.

'They were unforgivable.'

'You see, I thought that I was the only person who knew what had happened.'

A bold thrust, and it drives home. Zeno stands there gawping at her like an idiot.

'To Rosetta?' he murmurs.

She corrects his mistake with an indulgent smile.

'To *Rosa*. Rosa Coin.'

He nods like a somnambulist. Ada sits down on the chaise-longue and indicates with a gracious wave that her visitor should take the rather less comfortable chair opposite.

'Of course, one had heard the most extraordinary rumours,' she continues smoothly. 'As though the Germans could possibly have mistaken a Venetian aristocrat for the offspring of some Jewish tradesman!'

In a vain attempt to look confident and relaxed, Zeno crosses his legs and clasps his knees with his hands.

'And . . . taken the wrong child, you mean?'

'The thing is clearly absurd!' Ada declares airily. 'But you know what people are. Once they've taken an idea into their heads . . .'

Nod, nod, goes the head opposite. It's not even a good likeness, she thinks dismissively. Giustiniana Zen's boy, if he were still alive, wouldn't look anything like that.

'For a time I suspected a man called Dolfin,' she goes on without faltering. 'He lived quite close by and Rosetta used to call at his house now and then. He bribed her, you see, with sweets and cakes and all that sort of thing. That's the only reason she went. I had no access to such luxuries at that time, but Dolfin had friends in high places and could get anything he wanted. That's the only reason she used to visit him, of course. It was pure cupboard love.'

As Zeno goes on nodding, Ada realizes with a thrill that this is all he *can* do. Her opponents are condemned to nod to her tune for ever.

She has outmanoeuvred them completely. After all these years of confusion and uncertainty, she sees her way clear at last.

'So when she vanished like that, I naturally suspected Dolfin of having a hand in it. It's not natural, a man like that, living all alone, inviting young girls into his house. And this was during the war, don't forget. In those days a body was just a body.'

Nod, nod. Ada nods too, but with an ironical edge of which her visitor remains ignorant.

'But then I got a letter, out of the blue! That's where she lives now. Apparently she had been hidden away until the war was over, and then spirited away to the promised land.'

She beams at her visitor triumphantly.

'I hope that clears the matter up once and for all.'

There is a long silence. Then Zeno stands up, awkwardly.

'I shan't be seeing you again, *contessa*.'

Ada frowns. She can hardly believe her ears. Are her opponents conceding defeat? Is her victory assured?

As though in answer to her questions, he adds, 'There's nothing more I can do here.'

A wave of sweet relief sweeps through her. She longs to sing and dance and openly exult, but good breeding has taught her never to gloat.

'I quite understand.'

He extends his hand.

'Goodbye, then.'

It is the final snare, but she is not such a fool as to touch him. Ignoring the outstretched hand, she leads the way back to the *portego*. At the top of the stairs, she turns to him.

Goodbye,' she says, gracefully but with finality.

He stares at her for a moment, then walks past her and down the stairs, out of the house, out of her life. Ada turns away, reeling against the tide flowing past. Her ghosts are deserting her, streaming down the stairs and out of the open doorway.

No longer haunted, the house settles, shifts and shrinks. For a moment, Ada feels a sense of panic. She's grown used to the cushioning effect of those spectral presences, to the ample dimensions and flexible boundaries of the unreal space they generate all around. This rigid, po-faced insistence on the facts at first seems unduly mean and constricting.

But she sharply tells herself to pull her socks up. The Zulians haven't stayed around as long as they have by sulking in a corner because life isn't perfect. Her madness has abandoned her and that's that. There's no point in whining about it. Sanity is clearly going to take some getting used to, but she'll manage somehow. After all, she always has.

He crossed a square in front of a gaunt, graceless church and set off along a back canal, watched by a clan of feral cats perched on the wooden crates which had been set up for them to shelter in. The darkness which had fallen seemed to have seeped into Zen's mind. Listening to Ada Zulian's pathetic attempts to both admit and deny the tragedy which had shattered her life, shadow-boxing with the intolerable facts, had been a deeply disturbing experience. For the first time, he began to wonder whether the truth about the mysteries which surrounded him was not merely unknown but in some essential way unknowable.

It was the nature of the place, he reflected. If Rome was a labyrinth of powerful and competing cliques, each with its portfolio of secrets to defend, here everything was a trick of the light, an endlessly shifting play of appearances without form or substance. What you saw was what you got, and all you would ever get. The fate of Ivan Durridge, like that of Rosetta Zulian and indeed his own father, would remain shrouded in mystery for ever, a subject for speculation, innuendo and senile ramblings. Zen felt like a fly trapped in a web woven by a long-dead spider.

If he had not had the prospect of seeing Cristiana in just a few minutes, this sense of futility would have been almost unbearable. But beside that gain, all other losses seemed light. What did the rest matter, since he had found his destined mate? How could he care about professional setbacks when his private life was about to be thrillingly renewed and made over? How ironic that the new should also be the old, that the woman with whom he would share his future should be a figure from his childhood, and live opposite the house where he had grown up!

A chill breeze had sprung up, infiltrating the city like a host of spies. Rounding the corner into the wedge-shaped *campo*, Zen was reassured to see light seeping through the shutters on the first floor of his house. His one anxiety was that Cristiana might have been delayed. Normally she didn't get home from work until seven o'clock, but she must have made some special arrangement in order to see him. He closed the front door gratefully behind him, shutting out the wind, and climbed eagerly upstairs.

There was no one on the landing. Zen hung his coat and hat on the rack and opened the door into the living room. He could see no sign of Cristiana there, either. She must be in the kitchen, he thought with a warm rush of emotion, preparing dinner. He was halfway across the room before he noticed the man lounging in the high-backed armchair with its back to the door. This was the chair in which his father had always sat, and which his son to this day had never presumed to use. Zen stopped dead in his tracks, his heart racing, his stomach knotted up.

'How did you get in?'

Ferdinando Dal Maschio got to his feet, smiling easily.

'My wife provided a key.'

He stood there, letting Zen come to him.

'I gather that you two have been seeing a certain amount of each other. Under the circumstances, though, I'm prepared to overlook that.'

He glanced at his watch. `

'There's an important meeting of the party later this evening. That's why I got Cristiana to arrange your little tryst earlier than usual. She agreed, of course, just as she did when I asked her to take a copy of that fax with the background to the Durridge case which you were sent by your crooked patrons in Rome.'

Dal Maschio's eyes glittered.

'Whatever you and Cristiana may have got up to, Zen, that woman belongs to me. All I need do is whistle and she comes running. The same goes for your friend Tommaso Saoner.'

He laughed mockingly.

'Tommaso told me all about the way you tried to shake his faith in the cause over lunch. I could have told you that you were wasting your time. Tommaso is one of my most trusted and trustworthy colleagues, the man I plan to name as my deputy when I am elected mayor. Besides, nothing you had to tell him would have come as any surprise. He was in on the whole thing from the very start!'

'He didn't know that Durridge was dead,' snapped Zen.

Ferdinando Dal Maschio acknowledged the point with an inclination of the head.

'It makes no difference. Tommaso would rather die himself than betray the movement. Just as Cristiana would rather betray you than disappoint this little whim of mine to surprise you in your own house. They're both mine, body and soul. That's the sort of devotion I inspire in people, Zen.'

Zen stared coldly at Dal Maschio.

'You're trespassing,' he said in a hard voice.

'You're the one who's trespassing, Zen.'

'This is my house.'

'It's my city.'

'No more than it is mine.'

Dal Maschio shook his head.

'The municipal election results will prove you wrong. The latest opinion poll gives the *Nuova Repubblica Veneta* a clear lead over our nearest rivals.'

'That may change when its leader is arrested on charges of kidnapping and murder,' Zen retorted.

Dal Maschio spread his hands wide.

'You want to talk about the Durridge affair? No problem. I'll tell you everything there is to know.'

He circled round to stand behind the chair in which he had been sitting and leant on it, using the back as a lectern.

'Let me say first of all that I wouldn't get mixed up in anything like that now. They say that a week is a long time in politics, but the things that have happened in the past few months have astonished even me. If you'd told me last November that we'd be looking at victory in the municipal elections and the very real possibility of achieving a presence at national level within a year, I'd have thought you were crazy.'

He smiled nostalgically.

'It's hard to remember now that at that time we were more of a debating club than a credible political force. The idea was to galvanize people into rethinking everything they had taken for granted for too long, to smash the mould and suggest radical new solutions to the problems confronting the city we all love. Part of our strategy was to establish contacts with like-minded groups on the mainland. We talked to the regional *Leghe*, of course, but also to the German-language separatist movement in the Alto Adige, and to various Ladino and Friulano groups. But our closest relationship was with the newly-independent Republic of Croatia, not only because of our historical ties with that region, but because the Croats had achieved what the rest of us could still only dream about – the dissolution of the spurious nation state and the reclamation of regional independence, cultural integrity and political autarchy.'

Zen yawned loudly and lit a cigarette.

'Save me the speeches.'

Dal Maschio looked at him intently.

'You're good at sneering, aren't you?'

There was no reply. Dal Maschio nodded.

'It's all right. I understand. I used to feel the same way myself. It's a way of protecting yourself against feeling, against action. If you admitted your identity as a Venetian, born and bred in these islands, speaking this dialect and conditioned to the core by those experiences, you would not only have to admit all the pain and pride which such an admission would bring with it, you would also have to act to preserve and defend those values. You would either have to be prepared to fight, or to admit your laziness and your cowardice. Much easier just to avoid the issue by sneering.'

'You said you were going to tell me about Durridge. Either do so, or fuck off out of here.'

Dal Maschio shrugged and smiled.

'As I say, the Croats were an inspiration for everyone in the separatist movement, but their successful struggle had a special significance for us Venetians. The Dalmatian coastline of the new Croatia was of course the first and last outpost of the Venetian empire. Its beautiful and historic towns were all built by our forebears, and one day, perhaps, our flag may fly there once more. However that may be, the Croat and Venetian peoples cannot be indifferent to each other. So when I was approached by one of the Croatian delegation with a proposal which promised to be mutually beneficial, I was naturally inclined to look on it with favour.'

Abandoning his pose, he walked round the chair and sat down in it, crossing his legs.

'They wanted Ivan Durridge, or rather Durìc. I'd never heard of the man, but my Croatian contact filled me in. Durridge was a Serb, from Sarajevo, and he was responsible for some of the worst atrocities committed during the war. I won't attempt to list the things he did. Some of them are too obscene to mention. I was shown pictures and eye-witness reports by the survivors. Can you imagine a woman and her daughters having their eyelids cut off, being repeatedly raped and then forced to watch their sons and brothers impaled? That was the least of Durič's crimes, and here he was living in luxury on his private island in the lagoon!'

He jabbed a finger peremptorily at Zen.

'And as if all that wasn't enough, he was also gun-running for the Bosnian Serbs in the current conflict. That's why the investigation into his disappearance was hushed up by the secret services. You remember the scandal over the Gladio organization which was set up to sabotage a possible Communist takeover after the war? Gladio had arms caches all over Italy, yet only a few have come to light. With things changing so rapidly here, the secret service chiefs wanted those dumps cleaned out as fast as possible, and of course they weren't averse to lining their pockets at the same time. Ivan Durridge satisfied both requirements. He took the guns off their hands and paid money into the Swiss bank account of their choice in return.'

'How much money did the Croatians pay you?' Zen demanded.

Dal Maschio shook his head sadly.

'You may find this hard to believe, Zen, but it wasn't actually about money. It was about establishing credibility and goodwill with a potential ally and trading-partner in the federal and regional Europe of the future.'

'And it didn't bother you that all those fine words cost a man his life?'

Dal Maschio got to his feet again and walked towards Zen, waving his arms to emphasize his words.

'That had nothing to do with us! The plan was to fly Durridge up to Gorizia, then "accidentally" stray over the border and land him at a prearranged spot just inside Slovenia. The Croatian commandos who had immobilized Durridge before I landed the helicopter would then drive him to Zagreb, where he would be put on trial for his war crimes. That's what I was told was going to happen, and that's what I believe.'

He sighed.

'Unfortunately Durridge had other ideas, and maybe he was right. He'd been pretty badly beaten up by the time I got there. Gavagnin said he reckoned they would have killed him if it hadn't been for that phone call from his sister. They held a gun to his balls while he talked to her, but that made them realize that they needed him alive and functioning until we took off, to prevent the alarm being raised. Unfortunately once we were airborne they made the mistake of relaxing their vigilance. The next thing we knew, Durridge opened the door and jumped out.'

Dal Maschio shrugged.

'As I've said, I wouldn't do it again. The stakes are too high to fool around with stunts like that now. On the other hand, I'm not ashamed of what I did. The Croats are our ideological and political allies, and Ivan Durridge was a war criminal.'

'While you're just a common criminal,' said Zen, tossing his cigarette butt into an ashtray.

'I've never been charged with any criminal offence, much less convicted of one. And I never will be.'

'We'll see about that.'

'Mere bravado,' exclaimed Dal Maschio contemptuously. 'If you had any solid evidence against me you wouldn't be standing here making empty threats, you'd have me under arrest. But there's nothing to connect me or any member of the movement with the Durridge kidnapping, apart from an unsubstantiated statement by some taxi skipper.'

'How did Giulio Bon get hold of Durridge's boat?' demanded Zen.

'He found it cast adrift in the lagoon.'

'One of your helicopters appears in the air traffic control records as flying from the Lido to Gorizia on the day Durridge vanished. The route passes over both the *ottagono* and Sant'Ariano. Is that supposed to be a coincidence?'

'Neither more nor less of a coincidence than the fact that the road to Verona passes through Padua and Vicenza,' Dal Maschio returned promptly. 'I was flying from the Lido to Gorizia. Which way did you expect me to go, via the Po valley?'

'Why were you going in the first place?'

'I was delivering a cargo of fish to a restaurant in Gorizia owned by a friend in the Friulano separatist movement. It was a genuine order, and I have the waybills and invoices to prove it.'

Noting the expression on Zen's face, he laughed.

'You've got nothing against me but scraps and rags of circumstantial evidence that wouldn't serve to convict a known criminal, let alone the city's mayor elect. And thanks to the Questore's prompt response to our article this morning about your disgraceful treatment of Contessa Zulian, your mandate for action expires in just a few hours. Francesco Bruno evidently has a very acute sense for the prevailing political realities. Face it, Zen, you're beaten.'

He stepped forward suddenly, gripping Zen's arms.

'But if only you will, you can convert that defeat into victory! You're one of us, Zen! You know you are! And we're the winning team. Already now, and increasingly in the future. We've got the little people with us already, because we speak the language they understand. Now we need to get the professionals on board, the educated middle class with managerial skills. People like you!'

Zen shook himself free.

'What are you doing in Rome?' cried Dal Maschio. 'The regime you serve is morally and financially bankrupt. It's exactly the same as working for the KGB after the collapse of the Soviet Union. The centre can't hold any longer, Zen. The periphery is where the action is. In the new Europe, the periphery *is* the centre. It's time to come home. Time to come back to your roots, back to what is real and meaningful and enduring.'

Zen turned away.

'Save the rhetoric for your meeting.'

'It's not just rhetoric, and you know it! Do you want a Europe that is like an airport terminal where every language is spoken badly, where any currency is accepted but there is nothing but soulless trash to buy and fake food to eat? You don't! You can't!'

'Neither do I want one where politicans conspire to commit criminal offences aided and abetted by corrupt policemen in the pay of the local mob.'

Dal Maschio shrugged.

'You probably won't believe me, but I swear I never had the slightest notion that Gavagnin was involved with a drugs racket. That was another part of his life altogether. He didn't confide in me and I didn't pry. In any case, given that there's a market in illicit drugs, why should the Sicilians make all the money? No, I'm only joking . . .'

Zen regarded him bleakly.

'I think you'd better go.'

Dal Maschio glanced at his watch and began to button up his coat.

'Sooner or later you're going to have to choose, Zen. The new Europe will be no place for rootless drifters and cosmopolitans with no sense of belonging. It will be full of frontiers, both physical and ideological, and they will be rigorously patrolled. You will have to be able to produce your papers or suffer the consequences.'

He leaned towards Zen, almost whispering.

'There can be no true friends without true enemies. Unless we hate what we are not, we cannot love what we are. These are the old truths we are painfully rediscovering after a century and more of sentimental cant. Those who deny them deny their family, their heritage, their culture, their birthright, their very selves! They will not lightly be forgiven.'

He walked out of the room and downstairs. Zen stood quite still, listening intently to the clatter of Dal Maschio's footsteps as though they were a message telling him what to do next. The slam of the front door seemed to release him from this act of attention. He strode to the landing and grabbed his coat and hat.

Outside, the wind had freshened. It skittered about the courtyard, banking off the angled walls and blowing back from fissures barely wide enough to sidle down. At the far end of the street leading towards the Cannaregio a man could be seen emerging from the shadows into the cone of yellow light cast by a streetlamp. Zen jammed his hat firmly on his head and set off in the same direction, the hem of his coat billowing about him.

Dal Maschio kept up a brisk pace until he reached the lighted thoroughfare crowded with commuters heading for the station. Here he slowed to a relaxed but still purposeful stride which allowed him to respond in the appropriate way to the many greetings he received. For a privileged few he paused long enough to exchange a few remarks and slap a shoulder playfully, but most received no more than a smile and a nod acknowledging their existence but indicating that he was a busy and important man who could not be expected to recognize everyone who recognized him.

Zen adjusted the distance between them to take account of the situation, closing in as the crowds became thicker, falling back again as they crossed the Scalzi bridge and entered the relatively deserted streets beyond. Here Dal Maschio was accosted less often, but he nearly always stopped to speak. An area like Santa Croce, with its ugly tenements, failing shops and ageing population, was the heartland of the *Nuova Repubblica Veneta*, and its leader could not afford to leave anyone feeling slighted or ignored.

Thanks to these constant interruptions it was another twenty minutes before they emerged into the sweeping vistas of Campo Santa Margherita. Dal Maschio strode the length of the square, past the row of plane trees tossing their branches in the wind and the isolated market house with its ancient sign listing the minimum legal length for each type of fish that could be sold there. Here he veered right, towards the church of the Carmelites, and turned in under a *sottoportego* bearing an almost illegible sign dating from the war, a stencilled yellow arrow beneath the word PLATZKOMMANDANT.

Zen turned back, seeking somewhere to wait and watch. There was only one bar still open, a dingy wine-shop thick with tobacco smoke and the sound of vigorous sparring in the local dialect. A number of figures were dimly visible in the dull fumed light, both male and female, all far gone in years and drink. They turned to gaze at Zen as he made his way to a table by the window. This vetting concluded, most of them resumed their previous heated exchanges, taking no further notice of the newcomer, but one couple continued to watch him.

Zen shot them a glance as he sat down. The man he recognized as Andrea Dolfin, but the woman – adrift and becalmed somewhere in her sixties – he had never seen before, although something about her looked familiar. The proprietor, a burly man with the air of someone who had seen every kind of trouble, and seen it off, marched over to Zen's table and asked what he'd like, in a tone which suggested that he'd also like to know what the hell he was doing there. Zen ordered a *caffè corretto alla grappa*. Lowering the net curtain which covered the bottom half of the window, he assured himself that the entrance into which Dal Maschio had disappeared was visible from where he was sitting.

When he turned back to the lighted room, Dolfin and the woman were still staring at him and talking quietly together in a furtive undertone. The old man pointed at him, without making the slightest attempt to disguise the fact. He murmured something to the woman, who smiled in a sad, absent way. Zen turned back to the window, knowing that the gesture was an evasion. No one would be leaving the meeting on the other side of the square for at least an hour. When he looked back, the two pairs of eyes were still gazing in his direction.

After all Zen had been through that day, this insolent scrutiny was the last straw. If even half of what Ada Zulian had hinted at was true, Andrea Dolfin ought to be afraid to show his face in public, never mind mock the police. Having been betrayed by Cristiana and humiliated by Ferdinando Dal Maschio, he wasn't in a mood to take any insolence from Andrea Dolfin. Rising to his feet, he crossed the foggy expanses of the bar towards his tormentor.

'What the hell are you laughing at?'

Dolfin looked up with a slight frown, as though noticing Zen for the first time.

'A joke,' he said.

'At my expense, apparently.'

Dolfin shrugged.

'Not in particular, *dottore*. On the other hand, we're none of us exempt.'

Zen sat down and looked the old man in the eyes.

'It doesn't surprise me that you only come out after dark,' he hissed. 'After what Ada Zulian told me this afternoon, I wonder you have the nerve to go on living at all.'

'The more I see of life, the more I wonder that any of us do.'

The proprietor brought Zen his coffee.

'Everything all right, Andrea?' he asked, glancing suspiciously at Zen.

'Fine, fine.'

Zen swallowed the coffee down at one gulp.

'Do you want me to tell you what she said?'

Dolfin smiled broadly.

'I've heard it many times before. Ada never made any secret of her views. On the contrary.'

The man's complacent tone infuriated Zen. He pointed to the woman sitting beside Dolfin.

'What about your lady friend? Does she know? Do you want me to tell her what Ada has to say about you and her daughter?'

Andrea Dolfin gazed back at him calmly.

'Why not?'

He stroked the woman's ravaged face with the back of his fingers.

'I don't think you two know each other, by the way. This is Aurelio

Zen, my dear. He claims to be the son of Angelo Zen, the railwayman, although I'd always understood that Angelo's only child was born dead.'

Dolfin looked back at Zen. He held out a limp hand towards the woman.

'And this, *dottore*, is Rosetta Zulian.'

Zen's initial reaction was one of disbelief, closely followed by anger. What did Dolfin take him for? The man's wickedness was matched only by his effrontery. The tale which Ada Zulian had told him earlier that evening had been rambling, oblique and full of lacunae, a rebus spelling out a truth too terrible to be put into words, but Zen had been left in very little doubt as to what must have happened in the nightmare period following the German invasion half a century earlier.

Alone of all her family, Rosa Coin had survived the operation to 'cleanse' Venice of its Jewish population. That much was certain from the police report which Zen had read. Her parents and siblings had been packed off to the death camps, but Rosa's name was struck off the list of deportees since she had been 'found hanged'. Yet just two years later a person calling herself Rosa Coin turned up alive and well in Israel, claiming that but for Andrea Dolfin she would have shared the fate of the rest of her family and hundreds of her friends and neighbours.

When Ada had suggested, if only to ridicule the idea, that the Germans might have been mistaken about the identity of the dead girl, Zen had realized that the apparent contradictions in her tale resolved themselves if one simply substituted the name Rosetta for Rosa. Ada Zulian still could not admit to herself that her daughter was dead, so she had told her story inside out. It was *Rosetta* who had been kidnapped and killed by Dolfin, who had lured her to his house with sweets and treats.

Thanks to his contacts, he would already have known that Rosa's family was to be included in the next group of deportees. Perhaps he had even arranged to have them included himself, so as to facilitate his evil scheme. That was the key to the whole plan. Once he was assured of it, he could do what he liked with the hapless Rosetta. Then, when she was dead, Dolfin had gone to the Coin family with a proposal which he knew they were bound to accept, hideous as it was. They and their other children were doomed, but their daughter

Rosa might live, her entry struck off the deportation list as already dead when the corpse of her lookalike friend was 'found hanging'.

What parent could refuse? Despite their horror, their outrage and anguish, the Coins could not refuse this gruesome exchange. No doubt Dolfin made it easy for them, pretending that Rosetta had died of illness or by accident. In any case, he was running absolutely no risk of being exposed. In the Nazi-occupied Italy of 1943, Jews were non-persons, bureaucratic data deprived of rights or civil status, mere apparitions awaiting their turn to be processed out of existence altogether. It was unthinkable for them to lay charges against anyone, never mind a powerful and influential ally of the puppet regime. The Coins had no choice but to accept, and thus Rosetta Zulian vanished from the face of the earth, leaving no trace of evidence against the man who had callously plotted and carried out her murder. Ada Zulian might suspect the truth, but neither she nor anyone else could ever prove anything. It was the perfect crime.

For Dolfin to have got away with that was loathesome enough. For him to be touted as a paragon of selfless heroism by the unwitting Rosa Coin was even worse. But to desecrate his victim's memory by parading this alcoholic doxy as Rosetta Zulian was a gesture of arrogance and contempt almost beyond belief. Zen felt a suffusion of fury suffocating him. On some level he knew that it had less to do with Andrea Dolfin, whatever his sins, than with Francesco Bruno and Carlo Berengo Gorin, with Tommaso Saoner and Giulio Bon, and above all with Cristiana Dal Maschio and her husband. But that insight was impotent against his overwhelming urge to lash out, to smash his fist into Dolfin's face and shatter that mask of serene detachment once and for all.

It was something in the woman's face that restrained him, a quality of rapt attention whose meaning was enigmatic but which was utterly compelling in its intensity. As he returned her insistent gaze, Zen realised why she had appeared familiar when he walked into the bar: the woman bore a quite astonishing resemblance to Ada Zulian. You had to be looking the right way to see it, looking beyond the seedy details, the quirks of dress and accidents of age, to the underlying genetic structure. Then, like a trick drawing, it suddenly clicked into place, bold and unmistakable.

As so often in this waterborne city, Zen had the sensation that the whole room was in motion, the floor undulating gently like the deck of a boat. But the instability was all internal. In a twinkling, all the ideas he had so confidently been rehearsing seemed as insubstantial as a dream on awakening. No amount of elaborate theorizing counted for anything beside Zen's abrupt conviction that the woman sitting opposite him was indeed Rosetta Zulian.

Noting the consternation on Zen's face, Andrea Dolfin smiled artfully.

'She was always a great favourite of mine. Weren't you, dear?'

The woman continued to gaze expressionlessly at Zen.

'Her mother pretended to think there was something unnatural about it,' Dolfin continued. 'Wishful thinking! The plain truth was less palatable. Rosetta simply preferred my company to that of her mother.'

He made a disparaging moue.

'Not that that was any great accomplishment on my part. *La contessa* was obsessed to an absurd degree with considerations of her family's lineage and gentility. The rest of us just laughed at her pretensions, but poor Rosetta had to live with them, day in, day out. Ada set rigorously high standards of behaviour and taste, but her conception of the aristocratic ideal didn't allow much room for maternal love. On top of that, she wouldn't permit her daughter to associate with the local girls of her age, whom she of course considered common. Since the Zulians scarcely mingled in the social circles that Ada might have regarded as acceptable, poor Rosetta was starved of both affection and company.'

He exchanged a glance with his companion.

'Her response was to come and visit me whenever she could, and to make a secret friend in the Ghetto, a world to which her mother had no access.'

The woman smiled elliptically. There was something bizarre about her continuing silence, and the way that Dolfin was discussing her as though she weren't present.

'It shouldn't be necessary to say it, but after what Ada has no doubt hinted I had better make it quite clear that there was never any question of carnal relations between us. Quite apart from anything else, my own proclivities in that regard – they have ceased to trouble me for many years – happened to be for my own sex. My lover was killed in 1941 fighting the British at Benghazi. He was the reason I joined the party in the first place. All that died with him, all the big ideas, the high hopes. I had to start again, like someone after an accident. I had to think about all the things I'd taken for granted. And that's where Rosa helped me.'

He looked at the woman and smiled.

'She says I saved her life, but she'd already saved mine.'

Zen looked at him sharply.

'I thought it was Rosa Coin whose life you saved.'

The woman looked at the old man and gestured impatiently. Then she spoke for the first time.

'That's enough bullshit, Andrea.'

The voice was pure Venetian, as turbid and swirling as water churned up by a passing boat. She turned back to face Zen.

'I am Rosa Coin.'

Zen searched her eyes for a long time without finding any weakness. He shook his head feebly.

'But she . . . she lives in Israel.'

'I used to. Some cousins of mine who lived in Trieste went out there after the war, and once they were settled they invited me to join them. I didn't know what else to do. Andrea had been hiding me in his house, but I couldn't go on living there once the war was over. I wanted to make a fresh start, to begin again, a new life in a new nation.'

Zen got out his cigarettes. After a moment's hesitation he offered one to the woman, who took it with a shrug.

'I shouldn't, but . . .'

'At this stage, my dear,' Dolfin put in, 'I can't really see what you have to gain by giving up.'

Zen lit their cigarettes.

'You were talking about moving to Israel,' he said.

She nodded.

'I lived there for almost ten years. It was a wonderful experience which I don't regret for a single moment, but I never really felt at home. At first I assumed that that would pass. Where is a Jew at home if not in Israel? It was a long time before I realized that I must give up the idea of ever being at home anywhere. I would always be an Italian in Israel and a Jew in Europe. And once I accepted that, there seemed no reason not to come back to Venice.'

Zen smoked quietly for a moment. Now that the fit of rage had left him, he felt dazed and drained.

'And Rosetta?' he murmured.

'Everything I told you about her was true,' said Andrea Dolfin. 'She had the run of my house, and came and went as she pleased. One afternoon I came home to find a note from her on the dining table. She apologized for putting me to so much trouble, but she said she knew I'd understand.'

He sighed.

'I did, and I didn't. In the end, it's impossible to understand something like that. Anyway, it made no difference. She'd been dead for several hours.'

Dolfin struck his fist hard on the table.

'She should have told me! At the very least I could have given her some practical advice. She must have thought it would be quick and painless, like an execution. She didn't know that without a drop, hanging is a form of slow strangulation. I could have told her. I'd seen enough partisans hanged that way, from lampposts and balconies. I knew how long it took them to die. She should have told me! She should have trusted me!'

He broke off, struggling to control his emotion. The woman covered his trembling hands with her long, slim, articulate fingers, like a benign insect.

'I'd failed Rosetta,' Dolfin went on in a low voice, 'so I decided to make amends by saving her friend. That meant concealing the truth from Ada Zulian. I could claim that that was a difficult decision over which I agonized long and hard, but it would be a lie. If her daughter had been driven to take her life, the *contessa* was at least partly to blame. If I'd failed Rosetta, what had her mother done? Perhaps it was just as well that she never knew the truth.'

He took the woman's hands in his.

'The main cause of Rosetta's despair was undoubtedly the fact that the Coin family were among those Jews who had been selected for the next round of deportations. The Ghetto had been cut off from the rest of the city, like in the old days, but with my position it wasn't hard to persuade the guards to let me take Rosa Coin out for a few hours on my personal recognizance. I told them that she had been my secretary, and that I needed her to help put my papers in order before she was deported. I did not tell the Coins about Rosetta. I only said that I would do what I could to save their daughter.'

The woman dropped her cigarette on the floor and stepped on it. She wiped her rheumy eyes on her sleeve.

'When the police came, they never doubted the identity of the corpse. I'd dressed it in Rosa's clothes, including the Star of David, and cut the hair to match. I told them she had hanged herself while I was out. They weren't surprised, given the fate in store for her. They took the body away and told the Germans what had happened. And meanwhile the real Rosa was hiding in my attic, where she stayed for the rest of the war.'

'I remember my father calling me,' the woman said in a dreamy voice, as though talking to herself. 'Andrea was sitting on the best chair, the one only visitors used. I had only met him once, when I was out walking with Rosetta, but she had told me how kind he had been to her since her father was killed. Papa said I was to go and stay with Signor Dolfin for a few days, until things got better again. He tried to make it sound casual, but his voice was hoarse and my mother was crying and I knew that something strange and terrible was happening.'

She started to weep.

'Afterwards, when Andrea told me the truth, I tried to imagine the unspeakable anguish they must have felt, knowing that they were seeing me for the last time, yet having to pretend that everything was all right so as not to scare me.'

Zen was staring out of the window, his attention drawn by a movement on the other side of the square. A group of men had emerged from the *sottoportego* and were now standing in a circle, talking loudly and gesturing expansively. The sound of their voices could be heard faintly even inside the bar. Zen got to his feet.

'I apologize for intruding, and for my rudeness. Please forgive me.'

Andrea Dolfin glanced out at the square.

'You're surely not going to meet that band of hooligans, *dottore*?'

Zen shook his head.

'My interest in them is purely professional.'

Dolfin raised his eyebrows.

'Don't tell me you've got something on Dal Maschio!'

'Would that surprise you?'

Dolfin laughed harshly.

'It would surprise me if you could make it stick.'

The men in the square had concluded their discussion and were leaving in different directions in twos and threes. Zen buttoned up his overcoat and threw a note on the table to pay for his coffee.

'After what you've just told me, I'm certainly going to try,' he declared grimly.

Dolfin frowned.

'What has that got to do with Dal Maschio?'

Zen looked at Rosa Coin.

'Nothing. Everything.'

The windswept expanse of Campo Santa Margherita was deserted when Zen emerged from the bar. He turned left, walking quickly. It was a clear night, the darkness overhead pinked with stars and a bright battered moon rising. In the distance, on the bridge over the canal, Zen could just make out the figure of Dal Maschio and his two companions. Slowing his stride to match theirs, he followed.

The three men walked at a leisurely pace past the church of San Barnabà, through the dark passage burrowing beneath the houses on the far side, along walkways suspended over small canals or jutting out from the side of buildings linked by clusters of telephone and electricity cables and a washing-line from which an array of teddy bears dangled by their ears. The sound of their voices drifted back to Zen, resonant in the narrow streets, more faint in the open, sometimes snatched away altogether by the wind.

They crossed the bowed wooden bridge over the fretful, jostling waters of the *canalazzo* and rounded the church blocking the entrance to Campo San Stefano, where the trio came to a halt. Concealed in the shadows cast by a neighbouring church, Zen looked on as they concluded their discussion and said good night. Dal Maschio saluted his cohorts with a last masterful wave and walked off down a street to the left. The other two continued on across the square. Deprived of their leader's inspirational presence, they walked more quickly and in silence, eager to get home.

Zen followed them along the cut to Campo Manin, past the hideous headquarters of the Cassa di Risparmio bank and into the warped grid of alleyways beyond. The bitter wind had sent the usual crew of fops and flâneurs scurrying for cover, clearing the streets for Zen and his quarry. By the church of San Bartolomeo the two men paused briefly to say good night. One turned up the street leading to the Rialto bridge while the other, with Zen in attendance, continued straight on towards Cannaregio.

Lengthening his stride, Zen gradually closed the gap between them, and when they reached the broad thoroughfare of the Strada Nova he made his move. Hearing footsteps close behind him, the man looked round. Shock and suspicion mingled in his expression as he recognized his pursuer. Then, as though by an intense effort of will, he smiled.

'How lucky we happened to meet! I was just going to ring you. I wanted to apologize for being so snappy at lunch.'

A trace of an answering smile appeared on Zen's lips.

'Dal Maschio told you to smooth things over, did he?'

Tommaso Saoner's cheek twitched.

'Don't try and provoke me, Aurelio. I've offered you an apology and as far as I'm concerned the matter is closed. Just get on with your life and leave me to get on with mine, and we can still be friends.'

Zen shook his head decisively.

'That's no longer possible, Tommaso.'

Saoner stared fixedly at him for a moment. Then he shrugged.

'So be it.'

He began walking again. Zen followed, a few paces behind. They passed through Campo Santa Fosca and rounded the corner of Palazzo Correr. Shortly after the next bridge, Saoner turned off to the right. When Zen entered the alley after him, Saoner wheeled round.

'This is not your way home!'

'Venice belongs to all its sons,' Zen declaimed rhetorically. 'The whole city is my home.'

Tommaso Saoner hesitated for a moment. Then he strode rapidly away, taking an erratic route through back lanes to the Ghetto Nuovo and across the San Girolamo canal, not pausing or looking round until he stopped in front of his house in Calle del Magazen. He was still fumbling in his overcoat pocket for his keys when Zen stepped between him and the door.

'You can't get away as easily as that, Tommaso.'

Saoner stared at him truculently.

'What the hell is that supposed to mean?'

'It wasn't just luck that we met this evening. I knew you'd be at the meeting and I followed you all the way from Campo Santa Margherita. We've got to talk.'

'I've got nothing to say to you.'

Saoner tried to push past Zen to the door. There was a brief scuffle, which ended with Saoner sprawling on the pavement.

'I wouldn't try and push me around, Tommaso,' Zen said quietly. 'I've dealt with much tougher customers than you in my time.'

Crouching on the ground, Saoner examined his glasses, which had fallen off.

'I'll have you charged with assault,' he muttered, getting to his feet.

'And I'll have you charged as an accomplice in the kidnapping and murder of Ivan Durridge.'

A silvery sheen crept over the walls and paving as the moon showed for the first time above the houses opposite.

'They didn't kill Durridge!' Saoner declared passionately. 'The man jumped out!'

'If he did, it was because he preferred to die quickly rather than suffer what the Croatians had in store for him. But you didn't know he was dead, did you? You thought Durridge was in Croatia awaiting trial for his war crimes.'

'Ferdinando explained the whole thing to me this evening. The only reason he hadn't told me before was that he didn't want to implicate me.'

Zen laughed in his face.

'Don't be so naive, Tommaso. The reason he didn't tell you is that he doesn't trust you. He thinks of you as another Massimo Bugno, a shallow, fair-weather vessel, useful for running errands around the city but not to be relied on when a storm blows up.'

'That's not true!'

There was real pain in Saoner's voice.

'It's of no importance,' said Zen offhandedly. 'The essential point is that Dal Maschio masterminded the kidnap of Ivan Durridge and piloted the helicopter from which he fell to his death. We're talking about the man who may be the next mayor of this city – and that's just the first item on his agenda. Dal Maschio is ruthless, cunning and ambitious. He's going to go all the way to the top, unless he's stopped now. And we've got to stop him, Tommaso. You've got to help me stop him.'

Saoner grunted contemptuously.

'You're out of your mind. Who cares what happened to Ivan

Durridge? The man was a war criminal, for God's sake. All the Croats wanted was to do what the Israelis have done in the past, to grab the beast and bring him to trial. And all we did was to help them. It's not our fault that the crazy bastard decided to jump out of the chopper. It's got nothing to do with us, and nothing to do with the fine, positive ideals that the movement represents, and which I will never let you destroy with these shabby, cynical manoeuvres. Now get out of my way!'

Zen stood aside. Surprised, Saoner hesitated for a moment, wary of this sudden capitulation. Then he stepped towards the door, groping in his pocket with an expression of growing puzzlement. A gentle tinkling sound drew his attention.

'Is this what you're looking for?'

Zen dangled a set of keys in the air.

'You dirty pickpocket! Give those to me!'

Zen slowly shook his head.

'You need to spend some time alone, Tommaso, thinking over what I've just said. I don't want you to rush your decision. You can have till morning if you like. But in the end you'll agree to testify. I know you too well to . . .'

Saoner struck him across the face.

'I'll never betray the movement! Never, no matter what you do to me!'

Zen regarded him steadily, rubbing his cheek where the blow had landed.

'I'm not going to do anything to you, Tommaso. You have to do it yourself.'

He dropped the keys into his pocket.

'You can go anywhere you like, apart from crossing to the mainland. The use of phones is also prohibited, as is any attempt to involve anyone other than me. I won't be far behind you, but as long as you don't try and break these rules I won't interfere.'

The two men stared long and hard at each other.

'You're crazy,' Saoner muttered at last.

Zen shrugged.

'One of us is. Some time between now and dawn we'll find out which.'

At first Saoner made no attempt to get away. He set off at a moderate pace, as though out for a stroll to settle his stomach or thoughts before bed. By now the city had been given over to its cats. They appeared everywhere, perched singly on walls and lounging on ledges, clustered in silent congregation at the centre of a square, viciously disputing a scrap of food or absorbed in a fastidiously conscientious ritual of grooming.

Saoner walked the length of one of the long straight canals which trisect the northern reaches of the Cannaregio, then turned down through the meandering passages leading to the Strada Nova. For a moment it looked as though he were retracing the route he had taken in the opposite direction earlier, but when he reached the Rialto bridge he turned right and crossed over to the market area. As Zen reached the peak of the bridge, the variously inclined roofs glittered in the moonlight as though covered in frost.

Saoner was now some way ahead, threading his way through the stripped framework of the stalls used for the bustling vegetable market and into the covered portico of the *Pescheria*. Here the cats were especially sleek and numerous. They massed like rats, lured by the lingering odour of the fish-heads and entrails on which they gorged themselves by day, when the counters were loaded with slithering heaps of red mullet, sea bass, sardines, plaice, eels, crabs, scallops, cuttlefish, clams, mussels and all the rest whose names Zen knew only in dialect: *branzin, orada, tria, barbon, peocio, passarin, dental* . . .

By the time he realized what was happening, the only trace of Saoner's presence was a distant clatter of running footsteps, so distorted by the echoing walls all around that it was impossible to tell where it was coming from. Zen closed his eyes and did a rapid mental scan of the district. The only exit which Saoner would have had time to reach led via a narrow bridge to a quay on the other side of Rio delle Beccarie. From there, two lanes led away from the water. No, there were three – but one was a dead end.

Zen started to run, not in the direction Saoner had taken, but straight ahead, through the tiny Campo delle Beccarie, across the angled bridge and along the alley beyond. If he did not find Saoner in the next few seconds it would be too late, as the number of variables became so great that a solution would be impossible.

On reaching the first of the two alleys his quarry could have taken, he stopped dead, listening intently. Apart from the distant lapping of water, all was still. Zen's eyes narrowed. He ran over his mental map again, satisfying himself that there were no other exits. The alley in which he was standing was lined with an unbroken succession of houses on either side. Zen crossed it and walked quickly to the next intersection.

In this street there were three openings, all to the left. Zen moved as quietly as he could to the first entrance and peered round the corner. This proved to be a short blind alley cut off at the next canal. He went on to the next opening, whose nameplate showed it to be the entrance to a courtyard behind the large *palazzo* which faced the street. Inside, all was dark. Zen took a hundred-lire coin from his pocket and tossed it into the passage, where it tinkled resoundingly. Seconds later, Tommaso Saoner scurried out of the other entrance and ran straight into Zen.

At first he made to turn back, then changed his mind and strode past without a word or a flicker of expression. Zen fell in behind him, keeping closer than before. The two men moved steadily through the fan tracery of alleys and canals centred on San Giacomo dell'Orio. A searchlight suddenly appeared in the darkness ahead, swinging this way and that like a stick. A moment later, a watertaxi rounded the corner and came burbling past them. As the noise subsided, a church bell struck midnight. Zen smiled grimly at this signal that his official tenure in the city was at an end. If his opponents had counted on him meekly packing his bags and going when told to go, they had seriously miscalculated. He felt a weight lift from his shoulders as the twelve ponderous chimes cut through the red tape and procedural minutiae in which he had been enmeshed. As a free agent, he was much more dangerous and effective than he could have been in his official capacity.

They eventually emerged on to the open quay opposite the long low façade of the railway station, where Saoner suddenly broke into a run. For the first hundred metres or so Zen managed to keep pace, but after that Saoner began to pull ahead. He leapt up the steps of the high bridge across the Rio Nuovo and disappeared, heading towards Piazzale Roma. When Zen reached the top of the bridge he had to pause for breath. Too much desk work had taken its toll of his physique. Nevertheless he forced himself to carry on, even though he now knew that he would be too late. He could already hear the engine of a waiting taxi ticking over to keep the driver warm. By the time he reached the rank, Saoner would be out of reach, roaring off across the Ponte della Libertà in some plush Volvo or Mercedes, having neatly escaped the psychological trap which Zen had prepared for him.

A short flight of steps lined with dingy bushes led up from the *vaporetto* landing-stage to the bare expanse of asphalt marked with lanes for buses and cars. At the far end, the neon sign of the multi-storey car park glimmered eerily. The entire place was deserted. A moment later, Zen realized that the engine he had been hearing was one of the water buses which maintained a skeleton service throughout the night. It grew to a roar as the skipper reversed the engines to hold the *vaporetto* in against the pier. Three young men disembarked and headed off, laughing and talking loudly, towards the car park. The deck-hand had already closed the gate and begun to cast off when a figure emerged from the bushes lining the steps and ran towards the boat. The gate slid open again and the man jumped aboard as the vessel started to move away from the landing-stage.

Zen sprinted for the steps, yelling to the deck-hand to wait, but his voice went unheard above the clamour of the engine. The gap between the bows and the quay opened rapidly as the skipper put the helm over, heading out into the wide basin between the car park and the railway station on the other bank. Zen ran straight down the pier and was just in time to leap on to the stern as it passed by. The deck-hand had disappeared into the wheelhouse at the other end of the cabin housing.

The whole craft lurched as the swell in the main channel caught it side on. Zen hung on grimly to the outside of the guard-rails aft as the propellers just below his feet thrashed the water until it foamed like spumante. Then a darkened figure appeared, silhouetted against the double glass doors of the cabin. The door opened and Tommaso Saoner stepped out on to the sunken afterdeck. Zen put his foot on the lower rail and started to clamber over, but he was still balanced precariously on the sloping grid of slippery metal when Saoner reached him, stretched out his hand and helped him to climb inboard.

Zen collapsed on one of the red plastic seats in the stern. He looked up at Saoner, nodding.

'You see, Tommaso? You'd like to be ruthless and dashing like your hero Dal Maschio, but you're not. You're weak and decent. Dal Maschio would would have pushed me in without a second thought, and left me to drown or be sliced up by the propellers. You couldn't bring yourself to do that, but you still think you can run with the people who can, and have, and will.'

Saoner looked at him emptily, then turned away and walked back into the deserted cabin. Zen lit a cigarette with trembling hands, sheltering the flame against the wind as the boat turned out of the main channel, under a series of wide metal and concrete bridges and out into a broad canal running between a railway marshalling yard and the port area. The deck-hand appeared at the top of the companion-way leading up from the cabin.

'Anyone for Santa Marta?' he called.

Saoner stood up. There was a bump as the boat went alongside. Zen threw away his cigarette and followed Saoner ashore. Santa Marta was a bleak area, one of the new quarters built on reclaimed land at the turn of the century. Disused railway tracks ran between the hulks of salvaged boats propped up on concrete blocks. In the distance were redbrick blocks of flats, built to house the dockyard workers.

Blinding lights razored through the darkness and a speeding bulk flashed past with a blare of noise, missing Zen by a whisker. The experience seemed so utterly abnormal that for a moment he thought wildly of aliens in flying saucers and the like. It was several moments before he recovered enough to notice that the stretch of ground he had been crossing was a road providing vehicular access to the port area. He located the receding figure of Tommaso Saoner and started after him, smiling ruefully. He had not only come within an ace of being killed, but in a way that would have ensured that his name would always bring a smile to everyone's lips. Aurelio Zen, the man who got run over in Venice.

On the graceful stone arch across the Arzere canal, Saoner paused briefly, perhaps uncertain which direction to take, or momentarily perturbed by the sight of the prison complex a little further along the canal. The reflection of the streetlamps rolled gently on the trace of swell carried in from the open waters of the lagoon. At the corner opposite, a man dressed in pyjamas was closing the green shutters of his bedroom window. He paused to stare at Saoner, who promptly turned right and set off at a cracking pace, as though he had decided upon a destination and was eager to arrive. But this appearance of purpose and urgency was contradicted by the circuitous course he took, weaving this way and that, first towards Campo Santa Margherita – where Zen closed up, fearing that he might try and rouse some of his NRV colleagues from their beds – and then east towards the Rio Nuovo, before finally doubling back by way of the gaunt church of Angelo Raffaele to emerge on the windswept shore of the Zattere.

The breeze had knocked the Giudecca channel into short, choppy waves which slapped resoundingly into the stone embankment, occasionally dumping swathes of water on the promenade. A faint mist dulled the light of the infrequent lamps, and the moon had disappeared behind a raft of cloud. To the right, the flares of the oil refinery at Marghera punctuated the darkness. As Zen followed Tommaso Saoner past the florid ocean terminal of the Adriatica line, he felt a sense of weariness and despondency creeping over him. He had been up since the crack of dawn, and it had not been an easy day. He began to realize that he couldn't keep this up all night, as he had planned. He had to find some way to force the issue, to try and shake Tommaso's blind devotion to Dal Maschio, if necessary by deceit.

As they rounded the curving prow of Dorsoduro, the lights of the Riva degli Schiavoni came into view on the other side of the broad channel of San Marco. Where they were, all was dark and deserted. The massive façade of the former Customs warehouses dominated the landward side, while to the right the expanses of the lagoon opened out into chilly vistas of windy immensity. Saoner seemed to have forgotten where he was, for he marched resolutely onwards until he was abruptly brought up short at the brink of the high stone quay forming the tip of the triangular island of the Salute.

Aurelio Zen caught up with Saoner as he looked down at the black water seething fitfully below. For a time they stood side by side in silence.

'It's a scam, Tommaso,' Zen said eventually. 'Can't you see that?'

'You think everything's rotten, because you're rotten yourself,' muttered Saoner.

Zen looked at him.

'Do you really think I'm rotten?'

Saoner nodded. He glanced at Zen.

'You've spent too much time serving the old system, the old masters. But things are changing at long last. You can't see that. When you look at someone like Dal Maschio, your first thought is to try and tear him down. He's too new, too threatening. If you allowed yourself to actually listen to what he says, you might end up realizing that it all makes sense. You would have to change the habits and ideas of a lifetime, and that would be too much trouble.'

He wagged a finger at Zen.

'You called me weak just now. Well, you're lazy. You'd rather have the devils you know than a man who, whatever his faults, is worth more than the whole of the old gang put together!'

At their feet, the unquiet water swirled and splashed.

'You talk of Dal Maschio like a lover,' Zen murmured.

'What the hell is that supposed to mean?'

'He's won your heart, and you can't understand why I can't see what you see in him.'

He shrugged.

'It's an old story, and harmless enough in private life. But this is a question of politics. Remember those Greek lessons we sweated through at school, when it seemed the bell would never ring? *Polis*, a city. *Polites*, a citizen. It's not your personal feelings about Dal Maschio that are at issue here, Tommaso. It's your public duties, your responsibilities as a citizen.'

Saoner barked a laugh.

'I don't need moral lectures from you, Zen,' he snapped, turning away.

The pursuit began again. At the same deliberate, purposeful pace, Saoner led the way along the other side of the Punta della Dogana, past the Salute church and into the tangled skein of alleys leading to the Accademia, where he crossed the bridge for the second time that night. When they reached Campo San Stefano, he stopped and seemed to hesitate. This was the spot where the leader of the *Nuova Repubblica Veneta* had taken leave of his acolytes earlier, and for a moment Zen thought that Saoner might try and make a dash to Dal Maschio's house, and moved to the left to cut him off. In the event Saoner turned the other way, towards the Piazza, bringing them into a district quite unlike any through which they had passed so far, into streets lined with banks, restaurants, hotels and a succession of shops and boutiques catering to the needs of the international shop-till-you-drop brigade.

But the water seemed to be calling Saoner, and when they reached the lugubrious monstrosity of San Moisè he veered right down a passage leading out on to the quayside. They walked past the ferry landing-stage and the harbour-master's office, beneath a grove of trees where a mob of starlings squabbled invisibly and along a broad promenade curving away as far as the eye could see. As though in response to these unfettered vistas, Saoner increased his pace until Zen had difficulty keeping up with him.

They crossed the bridge over the canal leading to the Questura, and then the Rio dell'Arsenale. Here the lighting was sparser and dimmer, and at moments Saoner's figure disappeared altogether into the rushing darkness. Zen began to lose all sense of reality, as though his night's dreams, denied, were seeping out to taint his waking consciousness. He dimly remembered what he was doing and why, but only as one remembers some fact about a country one has never visited.

'Tommaso!'

There was no response. Zen broke into a run.

'Stop, Tommaso! Let's talk!'

Saoner neither turned back nor changed his pace. Zen kept on running until he caught up with him.

'This is ridiculous, Tommaso! Let's not go any further.'

Like an automaton, Saoner kept striding on. By now they had reached the area laid out by the invading French as a formal public garden with walks, fountains and statues in a vain attempt to make an honest city of the *Serenissima*. In the depths of winter and the dead of the night, the place looked even more bizarre than usual. Zen grabbed Saoner's arm and pulled him to a stop. The moon slid out from behind the cloud again, turning the darkness to dusk. The two men stood there breathing fog into the silvery air. The serried trees lining the promenade had been pruned back to an equal height, making them look like giant candelabra.

'All this talk of morality!' Saoner exclaimed bitterly. 'You hypocrite!'

Zen stared at him, genuinely surprised.

'What do you mean?'

'I know why you're out to destroy Dal Maschio! Because you've got the hots for his wife, that's why!'

'That's bullshit!'

'She spent the night at your place on at least two occasions, according to my informants. They say you were fucking so hard it made waves in the canal.'

Forcing himself to remain calm, Zen took out a cigarette and lit up.

'That's very flattering, Tommaso, but unfortunately not true. Signora Dal Maschio and I met socially on a number of occasions – our mothers are close friends – but I'm afraid to say that her only interest in me was as a spy acting on her husband's instructions to find out what progress I was making in the Durridge case.'

He released a rippling ribbon of smoke.

'Mind you, in the course of our conversations she did let fall a few stray bits of information herself. I vividly remember her telling me some of her husband's unguarded comments on his associates in the *Nuova Repubblica Veneta*. Would you like to hear what he thinks of you, Tommaso?'

Saoner stamped his feet, as though to warm them.

'I know what Ferdinando thinks of me.'

'I have to say that he was fairly dismissive of his supporters in general. "Clerks and shopkeepers hitting their mid-life crisis. The ones with balls have affairs, the rest give themselves to me." '

'Ferdinando would never talk like that,' snorted Saoner.

'As for his views on you in particular . . .'

Saoner turned brusquely away.

'I don't want to know!'

'It's not that bad,' Zen chuckled, pulling him back to face him. 'Cristiana told me that he's very appreciative of all the work you've done so far. "We would never have got where we are today if it hadn't been for men like Tommaso, simple and strong, dull but dependable, incapable of independent thought but quick to follow orders." He's aware of your shortcomings and limitations, you see, but he also fully appreciates your merits. That's why he was initially so reluctant to get rid of you.'

Saoner flinched.

'What the hell are you talking about?'

'I'm talking about the reshuffle he's planning if he wins the election. Assuming the party does as well as expected, Dal Maschio's whole political position will change completely. He'll no longer be the leader of some fringe group, but mayor of one of the most important European cities, with a national and international profile and immense powers of patronage and persuasion. To deal adequately with that, he's going to need a new set of men around him, men of vision and imagination, with quick wits and a nice television manner.'

Zen let his cigarette fall to the pavement and stepped on it carefully.

'Mind you, I'm sure he'll find some suitable role for people like you,' he went on quickly. 'Something which matches your talents and skills. Cristiana mentioned the possibility of a post with the department responsible for dredging the canals.'

'This is all lies!'

Zen looked at him steadily and said nothing.

'You're making it all up!' Saoner exclaimed in a tone of desperation.

'You're the ones who are making it up,' Zen replied quietly. 'You've made an inspirational leader out of an opportunistic mob-orator and you've remade the history of the city to fit in with his nonsense about a Venice cut off from the rest of Italy and Europe, inhabited by pure-blooded, dialect-speaking, one-hundred-per-cent Venetians.'

Saoner clenched and unclenched his hands in desperation.

'That's enough! I can't bear any more. Why are you tormenting me like this?'

He started to walk away, mumbling to himself.

'We were only trying to change things for the better. There's nothing wrong with that, is there? I never meant to get mixed up in anything illegal. I don't remember how that happened. I just don't remember . . .'

He broke into a run, sprinting through the public gardens and across a bridge into a neighbourhood of turgid nineteenth-century apartment blocks like a chunk of Turin dropped down in the lagoon. Zen followed, calling out to him to stop. Down the broad, straight, eerily vacant moonlit streets the two men ran, their footsteps hammering on the flagstones. But Zen's lungs were still raw from the cigarette he had just smoked, while Saoner was running with manic energy, like a man fleeing some unimaginable horror. As his quarry vanished over a bridge on to a grubby islet where the metal scaffolding of the football stadium reared up in the darkness, Zen gave up the chase.

Breathless and cold, he walked slowly back through the deserted streets of Sant'Elena and across the strip of scrubby pine forest to the *vaporetto* stop. An immense weariness overwhelmed him and he sank down on a bench. Scurries of wind plucked at his clothing like invisible fingers. He felt utterly despondent. He had done all he could do, and it had not been enough. He had lied to Tommaso in the most blatant and hurtful way about Dal Maschio's opinion of him, but all to no avail. He had underestimated the hold a man like Dal Maschio could exercise over his followers, and the potency of the atavistic cravings from which he had concocted his ideological designer drugs.

The noise of an approaching ferry roused him from his stupor. Reluctantly he hauled himself to his feet and hobbled stiffly down the path to the landing-stage. Someone was already waiting there. Then Zen saw that the *vaporetto* was going to the Lido, not to the city. He was about to return to his bench when the waiting figure was caught in the boat's lights as it nudged in alongside. It was Tommaso Saoner.

Zen hurried down the gangway just in time to climb aboard. Saoner had already gone below. The helmsman reversed engines to clear the landing-stage, then eased the craft out into the deep-water channel, passing astern of a car ferry also bound for the Lido. Zen edged round the deck until he came to a window with a view of the cabin. Tommaso Saoner sat bolt upright on his seat, staring straight ahead, seemingly oblivious to the tears streaming down his cheeks. Zen drew back into the darkness, wrapping his coat tightly around him. The wind had eased, but it was colder than ever. A shattered image of the moon tossed and bobbed on the lumpy seas, permuting its scattered fragments like a shaken kaleidoscope.

The wind dropped away as the ferry drew into the lee of the island. Zen waited to let Tommaso Saoner get off first, but it was not until the deck-hand went down to the cabin to rouse him that Saoner rose to his feet. At first he seemed unwilling to budge, but after a brief exchange with the mariner, who pointed out that the boat was going out of service, he climbed up the steps and went ashore.

Of all the topographical freaks in the lagoon, the Lido had always seemed to Zen the most disturbing. In summer, its vocation as a seaside resort lent the place an illusory air of normality, but in the bleak depths of February its true nature was mercilessly exposed. Here was a perfectly normal contemporary urban scene, with asphalt streets called *Via* this and *Piazza* that, complete with road signs and traffic lights. There was the usual jumble of apartments and villas, offices and hotels, the usual roar of cars and lorries, scooters, bikes and buses. Everything about the place was perfectly banal, in short, except that it was built on an isolated sandbar a few hundred metres wide between the shallow reaches of the lagoon and the open expanses of the Adriatic.

By the time Zen got ashore, Saoner was already fifty metres ahead, striding down the wide central avenue which led to the sea. Zen almost let him go, but at the last moment his curiosity got the better of him. A pair of headlights split the darkness at an intersection ahead. A car appeared and paused briefly before crossing the main street and disappearing to the right. It was immediately followed by a delivery van, three more cars, a lorry, and finally a milk tanker. Zen loped along the tree-lined pavement, trying to work out some rational explanation for this mysterious nocturnal convoy. Such was the state of his brain that it took him about a minute to realize that all the vehicles must have disembarked from the car ferry he had seen earlier. Satisfied, he scanned the street ahead to find that the figure he had been following had disappeared.

Despite his immense fatigue, he ran all the rest of the way to the huge piazza where the avenue joined the *lungomare*. During the summer this was the heart of the fashionable tourist area, but now the gardens looked drab and tatty and the wind made the trees shudder as though in pain. Zen looked all round, from the moth-balled hulk of the *Grand Hotel des Bains* to the gleaming strip of the boulevard skirting the beach where surf foamed dimly at the limit of vision.

'Tommaso!' he shouted.

The wind dismantled the word and flung the pieces away, but he called again and again.

'Tommaso! Tommaso!'

He walked all around the piazza and along the road in both directions, but there was no sign of any other living soul. Fugitive traces of light were beginning to appear in the east before he finally gave up and turned away to begin the slow journey back to the city.

Winter sunlight, hard and brilliant, searched the grimy window and marked out a skewed square on the floor. Some vestige of childhood superstition made Aurelio Zen avoid setting foot in it as he went to and fro, collecting his belongings from all over the flat and returning them to the battered leather suitcase which had been the companion of his travels for almost thirty years.

The chore did not take long. He had brought only the bare minimum with him, and much of that he had never got around to unpacking in the first place. At a loss again, he sank down in a chair, gazing down at the glaring patch on the tiled floor. It was a beautiful day, everyone agreed, for the time of year. Overcome by exhaustion, Zen closed his eyes. The sun-struck square was still visible, branded on his retinas as a throbbing block of darkness.

He opened his eyes again, reached out a hand for the phone and dialled. Once again, no reply. He let it ring a long time, seeing the deserted apartment in Rome, hearing the bell shrilling periodically in the traffic-troubled stillness. At length he replaced the receiver and glanced at his watch. There were still almost two hours before his train left. He felt like a child again, waiting for school to end, for the bell to sound and real life to begin.

As if in response to his thoughts, a bell did ring, gurgling throatily in the stairwell. Zen looked up apprehensively. On the wall opposite hung a large canvas supposedly painted by his mother's uncle. He realized for the first time that he had no idea what, if anything, the turbid whorls of colour were supposed to represent. It had never occurred to him to ask. He had taken the thing for granted all his life, as though it had come with the wall.

The bell rang again. He stood up and walked over to the window, but there was no one to be seen. He opened the window and dipped his face into the cold, clear air outside. On his doorstep, dressed in a grey tweed coat and a green headscarf, Cristiana Morosini stood gazing up at him. They looked at each other for a time without speaking. Then Zen turned back inside and pushed the door release button.

When she entered the room, he was still standing by the window, facing the door. Cristiana hesitated in the doorway for a moment, then walked a little way into the room, coming to rest with her feet in the patch of sunlight. She looked around nervously, opening and closing her lips several times without any sound emerging. Then she saw the open suitcase.

'You're leaving?'

Zen eyed her in silence for a moment.

'Why didn't you use your key to get in?' he asked. 'Or has your husband still got it?'

Cristiana waved her hands vaguely. Zen felt a sentimental stab of pity for those plump white fingers which had explored his body so thoroughly and so satisfyingly. Whatever had happened certainly wasn't their fault.

'I was going to phone and let you know he'd be here,' Cristiana faltered, 'but Nando said he wanted it to be a surprise.'

'And what Nando wants, Nando gets.'

Her expression hardened slightly.

'He's still my husband.'

'And what does that make me, Cristiana? What does it make you?'

His voice was so strident that it made the windowpane shiver. Cristiana shrugged peevishly.

'I don't know what to say, Aurelio. I thought it was just a fling. I liked you, and Nando had hurt me badly. I thought I deserved to get my own back, and to have a little fun too.'

Zen looked away, shaking his head in simulated disgust.

'Oh come on!' Cristiana exclaimed with something like anger. 'Imagine what you'd be saying now if this had turned out the other way round, and I was being possessive and clingy when all you wanted was to go home and forget it ever happened. I knew all along you had someone in Rome. It never occurred to me that you were taking it seriously.'

'Of course I wasn't!'

He looked back at her with a fixed smile.

'Apart from the sex, Cristiana, my interest in you was purely professional. I hoped you might let drop something about your husband which would be helpful to me in my investigation.'

She gazed numbly at him.

'No doubt you cultivated me for precisely the same reason,' Zen went on, 'to keep dear Nando informed about the progress I was making. We were each using the other. No one got hurt and neither of us has any right to complain.'

'That's not true!' Cristiana retorted. 'You told me you were investigating Ada Zulian's problems. Why on earth should Nando care about that?'

Zen shrugged.

'Have it your own way. What does it matter, since you've won? I went to see Mamoli this morning. The judiciary is dropping the case. Bon and the others have been released. Your husband's election triumph is assured and you can look forward to being Signora Dal Maschio, loyal wife of the local political supremo. Only you and I will know that you're married to a kidnapper and a murderer.'

'What?'

Her face was rigid with shock.

'Didn't he mention that little exploit?' murmured Zen. 'How odd. I'll bet he tells all his *other* women. Just the sort of thing to get them going.'

Cristiana walked towards him.

'What are you talking about? What are these horrible lies?'

Zen held up his hands.

'Since you've branded me a liar, there's no point my saying any more. Why don't you ask Tommaso Saoner? He knows all about it.'

Cristiana stopped and stared at him, shaking her head slowly.

'That's an appalling thing to say.'

'It was an appalling thing to do, Cristiana. Durridge may have been a war criminal, but . . .'

'To joke about Tommaso like that, I mean!'

He frowned.

'Like what?'

They confronted each other in silence.

'Haven't you heard?' she said at last.

'Heard what?'

'It's been on the local news and . . .'

'What are you talking about?' snapped Zen irritably.

Cristiana lowered her head.

'He's dead.'

'Dead? Who's dead?'

'Tommaso Saoner.'

He laughed.

'Don't be ridiculous! Why, I saw him only . . .'

His voice trailed away.

'The body was washed up at the Lido this morning,' said Cristiana. 'Nando is devastated. Tommaso was one of his closest and most trusted associates. They met just last night. Nando even walked part of the way home with him.'

She looked at Zen.

'When did you see him?'

He turned to the window.

'Oh . . . before that.'

There was a long silence.

'What happened?' he muttered almost inaudibly.

'It looks like suicide. The body was fully clothed, and there was no sign of violence. But Nando says he seemed perfectly normal last night. He even made a joke about you.'

She shivered.

'What could have suddenly driven him to do something like that? And what was he doing on the Lido in the first place? It doesn't make sense!'

There was a long, sombre silence. Cristiana looked at Zen, who was still facing the window.

'I thought he was supposed to be a friend of yours,' she remarked sharply.

'He used to be.'

'Well you don't seem to care particularly that he's dead!'

This time the silence was even more oppressive.

'I'm not sure I really know you,' Cristiana muttered. 'I'm not sure I really like you.'

Zen turned slowly and looked at her.

'Neither am I,' he said.

They exchanged a long glance, then Cristiana abruptly turned and walked out. The front door slammed shut. Zen stood gazing down at the quadrilateral of sunlight on the floor. It had moved slightly to the left, and was shorter and squatter than before. Zen stepped carefully around it and picked up the phone.

'Mamma? At last! It's me, Aurelio. I'll be home this evening. In time for dinner, yes. Can you get Maria Grazia to make something really nice? I haven't eaten properly all week. Rosalba? I ate there the first day, but since then . . . She's fine. Who? Cristiana? She's the daughter, isn't she? I met her briefly. Anyway, how are you? Good. Are they? Glad to hear it. I'm looking forward to seeing you both this evening. You and Tania. What? What? Moved out? Where's she gone? Why did she leave? I thought you two were getting on well together . . .'

He sat down on the sofa, the receiver clamped to his ear.

'Me? What did I do? I wasn't even there!'

His face gradually grew hard as he listened.

'Sorry, Mamma, but I've got to go or I'll miss my train,' he said in a different voice altogether. 'Goodbye. Yes. Goodbye. And you. Goodbye.'

He got out his crumpled pack of *Nazionali* and sat there smoking one cigarette after another until the packet was empty and the ashtray full. Then he put on his coat and hat, closed his suitcase, and left.

Out of the sun, the air was still chilly. Zen walked the length of the triangular *campo* without looking back, hefting his suitcase in his right hand, his shoulders hunched and his head lowered. As he rounded the corner into the long alley leading to the Lista di Spagna he collided with someone coming the other way. Zen muttered an apology and was about to pass by when the man spoke his name. Zen set down the heavy suitcase and looked at him, taking in the greasy grey hair, the shabby suit, the tartan carpet slippers, the nondescript mutt trailing along at the end of a rope.

'Daniele,' he murmured without enthusiasm. 'You must excuse me. I'm late for my train.'

'You're leaving?'

'As you see.'

'So soon?'

Zen picked up his suitcase again.

'I should never have come in the first place.'

Daniele Trevisan scuttled up to him with amazing rapidity and grasped him by the arm.

'You can't go yet!'

Zen looked down at the elderly face, as shrivelled as an old nut.

'Ever since I saw you last week, I've been wondering whether or

291

not I should say anything,' Trevisan went on hesitantly. 'God only knows when you'll be back, and whether I'll still be alive.'

He shook his head helplessly.

'I just don't know what to do, Angelo.'

Catching sight of Zen's expression, the old man hastily corrected himself.

'Aurelio, I mean.'

Zen tried to tug himself free of the man's fierce grip.

'Let me go!'

'Stop! Wait!'

Zen turned on him with a menacing glare.

'Why can't you leave me in peace?' he shouted.

The old man stared back at him mutely.

'What do you want with me?' demanded Zen.

'Why, nothing! I just . . .'

An ingratiating smile appeared on Daniele Trevisan's face.

'I only wanted to offer you a glass at Claudio's new bar. Come on, Aurelio! You can't leave Venice without having a last *ombra*.'

Zen looked at him.

'Please!' the old man added unexpectedly.

Zen glanced at his watch.

'We'll have to hurry. I've got a train to catch.'

When they reached the bar, Zen found to his surprise that he recognized it. He had been taken there many times by his mother to watch television, at a time when only the super-rich could afford a set of their own. By stretching his credit to the limit, a *barista* in the Lista di Spagna had managed to acquire a set and thus transform what had previously been a perfectly ordinary wine-shop, frequented solely by elderly males, into the social hub of the community, where men, women and children from all over the neighbourhood flocked to watch Mike Bongiorno's quiz show 'Double or Quits?' – having paid the exorbitant surcharge on drinks ordered during the transmission.

The television, in a more modern incarnation, stood on the same shelf at the end of the room, showing an American police series crudely dubbed into Italian, but the old magic had fled. The bar was empty but for scattered groups of foreign tourists who looked askance as Daniele Trevisan sidled up to the bar dragging his flea-ridden dog. Nor did Claudio seem particularly pleased to see them. He looked blank when Daniele introduced Zen.

'Angelo's son,' prompted Daniele Trevisan.

Claudio shrugged.

'You drink too much, Daniele.'

He set two glasses on the bar and filled them with the contents of an open bottle.

'Take it down the back,' he told them. 'You'll scare away the tourists.'

They made their way to a dim, grubby area at the rear of the premises, stocked with damaged chairs and tables and crates of empty bottles.

'It was just like meeting you today,' Daniele said once they'd sat down. 'I'd popped round to see if Ada was all right, when suddenly there he was, walking along the canal towards me.'

He risked a smile.

'*He* wasn't watching where he was going either. Must run in the family.'

The old man bit his lip.

'I knew at once it was Angelo.'

Zen's arm jerked convulsively, knocking his wine over. The glass rolled across the table and fell to the floor, bursting like a bulb. A moment later Claudio appeared, marching towards them with a furious expression.

'Right, that's it! Out!'

Zen got out his wallet and handed over a two-thousand-lire note.

'It was an accident. That should cover it.'

'I don't want your money! I want you out of here! I'm not running a refuge for drunken louts!'

'No,' Zen retorted, 'you're running a cheap scam whose sole purpose is to rip off tourists who don't know any better by selling them shitty sandwiches at ten times the proper price and wine that tastes like bat piss.'

The barman looked as though he were about to have a fit. He kicked away Trevisan's dog, which was sniffing at the seat of his pants.

'If you don't get out of here right now I'm calling the cops!'

Zen flipped his wallet over, revealing his police identity card.

'They're already here.'

293

The barman's shoulders slumped. He turned away, hastily palming the banknote. Zen plucked it back again.

'People might think I was trying to bribe you,' he smiled sweetly.

'For a lousy two thousand lire?'

Zen shrugged and handed the note back.

'You're right. I could buy four like you for a thousand.'

Daniele Trevisan burst into malicious cackles as Claudio retreated.

'That's the way to treat them!'

The spilt wine had formed a puddle which was inching imperceptibly across the table towards Zen. He dipped his finger into it, creating a canal through which the liquid emptied itself safely over the opposite edge.

'You were saying something about having seen my father,' he said quietly. 'That's impossible, of course.'

His eyes averted, Daniele Trevisan shook his head.

'It was him all right. Two years ago. Two and a half actually. July, it was. The city was sweltering.'

His eyes became vague and distant.

'I spoke to him in dialect. At first he didn't seem to understand, and answered me in some strange language. Then he began to speak, haltingly at first, like a child.'

Zen stood up.

'You're either mad or mischievous. Either way, I'm not going to listen to this pack of lies a moment longer.'

He picked up his suitcase and buttoned his coat, glancing from time to time at Trevisan. The old man did not look at him. After a moment Zen sat down again.

'You've got ten minutes,' he said coldly.

Trevisan stared into his wineglass as though it were a clairvoyant's crystal ball.

'He asked about you and your mother. I explained that you'd both moved to Rome. "We've already been there," he said. He was with a group of Polish tourists on a cultural and religious trip. The borders had just been opened and they were taking advantage of the new freedom to visit Italy and see the Polish pope. "Don't tell me you've turned religious, Angelo!" I said, but he said it was just that the tours organized by the Church were the cheapest. They'd driven all the way from some city with a name I forget.'

'This is absurd!' exclaimed Zen. 'What has Poland got to do with it?'

'That's where he lives.'

'Don't be ridiculous!'

Daniele Trevisan consulted his wineglass once more.

'It seems he deserted from the army in the Ukraine. He and a couple of other lads from the city decided they'd had enough. Do you remember Fabio Fois and what's-his-name, the elder of the two Vivian boys? I suppose you'd have been too young.'

He sighed.

'They didn't make it, of course. The other two died. Angelo was taken in by a peasant woman whose menfolk had all been killed. He stayed there, lying low, helping to work the farm, until the war was over. By that time the woman was pregnant. Later on they moved to the city. The Communists were in control and the borders had been sealed. That's when Angelo learned that he was in Poland. And there he had to stay.'

Zen smiled in a superior way.

'Even supposing this preposterous story were true, as a foreign national he'd only have needed to show his documents and they would have had to let him out.'

'He'd destroyed his Italian papers when he was on the run, for fear of being shot as a deserter. He was passing as one of the woman's dead brothers.'

Zen slapped his palm on the surface of the table.

'He could have gone to the Italian embassy in Warsaw! He was a displaced person, for God's sake, a refugee. He could have come home any time he wanted to!'

Daniele Trevisan looked at Zen for the first time.

'Perhaps he didn't want to.'

Their eyes clashed briefly.

'I don't believe any of this,' Zen muttered in an undertone. 'You're making it up.'

'It's true, Aurelio. I swear it.'

'So where is this person now?'

The old man shrugged.

'Back in Poland, I suppose. The tour group was leaving that afternoon. I asked if he'd be coming back, but he said no. "It's been too long," he said. "It's another life." Then I asked him if he was going to . . .'

He broke off, fiddling with stem of the glass.

'Going to what?' demanded Zen.

Trevisan gestured awkwardly.

'If he was going to get in touch with you and your mother. But he said he wouldn't. "They think I'm dead," he told me. "It would only cause trouble." I tried to argue with him, but he wouldn't listen. He made me swear on my mother's grave never to tell you or Giustiniana anything about this. And I wouldn't have if I hadn't seen you . . .'

He looked at Zen and nodded.

'You're right. You shouldn't have come.'

Zen held the old man's eyes for a long time. Then he picked up his suitcase and walked out. The street was packed with people heading to and from the station. Zen was immediately caught up in a large group calling animatedly to each other in some language which was opaque to him. A counter-current flowed back along the other side of the street. Where the two met there was an area of turbulence and confusion, while the drag caused by the shops and houses to either side created a further set of whorls and eddies. Several times a blockage momentarily slowed the progress of the human current, with a consequent backing-up and an increase in pressure which made everything move faster when the obstruction was finally swept aside.

At length the walls fell back. The crowd lost its cohesion and impetus, spreading out across the courtyard in front of the station. People wandered about, seemingly at random, looking bewildered and lost. Somewhere in the distance a massive, muffled voice read out a succession of unintelligible announcements. A gypsy beggar hunched over an accordion played a snatch of a military march over and over and over again. An excess of sunlight had blinded the clock. A child cried.

'Excuse me!'

A middle-aged couple, oddly but neatly dressed, stood beaming at Zen. The man said something incomprehensible. Zen shrugged and shook his head. The man repeated the phrase more slowly, pointing to a map in the guidebook he was holding. Zen understood only that he was asking directions to somewhere in English. He closed his eyes and tried to summon up a few words in that language.

'I'm sorry,' he replied with an apologetic smile. 'I'm a stranger here myself.'

BOOKS BY MICHAEL DIBDIN

"Dibdin has a gift for shocking the unshockable reader. He writes the unmentionable calmly and with devastating effect." —Ruth Rendell

DEAD LAGOON

In this stylish novel, Michael Dibdin's urbane and skeptical Italian detective Aurelio Zen returns to his native Venice to search for a vanished American millionaire. The result is a mystery rich in character and deduction, and intensely informed about the history, politics, and manners of its Venetian setting.

Fiction/Crime/0-679-75311-7

THE DYING OF THE LIGHT

The setting in this brilliant and haunting variation on the classic drawing-room murder novel is Eventide Lodge, where guests have gathered for tea. Colonel Weatherby is reading by the fire. Mrs. Hiram Hargreave III is whiling away her time at patience. And Miss Rosemary Travis and her friend, Dorothy, are wondering which of their housemates will be the next to die.

Fiction/Crime/0-679-75310-9

THE LAST SHERLOCK HOLMES STORY

Michael Dibdin pits the sleuth of Baker Street against the Butcher of Whitechapel—the archfiend Jack the Ripper. And in doing so, he gives us a Holmes possessed of greater and more disturbing depths than the one we thought we knew.

Fiction/Crime/0-679-76658

RATKING

In this chilling masterpiece of police procedure and psychological suspense, Dibdin introduces us to Aurelio Zen, sending his stoic Italian police commissioner to investigate the kidnapping of Ruggiero Miletti, a powerful Perugian industrialist.

Crime Fiction/0-679-76854-8

VINTAGE CRIME/BLACK LIZARD
Available at your local bookstore, or call toll-free to order:
1-800-793-2665 (credit cards only).

Praise for *Shelter in the Storm*

"With lovely, evocative writing, Laurel Blount brings to life a tender story of two wounded hearts healing and finding lasting love in the wake of tragedy."

—Marta Perry, national bestselling
author of *A Springtime Heart*

"Laurel Blount's *Shelter in the Storm* is the perfect mixture of sweet romance and family drama. Naomi is a fully fleshed[-out] character who will win your heart with her sincerity and wisdom as she and Joseph face an unthinkable tragedy. Their Amish world is as fascinating as their struggle to remain grounded in their faith. Readers will relate to their unflagging efforts to hold on through a season of storms. As Joseph's father says, 'When our world goes dark, then we must hold hard to the rope of our faith, and trust Gott to lead us out.' This is the kind of hope-filled story that readers are hungry for."

—Dana Mentink, national bestselling
author of *Secrets Resurfaced*

"I couldn't stop reading *Shelter in the Storm*. Laurel Blount mixes comforting, homey Amish romance with exciting suspense and cliff-hanger chapter endings. Her characters are real and appealing, and I was rooting for them from start to finish. I'm so glad there will be more books in the Johns Mill series. It is off to a wonderful start!"

—Lee Tobin McClain, *USA Today*
bestselling author of *Cottage at the Beach*

"Two very different worlds clash in this heartfelt story of faith, family, forgiveness, and love. Endearing characters warm the heart in this hopeful love story."

—Tina Radcliffe, author of *Ready to Trust*

"This is a very good book. Laurel Blount's *Shelter in the Storm* had me hooked from the first line. . . . This sweet, tragic story is touching and honest and beautiful. I highly recommend this book, and I can't wait for the next book in the Johns Mill Amish series by the amazing Laurel Blount."

—Lenora Worth, *New York Times* bestselling author of *Seeking Refuge*

Also by Laurel Blount

SHELTER IN THE STORM

STRENGTH IN THE STORM

Laurel Blount

JOVE
New York

A JOVE BOOK
Published by Berkley
An imprint of Penguin Random House LLC
penguinrandomhouse.com

ISBN: 9780593200223

First Edition: February 2022

Printed in the United States of America
1 3 5 7 9 10 8 6 4 2

Book design by George Towne

CHAPTER ONE

❧

THE LITTLE, EVERYDAY MEMORIES ALWAYS HURT THE most.

Emma Hochstedler knew that well enough. Ever since the shock of her parents' deaths six months ago, she'd gone teary-eyed over the strangest things.

Like today. Here she sat on a busy June morning, sniffling over a battered egg basket. It was a foolish waste of time, she knew, but still, she couldn't help it.

She hadn't seen this one coming. She'd passed the daily chore of chicken tending to her younger sister, Miriam, years ago, and to be honest, she hadn't given the egg basket much thought since. But just now when Emma had pulled it from its shelf, the handle had fit her hand with such heartbreaking familiarity that she'd been brought up short. For a finger snap of time, standing there on the back porch of the farmhouse, she'd been a happy little girl again, her sheltered world still shining and unbroken.

The doorknob rattled behind her, and she blotted her

eyes with the back of one hand. She couldn't let the family see her crying. It would worry them. The least she could do—the very least considering the circumstances—was not to add to their pain by giving in to her own.

"Emma? *Vass is letz?*"

Her new sister-in-law stood in the kitchen doorway, a broom in one hand and a concerned look on her kind face.

"Nothing's wrong, Naomi." Emma forced a smile. "Except that I'm sitting here woolgathering when we have such a full morning ahead of us." She brandished the basket. "I'm off to the coop, and then I'll be ready to help you pick the cucumbers."

Naomi's brow puckered. "You're seeing to the chickens?"

"*Ja.*" This time Emma's smile came more easily. "I thought I'd take the job off your hands. You're doing more than your share already." That was true. Her brother Joseph had chosen well. Not only was Naomi sweet-hearted and devoted to her new husband, but she was patient and hardworking, a welcome addition to a family who'd weathered so many troubles. "Since your heart operation, I've had to scramble to find any chores left to do."

"I like to work," Naomi said. "After so many years of being sickly, it's a real blessing for me to finally be able to do for other folks." She glanced over her shoulder. "But it used to be Miriam's job to tend to the hens, ain't so? Back . . . before, I mean. Joseph told me it was her favorite chore."

"*Ja*, it was." Emma's lips curved at the memory. "It wasn't mine, so I was happy enough to pass it off to her, once *Mamm* said I could. They're a messy job, the chickens, but Miriam never minded. She knew all the hens' personalities, and she liked to name them after our friends. *Mamm* fussed about that. She didn't think it sounded kind when Miriam would suggest we stew Mahlon's Betty for supper because she'd started pecking eggs."

Naomi laughed, but Emma's answering smile halted half formed. Her twin brother, Caleb, had laughed, too, and *Daed* had smothered a smile. Now *Mamm* and *Daed* had passed, and Caleb—well, Caleb was lost to them, too.

Naomi stepped fully onto the porch and shut the kitchen door. "Emma," she said, lowering her voice, "I think we should ask Miriam to take the chickens over again. A job like that, something she used to enjoy so much, it might be a way to coax her outside of the house."

Emma shook her head, alarmed. "Not yet, Naomi. Yesterday she couldn't even step out to get the mop you needed, and it was just beside the door on the back steps. She'd never manage to go all the way across the yard, and it would upset her to try. It's all right, truly. I don't mind doing the outside chores until she's better."

"Oh, *ja,* I know you don't mind taking over her work, and of course, I don't mind, either. The problem is . . . I'm not sure all our helping is *gut* for Miriam." Naomi hesitated, her forehead crinkled with concern. "I am new to this family, Emma, and I don't want to make trouble. It's only that being sick for so long myself, I know better than most folks how tempting it can be to stop trying, especially if people around you make it easy to stay where you are."

It was plain how carefully Naomi was choosing her words, trying not to cause offense. Still, Emma felt stung. Since returning from her stay in Ohio, she'd taken on the job of Miriam's care, making certain that her sister wasn't upset or troubled, hoping that plenty of love and calm would speed her healing.

"Well, but your sickness was a physical one, Naomi. Miriam saw our parents killed right in front of her. It's no wonder she's fearful, and I don't think it's wrong of us to be gentle with her."

"We should be gentle, *ja.* But we must help her see that she's not only loved but also needed. Otherwise, I'm afraid her fears about going outside will settle in and be that much harder to get shed of."

Now it was Emma's turn to choose her words carefully. She loved Naomi dearly, and she didn't want to quarrel. They'd done real well since the wedding. It wasn't always easy, two women sharing a house and a kitchen, and there'd been a bump or two over the past few weeks, but nothing big. Naomi was a kindhearted, reasonable woman, and Emma was willing to give way to her brother's wife in most things. But Miriam's care was a different matter.

She cleared her throat. "Joseph doesn't want Miriam forced, Naomi. He has said so, and I agree with him."

Her sister-in-law frowned. "*Nee*, of course he doesn't want her forced! Neither do I." For the first time, Naomi's soft voice took on a bit of sharpness. "Only nudged a little. Emma, I hope you'll forgive me if I speak plain. Ever since you came home for our wedding, you've been rushing ahead of Miriam, carrying and fetching for her, doing her work before I can even suggest that she do it herself. She loves and trusts you, and since you don't seem to believe she can do anything, she's starting to think that, too. She's been staying in her room longer every day. Haven't you noticed?"

Emma's heart sank. *Ja*, she'd noticed that. It was one of the reasons she'd redoubled her efforts to help, because it seemed her younger sister was slipping backward rather than improving. "You think that's because of me?"

"Oh, *schwesdre*." Naomi put a gentle hand on Emma's arm. "You meant only to help. Neither of us are blaming you—not for this nor anything else. Maybe you should stop blaming yourself, *ja*? Then it may be easier for you to stop coddling Miriam."

Neither of us.

Of course, Naomi and Joseph would have talked over Emma's situation privately, like any married couple. Her sister-in-law's words shouldn't have bothered Emma, but they did, a little, reminding her that her brother's heart had settled in a new direction.

When Emma didn't answer, Naomi smiled. "Never mind. We will let things lie for now. As you said, it's a busy day today with the pickling to do, and we've enough on hand without fretting ourselves. Speaking of that, I've a favor to ask, if you're willing. The cucumbers have done so well this year that we're almost out of some of our spices. The vinegar's getting low, too. Joseph's got a good bit of work out in the shop today, so I wondered if maybe you could drive in to Zook's."

Go to town? By herself? Emma lifted her eyebrows, distracted from her worries about Miriam.

This was unexpected.

She hadn't been to town much since she'd come home, and on the few occasions she'd needed to go, Joseph had stopped his work to drive her. It was frustrating, having to be taken here and there like a child, but she'd understood her brother's caution.

After her parents' murders, the *Englisch* media had swarmed Johns Mill, anxious for photographs and details. Since it was Trevor Abbott's obsession with Emma that had led the troubled young man to attack her parents in their general store, the reporters had been obsessed with her as well.

In fact, they'd made such nuisances of themselves that her hot-tempered twin had ended up punching one of them and disgracing himself in the eyes of their church. In the heartbreaking days that followed, Caleb had turned his back on his faith, and Emma had fled to her uncle's more secluded community, hoping everything might calm down if she was gone.

The plan had worked—mostly. In spite of the unsettling news that a movie was being made about the tragedy, things seemed much quieter now.

"If you'd feel comfortable going by yourself," Naomi was saying, "I could get the cucumbers picked. I'm sure Miriam will help me wash and slice them up, so we'll be all ready when you get back. While you're in town, you might stop by Yoder's, too. Miriam's nearly done with her quilt, and she needs fabric for the backing. Like I told Joseph, I'm never much good at figuring what looks nice with what. You'll do a much better job picking out the material. But only," she repeated, "if you're comfortable about it."

"Of course! I'm happy to go, Naomi." And she was. A trip to town all by herself, just like the old days. Emma felt a rush of anticipation at the thought of clopping peacefully along in the buggy, of taking her own sweet time in the stores without worrying about keeping Joseph from his work.

Her sister-in-law nodded. "It'll suit," she said simply. "I'll make a list of everything we're short of, and I'll ask Joseph to hitch up the buggy so you can leave as soon as you're done with the chickens."

Emma smiled. "*Ja*, you ask. If I ask him, he'll likely remind me I've been hitching buggies up since I was twelve and make me do it myself! But he can't deny you anything."

Naomi blushed and waved her away. "Get on with you, then! We've both got plenty to do."

As Emma walked toward the chicken coop, her heart felt pounds lighter. Today might turn out to be a good day after all. The air smelled of summer, and there was only a hint of the heat that would settle in later. The vegetable garden looked promisingly green over by the barn, and *Mamm*'s orange and yellow daylilies nodded brightly around the wash shed. All in all, it was a real pretty morning for an unexpected jaunt into town.

Emma lifted the wooden latch and slipped into the coop. The hens chirred and clucked contentedly as she tossed pellets and scratch from the covered metal bin stored in the corner.

In the old days, the chicken's grain had been kept in the barn with the horse rations. Moving the bin was one of the many changes her older brother had quietly made since he'd taken over the farm. Another had been repurposing the abandoned family dairy building for his growing woodworking business.

Those changes hadn't disturbed Emma in the least, but now that Joseph and Naomi were married, adjustments were happening inside the house, too. Naomi had rearranged the kitchen cupboards, changing the way *Mamm* had organized things into something that suited her better. A few days after the wedding, Emma had opened a drawer expecting to see the family flatware where it had always been, only to discover measuring cups and spoons nestled there instead.

Naomi had been apologetic. "I hope that's all right, Emma. It just seemed handier to have the cups and measuring spoons nearer the counter where I do most of my mixing, and the silverware closer to the table."

Emma had assured her it was fine, and after a week of opening the wrong drawer, she'd adjusted. Naomi was Joseph's *fraw*, and as such, the kitchen was now hers to arrange as she saw fit. It was the natural way of things, and Emma understood that.

Still, it was hard to see *Mamm*'s familiar kitchen slowly being remade into Naomi's. It made Emma feel unsettled. As the last traces of her mother's preferences were gently erased, Emma couldn't help wondering how she herself would fit into her brother's new household.

While the hens scratched, Emma rinsed and refilled their water containers—always such a dirty job—then turned to the straw-stuffed nesting boxes mounted on the wall. She tucked smooth brown eggs into her basket with quick fingers, thinking about the unexpected turns her life had taken.

She'd never expected to be living with her brother at twenty-three. Nobody had expected that for her—Emma had always had plenty of fellows hanging around. In fact, her first proposal had come when she was still a schoolgirl. It was the only time she'd ever said yes.

That was partly because Sam Christner had taken her completely by surprise, and partly because the two of them had been such wonderful *gut* friends at the time. She'd liked the idea of marrying Sam—one day, when they were both grown up. They'd settle down cozily in Johns Mill, the two of them, and raise a big brood of children, half fair-haired and blue-eyed like herself and half with Sam's reddish-brown hair and hazel eyes. It had seemed such a natural thing to do.

Of course, it hadn't stuck. They'd been far too young to know their own minds, and in a couple of years their silly agreement had ended with an embarrassing squabble. Since then Sam had kept right on being kind to Emma and her family—that was his way—but they'd never been quite such good friends again.

She'd had other offers since, but she'd never said yes again. None of the fellows asking had seemed exactly right, and before she'd found one who did, Trevor Abbott had come along. Emma had felt sorry for the sad-eyed *Englisch* boy who'd hung around her parents' store, and so she'd tried to show him kindness.

In return he'd broken her world to pieces.

Emma left the coop, latching the door carefully behind herself. Naomi must have had a word with her new husband because Joseph was in front of the barn, hitching Titus to the smaller of the family's two buggies. He glanced up as she approached him, the morning sun glinting off the new-married beard stubble on his cheeks.

"Well, you've timed it right. I'm near done," her older brother teased.

"You shouldn't have been so quick with the job if you wanted my help, *bruder*." Emma ran light fingers down Titus's nose. The horse considered her calmly as Joseph tightened the straps.

"No point in my being quick, that's for sure. I could probably hitch Titus up again twice over in the time it'll take you to get ready. I don't see why girls always want to switch clothes before going to town, especially now. It seems to me that one black dress is much like another."

Spoken like a man, Emma thought ruefully. "It's not about the color, Joseph. If I walked into Zook's with smelly chicken muck on my skirt hem, I'd run all their other customers out!"

"Might not be so bad if you did," Joseph muttered. "When Naomi asked me about you going to town by yourself, it seemed all right, but now I'm wondering." He glanced sideways at his sister and smiled sheepishly. "She can near about talk me into anything, Naomi can. I thought I'd gain my wits back once the wedding was over, but it seems marriage only makes a fellow more featherheaded."

Emma smiled back. It did her heart good to see her serious-minded brother so happy. That mattered more than spoons any day.

"I wouldn't be expecting your good sense to come back anytime soon. But as it happens, I think your first decision was sound enough. I can manage town on my own just fine."

"I figured you'd be raring to go." Joseph finished fastening a buckle and slapped Titus affectionately on the side before moving to the next one. "I can't say my mind is easy about it, but I suppose you'll need to try it sooner or later. Naomi says I've been acting like an old woman, keeping you hemmed up the past weeks, now that the reporters are mostly gone. You've not complained, but I know it's been hard on you."

"Staying out of sight was a small enough price for me to pay," Emma replied quietly.

Joseph shot her a look over Titus's rump. "You owe no debts here, Emma. I've said so every way I can think of, but I don't guess you'll believe me until you can believe it yourself." He stepped away from the buggy and nodded. "It's ready."

"All right. I'll be back out in a minute." Emma started toward the house.

"Emma." She turned to find her brother looking uneasy. "Be careful, *ja?* I don't think you'll come to any trouble. If I did, I'd go with you, work or no work. I know you'll want to visit with folks, but remember that Lydia Zook, nice as she is, does plenty of business with *Englischers*, including those reporters. She'll talk the hind legs off a donkey, that one. I'd be cautious about what I said to her because she'll be repeating it to everybody who comes in the store. Things are better now, but we don't want to draw attention. The truth is, I'd rest easier in my mind if you did your shopping quick and got on back home."

"Then that's what I'll do." When he continued looking at her, she added. "And I'll be sure to mind my tongue around Lydia. Anything else?"

"*Nee.*" He shook his head. "You just never used to be so easy to boss, that's all. I kind of miss arguing with you."

He sounded sad, so Emma made a face at him. "Naomi's right. You *are* acting like an old woman."

She waited until she was sure of his smile. Then she headed inside to change her dress.

Chapter Two

SAMUEL CHRISTNER HALTED WITH ONE BIG HAND on the doorknob of the hardware store. He squinted at the slim woman stowing a bundle of fabric into the box strapped to the back of Joseph Hochstedler's buggy, and his heart did an all-too-familiar flip.

Ja, sure enough, that was Emma. What was she doing in town all by herself?

He scanned the street, relieved to see it was clear of *Englischers*. That didn't mean it would stay that way. Like most sorts of trouble, the reporters came in waves. There'd be none for a few days, maybe a week or two. Then a fresh gaggle of the nuisances would appear, pestering folks, asking pushy questions, taking pictures.

That was one reason Sam had driven into Johns Mill to place orders and buy nails at the hardware store himself instead of sending one of the apprentices on the construction crew he supervised. He'd wanted to have a look-see, make sure everything in town was calm. Since the Hochstedler tragedy, he did that every once in a while. At six and a half feet, Sam was the tallest, broadest man in Johns Mill. Generally, when he placed himself in the middle of some disturbance, his sheer bulk was enough to settle the troublemakers down.

His faith prohibited him from settling them any other way, but lots of times *Englischers* didn't know that. Sam sure wasn't going to be the one to tell them.

Sam weighed the hefty bag of nails in his hand, wondering if Joseph knew where his sister was. Since she was driving his buggy, likely he did. That meant this was none of Sam's business, and he could get back to his crew. They were working on the expansion of the veterinary office just outside of town, and Sam was responsible for keeping the project on schedule.

He wasn't responsible for Emma, and she'd made herself plenty clear on that point, long before today.

On the other hand, Joseph Hochstedler was a *gut* friend and a decent fellow who'd had more than his share of sorrows. The last thing he needed right now was more trouble, and if any reporters noticed Emma alone on the street, they'd pounce like ducks on a grasshopper.

Sam waited to see if she'd head home, now that she'd got her shopping done. If she did, then he could get back to his work with a clear conscience.

But when, instead of climbing into the buggy, she left the parking area and headed purposefully up the street, he wasn't surprised. He'd known Emma since they were schoolmates together. For a time, they'd even been . . . maybe not sweethearts. He'd sure believed so at the time, but they'd been too young for that. They'd been real *freindlich*, though, for sure.

He'd cared a great deal about Emma in those days. Too much, his family said. Maybe they were right, because he couldn't remember a single time when she'd made his life easier. More interesting, *ja*. And for a time, sweeter. Never easier. Generally speaking, things went the opposite way where Emma was concerned.

Sam started across the street. He'd best see to her. If she stayed in town long, somebody would be bound to notice. She couldn't hide that face of hers, not even in the depths of her black bonnet. Men especially were always quick to take notice of Emma, and it caused all kinds of trouble when they did.

Nobody said it out loud, but everyone in the Johns Mill Amish community knew that if Emma Hochstedler had been less pleasing to look at, the *Englischers* would likely have lost interest by now. But instead, Emma's beauty was the kind that caught a man's eye and then worked its way into his heart like a splinter.

Sam trailed behind her now, keeping watch. She made it up the sidewalk with no trouble and ducked safely into Zook's store.

He halted outside and thought things over. The bulk grocery was owned by a Plain couple. It catered mostly to Amish needs, but plenty of local *Englischers* shopped there, too. Eben Zook would do his best to keep Emma from being bothered, of course, but the storekeeper was a slight, stoop-shouldered fellow. He usually worked in the storeroom anyhow, leaving his talkative wife, Lydia, to handle the customers.

Shading his eyes with his hand, Sam peered in the window, but it was no use. Emma had disappeared into the maze of high shelves stacked with spices, grains, and other pantry staples.

He shifted his boots on the sidewalk and considered his options. His widowed sister, Leah, could spend half a day in Zook's, seemed like. No telling how long this was going to take, and the morning was wearing on. He needed to get to his jobsite, but he didn't much like the idea of leaving

Emma in town un-seen-to. She might be all right in Zook's, but there was the walk back to the buggy yet.

Maybe if he went inside, he could hurry her up. Emma liked to keep her distance from him, and generally, the quickest way to get her out of any room was for him to walk into it. Decision made, he reached for the door handle.

He caught up with her in the spice aisle, standing on her tiptoes. She was straining for a plastic container of mustard seeds, high on the top shelf. She couldn't quite manage, so he reached over her head and retrieved them for her.

"Oh!" Emma dropped down flat on her feet and scooted sideways. She whirled to face him, and the fear on her face shifted into annoyance. "Sam, for mercy's sake. You nearly scared me to death coming out of nowhere like that! You should have spoken."

"Sorry. People usually hear me coming." He held out the little tub. "Here."

"*Denki.*" She accepted the spice politely enough, but she looked uncomfortable.

She wasn't the only one. The last time he'd been this close to Emma had been at Joseph's wedding, and that hadn't gone so well. She'd popped out on the Hochstedler porch just when a crew of reporters had arrived, and he'd hustled her back inside to keep her from being mobbed.

Emma hadn't much appreciated his attempt to protect her. In fact, as he recalled, she'd said some real sharp words.

Then again, in his hurry, he hadn't been very gentle. That was one of the problems that came alongside being so big-built. Sometimes he forgot just how strong he was.

"Anything else up top you need?" he asked her now. "I'll reach it down."

"*Nee.*" Emma fiddled with the items in the basket she'd looped over one arm. "I managed the rest all right. I don't know why Lydia puts the mustard seeds up so high anyhow.

It makes no sense. It's women who buy those, not great, tall men like yourself. In our store, we always made sure to—" She stopped short, and her face paled a few shades.

Sam knew why, of course, as would anybody else. Levonia and Elijah Hochstedler had been killed in their store only a few months after they'd opened it. As if that hadn't been bad enough, shortly afterward the family had been swarmed by pushy outsiders, all fascinated by a juicy story and a well-shaped female face.

Trouble had piled upon trouble for the Hochstedlers, certain sure, and all of the Johns Mill Plain community felt for them.

"Well, it is *gut* to see you, Samuel, but I'd best get on with my shopping," Emma was saying. "Naomi's waiting for me to come home with the vinegar and spices. We've got a lot of cucumbers ready for pickling."

He was glad to hear she wasn't planning to linger. The quicker she left town, the faster he could return to his own work. Before Emma could protest, Sam slipped the basket off her arm. "A jug of vinegar's heavy and clumsy to carry, and you left the buggy a fair bit off. I'll help you."

"Don't trouble yourself. I can manage." She tilted her head and frowned up at him. "And how do you know where I left the buggy?"

He ignored the question. "It'll be quicker if I carry your things."

She made an irritated noise. "Don't you have any business of your own to tend to?"

"*Ja*, plenty, but I can help you first." When she hesitated, he added, "The morning's getting on, Emma. More folks'll be coming into town soon, and no telling who you might bump into. No sense asking for trouble, ain't so?"

She glanced at the clock ticking on the store wall and bit her lip. "I took longer in Yoder's than I should have. I was having such a nice talk with Mary, and it's been so long since I've been able to shop by myself. I lost track of the time. Joseph will be worried, likely." She shook her head. "I should have paid better attention."

She sounded as if she was talking more to herself than to him. He felt sorry for her, but that didn't change anything. "We'd best move along, then. Didn't you say you needed vinegar? Pick out the kind you want, and I'll take everything to the counter."

Emma considered him through narrowed eyes for a second or two. Then she sighed. "All right. It'll be quicker than arguing with you, I suppose. Come on."

She wove down the aisles with the sureness women all seemed to show in stores like this, making a beeline for a section stocked with jugs in varying sizes. She reached for a gallon of the white vinegar, but Sam stepped forward and snagged it first. He couldn't fit his thick finger through the dainty glass loop at the top of the jug, so he snugged it against his side, keeping his hand free.

"That all you needed?" He waited for her nod, then he headed toward the checkout counter.

Middle-aged Lydia Zook stood behind the counter, swathed in an oversized storekeeper's apron, absorbed in transferring freshly ground wheat flour into plastic baggies. She glanced up and smiled as they approached.

"*Guder mariye!*" She dusted her floury hands on a towel, watching as Emma took the basket from Sam and unloaded her spices onto the wooden countertop. "You must have some pickles planned, *ja*, Emma? Such a nice year for the gardens! I can hardly keep these spices on the shelf." She lifted one eyebrow when Sam heaved the jug of vinegar up alongside the other things. "This is all together, then?"

When Emma nodded, Lydia's brown eyes darted between her two customers with sharp interest. "Well, that's something, ain't so? It's been a good many years since I saw the two of you so *freindlich.*"

Emma turned a rosy pink, and when Lydia's attention was on the register, Emma cut a narrow look at Sam. It was clear that remark had ruffled her feathers, and no doubt she'd have something to say about it once they were alone outside.

That was fine by him. He'd always appreciated Emma's straight way of talking, even if he did find himself on the sharp side of her tongue now and then. At least she'd let a fellow know right off when he'd stepped wrong, so much better than those girls who got their feelings hurt and then wouldn't say why so a man could try to avoid making the same mistake again. It was frustrating to bumble over and over again, with no clue as to what the rules were.

That was why he'd slacked up on courting—mostly—no matter what his sisters might think. He'd always been more comfortable working with his hands than with his brain, and he'd found women—apart from Emma—too hard to figure.

That sure hadn't changed. Ever since his sister Leah's husband had passed, and she'd moved in with Sam, he'd been floundering like a landed fish. His sister was grieving hard, and he was worried about her, but he wasn't sure how best to help. An idea occurred to him.

"Lydia?" Sam spoke up as Emma rummaged in her bag for money. "You wouldn't be looking to hire on any help this summer, would you?"

Lydia glanced up from her cash register and laughed. "You looking to give your hammer a rest and get back behind the counter, Sam? Any storekeeper in town would hire you in a minute. No worries about shoplifters with you about, for one thing. And you did a real *gut* job running the Hochstedlers' store during your stint of it, didn't he, Emma?"

Emma automatically glanced through the big window, where Hochstedler's General Store stood empty and silent just across the street. Her lips trembled, and she looked down and became very interested in smoothing out her cash. "From what I heard, *ja*, he sure did. We were very thankful for the help."

The pain on her face made Sam grit his teeth. Now, why did Lydia have to go bringing that up? Lots of the men had taken their turns behind the Hochstedlers' counter over the past months. They'd sold out the store's inventory for Joseph so that the family could stay away from all the publicity nonsense in town. The help had been necessary and appreciated, but it wasn't something to be talking about in front of Emma.

"No danger of me taking up storekeeping. I'd rather build things than stay cooped up indoors. I was thinking of Leah."

"Oh." Lydia's expression changed from teasing to sympathetic, as everybody's did whenever he mentioned his sister. It had been a sad surprise, her Milton getting sick like he had and dying so young. Folks felt bad for her. "Leah's looking for work? I thought I'd heard she was helping out your aunt after her hip surgery."

"*Ja*, she has been, but I think she's ready for a change."

"I wouldn't doubt that." Lydia chuckled. "I don't expect Ruth makes the easiest patient."

Sam didn't answer. Ruth could be a hard one to get along with sometimes, but she was family, and ever since her younger brother, his uncle Davey, had died last year, she'd lived alone. Davey had been born special, and Ruth, who'd never married, had cared for him faithfully all his life. Now that he was gone and Ruth was getting older, she was making plans to join her older brother Robert's family in Pennsylvania. Apart from some elderly cousins, Leah and Sam were the only family Ruth had left in Johns Mill, so until she moved, it was their job to see to her.

And a job it was. Lydia was only telling the truth. There

was nothing easy about his sharp-tongued *aent*. Leah had nearly reached her limits, and Sam was worried. If she could get a job here, maybe they could hire a local woman to help out with Ruth. Besides, working in a store like this might be *gut* for Leah. She'd been keeping to herself far too much since Milton died.

"So?" he nudged. "Are you hiring?"

"*Nee*." The storekeeper shook her head. "I'm sorry, Sam. We always hire *youngies* for the summertime anyhow 'cause they're willing to work an hour or two here and there. That's all we need." She handed Emma's change to her. "Remember that summer you helped us out, Emma? You must've been, what, sixteen, I'm thinking? Always a lot of fellows stopping by whenever you were behind this counter, boys we never saw hide nor hair of otherwise."

Sam frowned, noticing how Emma's cheeks flushed as she stowed her change in her bag.

"That was a long while ago," she murmured.

"*Ja*, true." Lydia cut Sam a sideways glance. "But it seems like some things haven't changed too much. I remember the first time I saw you two together, I told Eben—"

"*Denki*, Lydia," Emma cut in. "I'd best be getting home. Naomi's waiting."

The older woman nodded. "Of course. *Mach's gut*, Emma." Lydia twinkled another meaningful glance in his direction. "You too, Sam."

Sam nodded, scooping the canning supplies off the counter before Emma could beat him to it. Emma pressed her lips together, but she didn't fuss.

At least, not until they were outside and several steps down the sidewalk. Then she stopped and turned to face him.

"I wish you'd left me to do my shopping on my own, Sam." A dangerous spark showed in Emma's blue eyes, and her chest was rising and falling quickly. "You know what a talker Lydia Zook is. Just imagine what she's going to be telling people!"

"Lydia likes to tease, and she can be heavy-handed with it sometimes. But there's not so much for her to tell. I was just helping you."

"She'll make more out of it. You know she will. When have you ever seen a man helping a woman shop? No wonder she thought we were . . . friends," she finished finally.

He knew what she meant by the spin she put on the word. She didn't like her name being coupled up with his. Nothing new there, but it jabbed sharply enough that he couldn't resist jabbing back.

"You can't blame Lydia for that. She remembers when we used to be *friends*." He put the same twist on the word as she had.

Emma flushed. "That didn't mean anything. We were just children."

Maybe it hadn't meant anything to her. It had meant plenty to him at the time. Still did, according to his sisters. When the Christners made up their minds about something— or someone—they stuck with it.

He remembered the day he'd made up his mind about Emma. They'd been walking together from the school-house to Zook's for a soda. He'd been thirteen and in his last year of school, already bigger and stronger than all the other boys his age. She'd been barely twelve, her beauty just starting to bloom. They'd passed a group of *Englischers* on the sidewalk, and one of them, a full-grown man, had turned to watch Emma after she walked by.

She hadn't noticed. She'd kept chattering on about something that had happened at school. But Sam had noticed, and he hadn't liked the look on the man's face. Sam had drawn himself up and looked the fellow straight in the eye. The stranger had taken Sam's measure with one quick up-and-down gaze, then he'd ducked his head and turned away.

Relieved, Sam had looked down at Emma's rosy face, so innocent and trusting, and something had occurred to him. Next year he'd be working alongside his *onkel*, learning construction. He wouldn't be able to walk around with Emma so much anymore, and no other Plain boy was near big enough to shoo *Englisch* men away with just a look.

And Emma was only going to get prettier. It had worried him, that.

He'd interrupted her chatter. "We should get married, you and me, just as soon as we're old enough." He'd cast another look behind them, making sure the man had gone about his business. Assured that he had, Sam had turned back to Emma and nodded. "That'd be best, I think. I could look after you all the time, then."

"Oh!" She'd stared up at him, her mouth round with surprise.

He'd braced himself for an argument. Emma was never shy about telling him off, even back then.

Instead, to his surprise she'd blushed and stuttered, "*Ja*, Sam. All right."

He'd been man-sized for months by then, capable of doing a man's work and expected to do it, too. But he'd never really felt like a man, not until that moment, when little Emma Hochstedler had promised she'd be his wife, once they grew up.

Now, the childish memory stung at him, sharp as a wasp.

He glanced at Emma. Her cheeks had passed from pink to rose red. Standing in the summer sun with that high color in her face, she was a sight to behold. Sam figured himself to be more or less immune to Emma's looks now, but even he felt the jolt of her beauty deep in his belly.

That annoyed him a little.

"I'm sorry if I've caused trouble. I'm doing my best to stave it off. That face of yours draws it like sugar draws ants, and I figured your family's had more than their share just lately."

His words brought something new in Emma's expression. Hurt. She held out her hands. "Give me my things, Sam."

He was looking into her eyes, preparing to argue, when he saw her gaze slip to something behind him. Before he could turn around, he felt two small arms go around his knees in a tight hug.

"*Onkel!*" His four-year-old niece, Janie, looked up at him, her green eyes sparkling with fun. "I sneaked up on you!"

"You did a good job of it!" He caught sight of Leah walking toward him, and his stomach fell.

He hadn't seen his sister in a few days, and she didn't look good. After their aunt's hip surgery, Leah had volunteered to stay with Ruth and help out. Sam hadn't much liked the idea. Ruth had an ill temper even when she was healthy, and Leah was still grieving for her husband. Sam had spoken out against the plan, suggesting they talk to Ruth's brothers and see if some other arrangement could be made.

But Leah was a big one for doing her duty, and she'd felt she was the likeliest person for the job. Over the years, most of their relatives had relocated to other communities in order to find work. There was nobody else close by who'd be up to the task. Besides, Leah had pointed out, she'd cared for Milton during his short illness. She'd be the best suited to look after Ruth.

In the end, Sam had told her to do as she thought best. It would be for only a few weeks. Maybe, he'd told himself, it would even do Leah some good to get out, to have something new to focus on.

He'd been wrong about that. Instead, just as he'd feared, being in Ruth's household seemed to be setting Leah backward. She looked bone weary, and the unhappy lines around her mouth and eyes were as deep as they'd been right after Milton's death.

Of course, that might be partly because of who was standing beside him. Leah, like the rest of his sisters, had some silly notion that Emma had broken his heart years ago, and they'd been cool toward her ever since.

"Hello, Sam," Leah said as she neared them. Then a little more frostily, "Hello, Emma. *Vi is dei family am du?*"

Emma's answering smile was much warmer. "They are all well, *denki*. It's real *gut* to see you, Leah. I was sorry you weren't able to come to Joseph and Naomi's wedding."

"*Ja*, I was sorry, too, but Ruth was just out of the hospital and couldn't be left by herself. They make a sweet couple. How are they settling in?"

"*Recht gut*. It's a good match, and Naomi's making herself right at home. Miriam and I are real happy for them both."

There was a determined brightness in Emma's voice that made Sam shoot a narrow look at her.

"Please tell them I said hello." Leah turned to Sam, and her polite smile thawed into sisterly affection. "This is a real nice surprise, *bruder*, catching you in town. Once Janie saw you, nothing would do but she run over to say hello."

"I miss you, Sam." Janie pursed her lips into a pout. "I don't like living at Ruth's. I want to come stay with you again."

"It is a sin to complain, Janie," her mother admonished quickly.

"I miss you, too, Butterbean," Sam said. "But you'll be back home before too long, I expect. Where's Ruth now, Leah?"

If he hadn't been watching close, he might not have seen the telling little twitch on his sister's face when he mentioned their aunt. *Ja*, Ruth was wearing on Leah, certain sure.

"She's across the street at Dr. Lipscomb's. She said her hip pained her all last night, and she wanted to come in and talk to him about it. They're having to work her in, and you know how that goes—there's no telling how long it'll take."

"How is her recovery coming along?" Emma asked.

"The doctor's been real pleased with her progress, but Ruth—" Sam watched his sister search for a polite way to describe the situation. "Ruth likes to be the one in charge," she finished tactfully. "She's having a hard time being a patient."

"She says things that make *Mamm* cry, and she never likes anything we do. I think she's a very mean old lady," Janie announced.

"Janie!" Flicking a horrified glance at Emma, Leah scolded her daughter again. "*Shemm dich!* That is unkind. And very disrespectful."

Janie ducked her head, but Sam had to clear his throat to cover up a chuckle. He'd felt the exact same way about Ruth when he was a boy, and he'd only had to visit her on alternate Sundays. He'd secretly felt sorry for his *onkel* Davey, having to live with such a fussy woman. Davey had been sunny-natured, though, and he'd never seemed much bothered by his older sister's snippy ways.

"It's hard for some folks to be sick," Emma was saying. "And just as hard for the person looking after them, especially when you're grieving yourself."

Sam sucked in an uncertain breath at Emma's directness. Since his sister had moved in with him eight weeks ago, they hadn't spoken much about her fresh widowhood. He knew Leah cried some at night, even though she tried to be quiet about it. When a man had lived alone as long as Sam had, he picked up on new noises in the house. But Leah always put a brave face on in the morning, and she didn't seem to want to talk about it, so he'd just let it lie. He'd figured maybe it was like picking a scab—best to leave it be and let some healing happen before scratching at it too much.

But at Emma's remark, Leah looked surprised and nodded. "*Ja*, that's so. I do try not to be selfish in my own sorrow and to depend on *Gott* to help me be patient with Ruth, but some days are just . . ."

"Awful." Emma finished the sentence quietly. Sam frowned, recalling that Emma had spent time up in Ohio caring for her *kossin* Henry, who'd been disabled in an accident years ago, and that her own aunt and uncle weren't known for their pleasant natures. Small wonder she understood Leah's troubles so well.

"I'll be praying for you, Leah," Emma added. "And for Ruth, too."

"*Denki.*" Leah's face crumpled, and Sam's heart dipped, thinking she was about to cry. Instead she firmed up her mouth and looked down at her daughter. "We'd best be getting back, Janie. Ruth doesn't like to be left alone too long."

Janie cast a longing look at Sam. "I hope we get to come back to your house soon."

Poor little *kind*. He tweaked her nose. "I hope so, too. You and your *mamm* have been good company for a lonely *schliffel* like me. I've hardly known what to do since you left me."

Janie beamed, and even Leah smiled faintly. "You don't look like you're suffering too much." His sister's eyes cut to Emma and narrowed. "Not just at the moment anyhow. But never you mind. We'll be back causing you trouble as soon as Ruth's better."

"I'll be looking forward to that."

Leah took Janie by the hand and headed across the street. When they were safely out of earshot, Emma said, "It was kind of you, Sam, to take Leah and Janie in now Milton's gone."

"There's no special kindness in that. I was glad to do it.

She's my sister, and it's my job to look after her. There's nobody else, now that *Daed*'s passed and *Mamm*'s moved into the *dawdi haus* on Vera John's farm up in Kentucky. I wish Leah didn't have to go help Ruth just now," he added, "but there was nothing to it. She would go, no matter what I said about it."

Emma nodded. "A person needs to feel useful. Speaking of that"—she held out her arms—"you'd best give me my things so we can both get about our day's work."

Sam hesitated. At least Emma didn't seem mad anymore. "I can carry these to your buggy first."

"You've wasted enough time on me. You've your own business to see to." When he didn't hand her bags over, she frowned. "Oh, for pity's sake. Don't worry, I'm going straight home. I won't be *troubling* anybody else today."

He sighed. "I didn't say you troubled people, Emma. Only that trouble seemed drawn to you. That's different."

"Not so very." She wiggled her fingers until he gave in and put the bags into her arms. "*Denki.*"

"*Du bisht welcome. Mach's gut*, Emma." Sam stood there for a second, watching her walk away, then blinked and came to himself.

He'd no business standing here like a lazybones. Emma was right enough about one thing. He'd his own work to see to, and he'd best get out to the jobsite. His men were good workers, but like most, they slacked off when he wasn't about. Besides, they'd be needing—

The nails.

He'd tucked the sack of nails in the top of Emma's bag from Zook's.

He turned around, intending to call out to her, but in spite of her load, Emma was walking fast.

Clearly, she was thankful to be shed of him, and it would be no great inconvenience to buy another couple pounds of nails. He'd use them sooner or later, and he could pick up the ones he'd forgotten when he headed out to talk to Joseph. He'd been meaning to do that anyhow, to plan out the final renovations to the old dairy barn Joseph used for his woodworking.

Sam lingered another minute, watching Emma hurry along. She was nearly to the spot where she'd turn into the parking lot. Once she did, he wouldn't be able to see her, but likely that was all right. There were hardly any *Englischers* out and about today anyhow. At the moment, he saw only one, a harmless-looking elderly fellow, leaning heavily on a cane, limping up the sidewalk toward Emma.

Sam narrowed his eyes as the two neared each other. Not much harm was likely to come from a grandfather like that, but there was something about him that made Sam's skin prickle. He'd stuck his nose in so much trouble over the years that he'd gotten pretty good at seeing it brewing, and right now his instincts were telling him something wasn't right.

The old man seemed to be trying to catch Emma's eye. She had her head down, mindful of her bag from Zook's and the vinegar.

Pass her by, he urged silently. Once the man had moved safely on, Sam could go see about buying more nails.

He should have known better. Men were never able to pass Emma by.

Sam saw the fellow speak to her, saw Emma stop, as of course, she would, for an old man with a walking stick. Emma was nothing if not softhearted.

That was what got her into trouble, more often than not. A woman with such looks needed to be more careful than most, but that was something Emma had never been so good at.

Sam waited, tense as a hound on a scent, watching. The *Englischer* was talking fast, leaning forward. Emma's bonnet blocked her face, so Sam couldn't read her expression, but as it happened, he didn't need to.

Emma took a quick step backward, putting more space between herself and the elderly man. Something the fellow was saying had upset her. Sam started down the sidewalk.

When the vinegar bottle slipped from her grip and cracked into pieces on the sidewalk, he broke into a run.

CHAPTER THREE

❧

"I'M SO TERRIBLY SORRY." THE OLD MAN WHO'D IN-troduced himself as Ian McMillan appeared genuinely up-set. "I've made you drop your vinegar. Perhaps I shouldn't have spoken to you at all. It's just that I've been hoping to bump into you. We really need to talk."

"I have to be going." Emma repeated what she'd been saying ever since the elderly *Englischer* had stopped to speak.

She hadn't been worried at first. He'd looked harmless enough, a stooped fellow with a short white beard, in his sixties as best she could tell. He leaned on a polished wooden cane as he walked, limping hard on his right leg, and he wore wide, black-rimmed glasses.

When he'd given her his name, she knew she'd heard it before, but she'd not been able to place it. He'd seemed expectant, no doubt waiting for her to give her own name, which she'd no intention of doing.

But she'd seen no harm in him. She knew plenty of old

men like this, lonely fellows who liked to talk, and her up-
bringing had schooled her to be respectful of them. She'd
felt no alarm at all, and so it had taken her completely by
surprise when he'd told her that he was the screenwriter for
the movie being made about her parents' deaths.

The pungent odor of the vinegar wafted around them. It
had splashed over her dress and shoes, and his as well, but
he seemed unbothered. The owlish eyes behind the glasses
were focused intently on her face.

"You are lovely, my dear," he murmured. "Your photographs don't do you justice. I'm glad I've seen you in person
at last. It does help me understand why things happened the
way they did. Now, I should buy you another jug of vinegar." He gestured at the puddle and the chunks of broken
glass. "It was too bad of me, pouncing on you like that. No
wonder you were startled. I did try other means of getting
in touch, but your bishop has been most uncooperative. I
truly do need to speak to you if this script is to have any
sort of balance to it. We can meet at your convenience,
and—oh!"

The man broke off, his eyes widening.

Emma didn't bother to turn her head. This time she knew
who was coming up behind her. Nobody else in town
walked that heavily. And anyhow, she just *knew.* She knew
it was Sam, just as she knew that it was summer. Because it
was, and there was no mistaking it.

She felt a sense of guilty relief. Sam would make short
work of this strange situation. That was the thing about
Sam. He took care of problems.

"Emma." Sam spoke in English so the man would be
sure to understand. "You'd best go on to the buggy. You
need to be getting yourself home, ain't so?"

"*Ja,* I do." She sidestepped the puddle and edged around
the old man.

"My dear young lady." To her astonishment and horror, the *Englischer* reached out and grasped her wrist. "Please, may we start over? I would so very much like to speak to you and ask you a few questions."

Before she could blink, Sam had stepped between them. His solid body butted against the man's forearm and broke the writer's grip on her arm, although Sam himself never put a hand on the fellow.

Now Emma could see nothing but a pair of immense shoulders, but she could tell by the set of them that Sam meant business.

"Emma's going on her way now." Sam spoke softly, but there was no mistaking the certainty in his tone. "You're going to stand here with me and watch her leaving, and you'll not be touching her again. We don't consider that polite."

"I meant no harm! I've muddled this up terribly. I only wanted to speak to Miss Hochstedler, to interview her, actually. For the movie, you see. It's vital, I assure you, or I'd never have troubled her."

Emma leaned sideways to catch a glimpse of the man's face. He was looking up at Sam, his face papery pale.

"Maybe that's so," Sam observed impassively. "But what you've said changes nothing that I can see. We've no interest in your movies." He glanced in her direction. "Go ahead, Emma, and you can tell your brother I'll be following shortly."

Following? Her? "Oh, but, Sam—"

"I need to speak with him about that job he's wanting done," Sam cut in firmly. "I've been meaning to get out your way. Might as well do it now. I'll bring you along some more vinegar, too." He put a foot out and nudged a jagged piece of glass to one side. "This fellow here will help me get this mess cleared up. Then he'll come to the store with me, and we'll see about buying you another jug. And after that he's going straight home. Aren't you, then?" He directed that question to the *Englischer*.

The elderly man's mouth worked like a fish brought to land. He wasn't able to get any words out for a minute, but then he stammered, "I am so very sorry to have offended."

Overshadowed by Sam, Ian McMillan appeared shrunken, as if all his confidence had puddled on the sidewalk with her vinegar. The old man almost looked as if he was going to cry. He was no danger to anybody, and Emma felt silly to have been so startled.

Besides, Sam, she knew, had his own work to get back to. He shouldn't give up even more of his morning driving so far out of his way just to be sure she got home safe.

"Sam," she whispered. "*Es shatt nix.*"

"*Ja*, that's so," he agreed. "There's no harm done. Nor will there be. Go on, Emma. I'll be following along behind. Tell Joseph to expect me."

Emma wanted to argue, but the set of Sam's jaw promised her it would be a waste of her time. She swallowed and nodded.

"I will tell him." She darted one last look at Ian McMillan. He started to speak, but then he glanced at Sam's face and went quiet.

Stepping around the broken glass, Emma hurried toward the lot where she'd left the buggy. She stowed her purchases in the back and settled into the seat. Flicking the reins on Titus's back, she drove him onto the highway toward home.

Once safely out of town, she tried to relax, but this drive wasn't nearly so pleasant as the one coming in. The morning had turned blazing hot, and being inside the buggy felt like sitting in an oven. She'd not been on the road five minutes before she was sweating under her many layers of clothing. The odor of vinegar coming from her shoes had her wrinkling her nose, and one of the straight pins securing her dress had worked loose. It pricked her sharply whenever she moved.

Like the air inside the stuffy buggy, Emma's happy day had soured, and it seemed everything—and everybody—had taken a turn needling her.

Including Sam Christner.

Emma shifted her position gingerly and sighed. Everybody else in Johns Mill got along with Sam just fine—unless they were up to something they shouldn't be. But as much as she'd appreciated his help back there, nowadays Sam jabbed at Emma worse than any loosened pin ever could.

It hadn't always been that way. Things had changed about the time she turned fourteen, when she'd realized that all the boys were treating her different than they used to—all of them but Sam. He'd just acted the same way he always had.

That had comforted her and frustrated her in turns.

She could still remember the day the friction between them had come to its head. It had marked the last day of a friendship that had lasted all their growing-up years—a friendship that she'd figured—that everyone had figured—would keep blooming steadily into something more.

She'd faced Sam down after school, her hands fisted on her hips.

Sam, what did you say to Amos Mast? He won't even speak to me.

Nothing much. Only that we've got an understanding, you and me, so he's wasting his time bringing you treats.

For the first time, it had irked her a little, that matter-of-fact claim on her future.

It was only some butterscotch cookies! You've made a fuss over nothing.

Sam had shot her a surprised look. *It wasn't nothing to*

Amos, and I just didn't want him pestering you when there was no point to it. Didn't you know he'd gone sweet on you?

She *had* known that, with a certain secret sureness, but being called out by Sam for it had flustered her. To make matters stickier, some of the other scholars leaving school had caught wind of their argument and were lingering within listening distance. Emma had flushed, and she'd pitched her next comment a little louder.

You know, just because you were born bigger than most, that doesn't make it right for you to boss everybody around.

Sam had frowned. *And just because you were born prettier than most, that doesn't make it right for you*—He'd stopped himself short and gone on in a calmer voice. *Look, Emma, let's not fuss. You've promised to marry me when we grow up, ain't so? All I did was let Amos know how things stand between us, figuring I'd save you some trouble and him some hurt feelings. If you're wanting scotchies, I'll bring you some myself."*

He'd spoken quietly, but one of the girls standing closest by had snickered, making Emma's cheeks burn. Sam shouldn't talk about their childhood pact right out in front of everybody. Now she'd be teased for weeks.

Well, maybe I won't marry you after all, Sam, and you can just keep your cookies!

His eyes had widened, and for a second she'd seen something in them that had caught at her heart. Then he'd set his jaw and looked away.

Suit yourself.

And that had been the end of that.

Looking back, she knew the squabble had been more her fault than his. Of course, the whole idea of them getting married had been silly to start with, and it would have been put aside sooner or later. But still, ever since that day, she'd felt . . . uncomfortable around Sam. Not because he'd been unkind. He'd gone right on being nice to her, but they'd never really been *freindlich* again.

A horn blared, and a white pickup whooshed past the buggy in a rush of hot air. Startled out of her memories, Emma jumped, wincing as the stray pin stabbed at her stomach. She tightened her fingers on the reins, but she needn't have worried. Titus barely flinched. He didn't like *Englischers* much, but he was used to their vehicles.

Emma brought her mind back to the present. As the Bible warned, she'd plenty trouble enough to deal with in the here and now without dipping back into the past for extra helpings.

When she got back to the farm, she turned the buggy into the drive, intending to take it to the barn. Instead when she passed the house, she reined up short just outside the kitchen door, her eyes widening with surprise.

Miriam was sitting outside—*outside*—on the back steps, rinsing cucumbers in a metal washtub. She glanced up as the buggy rolled to a stop. Her face was pale as milk, but she managed a wobbly smile when she saw Emma looking.

"Miriam!" Emma waved. "Good for you! Hang on a minute, and I'll come help."

"Emma!" Naomi was walking up from the garden. She carried the egg basket looped over one forearm, heaped with cucumbers. "Let me just hand these over to Miriam for washing, and I'll help you unhitch. Joseph had to walk down to the phone shack."

Her sister-in-law hurried toward the steps. Just as she reached Miriam, the handle on the basket broke completely away, and the cucumbers tumbled around Miriam's feet.

"Oh, my!" Naomi exclaimed. "I knew I was stuffing this old basket too full, but there were so many cucumbers, and I hated to make another trip. Well, this is what I get for being lazy. I'm sorry, Miriam. I've made a bigger job for you, haven't I?"

"*Sell is awreit*, Naomi," the younger girl murmured, but she looked nervously at the cukes that had rolled down the steps into the yard. The idea of venturing away from the house to gather the spilled vegetables was obviously more than Miriam felt capable of. Her mouth started to tremble.

Emma set the brake. "I'll help—" she started, but Naomi cut her off.

"We'd best get Titus unhitched. Joseph doesn't like for him to stand in harness. I'll come help you, and then we'll carry the groceries into the house."

Emma felt a flash of annoyance at Naomi's bossiness, but she squashed it down.

Family harmony depended on everybody cooperating— and giving in with good grace when called for. The church taught that, and Emma had seen that truth played out in her own family and others many times.

That didn't mean it was always easy.

She cast one last, worried look at Miriam. Then she drove the horse into the barn and began the routine of un- fastening the harness. When Naomi came in, Emma spoke without looking up from the buckle she was working loose.

"It won't take me long to unhitch. If you want to go ahead and carry the spices and things into the house, I'll follow along in a few minutes."

"*Ich binn sorry*, Emma." Naomi approached and laid a gentle hand on Emma's arm. "Please forgive me for speak- ing sharp. It's just . . . Miriam was doing so wonderful *gut*. After you left, I was able to coax her out onto the back stoop, and I really wanted to see if maybe she could step down into the yard to gather up those cucumbers on her own."

"Ah." Realization dawned as Emma looked into her

sister-in-law's worried eyes. "And I was about to ruin everything by doing it for her."

Naomi made a soft noise of protest, but Emma knew she was right. It was no accident that Miriam had taken such a big step forward while Emma was away. "You were speaking the truth this morning. I really am making Miriam worse." She frowned. "Was that why you came up with the idea of me going to town by myself today? Because you knew you had a better chance of getting her outside if I wasn't here to interfere?"

Naomi was too kindhearted to agree. "You mean only good, Emma. You love your sister, and helping people comes naturally to you. It's not that I am right, and you are wrong. It's only that because I am one step removed from it all that I can see things a little more clearly, maybe." She patted Emma's arm before turning her attention to the leather straps in front of her. "The important thing is, Miriam is having a good day today. We'll both be happy for that." She sniffed and wrinkled her nose. "Do you smell vinegar? I think maybe it's spilled in the buggy."

"*Ja*, it spilled, all right, but not in the buggy. It's all over me. I dropped the jug on the sidewalk when I was walking back from Zook's."

She braced herself for questions, but Naomi only made a sympathetic noise. "Well, that's a pity, ain't so? But these things happen, and vinegar's cheap to buy."

"That's true," Emma agreed with some relief.

Together the women finished tending to the horse before unloading Emma's purchases. Naomi poked through the bag from Zook's as Emma removed the quilt material from the box strapped to the rear of the buggy.

"Emma?" Naomi held out a crumpled brown sack. "Did Joseph ask you to get these nails?"

"*Nee*. I didn't buy those." Emma frowned for a second

before realization hit. "They'll belong to Sam Christner, likely. He helped me carry my things."

"Did he now?" Naomi spoke lightly, but something in her tone made Emma glance at her. "That was kind of him."

Emma forced a laugh. "Maybe not kind so much as bossy. You know how Sam can be. Anyhow, he probably set that bag in mine for easy carrying and then forgot about it. It's all right. He said he was heading out this way anyhow, to speak to Joseph about a job?" She lifted her voice carefully at the end. Part of her had wondered if Sam had been stretching the truth a bit, for Ian McMillan's benefit. Maybe he wasn't actually planning to drive out at all.

She sort of hoped he wasn't. It had been such an unsettling day already, and being around Sam always rattled her nerves.

But Naomi was nodding. "There are some changes Joseph wants to make to his woodshop."

"I thought all that work was done already." Converting the old dairy into a woodworking shop had been the focus of many weeks of work. Sam hadn't been able to help with that—his crew had been committed to another job.

"It mostly is, but you know how that goes. You think everything is finished, but then something doesn't work as well as it should, or you see an improvement you'd like to make. There are only a few things left to do, but he'd spoken to Sam about tending to them. Joseph figured it was a *gut* time to ask, since Sam will be looking for side jobs now that Leah and Janie are with him. He figured maybe they can work out an arrangement that will suit them both."

Emma hadn't thought about that. Of course Sam would have extra expenses now that his sister and her daughter were depending on him for support. Milton and Leah's house had been sold to pay for the doctor bills, but from what Emma gathered, there were still some debts outstanding.

She remembered how pinched and tired Leah had looked in town, a far cry from the lighthearted girl she'd been before her marriage. Emma had never been close friends with Sam's sister, but she felt deeply for the other woman. Being widowed so young was a heavy sorrow.

"Well, he's coming along this afternoon to talk about it, so I hope Joseph gets back from the phone shack quick. Oh! And he saw me drop the vinegar and said he'd bring along another jug."

Naomi raised an eyebrow. "Did he?" There it was again, that strange, thoughtful note in her voice. "Sam was a *gut-maynich* fellow today for sure."

"*Ja*, he was very kind." Emma averted her eyes. She should tell Naomi the whole of what had happened in town. She wasn't sure exactly how to go about it, though, and it was sure to upset everybody.

Carrying the purchases, Naomi and Emma walked across the yard toward Miriam. She had managed to collect all but the very farthest cucumbers, Emma noticed. Would Miriam have done so well if her older sister had been hovering over her?

Likely not.

She heard a noise and looked to see Sam turning into the drive.

Emma's gaze flicked to Miriam, who'd frozen, one hand clutching a cucumber, ready to bolt back into the kitchen. But after only a second, she relaxed and went back to her scrubbing. That was Sam, and he didn't frighten her.

Everybody knew Sam's buggy at a glance. It was taller and broader than most others—much like he was himself. An old Percheron named Dobs pulled it, a much larger horse than was usually used with carriages. Sam and his uncle had relied on Dobs for years to pull heavy wagons full of construction supplies. When the horse had grown too old for such work, Sam had switched him to the buggy.

At first, a few folks had made fun, joking that Sam needed such an oversized horse to haul him about, big as he was. Sam had only shrugged and said he'd no mind to waste such a well-trained animal.

Since Sam himself had done the hard work of training half the horses in Johns Mill, people accepted his explanation easily enough, but Emma suspected there was more to it than that. Sam was more softhearted than most folks knew.

"I'm glad he's come on so quick. It gets us out of a pickle for sure." Naomi laughed at the accidental play on words. "Or back into a pickle, I should say. I didn't like to say before, but I was careless, and I let the vinegar get low. We didn't have enough left to do even one batch of bread and butters without a fresh jug."

Emma noticed Joseph walking across the fields on his way back from the phone shed. He tossed up a hand at Sam, who waved back. Her brother altered his course, heading in Sam's direction.

Emma's heart fell. Of course Sam would tell Joseph what had happened in town. Not only would that worry her brother, but Naomi would wonder why Emma hadn't mentioned it straight off when she was explaining about the vinegar.

"There was something in town," she admitted hurriedly. "It wasn't much of anything, really, but I expect Sam's going to make a fuss about it, so I'd better tell you. A man grabbed my arm on the sidewalk." Emma swallowed, her eyes fixed on Sam's buggy as he slowed to a stop and set the brake. "It was that Ian McMillan, the *Englischer* who's writing the movie about what happened to *Mamm* and *Daed*. I don't think he meant any real harm, but he startled me for a minute, and that's why I dropped the vinegar. Sam came over and ran him off, and—"

A clanging noise interrupted her, and belatedly, Emma

glanced toward the steps. She'd been so intent on Sam and Joseph that she'd forgotten about Miriam, sitting well within earshot.

Her sister had risen to her feet, knocking the big pan of clean cucumbers on its side. Her breathing was coming too quick, and her face had the startled, pinched look that always came just before one of her attacks.

Naomi made a concerned noise and hurried up the steps. She murmured comfortingly to the younger woman in *Deutsch*, but Miriam's gasps only got louder. Emma started toward them, but Naomi put up a hand, motioning for her not to approach.

"Everything's all right now, Miriam. Emma's home safe, and Sam's even come along, too, making sure of it. See? There he is."

Miriam's eyes darted over Emma's shoulder. Following her younger sister's gaze, she half turned to see Sam watching them from the buggy seat. He set the reins, then jumped down in one easy movement. He straightened and stretched, bulky muscles moving under the fabric of his coat. His gaze slid from Emma to Miriam, and he nodded.

That one nod was all it took. Right away Miriam's breathing grew a little slower. Sam was the strongest man they knew, stronger than Joseph and Caleb, even. He tolerated little nonsense from *Englischers* or anybody else, and he was here with them now. On their side, like always.

Miriam swallowed and blinked, always a good sign. When she was truly panicking, her eyes were wide open and fixed. Her gaze slipped upward to Naomi's face.

"I think I'd like to go inside now."

"Of course." Naomi spoke brightly, as if everything were perfectly normal. "We'll need to get started on the pickles soon anyway. Emma, will you bring in the cucumbers when you've got them rinsed off?"

Emma swallowed. "*Ja*, I will."

She watched as Naomi and Miriam walked into the house, her sister clinging to Naomi's arm. Then she crouched to gather the cucumbers. Bits of wet grass clung to them, but a quick rinse at the outside pump would fix them up.

She also picked up the old egg basket from the ground, although it was plainly beyond repair. For just a second, she wrapped her fingers around the handle, willing it one last time to take her back to the past. But the handle had split, and it pinched. So she set it gently inside the broken basket, to be thrown out.

CHAPTER FOUR

❧

INSIDE JOSEPH'S WOODWORKING SHOP, SAM LISTENED as his friend described what needed doing to complete the conversion of the old Hochstedler dairy. Sam hadn't brought paper or pencil with him. He didn't usually write anything down. He'd only misplace the notes, most likely, so best to focus and remember.

He ran a finger down the side of a doorframe. It had been put in straight and true, and although he'd looked around the shop closely for signs of slipshod work, he'd seen none.

"The men you had in did *gut* work for you, Joseph, work that will stand up fine. I wonder that you don't just have them back to finish it off. You can, if you'd rather. I'll take no offense to it."

He figured that at least some of this offer was kindness. Joseph knew, like all the rest of the community, that Sam had taken on Leah and Janie's care, along with what part of Milton's medical bills the community hadn't already cov-

ered. Folks had been throwing him jobs like this here and
there, work that he could do in the evenings after his regular job was finished for the day.

It was kind of them, and Sam understood their thinking
and appreciated it. He'd have done the same himself if any
of them had been put in a similar situation. Still, Sam recognized quality work when he saw it, and the construction
crew Joseph had hired had served him well. It was only fair
that they should get any additional work, too, at least the
way Sam reasoned it.

Joseph looked uncomfortable. "*Ja*, I thought they did all
right, but I didn't much like using them, Sam. I'd rather
have had you to start with. It was just that your schedule
was full up at the time we needed the job done."

Sam shrugged. "I know that. A man has to get his work
done as he can, and you were taking on a wife. You needed
your livelihood up and running. But I wouldn't feel right if
I didn't tell you straight out that they did solid work here,
and you'd not go wrong if you wanted to have them back to
finish the job."

"I'm glad to hear it, but I'd rather have you, if you've the
time. Truth is, it made Miriam uncomfortable to have them
here. There were several *Englischers* on the crew. They
seemed nice enough men, and they gave no trouble, but you
know how she feels about that."

He did. Poor *maidel*. "Then I'll see to it myself, and I
thank you for the work."

"Once you get it figured up, let me know how much the
materials will be, and I'll pay you for that part up front. I
know you'll have to fit this job in as you can, and I don't
want you waiting on your money. *Denki*, Sam, for coming
out so soon. I wasn't expecting you to take time out of your
workday. I figured you'd come out of an evening."

That's what Sam had figured, too. He hesitated, wondering if he should let Emma have the telling of what had

happened in town. But no, being as how he'd had to step in, it would be less than honest not to tell Joseph about it. So he did.

Joseph kept his eyes on his boots as he listened, but Sam knew from his friend's tense stance that he was paying close attention. When Sam had finished, Joseph blew out a long, weary breath.

"I figured we might have some trouble from that fellow. I've had no dealings with him myself, not in person anyhow. He tried to rent this farm, you know, when we were planning to move to Ohio. He wasn't too happy about it when I found out who he was and put a stop to it. I had to ask a lawyer to speak to him before he gave up the idea." Joseph's expression told plainly what he'd thought of being pushed to that extreme. "I think this Ian has a muleheaded streak."

"Might be so," Sam agreed, remembering how the man had taken Emma's arm. "He backed down easy enough once I spoke to him, so that's something."

Joseph nodded slowly. "It seems awful strange to me that he just happens across Emma the first time she goes to town alone. I know he's been out to see Isaac, hoping, I guess, that our bishop might have some sway in getting her to speak with him."

Sam laughed. "He doesn't know Isaac so well, then. Isaac's a soft-spoken man but he doesn't push so easy."

"*Ja*, from what Isaac told me, this Ian fellow left their meeting disappointed. Isaac hoped that would be the end of it, but I wasn't so sure. It bothers me a bit, him meeting up with Emma, but likely it was just a coincidence. I can't think how he would've known she was going to town. We didn't know ourselves she was going until this morning. It was a mercy you happened to be in town yourself and saw what was happening."

"*Ja*, I figured it'd be best if I followed her out here so

he'd know she wouldn't be alone. He was mighty excited to talk to her, and even though I did my best to discourage him, I wasn't any too sure that he'd leave it lie."

Joseph clapped him briefly on the shoulder. "We're never any of us alone when you're close by, Sam. You're a great help, and I'm thankful to *Gott* for that, and to you yourself. You've been a good *freind* to this family, and I'll not soon forget it."

Sam shrugged, uncomfortable with the gratitude. There was no need for it. "*Du bisht welcome*," he said. "You've been a friend to me in times past, too, so you owe me no debt." He paused, but then he figured he'd already meddled in this family's business a good deal today. He might as well finish the job off. "I'd not send Emma to town alone anymore, though, Joseph. Not for a while. I ain't always there."

"*Nee.*" Joseph sighed. "I'd thought of that already. She was that happy about getting to go, too. It's a shame. It's hard on her being cooped up here at home. I think it's wearing on her. She doesn't seem the same. Of course, none of us are." Joseph seemed to be struggling to find the right words. "But Emma's change runs deeper. She's lost her spirit, seems to me. She's quieter, she hasn't got so much fire to her as she used to have."

"Didn't seem so quiet to me," Sam observed ruefully. "She gave me what for, just about the same as always."

Joseph smiled. "Going to town must have done her some good then. I figured it was the time she'd spent with Melvin. He's enough to squash anybody's spirits. I thought she'd perk up, but she seems worse the longer she's home." Joseph hesitated. "I forget sometimes how it must feel to her, being back home. She left the day after the funerals, you know, going to Ohio with Melvin, and only came back in time for the wedding. I had my time here to . . . get used to things without *Mamm* and *Daed* and with Miriam not being well. Of course, I had Naomi to ease all that for me." At the mention of his wife's name, Joseph's face brightened. "Emma's still getting used to it, I think, the way things are different here. It's a slow pain, that, and it takes its time."

Sam couldn't think of anything useful to say, so he said nothing. The idea of Emma hurting like that troubled him, the same way Leah's grief did. He didn't like seeing women suffer. It made him want to fix things.

But, of course, in this case, there was nothing anybody could do. Sometimes, as Joseph pointed out, pain just had to take its time.

After making arrangements to start work on the woodshop the following afternoon, Sam left Joseph starting up his lathe. He'd climbed into his buggy, picked up the reins, and was just about to cluck to Dobs when he noticed the jug of vinegar resting on the floor.

He'd near about forgotten that. He picked it up, climbed back down, and headed for the house.

He didn't think of knocking on the back door. He never had done, and the family already knew he was there. In any case, it wasn't like he was a quiet man. Like he'd told Emma back at the store, people generally heard him coming. But when he approached the kitchen door, set ajar to get what breeze might blow in from the yard on this stuffy day, Emma didn't seem to realize he was there.

He halted in the doorway. She was alone in the kitchen and half turned from him, standing at the table, the cucumbers set in front of her in rows. She was slicing them into rings, one at the time, and tossing them into a stock pot at her elbow.

That was nothing unusual, but Sam could tell right off that she was upset. It was in the rigid set of her narrow shoulders, and the way she moved—quick and hard. As he watched, she scooped a handful of rings from her cutting board and chucked them at the pot. A couple of them missed and rolled onto the floor, and Emma muttered something he couldn't quite hear, then brought her hands up to her face.

It took Sam a minute to realize what was happening because there was no noise. But then her shoulders shook, and when she sucked in a shuddering breath, he knew that she was crying.

He came into the kitchen then, striding toward the table. When he got there, he was brought up short, unsure what to do next. Emma looked up at him through her fingers, startled, her sky-blue eyes red-rimmed and wet with tears. She sniffed hard and wiped hastily at her cheeks with the dishtowel she'd flung over one shoulder.

"Emma." He spoke her name warily. He had sisters aplenty—Leah was one of five girls, all married now, and he'd learned that crying girls were unpredictable. He couldn't count the times he'd butted in on one, only later to wish he'd had the sense to keep his distance.

He'd never been much good at that. There was something about seeing a woman with tears in her eyes that stirred him up inside. He'd do most anything to make them stop. His sisters had figured that out early. If they wanted Sam to do anything, a few tears would get the job done quicker than most anything else.

Emma, though . . . Emma had never been a crier. That made her tears all the more bothersome. Things must be awful hard for her to be brought to this.

Now she swallowed hard, avoiding his gaze. "Onions," she explained, gesturing toward the four white globes that sat peeled but uncut on the side of her cutting board.

Sam set the vinegar on the table with a thump.

"*Nee*," he said. "It isn't onions, Emma. What's wrong? If it's about that fellow back in town bothering you, don't worry over him. He—"

"It's not that." Emma leaned over and retrieved the cu-

cumber rings that had fallen to the floor. She tossed them
into her scrap bowl and went to wash her hands. She glanced
at the vinegar jug. "Did you make him pay for that?"

"I didn't have to make him. He was only too happy to
replace it for you. Kept apologizing the whole time. Lydia
Zook was about to die of curiosity to know what happened." He grinned at the memory.

Emma made an irritated face. "It's not so funny. There's
no telling what a story she'll make of it, and that's the last
thing I need, ain't so? I'm tired of being talked about. It
would have been better if you hadn't dragged him back to
the store. You should have just let him go on his way."

"You're angry with me over this?" Fine with him if she
was, especially after what Joseph had told him. He'd a whole
lot rather have Emma spitting mad than crying. This Emma
he could deal with. "Well, next time some *Englischer* comes
up and grabs you by the arm, maybe I'll just leave you to sort
things out for yourself, then."

He wouldn't, of course. But it wouldn't hurt her to
think so.

"Oh, I know you mean well, Sam, but you're heavy-
handed sometimes, and it just makes things worse than
they already are. Anyhow, it doesn't matter. I'll likely not
be going to town anymore after today. I'm sure you told
Joseph about what happened."

"I did. I'm sorry, but I wouldn't feel right about keeping
such a secret from your brother."

"It's not a matter of keeping secrets!" Emma argued
sharply. "It'll *worry* him, Sam. It worries them when things
like this happen—all of them. Joseph, Miriam, and Naomi.
I don't like being a bother, and lately that's all I seem to be.
There seems to be no end to the grief I can bring on this
family. Do you know where Naomi is right now? She's upstairs with Miriam because it upset her to hear that I had
some trouble in town. And I can't even go upstairs and

comfort her because—" Emma's voice broke, and Sam watched her fight to finish her sentence. "Because I make her *worse*, Sam. I came home to help my sister get well, and instead all I'm doing is making her worse!"

Emma slammed the knife down flat on the cutting board, so hard that Sam jumped. And then she buried her face back in her hands and sobbed.

"*Ach*, now," Sam said helplessly, shifting his weight from one boot to the other. "Everything will come right, Emma, sure enough." He wasn't sure what he was supposed to do, but he couldn't stand by and do nothing, so he reached out and put one large hand gently on her back.

He'd meant only to comfort her, to reassure her somehow, the way he would soothe a horse, with a touch. But to his astonishment, she turned and buried her face against his chest.

He froze, stunned.

Joseph was right. Something was wrong, because Emma didn't fall apart like this. That was something he'd always liked about her—that she had more spunk than most other girls. She was softhearted, true, but there was a steely strength behind her sweetness. If you pushed her too far, she'd pop back at you like a string of barbed wire that had been stretched too tight.

In fact, back in their schooldays, he'd goaded her on purpose more than once, just to see her snap at him, her eyes spitting blue sparks. That was a sight to behold.

Now that same girl was crying against his chest—he could feel the warm wet of her tears seeping through his shirt.

"It's all right," he repeated desperately.

"It's not all right." She shook her head against him, her voice tight with tears and frustration. "Everything has gone wrong, and I want to fix it, but *Ich kann naett!*"

Oh, *ja*, he understood that—the desire to help, to make

things right—and the frustration when, instead of helping, all you did was muddle things up more. How many times had people looked at him with exasperation? *Mind yourself, Sam*, they'd say. *You don't know your own strength.*

He patted her back awkwardly. "*Ich helf dich*," he assured her firmly. He closed his fingers around her forearms, mindful to be gentle, and pulled her a little away so he could look into her face. "I will help you, Emma," he repeated.

"There's nothing you can do, Sam." She snuffled a sad laugh and used her sleeve to blot her wet cheeks. "Nobody can help me. I can't even help myself. I'm sorry. I don't mean to be such a baby."

She stepped back, away from him. As strange as it had felt to have her in his arms, it felt strange again to have her out of them. His heart swirled crazily, like a leaf dropped into the current of a rushing stream.

"It might have been better for me to stay up in Ohio," Emma was saying. She cleared her throat and picked the knife up again. "At Melvin and Nella's, helping look after Henry. But their daughter moved back close, and they don't need me anymore."

Sam frowned. He'd met Melvin, and Emma's *onkel* was the sort of fellow folks crossed state lines to get farther from, not nearer to. "Were you happy there?"

Emma started back slicing the cucumbers. "What difference does that make? I was useful in Ohio, and that's more than I've managed to be here." She glanced toward the stairs leading up to the bedrooms. "I'm good at looking after sick folks, generally. I thought I could be a help to Miriam, but she does better when I'm not even in the house. Naomi thinks it's because I'm too close to her, that I step in too soon. I suppose that's true. I just can't stand to see my sister suffering."

"I know how that is. I'm worried about Leah, too. Our

aunt, the one Leah's been looking after, is a lot like your uncle." Sam struggled to find a way to tell the truth without being disloyal. "Ruth's always had a sharp tongue, but she's been harder to deal with than ever since my *onkel* Davey died."

Emma paused in her slicing and considered him. "Leah did look worn out, didn't she? It must be hard on her, looking after your aunt when her grief for Milton is so fresh."

"I told her we ought to hire a helper." He didn't want Emma to think that he didn't care about his sister's well-being. "Leah worried about the cost of it. And she didn't believe any of the young girls around here would be up to the job because Ruth is . . . particular . . . even when she's not getting over an operation."

"Particular." Emma twisted her mouth into a half smile. "You needn't mind your words around me, Sam. I've known Ruth all my life, and she's sharpened her tongue on my hide more than once. I understand how she is, but she doesn't bother me." Emma stopped and lifted her eyebrows.

"That's right." She spoke thoughtfully, staring into space. "Ruth doesn't bother me nearly so much as she'd bother somebody else. I'm used to cantankerous folks, goodness knows." Her eyes darted up to Sam's, sparkling now with excitement. "And I'm a good nurse, truly I am, Sam. I would do it for nothing, too, you wouldn't even have to pay me."

"Emma." Sam was already shaking his head. "I don't think—"

"But it would work!" Emma's face was lighting up. "I could live with her, couldn't I? Temporary like, until she's a good bit better? And Leah could go home with you and Janie. It's the perfect solution for everybody!"

Once, years ago, Sam had stepped out in an *Englischer*'s attic to take a measurement, and halfway across he'd felt the beam under his boots crack and sag. He'd stood frozen, uncertain about which direction to move, afraid that the wrong decision would send him plummeting through his customer's living room ceiling.

He felt much the same way now with Emma, unsure of which way to go, his nerves humming like angry bees.

"I'd have to talk to Leah."

"She'll agree if you want her to," Emma said immediately. "And she won't, if she has any feeling that you're against the idea. Ruth won't be happy no matter what you do, so that's no matter. So really, it's up to you, ain't so? Think, Sam, what a relief a break like that would be to Leah. And living with Ruth can't be pleasant for Janie, either, I wouldn't think."

Nee, it wasn't pleasant. Janie hadn't seemed her usual sunshiny self since she and her *mamm* had moved to Ruth's. And Emma was right. Leah needed a break from their aunt. He hadn't liked the look of his sister's face today. He'd already been worried that she'd grieve herself sick over Milton's death, and the stress of caring for Ruth had only made things worse.

He glanced up to find Emma watching him. He recognized the tense, hopeful expression on her face—he had too many sisters not to. She was working him, the same way he'd work a stubborn horse. Gently nudging, trying to get him to give in to what she wanted.

Well, he'd give her credit—she was a dab hand at it. *Schmaert* of her to bring Janie up, especially. Much as he wanted to help his sister, Leah was a grown woman and entitled to make decisions for herself. But Janie was only little, and now that her *daed* was gone, Sam had privately made up his mind that he'd look after the *maidel*, best he could.

"All right," he decided. "I'll speak to Leah. You can take over with Ruth for a couple weeks anyhow." By then, Emma would probably be more than willing to head back home.

"If you're certain, I can give you a ride over tomorrow evening. I was coming by to do a little prep work on your brother's woodshop."

Emma smiled, some of the lines smoothing off her brow. "Good!" she said firmly. "I'll speak to Joseph and Naomi and get a few things packed up. I'll be ready."

"I'll see you tomorrow then."

Sam left the house, squinting up at the sun as he crossed the yard to his buggy. The workday had nearly gotten by him. His men would be irritated and likely loafing by now. The project was already running behind, and today's delay wasn't going to help.

Sam didn't like to miss deadlines, and he almost never did. But still, the damage done to his schedule weighed less heavily on his mind than the prospect of sticking Emma with his *aent*. Emma might be pleased enough right now that she'd gotten her way. Sam didn't think she'd be near so pleased by the end of it.

He turned the worrisome situation over and over in his mind as Dobs plodded back toward town. It wasn't until he passed the Johns Mill city limits sign that he realized he'd forgotten his bag of nails again.

CHAPTER FIVE

❧

THE NEXT EVENING AFTER SUPPER, SAM BROUGHT
over a load of material and spent an hour's time working in
the woodshop. When he was done, he walked up to the
house, ready to drive Emma over to his aunt's. Emma didn't
want to keep him waiting, and she hurried as best she
could, but there seemed to be a hundred last-minute things
to see about.

By the time she made it to the back door, he'd been
standing beside his buggy for a good ten minutes. To her
relief, he didn't look annoyed.

He was murmuring to Dobs, and the horse's massive
head was bent over his owner's hand, slobbering over some
small treat. A sugar cube, most likely. Sam had always been
fond of his horses, and he usually had sugar or a bit of car-
rot tucked away.

He glanced up when the screen door slapped shut behind her. "You're ready, then?"

"*Ja*. I'm sorry I was so slow."

"No hurry. Whatever time we arrive at Ruth's will be soon enough." He shot her a meaningful glance. "Too soon, maybe. Here, I'll take that for you."

Sam took her suitcase and heaved it into the back of the wide buggy. Then he turned back to offer her a steadying hand so she could boost herself more easily into the seat.

Surprised, Emma hesitated a second before placing her fingers in his calloused palm. Mostly, Plain women managed such everyday things as climbing into buggies on their own.

Sam wasn't the first fellow to offer her such help, though. Her *daed* had been a gentle and considerate man, and he'd trained his sons to look to their *mamm* and to their sisters. And of course, there were the fellows who'd liked finding an excuse to touch her. They'd offered courtesies like this because she'd not have allowed it otherwise.

Sam was only being practical. These seats were set higher than most, and likely he was used to giving women a boost into them. As she settled into her place and smoothed her dress, Emma found herself wondering how many times Samuel Christner had helped girls into this oversized buggy of his. He'd never come much to the singings, not after the first few, and he was still unmarried, so maybe not so many.

"*Denki*," she murmured.

Sam nodded shortly. As he rounded the buggy, he gave Dobs a quick stroke on the nose, then he climbed into the buggy and dropped heavily onto the bench seat. The springs squawked and sagged, causing Emma to bob up and down on her end like a cork on a fishing line. She gasped and scrabbled to grip the side of the buggy and steady herself.

"Sorry." Sam's cheeks turned the shade of a brick. "I forget sometimes what happens when I move around too much. I've been meaning to take these springs out and put in a regular fixed seat. Last time Leah rode with me, she made me stop the buggy so she could get in the back with Janie. She said I made her seasick, shifting around so."

"That's all right," Emma said quickly. "You'll hear no complaints from me. I'm too thankful for the ride and for the chance to work for your aunt."

"We'll see how thankful you're feeling in a week's time." After looking to be sure she was well settled, Sam flicked the reins lightly against Dobs's back. It seemed more a gentle suggestion than a command, but the massive horse moved forward, pulling the big buggy as if it were no heavier than a pony cart.

"I'm not worried," Emma assured him. She wasn't, no matter how many gloomy hints Sam dropped. She'd dealt with ill-tempered people before—Melvin, her uncle in Ohio, being one of the worst.

"Well, I am," Sam muttered. "There's just no telling what Ruth might say when we get there. She's none too happy about this idea. She says family should take care of family instead of hiring it out. She only agreed to give it a try because I told her I'd finish up some odd jobs on her place she's been wanting done. I was going to do them anyway," he added hastily. "Soon as work slowed down a little. But she always wants things tended to yesterday. Ruth can be a hard woman to please."

Emma firmed up her mouth. "Well, I can be a hard woman to get rid of, so she'll have her work cut out for her scaring me off."

Sam chuckled, and his expression relaxed. "You look just like Caleb when you set your jaw like that. He always was a *schtubbich* one, your brother. Once he dug in his heels, there was no budging him, not even—" Sam cut his words off abruptly. "Get up, Dobs," he said, flipping the reins against the horse's wide back.

Emma clenched her fingers together. "It's all right, Sam.

Caleb's only shunned, not dead. Besides, he'll be coming back before long to set things right."

"That's good news. You've heard from him?"

"No," she admitted.

She hadn't heard from him. Not so much as a word for months now, which was strange.

And a little worrisome.

Not long after she'd gone to Ohio, Caleb had left Johns Mill as well, determined to find Trevor Abbott and bring him to justice for their parents' murders. In doing so, he'd abandoned not only the faith he'd promised to follow, but also Rhoda, the young wife he'd married only a few weeks before the tragedy.

"Did he get in touch with Rhoda, then?"

"No. She said he wrote her one letter, telling her how to reach him if she wanted to join him, but there's been nothing since."

"It's a shame, the fix he's left that girl in," Sam muttered. "I'd never have matched the two of them up in the first place, maybe, but it wonders me that he could do such a thing, even so."

Sam wasn't the only one in the community who'd been surprised by Caleb's marriage. Her twin was known for playing fast and loose with their rules, and some, including their own parents, had wondered if he planned to join the church at all.

But then Rhoda Lambert, Emma's best friend and their bishop's only daughter, had caught Caleb's eye—and then his heart. There'd been some worried talk over the odd match. Rhoda was as sensible and devout as Caleb was wild. But in the end, they'd all celebrated the unlikely marriage and hoped for the best.

Instead their worst fears had been realized, and Rhoda was left bearing the brunt of her husband's decisions. Since divorce was unheard of, she could never remarry while Caleb was alive, but since he was actively shunned, she wasn't allowed to accept any support from him. It was a heart-breaking fix for any young woman, and everyone agreed that Rhoda deserved much better.

"He would never have done it if he'd been in his right mind," Emma said now. "He loves Rhoda with all his heart." She knew that was true, because she knew her brother. She'd stood up with Caleb and Rhoda at their wedding. She'd heard the telling shake in her brother's voice when he'd promised to care for Rhoda all the days of his life, and she'd seen the look on his face, in his eyes.

"He has a funny way of showing it." Sam's words weren't unkind, but his tone made it clear enough what he thought of Caleb's choices. Sam had never had much patience with men who caused pain to women or children, and it was plain to see he'd now lumped her brother into that group.

Emma frowned. "Like I said, he's not thinking straight. I wish I could talk to him. If I could, I know I could make him see reason."

Sam lifted an eyebrow. "I don't see how, if neither the bishop nor Rhoda could manage it."

"Caleb was never much on listening to the bishop. And I'm not nearly as soft-spoken as Rhoda."

Sam chuckled. "That's true enough."

"Besides, Caleb's my twin. We've always had a special connection, and lots of times he's listened to me when he wouldn't listen to anybody else. It's like old Dobs there." Emma nodded to the horse plodding steadily along in front of them. "He's so strong, he could cause a lot of trouble if he wanted to, but he always does just what you want him to do, ain't so?"

"Always has." Seeming relieved at the change of subject, Sam clucked his tongue and flipped the reins again, speeding the old horse up a little. "Dobs isn't so strong as he was, though. The truth is, I'm looking around for a new horse, if I can find a bargain."

"Oh, no, Sam! Really?" Distracted from her thoughts about Caleb, Emma sighed. Sam and Dobs had been a fixture around Johns Mill for a long time.

Everywhere she looked, something else was changing.

"*Ja*, it's past time. Dobs is about twenty-five now, and he's not so good at pulling the wagons anymore, not when I've got them loaded up heavy. Even this family buggy tires him if it's full of folks. He still manages my two-seater all right, but I don't use it as much now that Leah and Janie have come to stay. There's an auction coming up in Ethridge, and I'm thinking I'll go have a look, if I can get away from work. There are some unschooled ones going up for sale, and those'll be cheaper. Plus, then I'll know I'm not buying another man's problems. I can train the animal up right from the start."

"I'm sure you'll choose a good one, but I still think it's a pity about poor Dobs."

Sam shot her a sideways glance. "If you want to pity somebody, pity me. I'll be the one who has the trouble of training the new horse, and that's always a right fine nuisance, especially when a man's got as much work on hand as I do right now. But it won't be such a bad deal for Dobs. He'll just go out to pasture, retired-like, and be waited on for the rest of his days."

"Oh, for true, Sam?" Emma smiled down at the old horse with an affectionate relief. "That's wonderful news! I was afraid you'd be selling him off to be butchered like most folks do."

"I probably should. It's foolishness, keeping on a horse like Dobs when he's of no further use. I can imagine what my old *grossdaddi* would say about that. He loved horses, but they were livestock to him. He treated them well, but he made certain sure never to lose money on them. The good of the family always came first. I've no business spending more money on Dobs, not with the bills I've got to pay yet.

But he's been such a faithful old worker, I just can't bring myself to send him to slaughter." Sam shook his head. "*Grossdaddi* would think I've gone soft in the head, footing a hefty feed bill just because I've taken a liking to a horse. I think so myself."

"Well, I don't think you're soft in the head, Sam. I think you're a real kindhearted fellow," Emma said earnestly. "You always have been."

"*Ach*, well." Sam looked embarrassed. "You'd say so. You always were one to worry over animals. No telling how many trees the other fellows and I skinned up over the years, putting blind baby squirrels or half-fledged birds back into nests, just because you wouldn't leave them be and let nature take its course."

Emma laughed. "You needn't pretend to be so hardhearted. You were the first one up those trees most of the time, and you'd—"

Suddenly she thought better of what she was saying. It was long years ago, true, but she remembered well enough why Sam had climbed so many trees with a squirming baby animal tucked in the neck of his shirt.

It hadn't been so much because of the creatures themselves. Sam would never willingly bring hurt to little wild things, but he'd grown up on a farm. He had a country-bred practicality about such matters.

He'd climbed those trees because she'd been the one asking him to.

She looked out over the summer fields rolling by the buggy, searching for something else to talk about, something that would paddle this conversation into safer waters. Maybe something about the gardens doing so well this year.

She glanced back at Sam.

He was hunched over the reins, his muscled arms bent at the elbows, his eyes scanning the road as he drove. A log truck started toward them in the opposite lane. Sam's expression never changed, but as soon as he saw it coming, he nudged Dobs gently over so that there was as much space as he could allow between them and the thundering vehicle.

Dobs was an experienced horse. He didn't startle at the truck, but he laid his ears flat as it roared by, clearly not liking it. When the truck had passed, Sam clucked his tongue.

"It's all right, Dobs," he muttered under his breath, his tone low and comforting. "All good now."

The old horse flicked one ear backward in Sam's direction, then lifted his head and jogged forward with a determined air.

Emma glanced from the horse to Sam and back again.

It's all right.

He'd said the same thing to her when she'd cried against his chest in the kitchen yesterday. And before, at Joseph's wedding, when he'd suddenly hustled her back inside the house when she'd started out the door. He'd startled her badly—her nerves were already on edge—and she'd fussed at him.

He'd held up his hands and spoke in the same soothing voice he'd used with Dobs. *Calm down. It's all right. Just some of those reporters hanging around outside with their cameras. Best you keep inside for now.*

Even when Sam didn't speak out loud, it was the same. Like when he'd first pulled up at the house, when Miriam had been on the verge of a panic. He'd only had to nod at her, and she'd calmed down.

It's all right.

Sam moved through their small world as slowly and deliberately as old Dobs, making things as right for his friends as he could. Soothing them, fixing things for them. Sheltering them. And he didn't get near enough appreciation for it.

Not even from her.

Especially not from her.

He glanced sideways to find her studying him. "What?"

Emma blinked. "Nothing. Except—" She fumbled to find the right words for what she wanted to say to him, words of appreciation and apology. "I think—"

He watched her for a second, and when she didn't go on, one corner of his mouth quirked. "*Ja?*" he prompted.

The buggy was facing into the sun, and the late-slanting light had dipped under the hood to shine on him. It lit up the beginnings of the weather wrinkles in the corners of his eyes, and the strong, firm line of his clean-shaven jaw.

He was still waiting for her to speak. Emma swallowed, and for some reason, she couldn't think of a single sensible thing to say. Except—

"Folks' gardens are doing wonderful *gut* this year, ain't so?"

CHAPTER SIX

❧

DAYLIGHT LASTED LONG THIS TIME OF YEAR, BUT the shadows were lengthening by the time Sam pulled into Ruth's yard. Emma examined the trim little house with interest.

She'd seen it before, of course. Johns Mill was a small community, and Emma knew most of the families and homes well. This house had been built years ago for the parents of the farmer who'd lived in the next house over, a different version of the traditional *dawdi haus* used for aging parents. Generally, those were attached to the main farmhouse, so that the older folks were handy by, easy to include in family activities and to care for. It was a good arrangement mostly.

This simple white house had been set apart, though, in a small, square yard fenced off from the surrounding fields. A buggy barn sat to the right behind it, along with a wash shed and a small garden. It was like a miniature Amish farm of its own, and Emma had always thought it a sweet place.

Other folks chuckled when they passed it. They joked that Robert Christner was no fool to choose such a place for his sharp-tongued sister, conveniently far enough from his own house that she couldn't pop in for easy visits.

Maybe it still hadn't been far enough. Robert had since moved his family up to Pennsylvania.

Emma shaded her eyes and peered toward the porch. Leah sat in a rocker, a bowl in her lap and a bag by her side. Shelling peas or snapping beans, likely. That sort of job was never ending this time of year.

Janie was keeping a lookout on the front steps. As soon as Sam slowed to a stop, she abandoned her own bowl of beans and flew toward the buggy.

"Sam! Sam!" the little girl shouted. Sam's face lit up.

"Hello, there, little one! Have you been a good girl today?"

Before Janie could answer, a fretful voice sounded from the shadows of the porch. "She's been a noisy girl, that's what she's been. In my day children were trained to be quiet."

Emma looked again. *Ja*, there was Ruth, sitting in a well-padded chair tucked in the deepest shade. The thin, elderly woman looked over the porch rail, her sharp nose wrinkled as if she smelled something unpleasant.

Sam hopped out of the buggy and scooped Janie up with one brawny arm. Before he could come around to help her, Emma had climbed down herself. She reached into the back of the buggy and retrieved her suitcase.

She suspected Ruth might have strong opinions about women who couldn't shift for themselves, and there was no point starting off on the wrong foot. Emma lingered on the far side of the buggy long enough to straighten her bonnet and dress with quick tugs. Then she walked briskly toward the steps, keeping a determined smile on her face.

"Hello, Leah," she called cheerfully as she mounted the steps to the porch.

"Emma." Leah's response was cool, and she didn't look up from her work.

Not the warmest welcome, but then when had any of Sam's sisters ever been friendly to her? Emma bolstered up her sagging smile and tried again. "Ruth, it's nice to see you doing so well after your surgery."

"I wouldn't call this doing well." The older woman considered her balefully, before turning toward her nephew. Sam was tugging the brim of Janie's bonnet down over her forehead to make her giggle. "My hip aches something terrible, especially at night. Not that anybody cares about that." She raised her voice and called out toward the yard. "Don't you let that great horse of yours stand for too long, Samuel. He ruins the grass. If you're bound and determined to leave, Leah, I suppose you might as well get your things and go. But before you do, you'd best show this one how I want things kept in the house."

"All right." Leah stood, setting her bowl of snap beans down on the seat of the rocker. She looked over Emma's shoulder at her brother. "Sam, you don't need to unhitch. This won't take me long."

"Take your time," he called back. "I'm in no hurry."

He might not be, but clearly his sister was. Leah strode through the living room, making Emma hurry to keep up.

She'd never been inside before, and she glanced curiously around the small home. Everything was neat as a pin and sparsely furnished to make the most of the limited space. This place would be easy to keep clean, and it was a real smart house for a woman living on her own.

Maybe someday she should try to find a place like this for herself, Emma thought as Leah turned down a short hallway. She was already past the age when most of the girls in her community married. By the time things shifted back to normal—if they ever did—she'd be older still. A house like this, with Miriam living with her maybe, might be the best she could hope for.

"Here." Leah pushed open a door, revealing a small bedroom. "This is where you'll sleep. There's only the two bedrooms, and Ruth's is just across there, so you'll be able to hear when she calls out in the night."

"Does she often need help in the nighttime?"

"*Ja.* She doesn't sleep well, and she doesn't seem to want anybody else to, either." Sam's sister flushed, darting a wary glance at Emma. "That was wrong of me to say. I shouldn't speak unkindly of my aunt."

Leah looked so bothered that Emma felt sorry for her. The Christners always had been a clannish bunch. Folks said they stuck together like burrs. For Ruth to inspire even this mild disloyalty from her niece and nephew, she must have pushed them to their very limits.

"You're not being unkind, not really. You're just letting me know what to expect. You needn't worry. I'll not be repeating what you say, and things will go better all around if you tell me straight out whatever you think I ought to know."

"Well, first off, she's not very happy about you coming here." Leah didn't look all that pleased about it, either, even though surely the prospect of going home must have been a relief to her.

"So Sam said." Emma set her suitcase on a wooden chair beside the door and unsnapped it. She'd go ahead and unpack. She suspected Ruth would keep her hopping as soon as Leah and Sam went on their way. "Don't worry. I don't get my feelings hurt easy."

Leah didn't look convinced. "I hope not, because my *aent*'s not shy about speaking her mind. She's likely to say something to you about . . ." Sam's sister left the sentence dangling, so Emma finished it for her.

"About what happened to my parents and my part in it."

Emma spoke matter-of-factly, but she turned aside so Leah couldn't read her expression. She gave her Sunday dress a shake and hung it in the small closet. "She can't say anything to me that my uncle didn't say while I was in Ohio. Besides, I know how folks can be when they're sick. I never mind them when they say or do things they shouldn't. It's a hard trial to feel poorly."

She finished setting her few belongings in their new places then drew in a deep breath. She'd only come here because she believed Naomi was right. Miriam might improve faster without Emma hovering around. She hadn't counted on feeling happy in this house, but in a strange way, she did. In spite of Ruth's crankiness and Leah's coolness, Emma already felt better than she had at home. At least here, she had a clear-cut purpose.

She glanced over to find Leah biting her lip. "Is there something else?"

"Only that I'm not sure how bad Ruth's hip really is. The doctor says she's fully recovered from her operation, but Ruth doesn't act like it. I've been wondering lately if she might be . . ." Leah trailed off again, this time helpless in the face of the Christner family loyalty.

Emma had no such problem. "Exaggerating a little? Could be. Maybe she's lonesome out here by herself, now that her brother has passed. He was special, *ja?* Likely he took up a lot of her time and attention, and she doesn't know what to do with herself. Plus she's still grieving him, I'd imagine, and grief is its own kind of sickness."

Leah sucked in a sharp breath, and when Emma looked back at her, the other woman's eyes had filled with tears.

"Oh!" Emma had been thinking aloud. She hadn't even considered Leah's own fresh loss. "*Ich binn sorry.* I didn't mean to—"

"It does feel like that," the other woman murmured. "Like a terrible sickness I'll never get over."

Emma's heart panged. She knew that feeling. She understood that despairing sense that nothing in the world would ever be right again.

She mustered up her courage and laid a gentle hand on the other woman's shoulder. "You will get over it, though, Leah, one day. Until then you must be gentle with yourself. Go on home to your *bruder*'s house and spend time with Sam and your sweet little *dochder*. That'll be the best medicine for you. And don't trouble yourself about your aunt. I'll see to her just fine."

Leah hesitated, then said softly, "*Denki*, Emma."

Emma smiled and gave her a reassuring pat. "*Du bisht welcome.* Now, why don't you show me the rest of the house and give me an idea of Ruth's likes and dislikes real quick? Then you can get on your way."

Leah smiled back—a sad smile, but a real one this time. "We'd best start with her dislikes because those will take the longest. Come on, I'll show you where everything is in the kitchen."

Like the rest of the house, Ruth's kitchen was small, but neatly organized, and Leah's tour didn't take very long.

When it was done, Emma nodded. "I think that's all I need to know. Except where the nearest phone shack is, in case there's an emergency. I don't expect one," she added, "but it's best to be prepared, just in case."

"There's a phone you can use next door," Leah said. "An *Englisch* lady lives over there in the old farmhouse this place used to belong to. Her name is Birdie Marshall. All the Plain folks around here use her phone when they need one. She even leaves the back door unlocked so that you can go in anytime, whether she's home or not. She'll take messages for you, too."

"She sounds very kind."

"Don't say so to Ruth. They got off on the wrong foot years ago, but Birdie still lets us use her phone whenever we need to. It's just a short walk through that pecan orchard there." Leah nodded toward the yard.

Emma looked out the window. She could see the orchard, just beyond the fence bordering the yard.

She could see Sam, too, and she smiled. He was once again standing by Dobs's head, this time showing Janie how to feed the horse a sugar cube. Janie giggled as the horse mouthed her tiny hand.

Sam leaned down to reposition her fingers, bending them back so the horse could get to the sugar on her palm more easily. Emma could hear the rumble of his deep voice. She couldn't make out what he was saying, but plainly he was explaining things to Janie. He was teaching a little girl, who would likely be around horses all her life, how best to tend them. Emma's own *daed* had given her many similar lessons, memories that were extra sweet to her now that he was gone.

She glanced at Leah. "Sam's *gut* with Janie, ain't so?"

Leah was smiling, too, as she watched her brother and daughter together, but at Emma's remark her expression chilled.

"Of course he is," she said. "Children love Sam. He's a gentle fellow, my *bruder*!"

For a second Emma didn't know quite how to answer. "I wasn't saying different, Leah. I've known Sam for years. I know how kindhearted he is."

"He's a hard worker, too, and he makes a real good living at the construction company. Any woman would be blessed to have a man like Sam for a husband."

"*Ja*, I agree. I'm surprised he isn't married already."

"He should be. If he had better sense, he would be." Leah muttered the last bit with a quick, cutting glance in Emma's direction.

Emma raised her eyebrows. Whatever softening Leah had shown toward her earlier was surely gone now. The other woman seemed irritated again. Emma was bewildered by the quick change and more than a little frustrated.

She didn't like to be rude, especially to a new widow, but she'd had just about enough of being cold-shouldered with no explanation for it.

"Leah, have I done something to upset you? Because if I have, I wish you would tell me what it was so that I could try and make it right. I'd like for us to be friends."

"It's not me you've upset."

"Then who?" Emma asked helplessly.

Leah didn't answer, but her gaze darted to the window. Emma frowned, more confused than ever.

"Sam? You think I've hurt Sam somehow?"

"I know you have." Leah was breathing faster now, and her face was a mottled red. "You could have had him years ago if you'd wanted him. But you didn't, and you hurt him. You hurt him so badly, he's never looked twice at any other girl."

Emma stared at her in blank disbelief. *That?* That was what these years of unfriendliness had been about? A broken romance from back when Emma and Sam were schoolmates together? But that was ridiculous.

Emma shook her head and hurried to explain.

"You're mistaken, Leah. Sam and me—there wasn't ever anything like that between us, not really. We were much too young to be serious. It wasn't like that at all."

A silence fell in the kitchen as Leah looked at her. Sam's sister was so upset that she was trembling from it, and she didn't speak for three long ticks of the clock up on the wall.

"*Nee*," she said. "I'm not mistaken. It wasn't like that for you, maybe. But it was like that for Sam."

Leah spoke with such absolute conviction that Emma's answering protest died in her throat.

"I just . . . I didn't know," Emma whispered.

"I don't see how you couldn't have. But I ought not to

have told you." Leah darted another look out the window and sighed. "He'd be ill with me if he knew. He's not admitted the truth of it even to himself, though it's been plain to all of us who know him best." She looked back at Emma, her face twisted. "It's just that . . . I want so bad to like you. I never thought I would, but you're a real nice person in lots of ways. I wouldn't mind us being friends. I could use a good friend right now, truth be told. But . . . please, Emma. Be careful of my brother. He's not so strong as he looks, not when it comes to you."

"Leah!" Before Emma could answer, Ruth called irritably from the front porch. "Samuel's horse just dropped a pile of *mischt* in my yard that's nearly as big as your daughter. If you're going to leave, *leave*."

"Don't tell him I said anything."

Emma blinked and shook her head. "No. Of course I won't."

She couldn't imagine having this conversation with Sam. And anyhow, surely Leah must be wrong.

"*Denki*," Leah whispered. "I'd best be going, then."

Leading the way back through the house, Leah picked up her suitcase, which she'd had sitting ready by the door, and walked out onto the porch. Sam had just finished shoveling the manure into the ditch by the road. He placed the shovel in the lean-to next to the small barn, then jogged back to take his sister's case and toss it into the buggy.

Sam gave Leah a hand up and then boosted Janie into the back seat. As he crossed behind the buggy, he glanced up at Emma, who was waiting on the porch to see them off.

"I was just telling Ruth I'd be along day after tomorrow to fix a few shingles on the back of the house. Some blew loose in that last storm we had."

"And high time that job was seen to," Ruth said from her

corner. "Should have been tended to right off. Roofs are nothing to play about with."

Sam glanced at his aunt, an amused exasperation in his expression. "They're only loose, Ruth. Not off entirely. I'll tack 'em down, and it'll be fine. Anyhow, Emma," he continued, "I'll be along then, so if you have any messages you want taken back home, you can send them by me easy enough."

Emma had to clear her throat before she could speak. "That's . . . kind of you, Sam."

Her voice sounded a little strange, and Leah shot her a worried look from the buggy.

Sam didn't seem to notice anything amiss at all.

"Be good to Emma, now, Ruth," he admonished. "Remember, she's trying to help."

"It'd be more fitting for you to tell her to be good to me," his aunt retorted. "But it's plain to see where your fancy lies—with the prettiest face, just like all the men."

Emma felt her cheeks growing bright red. Sam halted beside the buggy, looking at her with one eyebrow raised.

"Ruth and I will be fine," Emma assured him, hoping to hurry him on his way. He still hesitated, so she added, "We will see you day after tomorrow."

He frowned, but he nodded. "All right. See you then."

He climbed into the buggy seat, which once again tilted heavily under his weight, provoking an alarmed protest from Leah. A moment later, the buggy rolled out of the drive and turned back toward Johns Mill. Janie waved furiously from the side. Emma waved back to the little girl with a smile before her gaze shifted to Sam in the front.

He was in the middle of saying something to his sister, but when he caught Emma looking, he half smiled and ducked his chin in farewell. Then the big buggy moved on past the house, rattling back toward town.

Emma sighed, squared her shoulders, and turned to face

her patient. She'd sort through what Leah had told her later, when she was alone in her room. Right now she had Ruth to look after.

"I expect you're ready to go inside. No doubt that hard chair is paining your hip by now, even with all the padding Leah fixed for you." Emma retrieved the aluminum walker, which had been set carefully to the side, and placed it in front of the elderly woman. "Now, just take hold of it to steady yourself, and I'll give you a boost up."

"You can put that thing right back where you got it. I'll let you know when I'm ready to go in." Ruth looked up, her gray eyes narrowed. "I've my wits about me yet."

"All right. If you'd rather sit out here awhile yet, that'll be good, too. The afternoon's cooling off well, and it's comfortable in the shade." Emma combined Janie's and Leah's bowls of half-snapped beans, dropped into the rocker nearest Ruth, and set to work. Busy hands and pleasant conversation were wonderful ways to keep a person's mind from wandering to places it shouldn't.

Of course, how pleasant this particular conversation would be—that remained to be seen. Still, she'd do her part to make it so.

"I like your house, Ruth."

"My brother bought it for me and Davey to live in," the other woman told her. "Not Sam's *daed*. My oldest brother, Robert. The one who lives up in Pennsylvania now."

"Well, it's a fine place. From what I see, it's set up just right, too. Everything's nice and handy."

Ruth made an irritated noise. "*Ja*, everything but the house itself. It's too far out from town. I told *my bruder* he was being foolish, putting me and Davey so distant from his own home, but Robert favored this arrangement and felt it would be best. Men don't see things like women do."

Ruth shifted in her seat and winced. Emma dropped her

glance to the beans in her lap and pretended not to notice. "Well, you've made the best of it, looks like."

"The house has served its purpose. I won't be staying here too much longer, I don't expect. Now that Davey—" The other woman's voice faltered, and she cleared her throat before continuing. "Now that it's just me, there's really no point in keeping up a separate household. I've already written to Robert, telling him to sell this place. I'll move to Pennsylvania with him. He'll be thankful to have my help, I'm sure. His wife, Louella, was never a good manager, always throwing out more with a spoon than Robert could bring in with a shovel. Once I'm there, I'll teach her a thing or two, for certain sure." Ruth sounded so grimly determined that Emma felt a flash of sympathy for Robert's Louella.

"It's always a blessing when family can be together," she agreed tactfully.

"That's what I told Robert when he came up with the plan to move to Pennsylvania in the first place." Ruth made a scornful noise. "Not that he listened. Leah and Sam don't seem to think much of family togetherness, either. I guess they told you that I didn't want them to hire you. I believe family should look after their own folks whenever they can."

"I don't blame you for feeling that way," Emma said mildly. "It would be more comfortable for family to look after you, I'm sure. But now that you're almost all better, Sam thought Leah could use a little rest, since she's still grieving Milton."

"Grief's no excuse for not doing the work *Gott* puts in front of you. The way Leah is carrying on is selfish. I'm grieving for Davey, but I'm still willing to do my part and help out Robert and Louella. A woman finds her purpose in looking after her family."

Emma wasn't sure what to say to that. She'd expected

Ruth to be outspoken, but she'd already lost count of how many folks she'd criticized in the last few minutes. "Well, maybe I'm not the same as family, but I'll work hard and do my best to take good care of you while I'm here."

"Your work's not what worries me. Any *dochder* of Elijah's Levonia would know how to work, pretty face or no. But from what I've seen, you bring trouble, sure as manure brings flies." The lines around Ruth's lips deepened. "They never caught that *Englisch* boy, after all, and we're all alone out here. What if he comes after you and shoots me like he did your parents?"

Emma snapped the bean in her fingers with a sharp twist, but she kept her voice calm and kind. "That's not going to happen, Ruth. Trevor's long gone from Johns Mill."

"How would you know such a thing?" The old woman pounced triumphantly. "Unless you'd been talking to him yourself. Same as before, likely," she muttered, "not behaving as you should and bringing grief on those around you."

Emma struggled to hang on to her temper. Sam and Leah had warned her, but even so she'd not been prepared for Ruth to be quite so direct.

"I haven't spoken to Trevor, Ruth. I know he's not likely to be in Johns Mill because the sheriff and the other officers have told me so. Besides, it just makes sense. With everybody around here looking for him and knowing his face, it would be foolish of him to come back. He'll keep far away, I expect."

"I wouldn't count on it. A fellow like that, troubled in his head, wouldn't be likely to show too much sense—nor give up easy. Now help me get inside. You've left me in this chair so long, my hip's likely to ache all night."

Emma bit her tongue so hard that she winced. Then she rose and helped the elderly woman stand and take hold of the walker. As she followed Ruth into the house, she looked back at the road, stretching out quietly in either direction. Her heart skittered a little at the emptiness of it.

This house was nice enough, but Ruth was right. It did seem awful far away from everybody else. Emma glanced toward the rows of pecan trees beyond the fence, thankful to remember that a friendly neighbor with a telephone was just a short walk away.

And, of course, Sam would be back tomorrow. But somehow, since her talk with Leah, that thought didn't calm Emma's fluttering heart much at all.

CHAPTER SEVEN

❧

"COME ON, NOW," SAM GRITTED OUT BETWEEN CLENCHED teeth, struggling to keep the light two-seater buggy on the correct side of the road. His new horse, Breeze, was fighting the bit and trying to dance sideways. Sam was starting to see why this particular animal had been such a bargain. He'd be thankful when he finally made it to Ruth's house.

Probably he should have waited and gone to the auction as he'd originally planned. But time was a precious thing right now, and when Daniel Yoder had suggested Sam might be interested in the young, half-broken horse he'd bought at the last sale, Sam had driven out to take a look.

"He's a rare one," Daniel had said as he and Sam had watched the young animal trotting around the pasture. "Too spirited for me, though. I've not the hand with horses you have, Sam, nor the muscle, neither. It was a mistake to buy him, but he was such a looker, I couldn't pass him by for the price."

Sam hadn't been able to pass Breeze by for the price, either, but now he knew that what his old *grossdaddi* had said was true. A cheap horse was an expensive lesson.

Still, Sam hadn't entirely given up hope. Breeze was a fine gelding, well bred and the right size and age for buggy work. Once he calmed down some and learned his business, he'd be a good horse. And if he still didn't suit, once he was reasonably safe, Sam could always sell him off to some young man looking for a pretty stepper to impress the girls.

Of course, he couldn't poke too much fun at a fellow like that, now could he? Given that he himself was on his way to his *aent*'s house, even though, as Leah had pointed out, there were plenty of roads closer by and better suited to train a raw horse on. But he'd had the idea of showing Breeze to Emma, and once the thought had occurred to him, nothing would do but that he head out this way.

He'd been coming by regular-like since he'd dropped Emma off a week ago. He'd stopped by to fix the shingles and again to nail up some loose boards on the barn. Last trip, he'd patched a spot on the porch, and now Ruth was talking about making some repairs on the wash shed. Little jobs, and none of them too urgent, but he'd not minded.

It was his duty to see to Ruth anyhow, now that his uncle and *daed* weren't here to do it. And, of course, he wasn't resting too easy in his mind about Emma.

She put a brave face on it, but she had to be lonely staying out here with nobody but Ruth for company. Emma told him that folks stopped by some, now and again, but as near as he could piece together, it wasn't often. The women of the community did their duty by Ruth as best they could, but there was no way around it—she was nobody's favorite, and Emma was used to being in a house with family.

That was probably why she'd been so extra friendly to him when he'd stopped by. When you were starving, any meal was welcome. Even so, it had been right pleasant to see Emma's face lighting up when he'd dropped by. Somehow he'd found it easier and easier to pull time away from his busy schedule to drive out this way and spend the evening.

He rolled into Ruth's driveway at a little too quick a clip. He was halfway behind the house before he wrestled Breeze to a stop, and when Sam saw Emma standing in the backyard, the reins went dangerously slack in his hands.

She stood in the back by the clothesline, unpinning sheets from the line. The white fabric billowed behind her as she turned to smile at him.

Sam's breath caught at the picture she made. Folks had always said that Emma Hochstedler had been given more than her share of the pretties, and that was true. But when a woman could look like . . . *that*, even in the middle of a hot laundry day, wearing a black dress that would have drained the color out of most girls . . . well, it was saying something.

She folded the sheet she'd just unpinned with a few quick snaps and tucked it into the laundry basket at her feet. Then she hurried toward the buggy, her eyes fastened on the heaving horse.

"Oh, my," she said as soon as she was within earshot. "Isn't he a nice one, though?"

"Hold up, Emma." Sensing the looseness of the reins, the horse had taken a step forward, testing his freedom. Sam tightened his grip, and Breeze halted, blowing out a sulky breath.

Emma had stopped when he'd spoken, well used to the caution one needed to take around horses, particularly when they were young and untrained. "Well, he'll sure be a change after old Dobs, won't he? How's he doing for you, Sam?"

"He's trouble," Sam said grimly. "Not an easy trainer. I

can see that already, and I've only had him a day and a half.
But he's smart enough. I've seen that, too. The smart
horses, they give you the trouble at the start of things, but
it's the dumb ones that will keep on giving it to you. So
sooner or later, I expect he'll be all right."

Emma lifted one hand gently, and Breeze let her touch
his cheek. Then he rolled his eyes at her and tried to nip her
fingers. She moved her hand to safety and laughed. "*Ja*,
you've got your work cut out for you with this fellow, but
he'll come right soon enough. You've always been good
with horses. Everybody says so."

Sam could feel the red mottling his cheeks at her praise.
Time to change the subject. "Where's Ruth?"

"Inside, taking a nap." Emma tilted her head up at him,
squinting against the late afternoon sunshine. "She always
sleeps for a couple of hours this time of day." A little smile
dimpled around her mouth. "That way she can keep me up
half the night. If you're here to do some work, she won't
appreciate you banging about, not for another half hour
or so."

"I'll run Breeze down the road and back a few times,
then, to pass the time. He needs the practice, and he'll do
better on the way home if he's worn out."

"Can I come?"

Sam frowned. "Breeze is a pretty horse, all right, but
he's raw-trained yet, Emma."

"I'm not skittish, Sam. You know that. Just a short drive?
I can't be gone long anyhow. Ruth will be waking up
shortly, and I still need to do some weeding out in the garden. Why don't you drive me down to the stop sign at the
end of that little dirt road and back? There's not likely to be
any cars—there hardly ever are. Please? It'd be fun."

She tilted her face up at him hopefully. Although Sam
knew that she wasn't trying to use her looks to talk him into
it, there was something about having a pretty woman look-

ing up at a man that did make him want to please her. He'd done more than one foolish thing in the past because Emma had glanced at him with her head cocked sideways like that, with a smile just promising to blossom if he said yes to whatever it was that she was asking.

He'd do a powerful lot to see that smile, still. Even today, after so many years of knowing better.

"All right." Sure enough, Emma's lips curved up, and a light sparkled into her eyes. His heart gave a hard, painful thump in response.

The good Lord knew His business, for certain sure, but sometimes one did wonder what He might have been thinking, making a Plain woman so pleasing to the eye.

"Go slow around the back, Emma, and climb in easy-like. I can't get down. I don't trust the brake to hold him, not if he's determined to go."

"All right." Emma's nod was controlled, but she was tense as a coiled spring—obviously more than ready for a little fun.

Sam sighed as he waited for her to go round the buggy. He wasn't really being so foolish, he told himself. Of course, Emma would want a ride in the buggy; most folks would. The older folks because they were interested in the horse and seeing how Sam handled him. The younger ones, like Emma, because Breeze was a pretty animal and because a ride with a half-trained horse was a bit of excitement that nobody would fault them for having.

Anyhow, if he was going to take Emma for a ride before Breeze was fully trained, this would be the time to do it. The horse was a bit tired from the long drive over here, and that made him less likely to cut up.

Emma climbed in and settled on the seat. She glanced over at Sam, mirth and anticipation dancing in eyes that were every bit as blue—or bluer—than the summer sky behind her. "I'm ready! Let's go!"

Sam turned Breeze around, and they started off.

After they went out of Ruth's driveway, he drove a short way on the two-lane road before turning off onto a narrow dirt lane that cut through some fields and dead-ended onto the busier state highway. There was little traffic on the paved road, but there'd be none at all on this one.

That was a good thing, because they hadn't been on the road two minutes before Breeze was fighting him. Not so hard as he had before but doing his best to see which of them was going to be the master. Sam held him in, using every one of the skills his father and grandfather had taught him—and they'd taught him plenty. The Christners knew horses as well as the Hochstedlers knew cows.

When Breeze shivered and tried to rear, Sam corrected him quickly, and Emma laughed. "You're right. He's a smart one. He's trying you, ain't so? Testing to see if you'll let him be the boss."

"And I can't, not even once. Otherwise, I'll have twice the work later."

"He wants to run."

Sam made an irritated noise. "He doesn't know what he wants, except to foil me. And it doesn't matter anyhow. What matters is what I want, and that's what he's got to learn."

"It's going to be a hard lesson for this one," Emma observed as Breeze fought Sam's guidance.

"If he makes it so."

"Let him run a bit, Sam. It's a fair way to the end of the road yet."

Sam laughed, but a quick glance at Emma's face told him she was serious. "You can't mean it. Let this horse have his head? That's just what I'm trying not to do."

"Well, it's not letting him have his head if you *want* him to run, is it? Then it'd be your idea. And it'd be fun."

Sam sputtered a laugh. "I knew staying with Ruth would

be a hard thing, but I'd no idea it would take away your desire to keep on living, Emma."

To his astonishment she laid her hand on his. "You've got it backwards, Sam. Staying with an unhappy person like your *aent* has given me more desire than ever to keep on living—to really live, and not spend my time mulling over the past. I want to enjoy whatever pleasant thing *Gott* puts in front of me at the moment." When he looked up from their hands to her face, she smiled. "Right now what's in front of me is a fast horse and the one fellow in the county who's able to let him run and stop him when he's a mind to. Let him go, Sam. Just to the end of the road. Let him run."

The one fellow in the county.

"Hang on tight, then," Sam said.

Emma laughed, took her hand off his, and grabbed on to the sides of the seat.

He checked to make sure her knuckles were white before calling out, "Hi! Hi, Breeze!" He snapped the reins down on the back of the horse and let him go.

Breeze didn't wait for a second invitation. He was off like a shot, barreling down the road with everything he had. Sam had his hands full keeping the horse under control. The buggy bounced a bit, but the dirt beneath the wheels was packed hard and smooth, and Breeze was a good runner.

Sam shot a glance in Emma's direction, then wished he hadn't. Her *kapp* had blown back off her head, and her golden hair was loosening in the breeze. Her face was tip-tilted up, and the joy in her expression hit him square in the chest.

He'd been kicked by mules and felt it less. For one bewildered instant he lost his bearings. He felt a bump as the buggy veered slightly to the right, and a wheel wobbled onto the rougher surface of the road's shoulder.

For a second or two it took all his focus to get the buggy back on the road where it belonged—going off at this speed wouldn't be good. When he had Breeze safely back in line, he looked ahead and saw the end of the road coming up fast.

He'd waited too long to start slowing the horse down. He knew it right off. There was nothing he could do. They weren't going to be able to stop, not in time, and this road ended when it met the highway running crossways. Even if there was no traffic coming, they were headed for the ditch across the road.

Sam resisted the urge to jerk on the reins. If he did that with a half-wild horse like Breeze, he'd only make things worse. So he worked the horse down steadily, fighting him, slowing him as much as possible.

Even so, they overshot and plummeted across the road. Sam pulled on the wisdom his grandfather had passed on to him. *Any horse with sense don't want to get hurt. If you're in a real pinch, let him have his head. He just might save himself and you both.*

He loosened his grip on the reins, and Breeze turned, making the buggy skitter crazily sideways in the road. Emma was flung hard against him, and he heard her gasp.

At least she was still in the buggy, and that was the main thing. He couldn't worry about anything else at the moment.

Fortunately, the turn had slowed Breeze down, and the run had winded him. Sam was able to regain control with only a short battle, and before long he had the buggy safely in the correct lane.

Sam sent up a thankful prayer for the empty highway and took advantage of a wide, flat shoulder to turn the carriage around. In only a few minutes, they were back on the quiet dirt road headed to Ruth's. Breeze clopped along at a respectable pace, only shaking his head now and then to let Sam know he still had a mind of his own.

Sam looked at Emma. She was breathing nearly as hard as the horse, but she had finally loosened her grip on the buggy to attempt to put her *kapp* back where it was supposed to be.

"Are you all right?"

"*Ja*." She nodded and swallowed. "I am all right." She was doing her best to smooth her hair, but not having much success with it.

Sam spent the rest of the short drive back to Ruth's trying his best to figure out what to say. When they finally rolled into the yard, he cleared his throat.

"I'm real sorry about what happened back there."

She turned in the seat. "There's nothing for you to be sorry about. It was my idea to run the horse, not yours. Besides." Although her face was a few shades paler than it should've been, there was a twinkle in her eye. "I was right. It was fun."

"Fun? He got away from me, Emma. If there'd been a car coming from either direction at that crossroads . . ." Sam trailed off, hardly able to think. "You could have been bad hurt," he finished finally.

"Well, I wasn't. And neither were you. Everything turned out fine." When he didn't answer, Emma leaned forward, making him look into her face. "Sam? Don't feel bad. Please. If this is anybody's fault, it's mine. Not yours."

She smiled, and her beauty pulled at him, drawing him in like the smell of a fresh apple pie. That was the trouble with Emma. She didn't mean it to be so, but there was something about her that made a fellow do foolish things. It wasn't her fault. Sam knew that. Emma would never on purpose hurt anybody. Somehow, that innocence made her all the more dangerous, like an oil lamp, lit and put in the hands of a toddler.

Emma didn't know the power she held in that face of hers. She never had, not really, although she'd played with it a little here and there, like a child playing with a match. She lit fires and didn't even realize what she was doing.

But he realized.

"*Nee*," he said shortly. "You're wrong about that, Emma. It's my horse and my buggy, and I'm the fellow holding the reins. Don't matter much what anybody else tempts me to do. In the end, it's my responsibility to do what's right. All you wanted was a little fun. You didn't know Breeze as I do. You didn't know what he might do. I did."

"No, I didn't know much about the horse," Emma agreed softly. "But I'll tell you what I did know, Sam. I knew whatever Breeze did, you would handle it and keep us safe. And so you did."

She spoke with a quiet confidence that jarred him backward in time—back to their schooldays, when he and Emma had been friends, before the problem of her beauty had made itself fully felt. She'd believed in him back then, too, and he'd always been the first fellow she'd turned to when she'd needed something. And he still remembered how that had made him feel, when Emma would ask him for help with careless confidence that he would always help her. That he always could.

"Emma!"

Ruth's voice made them both turn. His aunt stood on the front porch, leaning heavily on her aluminum walker. She peered at them suspiciously.

"What are you doing in that buggy? And with no bonnet on!"

"I was taking in the laundry from the line when Sam drove up, and I asked him to give me a ride down the road. Isn't his new horse a beauty?" Emma hopped down from the buggy as she spoke. "I'm sorry, Ruth. I didn't think you'd be up quite yet. Are you ready for a cup of tea and a snack?"

"I'm ready for you to finish taking that laundry down. I

was taught not to run off and leave a job half done, but I suppose you *youngies* have different ideas. Sam, tie that animal off and come up here. I want a word with you."

Emma winked at Sam as she headed for the backyard. "*Denki* for the ride, Sam."

He only nodded, then busied himself tying Breeze off securely to the hitching post by the barn. He was as quick as he could be and still do a careful job of it, but Ruth's frown had deepened by the time he jogged up the cement porch steps.

Ruth wasn't the sort of woman who liked to be kept waiting.

"What do you need?" he asked her. Likely she'd come up with some more busywork for him to do.

"I need a young man to listen to reason," she said tartly. "And I'm old enough to know how likely that is. But I wouldn't be doing my duty by you if I didn't speak up, so I will. You need to stop making calf eyes at that girl. No good will come of it."

Sam frowned. "You're mistaken, Ruth. Emma just liked the look of Breeze and wanted to go for a ride, that's all."

"I may not have the eyesight I used to have, Samuel, but I know what I see when I see it. Ain't it always the way?" Ruth clucked her tongue. "Always go for the pretty ones, the fellows do, and they pay no mind to the trouble such girls always bring along with them."

Her voice was bitter, and Sam remembered suddenly that his aunt had never married. He'd never thought much about it. Ruth had just always been his spinster aunt. There was one in most every family. But once, of course, she'd been a girl, like Emma. It had never occurred to him that maybe back in her day, Ruth had wanted to be married— and hadn't been asked.

He spoke gently. "There's no trouble brewing here, Ruth. It was just a buggy ride."

"That's how it starts. That and the looks like you two were giving each other. Now, don't mistake me. It's high time you were married, Samuel. You're depriving some woman of a family of her own, staying single, and that's naught but selfishness. In my day, the young men were spoken to about that, reminded by the church to do their duties and take wives in due season. So, by all means, find yourself a *fraw*. But when you go looking, you'll do better to look away from that one there. Think on the grief she's brought upon her own family! All because she didn't behave herself as she should. Spoiled, likely, like all the girls with such faces. You don't want anybody like that, Sam, and you mustn't be *dumm*. From what I've heard, that one didn't want you when you were sniffing around her before. Likely she wouldn't look twice at you now if she hadn't landed herself in such a mess."

That stung a bit, because like so many of Ruth's barbs, there was a drop of venomous truth to it. Emma hadn't wanted him, back in the brighter days, when she'd had her choice of fellows. He couldn't argue with that, and it pricked him a little to think that he was making himself look foolish now.

"I've no notion of courting Emma Hochstedler, so you can—" He'd been about to say *rest easy*, but he stopped short. Something about his aunt's expression tipped him off, and he inched his head just a little to the side so he could look behind himself.

Emma stood at the porch steps, the basket of folded laundry clutched in her hands. Their eyes met, and the look in them went straight to his heart and slammed it flat, like the careless stroke of a hammer on a misplaced thumb.

He cut a suspicious glance back at his aunt, and sure enough, there was a gleam of satisfaction in her gray eyes. But all she said was, "I hope you've folded those well, Emma. If you haven't, you'll have to do them again. I don't hold with slipshod work."

Emma's throat flexed as she swallowed, but when she spoke, her voice was calm and even. "I've folded them the way my mother taught me. You can look them over, Ruth. If they don't suit, you can show me how you'd rather they be done."

She walked up the steps, edging past Sam, careful not to brush against him. "I'll put the basket inside and come back out to help you."

"I can help Ruth in," Sam offered miserably.

"*Nee*, Samuel." His aunt's voice was almost pleasant. "I got myself out here. I'll get myself back inside. You'd best be going along. I've no work for you to do here today. I've got a headache, and I don't want any hammering about the place. You can come back in a couple days. Or better yet, a week. We'll see what needs doing then."

As Ruth was speaking, Emma slipped through the door and out of sight. Sam stared after her, wishing he knew some way to undo the last few minutes.

"Mind what I said, Sam," his aunt murmured, her eyes narrowed. "Now, get on with you before that horse of yours finishes breaking my hitching rail."

CHAPTER EIGHT

❧

"ARE THE ROLLS READY, EMMA?" JANIE BOUNCED ON her heels as Emma opened the oven and peeked in at the baking bread. "I'm hungry!"

"We shouldn't pester, Janie," Leah admonished.

"Nobody's pestering," Emma assured her. "I'm enjoying the company." She was, too. Janie brightened up the kitchen with her smiles and her chatter, and even Leah seemed friendlier since they'd had their talk three weeks ago. "The rolls are not ready yet, but they will be soon. They just need to brown a bit more on top."

Janie huffed out a sigh, and Emma smiled.

She didn't blame the little girl for being impatient. The sourdough rolls did smell wonderful. "I'm so glad Sam remembered to ask Naomi for some of her starter last time he worked on Joseph's shop. If these don't win Ruth over, I don't know what will."

"I wouldn't count on it." Leah chuckled. "But if it comforts you, Ruth didn't like my cooking any better."

"She didn't like me, either," Janie announced cheerfully. "I'm too loud."

"And when we come back, you must try to be quieter," her mother instructed. "We should respect Ruth and be careful to follow her rules when we're visiting in her home."

"Do we have to come back here?" Janie's whole body drooped at the thought. "I want to stay at Sam's."

Before her mother could answer, Emma spoke up. "Janie, why don't you run outside and let Sam know that this bread is just about to come out of the oven? He might like a hot roll with some butter."

The little girl's gloomy face brightened at the mention of her beloved *onkel*. "All right!"

As soon as Janie had pattered out of the kitchen, Leah said, "I hope she's not getting on your nerves, Emma. I have been too gentle with her since Milton died, I think, and I'm afraid she is getting spoiled."

"*Nee*, Leah. Not at all. I enjoy having her close by. She's a little splash of sunshine, and this house can use all of that it can get."

Leah sighed. "I wish Ruth saw it so. You saw how quick she left the kitchen once Janie came in."

"That," Emma murmured, "is another reason I like having Janie close by."

Leah's eyes widened, and she smothered her laugh with a cautious hand. "Well, I can't say that I blame you."

Emma opened the oven again. The tops of the rolls had browned nicely, so she removed the baking sheets and began transferring the hot bread onto a rack for cooling. As Leah stepped forward to help, Emma tried to think of the best way to say what she'd wanted to say while Janie was outside.

Best, she decided, to simply come out with it. "Leah, if you'd be happier staying at Sam's awhile longer, I'm perfectly willing to keep on here."

Leah looked up in surprise. "But our agreement was for three weeks only. Aren't you ready to get back home?"

Emma thought of the note Sam had brought from Naomi along with the starter, detailing all the wonderful progress Miriam was making in Emma's absence. She'd been happy to hear that her sister was doing so well—but a little sad at the same time.

She managed a smile. "I'm not needed at home just now, so if I can help here, I'm more than happy to stay."

Leah slid the last of the rolls onto the rack to cool. "It's not that I don't appreciate the offer, Emma." She cast a quick glance at the door behind them and lowered her voice. "I've so enjoyed being at Sam's with Janie for the past few weeks. You've no idea what a relief it's been. I was just about at the end of my rope. Ruth *needles* a person so."

Emma started to agree but decided to keep quiet. She'd already said enough. If Leah wanted to criticize her aunt, she could, but Emma wasn't about to risk offending that well-known Christner clannishness by chiming in.

Leah was right about the needling, though. Ruth was the sharpest-tongued woman Emma ever met. Most Plain folks she knew were good-hearted believers who followed the guidelines of their faith as sincerely they could. Of course, they were also human, and they had their faults, like everybody else. She'd certainly encountered her share of difficult people, her own uncle included.

But she had to admit, Ruth took difficult to a whole new level.

Still, that didn't change Emma's situation any. It was best for Miriam if she kept away from home a little while longer, and that's what mattered.

"It would suit me to stay on," Emma repeated, "if it would be a help to you."

"Well—" Leah started, and Emma could see relief and hope dawning in her eyes.

"My niece is not the one you're supposed to be helping." A tart voice spoke from the doorway. "I am. And it doesn't suit me for you to stay, not at all."

Ruth stood behind them, her mouth tight with disapproval. That was another bothersome thing about Ruth. She'd perfected the art of sneaking up on people, even with her less-than-perfect hip. Emma couldn't count the number of times she'd been busy with a task, then nearly jumped out of her skin when she found Ruth standing behind her, looking for something to criticize.

"Ruth," Leah was saying gently. "Emma has been such a big help to us all. Please, be kind."

"It's no kindness to speak untruths." The older woman lifted her chin. "It's wrong for family to foist the care of one of their own off on others when they're perfectly capable of doing the work themselves. That girl there"—Ruth nodded at Emma—"needs to go back to her own people, and my folks need to be looking after me."

Ruth sounded as unpleasant as ever, but Emma noticed a telling quaver in the older woman's voice.

She's more hurt than angry, Emma realized. *She's hurt that her family, a family well known for looking after each other, seems so willing to pass her care along to somebody else. She's no husband nor kinder of her own, and now she feels as if she has no real place in her own family.*

And that, Emma knew, was a very unsettling feeling to have.

"I'm sorry I'm not suiting you, Ruth," Emma said quietly. "I'll try harder, *ja?* Your family cares about you very much. It's just that Leah's a recent widow, and—"

"You don't need to keep telling me my own family's business. I know well enough what Leah's situation is. I also know that husband of hers left her with a pile of bills. Samuel's having to pay them off, so they've little money to waste on hired help. In my day, when a man got sick, he accepted *Gott*'s will and died at home. He didn't go run up big debts at an *Englisch* hospital."

Horrified, Emma glanced at Leah and saw hurt glimmering in the other woman's eyes.

"I was the one who wanted Milton to get the treatments," Leah whispered. "Me and his parents, too. We asked him to try, for Janie's sake."

Ruth didn't budge. "Then his parents should be helping to pay off the bills, but I haven't sure heard anything about that."

"Milton's parents have helped as they could, but they've still got four girls living at home, and his *daed* doesn't make so much money now that he's gone to work at the factory."

"They could help other ways, couldn't they? They could take that child in for a while, for one thing. That would likely be best anyway. She's ill-mannered, and she needs a far firmer hand than you've got. She's going to grow up wild if you're not careful, and then where will you be? Milton's *mamm* raised eight children of her own. No doubt she'd settle Janie down quick enough. And you could stay here and look after me until Robert makes the arrangements for me to come to Pennsylvania. It wouldn't be more than a few months, likely."

Emma looked at Leah, expecting her to argue, but to her astonishment, the other woman's eyes were filling with tears. Emma remembered Leah's earlier remark about being too soft with Janie.

Ruth had put her finger right on Leah's weakest point—and pressed hard. In another minute, Leah would agree to it, feeling that she was doing her own daughter a service.

Emma spoke up quickly. "*Nee*, Ruth. A child belongs with her *mamm*. Janie is Leah's first responsibility, especially since the child's still adjusting to the loss of her father. I know you're not happy about it, but for now, at least, I think you'll have to keep putting up with me."

Emma's words seemed to lend Leah courage. "Yes, Ruth. Sam and I will help you all we can, of course, but I think it's best if Emma stays on for the time being."

Ruth's face turned beet red. She didn't like to be thwarted. Emma had learned that well over the past weeks. In many ways, Ruth behaved like a spoiled child herself—she often asserted her will just to show that she could. She didn't like to give in even on small things, and she certainly wasn't going to be happy about not getting her way in this.

"You're making a mistake, Leah," Ruth said darkly, "listening to that one." She jerked her head in Emma's direction. "She's not interested in helping you or me. She's set her sights on your brother. Samuel wasn't good enough for her back in the day, but now that she's disgraced herself, he's looking better, seems like. I've seen her out there laughing with him, getting him to take her for buggy rides. Coming back all mussed and flustered."

Leah looked wide-eyed at Emma, who hurried to explain, "It was only the one ride, Leah. When Breeze ran away with the buggy. Surely Sam told you about that."

From the expression on Leah's face, he hadn't.

"You see?" Ruth went on, "I tried to tell you bringing her here wasn't a good idea. She's too pretty for her own good. Girls like that always end up causing trouble, and this one's surely proven that. I think—"

"We've heard enough of what you think." Sam stood framed in the doorway, holding Janie by one hand. His broad face was set in hard lines as he scanned the scene in front of him. "Emma, I'm needing to have a word with my aunt. Could you take Janie out on the porch for just a minute?"

"But I wanted a roll," Janie protested.

"Janie!" Leah choked out, her eyes round and worried.

"That's all right. We'll take one with us." Emma picked up one of the hot rolls with trembling fingers and wrapped it in a paper towel. Then she beckoned to Janie with a shaky smile. "Come along."

Out on the porch, Janie plopped down on the steps to devour her roll. Emma lowered herself into the rocking chair, feeling sick to her stomach.

It shouldn't bother her so much, those mean-spirited remarks of Ruth's. Goodness knows, she'd made plenty of them over the past few weeks, criticizing everything from Emma's way of wearing her *kapp*, to her cooking, to the way she watered the garden. Emma had tuned them all out, but these digs—especially the ones about Sam—these had found their mark and dug in deep.

Maybe because there was a sharp sliver of truth in them. Ever since Leah had suggested that Sam might have taken their childhood attachment more seriously than she'd imagined, Emma had been looking at him with different eyes.

And the truth was, she'd liked what she'd seen. In fact, as they'd spent more time together, her old-time fondness for Sam had started to bloom again. It felt fragile, like a soap bubble floating in the air, something needing not to be bumped or jarred too much if it was going to survive. But there was something new there, a feeling she hadn't sensed between them for a very long time.

A time or two—although she was probably imagining things—she'd thought she wasn't the only one noticing. She'd turn her head and catch Sam watching her, and he'd look quickly away. Or when they were talking, and she'd laugh or say something funny, his strong face would relax, and there'd be a gentling deep in his eyes that went straight to her stomach, turning it warm and soft.

Maybe Ruth was right. Emma bit down hard on her lower lip, welcoming the sharp pain. Could be she *had* been flirting with Sam a little, trying to coax something more from him than just a friendship. Testing the waters to see if maybe what Leah had said was true.

"Emma?" As if on cue, Leah pushed open the screen door. The other woman's face was worried. "Sam would like to speak with you, if you don't mind. He's in the kitchen."

"Of course." Emma rose and started toward the door. Leah moved aside to let her pass, keeping her eyes down.

Emma's stomach turned over. So much for their new-found friendliness.

She found Sam standing by the kitchen table, drumming his fingers on its smooth surface. He was alone.

"Where's Ruth?" she asked.

"I had a word with her about minding her tongue. I told her she was the one disgracing her family, behaving so un-kindly toward you. Now she's taken to her bed with a head-ache." He rubbed his chin and sighed. "I didn't like speaking to her so sharp. She's my elder, after all, but she was so far out of line that I didn't know what else to do, short of calling on one of the deacons to speak to her, and I hated to do that to a member of my own family. She's been getting harder to deal with over the years, and she was never so easy to start with."

"Getting old is like any other kind of trouble, I suppose," Emma said quietly. "Whatever faults or virtues a person has, it brings to the surface. *Mamm* used to remind us that we should work on filling our hearts with all the good we could, because whenever a bucket gets jostled, it's what-ever's inside that spills out. And usually it splashes on who-ever's the closest."

"I wish Ruth's *mamm* had told her the same. I feel for her, and we want to make sure she's well looked after. But she does make it hard."

Emma took a breath. Best for her to make her apology now. Such things only got harder if you waited too long. "I'm sorry, Sam, if I've caused more trouble for you. I'm afraid I've—"

"*Nee.*" Sam held up a hand, signaling for her to stop. "You've no need to be apologizing, Emma. Ruth was just trying to embarrass you, that's all. You've done nothing wrong."

"I don't know about that. Ruth's exaggerated things, but there's some truth in what she said." Emma glanced up to find Sam's face blank with astonishment. "Oh, she's wrong about most of it. But I can see how I might have given her and Leah some cause to worry because of how I've been acting when you come by."

Sam let the silence stretch taut between them before he spoke.

"How do you think you've been acting, then, Emma?"

Emma flushed. "Well, real glad to see you, I guess. And of course, I have been," she hastened to add. "You probably noticed that yourself."

The corner of Sam's mouth twitched. "I figured that was because you were stuck out here with only Ruth for company."

"It wasn't only that," Emma admitted. "Although you're right about Ruth not being the friendliest company, and it was nice to spend time with somebody pleasant. You've been very kind, bringing word from home and stopping by so often. I know you're busy at work and with your extra jobs so I was grateful, but I feel bad for taking up such a lot of your time. "

"Nobody can take my time unless I'm willing to give it," Sam said slowly. "And from what I've seen, you've little cause to be grateful to me, Emma. I've done you no favor bringing you here."

"Oh, but you have, though! And not just me, either. Remember the letter you brought me from Naomi? She wrote me that Miriam walked to the chicken coop a few days ago. Naomi went with her, and she made it the whole way and back."

Sam smiled. "That's real good news, ain't so?"

"It is." Emma swallowed. "Naomi doesn't say so—she's too kind—but it wouldn't have happened if I'd been there."

"Aw, now," Sam protested, but Emma shook her head.

"*Nee*, it's true. I told you before. There's something about me being around that holds Miriam back. Maybe I coddle her too much, maybe seeing me reminds her of— what happened. I don't know, but she does better when I'm not there. So I'm thankful, Sam, truly, for this chance to stay here and help your aunt." Emma swallowed. "I wrote Naomi a while ago and asked her to look around and see if there might be some other people who needed help. But there weren't. Or rather"—Emma paused—"there weren't any who wanted *my* help. Naomi said everybody was very sorry, but it seems that screenwriter has been asking questions around town, and people are worried that all the fuss is starting back up. Nobody wants to deal with that, especially folks with a sick relative to think about. But I don't want to cause any trouble for you, either."

Sam stood silently for a moment. He made a kitchen feel a bit crowded, Sam did, even being still like he was now, with only his broad chest moving with each breath.

"You," he said finally, "are not the one causing me trouble, Emma." He paused. "But that's true, then? That you've been happy to see me when I've come? I've thought so, but . . ."

There was something so hesitant and hopeful in his eyes that her heart skipped a beat.

"Yes," she answered honestly. "I've been real glad to see you, Sam, every time. It's been . . . sweet spending time with you. It's reminded me of better days."

"Better days."

"*Ja* . . . back before everything changed. Our happy times in school when you and I were such *gut* friends. I can't tell you what a comfort it's been to me, having our friendship back."

"Because that's how you think of me, ain't so? As a friend." He flexed his shoulders and steadied himself, almost as if he were preparing for a blow. "Only a friend."

Emma started to say yes, but she found herself stuttering over her answer. Why, she wondered, was Sam asking? Was he just making sure that his aunt was wrong and Emma wasn't hoping for something he'd no intention of offering?

Or could this possibly have something to do with what Leah had told her?

Sam watched her fumble for a second or two. "I'm sorry, Emma. Maybe I shouldn't have spoken so plain, but it saves trouble later, I've found, if you just ask things straight out. You said Ruth wasn't wrong about everything, and I wondered if you were expecting that . . . if you were thinking maybe . . ." Now Sam was the one stuttering.

Emma, on the other hand, knew exactly what she was supposed to say. "You can rest easy, Sam. I've no expectation of anything but friendship from you."

"You've no expectation, then, that I'd ever think of courting you."

This was uncomfortable—and a little embarrassing. Did Sam really have to make her spell it out? "*Nee*, of course not."

"I see." Sam studied her. "But what if I did think of it? What would you say?"

Emma's eyes widened. "If you—what would I—*what*?"

Sam lifted an eyebrow. "It's not such a surprise, is it? You and I have talked about courting before, back when we were scholars together. But you've made it clear enough since that you'd no thought of being anything but friends with me, so I gave up on the idea. I never changed my mind about you, though, and lately . . ." Sam shifted his weight from one boot to the other. "I've been wondering if maybe you'd changed yours about me. I figured I probably wasn't thinking straight, but then after what Ruth said today . . . I thought I'd check and see how far off I am."

So Leah was right, after all.

As Emma looked at Sam, her heart sped into a crazy rhythm she hadn't felt for years.

"So?" He took a breath and looked away from her, out the kitchen window, as if they were talking about nothing particularly important. Only the tension in his shoulders gave him away. "You might as well tell me. How far off am I, Emma?"

She swallowed. "You're not so very far off, Sam. But I can't . . . tell anything for sure yet."

He turned to face her then, straight on, checking to see if she meant what she was saying. She looked right back at him, and she saw the smile starting in his eyes long before it made it to his mouth.

"Fair enough." Now there was something lighter in his voice, something that made her feel suddenly lighter, too. "We do tend to butt heads, you and me."

"That's true." She wasn't the only one being honest, it seemed.

"But," Sam went on, "I'm willing to give courting a try, if you are."

Something about the absolute practicality in his tone struck her as funny. She fought down a silly grin. "*Ja*, I'm willing, Sam. I think it might be fun."

Sam's smile dimmed, and he shook his head. "I've never been one to court just for fun, Emma. This is serious to me. I may as well be clear about that from the start. If this works out, I'll be looking to marry you and pretty quick, too. You should think this over real careful."

Ja, he looked serious, all right. So serious that Emma couldn't resist poking him just a little bit.

"Oh, I will. Don't worry about that. Although it seems to me you're the one who should be thinking everything over carefully, Sam."

One eyebrow flicked. "Why's that?"

"Because when word gets out we're courting, it's likely to put your aunt right back in the hospital."

"*Ach*, well." Sam's lips twitched. "That's a risk I'm willing to take."

CHAPTER NINE

❧

AFTER SUPPER THAT EVENING, EMMA WALKED THROUGH the pecan orchard on her way to Birdie's house to use the telephone. Naomi had requested the call in her note and had promised to be waiting in the phone shack at the appointed hour.

Emma had left Ruth's in plenty of time, so she didn't hurry. She planned to make the peaceful errand last as long as possible. She'd learned this coping skill during the long months in Ohio when she'd spent a lot of time lingering in a drafty phone shack. That tiny building had been as bleak and as uncomfortable as the Oak Point community itself, but compared to Melvin and Nella's home, it had been a welcome haven.

The home of Ruth's *Englisch* neighbor was far more comfortable, and on the few occasions Emma had come to use the phone, Birdie had been as friendly as she could be. Of course, Ruth had said little good about her, but then Ruth said little good about anybody.

"Thinks too much of herself, that one," Ruth had grumbled. "She's had three husbands, so they say, and you can make of that what you will. She outlived the last one, and I've been hoping maybe she'll sell the house and move off."

After meeting Birdie, Emma suspected she understood the problem. Birdie was kindhearted and generous, but she spoke her mind and stood her ground, and—apart from herself—Ruth had little use for people who did that.

That was another reason Emma was grateful to have this errand to run. Ruth had been in an especially dark mood ever since Sam, Leah, and Janie had driven away earlier that afternoon.

Emma had been feeling a bit let down herself. When Sam had been getting everybody loaded up, he'd glanced over at her. The look on his face had made her suddenly wish she could jump in the buggy and ride away with them.

She'd have liked a chance to ride behind Breeze again, even though it probably wouldn't be nearly as exciting as the first time. Sam had the young horse pretty well in hand now, but he was still a lively high-stepper. And while everyone was loading up, Janie was coaxing her uncle to stop for ice cream on the way into town.

Leah had once again warned Janie against being a pest, but Emma could tell from the softhearted look on Sam's face that there would be ice creams all around, sure enough. It would have been *wunderbaar* fun to ride along with them.

Well, that would have to wait for another day. Hopefully by then, Sam would have explained to Leah how things had changed.

And so they had, in more ways than one. This felt nothing like it had back years ago when Emma and Sam had secretly considered themselves matched up. They'd only been children, then. But earlier this afternoon, when Sam had talked about marriage, she'd realized this wasn't a boy playing at courtship with a schoolmate. Sam was fully a man now, and he wasn't playing anymore.

That shouldn't have been much of a surprise, given that the fellow in question was as tall and as solidly built as a barn. Still, the change was startling—like wading along in a shallow creek and suddenly stepping off into a hole.

The path to Birdie's house was a bit of a walk, but long before Emma got to the yard, she knew exactly what Ruth's neighbor was up to. She smelled woodsmoke. Birdie must be dealing with the pile of sticks and dried limbs that she'd dragged over to the edge of her yard.

Sure enough when Emma came through the azaleas, Birdie stood beside a crackling fire, her shoulder-length gray hair tied back in a red bandanna, a rake in one hand and a glass of iced tea in the other. She glanced up when Emma approached.

"Emma, darling! What a pleasure to see you." Birdie's voice had a throaty sound to it. She purred as much as her elderly golden tabby cat, Moses, who was currently basking in the last of the afternoon sun on her back steps.

"I thought you'd decided to wait until the fall to burn all this," Emma said.

"Oh, I know," Birdie said, making a face. "Fall is the best time for bonfires. Silly me. But I was feeling so lonely and irritated, and I just had to set something on fire. Don't you ever have days like that, Emma, dear? Never mind," she said with a wink, "don't answer that. You don't have to. You're sharing a house with Ruth Christner, so I'm quite sure you do."

Emma laughed. "It's not as bad as that."

"Of course not, darling." Birdie took a sip of her tea then leaned in closer to Emma. "It's worse." The older woman straightened, sly laughter twinkling in her blue eyes. "You've got that admirable Amish stoicism, my love, but you can't fool me. I've lived next door to that woman far too long. It's a wonder I haven't set *her* on fire." Birdie took another long drink, studying Emma over the rim of her glass. "For somebody who's dealing with such an objectionable old toot, you don't look nearly as run down as one would suspect. In fact, today you look quite chipper. That means one of two things. Are you leaving Ruth to stew in her own juices and going happily home?"

Emma laughed. "No." Even though Emma herself could never say the things Birdie said, it was rather satisfying to hear them spoken out loud, especially on days like today, when Ruth had been particularly difficult. "As a matter of fact, it was just decided that I'll be staying on for a while longer. I've come to telephone home to let my family know, if that's all right with you."

Birdie waved an impatient hand. "Oh, of course. You know you're welcome to use the telephone anytime you like." She cocked her head, considering Emma with a teasing glint in her eye. "Selfishly I'm glad to hear you'll be around awhile longer, although I'm afraid that's a bit nasty of me—like rejoicing when a prisoner's sentence is extended. But never mind. Let's get on to the juicy stuff. If you're not glowing because you're going home, you must be glowing because of a man. Oh, look at her blush. It *is* a man."

"Birdie, you're impossible," Emma stammered. Birdie's outspoken bluntness was all very well when it was confined to Ruth—but this *Englisch* woman spoke her mind about everything.

"Don't bother to argue. There's no point in it. I've been expecting this to happen. A girl who looks like you? Of course there are going to be men. Scads of men, likely." Birdie laughed her throaty chuckle. "I know because I was a beauty myself in my youth. Not quite so spectacular as you, I'm sad to say, but I broke my share of hearts in my time. So who is it? That nephew of Ruth's? The big, broad-shouldered fellow? Must be. There hasn't been another eligible man near the place since Moses there was a kitten, and that was at least eight lives ago now."

Emma flushed. She was saved from having to answer when the wind shifted, blowing the smoke from the fire directly into her face.

Coughing and with watery eyes, Emma retreated up the steps. Birdie smiled up at her. "You should take that as a compliment. Smoke always follows beauty, my mother used to say." She sighed. "There was a day when any smoke around—or any fellow, for that matter—would have followed me. Now, not so much, I'm afraid, and oh, how I miss it." She batted her eyes playfully. "I'd have given you a run for your money with that Amish muscle man of yours, I'll tell you that." Birdie gave Emma a quick up-and-down look and sighed again. "I'd have lost, but I'd have enjoyed the try. Darling, it's a good thing we weren't girls together. I'd have been absolutely green with jealousy."

Emma cleared her throat. All Birdie's easy talk about beauty made her uncomfortable. She knew, of course, that the people in her community had their opinions about her looks—especially the boys. She'd figured that out years ago. But among the Plain, nobody praised such things openly. Their official position was that beauty wasn't something to be admired. Character was what counted.

Birdie was under no such restrictions. The very first time she'd laid eyes on Emma, she'd exclaimed over her looks at length, and she hadn't stopped since. It made Emma uncomfortable, but she knew the other woman meant well.

"May I—" Emma gestured toward the back door. "I'm sorry, but Naomi and I arranged a time and—"

"Of course! You've set up a time to call, and I'm blathering away and making you miss it. I always forget how difficult this all is for you folks. I couldn't be Amish for a minute. Go on inside. You know where everything is. I need to stay out here and mind this fire."

Emma slipped inside Birdie's neat laundry room, carefully wiping her shoes on the mat by the door. Then she went through to the phone in the kitchen and punched in the number for the phone shack closest to the Hochstedler farm.

She was a few minutes late calling, which was always a bit of a chance, but to her relief, Naomi answered on the first ring.

"Emma?" Her sister-in-law spoke breathlessly. "Is that you?"

"*Ja.*" The one word was all Emma managed before Naomi rushed on.

"Isn't it awful? Have you and Ruth heard anything? How are they doing? There's been no news here, nobody's heard anything for hours, not since the very first."

"Naomi, what are you talking about?" Emma clenched the phone in her hand. "Heard anything about what?"

Silence fell on the other end of the phone, and when Naomi spoke again, it was more slowly. "I'm sorry, Emma. I shouldn't have rushed into it like that. We felt sure you'd know more than we do. Ruth's a member of the family, after all. There's been an accident."

"No."

Emma sank onto the chair by the phone. She didn't have to ask who was in the accident because somehow she knew, even before Naomi spoke again.

"Sam and Leah and Janie. It was that new horse of his that did it. They were stopped at an intersection, and something spooked him. He must have caught Sam by surprise because somehow Breeze pulled them right out in front of a truck. It hit them broadside."

Bad. The meaning of Naomi's words filtered slowly into Emma's brain, like liquid dripping through a jelly bag clogged with fruit. Broadside was very, very bad.

"How—how—" She didn't know what question she was

trying to ask. Thoughts weren't coming in complete sentences. They weren't coming at all. She could only sit there, dumb and quiet, holding the phone so tightly in her hand that her fingers ached with it.

"They're all alive." Naomi spoke the reassuring words quickly, and Emma could breathe again. "They were taken to the hospital. We know that much, at least."

Emma swallowed. "What else do you know?"

"Not a lot. Leah was the least hurt, although that's not saying much. She was in the back of the buggy for some reason. Janie and Sam got the worst of it. Poor little Janie was pretty torn up, they said. And Sam . . . Sam was struck in the head. There's some trouble with his eyes, but that's all we know. Leah's still at the hospital in Knoxville, but they've flown Sam and Janie to Memphis."

Memphis. Too far for Emma to go to see them. She would have to wait for news. Wait and pray.

"Call if you find out anything else. Tell Birdie. She'll let me know. Please, Naomi. If you hear anything else. All right?"

"All right. Of course. Hopefully somebody from the family will be coming out to tell Ruth all the details. I was sure they already would have, but I suppose nobody's thought of it yet."

Ruth wouldn't be high on anybody's list, but *ja*, sooner or later somebody would come by. "But you'll call me if you hear anything at all," she pressed.

"*Ja*." Naomi paused. "Oh, Emma, I'm sorry to have dropped it on you like this. I know you and Sam were old friends."

Suddenly Emma couldn't take any more. Without even saying goodbye, she hung up the phone. She looked up to find Birdie standing in the doorway, her face smudged with smoke, and her eyes sharp and concerned.

"I heard a bit of it," she said. "Enough to get the gist. Buggy accident."

Emma nodded.

"I'm so sorry, darling. If you need somebody to drive you to the hospital, I'll be glad to do it."

"They took them to Memphis."

"I see. It must be bad then. Sorry," Birdie said quickly when Emma winced. "I'm afraid I've never seen much benefit in sugarcoating things. Memphis is the best place for them to be. It's a fine hospital, one of the best in the country. My second husband had his bypasses done there. Quite successful."

"I should walk back and tell Ruth." Emma stood.

"No, of course you're not walking back. I'll drive you. Just let me spray this ridiculous fire with the garden hose, and I'll run you right over. Won't take a minute." Birdie paused at the door, her eyes compassionate. "I truly am sorry, darling girl, and I hope your fellow will be all right."

Her fellow. That did it. Emma pressed her hand against her eyes hard, trying not to cry, but her shoulders shuddered.

"I'm sorry," she managed. "It's just a little too much."

In a second, she was enveloped in a warm, smoky-smelling hug. "Oh, darling," Birdie said, and she felt the older woman's chin resting on the top of her head. "Of course it is. It's just so terribly unfair, isn't it? First your poor parents and now this. I suppose it's not only smoke that follows the beauties, my dear. Trouble follows them, too."

CHAPTER TEN

❧

SAM SHIFTED HIS POSITION ON THE EDGE OF HIS
second cousin Bessie's spare bed, feeling the mattress dip
and sag under his bulk. He'd lost weight during his two
weeks in the hospital. He could feel it in the loose fit of his
clothes, but even so, he was too heavy for this old bed. He'd
only been back in Johns Mill for three days, but he'd heard
some warning creaks and pops from the bed's wood frame
already. Likely a few more nights of his tossing and turning
would destroy the thing, and that would make another trouble for his family to cope with.

As if having a badly injured little girl and a big, blind,
fool-headed fellow on their hands wasn't bad enough.

Sam clenched his fists on top of his knees, measuring
the pain as the torn skin on his hands and arms stretched.
It hurt, but not as much as it had to start with. His body was
slowly healing—except for his eyes. He still couldn't see
anything but a mottled darkness.

He'd woken up to it in the hospital, this black nothingness in front of his face. He'd flailed, confused, trying to pull off whatever was covering his eyes. He remembered little else of that now. They'd given him something to calm him down, he suspected. And when he'd finally been clear-headed enough to ask questions, they'd dodged most of them.

The doctor had used big words, and he'd seemed in a hurry. After he'd left, Sam had asked the nurse with the kindest voice to tell him again, using plain words this time, why he couldn't see. She'd explained that the knock he'd had on his head, the one that had put him senseless on the ground, had done something inside his skull to the nerves in his eyes. It was real unusual, she said, so likely more doctors would be coming by to see him.

And so they had, although he didn't know why, since they admitted, one after the other, that there was nothing much they could do. Watch and wait, the doctors had said. In time they would know. His sight would probably come back, but they weren't promising anything.

Sam wasn't asking them for promises—not for himself anyhow. He only wanted promises for Janie. Unfortunately, nobody seemed willing to give him any of those, either. In fact, they were being very closemouthed about her, and that worried him most of all.

He remembered little about the accident. Only a split second of horror when Breeze had started off at the intersection, spooked by a horn. Sam had been holding the reins one-handed, talking to Janie, and thinking about Emma. He'd held a dripping ice cream cone in his left hand, trying to keep ahead of it so it wouldn't drip all down his sleeve.

His attention had been everywhere but where it should have been.

Then some *Englischer* had blown his horn as he'd passed by, Breeze had bolted, and Sam had flung down the cone and grabbed at the reins.

He hadn't been quick enough. He'd realized it, and he'd reached for Janie, hoping to throw her clear. That was all he remembered.

Leah and Breeze had been the least hurt. The truck had hit the front of the buggy, but the back had taken less of the blow. Breeze had been dragged, they said, and the vet had done two surgeries on him, giving his services for free as he often did in circumstances like these. The horse would never be a pretty stepper again, but he would live and could still be useful. The vet had sent word to Bessie's yesterday asking where Sam wanted the horse sent.

Sam didn't blame Breeze for the accident, but it would suit him well enough never to deal with the animal again. He'd sent word back, telling the vet to do whatever he liked.

Leah had suffered a broken arm, and some other minor issues, but overall, she had fared the best of them all.

Or the worst, depending on how you looked at it. Sam couldn't bear to think about the pain his sister must be in right now.

The impact had hit on Janie's side. As badly hurt as Sam had been himself, he could only imagine what must have happened to his niece. And he had imagined it, over and over again in his head, each picture worse than the one before it, because nobody was telling him much.

Janie was still in the hospital in Memphis. That much Sam knew, but nobody would give him any details. They only said not to worry, that she was improving slowly, that the doctors were sure now that she would live. That he should focus on getting better himself.

He was thankful for those things, but he knew they were keeping something from him. He heard it in the gentleness of his family's voices, in the way they sidestepped his questions, going silent and annoyingly patient when he grew short-tempered. He suspected Leah had asked them not to tell him the whole of it, and they wouldn't go against her request. Maybe his sister thought she was sparing him, not telling him the worst, but she'd done him no kindness.

Whatever it was they were keeping from him, he already knew it must be bad. With each day that passed, his nerves stretched thinner, wondering what it was and expecting the worst.

As long as Janie was all right, then he could accept whatever *Gott* gave him—even if he were to be blind forever. That was no better than he deserved anyhow, for being so stupidly careless.

It was a harsh thing to think about, though—living in this darkness for the rest of his life. He'd not be able to do his work, and that changed everything. He wouldn't be able to help Leah and Janie.

And he sure wouldn't be able to support a wife.

He hadn't gone much further in his thoughts than that. He couldn't stand to.

Sam tilted his head, listening. A murmur of voices was coming from downstairs. A woman's voice, he thought. He hoped it was Leah.

And he hoped it wasn't.

She'd been spending all her time at the hospital with Janie. She'd visited his room before they'd released him, saying she'd come to see him again when she could. In the meantime, their sisters were taking shifts with her at the hospital, along with Milton's family.

Sam's care had been assigned to Bessie and the women of the church. He tried to be a grateful patient, but it was hard. It set his teeth on edge to be helpless. He wasn't used to it.

He needed to be working, to be looking after his sister in this hard time. He ought to be taking her burdens onto his shoulders, making sure that Janie was well cared for and that the bills that were surely mounting up had some hope of being paid.

Instead he was stuck here, being a trouble to his family and his church, and led from place to place like some old dog.

He heard the bedroom door creak open.

"Sam?"

For one instant, his heart lifted like a bird launching itself from a branch, but then it shot downward. His fingers clenched tight on the soft quilt covering the bed. "Emma?"

"*Ja*, it's me."

He froze. He didn't know what to do or say. She'd asked to come to see him before, and he'd made an excuse.

He'd needed to wait. Partly because he hadn't wanted her to see him like this, but it was more than just that. Emma just . . . mattered too much. He hadn't wanted to see her until he'd known for sure which way this storm was going to blow.

He pushed up to his feet, trying to orient himself toward the door. It was hard to remember where things were. He tried, but he wasn't familiar with Bessie and Leman's house, and more often than not, he blundered.

He heard her moving toward him. Cool, firm hands took his sweaty ones. He could smell her—a scent of clean laundry and soap that snatched him backward. A memory of Emma flashed into his mind—the way she'd looked that last afternoon when he'd finally gotten the nerve to ask her about courting. He'd been wondering for days how to bring it up, every time Emma had glanced at him with those blue eyes of hers. Emma had the prettiest eyes, like the water of Miller's Lake on the finest day of the summer, reflecting the sky.

And for one sweet moment, she'd been looking up at him—at *him*, Sam Christner—while all his hopes clicked into place like the planks of a dovetailed floor.

"I wanted to see you sooner," Emma was saying. "But I couldn't get to Memphis. The first day you were home, I came by, but Bessie said you were too tired for visitors."

He heard the gentle confusion folded into the question. *Didn't you want to see me, Sam?*

"Today I just pushed myself in," she was saying. "I had to see you—to talk to you. I've been so worried about you. About all of you. You don't look bad at all, Sam." He felt a gentle touch high on his cheekbone, and he flinched. "I'm sorry," she said. "You're bruised a bit on your face, but those are fading."

She didn't fool him any. She'd only touched his face as an excuse, to find out if he could see anything. People did that a lot. Maybe the doctors had told them to. He didn't know.

"Do you want to go out on the porch?" Emma asked. "It'll be cooler out there in the shade, and I expect you'd like a change from this stuffy bedroom. You can hold on to my arm, and I'll help you down the steps."

Steps were hard, and going down them was the worst. He'd never thought much about stairs before, but there was something about stepping off into nothingness that made his head swimmy. The first time, even with Bessie's help and holding on to the rail, he'd nearly lost his balance.

It had scared Bessie to death. *Ach, Sam, maybe we'd best wait for Leman next time. If you fall, big as you are, you'll likely smash me and this old staircase both to bits!*

Since then, he'd learned to take it slow, feeling out for each step carefully, putting one foot down before bringing his other down to join it. Sam suddenly hated the idea of Emma seeing him hobble down the stairs like an old man.

"I don't feel like going anywhere," he said roughly. "If it's too hot for you, you'd best go on outside. Bessie was right in what she said. I'm not up for visitors."

There was a pause, and he felt Emma's shock in her fingers. They loosened, and when they regripped his, they held him more lightly. Cautiously, as if Emma was no longer so sure of her welcome.

"I'm not just any visitor, though, Sam. At least I didn't think I was." When he didn't answer, she sighed. "Sit down then. I suppose we can talk just as well here. Better maybe because we won't be overheard. Sounds like you and I have a few things to work out." She turned loose of his hands, and he flexed his fingers. He didn't know what to do next, and that made him irritable.

"The bandage on your arm looks to need a change," Emma said after a few seconds. "Why don't I tend to it for you while we talk? Bessie's got all the supplies handy."

He touched the gauzy bandage. It hurt, but he didn't care about that. "It's fine."

"*Nee*, it isn't fine." Emma's voice sounded sharper now. "It looks like you've broken it open somehow. There's blood seeping through."

"It's not bothering me."

"Maybe not, but it'll bother Bessie plenty if you get blood on her quilt." He heard the scraping of a wooden chair as Emma dragged it closer. "Now, here." She placed her hands gently on his upper arms and tried to nudge him. He didn't budge. She made an impatient noise. "Move a bit sideways, Sam, won't you? I need you to sit down if I'm to see to this."

"Emma." He didn't like being looked after. It was bad enough with the others, but they'd all been older women. Old enough to be his *mamm*. This was Emma. "Leave me be."

"Sam!" Exasperation was plain in her voice now. "I'm trying to help you. Bessie said you've been acting like a wounded bear since you got here, and so you are! Now, *sit*, and let me get that dirty dressing off."

She sounded so normal, fussing at him, not giving him an inch, just like always. Emma was kindhearted to a fault, but she didn't put up with much nonsense. Lots of bluster, but underneath it, all the sweetness a man could wish for—

like those crunchy candies with the soft, melty centers his *grossmammi* had made at Christmastime.

Those had always been his favorite.

"Sam, I mean it, now. Stop being muleheaded."

Emma's voice was firm, not like the hesitant, sympathetic voices that had been murmuring around him lately. He reached behind him and fumbled to find the location of the chair. Once he had it, he sat.

"Good." He heard soft steps, and a puff of Emma-scented air hit him as she moved past on her way to the table for a clean bandage. She started clinking things around. "Now. I'm going to unwrap the one that's on you. It looks like it may stick a bit. When was the last time it was changed?"

"I don't know." He honestly didn't. Time blurred for him. One of the women had wanted to change it; he'd told them not to bother. Maybe he'd been a bit rude, which he shouldn't have been, but he'd asked again for news about Janie, and all he'd gotten was a lot of soothing words.

He suddenly straightened on the chair, and Emma made a worried noise. "You'd best keep still, Sam. I don't want to hurt you, and this isn't coming off easy."

Emma would have made it her business to know about Janie, and folks would have had no reason not to tell her. No matter how bad it was, he was sure Emma would tell him the truth.

He opened his mouth to ask and stopped. He'd never been afraid of much in his life, but he had to admit, he was afraid of what Emma was likely to tell him.

"There." He heard her sigh in relief as the last of the bandage peeled away. "Oh, my. They should be changing this more often, Sam. It's a bad scrape, and it's got a bit of infection starting. I'm going to clean it up good and put some medicine on it." There was a pause. "It's likely to hurt a bit."

"I don't care about that." He braced himself. "Emma, what have you heard about Janie?"

"She's still in the hospital." He felt Emma's fingers, light and careful, dabbing at the area on his arm where his skid along the road had rubbed away a long strip of skin.

"How bad hurt was she?"

Emma's hands went still. "She's improving, Sam, from what I hear. Every day. And that's real good news."

"That didn't answer my question. I want to know how bad she's hurt, Emma."

"Oh, Sam." He heard the pained sympathy in Emma's voice, and it stung worse than the stuff she was dabbing on his wound. "Leah should probably—"

He jerked his arm roughly away from her.

"Sam!"

He stood up clumsily, and he heard the wooden chair clatter backward onto the floor. "I need to know, Emma!"

"All right! Sam, all right. I'll tell you everything I've heard. Now, sit down. No." He felt her tugging on his arms. "Sit here." He sat and felt the bedsprings sagging under him. "We'll just have to be careful of Bessie's quilt."

"Emma." He couldn't take much more of this dithering. His nerves were stretched past their breaking point already.

He heard her take a breath. "Sam, I don't know too much about Janie. I haven't talked to Leah for myself, so I only know what I've been told."

"Tell me that, then. All of it, mind."

"Her legs were broken, both of them, badly. I believe there was some damage to her hips, and that's why she's still in the hospital. They're being real careful."

"Will she walk again?"

"*Ja*, they say so."

He couldn't see her face, of course, but Emma's answer had come quickly enough that he believed it. He rushed on to the next question that had been fretting him. "There's no problem with her eyes, like I have? She can see all right?"

"Yes, she can see fine from what I hear."

He swallowed hard as he came to the stickiest question. "Is her head all right? She's not . . . damaged? She's still able to think and talk the same? She's still Janie?"

"Yes, Sam. Her brain swelled a little to start with, but that went down. From what I hear, nobody's concerned about there being any of that kind of damage. She's been awake and talking to her *mamm*."

Sam sat very still as Emma gently coated his arm with a cold, slimy ointment, his brain sifting through what he'd heard.

The broken legs were bad enough, for certain sure, but the answers to the worst questions had sounded all right.

"How long until she's better?"

"They don't know."

"Emma."

"Sam, they don't. She's doing well, they say, but it was a nasty accident. They seem to think she'll be out of the hospital in another week or so. She'll have to have physical therapy, and there'll be another operation or two in her future, but she'll recover."

Sam sat quietly, allowing Emma to finish rewrapping his arm as he thought about what she'd said.

His first feeling was relief, but something still didn't make sense. He knew Emma wouldn't lie to him. If this was the worst of it, though, he didn't see why people wouldn't have told him.

"What are they worried about, Emma? What aren't they telling me?"

Emma sighed. "I expect they're mostly worried about you, Sam. You're every bit as bad hurt as Janie is, don't forget. They don't want you upsetting yourself."

"Upsetting myself over what, then?"

Emma had done with his arm, and he sensed her preparing to move away. With an instinct he didn't know he had, he reached out and captured her wrist.

"I'd tell you, Emma. If you were the one sitting here instead of me, asking. Even if the whole world warned me not to, you know I would tell you."

She hesitated, and he could feel her pulse throbbing in her slim wrist.

"*Ja*," she murmured finally. "You'd tell me, Sam. And I remember what it was like, folks tiptoeing around, afraid to say things for fear you'll feel worse than you already do."

"I couldn't feel worse than I already do." He lifted his chin. "I'll know the whole of it, Emma. Please."

"She'll be scarred, Sam."

"Scarred." He repeated the word. "Where?"

"On her arms and her chest, mostly." There was a pause, and he felt Emma's muscles tense. "She got dragged a bit. Along the road. That's why."

"Will she be scarred on her face, too?"

"*Ja*." Emma spoke softly.

Ah. There it was.

"Bad?" When she didn't answer, he prodded sharply, "Emma."

"Bad enough," she said. "They won't know anything for sure until later, but they've cautioned Leah about it."

Sam's breath was coming quick, but he couldn't seem to get it deep into his lungs. Scarred, his Janie. She'd always been a sunshiny *maidel*, with such a sweet smile. So pretty, too, like a bright little flower just starting to bud.

But now she would be scarred bad enough that they'd warned her *mamm* about it. All because of him. Because he'd not respected the danger in that wild, half-trained horse. Because he'd been holding an ice cream instead of holding the reins.

And because he'd been daydreaming about Emma instead

of paying attention, as he should have been. He'd have seen it coming, otherwise. He had a sense of horses, like all the men in his family. He'd always been able to read them. He'd have seen that bolt coming, certain sure, if he'd had his mind on the job at hand, as he should have.

"It's a shame, Sam, but remember, it's not near as bad as it could have been. How she looks doesn't matter. We must be thankful, and we must trust *Gott*. He loves Janie better than all the rest of us, and—"

He wasn't in the mood for a sermon. He interrupted her. "I want to be alone now."

"Sam—"

"Emma, I thank you for telling me the truth of it. But please. Leave me be."

He heard her breathing, soft and quick. Then, "All right, Sam. I'll go, for now. But I'll be back. We'll talk again, later, you and me."

He didn't answer. After a few reluctant seconds, Emma left the room, closing the door quietly behind herself.

Once he'd heard her start down the steps, he lowered his head into his hands and wept.

CHAPTER ELEVEN

❧

ONE FRUSTRATING WEEK LATER, EMMA SAT ACROSS from Bishop Isaac Lambright in Bessie's spotless kitchen. Bessie hovered like an anxious bee, pouring tea and nudging a plate of cookies toward Isaac's elbow. Her quiet husband, Leman, had chosen a chair in the corner by the stove and was watching the proceedings from a safe distance.

"*Denki*," Isaac said politely. "This is very nice. Now, please, sit down, and let's talk this matter over. Emma here is worried that our friend Samuel is struggling. Do you agree, Bessie?"

"*Ja*." Bessie sank into her chair and folded her hands on the table, nodding nervously. "We've tried our best, Leman and I, but Samuel isn't doing well. He won't eat hardly anything, no matter what I put in front of him. That's not like Sam. You've seen him eat at church, Isaac. Like a horse, usually. But now he won't even join us at the table. He just wants to sit in that room all by himself. I've tried to encourage him to come out amongst us, but he gets right short when he's pushed."

Bessie twisted her fingers together, shooting uncertain looks between Isaac and Emma. She'd agreed to this meeting at Emma's urging, but inviting the bishop into her kitchen clearly made her uneasy. She'd been up and scrubbing for hours—the strong scent of lemon cleanser mixed with the scent of tea.

"I am sure you have offered good care to Samuel," Isaac reassured her. "This is not your fault. It sounds as if despair has gotten a grip on our friend, and that can be a hard thing."

"The only thing he shows any interest in is how Janie is doing," Emma volunteered. "The news isn't always good, so that hasn't helped. I know this plan of ours is a little unusual, but nothing else seems to be working."

Emma had tried her best to talk to Sam without calling in reinforcements, but he was shut away inside himself. He barely spoke back, and when he did, his answers were short and vague.

Lately, he'd gotten worse. Janie had developed an infection, and she would be staying in the hospital longer than expected. Yesterday had come word that the date of her discharge had been pushed out again. With each bit of discouraging news, Sam slipped deeper into a darkness that had nothing to do with his vision.

Bessie and Leman were doing their best, as they'd said, but they were no match for Sam's grief and guilt. That was clear. So, in desperation, Emma had come up with a plan, and she'd called on the church for help getting Sam to agree with it.

The bishop steepled his fingers together and studied the tea remaining in his cup, his brow wrinkled in thought.

Isaac looks a good bit older, Emma realized. There was

more salt than pepper in his beard now, and the grooves in his forehead were much deeper than she remembered.

Small wonder. As leader of the local church, Isaac had been tasked with shepherding his community through both the Hochstedler tragedy and the *Englisch* media's fascination with it. That would have been difficult enough, but her family's sorrows had spilled over into the laps of the Lambrights in some very personal ways, too. As a result, Caleb, Isaac's son-in-law, was shunned, and his only daughter was living far away with relatives. Looking at the bishop now, Emma could see that these troubles had taken a heavy toll.

"I am sure Sam's loss of sight is not helping matters any," Isaac said after a few moments of thought. "What do the doctors say of this?"

"They say that it is too soon to tell if his sight will return." Leman spoke from the corner of the kitchen. "We have taken him to one doctor in Knoxville for a checkup. This man said that the longer Sam goes without seeing, the less likely it is that his sight will return, but there is some hope yet."

"Some hope," Isaac repeated and sighed. "Sometimes that is hardest. When we know *Gott*'s will, then our duty is plain. We must resign ourselves and go down whatever path He in His wisdom has assigned us. But when we do not yet know, when there are two paths laid out and we must wait . . . that is the more difficult thing. Especially for a man like Sam, who is used to action. I will speak to him."

"Talking to him isn't likely to help," Emma argued before she thought. "Sam can be very stubborn."

Bessie and Leman looked at her in disapproving horror, but Isaac only lifted his bushy eyebrows a notch, a little smile flickering above his beard.

"I will not argue that point with you. What of Ruth? What does she think of this plan you've come up with?"

No surprise that the word *stubborn* had brought that question to Isaac's mind. Emma hesitated, but she had to be honest. "She is not too happy about my part in it, but she says she will agree if you believe it is best."

There was a long silence, then the bishop nodded. "I will see Sam for myself. Then I will decide."

He rose. When Emma stood, too, Isaac shot her a surprised glance.

"I thought I should come with you, maybe," she said. "In case there are any questions."

For a second, the bishop looked as if he might protest, but then he seemed to think better of it, and nodded. "*Ja*, you should come. It is best for everything to be clear from the beginning."

Upstairs in his bedroom, they found Sam hunched in a straight chair. He turned his head in their direction, but his gaze slid past them.

Emma swallowed. It was hard, seeing Sam like this. Not just the blindness, although every time his eyes slipped past her face without stopping, it hurt her heart. But worse were the lines of pain and grief she saw etched in his expression, deeper every time she came. And each time she'd visited, there'd seemed to be less left of what had made Sam himself.

Bessie fretted endlessly about the weight Sam was losing. Emma was more worried by the hollow expression on his face and the flat tone he used when he spoke. All so very different from the strong-hearted man she'd known all her life.

The man she'd been on the tip edge of falling in love with.

That was why she'd pushed for this meeting, for this plan. Sam needed to be jostled out of this despair he'd fallen into—and soon. Emma felt the urgency of it, although she'd fumbled trying to explain it to the others.

"Sam, Isaac has come to see you," she said now.

Sam's expression shifted into a weary resignation. "Isaac," he greeted the other man quietly.

"Sam." The bishop looked around at the small, hot room. The smell here was definitely not of lemon. It smelled of an unbathed body, and the bedclothes were rumpled. Sam's hair badly needed trimming—and washing, from the look of it. Isaac glanced at Emma and sighed.

"Why have you come?" Sam asked. "Is there news of Janie?"

"No, this isn't about Janie. We've come because we are worried about you, my friend."

Sam slumped back in his chair. "There is no need to worry over me."

"*Ja*, you are right." The bishop pulled a second chair close to Sam's and sat. "Worrying does no good. Wiser to trust *Gott* and take action, ain't so? Speaking of that, we have talked it over, and we feel that you may do better in another household. Bessie and Leman have done their best for you, but we think it is good now that you leave them and move to the home of another relative. What do you say to this?"

Sam didn't answer immediately, but after a second or two, he shrugged. "All right." Emma waited for him to ask questions, but he said nothing more. He just sat.

Finally she couldn't stand it. "Don't you want to know where you're going, Sam? Or who's going to be taking care of you?"

He lifted his head at her voice, but his expression stayed stony. "That's not for me to choose, is it?"

Emma opened her mouth, but Isaac shot her a warning glance. She shut her lips together and waited.

"*Gut*," the bishop announced. "That is the right attitude to have. We must be cooperative when we are ill, to make it as easy as possible for those who are entrusted with our care. Bessie will help get you packed up, and you will be moved to Ruth's this afternoon. I can drive you myself."

"Ruth's." Sam repeated his aunt's name with some alarm. "She's got the care of me?"

"*Nee*, at least not entirely. You'll be living there, but Emma here will be looking after the both of you."

Sam stiffened, sitting bolt upright. "Emma?"

"*Ja*. She's offered to take you both on." The bishop leaned back in his own chair, making it creak. "She's a brave woman, I think. From what I hear, you've been none too easy to deal with. And of course, Ruth . . ." Isaac left that sentence unfinished. Everybody knew Ruth. He didn't have to explain.

"Isaac." Sam's voice sounded stronger now, more like himself. "I'll go wherever you say. I'm . . . sorry about Bessie and Leman. I've cut up a little rough, I know, and it was selfish of me. But this is not a good idea."

Emma shot an alarmed glance at Isaac, but the bishop's expression didn't change. "It's been decided, Sam. Ruth can be a challenge, but I am sure you two can find a way to get along, since she's being gracious and opening her home to you. It'll be good for her, I think, to be given the chance to give back to her community. That's a precious blessing, and we've not given her enough opportunities to serve others since Davey passed on."

"It's not that." Sam shifted in his seat. "Emma, can you leave us a minute, please?"

"*Nee*, Emma," the bishop countermanded quietly. "You can stay. She's a part of this, Sam, and there's no point in secrets."

Sam lifted his chin. The purple bruises on his face had faded into yellow, and the cuts were reddened stripes that would heal into scars. "I don't know if Emma told you, but I'd . . . spoken to her . . ." His throat moved as he swallowed. "Before all this."

"She mentioned something about that, *ja*." Isaac looked at Emma. "That you two were thinking of courting. I was interested to hear."

Sam's brow furrowed. "That was . . . before. Things are different now, but still, it might make a problem."

"Oh, I don't see that, no. Emma won't be living there. She's asked for a special permission to stay with the *Englisch* neighbor, to rent a room for a few weeks. It is unusual, but no different, I think, than staying in a hotel when traveling. As Emma has pointed out, she will only sleep there. She will be spending the rest of her time looking after you and Ruth. And you require no personal care, from what I understand, only the more general things. You just can't live alone for the time being." Isaac got up from his chair and laid a hand on Sam's shoulder. "I think this will suit."

"It will not suit me." Sam bit out the words, and his hands fisted against his knees.

"From what I have heard, being here hasn't suited you, either. This will be a good exercise for you, Sam, in patience. Obedience and humility, too, maybe. We can always benefit from such lessons. Anyway, this arrangement is only temporary. There is still good hope that your vision may return."

"Do you think, after what her brother has done, Emma should be permitted to stay with an *Englisch* woman?"

Emma froze. She couldn't quite believe that Sam had said such a thing, had cast up her twin's choice not only to her, but to Isaac, who'd also been hurt deeply by it.

"I am not Caleb," she began hotly, but Isaac held up a silencing hand.

"I have no concerns about Emma's faithfulness, Sam. If you were thinking of courting her, I wouldn't believe that you'd have had any such concerns yourself. Now, you'd best get ready for the move. I'll send Bessie up to help you. Emma and I need to talk about arrangements."

"Isaac," Sam protested, but the bishop walked out the door as if he hadn't heard. He beckoned for Emma to follow.

She followed him into the hall, shutting the door behind them. A loud bang came from the bedroom, and Emma's eye widened. She reached for the doorknob, but Isaac shook his head and motioned her farther down the hall.

"He kicked the chair over," Isaac said when they were out of Sam's earshot.

Emma bit her lip. "Maybe I should go back in—"

"*Nee*, I think not. Let him wrestle with his will in peace. We have done what we came for."

"Maybe I was wrong to suggest this. I knew Sam might balk a bit—but I'd no idea he'd be so . . ." Emma struggled for the word. "Upset," she finished, although that didn't quite cover it. Mean, more like. She still couldn't believe he'd cast Caleb's leaving up to them. That was so unlike kindhearted Sam—it had shaken her.

"You were not wrong, Emma. This was a very good idea."

To her astonishment, the bishop was smiling. "What?"

"Did you see how angry he got? And so quick, too. Like lightning. *Ja*, this is good. It's not Sam's anger that we should fear. That we can overcome. It's what we saw first—the sitting, the staring. Not caring what happens to him. Despair—that's what destroys a person, if they're allowed to stay in it for too long. But we got his blood up, you and I. He doesn't want to be helpless around you, that's plain to see. With you around all the time, he'll start trying again, and that's just what we want him to do."

Emma had hoped so, too, but now she wondered. "Are you sure?"

"Sure?" Isaac shrugged as they started down the steps. "Who among us can be sure of anything, except *Gott*? But I think it's a good sign. We will try this, Emma, and we will see. That is all we can do."

"Isaac, what he said about Caleb. I'm truly not going to—"

Isaac stopped halfway down the steps at the sound of his son-in-law's name. He didn't look directly at her, but a spasm of pain passed across his face. "I know this, Emma. You two may be twins, but you're cut of different cloths. I've no fear of your faith failing you." He glanced up at her then and smiled. "And that's a good thing. You'll be needing *Gott*'s help, with Ruth and Sam both on your hands."

Emma glanced back toward the bedroom and squared her shoulders. "I will do my best," she said.

"Then," Isaac said with a smile, "I have good hopes that this plan will succeed."

Two hours later, Emma was turning Ruth's elderly mare into Birdie's driveway. She'd driven by Ruth's house at a trot, hoping that Ruth wouldn't notice them going past. Isaac would be bringing Sam out after supper, and she had a lot to do in the meantime. First she needed to let Birdie know that their plan had been approved.

She hurried in the back door. "Birdie?"

"Up here!" Birdie's call came from the front of the house, so Emma walked quickly in that direction. Birdie was sitting in a plush, plum-colored armchair in her living room. She rose when Emma appeared and nodded toward the couch. "Darling, we have a visitor."

"Oh!" Emma stopped short in the doorway. She glanced toward the sofa, and her heart rose into her throat.

Ian McMillan used the arm of the couch to boost himself to a standing position. He smiled at her.

"My dear," he said. "I hope you'll forgive yet another intrusion."

Emma wasn't sure what to do. She looked at Birdie helplessly.

The other woman was watching Emma closely, reading her discomfort. Birdie frowned, and a certain spark came into her eyes. But when Birdie spoke again, her voice was even and pleasant.

"Mr. McMillan here dropped by," she explained. "Unannounced. He said he'd heard you were staying nearby, and he'd hoped to have a word with you. To follow up on your meeting in town, he said. He stopped next door first, but apparently Ruth packed him off with a flea in his ear."

Good for Ruth, Emma thought. But not so good for her. She'd hear about this, for certain sure.

"A very forceful woman," the screenwriter said, shaking his head. "She doesn't seem to hold to the more peaceful tenets of your faith, does she?"

"So he came here." Birdie spoke lightly, but her eyes were sharp and questioning. "As you can imagine, anybody coming here with a tale of woe about Ruth . . . well. I'm afraid I felt a certain kinship. And then, he said he felt the need to apologize to you, so I saw no harm in letting him wait." She flashed a tight smile. "I do have a soft spot for groveling men."

"Yes," Ian hurried to interject. "I'm afraid our chance encounter on the street didn't go well, Miss Hochstedler. Your gentleman friend didn't give me ample opportunity to explain myself and express my sincere regret at having startled you. I'm so terribly sorry."

"You're forgiven." Emma said the words quickly.

The man offered a charming smile. "You're very kind."

"Yes." Birdie's eyes narrowed. "She is. Still, she has no choice but to forgive you, you know. Her religion requires it. But I'm not Amish, Mr. McMillan, and I can bear a grudge with the best of them. The fact is, the longer I stand here, the more I'm getting the feeling that you finagled your way into my house under false pretenses. If you have any intention of causing trouble for Emma here, let me assure you, I can be more forceful than Ruth Christner ever thought of being."

The *Englischer* looked alarmed. "Oh, no, my dear woman. I assure you, my visit today is motivated by concern. I have only this young lady's best interests at heart."

"I am not your dear anything," Birdie said. "I think you'd best state your *concerns* as quickly as you can. And then," she added ominously, "we'll see."

"Of course. I wanted to apologize again, as I said. And I admit, I also wanted to talk to you about the script." His gaze moved past Birdie to fasten hopefully on Emma. "I didn't have the chance to explain before. I really do need to interview you. It's the only way the story can possibly be balanced. As it stands now——"

"What script?" Birdie interrupted.

"Mr. McMillan is the man writing the movie about what happened to my parents," Emma murmured.

"Out of my house," Birdie ordered. "This minute. Out." She crossed to the front door and pushed it open.

"No, no, you don't understand. I'm not trying to cause any trouble. It's just that the studio set up interviews with the Abbotts, and the story they're telling . . ." The man shook his head and turned back to Emma. "I need to talk to you, too. I have to get a sense of what's real here. Otherwise——"

Birdie spoke before Emma could. "You're going to get a sense of something if you don't get out of my living room this instant."

"But——"

"Do I need to call the sheriff's office, Mr. McMillan?"

The *Englischer* shut his mouth with a snap. "No, Mrs. Marshall. You do not. I'll go." He took a card out of his pocket and placed it on the coffee table. "Here is my number, Miss Hochstedler. I very much hope you will think this over and call me. I truly mean you no harm, and I do believe it would be to your advantage—and to the advantage of your family—to have your side of the story told accurately." He picked up his walking stick and clapped a floppy cloth cap on his head. "I'm deeply disappointed, but at least my conscience is clear. I've done what I can. Once again, I must apologize for upsetting two very delightful ladies, and I wish you both a good afternoon."

He went through the door Birdie was holding open. Emma came up to stand beside Birdie, and the two of them watched the screenwriter limp down the walkway toward a small silver car parked in the front yard. Caught up in her plans and worries about Sam, Emma had driven right past it without even noticing.

She was going to have to start paying more attention.

Birdie shut the door firmly, but they lingered at the window until he'd driven out of the driveway. Then Birdie turned to Emma with a worried expression.

"Oh, darling girl, I'm sorry. I'd no idea who he really was, and he seemed so charming. I've always been a fool for a silver-tongued man, more's the pity. And the story he told about Ruth . . ." She shook her head. "If it hadn't been for that, I'd never have let him in, but that softened me right up. I'm just terribly sorry."

"That's all right, Birdie. You couldn't have known. He took me by surprise, too, that first time in town. But I'm glad you made him leave. I've no interest in talking with him, and that's already been made plain. He was wrong to come here and bother you."

"I'm not worried about myself. I just hate that he upset you." Birdie crossed over to the sofa and began straightening the throw pillows. "Although—not that I approve of the man's tactics, mind you, but are you absolutely sure you shouldn't talk to him? Give him your side of the story?"

"No. We aren't in favor of this movie, and we don't feel we should contribute to it."

Birdie tilted her head sideways. "Darling, you know I speak my mind, so I'm going to go ahead and say what I think. That movie's going to be made whether you talk to Mr. McMillan or not. If the Abbotts are the only ones providing information . . . well, I can imagine the sort of nonsense they're spouting. They always did spoil that son of theirs—when they weren't ignoring him altogether." She shook her head. "You know, sometimes when we don't speak up against lies, it's every bit as bad as lying ourselves. Keeping silent isn't always the best policy."

Emma blinked as a memory stirred. What was it that Isaac had said earlier? Something about Sam's silence being more troubling than his anger?

Of course, that had nothing to do with this. Anyway, she'd already made her decision about Ian McMillan and this script of his. Hadn't she?

"People believe untruths all the time, Birdie. About far more important things than a silly *Englisch* movie. No matter what I say, I expect folks will believe what they want to believe."

"Maybe you're right." Birdie drew a deep breath. "All right. I've said my piece. You do as you think best. Now, let's get on to something more interesting. I've been on pins and needles all morning waiting to hear how your meeting went. What did the bishop say?"

Emma smiled. "He has approved my staying here."

"Wonderful!" Birdie gave a pillow a last good thump and turned, her face alight. "I'm absolutely delighted, darling, and I'm sure this arrangement is going to prove to be just what that poor Sam of yours needs. And don't you worry. I know this is a special exception they're making, so I promise to behave myself while you're visiting." She winked. "Or I'll try anyway. You'd think that'd be getting easier at my age, wouldn't you? But anyhow, I'll do my very best. Now come on." She looped her arm through Emma's. "I'll show you your room."

CHAPTER TWELVE

"SAM, YOU HAVEN'T EVEN TOUCHED THAT SUPPER tray."

He raised his head. Near as he could tell, Emma was standing in the doorway of Ruth's spare bedroom. She sounded frustrated.

Well, fine. He was frustrated, too.

He hadn't wanted to be driven here this afternoon, but his protests had fallen on deaf ears. So here he was, delivered by Isaac like an oversized sack of potatoes.

"You have to eat," Emma went on fussing.

"*Nee*, I don't." Maybe he'd been dragged into going along with this embarrassing setup, but that didn't mean he had to go along with everything. He was too mad to eat anyhow. The smell of the food made his head hurt and his gut churn, and even the thought of swallowing it made a sour bile rise in the back of his throat.

"You should at least try. Your pants are just about falling off of you."

Now, that was a picture, wasn't it? Sam felt his face heating up, and he set his jaw.

"Emma, I have already said no." He kept his voice low—and firm. "Just take the tray back to the kitchen and leave me be."

Of course, she didn't leave. Nothing was that simple with Emma. Instead she shut the door and walked in closer.

The bedroom was cramped, and there wasn't much space between them. He could hear her breathing, soft and just a little too fast, and he could see in his mind's eye what she must look like, plain as day.

Who knew that over the years, his memory had saved so many pictures of Emma? He seemed to have one for her in every possible mood. The smallest trigger, like the sound of her breath right now, and the matching image of her rose up in his head, just as clear as if he could really see her.

She'd be flushed, and the pink in her cheeks would make her eyes look even bluer. Her mouth was probably trembling just a little, as her bosom rose and fell under her apron. Sam had learned over the years that the tremble didn't always mean Emma was about to cry. It might, sometimes.

It might also mean that she was fighting mad and about to give him a generous piece of her mind. He was pretty sure which way the wind was blowing today, even without his eyesight.

"I won't leave you be, Sam. So you might as well put that idea straight out of your head." Emma's voice was low, too, but it shook with feeling. "I want to help you, but you have to at least try."

"I don't want your help." His own breathing had sped up in rhythm with hers, and he could feel his temper sliding away from him.

Having Emma here so close by—the very thing he'd daydreamed about for years—was killing him now. She was a constant reminder of how temptingly close to reality those dreams had come before flitting back out of reach.

For the first time in his life, he wished Emma Hochstedler would go away and leave him alone.

"Well, too bad," she was saying. "You've got my help, whether you want it or not."

He firmed his mouth and stood. "I'm a full-grown man, and I'll decide for myself whether I want to eat my supper or not."

"For pity's sake, sit back down. Nobody's going to argue that you're a full-grown man, Sam." Emma's voice was sharp. "Least of all me. Not when you're standing there six feet and over in your sock feet. But you're not acting grown-up. You're acting like a spoiled child having a fit because he doesn't like what's been put on his plate."

Sam felt that sense of sliding again—of moving toward something he didn't want to hit. Like the way the buggy had slid, just before the truck had hit them. He could hear Janie's short, scared cry, and the blare of the truck's horn.

The pain that hit him alongside that fragment of memory pushed him right over the edge.

He needed to be alone. Right now, before he said something or did something he'd regret.

"Get out, Emma." It took him a minute, but he finally managed to add, "Please."

"No."

That one stubborn word was all it took. Sam's frustration met his pain and rose up in a towering wave. His fingers clenched over the back of the chair, and in one smooth movement, he picked it up and flung it hard against the right-hand wall. He heard it hit, heard a tinkling shatter, then heard Emma's shocked intake of breath. The room was suddenly thick with the smell of lamp oil.

"Emma!" His aunt's worried call came from the kitchen. "What happened?"

"It's all right," Emma answered quickly. "Sam just knocked over a lamp."

"Oh, for goodness' sake!" Now Ruth sounded irritated. "See there? I knew something like that was bound to happen."

"Well, it did, so you'd best stay where you are and start eating your supper. There's glass everywhere in here and oil. Don't worry, though. I'll get it cleaned up." He could tell Emma was trying to sound calm, but her voice shook.

Sam's anger congealed into a cold miserable lump in his stomach. He'd scared her, showing his temper like that. Sam had never wanted to be the kind of man who used his size and his strength to frighten innocent people. But look at him now.

Tears came to his eyes, and he was both embarrassed and horrified. He could imagine what *Daed* would have said about Sam standing here, a great hulking fellow, crying like a baby in front of a girl.

"I'm sorry." He ground the words out. "I shouldn't have— I'm sorry."

"It's all right, Sam." He felt her touch his arm, could feel her hand shaking, making a lie out of her words. "It was only a lamp, and an ugly one at that. You've done no real harm."

No real harm.

"That's not so." It poured out of him now, the feelings he'd been bottling up, afraid to share, afraid to speak out loud for fear that saying them would make them truer than they already were. "Janie broken to bits and all scarred up, that's harm I've caused. Leah's arm broken, too, and a horse was hurt, that's harm. And me here blind and not able to help my own family out of the trouble I've brought on them with my carelessness. And now . . . yelling at you . . . breaking things . . . I've done plenty of real harm, Emma."

"*Nee, nee.*" Her hand ran up and down his forearm, gently, reassuringly. For all her earlier words about him being a man, she soothed him like a child. "It was not your fault, Sam, the accident. Everybody says the same."

"They can say what they want. It doesn't change the truth. It was my fault."

There was a short pause. "It wasn't, I don't think. But I know that what I say about it doesn't matter." Emma's voice was thick with feeling. "I know because it doesn't matter to me, when people tell me that what happened to *Mamm* and *Daed* wasn't my fault. People can't take away the guilt from us by saying such things, no matter how kindly they mean them. It doesn't work. The terribleness, it just sticks inside our hearts like hot tar. I can't help you with that. Only *Gott* can help and He will, if you'll let Him. But I know how you feel, Sam, if that helps you any. I know how much it hurts. I *know*."

Ja. The truth of it sank slowly in. She knew, all right.

In fact, Emma was probably the one person who could truly understand what it felt like to single-handedly destroy your own family.

She was trying to comfort him, pointing that out. It didn't work. It pained him more, somehow, thinking of Emma suffering like he was now. Only worse, because he'd been suffering for a few weeks. She'd been enduring this pain for months.

And her folks hadn't just been injured. They'd died.

Sam clenched his fists at his side. If Janie had died . . . or Leah. He knew it would have been *Gott*'s will—that nothing like that happened unless the Lord allowed it. The church had taught him that. But for such a thing to have come through him?

He was almost out of his mind with the pain and guilt he was bearing now. That would have turned him savage. And yet Emma had been forced to bear that awful burden. Emma with her sweet smile, and her habit of looking up at a fellow and tilting her head in a way that made him go all warm and foolish inside.

Sam cleared his throat roughly. "What happened that day . . . it wasn't your fault. You didn't pull that trigger. Trevor Abbott made that choice. You can't hold yourself responsible for somebody else's doings."

"But you can make yourself responsible for a horse's doings?"

"That's different. I was driving one-handed. That's why Breeze got away from me when the horn blew. He wouldn't have otherwise. He always gives hints about what he's going to do. I'd learned to pick up on them. But that day I wasn't watching him close enough. I was thinking about— something else."

Emma said nothing for the space of four heartbeats. Sam knew because he counted them, one after the other. "About me. You were thinking about me, about the talk we'd had, just before."

He started to deny it, then stopped himself. People had been sugarcoating the facts for him ever since the accident. Sometimes he wished they would just admit the truth and stop trying to protect his feelings. Better to deal straight on with a mess than keep trying to cover it up and pretend it wasn't there.

"*Ja*. I was." He couldn't resist adding bitterly, "Not that it matters anymore."

There was a longer pause this time. Five heartbeats. Then six.

"It still matters to me, Sam."

Still? His heart thudded hard. "But everything's different now. With my eyes like they are . . ."

"Only *Gott* knows what's going to happen about that, Sam. You'll have to wait to find out, and so will I. But I see no reason why we can't wait for His answers together. Hope together and pray together, you and me. The truth is . . . I think we're meant to."

"Meant to." He was listening to her closely now, straining for every word, like a drowning man reaching for a rope.

"*Ja*. I don't know what the future will bring any more than you do. But I do think maybe *Gott* has put us together for this hard time. Because of what I said earlier. Because I can understand what you're feeling. Because we can help each other in ways nobody else can."

He shook his head miserably. "How can I help you—or anybody else—now?"

To his surprise, Emma laughed softly. "Well, the same way you always have, Sam. By being strong. There are different kinds of strength, ain't so? You will have to learn to use some new muscles, that's all. Now, you'd best sit down on the bed while I get this mess cleared up. The lamp oil is spreading everywhere, and you're in your sock feet."

She took him by the arms and pushed at him gently. And he stepped backward without argument and sat down on the edge of the bed.

"Good." Emma sounded surprised—and relieved. "Now, don't move, *ja?* There's broken glass. Just wait. I'll get some rags and have it cleaned in no time."

"All right."

"And while you're sitting there, try to eat some of your supper." When he didn't answer, she added, "Please, Sam? For me?"

He'd heard that particular *please* from Emma half a hundred times over the years, and it had rarely failed to move him. But right now it was a different word, a word she'd spoken earlier that kept playing itself over and over in his head.

Still.

It still matters to me, Sam.

He was being foolish, setting his heart on the slim hope in that word. He knew it. But then, he'd never really stopped being foolish over Emma, had he? Not even after all these years.

And he already knew he wasn't going to be able to stop now.

"*Ja,*" he said quietly. "I'll try."

For you.

Chapter Thirteen

❧

THE NEXT MORNING, SAM KNEW THE MOMENT EMMA left the kitchen and started down the hall. Ruth's house was small enough that he could hear everything that went on.

Folks were always talking about how efficient this little house was, so well suited for Ruth and Davey, but Sam had always felt cramped here. Even as a boy, he couldn't move a muscle without knocking something over, and he'd dreaded coming for visits.

Of course, that probably had as much to do with Ruth herself as with the house. She wasn't a good hand at making folks feel welcome.

Emma knocked softly. "Sam?" He heard the door open. "Breakfast is ready."

He'd known that, too. The scents of frying sausage, eggs, and coffee had been teasing his nose for the past half hour.

The door squeaked as Emma opened it wider. The

hinges needed oiling. If things had been different, he'd have seen to that. As it was, he'd only make a mess with the oil, and send Ruth through the roof, so best not.

It was a strange thing to think of—not even being able to do such a simple job. He seemed to be finding more and more things he couldn't do.

"You must be starving by now. You only picked at your supper last night," Emma said.

"I wasn't hungry last night. I'm not now, either."

"That happens when you don't eat for a while. Your stomach's given up hope, but one really good meal should wake your appetite up."

Sam sighed. He wasn't up to having this argument again. "Bring the tray in, then. I'll eat what I can."

"Oh, there's no need for a tray anymore. I've got everything ready for you in the kitchen."

He frowned. "I'd rather eat in here." He'd rather not eat at all, but one thing at a time.

He heard her walking across the floor, and he tensed. He hated not being able to see people coming. He felt a soft flutter of air as she stopped beside him, and he smelled soap, starch, and sausage.

"It's not healthy for a person to eat alone. Come have breakfast with Ruth and me."

He started to say no. He meant to. Then she laid a hand on his shoulder. He felt each one of her fingers through the material of his shirt, felt the warmth of her touch.

"Please, Sam." He recognized that coaxing tone in her voice. He should because he'd almost never been able to resist it. He'd always thought it was Emma's pretty face that made men softheaded around her, but maybe not. Even now that he couldn't see her, he still felt himself weakening.

"Emma." The frustration he felt came out in her name. "Leave me be. I don't want to eat at all. I don't want to eat in the kitchen, for sure." *In front of you, making a mess of myself.* He'd gotten better at managing, but he still spilled, still got things muddled up.

"I know you don't want to, and I don't want to make you mad." She paused then added, "But does that really matter, Sam? What either of us want?"

He'd been all ready to argue, but the question stopped him short.

He knew the answer. He'd cut his teeth on this teaching. No, it didn't matter what he wanted or how he felt. What mattered was what was best—not for himself—but for others.

So he stood. "All right. I'll eat in the kitchen."

He was sure that, if he could have seen her face, he'd have seen surprise that he'd agreed so quickly. He couldn't see her, but the little pause before she answered told him the same.

"*Gut!* Come on, then." As she spoke, she tucked his arm through hers. "I'll walk with you."

There was something about that, feeling her slim arm resting against his, that made his belly churn uncomfortably. He liked the feeling—and he didn't like it—all at the same time.

He wanted to walk arm in arm with Emma, but he didn't want her leading him around.

He pulled his arm away. "I can walk by myself."

"But—"

"I know the house well enough to find my way." To prove it, he walked to the door. He found that easily enough and turned down the hallway toward the kitchen. He tried to walk same as always. No doddering and feeling the walls, not when he could sense Emma standing behind him, watching.

"Sam!"

Her warning call came just as his right boot hit some-

thing. He stumbled, and there was a loud clatter as whatever it was skidded down the hall. He leaned down and felt
with one hand but found nothing.

"It's all right. It was only a chair." Emma brushed past,
and he heard the scraping noise of the chair being set right
again. He remembered now that Ruth kept a wooden chair
in the hallway just outside the kitchen doorway. Supposedly
it was kept there in case of an extra guest who needed a
seat, but of course, Ruth almost never had that many guests.
In Sam's memory, it had mostly been used for punishment.
He'd been banished to it numerous times for not behaving
exactly right during a meal. Ruth was particular about table
manners.

Emma had better keep that chair handy. He'd likely be
needing it.

"I'll thank you to be more careful." Ruth spoke sourly as
Sam came through the doorway. The kitchen was warm
with the heat from cooking and smelled strongly of coffee.
"I don't have the money to be replacing my furniture because you're kicking it to pieces."

"He stumbled, Ruth. I doubt you or I would manage half
so well if we couldn't see. Here, Sam. Sit down." A chair
scraped, and he felt Emma's gentle hands helping him to
his seat.

"Oh, he was always like that. He was clumsy as a five-
legged calf growing up. Had feet the size of boats when he
was just a boy, and he couldn't walk across a room without
breaking half the things in it." Sam heard the clink of a cup
on a saucer. "No wonder the family's sent him here for me
to look after. Same as they did with Davey. Nobody wants
to take care of me, but they certainly do like for me to take
care of other folks, I notice."

"Ruth, that's unkind and untrue. Your family did take
care of you," Emma was saying.

Sam was barely listening to Emma's protest. He was

focused on the peculiar note in Ruth's voice when she'd talked about being stuck with him. He couldn't put his finger on it, but there'd been something different in his aunt's voice.

He heard the scrape of spoons against dishes, and the thump of a plate being settled in front of him.

"There's your breakfast," Emma said. "Sausage is at the top of the plate, bread's on the left, and the eggs are to the right. Your coffee is—" She took his hand and cupped his palm around a hot cup. "Here."

It smelled even better close up, but Sam didn't move, unwilling to pick up his fork and make a fool of himself in front of Emma. He could manage eating, just not too well. And he wasn't hungry most of the time anyway. As embarrassing as it had been to hear, what Emma had said yesterday was true enough. His pants were getting so loose that he had to hitch them up when he walked.

He bowed his head to return a silent thanks, and he couldn't resist adding one desperate plea.

Please don't let me make too much of a mess.

"Go on," Emma prodded when he lifted his head. "Try the sausage. The Millers sent it from the café, and it's good. Not up to my uncle Melvin's, mind. Sausage is the only thing he's really good at."

"Melvin." Ruth huffed. "I wouldn't eat that fellow's sausage. There's no telling what he'd grind up in it, thinking he was saving a nickel."

Was the sausage in links? Sam wondered. Or patties? If he'd been alone, he'd have run a hand over his plate to see. He hadn't eaten at a table with other folks since before the accident, and he felt self-conscious and strange.

He heard the noise of Emma settling herself beside him at the table.

"You'd best eat," Ruth observed sternly. "Big-built men like you shouldn't be skinny. It doesn't look natural. Besides, I won't have folks saying you're not getting enough food from my table."

"Ruth." Emma's voice had a dogged pleasantness to it. Ruth was getting on her nerves. "I need to take the buggy into town this morning. You and Sam can manage all right here by yourselves, can't you?"

Sam frowned. Emma going to town by herself? He didn't much like that. He tensed and started to object, but then fell silent. What could he do about it? Nothing. He'd be no good to her, even if he did ride along.

He sagged back into his chair. He was no good to anybody these days.

"I'll manage him all right." Ruth snorted. "Didn't I manage Davey all those years? Go on, do your running around if you're bound to."

There was that strange note in Ruth's voice again. Sam tried to put a name to it as he felt for his coffee, slowly, carefully.

"I'll be back well before lunch," Emma said.

"I'll believe that when I see it," Ruth retorted. "I'll end up fixing lunch for the both of us, likely as not."

Emma started a mild protest, but Sam wasn't really listening. He was focusing hard on Ruth's voice, and suddenly, it clicked.

Happy.

That was it. Ruth was happy. No wonder it sounded off. He'd never heard Ruth sound pleased before.

His mind on that, he forgot to be careful. His fingers bumped his coffee cup and hot liquid splashed out over his hand.

"Oh!" There was a scurrying, and then Emma took his hand, dabbing at it with a towel. He felt the usual heart-jump at her touch. That, combined with the fact that he couldn't even eat at a table decently, pushed him past his limits.

"*Schtopp!*" He snapped out the word, pulling his hand away from hers.

"Sam, that coffee was fresh-poured and hot. Let me see if you've burned yourself."

"I can't see, Emma, but I can feel." He could, and his feelings were smarting more than his hand. "I'd know if I'd burned myself." He stood. "I'm going back to my room."

"Emma, you need to go get the horse hitched if you're going to town." Ruth spoke up tartly. "Sam, you sit back down."

There was a short silence. He sensed something pass between his aunt and Emma. The air felt itchy, like it did just before a thunderstorm.

"All right." Emma's voice was carefully even. He heard more rustlings, and then the sound of the door shutting.

He knew Emma was gone. The room felt emptier.

"Sit, Sam," Ruth repeated from someplace beneath him.

"I'm not hungry."

"I didn't ask you if you were hungry. Although I was taught as a child that it was a sin to waste good food once it's been put on your plate."

"I didn't ask for this food."

"Ain't the first time you've had to deal with something you didn't ask for. Won't be the last. Sit." When Sam didn't comply, he heard his aunt make an impatient noise. "You're in my house now, Sam, and I'm not so softhearted as Bessie. Don't make yourself more of a chore than you have to be. Do as you're told."

He stood frozen, pondering her words. He'd known, of course, that he was a chore to people now, even though they wouldn't say so.

But Ruth had never been shy about speaking her mind, and there was a strange relief in that. Somebody—finally—was speaking honestly to him. It occurred to him that Ruth might be able to tell him the truth about a lot of things.

He sat.

"Now eat. You can't keep on like you are. You'll be falling down next. That's what I thought had happened when you tripped over that chair. Probably broke it to bits."

Ruth wasn't the only one who could speak the truth straight out. "Small loss if I did. It's an ugly chair."

Ruth's snort was muffled. Likely she had her pointed nose stuck in her coffee cup. "You're like all men. Thinking the looks are all that matters. They ain't. That chair's useful. That's what matters. Now, eat your breakfast. It's gone cold, likely, but that serves you right. Don't ask me to warm it up for you."

"I'm not asking you to do anything for me."

"Ha. You're asking plenty. You're expecting me to take you in and look after you. They all are." There it was again, that self-congratulatory note in Ruth's voice. It made no sense to Sam, but it was definitely there.

"You didn't have to agree."

"Sure I did. In my day, when you were asked to do something by your bishop, you did it, whether it suited you or not. Besides, it'll be the quickest way to put a stop to all this nonsense between you and that one outside. You needn't think it's you yourself she's so interested in. She likely thinks if she makes a show of looking after people, folks will forget about the trouble she's caused. Once the new wears off, she'll lose interest right quick, you mark my words. If you want a wife with good character, look for one with a plainer face."

Sam managed to take a sip of what was left of his coffee. Ruth herself sure didn't offer much proof to that idea. His aunt was as plain as a white hen, but Sam had never heard anybody praise her character.

Still, like always, Ruth's barbs stuck in a man's hide and stung like hornets. Emma did like looking after people. She always had. Could that softheartedness be behind what she'd said last night? The idea made him irritable. "You can give your tongue a rest, Ruth. It doesn't look like I'll be marrying anytime soon."

"Well, that's true. You're pretty poor husband material right now. Unless your sight comes back—and I don't have any confidence that it will, by the way—you won't have any way of making money, will you? Mind yourself, Sam! You're dribbling egg yolk everywhere."

Sam stopped in mid-chew. Somewhere along the way, he'd picked up his fork and started eating. He'd been so busy feeling annoyed with Ruth that he'd barely noticed it.

He started to set his fork down, but realized that he was hungry—really hungry. The food had gone stone cold, but it didn't matter. And maybe he was dribbling egg, but Emma was outside hitching up the horse, and he didn't care if Ruth saw him make a mess or not. He took another mouthful. Then another.

Ruth sighed loudly, obviously wanting him to hear. "It's a good thing the Zooks sent over plenty of that sausage, and that Joseph's Naomi is sending food, too. Otherwise you'll be likely to eat me out of house and home."

There it was again. That self-satisfied note. For all her complaining, Ruth wasn't near as displeased with this setup as she was trying to make out. It made little sense, that. Maybe if he could see her face, he could puzzle it out, but since he couldn't, there was no telling.

He decided not to worry about it. He had plenty other things to fret over. Speaking of that, there were some questions he wanted to ask his outspoken aunt while he had the chance.

"What's the news of Janie? Is she walking any?"

"They say so, but only with help, and it causes her a lot of pain. That foolish horse." Ruth clucked her tongue.

Sam shook his head. "It wasn't so much Breeze's fault as mine."

"If you mean because you bought the skittish animal to start with, I'd agree with you. Another example of a man prizing looks over character, I'd say."

Sam ignored the jab. "Is there any word about when she'll be able to leave the hospital?"

"She already has. Day before yesterday, I believe Emma said. Leah took her over to Milton's parents. They're going to stay there for now. Maybe for good. Janie's still got a long road ahead of her, and your sisters have to get back to their own families. Leah will need all the help she can get."

"What?" Sam turned his head toward his aunt swiftly, and for a second—he almost thought he saw her—or the outline of her. Then he blinked, and only the foggy darkness was there. "Janie's already out of the hospital?" And Emma had known about it?

"Yes," his aunt answered. "Samuel? Where are you going?"

Sam had risen to his feet. He fumbled for the edge of the table and walked toward the door, feeling ahead with his hands. His foot caught on the leg of a chair and sent it sliding.

"Sit back down before you fall down, Samuel!" Ruth clucked behind him like an agitated hen. "Or wait, and I'll walk with you."

"I'll go by myself. I can find the barn. I need to talk to Emma alone."

He stepped out the door and onto the steps. He hadn't been outside much lately, and the air hit him in a warm, fragrant swirl, bringing with it a rush of memories that shocked him into stillness. For a second, he could almost believe that he could still see—that he'd only closed his eyes to breathe deep of a summer's morning.

He could smell the grass and the tea olive blooming beside the steps. He also smelled the horse manure from the barn—Maude's stall must need mucking out. The morning breeze cooled his cheeks, but he could feel a building warmth coming from the sun. In a couple hours, it would be hot as blazes, but it was nice now.

This was the time of day he'd always liked best. There was a lot of promise in the mornings. A man's work lay ahead of him, plenty to keep busy, plenty to do. He'd always felt a little let down in the evenings, coming home alone. Evening times were for family, and once his parents had moved off, he'd had none. Of course, when Leah and Janie had come along, it had been some different. Even though they'd come sorrowing, they'd sure made his life happier.

In return, look what he'd done to them. A car rushed by on the road, and Sam's fingers clamped on to the handrail.

"Sam!" Emma's voice spoke from a distance, then closer. "It's so nice to see you out of doors!"

"I need to talk to you."

"Is something wrong?" Her voice came closer. "Did Ruth say something? I do wish she'd try to mind her words."

"Ruth doesn't bother me. I'd rather talk with somebody who doesn't mind her words than somebody who keeps things from me. She just told me about Janie, about her being out of the hospital. She said you told her that Leah and Janie were staying with Milton's family. That's only an hour's drive from here."

Emma didn't answer him. The summer breeze blew fitfully against his cheek. He could feel it ruffling his hair, hear the leaves around him rustling. A bird sang loudly nearby.

"Why didn't you tell me, Emma? You knew I wanted all the news of Janie. And you knew I planned to go visit her as soon as she was home from the hospital."

"*Ja*, I knew." Emma sounded tired.

Sam told himself he didn't care. "Then you should have told me."

"Janie is getting good care from people who love her.

And you are going through your own troubles right now, Sam."

"That doesn't matter—"

"Of course it matters. Folks are concerned about both of you."

"Folks." Sam repeated the word slowly. "Do you mean my sisters?" An idea occurred to him. "Emma, did Leah ask you not to tell me about Janie? Does she not want me to come?"

There was another silence. He could hear Emma's breathing. This conversation was upsetting her.

Fine. That made two of them.

"Emma?" he prodded.

"Leah just"—Emma hesitated—"sent word that she thought it best to wait on a visit. That's all."

He scrubbed a hand roughly over his face. "Why?"

"Sam," Emma pleaded gently.

He took his hand away from his eyes, and for a second, like he had back in the kitchen, he thought he saw something. A glimmer of light in the muddled darkness, outlining a blurry shape.

It was quickly gone again. He swallowed and braced himself. "Just tell me, Emma. Why doesn't Leah want to see me?"

"It's not that, Sam! She just doesn't want you upset. That's all. She thinks that it would be best for you to . . . find your feet a bit before you come to visit Janie."

He felt like an ox was sitting on his chest. "She thinks I'll do something . . . say something to upset Janie?" He remembered the chairs he'd flung in a temper, and his heart sank.

Maybe his sister was right.

"Sam." He felt Emma touch his arm lightly. "Try to think it through. Remember, Janie's adjusting to things, too. Leah doesn't want her unsettled, either. The way you're feeling just now . . . can you really be sure you could handle a visit without showing your grief over what's happened? Without making things worse for Janie, even though you'd never mean to? The way I did with Miriam, maybe?"

Sam frowned. He hadn't thought about that. He clenched his jaw. "I don't want to upset Janie."

"I know you don't. And it's not forever. Just wait for a little while longer, Leah says. Until they've settled in well with the Troyers. A couple weeks maybe. Then of course she wants you to come." Emma paused. "And I'm sorry I didn't tell you that Leah had called. I didn't know how to."

That still bothered him, a little. He lifted his head. "Well, you've told me now. That'll have to be good enough, I reckon. I guess you'd best get on to town, if you're going."

Emma took her hand away. "I'm not going. When I went to hitch up, I noticed Maude favoring her left back leg. I'm not sure if I should drive her or not."

"Oh?" Sam's brain latched on to the new problem with some measure of relief. He'd mull over the rest of it later. "She's an older horse, and she's been driven more lately than she's used to. Might be nothing but a little morning stiffness. Maybe I should—" He broke off mid-sentence. He'd been going to say he'd take a look at his aunt's old mare, but of course, he couldn't do any such thing.

"You know." Emma's voice sounded thoughtful. "You should come to the barn and check her."

He blew out a scoffing breath. "How am I to do that, when I can't see my hand in front of my face?"

"What did you tell me back in the kitchen? Just because you can't see doesn't mean you can't feel. You could tell with your hands, maybe if the leg's swollen, or where the problem is. You might be able to get an idea if she's okay to drive or not."

"I doubt it."

"You won't know until you try. You can't do anything

for Janie, Sam, not right now, much as you want to. But that's no excuse for not doing what you can do, is it?" He felt her take his arm again—and tug. "Come on."

He didn't want to go out to the barn and fumble around with a horse he couldn't even see. But again, what he wanted didn't much matter.

He nodded wearily. "All right. Take me to her."

CHAPTER FOURTEEN

✒

AS EMMA GUIDED SAM ACROSS RUTH'S SMALL YARD
to the barn, she realized that leading him was easier than it
had been. He didn't resist so much, and he paid closer attention to her little nudges and pulls.

Sam was getting better at being blind. Emma couldn't
decide if that made her feel better or worse.

Nowadays, Emma didn't allow herself to question *Gott*
too much. She'd fallen into that kind of dark thinking for a
while after her parents' deaths, but it hadn't led her any-
place she'd wanted to go. Trusting was a big part of her
faith, and Emma had learned the harder it was to trust *Gott*,
the more important it was to do so.

Important, but not easy. It was an act of the will, trusting
in the dark, and it took courage. She'd learned this lesson
the hard way, much, she realized, as Sam was doing now.
He had to follow without being able to see the path for
himself, to trust in the character of the one leading him.

Once inside the horse's stall, Sam stepped away from

Emma. Speaking softly in *Deutsch* under his breath, he ran
his hands along the old mare's body until he found the leg
she was favoring.

"*Ach*, now. That hurts, ain't so? We'll see to it," Sam
murmured. "Don't worry, old girl."

"So?" Emma watched Sam's face closely as he felt along
the leg. "Can you tell anything?"

"It's paining her," Sam answered. "I can tell when I
touch it. She's fearful and she tenses up. But she's not kicking, so I don't think it's too bad. It's hot, though, and I think
a little swollen. We can let her rest it a day or so and see. If
it's no better, we'll best call the vet in."

"No trip to town for me, then."

"*Nee*, not today. Not with old Maude." Sam hesitated,
then said, "You could ask if somebody would bring Dobs
out here. He'd be good to have on hand, and you could drive
him easy enough."

Emma laughed. "Can you imagine what people would
say if they saw me driving Dobs around town?"

Sam's face went still. "I don't think you need worry
they'll make anything much of you driving my horse, Emma.
Not seeing the state I'm in now."

"I didn't mean that, Sam. I only meant how funny I'd
look driving that huge horse of yours. The two of you sort
of balance each other out, but I'll look like a little mouse
driving an elephant."

Her feeble attempt at a joke didn't help much. Sam didn't
even smile. "Dobs might as well get some use, seeing as
how I can't drive him myself. Not right now anyhow. Maybe
never, if this blindness keeps on." He spoke so matter-of-
factly that Emma hastened to argue with him.

"I expect you'll be driving Dobs again yourself, soon
enough."

"Nothing's expected, Emma. Hoped for maybe. But not
expected. The doctors aren't telling me much, but at least

they've told me that." He shrugged. "Even if they hadn't, I'd have figured it out for myself by now. I can't provide much help to anybody nowadays, but at least maybe I can give you a way to get to town." He paused. "What were you going in today for anyhow?"

"I had plans to talk to Isaac." That reminded her. "I'd best run back to Birdie's and telephone over to The Bakery. I'll need to let him know I won't be coming in to see him today after all."

"What were you wanting to talk to Isaac about? Is something wrong?"

"*Nee*, not wrong exactly. I just needed his . . . guidance on something."

"On what?"

She hesitated, and Sam's expression shifted.

"Never mind. There's no point telling me. No matter what it is, there's likely nothing I could do to help you with it. If you want to go on ahead to Birdie's, I can find my way back to the house." He rubbed his stomach and winced. "I'd best hurry. Breakfast doesn't seem to be setting well with me. Too much food after having too little, I guess. Speaking of that, don't give Maude any grain, but keep her in plenty of hay and let her rest up. We'll see how she does."

He turned away, his big hands gently coasting over the splintery slats of the stall, feeling his way out. It made Emma's heart ache, seeing Sam move like that. He'd rarely moved fast—although he'd startled her more than once by stepping in quick when he thought his help was needed. But before, even when he'd moved slow, Sam had always moved sure.

She'd hurt him, she realized, not being willing to tell him about her reason for meeting with Isaac, even though she'd only meant not to add to his worries.

"I've time to walk back with you before I go, Sam," Emma offered around the lump in her throat.

He stopped with his back to her, and his shoulders stiffened. "I've got to learn to do for myself, best as I can, Emma. I know you're trying to be kind, but I'm not used to being looked after."

She closed the small gap between them and laid a hand on his arm. "I know. You've always been the one taking care of everybody else. Me included."

"I did what I could. Those days look to be over now, but even if I'm not able to be much help to other folks, at least I can try to help myself. Learn to walk without falling on my face maybe." He made an attempt at a smile.

Emma opened her mouth to answer, but the words wouldn't come. What Sam had just said—about the days of him helping folks being over—that was something she'd never thought she'd hear him say. Sam Christner had always taken care of the people around him—whether they liked it or not.

He could be overly generous with that help sometimes, and he didn't always wait to be asked, either. She'd fussed at Sam many a time over the years for stepping in too fast and for making his own decisions about how other folks' troubles should be settled. Of course, she'd known she was wasting her breath. Sam would never change. All that rough-around-the-edges helping was too much a part of who he was.

Or it had been.

"Ian McMillan." Emma blurted out the words to Sam's broad back. "The screenwriter who stopped me in town? He came to Birdie's the other day, asking again to speak with me. That's what I want to talk to Isaac about."

"What?" Sam jerked around. She knew he couldn't see, but for a second, she thought his eyes snagged on her face. "That old fellow came all the way out to Birdie's? He's persistent, I'll give him that." His mouth tightened. "If I wasn't in this fix, I'd set him straight quick enough. But since I can't, you're doing right to speak to Isaac. He's already told this Ian no. I expect he'll tell him again, and maybe even have a word with Sheriff Townsend about him pestering you."

"I'm thinking maybe I should talk to Mr. McMillan." Sam's expression changed to disbelief, and she hurried on. "He says the Abbotts are talking, and they're making the truth over to suit them. All he wants is to hear the other side of things so that the story isn't one-sided. Birdie thinks I should meet with him."

"Birdie is *Englisch*. She may mean well, but you shouldn't take advice from her. This isn't a good idea, Emma. The fewer dealings you have with these movie folks, the better off you'll be. I'm sure Joseph would tell you the same."

"I think my brother would tell me to pray about it and ask the bishop for advice. And that's what I'm doing. But if Isaac agrees, I'm going to meet with him." She hadn't been entirely sure of that in her own mind, not until now. "There's nothing wrong with telling the truth."

"I'd say that depends on your reason for telling it. There are plenty of truths best left unspoken. Why do you want to talk to this fellow anyhow? Let him write his story however he wants—nobody expects the truth from such a movie. Nobody among us will believe anything the man writes about you, and the folks that will believe such nonsense are not our concern. You should keep yourself clear of it."

"I'm not worried about myself, Sam. He can say what he likes about me. But what about *Mamm* and *Daed*? You know what the Abbotts have been hinting—that they were somehow in the wrong in this."

"Nobody thinks that."

"Some of the *Englischers* do—and more will, if it's put into a movie."

"What they think doesn't matter to us."

"It matters to me!" The words burst out of her. "It isn't fair!"

Sam's face tensed, and he took a moment before he answered her. "You're talking like Caleb. It's not our place to worry about such things. *Gott* will have to settle that as He sees fit. If you stick your oar in, you're only going to muddy up the waters."

"Seems to me the waters are plenty muddied up already. I'm trying to clear things up."

"Your parents aren't here to be hurt, Emma. Besides, I knew them, near about as good as I knew my own. They'd never have worried themselves much over what any *Englischers* thought of them. You won't be helping them any by getting mixed up in this movie mess, but you're likely to cause a lot of trouble for yourself."

Emma's heart was pounding and her breath was coming too fast. "Sometimes trouble serves a purpose, Sam."

"And sometimes it doesn't!" Sam's frustrated shout made her take a surprised step backward. Sam spoke forcefully sometimes, but he'd never yelled at her. "Like this—" He gestured roughly toward his unfocused eyes. "Like Janie, being scarred up and having to learn how to walk all over again. Sometimes trouble's just trouble. We've all got to suffer through our share of it, but you'd better quit running out to meet it. If things go sour, I won't be able to step in and help you."

Her heart thudded painfully. "You're not the only one who can learn to look after himself, Sam. I can do the same." She kept her voice low and fierce, struggling not to let her hurt feelings vent themselves in anger. "Don't worry. The next time trouble comes, I won't ask for your help."

Sam clenched his fists, his face flushing hot. "You've never had to ask me, Emma. I didn't wait long enough for that, not if I knew you were in trouble. I've stepped in and looked after you and the other people I care for because I need to do it. *Gott* built me to do it. That was my job, as much as the construction work. If I didn't . . . it's the only way I could sleep at night, knowing I'd done what I could. But now what can I do? Stand by and wait for you to get hurt, and not be able to do a thing about it. Better *Gott* had taken me in the accident than leave me here like this."

"Sam!" Emma was aghast. "You mustn't talk so! It's wrong even to think that way. It's—" Before she could finish her thought, he doubled over and was violently sick.

She hurried to him, laying a hand on his back as he retched, murmuring softly. When he'd finished, he leaned his head against the rough post, his eyes closed.

"That breakfast really didn't set well," she said. "I'm sorry, Sam."

"*Nee,* I'm sorry," he mumbled. "I lost my temper. I shouldn't have shouted at you—shouldn't have said what I did."

"That's no matter," she assured him. "*Gut* for you to get the bad out, maybe, just as your stomach will likely feel better now."

"Maybe." He straightened and rubbed at his face. "I shouldn't have eaten so much."

"Sausage wasn't the best thing to start with, probably. I meant to tempt you, but I guess that worked a little too well. I don't think it'll be working a second time. It'll likely be a long while before you'll be able to face a plate of sausage again. Wait here, and I'll run get some water so you can rinse out your mouth." She went to the door and pushed it open. Bright morning sunlight spilled into the barn.

"Emma." There was a strange note in Sam's voice. She hurried back to stand behind him. He coughed, and his breathing picked up. She took a prudent step backward.

"It's all right. Go on and get rid of it all. It's the only way to feel better. I'm sorry. The food I fixed was too rich for a fellow who's barely been eating. It'll be toast and tea for you tomorrow."

"Emma," he repeated. He lifted his head off the post and turned toward her. For the first time since the accident, his eyes found her face—and stopped.

She stood, staring. Hoping. Then a slow, incredulous smile began to break across his face.

"I can see, Emma." He raised his hand in front of his face and flexed his fingers. "Not too *gut*. Everything's foggy, even close up. But the darkness has given way."

CHAPTER FIFTEEN

❧

"I'M TELLING YOU, THIS IS A BAD IDEA, SAMUEL. NO good comes from mixing up with *Englischers*. We've certainly all seen proof enough of that." He heard crisp snaps as Ruth broke a green bean, then the sound of her flinging the pieces in the bowl in her lap.

His aunt had been complaining since Emma had announced her plan to meet with Ian McMillan over at Birdie's house this morning. Emma had just gone inside to get ready, but Ruth's fussing was still going strong.

He wasn't any too happy about this, either, but at least Emma had agreed to let him come along, and he was thankful for that. He couldn't do much to help her, but now that he could see a little, he could do more than nothing. This elderly *Englischer* seemed awfully good at getting his own way, and folks like that bore watching.

"Isaac has said it's all right." Sam shifted his weight in the porch rocker and squinted, trying to make out the outline of the geraniums in the pot at his elbow. He could see them—sort of. The flowers were a cloudy red smudge. He could catch only the colors and the general shapes of things, nothing more. He only knew they were geraniums because he'd felt the fuzzy leaf and because he could smell them. They had a funny scent, geraniums. Reminded him oddly of tomatoes.

"Isaac says." There was another series of crisp cracks, followed by more metallic pings as Ruth hurled the bits into her bowl. "Isaac hasn't been the same since that daughter of his left for Pennsylvania. He and Ida have always been foolish about that girl—it's what comes of having only the one child, I suppose. They've spoiled her, and we can see how it's worked out for them." The rocker creaked as Ruth rocked herself back and forth. "Everybody warned the girl against taking up with Caleb, but nobody would do for her but him. Now look what's happened."

"Rhoda can't be blamed for Caleb's doings."

"A *schmaert* wife could have stopped him." Best he knew, his aunt had never had a chance to be a wife herself, but he noticed that she had plenty of opinions about how married folks should conduct their business. "When Bessie was here visiting, she mentioned that the Lambrights are thinking of moving to Pennsylvania, too. We'll have a new bishop if that happens, and if you ask me, that's *Gott*'s provision. Isaac's far too slack. We need a firmer hand around here, what with all this trouble the Hochstedlers have stirred up."

Sam cast a wary look at the door. Emma would be back any minute, and he wished his aunt would take up a different topic. "Maybe you'd best do less talking and more snapping, Ruth. Emma means to can those beans soon as we get back, and from the sound of it, your bowl is still near empty."

His aunt made an irritated noise, followed by two more snaps and pings. "You're a fine one to lecture me about working. A great big man sitting there doing nothing."

That was Ruth. She always knew just where a fellow's sorest spot was—and she never missed a chance to jab at it.

"I wouldn't be sitting here if I had a choice in it. The sooner I can get back to my work, the better it'll suit me." After his sight had returned—or some of it anyhow—Emma had phoned the eye doctor from Birdie's house and made an appointment with a specialist. Sam was going in next week for an exam. He was hoping his eyesight would have improved even more by then, so he could get back to his construction crew.

Jeff Branton, the owner of the company, had made it clear more than once that Sam would be welcomed back with open arms the minute he was able. Business was booming right now, Jeff said, and nobody could keep a crew on task like Sam.

"You don't want to rush back." Ruth sounded alarmed. "You need to give your eyes plenty of time to heal up, or they'll likely worsen again."

"I expect it'll be all right. I work more with my muscles than my eyes. Soon as I can see well enough to hit a nail, I'll go back. I've bills to pay." His doctor's bills and Janie's would cost plenty, not to mention the balance still left on Milton's. Sam meant to start paying those down the minute he was able to start bringing in money again. He counted it the least he could do.

"The church will help. I've already heard that the women are doing a supper for you. Those bring in good money." There was more creaking. Ruth had sped up the pace of her rocking, proof that she was agitated. "Even if you are able to work, it won't be smart for you to live alone, not for a while anyway. From what I hear, Leah's planning to stay with Milton's parents, and you won't look after yourself near well enough. Men never do when they're left on their own. Your eyesight would likely fail again, and then where would you be?"

Sam frowned. There was a pleading in her voice, buried

underneath the sharpness. As hard as it was to believe, Ruth didn't want him to leave.

His aunt hadn't exactly gone out of her way to make him feel welcome. In fact, she'd pointed out what a trouble he was to her at every possible opportunity. And yet she wasn't looking forward to him leaving. He could tell it just as plain as if she'd said it straight out.

"Maybe I'll stay on here awhile," he said, testing the waters. "Even after I go back to work. For a couple weeks, just until I have my feet under me. If it suits you."

"Doesn't matter what suits me," Ruth retorted. "Only what's right to do. I've always been one to do my duty. Nobody can say different. Look how I stood by Davey. Took care of him all his life like he was my own son. I hardly had a moment to myself, all those years. I'm used to sacrificing for others."

She wasn't fooling him. He heard the relief in her voice. It shouldn't surprise him. The church's teaching was clear. A life without work was a life without purpose. Caring for Davey had given his aunt a purpose, and of course, she'd found herself at loose ends since his *onkel* had passed.

Sam felt a stirring of sympathy. He knew what it was like to have your purpose taken away from you. He and Ruth had that much in common, at least.

The screen door creaked open.

"Sam?" Emma said. "Are you ready?"

"*Ja.*" He stood and turned in her direction. He could see only the blurriest outline of her—the blackness of her dress and bonnet, and the pale oval of her face.

"We won't be gone long, Ruth," Emma was saying.

His aunt clucked her tongue. "You shouldn't be going at all. You'll find that out to your sorrow, I expect, since you won't listen to anybody. Just like that hardheaded brother of yours," Ruth added under her breath.

Emma stiffened, and for a second, Sam thought she

would speak. Instead she walked silently down the steps, pausing at the bottom to wait for Sam.

He followed a bit more slowly. The bottom step, which was a different height than the others, gave him a bit of trouble, and he stumbled before catching himself on the railing. He heard Emma suck in her breath, but she said nothing until they were beyond earshot of the porch.

"It's such a nice day for a walk." She slipped his arm through hers. "You don't mind, do you, Sam? Nobody will see if we walk arm in arm." Emma tried to sound casual, but he heard the worry in her voice. Funny how often folks said one thing when they really meant something different. He'd never really noticed that before.

Sam hesitated. He knew Emma only meant to help, but he didn't like being led about. On the other hand, the pecan orchard hadn't been kept up well, and he didn't want to make a fool of himself by falling.

And he didn't exactly mind the feeling of Emma's hand curved into the hollow of his elbow.

"All right," he agreed.

He still couldn't see well enough to tell exactly where he was, but he knew when they'd crossed out of the yard onto Birdie's property. The smells and the sense of shade brought up a picture in his mind. The orchard was an overgrown patch of trees, badly needing tending. Pecans brought a decent price, but like everything else, they required work to turn a profit. Birdie apparently didn't need the money because she'd chosen to let the orchard go.

Sam counted that a shame. Pecan trees took years to even start producing, so to his thrifty Amish mind, this was wasteful. But then *Englischers* often were, and Birdie was a woman on her own. Unlike an Amish widow, she had no community of menfolk who'd take on her chores as a matter of course, so maybe looking after such a big property was more than she could handle.

Emma walked him through the maze of sticks and stumps, helping him step around tangles of blackberry briars. Even so, careful as she was being, they had to pause when a thorny bush snagged at her dress. The underbrush was getting out of hand, which would make the orchard even more useless. There'd be no way to find the nuts with all these briars and limbs cluttering the ground.

"Once I'm able, I'll clear this place out, if Birdie's willing," Sam said. He lifted his face, trying to see what he could. It wasn't much. He could make out the grayish-brown trunks of the trees, and the green covering of the leafy branches arching over him. It was already hot today, and not much breeze stirred, not even in the treetops. He couldn't hear the movement of the leaves, only the songs of the birds and the skitterings of small animals up in the branches. This place would be heaven for squirrels, what with the nuts dropping ungathered every fall.

"She'd likely appreciate that, if you have the time."

He wouldn't have much time to spare, not if *Gott* willed him well. He'd need to focus on paid work, but that didn't matter. It was a man's job to look after widows. The Bible was clear on that. "I'll make time. She's been kind, letting us use her phone, letting you stay there. It'll be a way of paying her back maybe."

He liked that idea—the thought of standing on his own two feet again, looking after other people.

Emma must have finished picking the thorns away from her dress because she straightened and put her hand in the crook of his elbow again. As she did, the length of her arm bumped gently against his own, and his heart stirred. He couldn't resist putting his other hand over hers, pressing her touch a little closer.

He liked this, too. He liked the feel of the two of them walking side by side. It was sweetly unsettling, but it also felt right, having Emma snugged up close beside him.

If his sight kept getting better, maybe before too long . . . Sam tried to tamp down the bubble of joy that thought shook loose. It was too early for hoping. He had that doctor's appointment to get through first.

But he couldn't help hoping a little. And wishing he had some way of knowing how Emma felt, walking along beside him now.

"Step careful, Sam. There's an ant bed just in front of us." She tugged lightly on his arm, shifting him to the left, and he followed easily. Emma's voice was just south of his ear, and a shiver ran up the back of his neck at the nearness of it. "I can tell you're seeing a good bit better."

"I'm seeing something at least, and that's better than it was. But nothing's too clear yet."

"Well, you're lots easier to walk with. Before, I had to push and pull, but not anymore."

Sam chuckled. "I think we've just found our rhythm, you and me, like two horses set in harness together. For a while they'll fight each other. But they learn how to move together well enough, once they get a sense of each other."

She didn't answer right away. Sam had never realized before how telling a silence could be. He sensed Emma thinking over what he'd said, and he wondered again if she felt the same tickle of sureness that he was feeling himself.

"We might make a matched pair yet." He spoke lightly, testing her to see what she might say.

"Matched?" She laughed. "Us? We're more like big Dobs and little old Maude. Can you imagine what those two would look like, pulling together?"

"Oh, you never know." He paused, then put another foot tentatively out. "I think they'd pull together real well once they settled."

"Maybe they would." He could hear Emma's smile in her voice. "Or maybe Dobs would drag poor Maude around behind him like a mop."

He chuckled. "*Nee*, Maude's got too much fire in her for that. I expect she'd hold her own just fine."

Emma stopped walking. "Sam?"

His heartbeat sped up, and he angled his face toward hers. She was close enough now that he could see the outline of her pretty face framed inside the bonnet. Not much was clear, but then again, he didn't really need it to be. He knew Emma's face better than he knew his own. Knew every line of it, every mood.

"*Is alles awreit?*" He didn't really think anything was wrong. He sensed she had something to say to him, that she wanted to say it out of earshot of others.

He leaned a little closer. He wanted to hear what she had to say—if he could manage hearing anything over the pounding of his pulse against his eardrums. They were standing so close now that if he lowered his head just a bit more, he could've kissed her. His heart stuttered at the idea.

She spoke softly, her voice a little shaky. "Before we get to Birdie's, I wanted to say . . . to ask you . . ."

"*Vass?*" he prodded gently.

"Please be nice."

Nice.

Sam straightened, turning his head away from her. The sweet tension he'd been feeling dissolved into disappointment.

And annoyance.

He'd been standing here, gap-jawed like some fool, thinking Emma was about to say something special to him—something sweet—and instead she'd spoken as if he were a child who needed to be reminded of his manners.

"Just because you have to lead me around like a *kind* doesn't mean I am one." He pulled his arm free and took a step away. "It's Ian McMillan's behavior you should be worrying about, not mine."

He wasn't touching her now, but he sensed her stiffen just the same.

"He only wants to talk to me."

"*Ja*," Sam said. "Wants it bad enough to track you like a deer, popping up wherever you happen to be. Enough to grab your arm in the street when you're trying to get away from him."

"He apologized for that. He's an old man and an *Englischer*. I don't believe he meant me any harm."

"You never do believe these *Englischers* mean you harm, even when it's clear to everybody else that they do. That's the trouble." He felt his patience slipping away.

"Sam," Emma said, her voice rising, "You're—"

"I'm right," he finished her sentence stubbornly. "That's what I am."

"*Nee*—"

"And whether this Ian means to cause trouble or not, he may very well do it. And not only for you."

She made a frustrated noise. He saw the blur of her, moving quickly toward him. Then to his astonishment, she planted both hands on his chest and pushed. Hard.

CHAPTER SIXTEEN

HE HADN'T SEEN IT COMING, BUT STILL, EMMA'S push barely budged him.

"What are you doing?"

"Stop arguing and move! You're standing in the middle of an ant bed. They're all over your boots and pants!"

He stepped quickly to the side. Emma followed, bending to slap at his legs—maybe a little harder than necessary.

"I can tend to myself." He leaned down too quick, his head knocking solidly against Emma's.

"Ow!" She stumbled a few steps backward. "That hurt. Sam, for pity's sake, why didn't you just let me brush them off for you? You can't even see them, and—" She drew in a sharp breath. "*Ach*, and now I'm in the ants myself!"

The next few seconds were spent slapping and brushing the stinging insects off. Sam did it mostly by feel, and none too well, either. As Emma had pointed out, he couldn't see the tiny things, and he pretty much only knew where they were when he felt their bite.

Sam finally gave up and straightened. He could hear Emma breathing hard, and he saw the blur of her arm reaching up to straighten her bonnet.

"Well," she said, "we'll both be itching plenty tomorrow, I suppose. Do you want me to walk you back home?"

"Why? Over ants? *Nee*. I'm all right." All right, but feeling foolish. After his blustering about not being a child, he'd blundered into an ant bed in his temper. If that wasn't childish, he didn't know what was.

Emma didn't answer, and once again, he sensed her weighing her words. She wasn't sure she wanted him along, he realized. She was probably thinking that getting swarmed over with ants wouldn't make him more likely to be patient with this Ian she felt so sorry for.

"I'll mind my tongue," he assured her grudgingly. "You needn't worry yourself."

"All right." She stepped close again. Her fingers found their place in the crook of his elbow, but it didn't feel the same. Between the argument and the ants, they'd lost something.

When they arrived at the house, the *Englisch* lady met them at her back door.

"Come on in." Birdie sounded breathless, Sam noticed, as if she'd been the one walking rather than them. "Thank goodness you're here. Mr. McMillan arrived ten minutes early, and he's been talking my ear off. He's waiting in the front room, and I've made coffee and cookies. Go ahead on in and get settled down, and I'll bring in the refreshments."

After being in the bright and spacious outdoors, walking into Birdie's house made Sam feel smothered. He'd thought Ruth's house was cramped, but this house, although bigger, was worse. There seemed to be so many things crowded about him that he felt uncertain moving. And the place smelled—not bad. Just different. Strong store-bought scents mingled with the ordinary smells of food and coffee.

He didn't see how Emma could feel at home here. If he'd

had to sleep in this house, he'd have ended up putting a blanket out on the porch or in the yard. Someplace where he could breathe.

Emma certainly seemed comfortable enough. She moved in front of him, leading him down a narrow hallway until they stepped into the front room.

Sam immediately sensed where Ian was, even though the fellow was only a blurry splotch. The other man rose slowly to his feet.

"Miss Hochstedler," he said. "I very much appreciate your agreeing to talk with me. And you've brought your friend."

"*Ja*, you've met Sam before. And please, call me Emma." She sounded uneasy.

Sam was feeling pretty uncomfortable himself. It was one thing meeting this fellow on a familiar street when he'd been able to see clear. Now he was in this fussy *Englisch* house, and everything was blurry. He didn't like the helpless feeling it gave him. He straightened his shoulders and stuck a hand out in the general direction of the splotch.

He had to hold it out just a second or two longer than felt right, but then the papery coolness of an old man's hand closed over his.

"Thank you for coming," Ian said quietly. "I know Emma will feel more at ease, having you here. It's generous of you, especially under the circumstances. I heard about your accident, and I'm sorry." He released Sam's hand. "But Mrs. Marshall says you're improving, so that's very good news."

"*Ja*, I'm thankful."

"Sit here, Sam." Emma helped him to a chair just as Birdie came back through the door. He heard the chitter of cups and saucers on a tray, and the smell of coffee grew stronger.

"Sam, may I pour you a cup?" Birdie asked. He shook

his head. The last thing he needed was to spill coffee all over himself.

"No, thank you." He tilted his head toward Ian, who was fiddling with his own cup. "You said you wanted to speak to Emma about what happened to her parents. What exactly is it that you want to know?"

"Well, everything she's willing to tell me, I suppose. Thank you, Mrs. Marshall. This all looks delicious." There was a soft thump as Ian settled back on the sofa. "The Abbotts were very eager to meet with me, and they've told me their version of what happened. They were quite . . . cooperative."

"They're *Englisch*."

"Yes." There was a careful pause. "But I don't think it's only the cultural or . . . er . . . religious differences at play here. I get the feeling that they have an agenda, and that they'd very much like my script to advance it for them. They've read the proposed storyline, and they had some very specific suggestions for changes and additions."

"To make Trevor look innocent," Emma said.

"Not exactly. They're a bit more ambitious than that." Sam heard a sigh. "I believe they're trying to make him look heroic."

"You folks pick your heroes strangely," Sam observed dryly.

"Not all of us. That's why I'm here. I'd like to hear both sides of the story."

"Why?" Emma spoke up, and Sam felt the attention in the room shift to her.

"Well, to make it fair, of course." Birdie jumped in first. "The script should be written from a balanced perspective."

"But this movie, it's not supposed to be the truth. Is it?" Emma persisted. "Mr. Abbott told my brother sometime back that you wouldn't be held to the truth in the writing of it. In fact, he seemed very pleased about that, Joseph said."

"As well he might be," Birdie muttered.

Emma continued as if she hadn't spoken. "So why do you care so much what the truth is?"

"I always care what the truth is, my dear, even when I have license to stretch it a little. Knowing the truth informs my writing. It gives it a depth it couldn't possibly have otherwise. I'm known for doing quality work, and I have my reputation to consider."

Sam tilted his head, sifting slowly through the *Englischer*'s high-sounding words, searching for the truth. "This really isn't only about being fair, ain't so? This is about you doing this job well enough to get the next one that comes up. Emma's story is the tool you need to do that. I notice you're making her no promises that you'll be any kinder to her parents if you do hear her side of the story."

"How can I make promises when I've no idea what she's going to tell me? For all I know, the Abbotts are telling the truth."

Well, that was reasonable enough. Sam had to give him credit.

"But," Ian went on, "I can make a promise of what will happen if I don't hear her story. Abbott will get his way. To tell you the truth, that's the primary reason I've been pressing so hard for this meeting. I very much dislike being manipulated, and I've no desire to pen propaganda for a coldhearted murderer."

"Trevor wasn't coldhearted," Emma said. "He was just . . . broken inside. I didn't have sense enough to see that. I thought I could help him by showing him kindness. He didn't seem to get a lot of that. But I wasn't helping him at all. I was only being selfish."

Selfish? Emma wasn't selfish. Sam frowned, but before he could protest, there was an eager rustling of paper.

"Why do you say that?" Ian asked.

"I liked the fact that he needed me." There was the tiniest tremble to Emma's voice. Maybe nobody else would have noticed it, but Sam did. "My brother—my twin—had just married. We'd been very close, and I suppose it left a hole in my life. It made me feel important to have Trevor so anxious to see me every day at lunchtime. To have him tell me his problems, as if I could solve them. Which, of course, I couldn't."

Neither of the two *Englischers* reacted, but Sam clenched his hands in his lap. Ian and Birdie couldn't know what it cost Emma to admit that. To seek importance; that was not good. Their faith taught that one should never seek such a thing; that to do so was prideful.

"It was wrong of me," Emma was admitting now.

"Wrong of you how?"

"In many ways. We'd been meeting at the café, but Trevor was uncomfortable there. He felt like people were watching him, saying unkind things. So we started taking our lunches out to the little park behind the hardware store. I knew my parents wouldn't approve. It was one thing to be polite and *friendlich* in a busy café, but another to meet an *Englisch* boy for lunch every day alone. So I kept it a secret from them. I was being deceitful and disrespectful of my parents' wishes."

"You were a grown woman by the world's standards," Ian said. "Most people would think you should have been able to make your own decisions, regardless of your parents' opinions."

"We do not follow the world's standards," Emma pointed out. "And as we see now, my parents' opinion would have been the wiser one to follow."

"Ah." More rustling of paper. "Of course. Point taken. You were going against your parents, then. How else were you wrong?"

"I was mistaken in thinking I could help Trevor with his troubles. That was pride. He said I was helping by talking

with him, but I didn't even really understand what his problems were. I knew he didn't get along with his parents, that
he had no friends at his school, and that he took a lot of
medications."

"He'd stopped taking some of them just before the . . .
the incident with your parents. Did you know that?"

Sam noticed the hesitation before Ian brought up her
parents' deaths, and how carefully he picked his words.
Seemed like the fellow was trying to mind his manners.
Sam relaxed a little into the softness of his chair.

"No." He heard the sound of Emma swallowing. "I did
not. I knew he seemed different there at . . . at the last. More
energetic. I thought maybe he was getting better. He said he
thought so, too."

"Tell me what he said."

Sam listened as Emma recounted her conversations with
Trevor. She was unflinching in her honesty, taking no
thought to protect herself.

He knew that after it had happened, Emma had asked
for forgiveness from the church. He'd heard of it. He also
knew that the bishop had, after due consideration, decided
that a full public repentance wasn't necessary.

There had been mixed reactions about that. Sam had
heard about them on the construction sites, from men who
normally didn't bother much with gossip. The community
was divided.

Some thought that Emma had erred enough that she
should have been on her knees before the church, asking
forgiveness as she'd offered to do. There were murmurs that
maybe Isaac's judgment was a little off, since he himself
was involved in the issue, thanks to his daughter's recent
marriage to Caleb Hochstedler.

Others had agreed with the bishop's stance. The Hochstedlers had suffered a terrible loss, and there was no point
compounding it by coming down harshly on a girl whose

only fault had been an innocent kindness. And, of course, being born pretty enough to attract the wrong sort of attention from men. That part wasn't said aloud, but plenty were thinking it.

Sam had agreed with the second group, but he'd known Emma hadn't. She blamed herself for what had happened. Joseph had mentioned as much and had been worried about it.

Maybe, Sam thought now, Isaac had made a mistake, not allowing Emma to make a public repentance. Maybe he should have let her ask forgiveness for the sin she felt she'd committed. Could be that would have helped her to forgive herself.

Because she needed to. That much was obvious to Sam as she quietly recounted the details of her meetings with Trevor. It was also plain to him that the boy had been lost in his darkness long before Emma had ever laid eyes on him.

She must have seemed like a lamp to him, all lit and shining. No wonder he'd clung to her.

After nearly an hour of answering questions, Emma cleared her throat. "I need to get back to Ruth's. We're canning a batch of green beans today, and that'll take a while."

"Of course." There was the sound of a notebook being closed, and of Ian rising to his feet. Emma rose, too. "Thank you very much. This has been a tremendous help. If I have any additional questions, may I contact you?"

There was a short pause. Then, "No, I don't think so. I have told you everything, and that is all the help I can give. But I will be praying for you and your work."

"Thank you, my dear. That's very kind."

"*Du bisht welcome.* Birdie, let me help you with these dishes before I go."

Birdie argued, but Emma insisted. Before long the women had gathered up the cups and the tray and disappeared into the kitchen.

Ian cleared his throat. "If you don't mind me asking, Sam, how much can you see?"

"Some." Sam was listening to the soft murmur of the women's voices, accompanied by the clatter of dishes. Near as he could tell, Emma was not upset. "Not too much yet, but I'm thankful for any improvement. There's hope it will keep getting better, so that's good news."

"I'm glad to hear it." Ian sounded relieved. "Especially because . . ." There was a soft thud as Ian sat on the end of the couch closest to Sam's chair. "I'm concerned about Emma."

Sam turned his head sharply in the other man's direction. "Why's that?"

"Well," the man hedged. "I don't want to be an alarmist. There may not be anything to worry about, but it's been weighing on my mind. I don't like to frighten the dear girl, but I did want to mention it to you, just in case."

Sam frowned. "If you've something to say to me, you'd best spit it out. Those dishes aren't likely to take long."

"All right." Ian drew in a deep breath. "I consulted a psychiatrist to better understand Trevor's mental state. He thinks it unlikely that such a troubled man, a man willing to go to such terrible lengths, would be willing to simply walk away from the object of his obsession. He very much believes that Trevor will come back to Johns Mill now that Emma's returned. Probably sooner rather than later." Ian paused. "The doctor pointed out that many people, after doing what Trevor did, for the reasons he did it, would have turned the gun on themselves. He didn't do that. He ran. The psychiatrist feels that means Trevor isn't finished."

Sam thought that over with a growing sense of unease. He didn't know much about psychiatrists, but what Ian was saying had the weight of truth to it.

"This doctor you talked to? Does he think Trevor means Emma harm?"

"He wouldn't rule out that possibility. And from some things the Abbotts said . . . I did wonder if they're being completely honest with the authorities. They didn't say anything definite, but I believe it's possible that they've been in touch with their son. Perhaps quite recently."

Sam's hands tightened on the padded arms of the chair. "You think Trevor might be someplace nearby?"

"I hope not, but I honestly don't know." The women's voices grew louder. They were coming back up the hall. Sam felt a hand pat his arm. "I did mention my concerns to the local sheriff, but he didn't seem to take the idea very seriously. That's why I feel better knowing that you'll be looking after her."

"Sam?" Emma spoke from the doorway. "Are you ready to walk back to Ruth's?"

"*Ja*, I'm ready." Sam rose, squinting at the blurry figure approaching him, trying to make her come into focus. It was no use.

And, he realized with a sinking heart, neither was he. How could he possibly look after Emma when he couldn't even see her?

Chapter Seventeen

✿

LATER THAT EVENING, EMMA WASHED THE SUPPER dishes while the loaded canner on the gas stove slowly rose to the correct pressure. Ruth sat at the table, fitting the last of the freshly washed beans into clean jars.

"We should have time to can one more load before bedtime," Emma said over her shoulder. "Are you sure you don't want to can this next batch in pint jars? It'd be a bit quicker, and handier, too, when you're fixing small meals."

Ruth had surprised her by refusing to use the pint jars Emma had unpacked and washed, insisting on canning her small amount of green beans in quarts. Emma had put the smaller jars away and prepped the bigger jars without argument. With Ruth it paid to pick your battles, and since these beans were intended for Ruth's pantry, she might as well have them as she liked them.

Still, it didn't make a whole lot of sense, canning in family-sized quantities for a woman living alone.

"No." Ruth said firmly. "You've seen how Sam eats now. There won't be any small meals around here this winter."

The older woman sounded almost pleased, and Emma's heart sank.

"Well." Emma struggled for a tactful answer as she dried the casserole dish. "You know, Sam's got that eye doctor appointment coming up in a few days. If his sight keeps improving, he's likely to get cleared for working."

Ruth's busy hands stilled for a minute, but then she shook her head and resumed fitting the beans into the jar. "Maybe. But maybe not. Anyway, Sam's said he won't be leaving right off, even if he does start back to work."

Emma smiled. She knew how ready Sam was to get home and throw himself into his work. It was sweet that he was willing to give his lonely aunt an extra week or two of his time, but that wouldn't solve Ruth's long-term problem.

"But sooner or later, he'll be leaving, ain't so? I will be, too. You've recovered real well from your surgery. I thought maybe you'd be ready to go to your brother's house, like you'd planned to do."

The kettle on the stove began to purr, signaling that her water had come to a boil. As she lifted it off the eye, Emma checked the canner's pressure gauge—not up to twenty-one pounds yet. She set the hot teakettle on a pot holder on the table and began adding salt to Ruth's newly filled jars.

"That was before. I had a letter from Robert, and he says it might be some time before he can get a place fixed up for me in Pennsylvania." Ruth shared that news in a carefully even voice. "So Sam can stay on here for as long as he needs to. There's no rush, and I've no confidence he'll be ready to go anytime soon. You get bad news just as often as good news at these doctor's visits. It's best to be prepared for disappointments." Ruth set the newly filled quart jar in line with two others, ready for boiling water to be poured over their contents. "Of course, that's harder to do when people are handing out false hopes right and left," she added.

Ah, Emma thought. That explained why Ruth had seemed a bit down lately. No wonder she was so eager for Sam to stay on. The letter from her brother must have been a disappointment.

"I don't think the eye doctor has given Sam any false hopes." Emma cast another quick look at the dial. Still not quite right, but rising steady. She'd need to watch it more closely now. *Mamm* had stressed to her that pressure canning was a careful chore. You didn't dare forget to keep an eye on the needle, or you'd likely end up scraping green beans off your ceiling.

"I wasn't talking about the doctor," Ruth said. "I was talking about you."

"What?" Emma glanced up from the teaspoon of canning salt she was leveling off to find Ruth frowning at her. "Me?"

"*Ja*. You should leave Sam be and stop filling up his head with ideas about the two of you ending up together."

"Ruth—" Emma didn't know what to say.

"Sam'll still come running every time you snap your fingers, just like a faithful hound. He can't help it. That kind of thing runs in our family. We've had our share of marriages that shouldn't have been made, all because a girl or a boy fell for a wrong 'un early on and wouldn't back away from it. You need to have enough sense for the two of you. He's got his own troubles now, and I'd think you'd have more kindness in you than to toy with him."

"I'm not toying with him."

"Ain't you? I may be old, but I've sense enough yet to see what's in front of my eyes. It's a pity, but men always do seem to pick the least likely girl to go foolish over. I'll admit, you're a better worker than I thought you'd be, but I still can't see you settling down as the wife of a blind fellow."

"Sam's not blind anymore."

"Well, he ain't the same man as he was, and I'll be surprised if he ever is again. It's not just his eyes, either. He's breaking his heart over what happened to that child." Ruth drew in a long breath. "The Christner men are hard workers and strong as oxen, but when it comes to loving they stumble, as often as not. And they generally don't get over it, either."

Before Emma could answer, Sam's heavy steps came up the hall. He stuck his head in the kitchen, narrowing his eyes as he struggled to locate her in the room.

"Emma," he said, "I've been thinking, and there's something I'd like to talk over with you, if you have a minute. Alone, if you don't mind, Ruth."

"It's a fine thing when a woman gets run out of her own kitchen," Ruth muttered. "But I've got these jars filled, and this hard chair is making my hip ache. I'm going to go sit in my easy chair and read *The Budget*. Make sure you get this next batch canned right, Emma. Like I told you, I'll be needing a deep pantry this winter."

After Ruth had left the room, Sam shut the kitchen door. Emma noticed how his hands fumbled on the doorknob. Even with what sight he'd gotten back, he still needed to rely on his hands to feel his way.

Please, Gott, let the eye specialist give him good news, Emma prayed silently. *Let there be something they can do to help him see better.*

She cleared her throat. "What do you want to talk to me about, Sam?"

He shifted his weight. "I've been thinking and praying over this ever since we got back from Birdie's. I finally decided I should speak."

Emma's heart sped up a little bit. "All right."

"I think Birdie should drive you back and forth every day."

"What?" Her heart fell so hard, she almost expected to

hear a *plonk*. "But that's . . ." She almost said stupid, but changed it. "Silly. And a waste of Birdie's time, too. The way the road curves, it's a shorter walk than it is a drive."

"It would only be for a little while. I'm near about ready to walk it myself—my eyes only have to get a little better. Then I'll be able to come fetch you every morning. I don't think you should be driving into town for groceries by yourself, either." He ran a hand through his hair, looking frustrated. "I don't know how we'll handle that. Birdie could go with you maybe, although I'd rather go along myself. Still, until my sight gets better, I wouldn't be much use."

Emma had been wiping the rims of the jars, but she set down her dishcloth and sank into the nearest chair. "Sam, what's wrong? What are you worried about?"

He looked down at her, his eyes on her face. She knew he couldn't see her clearly, but for a minute, it almost seemed as if he could. "It's just for the best, Emma."

"And you expect me to agree to ask Birdie for these favors without telling me why it's necessary?"

He was silent for a minute. Then he sighed. "*Nee.* I know you too well to expect such a thing. That Ian fellow . . . he's been talking to doctors, and they think Trevor's likely to come back around. And sooner rather than later."

"Oh." The word slipped past Emma's lips on a whisper. She listened as Sam went on, repeating what some doctor had said.

"Now, mind," Sam went on, "this fellow's never talked to Trevor himself, so he's only guessing. But—"

"I think he might be right." Emma's heart was pounding at a dizzying speed, and her mouth had gone dry. "Trevor was always like that . . . he kept going with things, even when common sense should have stopped him." She paused and swallowed. "Like with the gifts."

"Gifts?"

"*Ja.* That was what finally drove me to talk to Caleb. Trevor started bringing me presents. First it was little things. A candy because I'd said I liked that kind. He just happened to have some in his pocket the next day. And then a flower or two that he said he'd picked from his mother's rosebushes. That kind of thing. Nothing special."

"No, nothing special for you. You were used to boys giving you presents."

Emma raised her head and shot him a look. "You used to give me apples yourself, as I remember."

"I did," Sam admitted with a rueful smile. "Prettiest ones I could find, too."

"To start with, Trevor's things were like your apples. They didn't mean anything."

Sam made a soft, scoffing noise. Something about it made Emma's mind skip back to what Ruth had said about the Christner men.

Maybe those apples had meant more than she'd thought.

She waited, eyebrows raised, for Sam to speak, but he stayed quiet. When she realized that he couldn't see her expression clearly enough to respond to it, she prompted, "Did you want to say something?"

"No. So what did Trevor give you that did mean something?"

"One day he brought me a—" Emma gestured with her fingers, then again realized Sam probably couldn't see what she was trying to show him. "A little thing, no bigger than a stamp. Made of gold. A locket. It opened up, and you could put pictures in it. Women wear them on necklaces. It was pretty, had little flowers carved in it. He said it had belonged to his grandmother, and he wanted me to have it. It had his picture in it on one side."

"Ah."

"I told him I couldn't take such a gift, and I gave it back

to him. He argued with me over it. It seemed real important to him that I accept it."

"Did you?"

"*Nee*, of course not!" She paused. "But that night when I got home, I found it in the bag I'd carried with me to the café."

Sam's eyebrows lowered. "Pushy."

"At the time, I thought it was more silly. But *ja*, Trevor liked to have his way, and he didn't understand much about being Plain. The next day I made him take it back and gave him a scolding. But . . ." She darted another look up at Sam. "He kept doing it. Slipping it in my bag again, or in a sack of doughnuts I was taking home. I started checking everything before I left him." She swallowed. "I tried to think of it as a joke, but the way he wouldn't give it up, no matter how often I asked him to . . . it bothered me."

Sam's frown darkened. "And then?"

"He mailed it to the house in a card. I hid it from *Mamm* and *Daed*. That was wrong, I know. But that's when I finally spoke to Caleb about it."

"You should have spoken to me maybe."

Emma looked up in surprise. Sam's face was grim and set.

"Telling Caleb brought trouble enough. I only wanted his advice about how best to handle it, but he got bossy and took over. At the time, I chalked it up to him being new-married." Emma sighed. "My *bruder* was so happy with Rhoda, and it was like he'd gone from boy to man overnight. He asked for the locket, so I gave it to him. He showed it to *Daed* and told him the whole story. Caleb told me—later—that he was going to return it to Trevor himself and have a word with him. *Daed* felt he'd be the better one to do it, because Caleb was so—"

"Hotheaded," Sam finished.

"But it didn't matter. I don't know what *Daed* said to

Trevor, of course, but I know my father. He'd have made himself clear, but he would have been very kind." She swallowed. "He was always very kind, and he always thought the best of folks, *Englischers* and Plain alike. He'd have given Trevor no reason to . . . do what he did."

"There could be no reason to do such a thing. Emma?" Sam cocked his head to one side. "That canner. Maybe you'd best check it. It sounds funny."

The canner! Emma whirled around and made an exclamation of dismay. The needle was well into the red zone, and the weight on the top of the vent was vibrating frantically. She hurried to the stove and lowered the heat.

"Is it all right?" Sam had walked closer.

She nodded, then realized that he might not be able to read the movement too well. "*Ja*, thanks to you. I can't believe I let it climb so high. *Mamm* would have fussed at me *gut*. She was always so particular about being careful when we were pressure canning. It can get dangerous fast, if you're not watching careful."

"'*S is nimmand vay gedu.*" Sam reached out a hand, his fingers fumbling against her arm gently before clasping it. "It is all right, thankfully. Nothing bad happened."

It is all right. For some reason, hearing Sam's once familiar words of comfort made tears well up in Emma's eyes.

"Does this doctor really think Trevor is going to come back?" Her voice shook. What would happen if he did? Who would he hurt this time?

For a few seconds there was no sound but the noise of the canner, calming down slowly over the lower heat. "Nobody can truly know what such a troubled man will do. Like I said, even the doctor is only guessing."

"I think he is guessing right. And you think so, too, or you wouldn't be so worried about me walking back and forth from Birdie's. I could go home, I guess. But what if he showed up there? What would that do to Miriam? I don't know what to do, Sam."

"You'll stay here." Sam's voice was firm. "Close by me so I can look after—" He stopped short, and his expression hardened. "I keep forgetting." He released Emma's arm and raised his hand to rub at his eyes. "I can't see," he muttered.

"You can't . . . Sam, are your eyes worse again?"

"*Nee*, I didn't mean that. They're no better, but they're no worse than they've been. I only meant . . . how could I look after you? I'd not see him coming, even."

Fear struck in Emma's heart as she considered Sam's words. She wasn't afraid for herself, although she had a feeling that Trevor would just as likely hurt her as anybody else. But fear for Sam.

Sam might not see Trevor coming, but what difference would it make if he did? Even if Sam's eyes were as good as ever, a man's strength would be little use against a gun.

"Maybe," Sam was saying slowly. "Maybe you'd best go back home after all, Emma. Joseph can look after you better than I can."

It cost him to say that. She could see it, see the pain on his face as he admitted it, and it pushed her worries about Trevor out of her mind.

"Can you see me, Sam?"

"What?"

"Can you see me?"

"Sort of."

She moved a step closer. "Bend down."

"What?" Sam repeated.

She reached up and put her hands on each side of his face. Gently but firmly, she angled his head down toward hers until they were barely a few inches apart.

"Can you see me any better now?"

"*Ja*." He only whispered the word, but that was all right. "Not much better. But a little."

She looked into his eyes, and the knot of worry in her stomach dissolved, melting right away into nothing. "Well, I can see you perfectly," she said.

Then she tiptoed and kissed him.

It wasn't Emma's first kiss. She'd been curious enough to kiss a boy or two when they'd driven her home from singings. Those kisses had been sweet, she'd thought, but not so sweet that she'd been tempted to repeat them. No boy had ever gotten more than one kiss from her, and most of them had gotten none.

No, this wasn't her first kiss, but it might as well have been. Because, it turned out that kissing Sam Christner was a different matter altogether.

His mouth was slack against hers for only a second. Then his arms went around her, and he kissed her back.

She'd known Sam was a big man. Everybody knew that. But everybody hadn't been held close to his wide chest, hadn't felt the strength of his arms curved around them. Emma had never lost her wits when those other fellows had kissed her. Her mind had stayed cool and untouched by the whole thing.

But now with Sam, she couldn't think at all. There was nothing in the world but him, blocking out everything else. It was as if she'd sparked a match—and the whole world had exploded.

When he finally lifted his lips from hers, he kept his arms around her, holding her close. He looked down at her, his eyes a darker and more dangerous shade of brown than they'd been before. "Why'd you do that?"

It was a second or two before Emma could think clearly enough to speak. "*Ich vays naett*," she managed finally.

"You don't know?" Something flickered across Sam's face. Hurt, she thought. Or disappointment. She couldn't tell—her mind still wasn't completely recovered. He tightened his fingers gently against her waist for a second, then released her. "Well, maybe you'd best think it through before you go kissing me again."

He started to turn away, but she put out a hand and stopped him. His muscle tensed beneath her touch, and he halted, tilting his head down and toward her, waiting.

"I've done enough thinking to know one thing, Sam. I don't want to go home. I want to stay here. With you."

He turned to face her, and his breathing sped up again. He leaned closer in, and for a second she thought he was going to kiss her again, but he stopped short of it. His eyes searched her face.

"I want you to stay, too." The corner of his mouth twitched. "I wanted it before. I want it more now. But, Emma . . ." He shook his head. "I should make you go."

"Make me? I've a mind of my own, Sam."

"You don't have to tell me that." She could see him wavering. "You've picked a bad time for this, Emma."

"You're wishing I hadn't kissed you then?"

"*Nee.*" The denial came fast, but it was followed by, "And *ja.*" He found her face with his hand and gently traced the curve of her cheek with one finger. "It's a hard thing for a fellow to see everything he's wanted just outside of his reach."

"I'm not out of your reach, Sam." She tiptoed again, but he stepped back.

"You'd better be. For now. Until I talk to that eye doctor, and I know better what I'm dealing with."

Emma felt a stirring of alarm. "But that doesn't matter."

"It does to me. We're not children now, Emma. I'm a man grown, and you're a woman. We're not playing anymore. And I—" He stopped, and the muscles in his throat flexed as he swallowed. "I have to do this right. I've seen what my mistakes can cost the people I care about. I'll not be thoughtless again, not when it comes to you."

"Sam."

"We'll wait, Emma, and we'll pray. We'll see what the

doctor says, and then we'll know what *Gott*'s will is for me." He paused. "For us."

"It'll be good news. I know it."

"I hope so." His mouth curved. "If it is, we'll talk again. And I won't be so quick to step back from you, either, I can tell you that."

She smiled up at him. "Good."

Chapter Eighteen

❧

"THAT *ENGLISCH* WOMAN'S FINALLY HERE." RUTH peered through the living room window as Birdie pulled her car into the driveway. "This is an important appointment. You'd think she could have been on time."

"She's only a few minutes late," Emma pointed out. "And she's being very kind to drive us all the way to Knoxville and back." She adjusted her bonnet and glanced down the hallway toward Sam's room. His door was still shut.

He'd been in the barn when she'd arrived, seeing to the horses. When he'd come inside to eat, he'd seemed frustrated. He'd had a hard time finding a bucket in the barn, and he'd reminded Emma and Ruth to please be careful about putting things back where he'd left them.

Emma had started to argue that she *had* been careful but then decided against it. Today was not the day for that.

He'd been quiet during breakfast, and she'd noticed he'd kept his head down longer during the silent prayer than was usual. She knew what he was praying for. The same thing she was. Good news.

And of course, there would be good news. Sam wasn't blind anymore. Maybe he wasn't seeing so well yet, but he was improving. *Ja*, she felt confident that they would be happy after they'd talked with the doctor.

It was the visit with Janie they'd planned after the appointment that had her concerned. The Troyers lived close to Knoxville, and Sam had asked his sister if they could come by while they were in the area. Leah had agreed, but Emma could tell she was still worried about how her brother might react to the reality of Janie's injuries.

Birdie rapped on the front door, and Emma went to open it.

"Here I am!" Birdie said. "Are you and Sam ready to go?"

"They were ready on time," Ruth pointed out.

"Oh, Ruth." Birdie wrinkled her nose. "I knew you couldn't resist taking a poke at me for being a little late. Well, I'm sorry, but I had to fix my face. Some of us prefer not to scare people. Sam! There you are!" Birdie's smile returned as Sam came out of his room and started down the hall. "I think you'd better ride in the front seat with me."

"That will be fine." Emma noticed that Sam's eyes went to Birdie's face but didn't quite settle correctly. Her stomach dropped. He had a general idea of where Birdie was, but he couldn't see her clearly.

Emma had been watching Sam closely over the past few days, trying to gauge what he could see and what he couldn't. Every time he reached for the salt and nabbed it on the first try, her heart soared. And every time he had to fumble to find a doorknob, it sank.

She tried not to do it, but she couldn't help it. She had to keep reminding herself that, whatever happened, whatever *Gott*'s will was for Sam's eyesight, it was out of her con-

trol. It was something she and Sam would simply have to
accept.

And she would accept what *Gott* decided, of course. But
Sam was going to have to accept something else as well.
Emma wasn't going to give up on the two of them, no matter what the doctor said today. She'd talk Sam around some
way, and they'd figure things out.

"I hate to separate you two lovebirds, but the back seat
of my car is so cramped, Sam's knees would be up to his
elbows," Birdie was saying.

"Lovebirds," Ruth scoffed. "You silly *Englischers*."

Birdie glanced at Emma and winked. "Looks like Sam
may not be the only one in this house who doesn't see
things too clearly."

Emma wished Birdie would keep quiet. She meant nothing but good, Emma knew that, but her tendency to speak
her opinions out loud wasn't going to go down well with
Ruth. Especially not on this subject.

"Samuel's got better sense than you think," Ruth muttered.

"*What* did you say?" Birdie's eyebrows rose, and she
puffed up like a hen whose chick had just been pecked on
the head.

"We'd best get going." Emma grabbed Sam's arm and
tugged him toward the door. "We're running late."

Unfortunately Birdie was blocking the doorway, and she
refused to budge. "Your nephew's a fine young man," she
said clearly. "I've been very impressed by how he's handled
all the difficulties that have been plopped in his lap. That
most definitely includes you, by the way. I suppose these
two children are too respectful to argue with you, but I'm
not. Sam couldn't do a bit better than our sweet Emma here,
and you know it."

"I know no such thing."

"We really need to go," Emma interjected desperately.

She looked up at Sam, hoping he'd chime in and help. To her astonishment, he looked as if he was about to laugh.

"You're just saying that because you're jealous." Birdie shot Ruth one last narrow look, then turned to Emma and Sam and beckoned them toward the door. "All right. Come on, my pets."

"I am not jealous." Ruth pronounced each word with a separate huff of air.

"Yes, you are, you old beanbag," Birdie responded coolly over one shoulder as she ushered Emma and Sam out the door. "And so am I. Who wouldn't be? Young love is the sweetest thing there is."

Ruth started to argue, but Birdie quickly banged the door shut behind them.

"For heaven's sake," she muttered, "let's hit the road before that woman thinks of something else nasty to say. Before I met Ruth Christner, I used to say I'd never met an Amish woman who wasn't sweet as pie. I'll tell you what— I sure don't say that anymore. Go on now, and hop in. I left the car running. I figured we might need to make a quick getaway."

The ride to Knoxville took about forty-five minutes. Emma had worried a little about accepting Birdie's offer to drive. She was an older woman, after all, and the city traffic could be a challenge. But she seemed to know just what she was doing, although Emma noticed that she seemed to regard speed limit signs as more of a suggestion.

Maybe because of that, they arrived at the doctor's office with a few minutes to spare in spite of their late start.

Emma had also wondered if Birdie would insist on going inside with them. The *Englisch* lady meant well, of course, but her understanding of boundaries could get a little blurry sometimes. Emma was relieved when the other woman pulled a romance novel from between the front seats and slipped on a pair of reading glasses.

"I'll be here when you get done," she announced cheerfully.

"Then you'll drive us to see my sister and Janie at Milton's family's home?" Sam asked.

"That's right," Birdie agreed. "I've already put the address in my phone, so it won't be any trouble to find the place. Go on, now. You know how these doctors are. They'll keep you cooling your heels in their waiting room forever, but you'd better not show up five minutes late, or they're giving your appointment to somebody else. Shoo."

Emma took Sam's arm as they exited the car. She'd watched him on the ride over, and he'd hardly looked out the window. He'd kept his eyes on Birdie or on his own hands, clenched in his lap. Probably in part because he was thinking and praying about the appointment and about seeing Janie for the first time since the accident. But also because he couldn't see anything of the passing scenery anyhow.

The inside of the eye specialist's office was bewildering. This must be a thriving practice because the spacious waiting room was crowded, and there was a huge half-moon of a reception desk with at least six people checking folks in. A television blared from one corner, and its constant noise mingled with the chatter of the patients, making Emma want to plug her ears.

She and Sam chose a line and waited patiently until it was their turn to speak to the worker at the computer.

"We have an appointment," Emma said.

"Which doctor?" The woman at the computer spoke without lifting her eyes from her screen.

Emma darted an embarrassed look at Sam. "I don't remember," she admitted. "I called your doctor in Nashville, and he set up this appointment. I wrote it down, but I left the paper at Ruth's."

"We've never been here before," Sam said. "Can you look it up for us?"

The iron-haired woman made an irritated noise and clicked a few keys. "Name?"

"That's what we're telling you. We're not sure," Emma repeated.

"*Your* name."

"Emma Hochstedler."

"Spell the last name."

Before Emma could start, Sam touched her hand. "I think she needs my name."

"Oh!" Of course! How *schtupid* of her.

The woman behind the desk was looking at them now and frowning. "The patient's name," she said slowly and deliberately, as if she were speaking to a slow-witted child.

"Sam Christner," Sam supplied quietly.

More clicking. "You're seeing Dr. Appleton, the neuro-ophthalmologist. Do you have an insurance card?"

"No. I will be paying in cash."

"Then you'll have to pay a percentage up front." Sam took a check out of his pocket and lowered his head almost to the paper to fill it out. It took him a while, and the receptionist looked irritated.

When it was done, more keys clicked, a machine whirred, and the woman handed them a printed receipt.

"*Denki*," Emma said. She took the receipt and folded it into pocket size before handing it to Sam.

"What?" The woman frowned across the desk.

"Thank you," Emma translated, blushing.

"Oh. You're welcome. Take a seat. He's on schedule, so you should be called back soon. Next!"

"I'm sorry," Emma whispered to Sam in *Deutsch* as they found seats together. "I bumbled that, didn't I? I don't seem to have my wits about me today."

Sam shifted in the flimsy plastic and metal chair. "Who could in such a place? Noisy, and the woman had a rude voice. But you did all right. Thank you for helping."

"You're welcome."

The woman at the desk was right. Barely fifteen minutes later, a plump young man appeared at the doorway, peering down at an electronic device in his hand. "Sam Christner?" he called, mispronouncing the name with a long *i*.

Sam and Emma got up and approached. The man had on scrubs with glasses printed on them, and Emma was relieved to see that he looked friendlier than the woman at the desk.

"Which one of you two is Sam?"

"I am Sam."

"Fine! Are you Mrs. Christner?"

"*Nee*. I mean, no." Emma fumbled. "I am . . . we are—"

"We're planning to get married. She can come back with me, *ja?*"

"Of course! And congratulations. Come on through. Dr. Appleton will be with you shortly."

Emma followed Sam wordlessly through the door and sat through all the tests and checks the nurse did in preparation for the doctor's arrival. She was glad that she wasn't expected to answer any questions. All she could do was think over and over again about what Sam had said.

We're planning to get married.

It seemed like forever until the nurse had finished up everything. "All right," the man said. "The doc will be with you in just a few minutes. Okay?"

"Thank you," Sam said.

The minute the door was shut, Emma said, "Sam?"

He shot her a shamefaced look. "I know. I told that man an untruth. It was wrong of me. But after how unkind the woman at the desk seemed, I wasn't sure you'd be allowed back here otherwise."

An untruth. Oh.

Before she could think of anything to say, there was a brisk knock on the door. A balding man of about fifty years stuck his head through and smiled.

"Sam Christner?" This one said the name correctly. "I'm Dr. Rodney Appleton." He held out a hand. "Good to meet you."

"*Gut* to meet you, too, Doctor. I thank you for seeing me." Sam put his own hand out and fumbled only a little before finding the other man's.

"You're quite welcome." The doctor nodded at Emma before dropping into a rolling office chair. For a second, his gaze snagged on her face, but he only smiled politely and glanced down to study his electronic tablet. "According to this, I should be very pleased that *you're* seeing *me*, huh? You've had some significant difficulties." He looked back at Sam, and Emma could see a gleam of sharp interest in the doctor's gaze.

"Yes, my eyes are better, but still not too good."

"Well, if you'll let me take a look, then we'll see what we're dealing with." When Sam nodded, the doctor clapped his hands together. "Okay! Let's get started."

Emma watched quietly from her corner as the doctor put Sam through a variety of tests. It took a long time, and the doctor's face was impossible to read. He simply performed test after test, noting the results and not changing his expression at all.

When finally everything was done, the doctor snapped the lights in the room back on and dropped down into his chair with a sigh.

"Well, Sam, I have to say, you're one lucky son of a gun."

Emma's heart soared. Lucky. That's not what she or Sam would call it, but it meant good things.

"I have been blessed, *ja*," Sam corrected him quietly.

"You certainly have. I've read Dr. Oscar's notes. As you probably know, what you suffered is called traumatic optic neuropathy. It's a pretty uncommon result from a closed head injury like yours, actually. So you didn't win that coin toss, I'm afraid. Things got worse from there. You lost consciousness after the buggy accident. Is that right?"

·

"I blacked out for a while. By the time I came to, I was in the hospital."

"That's a poor prognostic factor for vision recovery in situations like this. You'd also experienced no improvement whatsoever after forty-eight hours. Correct?"

Sam shook his head. "I couldn't see anything then."

"And you were completely blind until about a week and a half ago. Is that right?"

"I could see like"—Sam gestured with one hand—"mottled up clouds sometimes. Like milk poured in coffee. But nothing else."

The doctor whistled through his teeth. "This is where we get to the lucky part. Those two factors alone—the losing consciousness and the lack of improvement in that critical forty-eight-hour window—put your chances of recovery way down. If I'd been called to make a bet at that point, I'd have said you'd be blind for the rest of your life. But you've defied the odds, my friend. Like I said, you're one lucky guy. Or blessed, as you say," the doctor amended.

"I am very thankful."

"So." The doctor leaned back in the chair and crossed his arms over his chest. "Let's talk about where we go from here. First off, I'm going to put you in touch with a social worker who can give you an idea of the resources available to you locally. We'll provide the documentation to certify you as legally blind so that you can receive whatever financial and social accommodations you're entitled to." He frowned. "I'm actually not sure how that will apply in your religious situation, but you should check it out just in case."

"Legally blind," Sam repeated the words slowly.

"Right. It's just the term we use to describe your current level of vision. You're obviously not completely blind now. You can see a little, but not well enough to say, drive a car. Of course"—the doctor laughed shortly—"that particular example won't be applicable to you, but you get the idea."

Sam was frowning. "Are you saying my eyesight won't come back completely?"

There was a long pause where the only sounds were the murmurs of voices and the shrill ring of phones outside the closed door. Then the specialist cleared his throat.

"Well, yes, Sam. That's exactly what I'm saying."

"But." Emma couldn't help herself. It seemed so . . . hard, after the rising hopes of only a few seconds ago. "You just said he was lucky."

"Right." The doctor swiveled his chair to face her. "Lucky to see at all," he explained gently. "That's a much better outcome than I would have expected for him given the circumstances, as I said earlier. I'm sorry, Sam. I guess I shouldn't have been so blunt. I wasn't aware that you were expecting a better prognosis."

Sam's face was tense, but he shook his head. "*Nee*, it's all right, Doctor. I was expecting *Gott*'s will, that's all. You've no control over that, and you've explained it to me real well. I thank you."

Sam was mostly silent after that, answering politely as arrangements were made about resources and follow-up appointments. Emma watched him closely, doing her best to guess what he was thinking.

Her guesses only made her worries grow.

When the appointment was finally over, they settled up the bill and headed out to the parking area. Emma pulled Sam to the edge of the sidewalk, anxious to have a private word with him before they got back into Birdie's car.

"Are you all right? I know this was a disappointment to you."

Sam lifted his face and squinted up at the sun. "It was not what I was expecting, this news, so it took me by surprise. I will have to think it over."

"It doesn't change anything. I want you to know that."

"*Ja*, Emma, it changes things. Whether we like it or

not." He looked down at her, and she could see the tired lines in his face. "I don't want to talk about this now. Like I said, I will have to think about it and pray about it. It takes me a while to figure things out, but sooner or later, I'll know what's right to do. Right now, though, I need to put my own troubles in the back of my mind until after my visit with Janie. All right?"

Janie. Emma's heart fell. After this disappointment, how would Sam handle that visit?

Not so well, she thought.

"Don't you want to postpone the visit until another day? I'm sure Leah will understand."

"No." His response was quick and sure. "We're not putting it off any longer. Don't worry. I'll keep this news to myself for now. We'll only say what the doctor said at first, that I'm blessed. I'll make sure Janie isn't upset, nor Leah, either."

It wasn't Janie or Leah that Emma was most worried about. But it was plain that Sam was solidly set on this course, and she supposed they might as well let this day do its worst.

"All right, Sam." She took his arm, and together they started across the parking lot.

CHAPTER NINETEEN

❧

ON THE WAY TO LEAH'S, SAM DISCOVERED THAT PUT-
ting his troubles to the back of his mind was easier said
than done. He and Emma rode in silence while Birdie carried on an argument with the mechanical voice coming
from her phone.

"No, I'm not going to turn there! It's a one-way street,
for goodness' sake. Honestly," she muttered, "you wonder
if the people who program in these directions have ever
actually driven a car. But don't you worry, Sam. I'll get us
to your sister's house eventually."

After a few seconds, Emma answered her from the back
seat. "That's all right, Birdie. We are in no hurry."

He should have answered himself, Sam realized. He had
a lot on his mind, but that was no excuse to be rude. "Leah
understands we could not come until we'd finished with the
appointment. She isn't expecting us at any particular time,
so it doesn't matter when we get there."

"Good!" Birdie lapsed into silence, apparently distracted by the traffic as she worked to get them out of Knoxville and to the small Amish community over in Leeds where Leah's Milton had been born and raised.

Sam was glad the *Englisch* woman wasn't as chatty as usual. He was trying to sift through the news the doctor had given him.

Like he'd told Emma, he'd not been prepared for it. He wasn't sure why he'd been so hopeful that the news would be more positive. He wasn't the kind of fellow who had his head up in the clouds, not usually. Life had taught him to take a realistic view of things, and he figured he did that mostly.

But today he'd gone into that office secretly believing he'd hear good news, and when the doctor had explained things, Sam felt as if his feet had been knocked out from under him.

And not only his. He was very aware of Emma sitting behind him, waiting for the talk they'd have to have sooner or later.

He'd made things worse, telling the lie about them planning to be married. It had been a fool thing to do. He'd blurted it out so she could go back with him, but deep down he knew there was more to it. In his heart, he'd meant it. He'd had it all settled.

He wanted Emma as his wife.

He always had wanted her. Only her. His family had teased him for years about being stuck on Emma Hochstedler, about being unable to move past her and find himself another girl. Over and over again, he'd shrugged and denied it—and half believed himself when he did.

But it seemed they'd been right all along.

Now the thing that he'd never thought possible had happened. Emma was feeling the same way about him, about big, slow-thinking Sam Christner, as unlikely as that seemed.

That, he realized suddenly, was why he'd felt so optimistic going into this appointment today. In a world where something like that could be true, he'd not believed anything very bad could happen to him ever again.

Well, he'd been wrong. He wasn't sure exactly where this news left them—he hadn't prodded it enough to know, not yet. But he knew it wasn't going to be good, once he did.

Different thoughts had been filtering in as Birdie wove her way through the traffic, fussing with her phone. He'd be no good on a construction site if he couldn't see better than this. In fact, he'd be a liability. He didn't know how to do anything else. He'd only been trained for this one thing, like most all the men in his family. What was a man without his job? His work . . . that was most of who Sam was.

Most, but not all.

Because it got worse than that, even. He'd never see Emma again, not like he had before. Not like he'd seen her that day of their crazy ride, standing by Ruth's clothesline, so lovely even in her black mourning dress that she made a man's breath catch in his chest. He'd not be able to read her face again, like he'd been doing since they were children together, guessing her feelings by the way she tilted her head or held her mouth.

Sam swallowed and turned his head back toward the window, though he could see nothing but a colorful blur going past. Almost immediately he felt Emma's hand touch his shoulder. Briefly, reassuringly.

"Are you sure about this, Sam?" She spoke softly in *Deutsch*, so Birdie wouldn't understand. "We do not have to go today. Maybe it would be better not to. I can explain to Leah. Nobody will be upset."

"*Nee*," he said. "We will go as we'd planned. I don't want to change our plans at the last minute. I can see well enough not to upset Janie too much, I think."

"It may upset you, though, being with Janie for the first

time since the accident." Emma's voice was quiet but urgent. "You've already been given a lot to think about today. It's all right to take a break between these two such hard things. Wise, even."

He stiffened under her touch. Two hard things? A tickle of fear threaded its way through his body.

Janie was getting better. She had scars, but she would live. She would walk. Everybody said so. They had been postponing the visit only because they hadn't wanted to upset her by Sam's blindness. Now he could see, a little. And since it was as good as it was likely going to get, there was no reason to postpone the visit anymore.

Yet Emma seemed worried—not about Janie but about Sam.

That made him uneasy. Had they been keeping something from him? Was Janie worse than they'd let on?

"All right." Birdie sounded happier now. "I think that stupid GPS finally has it figured out. This looks right, doesn't it?"

Sam had no idea, but Emma answered. "*Ja*, those are Plain houses. We are in the right area, at least."

"It is a white two-story house, with two big barns behind," Sam said. "One on each side of the house."

He'd only been to the Troyers' home once or twice, but he'd remembered those barns. They'd been built a hundred years ago, and he'd admired their craftsmanship. He and Milton had talked about them. His late brother-in-law had worked in a factory that built RVs, and he'd appreciated good construction as much as Sam had.

"This must be it right here, then." He heard the clicking of Birdie's blinker as the car slowed down. "My, would you look at those flowers? Just lovely. All you Amish women have such green thumbs!"

"Not as much green thumbs as muddy knees," Emma said. "It's a lot of work to keep up the flower beds, but they do make a house look real cheerful. The children help a lot, too, of course."

"Well, it's a beautiful farm. Just like a picture." The car rolled to a stop.

"Will you come in?" Emma asked politely. "I am sure Leah would be happy to fix you a glass of tea, and you can rest while we visit with Janie."

"No, no. I'm going to drive back to that little restaurant we passed on the way in. Did you see it? The one with the antique store attached? I'll have a lovely time browsing around in there. What say I come back in about two hours? Will that give you enough time? I don't want to rush, but I'd like to get back through that awful Knoxville traffic before dark."

"That will be fine," Sam said. "Thank you, Birdie."

"You're very welcome."

Sam pushed open the car door, but waited for Emma before stepping out. He didn't remember the Troyer farm too clearly—definitely not well enough to walk to the house without some help.

"Sam!" His sister's voice called from the porch before Emma had even pushed the door closed.

"Hello, Leah!" Sam made himself smile and waved in the direction of the call.

"There's a walkway to the porch," Emma murmured. "Nice and smooth, all paved, but it's narrow, and there are flowers on both sides of it. We can't walk side by side. I'll go first, and you can follow right behind. Okay?"

"*Ja*, I can do that."

Emma stepped to the side when they reached the porch just a split second before Leah flung herself into his arms.

"Sam, it's wonderful *gut* to see you!" His sister spoke into his ear. "I've missed you so! I wanted to come and visit you, but—"

He patted her back. "That is all right. I am glad you

didn't waste your time on me. Looking after Janie was your job. Where is she?"

"Upstairs." There was the tiniest hitch in his sister's voice, and Sam frowned. Back when he'd been able to see, he probably wouldn't even have noticed it, but now his ears picked up on things like that.

He also noticed that the place was awfully quiet. "Where is everybody else?"

"They've gone to town, the whole family. They said they had errands to run, but I think they just wanted to give you and me and Janie some time alone. They should be back before long, though, and they're looking forward to visiting with you before you leave."

"I'll sit out here on the porch and wait for them," Emma said. "It's a real pretty day."

Again, Sam had that feeling of something running under Emma's words. Leah had taken his arm and was leading him toward the porch, and he felt his sister tense and turn toward Emma.

He couldn't see well enough to read their faces, but he suspected some sort of unspoken communication was going back and forth.

"All right, Emma. Make yourself at home," Leah said. "We'll be back down in just a little while. Milton's *mamm* made some lemonade and gingersnaps for us."

"That was kind of her." Sam followed Leah as she led him up the steps and across the porch to the door.

"They've all been nothing but kind, the whole time." He heard the soft slam of a screen door as Leah took him into the house. He got a sense of space. The Troyer house was an older one, and the ceilings were high, he remembered—a nice feature in summertime. "After Milton died," his sister continued, "they invited me to come here with Janie, but I felt it would be too hard, being here with Milton's family without him. Everywhere I looked, there would be another memory. Hard, too, to see them grieving for him just as I was. I couldn't stand the thought of dealing with their sorrow as well as my own. I didn't think I could handle it, but maybe it's what I should have done."

"Do you think so?"

"I don't mean that I didn't appreciate spending time with you, Sam. But it's just . . . I guess I thought maybe I could run away from my grief. That being away from my memories and Milton's family would somehow make things easier. But grief doesn't work like that. I should have remembered what folks say—that joy doubles when you share it, but sorrow is halved. It's been a real comfort being here with Milton's parents, seeing his brothers and sisters. There's a lot of him in them, you know? I feared that would make things worse, but instead, it makes me feel better."

Leah did sound better, Sam thought, in spite of everything. "Do you think you will stay on here, then?"

"Watch the steps here. They are old and kind of steep. Take hold of the handrail there on your left." Leah waited until Sam managed the first step before answering, "That depends. I am happy here, and Milton's *mamm* and *daed* have said that we may stay as long as we like. And it's real convenient to Janie's doctor's appointments, for the time being. Which they've insisted on paying for, by the way. The church here is going to help, too. So you needn't worry about that."

Sam swallowed. Those bills should have been his to see about. "That's good of them."

"*Ja*, they've all been very good to us. But whether we stay here depends on other things. Like you. Here now, we're at the landing. Wait just a second, and let's talk."

"All right."

"What did the doctor say about your eyes?"

"That I was lucky," Sam said promptly.

"Lucky."

"To see again. It is a real blessing because he normally would not have expected my eyes to improve."

He could see a flickering of movement. Leah was checking his eyes by wiggling her fingers. "That's a blessing for sure. How well do you see now, Sam?"

"Well enough to see that you're flapping your hand in front of my nose. Better up close."

"Can you see my face?"

Sam hesitated. "Not too clear."

"Sam, today wasn't good news. Was it?" His sister's voice was heavy with sorrow. "Is your sight going to get any better at all?"

Sam cast around in his mind for the right thing to say. He didn't want to add to Leah's troubles, not now, when she had Janie to look after. "Leah, if it's *Gott*'s will for me to see better, I'll see better. If it isn't, I won't. It doesn't much matter what the doctors say. I'll have to accept whatever happens and go on from there." He paused. "You understand that."

He felt his sister's hand tighten on his arm. "*Ja*. I do understand. And I know how hard such acceptance can be. If you need me to come back home, I can—"

"*Nee*. I am all right where I am. Emma is helping, and Ruth is recovered. It is fine."

"Yes, Emma. I'll want to talk to you about her, too, *bruder*. But first, we'd better see Janie. She's playing in her room."

"How is she doing?"

"Lots better. The doctors call her lucky, too. She's walking pretty well now and only limps a little. She should be able to get around fine in just a few more weeks. But—"

"But what?"

"They told you already that she's got some scars on her

face." Leah spoke lightly, but he'd heard that note in his sister's voice before, back when she'd been assuring him that looking after Ruth was not so terrible, after all.

"Emma told me." A lump of dread was forming in his stomach. "So they're bad, then?"

"Oh, well." Leah started up the next section of stairs, tugging Sam along with her. "Scars are scars. Maybe we don't like the look of them, but they are signs that the body has healed, and that is good. I just didn't want you to be surprised."

The weight in Sam's belly grew heavier. Before he could ask any more questions, Leah pushed open a door. The room must have had a lot of windows because a bright light washed over him, making him blink.

"Look who has come to see you!" Leah said cheerfully.

"Sam! Sam!" Janie's voice was followed by a scuffling. Sam knelt and held out his arms. It took longer than it should have for the little girl to make it to him, but when she did, she flung her arms around his neck and hugged him as tight as ever.

"It's wonderful *gut* to see you," Sam managed to say. His voice didn't seem to want to cooperate. He could feel the starch of Janie's *kapp* against his cheek and see her shoulder. She was wearing a blue dress. She'd always looked real nice in blue.

"*Can* you see me?" Janie drew back, but she kept her hands on his shoulders. "*Mamm* said you might not be able to."

"I can see you a little bit. Not real good, but I'm lots better than I was."

"I'm better than I was, too," the little girl said matter-of-factly. "Your eyes are different," she added after a minute. "And you're skinnier. But other than that you look the same." She paused. "I don't look the same anymore, but that's all right. How we look on the outside doesn't matter very much anyhow. It's the inside that counts."

"That's true. I am glad to see you, Janie, inside and outside. You know, if you come real close to my eyes, I can see you even better maybe," he added. He heard Leah make a protesting noise, but Janie answered before her mother could speak.

"Okay."

A split second later, she was nose to nose with him.

Even with his poor vision he could see the wide, angry pink stripe of scarring cutting across Janie's left cheek. He sucked in a startled breath.

It was bad, for sure. Much worse than he'd imagined even. No wonder the doctors had warned Leah about it.

"Sam." His sister's voice cut into his pain. "I think we've left Emma by herself long enough, *ja?* We should go downstairs. Janie, come here. I'll help you down the steps and come back up to help your *onkel.*"

"All right," Janie agreed cheerfully. Her face drew away, then came back, her small nose almost touching Sam's. "I almost forgot to tell you," she said in a more somber tone.

It took him three tries to get the words out. "What, Butterbean?"

"That I'm sorry Breeze got hurt. He didn't mean to run into the road. He just got scared. He's a real pretty horse, and I know you like him a lot."

"I'm sorry, too, Janie." Sam whispered the words. It was the best he could do. "I'm very sorry."

"Janie. Come on. Let's go downstairs." His sister sounded worried. "Sam, I'll be right back, okay? Just wait here."

He nodded without speaking. When he was sure they were out of the room, when he heard them starting slowly down the stairs, he pressed his hand hard over his eyes and set his jaw, praying for the strength to keep his feelings under control.

He had to get hold of himself. He couldn't let Janie see how upset he was.

For pity's sake, he'd already caused enough damage.

CHAPTER TWENTY

❧

"HELLO!" EMMA TURNED TO SEE JANIE FRAMED IN the doorway of the house smiling and waving. Leah stood behind her. "*Mamm* says it's time for cookies!"

Emma smiled back, taking care not to allow her expression to change when she saw the thick, raised scars crossing the little girl's cheek and running down her neck.

"Well, hello," she said, getting up from the swing. "It's so good to see you, and I was just sitting here thinking how much I'd enjoy a gingersnap." She glanced behind Leah, but the hallway was empty. "Where's Sam?"

"Upstairs still." There was a forced brightness to Leah's voice, but Emma noticed the worry in the other woman's eyes. "Janie's doing real well on her feet now, but she still needs some help down the steps. I was just about to go up to get him."

"I can go." Emma made the offer quietly, watching Leah to see how it went over. "While you get the snacks ready. I've had a lot of practice helping him."

Leah started to refuse, but then she looked at Emma. Tears sparkled in the other woman's eyes as she nodded. "*Denki*, Emma. I think you should go. You've spent more time with him than I have lately. You'll know best how to help him now."

The two women's eyes met, and Emma understood two things. Seeing Janie had been hard on Sam.

And now Leah was trusting Emma to tend her brother's hurts, inside and out.

Emma lifted her chin. "I'll do my best."

"Come on, Janie," Leah said. "You can help me in the kitchen. We'll go ahead and get enough plates and glasses out for the rest of the family. I expect they'll be here any minute." Leah led her daughter toward the back of the house.

Emma went up the steps. All the bedroom doors upstairs were open except for one, which was almost closed. She went to that door and knocked.

"Sam?"

"*Ja.*" He answered quickly, but there was a suspicious thickness to his voice.

She pushed the door wider. Sam stood by the window, looking out. She doubted he could see much of the farmland stretching outside the Troyers' home. She suspected he just wanted a reason to keep his back to the door.

"Janie and Leah are fixing our snacks in the kitchen. They sent me to get you." She walked up beside him and lay a hand on his arm. The muscle, still firm, even after all these weeks of rest, flexed under her touch. "Are you all right?"

"You've seen Janie?" He didn't look down at her, staring off instead into the distance.

"I have."

He nodded slowly. "So have I, as best I could. I saw enough anyway. I tried not to . . . let on, and I don't think Janie noticed. But I think I upset my sister." He sighed. "No wonder she didn't want me to come here."

"I don't think Leah's upset with you at all. I think she's more worried. She knows how you've been fretting over Janie, and she didn't want to make things worse. She was afraid it would slow down your own healing."

"It's all right, Emma," he cut in quietly. "It doesn't matter. I could have done no good by coming earlier anyhow. I could not have helped her, nor Janie."

I could not have helped her. There was so much regret in those words that Emma's heart twisted itself into an aching knot. "There's a difference between helping and being able to fix things, Sam."

"It seems I can do neither, but at the least I can try not be a hindrance, I guess." A muscle was jumping in his cheek. "There's nothing to say about it that wouldn't be a waste of time now. It is what it is. I have to live with what I've done." Swiftly, as if he were ashamed of it, he raised the back of his hand to scrub at the corner of his eye. Emma tightened her grip on his arm.

"But you didn't do it, Sam."

"I did enough. My sister trusted me, and I nearly got her and her daughter killed. That sweet little *maidel*. Those scars on Janie's face, those go on my debt. Do you know what she said, just now? She told me she was sorry about Breeze getting hurt because she knew I liked him. She tried to comfort me."

"Oh, Sam." Before she could say more, she glimpsed movement through the window. A wagon loaded with Troyers was pulling into the yard. The family swarmed off, talking and laughing, and in a few seconds, the house was ringing with their voices.

Sam's face tightened. "I should go down. Milton's folks have been kind to Leah and to Janie. They've even taken on their bills to pay, although it'll be a hardship for them. I owe them my thanks."

This would be difficult for him, Emma realized. Harder,

maybe, for Sam than for most. He was always so quick to help other people with their troubles, but when he was wounded himself, he craved time and the privacy to hurt alone.

"Stay up here awhile longer if you want," she said. "Birdie will be back soon, and people will understand."

He shook his head. "Janie's been looking forward to seeing me, Leah said. So she'll see me for as long as I'm here. I can't change what happened, but that much I can do. You'd better help me down the stairs, though. It won't do anybody any good if I fall and break a leg."

The minute they reached the bottom of the stairs, Sam was enveloped in a friendly crush of Milton's male relatives. He was swept away to the living room, and soon the men were talking and laughing together. Emma went with the women to the kitchen to help unpack groceries and finish getting the refreshments ready. As she worked, she strained to catch snippets of the conversations going on in the living room. Every now and then she would hear the low rumble of Sam's voice. She'd never noticed, really, how much deeper his voice was than most other men's, but that meant she was able to pick it out easily.

He seemed to be carrying his end of the conversation all right, but to Emma's ear, there was something subdued about him.

"They are trying to be kind." Leah leaned over and spoke quietly while two of Milton's younger sisters had an energetic discussion about whether soft drinks should be offered alongside the lemonade. "To Sam, I mean. They want him to feel he is welcome here. They were the same with me at first. Everybody talking to me at once, rushing to do things for me."

"Milton's family are nice folks."

"*Ja*, they are. Sarah," Leah called to her mother-in-law, "I am going to take Emma out to see the new calf. We will be right back in."

"Sure," the older woman answered easily.

"I'll come, too," Milton's sister Betta said, but her mother shook her head.

"*Nee*, I'll be needing your help inside. You go on, Leah."

"She knows I'm not really excited about the calf," Leah said as soon as they were safely out the door. "She's giving us the time to speak alone. Like you said, they're real nice people. They want us to stay on, me and Janie. For good."

"Oh." Emma wondered how Leah felt about that offer, but she didn't like to ask.

"I want to stay," Leah admitted. "Being here while Janie was so sick, it showed me how strong this family is and how much they love us. I thought after Milton died that maybe I wouldn't feel so much a part of them, but I do. I feel more at home here than I have anywhere since Milton passed."

Emma nodded. "That feeling is a precious thing."

"It is. But I've other family to think about, too. So tell me quick. What did the doctor say about Sam's eyes, really?"

"You should ask Sam."

"I did. He didn't tell me much. Has he asked you not to talk about it?"

"Well, no. Not exactly."

"He doesn't want me worried. That I know. But I'll worry more if I don't know the whole of it, so you might as well tell me." When Emma hesitated, Leah stopped and turned to face her. "I've handled worse things, Emma. I can handle this. Whatever it is."

Emma looked into the other woman's face. There was sorrow there, and concern, but there was a new strength, too. Staying here with Milton's folks had helped Leah. Family drew strength from family.

"I know you can handle it." She drew in a breath. "Sam just didn't want you to have to, but I don't suppose that's up to him." She outlined what the doctor had said. Leah listened silently until she was finished, then sighed.

"That's not so good. If he sees no better than he does now, he won't be able to go back to his job." She shook her head. "He's going to have to change directions, and my *bruder*'s like most of the men in my family. Change doesn't come easy to any of them." Leah looked up at Emma and cocked her head to one side. "So where does this leave the two of you?"

Emma stuttered, and Leah shrugged.

"I'm sorry. I know it's rude of me to ask such a thing. But after everything that's happened, I don't have the time or the patience to play the usual games. It's clear you two have feelings for each other. Are you and my brother planning to get married or not?"

Emma blinked, but she decided she might as well answer Leah's honesty with an honest answer of her own. "I don't know."

Leah lifted an eyebrow. "Hasn't he asked?"

"No." Emma could feel a heat creeping up her cheeks that had nothing to do with the summer sunshine. "Not in so many words. He's hinted at it some. But that was . . . before today." Emma couldn't quite believe she was having such a frank conversation with Leah. "I'm not sure what he is feeling now."

"About you?" The other woman laughed shortly. "The same thing he's been feeling all along, I'm sure."

Leah spoke with such certainty that a flicker of hope stirred in Emma's stomach. "You think so?"

Leah laughed again, but there wasn't much humor in it. "Didn't you hear what I just said? The men in my family don't change. Sam made up his mind about you years ago. The more important question is, have you made up your mind about him?"

"I have."

Leah studied her for a few seconds. "Even now, after what that doctor said?"

"Even now."

Leah started walking toward the barn again, her face thoughtful. "I don't know whether to be happy or worried. You're going to have trouble with him. My brother can be stubborn."

It was Emma's turn to laugh now. "That's no surprise to me."

"He's not going to see any way he can work this out without causing you some hardship. He's not going to want to do that, and he's likely to dig in his heels."

"I know." Emma could already see that coming. Sam would want to protect her from the trouble that lay ahead for him. "I can be stubborn, too."

"You'll need to be." Leah pushed the barn door open. "I suppose you'd best come on in and look at the silly calf. The girls will ask."

She led the way to a stall, and Emma peeked through the rough boards. A doe-eyed Jersey cow looked at her suspiciously before bending to lick the calf curled up in the straw. The little creature was a duplicate of its mother except for a blaze of white across its forehead.

"Is it a heifer or a bull?"

"A heifer," Leah responded absently.

"Oh, *gut*. That's always a blessing."

"*Ja*." Suddenly Sam's sister turned to face her. "Emma, I need to ask you for forgiveness. My sisters and I have thought poorly of you for a long time. We blamed you for Sam's hurt, and that wasn't fair."

"Oh, you don't have to—"

"Yes, I do. It wasn't your fault. Sam . . . well." Leah shrugged. "It was unwise of him to fall for you so young, and to hold on to those feelings like he did after you made it clear you weren't interested. But we felt sorry for him, because he was our brother. Our thickheaded, *schtubbich* brother maybe." A smile flickered across Leah's face. "But ours, and we didn't like seeing him hurt. Nor alone. And nobody would do for him but Emma Hochstedler, and she didn't want him. So we weren't too friendly to you. I'm sorry for that."

"I can understand, Leah. And, of course, you are forgiven."

"You're a kind person, Emma. Everybody has said that all along. Sam especially, but I only saw what I expected to see, I guess." Leah's hands strayed up to toy with the strings of her *kapp*. "I'm not just saying this because you've changed your mind about Sam. You've been real generous to my family in their pain, even in the middle of your own problems. It's shamed me and shown me how wrong I've been to judge you." She sighed. "When big troubles come to us, they have a way of melting away the silly disagreements we have, ain't so? Seems like I can understand people's hearts a lot better. There've been some surprises in that, good and bad."

"I know what you mean." Her parents' deaths and Caleb's shunning had sifted people into different groups. A few folks who'd always seemed kind before had turned judgmental once her family had trouble, implying in little ways that the Hochstedlers had brought their sorrows on themselves. Others, even some they'd had some differences with, had gone to surprising lengths to be helpful and had shown her family only compassion.

The cow left her baby and came to the gate of the stall to get a closer look at her visitors. Leah reached through the rough planks and stroked the animal's nose. "Before Milton died, I liked his family well enough, but I wasn't real close with them. They're loud, and they show their feelings so easy. They weren't like my family at all, and I felt out of place among them. But now—and especially after the

accident—I've seen how much goodness is in them all. It's
made me love them better. And you—you've been very
kind, first to Ruth, and then to Sam. There's a lot of goodness in you, too, Emma. I didn't see it before. I couldn't see
past how you looked on the outside, I guess." Leah gave
Emma a wry look. "I've spent a lot of time lately making
sure Janie understands that our looks aren't near as important as what's in our hearts. That's because of her scars, of
course, but I can see that me judging you because you happened to be born good-looking is just the other side of the
same coin. There are different kinds of beauty." Leah
smiled. "You have a real pretty heart, Emma."

Emma's answering smile wobbled with feeling. "So do
you," she said.

Leah smiled, then glanced toward the barn door. "If we
don't go back in soon, somebody will come looking for us.
But first, I'd like to ask you a favor, if you don't mind me
meddling in your business just a little bit more."

"Go ahead."

"Sooner or later, you're going to have a talk with my
bruder about the future. When you do, will you try to remember what I've told you? That nobody will ever do for
Sam but you? Whatever reasons he gives you why you can't
be together, just remember—he'll never change on the inside, whatever he says or does on the outside."

Emma gave a short nod. "I'm counting on that."

Leah smiled, then—a big, real smile. "I think I'd like
having you for a sister, Emma," she said, just as a noisy
group of young Troyers burst into the barn with the news
that the refreshments were ready.

Back in the house, Emma could see that Leah's description of her in-laws was right on target. They were as loud
as they were loving, and they wore their feelings on their
sleeves. They were an endearing bunch, but Emma was relieved when Birdie drove up, and it was time to go home.

She watched with her heart in her throat as Sam said goodbye to his sister and to his niece, noticed how he cupped Janie's face in one big hand, his thumb gently stroking the angry red of the raised scar. But his goodbyes were cheerful, and there were lots of promises to see one another again when Sam came back in a few weeks for his follow-up appointment.

Once safely in the car, though, Sam seemed to deflate. Birdie picked up on it before they'd even pulled out onto the two-lane road.

"You look completely pooped out, Sam," she said.

He shot her an uncertain glance. "Pooped?" He repeated the odd expression with a wrinkled nose.

Birdie chuckled. "It just means tired."

"Oh. *Ja*, I am tired."

"Those Troyers would tire out anybody," Emma supplied from the back seat. "They're so nice, but they're a lot of them. I'm a little worn out myself."

"Well, don't you two worry about a thing. Just close your eyes and take a nice nap, if you want to. I had a real strong cup of coffee at that shop, and I'm wide awake enough for all three of us. I'll get us home all right."

"Thank you, Birdie," Emma said.

Sam murmured his own thanks, leaned his head against the car window, and closed his eyes. Emma quickly followed suit in the back seat.

She didn't believe for a minute either of them would truly go to sleep, but at least this way, they could both avoid being peppered by Birdie's well-meaning questions during the long drive home. She was surprised when, a few minutes later, she heard soft snores coming from Sam.

She opened her eyes and saw Birdie looking at her in the rearview mirror. The other woman winked.

"Men," she said quietly. "They can fall asleep faster than scat, no matter what's going on. We women aren't so lucky. You two have had a hard time today, haven't you? You haven't said much, but I can tell."

Emma glanced at Sam. Only part of his face was visible, and the tense lines were relaxed in sleep. Her heart stirred.

"Maybe we'd best not talk right now," she suggested. "Let him rest."

Birdie looked disappointed, but she nodded and refocused on the road. "You should shut your eyes, too. After all, when we get to the end of this trip, you're going to have Ruth to deal with."

"You're probably right." Emma closed her eyes and followed Sam's example, leaning her cheek against the smoothness of the car window.

"I expect Ruth will be in rare form," Birdie muttered. "Being alone all day long, no doubt she'll have saved up all sorts of things to fuss about. You'll have a battle on your hands, I'm sure, so rest up while you can."

Birdie was right. There was a battle looming ahead for sure. But for once it wasn't going to be with Ruth.

CHAPTER TWENTY-ONE

BY THE TIME THEY GOT BACK TO JOHNS MILL, THE sun was setting. When Birdie bumped her car into Ruth's driveway, Emma unbuckled her seat belt, but Sam half turned in the seat and shook his head.

"Don't get out, Emma," he said. "You may as well go on home with Birdie. It'll save her a trip to pick you up later."

"Oh." Emma had hoped to find a chance to speak alone with Sam tonight. She'd known it would be a challenge to manage it around Ruth. She could already see Sam's aunt peeking through the living room curtains. Still, they needed to find some way to talk everything over between themselves.

Birdie glanced between them, her face puckered into a concerned frown. "I don't mind running back over."

"Thank you, but we've troubled you enough for one day," Sam said. "Although, if you're willing, I could use a ride into town tomorrow morning."

"Of course, Sam," Birdie agreed immediately. "I'll be happy to take you."

"If it's convenient, maybe we could go after you drive Emma over in the morning. I need to go in and have a word with my old boss. I told him I would, once I'd met with the doctor." A muscle twitched in Sam's jaw. "Our talk won't take long, I'm sure."

"Would you like me to go with you, Sam?"

"*Nee*, Emma, this is something I'd rather do by myself." He pushed open the car door.

"Wait, I'll walk you to the house, and—" Emma started.

"I can manage myself, *denki*. But I'll see you in the morning."

She considered arguing but decided there wasn't much point in it. They were both tired, and it had been a long, emotional day. She sank back into her seat. Maybe it would be best for them to talk when they were both fresher. "All right, Sam."

Birdie drove the short distance home in an uncharacteristic silence, darting frequent looks at Emma in the mirror. When they pulled up behind her house, the older woman made an exclamation of dismay.

"Look at that. I've left the kitchen light burning all day, and I'd have sworn I turned it off before I left the house this morning." She shook her head. "I'm turning into a forgetful old lady."

Emma managed a smile as she got out of the car. "I don't think you'll ever be an old lady, Birdie."

"Well, I've certainly been doing a good impression of it lately." She wrinkled her nose. "For instance, right now I'm feeling an overwhelming urge to give you motherly advice, and that's an old lady habit if ever there was one."

The only thing Emma really wanted right now was solitude and her bed. That defeated look she'd seen on Sam's face had worried her. She needed to spend some time in prayer, settling her soul down, bringing her hopes and her fears in line with *Gott*'s will.

Whatever that turned out to be.

But she couldn't be rude, not after all Birdie had done for her today, so she mustered a smile. "I am always happy to hear advice."

"See?" Birdie chuckled as she led the way into the kitchen. "That's what I admire about you Plain folks. So tactful. You're always happy to hear advice, you say, but you don't mention anything about actually taking it." The other woman reached into a cupboard and removed two beflowered teacups. "I don't use these very often, but they seem appropriately motherly, don't they? I'm going to fix us both a cup of decaf tea, and we'll chat for a minute."

Ten minutes later, they were seated at Birdie's round breakfast table, cups steaming in front of them, scenting the air pleasantly with mint.

Emma raised her cup to her lips, blew on it softly, and took a sip. "So?" she prompted quietly.

"So." Birdie stirred her own cup for a minute, then sighed and looked straight at Emma. "I'm not going to ask you what that specialist said today because I don't need to. It wasn't good news; that was plain to see. And Sam looked even worse after the two of you finished that visit with his sister, so that didn't go too well, either, I'm guessing."

"It was a hard day."

Birdie set her spoon on her saucer. "You know," she said, "I've been married three times. Divorced once, widowed twice. And don't be shocked, but I haven't completely given up hope that I'll find another fellow." She winked. "I suppose you could say I've got a soft spot for romance, and I can't help rooting for you and Sam."

"Oh." Emma fastened her gaze on her teacup, feeling uncomfortable. Today seemed to be the day for talking about her personal feelings. First Leah, and now Birdie.

"I know. It's none of my business and not something you Amish folks like to gossip about, though I've never understood why. Love can really put a shine on life. Why not talk about it?"

"We do talk about it some. It's just considered to be a private thing, I guess, so people keep the details of their plans to themselves, mostly, until things are well along."

"And your plans—yours with Sam, I mean—aren't well along yet? Is that it?"

Emma glanced up, unsure how to answer. Finally, she just shook her head.

"And this news he got today hasn't helped any with that." Birdie's voice had gone uncharacteristically serious, and sympathy shone softly in the older woman's eyes.

"We've hit a bit of a snag, *ja*. But nothing worth having is easy," Emma said carefully.

"No, that's true." Birdie folded and unfolded her paper napkin. "You know, I think the world of Sam. Not only is he a fine-looking fellow—and I've always liked men who are easy on the eyes—but he has a good heart, too."

"Yes, he does."

"It seems unfair that he's been dealt such a rotten hand of cards, Emma. But it doesn't sound like things are likely to get better, not anytime soon. If ever." She sighed. "Maybe I shouldn't say this . . . but the truth is, he reminds me a lot of my first husband, James. James was a big, strapping man like Sam. He was a pilot, and oh, he loved flying his 'birds,' as he called them." Birdie smiled sadly. "I used to tease him that he married me for my name more than anything else. But then, the airline downsized, and they offered him early retirement. It wasn't a choice, really, and James wasn't the only one in that position. Lots of other pilots were displaced, too, and the market was flooded. He couldn't get another job for love or money." Birdie drew in a breath and leaned back in her chair. "I tried everything I could think of to cheer him up. I told him we'd travel. We'd take up gardening. I'd do whatever it was he wanted to do. Nothing worked. He stayed miserable right up until the day he died, which was less than a year after his retirement. I honestly think losing that job killed him, Emma. It cut out a piece of his heart, and he couldn't live without it."

Emma shifted uncomfortably in her chair. She knew Birdie was trying to sympathize, but this conversation wasn't doing much to help her worries about Sam. "Men do often feel strongly about their work," she admitted. "Although, of course, women can feel that way, too."

"Can't we? For me, though, it wasn't work. It was my looks," Birdie supplied promptly. "And my youth, of course. I just despised getting older. Darling, you should have seen me when I turned sixty. I pitched a fit for two months straight. Of course, then I went and had a tummy tuck, and I felt loads better."

Emma laughed. "With us, it is often our children. We have big families, mostly, and that takes up a good deal of our time. When the youngest ones are old enough to look after themselves, some women feel like they've lost an important part of themselves. Of course," she added with a smile, "the good news is that there are usually plenty of grandchildren to spoil by then. If not, in our community there's always some young *mamm* with a houseful of children who is thankful for a helping hand."

Birdie chuckled. "Yes, I suppose there would be."

"The truth is, I think we all have things that try to come between us and *Gott*, things we think we can't live without. But we can live without them if we have to. Sometimes it takes a little while for us to realize that." She paused. "Sam just needs some time. That's all."

"Well." Birdie finished pleating her napkin and set it aside. "I'm sure you're right. Here I thought I was going to give you advice, and you turn out to be the wise one. That'll teach me, won't it? Maybe if James and I had been part of a community like yours, he would have found his way, too. All right. I suppose we should get ourselves to bed." She rose and reached for Emma's cup.

"I'll wash up, Birdie."

"You'll do no such thing. Although maybe you'd best be in charge of turning all the lights off, since I don't seem to be able to remember to do it. It worries me that I'm getting so forgetful. I didn't like to admit it to Ruth, but the real reason I was late this morning was because I couldn't find my car keys."

"Your keys?" Emma frowned. "You always put them in the dish there on the counter."

"Yes." Birdie turned on the water. "But they weren't there this morning. I turned the house upside down looking for them."

Emma had picked up the sugar bowl, intending to return it to its spot in the pantry, but she paused. "Where were they?"

"Would you believe it? I'd left them in the car after driving you over to Ruth's that morning." Birdie shook her head. "I never used to be so forgetful. One of the side effects of getting old, I suppose."

A chill tickled its way up Emma's spine. She hadn't noticed Birdie forgetting things. In fact, she'd thought Birdie seemed remarkably sharp.

She remembered what Sam had said the other day, when he couldn't find the bucket in the barn—about it being moved. She knew she hadn't moved it, and she doubted Ruth had, either.

The chill shivered up her backbone again.

Her mind flickered to the suspicions Mr. McMillan had confided to Sam. Then she shook her head.

She couldn't give in to fear. An older lady leaving a light on and forgetting her keys was normal enough. And Sam

STRENGTH IN THE STORM

hadn't been alarmed by the bucket being out of place, only annoyed. Things did get moved around some in a barn.

Still, after Birdie had said good night and headed to her bedroom, Emma went to the back door and clicked the seldom-used lock into place. She twitched the curtain aside, looking out over the empty, moonlit yard. Everything appeared perfectly peaceful.

But as she turned to head off to bed, she mentally added another item to the list of things she wanted to talk about with Sam tomorrow.

Unfortunately, it was midafternoon the next day before she found an opportunity to speak to Sam privately. He left with Birdie as soon as Emma arrived in the morning. To her surprise, he'd returned from his errand in Aaron Lapp's buggy, with Dobs trotting along behind.

Aaron had visited for a good while, sharing news about Katie and their little Sarah. And after Aaron had gone, Sam seemed to do his best to avoid being alone with her. After lunch, when Ruth announced her intention to take her usual nap, Sam rose from the table as well.

"I'm going out to the barn. I've been wanting to clear out the extra stall. It's been used for storage, but with two horses here now, we'll need it if we have a visitor." He was out the door before Emma had taken the first plate to the sink for washing.

He didn't want her to ask him about his trip to town, Emma guessed. His meeting with Jeff Branton must not have gone well.

When the kitchen was all cleared up, she glanced at the back door and considered her options. She'd been waiting since yesterday to talk with Sam, and she didn't want to put it off much longer. Sam didn't seem in the mood for a conversation, but she knew he was thinking everything over in his slow, methodical way. Once he'd made up his mind about their future, he'd be nearly impossible to sway—

Leah was right about that. If she didn't say her piece soon, there'd likely be no point in saying it at all.

After a moment's hesitation, she walked outside and headed for the barn.

It hadn't taken her all that long to finish up the dishes, but Sam already had the stall nearly cleared out. The items that had been stored there, odd buggy parts, a few garden tools, and some old wooden crates, were stacked neatly against the side wall. Sam had a shovel and was running it along the ground inside the stall, no doubt checking for anything small he might have missed. Just as Emma walked in, the shovel clanked on something. Sam bent over, felt around with his hand, and picked up the metal end of a hoe.

"If you've come out to check on me, I'm fine." He turned and walked out of the stall to put the hoe blade into a crate with other small, rusty items. "I don't need any help."

He didn't seem to. He walked around the dusky barn as if he could see perfectly well. But Emma noticed as he headed back toward the stall how he jutted out his elbow, letting it run along the wooden wall, checking for the opening.

That was smart to do, and Emma felt a sad spark of admiration. Sam was adapting to his situation, little by little. She cleared her throat.

"I didn't come here to help. I want to talk to you." Not sure how to begin the conversation, she inspected the items he'd removed from the old stall. A dusty children's ball was perched on top of the odds and ends in the crate. Emma picked it up. Once upon a time, it had been a cheerful red, and there had been a white star printed on its top and bottom. "Who did this ball belong to, do you think? Ruth? I can't imagine her ever being a little girl playing with toys, can you?"

"That was likely Davey's," Sam replied. "He was like a

child in his mind, and Ruth always made sure he had something to play with. He liked balls and tops and things like that, right up until the day he died. She said it was to keep him busy and out of trouble, but I think she tried also to make him happy, as best she could. I was about to throw it out, but then I thought that she might have tucked it in here for memory's sake, so I left it."

"That was thoughtful of you." Emma bent to poke around in the crate.

"Don't move things," Sam said sharply. Then he sighed and added, "I know where things are, as long as they're left where I put them. If you move them around, it makes it harder for me to find them later."

"I'm sorry." Emma carefully replaced the ball exactly where it had been. "I'll be more careful."

"That's all right. I'd not have thought of it, either, not until I had sight problems of my own. One thing this affliction has done for me, it's made me sorry for every time I spoke sharp to a worker for being slow or fiddle-fingered on a job. Now I'm the slowest and clumsiest fellow of all. I reckon that's a fitting punishment." He paused. "I guess you came out to hear what Jeff said about my job."

Not only that, but it was a place to start. "What did he say?"

"What I expected. That he has no work that I could do with my eyesight as it is. He was sorry, but he has to think about his insurance, things like that. I'd be a risk on a jobsite."

Emma's heart twisted at the self-disgust in Sam's voice. How hard it must have been for him to hear those words when such a short while ago, he'd been Jeff's right-hand man. "I'm sorry. You're getting so much better, though, Sam. Every day you are. You'll find your way through this."

"Well, I'm trying, with *Gott*'s help." Sam leaned on his

shovel, keeping his back to her. "Was there anything else, Emma?"

She hesitated. She wanted to talk to him about their future. She wanted the two of them to figure out some way to go forward together, in spite of the disappointments they'd had to face. Something about the set of Sam's shoulders warned her not to go there. Not today, so fresh on the heels of his talk with Jeff.

So she cleared her throat and went in a different direction. "Birdie and I had a conversation earlier that I thought I should tell you about."

Halfway through Emma's description of Birdie's sudden forgetfulness, Sam turned to face her. His whole body tensed as he listened, but he didn't interrupt.

"So," she said, "I thought I should mention it. Maybe Birdie's right, and she's just getting absentminded, but it seems strange to me. And when I remembered about that bucket being moved the other morning . . ."

"You're wondering if maybe it's Trevor." Sam seemed to be thinking over what she'd told him. "I figured I was hearing things," he muttered. As she watched, he tilted his head toward the horses' stalls, and then toward the hole where the ladder disappeared into the loft. Emma looked, too, but she saw nothing except the dark square leading up to where the hay was stored.

"What do you think?"

Sam's jaw tightened. "I think somebody needs to stop playing games and show himself." He turned around to face the ladder. He stood in front of her, tall and wide, his shoulders blocking her view. "All right!" His voice echoed against the rough eaves of the barn. "I've no patience for this nonsense. We know you're up there. You'd best come down."

"Sam—" Emma started. Then she heard it. The sound

of footsteps on the boards overhead, moving toward the ladder.

Trevor. Her breath caught in her throat.

"No!" The word blew out on a frantic burst of air as she pushed herself between Sam and the young *Englischer* jumping out of the loft.

CHAPTER TWENTY-TWO

SAM NEARLY JUMPED OUT OF HIS SKIN WHEN EMMA
rushed around him. "What are you doing?" He reached out
to catch her, but his fingers closed on empty air.

Then he saw her slight outline in front of him, and he
understood. Scared as she was, Emma was trying to protect him.

Which meant she didn't believe he could protect himself.

A sick hurt dropped into his heart, just as he heard Emma's startled gasp of recognition. She ran forward, straight
toward the man who'd jumped down from the loft.

Sam stood silently, crossing his arms over his chest.
He'd been right then.

Good thing, or Emma's bravery could have caused a
problem for both of them.

"Sam! It's all right! It's Caleb." Emma could barely get
the words out. She was laughing and crying at the same
time. "For true, Sam. It's my *bruder*!"

"*Ja*, I thought it might be."

"Hello, Sam." A familiar voice answered back. "How'd you know it was me up there?"

"The horses told me. They don't much like *Englischers.*" Sam squinted. Even with his limited sight and the dim light, he could tell that Caleb wasn't dressed Plain. "You might look like one, but you must not smell like one yet. You didn't worry them."

"I probably smell more like another horse than any kind of man by now." Emma wasn't the only one struggling to speak. Caleb's voice sounded a little thick, too. "I've been in and out of this barn for a week or so. Over to that *Englisch* lady's, too, some, keeping an eye."

"For pity's sake!" Emma's voice wobbled, but there was a teasing lilt to it. "That was a silly thing to do, and you worried Birdie to death, leaving lights on and moving her keys."

"I'm sorry about that. I needed to charge my phone, and I didn't like to linger in the house for as long as it would take."

"You should be sorry, sneaking around like that! You should have come right up to the door the minute you got back into town."

"I thought it would be best if nobody knew I was here."

"Not even me? But Caleb, why? If it's about the shunning, you needn't have worried. You should have known we'd all be happy to see you. It's the answer to our prayers, having you back. We've missed you so. Rhoda, too." Emma paused. "Have you talked to her already? Or are you planning to speak to Isaac first?"

Sam sensed the change in Caleb as soon as Emma spoke his wife's name. Her brother said nothing, but his silence seemed harder somehow.

No, Sam realized, Caleb hadn't talked to Rhoda, and he wasn't planning to talk to the bishop, either. He might be standing in an Amish barn, but Caleb wasn't truly back home at all, at least not in the way that mattered to his sister.

Sam's heart fell. Emma would be grieved.

"You'd best tell her," he muttered. "No sense keeping her hopes up."

The younger man moved restlessly. "Her hopes wouldn't have gotten up in the first place if you'd not started yelling. I figured I'd better come out before you pulled the whole barn down over my head."

"Tell me what, Caleb?"

Again her brother didn't answer, and Sam felt a surge of impatience. Caleb was only drawing this pain out. Kinder to say what he needed to quick and get it over with. "He didn't want you to know he was here because he's not come back to stay. Have you?"

Likely Caleb was staring daggers at him, but Sam was too annoyed to care. This was going to hurt Emma, and she'd already been hurt more than enough.

And after yesterday, he could see still more pain coming in her direction.

Since Caleb obviously wasn't in any hurry to tell Emma the truth, Sam did it for him.

"Unless I miss my guess, your brother's come here hunting."

"Hunting." Emma repeated the word. "Is that so, Caleb?"

"I heard rumors that Trevor was headed back to Johns Mill . . . something that movie writer has been saying to people in town. I've been staying close by for the last few days, keeping an eye. I didn't mean to show my face nor cause any trouble for the family. I was doing all right, slipping around without being noticed, until today. You may not be able to see too well now, Sam, but you have ears like a hound. I thought I was being quiet."

Caleb's attempt at distraction didn't work. Emma wasn't ready to turn loose of this. "Surely you weren't going to leave without so much as speaking to me? Without letting me know, even, that you're all right? Do you know how worried I've been over you, *bruder*? How worried we've all been?"

"I'm sorry, Emma. But I knew if you saw me, you'd only try to talk me into staying."

"Well, of course I would." Emma's voice caught. "You're breaking all our hearts with this foolishness of yours, Caleb. Joseph's, Miriam's, and mine, all three. And we're the least of it. Do you have any idea what you've done to Rhoda?"

"I'm not going to talk about Rhoda." On the surface, Caleb's refusal only sounded surly, but Sam heard the hurt underneath his words, an ocean of it, deep and dark.

Trevor Abbott had better watch himself, Sam thought uneasily. Bearing that much pain would make even a quiet man dangerous, and Caleb Hochstedler had never been a quiet man.

Emma pushed on stubbornly. "Well, I'm going to talk about her. She's your wife, Caleb, and you walked out and left her. You know what that means. She can't marry again, not as long as you're living, but she can't take support from you, nor live with you as your wife, or—"

"I know what it means, Emma," Caleb cut in shortly. It didn't slow his sister down.

"Then you also know it was selfish and wrong to do this to her."

Sam frowned. This conversation wasn't going to help, not in the direction it was going. It would only end up causing more *druvvel*. Sam could see that plain enough, even if these two, caught up in their feelings, couldn't.

"Leave it, Emma," he suggested quietly. "The grief he's causing his *fraw* lies between them two. It's not for others to remark on."

"Sam's right. This is not your business, *schwesdre*, but

I'll tell you this much. I asked Rhoda to come with me before I left. And I wrote her after. Asking her again. She said
no." Caleb paused, then went on roughly. "And she made it
clear that she didn't want to hear from me again until I was
ready to make my repentance before the church. She's
made her choice, Emma, or she's let her father make it for
her. Rhoda's the bishop's daughter, through and through,
more than she's ever been my wife."

"Rhoda's both of those things, Caleb, don't you see?"

"Emma," Sam warned again, but she ignored him and
rushed on.

"She can't be one or the other, and it's unfair of you to
ask it. You asked her to turn her back on *Gott* for you. On
her family and her faith. I think—I'm sure—she'd have
done anything else you wanted. But she couldn't do that."

"I would have done it for her. I did do it. I only joined
the church because of her."

"And by doing that, by pretending to believe something
you didn't, you've put both of you in a terrible position.
Please, Caleb, think about what you're doing. Rhoda is a
sweet, kind person and my good friend, and you're ruining
her life."

"She's your friend, *ja*, but she's my wife!" Caleb spoke
so sharply that Sam frowned. "Emma, I know you always
want to fix things, but Sam's right. This isn't your trouble
to fix. What passes between me and Rhoda is our personal
business, and I'm done talking about it. And, Sam, you can
loosen up. I'm not going to hurt my sister, no matter how
mad she makes me."

Sam blinked and relaxed. He hadn't realized he'd tensed,
but he had. *Nee,* Caleb wouldn't ever hurt Emma. Sam
knew that. On the other hand, if Trevor Abbott had shown
his face in this barn, the *Englischer* wouldn't have walked
away undamaged. Sam knew that, too, and it chilled him.

"Have you seen any sign of Trevor around here, then?"

Sam asked. He'd stepped closer to Emma while she and her brother were arguing, and he could feel her trembling. Somebody needed to steer this conversation into safer waters.

"*Nee*. It was a goose chase, coming here," Caleb said. "I found out that the Abbotts have a cabin up north, so I'll be looking there next."

Emma made a frustrated noise. "You're just going to leave again?"

Caleb shifted in her direction. "For now at least. Until I see Trevor in jail where he belongs and things set right for *Mamm* and *Daed*."

Sam heard Emma swallow. "This," she whispered, "this is not setting things right, Caleb. You know that. And *Mamm* and *Daed* would be the first ones to tell you so."

"Maybe. And if they were here, I'd listen to them, but thanks to Trevor, they're not."

There was another short, painful pause before Emma spoke again. "Will you at least write to me?"

"I'm not much for writing, Emma, and I move around so much that you could never write back. But here. Use this." Sam squinted, but he couldn't see well enough to know what Caleb was holding out toward her.

"A phone?"

"Take it. It's not a pricey one, and I can get another easy enough. That's its charger wrapped around it. You'll have to find a way to keep the battery up, but then I can call you sometimes. You could call me, too, if anything happens I should know about." He sounded hopeful, but Emma took a step backward.

"Come on, Emma," Caleb said impatiently. "You know, as well as I do, that plenty of Plain folks have phones for businesses and other things. This is at least that important, ain't so? Anyway, nobody has to know."

"I would know. Besides, I can talk to you, Caleb," she said, "but I can't take anything from your hand, not while you're shunned. You know that. Not until you've come home and made things right. Won't you?"

"*Nee*," her brother said stubbornly. "I'm seeing this through."

"Caleb, please. What you're doing—it's dangerous. Anything could happen to you. And if something did, I don't think I could stand it."

Emma's voice broke on the words, and Sam clenched his jaw. The only thing he hated worse than hearing those tears in her voice was knowing that there wasn't a thing he could do about the pain she was feeling.

"I'm sorry, Emma." There was no yielding in Caleb's voice. "I don't mean to hurt you, nor . . . anybody else. But this is something I have to do."

Emma was crying now. Sam could hear the soft, shuddering sounds of it. He gritted his teeth. If this were any other fellow . . . but this was Emma's twin, her other half, she'd called him growing up. Much as he'd like to, Sam couldn't stop Caleb from bruising the part of Emma's heart that belonged only to him.

But he didn't have to stand here and listen to it, either.

"I'll go in the house and leave you to talk," Sam muttered. "This is family business."

"*Nee*," Emma corrected. "It isn't. My *bruder* has left our family. And by doing that, you *have* hurt me, Caleb. You're going to keep right on hurting all of us who love you until you give up on this idea about finding Trevor. I'm going inside. When you are ready to come home, and make things right, then I will welcome you with open arms. If not—" Emma's voice broke. "If not, then know that I'll never stop praying for you. Maybe *Gott*'s love will break through that stubbornness of yours, even if ours cannot."

She brushed past Sam, and headed for the door. Neither he nor Caleb spoke until it had thumped shut behind her.

"And folks think I'm the one with the temper," Caleb mumbled.

"She's upset," Sam replied sharply. "You've put her through the wringer with your doings."

"And that's making you mad as a bull." Caleb blew out a short, tired breath. "You always did keep a special look-out for my sister, but something's shifted now. You may as well admit it. I had a bird's-eye view of you two through the crack up there."

Sam wasn't sure what to say, so in the end he just stayed quiet. It was too complicated to explain anyhow.

"It's true, then. Emma's gone sweet on you, after butting heads with you for years. I'd never have seen that coming, and I'd have a real good time teasing her about it if things were different. Maybe it's because you're needing help now, with your eye trouble. You know how she's always been foolish about anybody who needed taking care of. I guess that made her look at you different. "

Sam frowned. "I don't need Emma to take care of me, Caleb."

"Maybe not, but she won't be able to stop herself. I saw how she pushed in front of you before she knew who I was. Don't ruffle up at me now. I'm just thinking out loud." Caleb fell silent for a few seconds. "Funny, ain't so? Me and Rhoda and you and Emma. Unlikeliest pair-ups anybody could ever think of. I hope yours turns out better than mine did."

There it was again, that deep thrum of pain in the other man's voice. "Yours could come right yet."

"*Nee*, Sam, I don't see how it could. I've done a lot of thinking over the past few months. Nobody thought Rhoda would ever look twice at me. I didn't think so myself, though it didn't stop me trying to catch her eye. That only made the game more fun, you know? But I'll tell you, when she did start riding home from singings with me, nobody was more surprised than I was myself. No man was happier, neither. It was the best time of my life, but now I wish it had never happened."

Sam had been at Caleb's wedding. He'd been as surprised as anybody when the bishop's daughter had taken the town troublemaker for a husband, but once he'd seen the newly married pair together, his doubts had faded away.

"You don't mean that," he said gruffly.

"*Ja*, I do mean it." Caleb's answer was quick and sure. "It's not my intention to spread my own pain around, but it's something you should think about yourself maybe. There's a reason some pairings are looked on as unlikely, Sam. People don't think they'll work out, and most of the time, they're right. It's like yoking a racehorse and a mule together and expecting them to pull a buggy. Hard to make that work at the best of times. And when the worst times come—and they always do sooner or later—well. Then there's just no way to make it work at all, no matter how much you want it to. Marrying Rhoda was the most selfish thing I've ever done, and if I could take it back and wipe the slate clean, I would."

"If you'd come home and get yourself in good standing with the church, maybe—"

"*Nee*," Caleb cut him short. "Marrying Rhoda was selfish, Sam, but me joining the church—that was *dumm*. I'm not cut out for the Plain life. I don't think the right way for it, and I never have. After I fell for Rhoda, I thought if I tried hard enough . . . But in the end, the trying just made everything worse."

"But if you . . . love her . . ." Sam struggled with the words. This topic wasn't the kind of thing much talked about, especially not between Plain men. But then, standing there in his *Englisch* clothes, Caleb wasn't really Plain anymore.

"I love her, all right, but you know what the church always

says. Loving somebody, really loving them, isn't about how you feel. It's all about wanting the best for them, even when it's not what's best for you. I don't agree with the church in most things, but they got that much right, I think. I'm not what's best for Rhoda. I never was. I never will be. I'm sorry for the trouble I've caused her, but as much as I'd like to change that, I can't. All I can do now is try not to cause her more."

Caleb was telling the truth as he saw it. Sam could hear the solid certainty in his words, could hear that the other man's mind was well made up.

Nee, Emma would not sway her brother off this course, no matter how hard she tried. And the sooner she saw it, the better off she would be.

"I'd best get going," Caleb was saying. "I was planning on leaving today anyhow, since there's no sign of Trevor around here. I left my truck parked off the road a ways back, and I've got a walk to get to it. Take this phone, and see if you can sweet-talk Emma into keeping it someplace handy. Soon as I pick up another one, I'll call so this one will have my new number in it." Caleb seemed to be fiddling with the thing. "I've set it on vibrate so it won't make any noise when it rings. I wouldn't want to get her in trouble. Here." Sam could make out Caleb's extended arm, but he made no move to take the phone.

The other man made an irritated noise. "You don't have to take it from my hand if that bothers you. I'll leave it someplace, and you can pick it up later, ain't so? I'll set it here, in this box, under this old bouncy ball so nobody will see it."

"All right."

He heard a rustling as Caleb set the phone in the box. "All right. Tell Emma goodbye for me. And, Sam?" Caleb cleared his throat. "I'm trusting you to look after my sister."

"I'm not such a hand at looking after people as I used to be, Caleb."

Caleb clapped him hard on the back. "I expect you'll find some way to look after Emma, though. You always have. You'll not let anybody hurt her, not if you can help it. Ain't so?"

"*Ja*." Sam lifted his chin. "That's so."

It was so, but there was more to it. Listening to Caleb talk about his regrets had made Sam that much more determined to have none of his own, at least not where Emma was concerned.

He wouldn't let anybody hurt Emma, and he wouldn't hurt her himself, not any more than he could help. And he wouldn't allow Emma to hurt herself, either, not on his account.

"*Mach's gut*, Sam." He felt Caleb clasp his upper arm briefly.

"*Mach's gut*."

The other man walked away. The barn brightened intensely as Caleb opened the door, and for a second, Sam could see the outlines of the things around him a little more clearly.

Then the door thumped shut, and the barn plunged back into a gloom that seemed far darker than it had before that brief, shining moment of light.

Chapter Twenty-Three

❧

EMMA DIPPED HER BRUSH INTO THE SOAPY WATER at her elbow and scrubbed hard at the discolored linoleum in front of Ruth's stove. The raspy sound of the bristles scraping the floor filled the kitchen but didn't do a thing to drown out her own thoughts.

Hard work is the best remedy for heartaches. Mamm must have said that a thousand times during Emma's childhood. When she'd returned from the barn, she'd wanted to shut herself in her bedroom, away from Ruth's prying eyes, and brood over her argument with Caleb. Instead, she'd filled up a bucket and set to work.

It was helping—a little. Now, if Ruth would just go away, maybe she could calm herself down enough to think straight.

"You're going to rub the pattern right off," Ruth complained.

"No, only the dirt. You've been fussing about wanting

this smudgy spot cleaned for days, Ruth. I'd think you'd be happy to see it finally getting done."

"Well, it's high time it was seen to, but you're scrubbing it too hard. See how the section you're washing is so much lighter than the square next to it."

Emma sat up and dunked the brush into the water again. "It only looks that way because it's getting cleaner," she said shortly. "The pattern's already worn off from folks standing here cooking, and the surface has gotten rough. That lets the dirt sink in, and it takes some pressure to get rid of it."

Ruth sniffed. "I've scrubbed floors since before you were born. I don't guess I need you giving me lessons on it."

Emma twisted around to look the older woman in the eye. "If you know better than me how to scrub it, you're welcome to get down here and do it yourself. Otherwise, I'll thank you to leave me in peace and let me get on with this."

Sam's aunt made a huffy noise and stalked out of the kitchen. Emma sighed and wiped her forehead on her sleeve. She shouldn't have spoken so sharply to Ruth. She'd have to apologize later.

For a second she stayed still just as she was, her eyes closed, her face pressed against the material of her dress. It smelled clean but oddly unfamiliar. Ruth favored a different kind of laundry detergent than *Mamm* had, and ever since coming here, Emma's clothing had carried a different scent.

Emma felt herself choking toward tears. Everything in her life was different now, and oh, how she missed the old familiar ways.

Even Caleb was different, and that was the strangest and most upsetting thing of all. When he'd jumped off the ladder and she'd seen him standing there on the barn floor, her heart had nearly burst right out of her chest. She'd been so fearful, afraid of what Trevor might do to Sam, but instead of seeing the man she feared most, she'd seen one of the people in the world she loved best.

The relief and joy of it had almost knocked her to her knees.

It had been *gut* to see her brother again, wonderful *gut*. And for a second or two, hugging him, everything had seemed—for the first time in a while—right in her world.

She should have known it wouldn't last.

She and Caleb had always been close. It was because they were twins, or that's what she'd always believed. Emma loved all her family, of course, but she and Caleb shared a special connection. At least, she'd always thought so, and she'd believed Caleb felt the same.

Finding that he'd been skulking around like a thief for a whole week, without even letting her know he was nearby . . . that had thrown her off-balance. And then, talking to him, seeing that hard edge in his eyes, hearing the difference in his voice. He already sounded more *Englisch* than Plain, as if in the time he'd been away, he'd lost something of the man he'd been.

Of the brother she'd loved.

That, she thought, was why she'd pressed him so hard to stay, to make things right with Rhoda and with the church. It had been a mistake. Caleb didn't take well to being cornered.

Emma wiped the wet floor with a ragged towel and checked her work. Then she angled the tip of the brush over a stubborn spot and scrubbed again.

Not long after she'd arrived in Ohio, she'd had a dream about her parents. By then, she'd dreamed about them several times. It was normal, she knew, and part of the grieving process.

But this dream had been different. She'd dreamed that she'd walked into Hochstedler's General Store, and her parents had been standing there, wearing their aprons, waiting on customers, just like it was any other day. After a moment of incredulous disbelief, Emma had rushed joyously toward them.

Mamm! Daed! They told me you were dead!

But then—and even though it had only been a dream, her heart still faltered at the memory—her mother and father had looked at her, those two most beloved folks, with no recognition, no love, in their eyes. They'd smiled at her in a vague, confused way and glanced at each other as if asking silently, *Who is this crazy girl?*

She'd pleaded with them, but they'd only shaken their heads and moved away, peeling off her clinging fingers. She'd woken up with tears on her cheeks, her grief freshly rekindled, like an ebbing fire when its coals are raked over. The horror of the dream had lingered far into the day.

It had felt like that today with Caleb. As if she were pleading with a stranger to remember who she was and what they'd once meant to each other.

She understood better now how Miriam must feel, struggling to keep her fears from sweeping her away. Seeing Caleb—and having him not *be* Caleb—had made Emma feel as if the last solid bit of ground had been yanked out from under her feet. Suddenly everything in the world seemed dangerously uncertain.

All the people she loved best seemed to be changing and cutting her adrift. Caleb had turned into someone new . . . not fully *Englisch*, maybe, but no longer Plain, either. Miriam, her sweet, shy little sister, was now closer to Naomi than she was to Emma. Joseph had shifted from brother to married man with concerns and plans of his own.

And then there was Sam.

At the thought of him, Emma's yammering mind went suddenly, dangerously still.

He was shifting away from her, too. She'd sensed it ever

since the doctor's visit, but she'd not wanted to face it. Her whole life, Sam had never shifted, not really, no matter how hard the winds blew, no matter what life threw at him. His strength had always carried him through.

But now, even though they hadn't yet talked about the future, Emma could feel him pulling away, little by little. He kept his face averted from hers, and he was practically camped out in that barn.

It was like the one time her parents had taken them to the beach. She'd stood at the edge of the water, awed by the rippling sea, and she'd felt a tickling. She'd looked down and seen the waves pulling the sand out from under her feet, washing it away.

She felt that same tickling now.

Emma straightened and dropped the brush into the bucket. The soapsuds were nearly gone, and the spot was as clean as she could get it.

She dried her water-wrinkled fingers on the damp towel and fought the urge to rush back out to the barn. She wanted to. She was tired of doubts—and afraid of them. Was Sam Christner going to break her heart? She needed to know. Right now.

She rose, carrying the bucket carefully to the back door. She walked out onto the steps, hot in the summer sun, and gently poured the dirty water on the tea olive blooming beside the stoop. She glanced at the barn and bit her lip.

She could go out there now and talk to him. But Sam didn't like being cornered any better than Caleb did, and rushing Sam . . . well. That never worked. Sam wasn't built that way. He needed his time, and probably the wisest thing she could do right now was wait.

But it wasn't the only thing she could do. She could also pray—for Caleb, and for Sam, and for herself.

The thought heartened her up. Everything and everyone around her might change, but *Gott* would not. She would take these problems to Him. Somehow, He would work everything out for His purposes. She'd pray for that tonight, and for Him to give her the patience to wait for His answers.

Unfortunately, the next morning, the only result Emma had gleaned from her night of prayer was a pair of sore knees—and those were probably just as much from the time she'd spent scrubbing the floor as from the time she'd spent kneeling by her bed at Birdie's.

Sam had been just as short and silent this morning as ever, and Ruth seemed filled with a strange, smug satisfaction that was grating on Emma's nerves.

She should have known better. *Daed* had always said that praying for patience was a dangerous business.

Pray for that, and you're sure to be put through your paces. You can only learn patience by being patient, and the Lord's never short of volunteers willing to help you practice.

It seemed Ruth was the volunteer *Gott* had chosen for Emma to practice on today.

Apparently, after Emma had left the night before, Sam had told his aunt what the eye doctor had said. Ruth's concern over her nephew's future seemed overshadowed by her pleasure at having her gloomy predictions proven right.

"I told you so," Ruth said as she and Emma washed up the breakfast dishes. "I told you that you wouldn't likely get good news from that doctor. Didn't I take Davey to doctor's appointments right and left over the years? It wasn't hardly ever good news."

"It wasn't terrible news," Emma replied briefly. She was thankful Ruth had waited until Sam had gone out to the barn before raising this subject. "Just not what we were hoping for."

"We?" Ruth raised a narrow eyebrow. "Sam's never going to be able to support a wife now. Surely you understand that."

"I understand no such thing." Emma plunged a cup into the dishwater and scrubbed at it a bit harder than necessary. "Maybe Sam can't see so well, but I expect in time he'll learn to manage all right. Look how he tends to Dobs and Maude now, all by himself. That's an improvement, ain't so?"

"Hardly much of one. A walk out to the barn and tossing some hay to a couple of old horses isn't the same as going to a job and earning a living. Of course, it'll be a help to me, Sam being able to do such things. Whatever he can't manage, we'll hire out or get the family to see to, same as Davey and I did. I expect we'll get along all right."

"Ruth." Emma drew in a measured breath as she up-ended the teacup into the drainer. "You really shouldn't plan on Sam taking Davey's place here. Not for long anyhow. If you do, I'm afraid you're going to be disappointed."

"Maybe." Ruth dried the teacup and set it in its spot inside the cupboard. "But maybe not. From what Sam tells me, Leah's happy enough with those Troyers, and she plans to stay on there. They wouldn't be my cup of tea, but it's fitting, I suppose, for her to stay out there with her husband's folks, just as it's fitting for an unmarried woman to stay close to her own family. Speaking of that, it's well past time you went home yourself. Sam said so last night, and I agree with him."

"What?" Emma turned to look at Ruth, the dishcloth dripping in her fingers. "Sam said that I should go home?"

"*Ja*, he did." There was no mistaking the gleam of triumph in the older woman's eye. "You've served your purpose here well enough. Better," she admitted grudgingly, "than I'd have expected. But we both decided that since you're not needed here any longer, you should go back home to your brother's house and be a help to them. The sooner you get out of that *Englisch* woman's home, the better anyhow. She's a terrible influence, and—Emma! Where are you going? There's more dishes to do!"

Emma left the kitchen without bothering to answer. If Ruth was doing as well as she claimed, she could finish the breakfast dishes by herself.

Over the past few days, Emma had discussed her personal life and marriage prospects with Leah, Birdie, and now Ruth, but she'd not swapped one word with the only person who really counted.

She'd waited long enough.

Emma strode out of the house into the hot summer morning, heading for the barn. It was time to have a talk with Sam.

CHAPTER TWENTY-FOUR

❧

SAM FELT AROUND IN THE FEED BIN SEARCHING FOR the metal scoop. The light in the barn was too dim—he should have left the door open so he could at least see outlines better.

He was used to pulling the door closed after himself, a farmer's habit he'd been trained into during childhood by his *daed*. A smart man always shut the barn door and fastened gates, even if he was planning on coming back through them in only a few minutes' time. If a fellow forgot and got delayed by something, he could lose an extra hour or so chasing escaped animals back into their pastures.

It was something else Sam would have to unlearn and do different now. That was getting to be a lengthy list.

As he ran his fingers through the grain, something furry skittered up his arm nearly to his elbow. Sam yelped and jerked upright, yanking his hand out of the bin and shaking it furiously. Whatever had decided to use his arm as a ladder—likely a mouse—scampered off to find a new hiding place.

Sam stood still for a second, letting his heart settle back down, then he leaned over and swept his fingers around in the feed until he located the scoop. Sticking his free hand down into Maude's bucket to keep track of the amount, he measured out her grain as best he could, battling a feeling of self-disgust.

Sam Christner, the same fellow who'd faced down a runaway bull when he was barely eleven years old, had just been spooked by a mouse. No wonder Emma had felt the need to push in front of him when she thought it was Trevor coming down out of the loft yesterday.

That had grated at him all night, keeping him tossing and turning in his bed. He'd replayed the moment over and over in his memory, and every time he felt the same stab of hurt—and fear.

He was thankful things hadn't gone worse. They could've. He'd been pretty sure it was Caleb up there, but he hadn't been positive. If he'd been wrong, Emma would have run straight toward a man who'd already killed two people.

It was a fool thing to do. A dangerous thing. And she'd done it to protect Sam.

He hadn't seen that coming. All his life, he'd been the one pushing in between other people and danger. But what Emma had done yesterday showed him better than any doctor's visit how much his life had shifted since the accident.

And how differently Emma saw him.

That was the truth that had kept him restless all night. Well, that, along with the regrets Caleb had shared about what had happened with Rhoda. Talking with a fellow who'd wrecked two lives by selfishly entering into a marriage he knew he wasn't cut out for . . . that had hit far too close to home.

Sam shared the church's view on selfishness, and he did

his best to winnow it out when he noticed it in himself. But every man had his weak spot, and Emma was Sam's. He'd known that well enough, so he should never have let his selfish hopes about her root in so deeply.

But he had.

Once the bucket was filled, Sam felt along the barn wall until he came to Maude's stall. The old mare wasn't pleased about having to wait for her breakfast, and when Sam fumbled at hooking the bucket in its spot, she jostled it with her nose. He heard a spattering sound as grain spilled down the planks.

At least maybe now the mice would stay out of the feed bin. No need to go to that much trouble when there was grain all over the floor. Sam bit back his annoyance, finished hooking the feed container in place, and went back to the bin to measure out Dobs's breakfast.

When he approached the old Percheron's stall, Dobs snorted impatiently.

"Calm yourself," Sam murmured, feeling along the planks for the right place to hook the bucket. "Maude wasted half her breakfast. You won't want to do the same. You and me both like our food too much for that kind of foolishness."

He got the bucket hooked on just before the horse lowered his big nose into it. Sam stroked the horse's forehead, listening to the crunching. "We're alike in more ways than just that now," he said. "Maybe I'm not so old as you, but I might as well be. My old *grossdaddi* could do his barn work quicker than this when he was in his nineties."

He stiffened at a noise behind him. He turned as the barn door opened, spilling brightness into the barn. When he squinted, he could make out the slim figure spotlighted in the opening.

"Sam, we need to talk." Emma walked in, banging the door shut behind her. The barn went shadowy again, and he had to rely on the sounds of her steps to gauge where she was.

Ja, they did need to talk, but he'd counted on having more time to think over what he needed to say and how to say it.

However, from the tone in Emma's voice, he probably wouldn't be doing much of the talking anyhow. She sounded more like her old self than she had in a while. If things were different, he'd have enjoyed teasing her a little.

But as things were now, best not. In fact, it might be a relief to get this talk over with. He'd been dreading it.

"Go ahead then." He felt his way back to the bin to put the cover on. He'd just as soon not be surprised by another mouse tomorrow.

"Did you tell Ruth it was time for me to go back home?"

Sam froze for a second, the metal lid in his hand. He should have known Ruth wouldn't be able to resist jabbing at Emma by repeating what he'd said.

For a second, he felt bad, then he remembered yesterday—and Caleb. He set his jaw. He clanged the lid into place, making the noise echo in the barn. "*Ja*, I did."

Emma didn't answer right away. She was mad. Or hurt maybe. Over the past few weeks, he'd gotten some better at figuring out people's feelings without being able to see their faces, but when they were quiet, it was harder.

"Why, Sam?" she asked finally. "Why would you say that?"

"Because it's time," he said more gently. "You've done all you can for us, Emma, and I thank you for that. But we can't ask you to stay here forever."

Another pause, and now there was a telling little hitch in Emma's breathing. She was hurt, then.

He hated that. It would have been so much easier on both of them if she'd just gotten mad.

"Can't you, though?" Emma cleared her throat. "Ask me to stay forever?"

And there it was.

He stood there with his back to her, wrestling with himself. It took a minute before he was able to answer her.

"*Nee.* I can't."

Emma wasn't the only one finding it hard to breathe. Sam kept swallowing, but the lump in his throat wouldn't go away. The air in the barn was so thick with unspoken words that it felt heavy.

"I see," she whispered.

He felt a sudden urge to kick something. He hated hearing that pain in Emma's voice and knowing that, once again, he couldn't ease it. Worse, this time he was the cause of it.

"Is this really what you want, Sam?" Emma's question sounded brittle, like the first thin ice of winter cracking under a man's boots.

Saying yes would have been the easiest thing. Maybe even the kindest thing. But he couldn't bring himself to lie. Not to her, and not about this.

"It's not what I want, no. But it's the way it has to be, Emma."

She laid her hand gently on his back. He jumped at the touch, knocking the lid back off the bin. It clattered to the ground, startling the two horses, who snorted and shifted in their stalls.

"Sam." Emma's voice was soft and pleading. He knew just the look that would be on her face. He could see it in his mind's eye, just as plain as day, and his stomach turned to jelly.

He shook his head. "There's no way around it. I won't be able to work, Emma."

That was the meat of the problem right there. He didn't see how he could support a family, not the way he was now.

In that way, he was no different than Davey had been, and his future was just as limited.

He remembered the indulgent tolerance he'd felt for his special uncle and was shamed by it. Davey had deserved more respect. Everything had been more of a challenge for him than for other folks, but he'd tried his best and been faithful to the jobs he was set. He'd always accepted his lot in life cheerfully, too, which was more than Sam could say.

He wasn't feeling very cheerful at all.

"Maybe you can't go back to your old job, Sam. But there are other jobs."

"Not so many around here nowadays, and none I'd be fit for. I work with my muscles, Emma. To earn a living that way, a man has to be able to see."

"Well, I'm sure I could find a way to earn some money if—"

And there she went again, rushing in between him and trouble.

Sam slammed the lid back into its place, jamming it down so hard that he knew he'd have trouble prying it back off. He didn't care. He was sick and tired of dealing with this lid. He was tired of dealing with all of this.

"You'll not be the support of me, Emma. I'm not one of your broken-down birds, to be fed and looked after and kept in a padded box. I'm a man, and I won't see the woman I—" *Love*. He almost said it, but he caught himself in time. "I won't see you living a hard life because of me."

"I don't think it would be so hard." Emma put her hand on his arm again lightly. "Not as long as I was with you."

Sam's world went completely still—and narrowed down to the spot just south of his shoulder where he could feel the trembling of Emma's hand through the material of his shirt.

How long had he waited to hear Emma say something like that? But she never had, not until now, when it was too late. To his shame, he felt a hot wetness stinging at his eyes.

"How we feel, either of us, doesn't change anything," he repeated doggedly. "It's a man's part to look after his family, and I can barely look after these two horses here. I couldn't take good care of you, or our—" He was going to say children, but somehow he couldn't get the word out.

Ach, the children he and Emma could have had together, if everything had turned out different. What a life that would have been.

He needed to get this over with. He turned to face her.

"Emma, I may not know much, but I know myself, and I'm built a certain way. It's more than my outside. It's my inside, too. I can't start a family I've no way to provide for, nor take a wife who'd feel like she had to look after me as if I were more her child than her husband. That would . . . it would break me down, Emma. I can't be a different man than I'm made to be, no more than Caleb could."

"But, Sam, it wouldn't be like that!"

"Wouldn't it? Don't forget, Emma. I know you nearly as well as I know myself. I've never seen you miss the chance to break your heart over somebody else's troubles. Well, I'll not see you breaking your heart over mine. No," he said when Emma started to speak again. "It's done. I'm not the right man for you, Emma. Maybe I could have been before. But I'm not anymore."

"Shouldn't I get a say in who's the right man for me, Sam?" Her voice shook with feeling. In the dimness of the barn, he could hardly make out the outline of her face, even though she was standing close enough to touch. That was probably just as well.

He squared his shoulders.

"You know, all the time we've known each other, you've never made things easier for me, Emma. I've not minded. You never meant to make things hard, and it wasn't your fault that I . . . cared so much. It didn't matter anyway, because to my way of thinking, you were worth it. You were worth every tree I climbed, every pushy man I stared down, all if it. But just this once . . ." He stopped and cleared his throat roughly. "Just this once, I'm asking you to have some mercy on me. And to let this—whatever it could have been between us—go."

He didn't wait for her answer. He headed toward the dim rectangle of light showing around the barn door and walked out into the harsh summer sun, leaving Emma behind in the dark.

CHAPTER TWENTY-FIVE

THE FOLLOWING MORNING, EMMA STOOD IN BIRD-
ie's spare room, her half-filled suitcase open in front of her.
She stared into space, her hands stilled in the motion of
tucking her Sunday dress into its place, thinking about
Sam. Her mind kept drifting to that awful conversation in
the barn, to the way he'd looked, and the things he'd said.

*It's done. I'm not the right man for you, Emma. Maybe
I could've been . . .*

"Now that's a sight I hate to see. I'm going to miss you,
darling."

Startled, Emma looked up to see Birdie standing in the
bedroom doorway. She'd been hovering ever since Emma
had announced her plans to leave. The other woman was
plainly curious about Emma's reasons, but so far she'd
stopped short of asking straight out.

Emma swallowed. "I will miss you, too."

"I'm so glad your bishop let you stay here. It's been a
real blessing to me, as you folks like to say." The older

woman twisted her fingers together. "Normally, I'm a pretty independent old fusspot. I don't think I realized how lonely I was until you came along, and I'm just miserable to think of you leaving."

Emma finished smoothing the dress, lowered the lid, and fastened the snaps. Birdie wasn't the only one feeling miserable, but it couldn't be helped. And that being the case, best she left as soon as possible.

All the arrangements were made. She'd called the phone shack and left a message for Joseph yesterday evening after her talk with Sam in the barn. Her brother had called her back this morning.

"You want to come home now? This afternoon, so quick?" Joseph's confusion had been clear.

"*Ja*. Please. If you can find the time to drive out here and get me."

There'd been a short, worried pause. "I will make the time," her brother said. "That's not a problem. But, Emma, is everything all right? Does Sam know about this plan?"

"It is Sam's plan, Joseph."

"Oh." Another pause, a thoughtful one this time. "I see." There was sympathy in her brother's voice, and also understanding. "Then, *ja*, I will come in the afternoon. Naomi will likely want to come with me." He cleared his throat. "She has some news she's anxious to share with you."

"What kind of news?"

"The kind of news I've been forbidden to tell you first, so you'll just have to wait."

Emma's grip had tightened on the phone. "Would this be . . . family news? Am I going to be an *aent* maybe?" Such things weren't usually discussed openly, but in this case, there were special circumstances. Naomi had confided in Emma that she wasn't entirely sure, given her previous health problems, that this would be possible, so Emma held her breath as she waited for Joseph's answer.

"No guessing!" Joseph instructed firmly. Then he chuckled. "For pity's sake, act surprised when she tells you."

"I will! Oh, for true, Joseph? There will really be a *boppli*?"

Joseph only laughed again, but that was enough. The answer to her question was the joy in her brother's voice.

That joy, as much as the wonderful news itself, felt to Emma like a special kindness from *Gott*. He'd given her something to be thankful for today, right in the middle of her own disappointments.

It was a lesson she needed to cling to. There was always something to be grateful for, even in the midst of sorrows. Like sweet, new babies, and a much-hoped-for joy for this brother of hers, who'd shouldered far too much trouble over the past year. And, of course, *gut* friends.

Holding that thought firmly in mind, Emma managed a smile for Birdie. "I'm sad to leave you, too. You've been so very friendly to me and so generous, too. I thank you for that."

Birdie made a rueful face. "Don't give me too much credit. You're an easy person to be nice to. Not like that old pain in the nose next door."

Pain in the nose. She was going to miss Birdie's unvarnished truth-telling. "Ruth's not so terrible deep down."

"You can say that because you're leaving today."

Emma laughed, but she answered seriously. "*Nee*, it's not just that. Now that I've gotten to know her better, I feel sorry for Ruth. You're not the only one who's been feeling lonely. I think she's had a hard time since her brother died."

"Oh." Birdie looked taken aback. "Yes, I suppose she would miss him terribly." Her face softened. "Davey was a sweet man. I used to give him candy bars now and again. I'd slip them to him on the rare occasions they came to use the telephone." Her eyes twinkled. "Partly to annoy Ruth, I admit. She thought they were bad for his teeth."

"It's a shame Ruth is so . . ." Emma struggled to find a word that wasn't too unkind. "Prickly," she said finally. "You two could've been *gut* neighbors to each other."

Birdie snorted again, but with less force. "I've tried. I baked her a custard pie when I heard Davey died. She left the dish on my back steps with a note that she thought the milk in it must have been soured. I can't imagine Sam staying on long out there once you've gone. She'll drive him crazy without you to be a buffer between them. Tell him if he needs to escape, he can always come over here. The same goes for that brother of yours if he happens to come back. I can't believe he was sneaking around here like a criminal. When you see him, you be sure to tell him that I'm not Amish, and I don't care if he's shunned or not. He's welcome anytime."

Emma set her suitcase on the floor and sighed. "I don't know if I will see Caleb again anytime soon. I let my temper get away from me, and I said a good many things to him I shouldn't have."

"Oh, darling. Don't be too hard on yourself. Men can be the most aggravating creatures in the world. Even your Sam. I've developed a real soft spot for that young fellow, but right now I could cheerfully thump him right on his hard head."

"Birdie!"

"Don't you 'Birdie' me. Even if you won't say so, I think he's the real reason you're leaving sooner than expected. I have a nasty feeling he's put a big dent in that sweet heart of yours."

Emma refused to respond to Birdie's fishing. Instead, she attempted a distraction. "Would it be possible to drive me over to Ruth's now? I know it's early, but there are some butter beans in Ruth's garden patch that need picking. I'd hate to leave that job undone, and I'd like to get finished before it gets too hot."

Birdie looked disappointed that Emma wasn't willing to talk about Sam, but she nodded. "Sure, I don't mind leaving now."

"That works out well then." Picking up her suitcase, Emma headed for the door. "I've a lot on hand today. After I finish in the garden, I want to give the house a good scrubbing. I plan to do a little baking, too, if I can squeeze it in before Joseph comes to get me."

"If I were you, I sure wouldn't be going to all that trouble, not after how Ruth's treated you. She doesn't deserve you, darling."

"*Mamm* said to always leave a blessing behind you when you end a visit, if you can. Speaking of that, I got up early and put together another of those little chicken casseroles you liked so much. You can eat it for your supper. It's in the refrigerator, and I wrote down how long to bake it."

Birdie's eyes filled with tears. "Well, aren't you just the sweetest thing? You didn't have to do that. You're already leaving plenty of blessings behind here." She sniffled and made an irritated noise. "Just look at me, acting like an old fool."

Emma smiled sadly and patted her shoulder. "Parting from friends is hard, and there's no foolishness in admitting it. You and I won't be saying goodbye forever, Birdie. We're friends now, and we will find ways to see each other when we can. Whenever I need a driver, I'll call you first, and that way we can have nice visits in the car, ain't so? And we can write to each other, and I can even call you sometimes from the phone shack, maybe."

"It won't be the same as having you close by," Birdie said sadly as she paused to close the back door carefully behind them. "But it'll be better than nothing, I suppose."

When, a few minutes later, they pulled up at Ruth's house, Birdie refused to pop the trunk of her car so that Emma could retrieve her suitcase.

"I'm holding it hostage. That way I'll have a good excuse to drop back by later and see you off. Ruth will have a conniption fit, but I'm not about to miss out on the chance to meet your brother and his wife. I've heard so much about them. I feel like I know them already."

"They would love the chance to meet you, too. I'll look forward to seeing you later, and thank you again for bringing me over early."

"Not early enough, I'm afraid." Birdie chuckled. "Somebody's beaten you to those butter beans."

Emma glanced across the yard. Sam stood in the garden, looking in their direction. He raised one hand in greeting then bent back over the plants.

"That's a good sign, isn't it?" Birdie said softly. "He's finding his way, getting back to normal."

Emma hesitated. She couldn't think how to explain to Birdie that a Plain man like Sam wouldn't normally spend time puttering in a vegetable patch on a weekday morning. That was work for *kinder* or for women, sparing the man for heavier labor. She swallowed and answered carefully. "I think he is making a new way for himself, *ja*."

A way that didn't include her.

After Birdie had driven away, Emma walked across the yard, hesitating at the garden gate. Sam was working at the far end with his back to her. He didn't turn around.

Likely he'd expected her to go on into the house, but she thought maybe it would be better for them to talk first out here, away from Ruth's nosy ears.

She took a deep breath, said a quick prayer, and started down the row Sam was picking. As she went, she scanned the little patch with a practiced eye. It needed another good watering, but midsummer gardens almost always did.

Early season gardening was much more pleasant. There was something hopeful and encouraging about digging in freshly turned earth after the shut-in days of winter. By this time of year, those hopes had been replaced by lots of hard work—and always some disappointments. Plants you'd counted on wilted or were attacked by bugs, weeds sprouted up overnight, rains held off too long or came too often.

Even in the best years, summer gardens never quite lived up to the sweet dreams of the spring. That was just the way it was.

For more things than gardens, Emma thought sadly.

Sam must have been working for a good while. He was at the far end of the last of the three rows of butter beans, and the plastic bucket beside him was three-fourths full. She watched him feel along the underside of the green bushes. A moment later he came out with a handful of plump pods and tossed them into the pail.

When she was halfway up the short row, Sam straightened, tilting his head in her direction.

"*Guder mariye*, Emma. You've come early."

That wary politeness in his voice had a familiar ring to it. He'd spoken to her just so for many years. Careful. Courteous. Cool.

And then, for a little while, things had been different. Emma's traitorous memory snatched her backward. For a second or two, she was standing with Sam in Ruth's kitchen, their first kiss only a whisper away, with him looking at her in a way that wasn't cool at all, but warm and deep and real.

There'd been no polite walls between them then. Now it was like the last few weeks had never happened.

She almost wished they hadn't.

Almost.

She cleared her throat. "I was planning to pick these." She bent and checked a couple of the plants. Sam had done a thorough job, and he was nearing the end of the last row. She straightened and sighed. "You probably should've let me. It must be an extra-hard job for you."

Sam's jaw tensed. "Not too hard. I can do this by feel. If the

pods are well filled out, I snap them off. It's simple enough."
He paused. "Even for me."

"I wasn't talking about your eyesight," Emma said. "Butter
beans are my least favorite things to pick because they grow
so close to the ground. All that bending over and crouching
makes my back ache, and I'm not nearly so tall as you."

"Ah." Sam's grim expression softened. "Well, there are
few enough jobs I can do that I shouldn't be choosy. At least
this one is outside. And since I'm not going by sight, I was
able to come out here as soon as I woke up. Doesn't matter
much to me if the light is dim."

"You're smart to work in the cool of the day." She
couldn't believe they were standing here having such a stupid conversation, as if they were strangers. Was this the way
it would always be between them now?

Sam tilted his face up to the strengthening sun. "*Nee*, not
smart. I couldn't sleep. The truth is, I'd give a lot to spend
another day working in the heat. I miss it . . . all of it. Sweating, getting sore, using tools and my muscles. That's real
work. Man's work."

"Work is work." She had to fight for the next words, but
she finally managed them. "And you're still a man, Sam."

His eyes went to her face. She knew he couldn't see her,
not clearly, not like he used to. But for a second there, it felt
as if he did.

His lips twisted upward. She wouldn't call it a smile.
There was too much sadness in it.

"A hard thing for any fellow to forget when you're standing next to him."

The hope she'd tried her best to give up on surged past
her self-control. Besides, she'd told Leah that she wouldn't
give up easily, no matter what arguments Sam made.

"Sam, please," Emma whispered in a broken rush. "Don't
you think—"

"Emma!" A familiar voice cut through the morning like a

blade. "Come to the house! It's time to get breakfast started!" Ruth was standing on the steps, and even from this distance, Emma could read the annoyance on the older woman's face.

"It's early yet, Ruth! I'll be there in a few minutes," Emma called, but when she turned back to Sam, he shook his head.

"Best go on in," he suggested gently. "There's nothing out here to keep you. Everything's finished."

Finished. Emma read the unflinching sureness on Sam's face with a sinking heart. He'd stick to his course with that well-known Christner stubbornness. There was nothing she could say or do that would change his mind now.

Without a word, she turned and walked back to the house.

CHAPTER TWENTY-SIX

IN THE KITCHEN, EMMA WENT ABOUT HER WORK
with a sense of numb apprehension. In a few minutes, Sam
would be coming inside to eat. She'd have to sit across the
table from him, under Ruth's sharp and critical eye, knowing it was probably the last time they would ever share a
breakfast together.

In fact, in the days to come, she and Sam would likely
not spend much time together at all. Oh, they would see
each other regularly at church and other gatherings. Johns
Mill was too small a place for that not to happen. But their
lives would slowly ravel apart until they were no more than
distant friends again.

That realization sat like a weight on Emma's chest. She
kept her head down and stayed busy, setting oatmeal to
cook and slicing up strawberries to stir into it. Then she
turned her attention to preparing some refreshments for Joseph and Naomi's visit.

As she mixed cake batter, she sensed Ruth's gaze on her.

Emma bit the inside of her lower lip, determined not to show any outward signs of being upset. She could manage this. She only had a little while longer, then Joseph would be here. A short, polite visit and she'd be headed home. All of this would be behind her.

That would be a relief, she told herself firmly. Things would seem much easier once she was back on the farm. Anything would be easier than being with Sam—and yet not with him—all at the same time.

"The oatmeal is scorching," Ruth announced sharply. She stopped slicing bread and walked to the stove to give the mixture a brisk stirring. She leaned over and peered into the pot. "I hope it'll be fit to eat. You can't walk off and leave oatmeal cooking like that, not on such a high heat. I don't know where your head is."

Emma looked up, her gaze straying to the view outside the kitchen window where Sam was finishing up in the garden.

Then she blinked hard and lowered her head. "I'm sorry, Ruth. I wasn't paying attention. I'm thankful you were."

"Well." Ruth seemed surprised by the apology. "You were distracted by the cake, I guess. It's hard to pay attention to two things at once . . . especially when you've got a lot on your mind." The older woman stood awkwardly by the stove, fidgeting her hands together as she watched Emma adding vanilla and almond extract to the bowl. "You're making pound cake?"

"*Ja*, I thought that would be the best choice. It won't need frosting, so it'll be easy to have it ready in time to share it with Joseph and Naomi."

"And it's one of Sam's favorites," Ruth pointed out dryly.

Emma refused to take the bait. She dipped a paper towel in lard and greased the circular Bundt pan carefully. "As soon as I get this in the oven, I'm going to give the house a good going over. If there's anything in particular you'd like me to see to before I leave, let me know."

"There's not much left to be done. You've done a good job keeping things neat."

Praise from Ruth? Well, that was a surprise—and rare as hen's teeth. Emma raised her eyebrows, but kept her eyes on her work. "I'm glad you've been pleased."

The clock ticked away on the wall, and Emma heard the slow scrape of the spoon as Ruth stirred the oatmeal a little more.

The other woman cleared her throat. "This is all for the best, you know."

"What's that?"

"You and Sam."

Emma froze then silently crumpled the oily paper towel tightly in her hand.

"It just wasn't *Gott*'s will for the two of you to end up together," Ruth went on.

Or yours, either. Emma was just about to speak those snide words when, against her better judgment, she glanced up. She'd expected to see smug satisfaction on the other woman's face. Instead when their eyes met, she saw a grudging sympathy.

In a stilted, clumsy way Ruth was trying to offer comfort. Emma blinked. First a compliment; now this.

Hurting people hurt people. Emma must have heard that old saying a million times, as her parents overlooked other people's sharp edges. Emma had never doubted the truth of it, but in the face of Ruth's constant needling, it was all too easy to forget, especially now when Emma was hurting herself.

Humbled by how close she'd come to responding unkindly, Emma spoke gently. "I agree that *Gott* always works things out for the best." She tilted the bowl and began to nudge the thick batter into the prepared pan.

"Sometimes it doesn't seem that way, but it's so." Ruth took three bowls out of the cupboard and began setting the table. "He gives us only what's right for us to have. Our job is to trust in that and do our best with whatever He sends, but it is not always easy."

Emma finished scraping out the batter and looked up. So Ruth did pay attention in church, after all. Isaac couldn't have said it better. "That's true."

Ruth's eyes darted to Emma's again, then back down at the table. "When I was young, I expected I would have a husband and children of my own one day, like all the other girls. But no fellow ever showed any interest in me. That's the menfolk for you. They go foolish over a pretty face, when a hard worker or a smart manager would be the better choice. Longer lasting, too." She lifted her chin and looked Emma in the eye. "There are more important things than being nice-looking, whether the men have sense enough to see it or not."

Emma considered the sharp little woman in front of her. "Yes, there are many more important things. The church is clear about that."

"The church is clear on a lot of things folks don't like to listen to. Anyway, when I was nineteen, with never so much as one buggy ride to my credit, *Mamm* sat me down, and we had a talk. Her health was failing by then, and Davey was only a little fellow. She said that since it didn't look likely that I'd be marrying anytime soon, she was going to put him into my care. From that day forward, Davey was mine, just as if I was his *mamm* instead of just his sister. So you see, *Gott* had a plan for me after all. It wasn't what I'd have picked out, maybe, but I had a lot of happiness looking after my Davey. Folks pitied me some because he was special, and they thought that made him more trouble to tend to. It did sometimes, but I didn't mind. And he never really grew up, so I got to mother him his whole life."

The wistfulness in Ruth's voice touched Emma's heart. "Your brother was blessed to have you."

"I hope so." The older woman pressed her lips together. "I did my duty by him, anyway, best I could. I didn't know what I was going to do with myself after he passed. Especially when Robert didn't seem to be in any hurry for me to come to Pennsylvania. I was real hurt by that, although I didn't like to let on. But see? Now there's Sam needing someone to look after him, same as Davey did."

Emma started to protest that Sam wasn't the same as Davey at all, but she bit her lip and stopped short. Sam had just made it very clear that his future was none of Emma's business.

She forced a smile and changed the subject. "Well, this cake is ready for baking, and that oatmeal is done. Will you call Sam in? I'm not very hungry, and if you think you can manage breakfast by yourself, I'll go ahead and get started cleaning the bedrooms."

She slid the cake into the oven and started for the door.

"Emma?" Ruth spoke from behind her.

"Yes?" Emma paused with one hand on the doorknob and turned with a smile.

Ruth stirred the oatmeal hard for a minute, as if struggling with what she wanted to say. Then she swallowed, and her mouth puckered back into its usual disapproving line.

"You be sure to sweep *gut* under the beds before you go. I think you've been skimping on that job."

Well, so much for Ruth's sympathy.

"I will be careful," Emma promised. Then she slipped into the hallway and closed the door behind herself.

It was good that she got a head start on her cleaning because Joseph and Naomi arrived earlier than expected. When Emma heard them drive up just after lunch, she tossed the dish towel down on the counter by the sink and hurried out to the yard.

Joseph stopped the buggy and set the brake, hurrying around to help his *fraw* down from her seat. Even if her brother hadn't spilled his happy secret, Emma would have guessed it. He treated Naomi as if she were made of glass. Emma smiled and blinked back tears.

Only when his wife was safely on the ground did Joseph turn his attention to his sister.

"It's good to see you, Emma." Her heart warmed at the genuine joy and welcome in his voice. "And it'll be good to have you home again, too. Should I unhitch?"

She understood the question. Her brother was discreetly asking how much hurry she was in to leave. For a second Emma wished she could just jump up into the familiar buggy and start back home. But Ruth and Sam were expecting to spend some time with Joseph and Naomi, and it would be wrong to disappoint them.

She swallowed and nodded. "*Ja*, best unhitch and turn Titus into the barn. Sam has a stall cleaned out and ready. I've made a cake, and I'm sure Ruth will want to visit before you go. Sam, too," she added belatedly.

Her brother studied her for a second. Then he nodded. "All right. I'll see to it. We can only stay a little while, though. Aaron's Katie came over to stay with Miriam, and she'll need to get back home before too long. Naomi, mind those steps there."

"I've been walking up steps by myself since I was a toddler, Joseph," Naomi pointed out with a long-suffering sigh. "I think I can manage these. Go tend to your horse." She waited until her husband had driven toward the barn before making a face at Emma. "Your brother is driving me crazy."

"Is he?" Emma asked innocently. "Why?"

Naomi narrowed her eyes. "You know already, don't you? And after I begged Joseph not to tell you, because I wanted the fun of telling you myself!"

Emma laughed and hugged her sister-in-law. "Don't be too angry with him. He didn't tell me—at least not on purpose. I guessed."

"I'm sure it wasn't hard. I've never seen a man act so foolish." The affection in her tone softened her words. "Our secret's not going to be a secret very long, I'm thinking. Well, it's too bad, because I was looking so forward to surprising you."

"It's wonderful news, surprise or not. A new *boppli* in the house! Miriam must be so happy."

"Oh, she is. She's already making a quilt for the crib." Naomi hesitated. "I hope you don't mind, Emma, but we were thinking of putting the baby in your old room. It's the closest to ours, and—"

"Of course!" Emma spoke brightly, in spite of the silly little pang in her heart. Another change. "I will move all my things out as soon as I get home, and we'll get it all fixed up. I could move into the boys' old room. Although"—she twinkled a teasing glance at her sister-in-law—"that room may be bespoke before too long, now that the family's starting to grow. Maybe I will scoot in with Miriam. The two of us can share her room easily enough."

"Oh, that's kind of you," Naomi said. "We can talk all that over on the ride home, *ja?* We have plenty of time to get everything arranged before our little surprise arrives. And speaking of surprises, I do still have one up my sleeve for you."

Naomi opened the cloth bag looped over her elbow and pulled out a folded letter. She handed it to Emma with a smile. "This came to the house the other day. Since I knew you'd want to see it right away, I brought it along. It's from Rhoda."

"Oh!" Emma took the letter, testing its thickness with her fingers. It had been a long time since she'd heard from Rhoda, and she was hoping for plenty of news. Maybe even some encouraging news. Had Emma's talk with Caleb done more good than she'd thought?

Naomi smiled. "You must be anxious to know what she

has to say. Why don't you stay out here for a minute or two and read it? I'll go on inside and say hello to Ruth and Sam."

That was like Naomi, always sensitive to other people's feelings. She knew that likely Rhoda's letter would carry news—for good or ill—of Caleb, and she wanted to give Emma time to read and react to it away from prying eyes.

Emma suddenly wondered if maybe Naomi already knew whatever news Rhoda was about to share. "Did she write to you, too?"

"No. Only to you, so I hope you will share whatever news you can with us. We have all been worried about her." Naomi leaned in closer. "But for goodness' sake, if there's anything she wouldn't want the whole town to know, you'd best be careful of sharing it with Joseph. It seems your brother can't keep a secret to save his life." Naomi winked and started up the steps.

Before her sister-in-law had made it to the door, Emma had ripped open the envelope and was devouring the letter.

She got only five sentences in before she stopped, her fingers tightening on the paper. She read Rhoda's words again.

And then again.

She heard the door opening, and she spoke without looking up. "I'm sorry, Naomi. I'm not . . . I'm not quite done yet."

"Emma? What's wrong?"

Sam was standing in the doorway, frowning down at her. He took hold of the handrail and started down the steps.

"Nothing."

"Something's troubling you. I hear it in your voice. What is it?"

Emma bit her lip. She probably shouldn't say anything. Rhoda mightn't want this news shared around, and Emma and Sam weren't so . . . close now.

But having him standing here, demanding to know what was troubling her—it felt so comfortingly familiar that the need to tell him her worries overcame her reluctance.

"Did Naomi tell you I had a letter from Rhoda?"

"She did not." Sam had reached the bottom of the steps now, and he stood only a few feet from her. "Is it bad news, then?"

"*Nee*. Not bad news. Good news. At least, I think it's good news." Emma swallowed. "Rhoda's going to have a baby. Babies, actually. The doctor says she's having twins, and soon. In another six weeks or so, they're thinking."

She watched the play of emotions across Sam's face. Surprise first, then a little uncertainty. In their community, pregnancies weren't often discussed. In fact, although everyone knew, of course, when a *boppli* was expected, the baby wasn't much talked about until he or she had actually arrived.

Then understanding dawned across his face, and he frowned.

"You're thinking your brother should know this."

"She hasn't told him. She says her father told her to wait, that Caleb needed to make his peace with *Gott* before she shared such news with him."

Sam's frown deepened. "Isaac said that?"

"So Rhoda says. But she has to know—and Isaac, too— that if Caleb found this out . . ." Emma looked up into Sam's face.

"He'd come to see her likely." Sam finished her sentence with a certainty that matched her own. "He'd not stay away, not after hearing news like that."

"*Ja*, he'd come, Sam, certain sure. And I think he'd stay. He'd never leave Rhoda to raise their babies alone."

"It wonders me then that Isaac would warn her against telling him. If this could draw Caleb back to the church, I'd think . . ." Sam paused. "Unless Isaac's looking at it different."

"What do you mean?"

"Maybe Isaac's thinking Caleb's not the only one whose mind could be changed by such news as this. Maybe he's thinking Rhoda's mind might be changed, too. That she might be more willing to jump the fence with Caleb if he came back and asked her again."

Emma thought it over. "It could be so. Isaac could think that he's protecting Rhoda's soul and the babies', too, doing this. Waiting to see if Caleb comes back willing to repent on his own first. Otherwise Isaac might lose his only child and his only grandchildren, not just for this life but for always."

"It makes sense that Isaac would see it so."

"It might make sense, but it's wrong, Sam!" Emma hesitated to say it, but she had to speak what she thought to be the truth. "This time Isaac is wrong. Caleb should be told."

"*Ja.*" Sam spoke heavily. "I think so, too. It's a husband's right to know such a thing."

"I wish I'd had this letter before I saw Caleb. I'd have told him myself. Rhoda doesn't say not to, only that she's not telling him." An idea occurred to Emma. "Maybe she wants me to tell him, Sam. Maybe that's why she wrote me about this. She'd have to know I'd tell Caleb if I could. But how can I? I've no way to get in touch with him."

Sam shifted his weight. "There might be a way."

"What do you mean?"

"He left that phone he brought, in case you ever needed to get in touch with him. It's out in the barn, in the box with Davey's old ball. He was going to call it from whatever new phone he picked up so you'd have his number."

Emma's heart was beating fast. "And did he call?"

"I don't know. I haven't fiddled with the thing. I probably couldn't see it well enough to figure it out anyhow, and he'd turned it down so Ruth wouldn't hear it ringing. But you could go out to the barn and take a look for yourself."

"I will!" Emma's excitement built, pushing her disappointments aside.

If Caleb would come back—if he and Rhoda returned to Johns Mill and they were all a family again . . . well. That wouldn't make up for losing the hope of a future with Sam. But it would bring some much-needed happiness into her life, for sure. And it would go a long way toward putting her family back on track again.

Caleb would come back. Emma believed that. Once he knew about the babies, he'd come back, and he'd stay. Deep down, Caleb had stronger ties to the church than he knew himself. He had his struggles with their faith, but fatherhood would change his perspective. He wouldn't want his children raised among the *Englisch*.

"Are you two waiting on me?" Joseph called from behind her. She turned to see her brother walking across from the barn. "Sorry. Titus wasn't feeling cooperative, but I'm finally done. Let's go in."

"I haven't seen Titus in a long while," Emma said lightly. "I think I'll walk out to the barn and say hello before I come inside."

Joseph chuckled. "Can you believe that, Sam? I haven't seen my sister except at church for weeks, but now she's more interested in visiting with my horse than with me. I never recall you being so eager to see Titus before, but all right. I'll walk back out to the barn with you."

Emma darted an alarmed look up at Sam's face but realized he couldn't see well enough to read her silent plea for help.

She needed to talk to her twin alone first. She knew her brothers loved each other, but they were opposites in temper and outlook. They'd always butted heads on a regular basis. She didn't want Joseph putting his oar into this pond until she had the boat pointed in the right direction.

"Joseph, I'd like a word with you." Sam spoke easily. "Real quick, if you don't mind."

"All right."

Emma pounced on the opportunity she'd been handed. "I'll just run out to the barn for a minute while you two talk. I won't be long."

As she hurried across the yard, she heard her brother ask, "Something wrong, Sam?"

"*Nee*," Sam answered so softly that Emma had to strain to hear. "At least, nothing wrong with me. It's just that . . . she's had a letter, Emma has."

"*Ja*, from Rhoda. Naomi told me she was bringing that along. Oh! She wants a minute to herself, then, to read it. Of course. I wasn't thinking—"

Emma slipped into the barn. The big door was open to catch the breeze, but she turned and slid it closed.

Titus snorted and moved uneasily in his stall.

"It's just me, boy," Emma murmured. She hurried toward the box containing Davey's old ball. Sure enough, Caleb's cell phone was tucked underneath it.

She turned the device over in her hands, looking for the power button. When she found it, she pressed it. Then again.

Nothing happened.

The battery must be dead. Emma made a frustrated noise. That made everything more complicated. She'd have to take it with her and find some way to charge it. It was one thing to make a quick phone call in this barn on the spur of the moment. It was another to have to plot and scheme to do it. She'd have to tell Joseph what she was planning and why, which would cause a whole set of new problems.

Maybe Birdie could help—if Emma could find a way to ask with nobody noticing.

Titus snorted again, and Emma glanced at him. "It's all

right," she said. "You haven't forgotten me already, have you?" Then she frowned.

The horse was looking up toward the loft, his ears swiveled forward intently. Emma stopped, listening.

There was a rustling noise, and something that might have been the sound of a boot on a plank. Her heart jumped hopefully.

"Caleb? Is that you?" Emma held her breath waiting. Sure enough, her brother's form appeared at the top of the loft. She squinted up at him. "Oh, what a blessing you came back! There's news from Rhoda. Wonderful news that changes everything. Come down, and we'll—"

She stopped short just as the man on the ladder jumped down to the packed earth floor and turned to face her.

"Hello, Emma," Trevor said.

CHAPTER TWENTY-SEVEN

❦

"I'M GLAD TO HAVE A MINUTE ALONE WITH YOU ANY-ways, Sam," Joseph said. "There's something I wanted to talk to you about."

"How about we go up on the front porch?" Sam started in that direction. It wouldn't be a bad idea to put a little more space between Joseph and Emma. From the porch, Joseph wouldn't be likely to hear her talking with Caleb on the phone.

Sam took the rocking chair closest to the barn side of the porch so that Joseph had to choose the one farther away. "So? What did you want to talk about?"

"Well." Joseph took a measured breath. "The truth was, I was wondering what plans you had."

Sam frowned. "Plans?"

"For work. I heard that you won't be going back on the construction crew. Jeff was talking about it at the café. He was sorry to lose you, he said."

Sam felt a stab of regret, but he shrugged. "He'll find another good man, soon enough. Jeff's a fair boss. He pays well, and he's careful with his crews. He'll have little trouble replacing me."

"That's not what he said. One man in a million, that's what he called you. He said even now that you're not able to see so well, you could probably outwork half the men on his crew. He said if it wasn't for his insurance troubles, he'd take you back just like you are."

Sam laced his fingers together in his lap. As he did, he realized that his hands were getting softer. Not so many calluses anymore. He sighed.

Joseph meant to be kind, repeating what Jeff had said. Sam knew that. But it felt like salt hitting a wound, being reminded he could no longer do what he'd once been good at.

"Jeff would change his tune quick enough if I actually showed up on a jobsite. I'd be little use to him," Sam said, trying to chuckle.

"Not so much use on a construction crew, maybe. But I was wondering . . . would you be willing to do some work for me?"

Sam turned his head in Joseph's direction. He couldn't see his friend clearly, only the foggy outline of his form. Whatever he was getting at seemed just as foggy. "That's kind of you, but I'd be no help to you, either, Joseph. I can't even hammer a nail straight these days."

"That's not the kind of work I meant. I was thinking about the store."

"The store?" Sam frowned. "Your parents' store?"

He could see movement as Joseph shifted in his chair. "*Ja.*"

"You want something fixed there?" Sam shook his head, "Like I said, Joseph, I can't—"

"I was thinking of reopening it."

There were a few ticks of silence as Sam digested this

unexpected bit of news. "You seemed real sure you wanted it closed before."

"I did." Joseph blew out a long, slow breath. "And to tell you the truth, it would suit me well enough to keep it closed. But you know the textile mill has cut down its crews again. A fair number of folks lost their work. I've had three fellows come by the house, asking if I was looking to hire on help at the workshop. I've already got all the help I need there, but Naomi mentioned that she'd heard some of the women talking after church. They were saying how they wished Hochstedlers was still open. Back after my parents died, when you and the other men ran it for us, their families made some good money selling different things there."

Sam nodded. "It was real busy, and folks sure didn't seem to mind what they paid. We couldn't keep stuff on the shelves. Of course, a lot of that . . ." He trailed off, unsure how to finish.

"Had to do with folks being curious about what happened. I know. And they're curious yet, especially with this movie being made."

"I suppose they would be."

"Naomi and I talked it over. I was never too happy about *Daed* closing the dairy and opening that store in the first place. You know that. And I've got my woodworking keeping me busy. But maybe it's wrong of me not to consider reopening, with so many people out of work and needing a place to sell their goods. I've been praying over it, and I think the Lord's leading me to go ahead with it."

Sam wasn't sure he understood his place in this plan. "What would you want me to do?"

"I'd want you to run it."

"Run it." Sam furrowed his brow. "You mean, keep the store? I don't know much about that, Joseph."

"You did all right with it before. You see well enough to get by, I think, especially if we hired you some help. And since I'd know I could leave everything in your hands, it wouldn't be a worry to me. You've got good sense, you're honest, and folks trust you. I think it would be a real good fit. I could pay you a salary and maybe a percentage of the profits, too. If it works out and you like it, we could even make it to where you'd end up owning the place if that would suit you. I'd be happy enough to have it off my hands. We'll figure all that out if you're interested. Are you?"

Was he?

"I don't know, Joseph. I thank you for the offer, but I'll have to think and pray on it a bit before I give you an answer." He'd never thought of himself as a storekeeper. But . . . if he could manage it . . .

At least it would be a living.

"All right." Joseph got to his feet. "You think it over. I'm going inside. You coming?"

"I will in a minute."

Joseph chuckled. "Waiting on my sister?"

Sam glanced up, but he couldn't read Joseph's expression. "What?"

"I figured you'd be wanting to talk this store idea over with her. You know," Joseph went on, "Emma was real well suited to storekeeping. Took to it like a duck to water, *Daed* said. Now that things in town have calmed down some, I don't think it would cause trouble for her to work there. Especially not if you were there alongside."

Sam got to his feet slowly. "Joseph, I don't know what Emma told you, but—"

"She told me nothing, and I've not asked questions, either. Like I said, I trust you, Sam. Whatever's between you and my sister, I know you'll do right."

"I'm trying to do right, *ja*." Although these Hochstedlers sure weren't making it easy. "I'm not the fellow for her, Joseph. She can do a lot better."

"The fact that you think that tells me you probably *are*

the fellow for her, Sam. The fellow I'd pick anyhow. But what I think doesn't matter. Why don't you go on out to the barn and have a talk with her? See what she thinks about this idea?"

Sam turned and looked toward the barn, not that he could see it clearly. He couldn't see anything else clearly right now, either. He'd thought he understood what his future held—and what it didn't. He hadn't liked it, but he'd been resigned to it.

Now, it was like a wall was coming down. Hope was starting to make its way back into his heart, like the smell of summer roses drifting through an open window.

The problem was, he wasn't sure what he should do with it.

But he knew what he wanted to do.

"Go ahead," Joseph said. He moved farther down the porch, and Sam heard the screen door creaking open. "Talk it over with Emma. Then bring her back up to the house if you can. That may not be so easy. I think I know what's keeping her, and it's got nothing to do with my horse."

"You do?" Sam shifted guiltily in his seat.

"*Ja*, I heard some noises up in the barn loft as I was getting Titus settled. Some kind of animal's up there. Titus sure didn't like the smell of it, so it's likely a stray cat. He's never been fond of those. Emma's probably trying to catch it to show Naomi, hoping between the two of them they'll talk me into taking the thing home with us." He sighed. "And I've got no chance of winning that argument. Just tell Emma to find a good, sturdy box for carrying. I don't want it getting loose in the buggy on the ride home. That happened with a half-dead raccoon Emma picked up off the road once. The thing came to in the buggy and went wild. I've still got scars."

"You heard noises in the loft?"

"*Ja*. Something's up there, all right. I just hope it's only *one* cat and not a mama with a litter of kittens." The screen door slapped shut behind Joseph. Sam stood on the porch, his mind fixed on what the other man had said.

Noises in the loft. Caleb must have doubled back. No wonder Emma hadn't reappeared. She'd be talking to her twin, telling him about Rhoda and the babies. That was good. Likely they'd walk up to the house together in a minute or two, and the process of Caleb's restoration to the community would begin.

Although if he'd been a smarter man, he'd have chosen a different place than Ruth Christner's house to begin it. She'd have plenty to say about all this, no doubt. On the other hand, given the heartache Caleb had put Rhoda and his family through, maybe he deserved a good dose of Ruth.

Sam scratched at his chin. It was funny, though. Caleb had sounded awful definite about his plans when he'd left before, and he wasn't usually one to shift his mind.

There was something else, too. What was it Joseph had said? Sam had been distracted by the notion of storekeeping . . . and Emma . . . but there had been something else, something that had jabbed at him.

In any case, he'd go out to the barn and check on Emma himself, just to be sure. He went down the steps carefully, holding the handrail to steady himself. Steps were easier now that he could see some, but they could still cause a problem if he got careless. He started across the yard, his mind turning back to what Joseph had said about the store.

Sam couldn't see how such a thing would work. Joseph was only suggesting the idea out of kindness—and maybe because Emma had asked him to. It would be just like her to try to fix things, to try to find Sam some job he could do.

He'd done all right when he'd kept the store before, but everything had been different then. It wasn't just his sight, either. He'd only been a place holder. His main purpose had been to stop people misbehaving, something he knew well how to do. He'd sold things, sure, and he'd done his best to keep good track of the money and all that, but he'd felt relieved to be done with it and back to his regular work.

He'd make a muddle if he tried to keep store on his own. Everybody knew—everybody had always known—that Sam Christner's best strength wasn't between his ears.

He was almost to the barn now. He heard the soft murmuring of Emma's voice and a man's voice answering. When the man spoke, Titus snorted, and there was a sound of shuffling as the animal moved restlessly in his stall.

Sam halted where he was.

Titus. That was what his brain had stumbled over back when Joseph had tossed off that bit about a cat being up in the loft because Titus hadn't liked the smell of it. And he'd said the horse had been uncooperative, too. Titus, who generally gave little trouble.

That made sense if it was a cat, but not if it was Caleb. Titus would know Caleb's scent, just as well as the horse knew Joseph's.

Instead, whoever was inside that barn with Emma was making Titus uneasy.

Trevor.

Sam lunged forward and caught himself just before he made it to the door. What was he going to do? In the dim light of the barn, he'd not even be able to see where the *Englischer* was standing.

He leaned against the door as quietly as he could and listened.

"I wanted you to understand, Emma." The boy's plea sounded shaky. "That's why I came back, so I could explain everything to you."

"Please." Emma spoke evenly, but Sam heard fear in her voice. His muscles tightened, and it took every ounce of his self-control not to shoulder through the door and take his chances. "Trevor, listen to me."

"I need *you* to listen!" Sam's stomach tensed at the panic in the *Englischer*'s voice. He didn't like panic. Panic made people unpredictable. "I've been waiting out here for hours, trying to catch you by yourself, so we could talk. You know, like we used to."

Say you will, Emma. Just agree with him.

"We will talk, Trevor. I will listen to what you want to say. But that gun frightens me. Give it to me, and I'll put it someplace safe so nobody will get hurt."

"You don't know anything about guns. I don't want you to hurt yourself. I'll put it in my pocket. See? You don't have to be scared, Emma. I wouldn't let anything happen to you. You know that, right? I need the gun because people don't understand. They don't know why I did what I did. But they will, though, before long. My parents are taking care of that. They're going to make sure people know the truth."

"Trevor, maybe you should talk to the police. You could tell them the truth, too."

"They wouldn't listen to me. They want to lock me up."

"I could go with you," Emma said. "To the police. If I were there, then they would have to listen to you."

"You would do that? You'd go with me? Right now?"

Sam heard Titus blowing out a breath and shifting again in his stall, reacting no doubt both to the strange smell of the *Englischer*, and to the tension the animal was sensing.

Sam's breath was coming quick, too. He knew what Emma was up to. Her mind wasn't on herself. It was on the people inside the house . . . Joseph and Naomi, Ruth—and Sam himself, likely. She'd do whatever it took to draw Trevor away from them.

"Of course! Don't you think that would be best, Trevor?" Emma was saying now. "Hasn't all this gone on long enough? You must be so tired of all the running and hiding. Let's go now and talk to the police together, you and me."

There was a pause.

"All right," Trevor said. "Let's go. Just you and me, though. Nobody else. I parked my truck on that dirt road just across the way. It's not far. I can drive us to the sheriff's office."

The boy was lying.

Sam heard it in his voice. If Emma left with him now . . . Sam took a breath, said the shortest prayer of his life, and pushed open the barn door.

Chapter Twenty-Eight

❧

EMMA KNEW IT WAS SAM. SHE KNEW THE INSTANT she heard the barn door creak, before he spoke or even stepped inside. It could have been Joseph, or Naomi, or even Ruth, of course, but Emma knew who it would be before she ever turned her head.

Trouble had come. And when trouble came, Sam was never far behind.

Trevor jolted around, fumbling frantically at his pocket.

"No!" Emma cried out. She started toward Trevor, intending to put herself between him and Sam.

"Emma." Sam's voice was calm, but there was a thread of steel in it. "Best you stay where you are. He's not going to shoot me."

She stopped short, her heart beating wildly, unsure what to do.

"Don't come any closer!" Trevor's voice shook, and when Emma glanced back at him, she felt the blood draining from her face. He had the gun out of his pocket and was pointing it in Sam's direction.

"I won't. I'll stop right here." Sam reached out and touched a post, patting at it with his hands. Having made sure of its position, he leaned one shoulder against it.

Emma bit her lip. Sam couldn't have made it any plainer that he couldn't see—all that fumbling around. That wasn't good. Trevor would know for sure now that Sam couldn't defend himself.

"You'd better not try anything!" Sure enough, Trevor's voice already sounded more confident.

"I'm not going to. There'd be no point in it. I can't see very well. In case," Sam added, "you couldn't already tell. I'm no threat to you. And you," he went on, "are no threat to me, either. You won't shoot a blind man. That's not the kind of thing you would ever do. I know that. You don't mind if I sit down, do you?" Now Sam felt around until he found a thick log that had been upended next to the post. He sank down on it.

Emma's eyes were flitting between Sam and Trevor. She thought she understood what Sam was doing.

"It's true," she said. "He can't see well, Trevor. He's not going to bother you."

"I'm not stupid, Emma. I know he can't see. I've been watching him." Trevor kept the gun pointed at Sam. "You should've stayed out of this."

"Maybe so. But I couldn't help hearing what you were saying just then. About nobody listening to you. And I thought . . ." Sam paused and scratched his forehead. "You know, that's the truth. He never did get a chance to explain himself because everybody was so upset." Sam tilted his head up at Trevor. "Although you have to admit, it didn't look too good, you shooting two unarmed people like that."

Trevor swallowed and darted a glance at Emma. "I wasn't planning on doing that."

"See?" Sam nodded. "That's just what I thought myself. No decent fellow goes in wanting to hurt a girl's parents. Not a girl he cares about anyway. Something must have happened after you went inside the store. What was it?"

"Sam—" Emma started.

"It's all right, Emma." Trevor's voice sounded even stronger now. Surer. "This is why I came here. To tell you what really happened."

"Go ahead, then. We're both listening." Sam leaned back against the post and stretched his legs out in front of him, for all the world as if he were talking with a friend.

Sam's working him, Emma realized. Gentling him, like he would a horse, wearing him down, waiting him out. Letting him think he's leading, so he won't fight so hard.

"When I went by the store that morning, I saw you weren't there." Trevor shot Emma a look. "I'd walk by soon as it opened, every day. Looking in to see."

"I know," Emma admitted. She'd seen Trevor do that in the mornings, walk by, glance in, and maybe wave at her. At the time it had seemed innocent enough. She hadn't thought much about it.

Because, she realized with a pang, she'd been well used to fellows going out of their way to get a look at her. Maybe if she'd been a little less vain, she'd have noticed and realized—

"You weren't there that day. Only your sister, and she never came to the store. So I went inside. I thought maybe you were sick or something."

"You were worried." Sam made it sound completely reasonable.

"I'd never really . . . talked to anybody else in your family before. I mean, your brothers had done some work for my parents, but I never had a conversation with them or anything. They were always jabbering to each other, talking so nobody else could understand."

"In *Deutsch*," Sam supplied. "That's the language we speak among ourselves. It's rude, though. To talk in front of folks who can't understand what you're saying. They should have been speaking English while they were with you."

"That's what I thought, too." Trevor sounded angry.

Sam shouldn't be throwing any kindling onto that fire, Emma thought in alarm. After all, Joseph was inside the house now. What if he were to come to the barn? He would, sooner or later. He'd come looking for her, wondering what was taking so long.

"I'm sure they didn't mean to be rude. We don't think of it always. Not when we're talking just to each other. It's what we're used to, and we forget sometimes, that—" She stopped. Sam had caught her eye.

She couldn't tell what it was about his face that warned her into silence. But something did.

"Go on, then," Sam said. "You went inside."

"I was going to ask your sister about you, but she wouldn't even look at me. She acted like she was afraid to. I mean, like terrified. And see?" Trevor's voice gained confidence again. "That's when I knew something bad must be going on."

Emma started to speak, but she saw Sam's hand twitch. A gentle movement, barely noticeable. *Stay still.*

"Ah." Sam nodded slowly. "And so?"

"And so I asked your father, Emma. Where you were, and he told me . . ." For the first time, Trevor faltered. "He told me that you wouldn't be coming back to work in the store for a while. That you'd be helping your brother and his new wife get settled. I said that maybe I could help, too. You see . . ." Trevor turned away from Sam to face Emma fully. His pale face was earnest. "I was trying to make a good impression. I wanted him to like me."

Emma could feel Sam's eyes on her, warning her to be careful what she said. But it was no matter. She couldn't speak now anyway. Somehow, this retelling of her parents' last morning had put her in a place beyond words. She could barely breathe.

After a second, Trevor went on. "But he said no, that it was best that you and I not see each other. I asked him why, and he said because he and your mother thought it best. And so, of course, I asked what you thought, and he said that was of no matter. No matter, Emma. Those were his exact words. That it had all been decided."

"Mmm." Sam made a thoughtful noise. He had his head ducked down, looking at his hands.

"I said it mattered to me. I mean, it was wrong, wasn't it, for him to think he could make all those decisions. Like what you wanted or what I wanted didn't even matter. And then . . ." The *Englischer* swallowed. "And then he . . . he *winked* at me, and he told me I should find another girl to talk to. He winked at me, like it was all a big joke to him. He didn't understand how I felt about you, Emma. He didn't understand anything."

Emma stood frozen in place. *Ja*, that was what *Daed* would have said. She could hear the teasing tone in his voice as he said it. He would have been trying to be kind, trying to soften the hurt of it a little by funning with Trevor, the way he'd often joked with his own sons.

She couldn't help it. A sob caught in her throat. She jammed her fingers against her mouth to stop the sound, but her shoulders shook.

"Emma?" Trevor's voice sounded uncertain now. "I didn't mean to . . . I was just really upset, and your father wouldn't listen. He was laughing at me." There was a note of childish outrage in his voice. "It was why I'd started carrying the gun around. People were always laughing at me. But I'd never planned to . . ."

He took a step in her direction, and Sam instantly rose to his feet. Trevor stopped and whirled around.

"You stay where you are."

"But see now? You've upset her." Sam's voice sounded low and calm. Emma squeezed her eyes shut and listened, holding on to the familiar sound of it desperately. "Best we not talk about it anymore now."

"I don't want to upset her." Trevor sounded like he was on the brink of tears himself now. "I never wanted to do that."

"I know." There it was again, that soothing rumble. She'd heard Sam use this tone a hundred times, mostly with horses, but with her, too, sometimes. "Because you care for her."

"Yes, I do."

"So, of course, you want her to be happy."

"Yes!"

"Then please, Trevor," Emma said, grabbing at the sliver of hope shining in the middle of this awfulness. "Turn yourself in to the police, so that—"

"He's not going to do that, Emma. Are you?" Sam turned the question to Trevor as matter-of-factly as if they were talking about the weather. "Tell her the truth now."

Trevor didn't answer. His eyes shifted between Sam and Emma.

"No. Of course you're not." Sam spoke evenly. "But now, you have to figure what you *are* going to do." Sam drew in a breath and raised one arm. Trevor flinched, but Sam only scratched thoughtfully at his chin. "That's the problem, ain't so? What to do now."

Trevor shifted on his feet. "I came back here to see you, Emma. My parents wanted me to talk to this writer. I did. On the phone, and he said he'd spoken to you already. And I could tell from what he said, that you didn't understand." He swallowed. "That you didn't know that I never meant to . . ."

Emma didn't know what she was supposed to say.

Sam answered for her. "You wanted to tell her that you were sorry that things happened as they did."

"Yes. Yes, that's right. I'm sorry, Emma." Trevor turned to her, his expression pleading. "I'm very, very sorry."

Sam turned toward her. Waiting. This time she knew what he expected her to say. What *Gott* expected her to say.

What was smart to say.

Even so, she had to take three breaths before she could say it. "You are forgiven, Trevor."

Trevor made a noise halfway between a hiccup and a sob and swiped at his face with the crook of his elbow.

Sam waited a beat or two before going on. "Now seems to me you've done what you came here to do. You'd probably better go now. There are other folks in the house there, and you wouldn't want them to see you."

Sam made it sound simple. Breathing brokenly, Trevor looked at Emma, and then back at Sam. Sam shook his head.

"You can't take her with you. You came here to set things right between the two of you, best you could. You've done that. If you try to take her with you, then you're going to mess everything up again. See, she doesn't want to go with you, Trevor. Do you, Emma?"

She shook her head. "No."

"And if you try to make her, then I'll have to do my best to stop you." Sam shook his head. "We both know how that's going to end. Badly for me, I'm thinking. But not so good for you, either. You'd be shooting a blind man, Trevor—or close enough to blind that it doesn't matter. And a friend of hers that she went to school with years ago, that she was always kind to. Just like she was kind to you. You don't want to do such a thing, cause her more pain than you have already, not when you've just set everything right again."

Trevor hesitated, and Emma could sense that everything—

absolutely everything that mattered to her—hung in the balance.

"I'll walk you down to the road," Sam said.

And suddenly, Trevor slumped. "All right. But you'd better not try anything."

"Oh, I won't." Sam chuckled. "You've got the gun, after all. Emma." Sam spoke evenly, lightly, but again she heard that steel in his words. "You wait here. Don't go to the house until I come back to get you, all right? When Trevor's well away."

"All right, Sam," she said, surprised by how steady her own voice sounded. "I'll stay right here."

"Come on then." Sam motioned to Trevor, and to Emma's astonishment, the other man moved in Sam's direction.

He stopped as he drew even with her, and he looked her in the eye. "Goodbye, Emma."

She nodded, swallowed, and ducked her head. "Goodbye, Trevor."

The *Englisch* boy hesitated there for a moment, and for a second she thought he was going to say something else. But finally he moved on with Sam toward the door.

There was a blinding flash of light as Sam shoved the big barn door open. Then the barn went dim again, and the two men were gone.

Emma raced to the door, peering through the crack, her heart pounding. There they were, walking down Ruth's graveled drive toward the road. They made a strangely mismatched pair, Sam in his Amish clothes and his hat, Trevor in his *Englisch* jeans and shirt. But it was more than that.

Sam stood head and shoulders taller, and he was twice as broad, but Trevor's hand rested inside his jacket pocket, where the bulge of the gun showed.

Sam seemed unconcerned, but Emma noticed that he'd placed himself between Trevor and the house. Her heartbeat skipped. If somebody were to step outside, or even glance out a window just now. If Joseph were to come looking for her . . .

She knew what Sam would do if Trevor pulled that gun out of his pocket. He would do the same thing he'd have done if he'd been in the store with her parents that awful day. The idea of it made her hand tighten on the barn door, and she started to push it open.

She looked back at Sam and stopped herself. There was an easy strength about him that made Emma's breathing quiet and slow. He walked slowly, casually, as if he were in no particular hurry. Trevor walked with a strange stiffness, as if he were in a dream.

Emma watched them, her face pressed hard against the crack, until they reached the end of the road. Then Sam stopped, and he seemed to be speaking to Trevor. The boy stood in front of him, slump-shouldered, listening. Sam held out his hand, and Trevor seemed unsure what to do.

Then he accepted Sam's hand.

After the handshake, Trevor sprinted across the road. Sam stood right where he was until the other man had turned down the dirt road where Breeze had run away with them.

Only then did Sam turn around and head back to the barn. But this time there was nothing slow or easy about his steps.

He made it to the barn so fast that Emma barely had time to step back before he shoved the door open.

"Emma," was all Sam got out before she threw herself into his arms.

CHAPTER TWENTY-NINE

❧

"IT'S ALL RIGHT," SAM SOOTHED HER, RESTING HIS cheek against her *kapp*. Even though it was all over, his heart was beating hard, and he was working to calm himself as much as Emma. "It's all right, now. He's gone."

"I was so afraid." She spoke in *Deutsch* against his chest. "I was so afraid for you."

"You did real well, though. You were *schmaert* and quick. You said all the right things."

"No." She pulled away from him, shaking her head. "It was you, Sam. You said everything right. How did you know what to say?"

"I listened to his voice. It told me what he was thinking. I'm sorry, Emma. I know you wanted to get him to the police, but he wasn't going to go. He was lying to you when he said he would. It was the best I could do, getting him to leave. If I could see clearer, maybe I could have—"

"You did wonderful, Sam. Nobody could've done better." He was holding her upper arms in his hands. He knew he should let her go, but he couldn't. He was just thankful to feel her here, living and breathing and safe. "Not so wonderful. He's gotten away. I heard the truck starting up just as I made it to the barn door. We'll have to call the police."

"We can't. Caleb's phone was dead, but Trevor took it from me anyhow and smashed it." She shivered, and he tightened his grip gently on her arms. "But Birdie will be here any minute, and she'll have a phone with her. We'll call then."

"All right." Sam swallowed. "We should go in now, I guess, and tell the others." He winced, imagining what the reaction inside the house was going to be. Everyone would be thankful that things had worked out as well as they had, but they would also be frightened.

"Can we wait, please? Just for a minute? Naomi shouldn't be upset right now. I need to be calm when we go in."

Ah. Sam's pounding heart lifted a little as he put two and two together. So Rhoda wasn't the only Hochstedler in the family way. No wonder Joseph had been so cheerful today.

The realization was followed by a quick chill of fear. If Emma hadn't trusted him and followed his lead, things might have gone very wrong out here. And there had been even more at stake than he'd known.

He sent up a quick, fervent prayer of thanks.

"How did you know, Sam?" Emma was asking. "When you walked into the barn, I was afraid Trevor would take you by surprise, but it was like you knew just what was going on, and what to do, right from the start. How did you know something was wrong?"

He didn't want to talk right now. He just wanted to stand here and hold her and be thankful. But it was calming her, talking it over. He could sense that, so he went along. "The horse. Joseph said Titus was restless, that something in the barn was spooking him. He thought maybe it was a stray cat, but I knew something was off."

"Of course." He heard a catch in Emma's breathing that

was almost a laugh. "It would be something to do with a horse. And Sam?"

"What?"

"You said something to Trevor. At the road. I was watching through the crack there. What did you say?"

"He stalled a little just there, and I said what it took, Emma. To make him leave." She waited, obviously expecting him to go on. He swallowed. "I told him that if he truly cared about you, he should leave you in peace, with your family." He hesitated then gave her the rest of it. "I told him . . . he should act like the kind of man who deserved somebody like you, even if he couldn't be with you himself."

"Oh." She drew in a sharp breath.

She was guessing the truth, likely—that Sam had been telling himself the same thing. He felt a flush of embarrassed warmth rising up his neck toward his cheeks. Maybe he shouldn't have been quite so honest.

"I had to play along with him, Emma, or we'd have had trouble. That's all I was thinking about, this whole time, just playing along, saying whatever it took."

That reminded him.

"And I'm sorry, Emma." Carefully and very gently, he raised one hand and felt for her face. It was still wet with tears, and he wiped them away with his thumb, best he could. "It must have been hard, listening to all that about your *daed*. Listening to me talking as if none of it mattered. I had to do it that way."

"I know," she whispered.

"Trevor's troubled in his head, and he doesn't think like we do. I had to talk in a way that made sense to him. I had to keep him calm, make him think I agreed with him."

"I know that," she repeated in a stronger voice. "You don't have to explain anything you said, not to me. I understand you, Sam, lots better than you think."

She turned her head and kissed his hand. He froze, feeling her lips, soft and warm against his palm.

"Emma." He cleared his throat and tried again. "Emma, I—"

"You love me, Sam. I know you do, even if you won't tell me."

He took a breath, but before he could speak, she put her hands on his cheeks and pulled his head down until they were nose to nose.

"I'll do this one more time, just to make my point. But next time, Sam, it's going to be your turn."

And she kissed him.

His turn came quicker than she might have expected. The minute her mouth met his, every bit of resolve he'd built up crumbled into nothing. He gathered her up into his arms and kissed her for everything he was worth.

When he reluctantly drew back to catch his breath, she whispered, "See? You do love me, Sam. You do. Nothing else matters, not what you do for work, or how we manage for money. We'll figure all of that out somehow, the two of us."

His mind flicked back to what Joseph had said about the store, a thousand years ago it seemed now. "Emma, listen. I—"

"No, I won't listen!" Emma's voice was shaking, but whether with tears or just plain old temper, he couldn't tell. "I've heard just about enough arguments from you, Sam Christner. Only one thing counts. Just you answer me this. Will I ever find a man who loves me more than you do? Is there one? Anywhere in this world?"

She made it sound like an accusation. He smiled. He did love this woman's fire.

"*Nee*, Emma." Sam spoke softly. He had no choice. His heart was swelling so fast, he could barely find room in his chest for breath. "There's no such man. No man loves you more than I do. No man ever could."

He narrowed his eyes, straining hard to see her face in the dim light. It was no use. He couldn't see it. But then he didn't really need to, did he? He knew every inch of Emma's face by heart.

"Then why should I settle for less than you? It's the love that makes the marriage, Sam. With everything else you can make do or do without. Only the love really counts. You're going to marry me." She spoke definitely. "Soon. This fall. You *have* to marry me."

His chuckle caught on the lump in his throat. "I don't think you should go putting it quite like that when you tell your family, Emma," Sam said. "I'm a good bit bigger than Joseph, but even so, it could get sticky."

"But you will, though," she persisted, "marry me. Won't you, Sam?"

Of course he would. A thousand times over.

"You know, you could at least let me be the one asking that question." He raised his hand and brushed his knuckles underneath the firm line of her jaw. "I think that's generally how it's done."

"No," she murmured, closing the gap between them and pressing her face against his chest again. "There will be no more questions between us, Sam. Not about this. Besides, you've had your chance. You asked me already, years ago, remember?"

He smiled at the memory. "So I did. And you said yes. But as I recall, you went back on it later."

"I've changed my mind."

"Fair enough." He rested his chin against the top of her head again and breathed in the scent of her. "But I'm not sure I can handle it if you change your mind again, Emma, so you'd best be sure."

"I am," she whispered.

Her lips stirred against his chest as she spoke. He reached under her chin with one finger and tipped her face up.

"My turn," he murmured. Then he kissed her again, more slowly this time.

"Oh!" she said when he'd finally lifted his mouth from hers.

He liked hearing the soft bewilderment in her voice. He liked it a lot. But he could also hear the crunch of tires on gravel outside the barn. Birdie had arrived, and now there was a phone they could use. They needed to tell the others about Trevor and call the police.

But before they left this barn together, there was one last thing he needed to make clear, while he still had wits enough to say it.

"I'll marry you, Emma, if you'll have me. And I'll make the best life for you I can. But," he said gently, "you'll have to trust me to do it in my own way. I'll not be babied. I won't have you looking after me as if I were your child instead of your husband. Not being able to see doesn't make me any less a man."

"Oh, for pity's sake, Sam! I've been the one saying that all along, haven't I?" Emma spoke with her old spark, and he grinned as she tucked her head back into the hollow of his neck. As they moved toward the door together, she went on, her voice muffled against him, "But remember what you told me? About how you're made a certain way and you can't change? Well, I'm made a certain way, too, and if you don't want me to baby you after we're married, you'd better give me something else to baby pretty quick." Just as his heart hitched in his chest, she added sweetly, "A kitten, maybe."

He chuckled and snugged her a little closer. "I think I can do better than that," he said.

They were still laughing when he pushed the barn door open, and they stepped together out of the dim and into the light.

EPILOGUE

❧

AT HER DESK IN THE STOREROOM OF HOCHSTEDLER'S
General Store, Emma Christner finished signing her name.
She tore the check from the register and held it out to Myra
Ropp.

"Here you go. And we can take as many more quilts as
you can bring, soon as you can get them to us. The lap
quilts Miriam made for us are selling especially well, but
any size is welcome."

Myra smiled. "I've had to slow down on my sewing with
the new baby to look after, but I've got my *dochders* working on half a dozen small quilts now. They'll be finished by
next week, and I'll bring them along to you." She folded the
check in half and tucked it in the pocket behind her apron.
"I've made up a new pattern that I think your customers
will like real well. I copied it after an old quilt my *grossmammi* gave me years ago, but I made some changes, too.
What I did was—"

Emma listened patiently, but her eyes strayed to the

open doorway leading out into the store. She'd heard the bell jangling just a minute ago, and that meant customers. Sam was behind the counter alone. Since they'd reopened the store two weeks ago, he'd figured out ways to handle most tasks without her help, but she still liked to stay nearby when she could.

That was natural enough. Her new husband was a fine-looking man. Emma's mouth tipped up. She loved being close to Sam, and she could already tell she was going to enjoy working in the store with him.

Whether Sam was going to love the work was another question, and one Emma had been praying over. He was not complaining. He never did. But she was watching him closely to see signs that being "cooped up inside," as he'd put it once, was wearing on him.

"I'm sorry, Myra." Emma interrupted the chatty woman's long explanation about her color choices. "But I really should get back to work."

"Ah, of course." Myra looked worried. "I've been keeping you. It's just I'm real excited about these quilts, and I truly want to please you."

"You're doing that already, so don't fret yourself. Your quilts sell almost the minute they come through our door, as that check I just wrote you shows. We couldn't be more pleased, Sam and I."

Myra's face relaxed. "I'm glad to hear it. I can't tell you what an answer to prayer this store has been to me and my family, Emma. I know it must have been hard for you to reopen it and come back after . . . after what happened here, but I'm so thankful. And I'm not the only one. Everybody says the same. It's been hard times making ends meet, and having this extra money coming in is such a help to us all."

Emma managed a smile. Myra was right. Reopening the store had been bittersweet, especially at first. That first morning, being here without *Mamm* and *Daed*, dealing with the customers with their curiosity and their awkward expressions of sympathy . . . that had been hard.

But Sam had stood right beside her, and that had helped. From her steady, unwavering husband she'd drawn enough strength to stand behind the wooden counter again. After a day or two, she'd even started to enjoy herself.

The overwhelming gratitude of Johns Mill's Plain community had helped, too. The store was serving a need; there was no doubt of it. Emma had been hearing the same thing over and over again, from so many people.

"You're doing *Gott*'s work here, Emma," Myra was saying now, "you and your *mann*. Turning your sorrows into such a blessing for the rest of us." The older woman nodded earnestly. "That's *Gott*'s good work, for certain sure."

"We have been blessed by all of you, too, Myra. We are only grateful if we are helping you in return." The bell jangled again. "I'm sorry, but I really should get back out front now."

Emma followed the woman into the store, scanning the display area. They'd barely been open half an hour this morning, and it was already busy with customers, most of them *Englisch*. A couple were mothers with young children, and a few other women were shopping alone. Her eye lit on one little boy who'd been left unattended in the toy area. He was making a jumble of the wooden tops all over the floor. She'd have to put those back on the shelf as soon as the child left, a never-ending job.

But, she reminded herself, an important one. Sam relied on her to keep things in order. It was one of the few things he let her do to help him, so she did her best, both here and at home.

After their wedding, Ruth had gone to Pennsylvania to be with her brother Robert. Before they left, Sam's uncle had handed him the deed to the little house, calling it a wedding present.

When Sam had protested, his uncle had shown both the Christners' trademark clannishness—and their stubborn streak.

"It's yours, Sam, and I'll hear no arguing over it. You've had the care of your *aent* for some time," Robert said. "And I can see the work you've done on this house over the years, though I've never seen a bill for any of it, not even the lumber. So take the place and welcome."

So they had.

After thinking it over, Sam had rented out the Christner family farm, and he and Emma had settled into Ruth's. For the time being, he'd said. It was a smaller place and would be easier to keep. And Birdie was nearby, with her phone and her car, should they have an emergency.

So they had their little nest, and Emma made a special point to keep it just so. It made life easier for Sam if he knew just where everything was.

He certainly liked to know just where Emma was, and he had an unfailing instinct about it.

She glanced toward the counter and smiled. Sam was ringing up a sale, using a calculator Birdie had ordered for him that said the amounts out loud. Sure enough, he paused in his work, tilting his head in her direction, even though she'd not made near enough noise to be heard over the bustling store.

Sam might stumble over a misplaced wooden toy, but he always knew just where his wife was at any given moment. She didn't know how he knew—but he did.

She approached just as he finished with the customer.

"Did you give Myra her check?" Sam asked.

"*Ja*, I did, and she seemed real happy to get it."

"I imagine she would be." Sam lowered his voice. "Her Paul was one of the men who got laid off from the mill last week. The money they make here will be their bread and butter until he finds a new job." Her husband nodded toward a pretty woven basket sitting on the table. "Paul dropped that off for us to think over. He learned basket making from his grandparents years ago and thought we might be interested in selling some, now he's got the time to make them."

Emma picked up the basket, feeling its tight, smooth weave and testing its heft in her hand. "Oh, I like it, Sam! Very much. It's beautiful. What do you think?"

"I think we'll sell as many of those as he can give us. I told him to get busy on them and bring them along as soon as he could."

Emma held the basket up, admiring it from every angle. "I'll check into what these are bringing other places so we'll get an idea of the price to set."

"I'll give you fifty dollars for it right now." The *Englisch* mother with the rambunctious little boys walked up to the counter, two of Myra's quilts folded in her hands. She plopped them down in front of Sam. "These, too. Do you have any more of that blackberry jam in the back? I want to give it for Christmas presents. I'll need at least a dozen jars."

"I'm sorry," Emma said, "but all we have of that is on the shelf. It's a real good seller."

The woman sighed impatiently. "Well, can you order in some more and ship them to me?"

"I'm afraid that's not possible," Emma said. "You see—"

"I don't understand the problem. I'm willing to pay to have them shipped priority mail. I want to be sure to have them by Christmas."

"The problem is not the shipping." Sam spoke up with a friendly firmness. "The problem is that blackberries do not grow this time of year. The ladies can't make any more jam until June." He smiled. "But we've a real good supply of this apple butter yet, and you can't beat that on a biscuit." He lifted the glass dome covering the cake stand they'd placed on the counter, displaying small squares of Emma's fresh-baked bread next to a chubby pot of apple butter, ready to spread. "Try it and see."

"Well, it smells good." The woman picked up a sample to taste. As soon as it hit her tongue, her expression changed. "Yes. I'll take all the blackberry you have left and another dozen of these."

"They're over on the shelf. There's twelve jars to a box, so they're a bit heavy. Good thing you brought help, *ja?*" Sam turned toward the taller of the two boys standing with their mother. He looked to be ten or eleven maybe, Emma thought. He also looked bored, and he was fiddling restlessly with a phone. "Go with your *mamm*, then, and help her bring the jars up to the counter."

"What?" The boy looked up and frowned. "Me?"

"Sure. A strong boy like you would not let his mother carry such a load on her own, I know." Sam spoke with utter confidence. Emma watched as the boy thought it over. He straightened his shoulders and slipped his phone back into his pocket.

"Wait up, Mom! I'll get them."

"I'll help, too," the littler boy said. Sam shook his head.

"*Nee*, not you. You wait here. I need a word with you."

The boy looked up at the towering man uncertainly. "If I have to stay here, can I at least have some of that bread you gave Mom?"

"Of course." Sam lifted the dome again and felt carefully with light fingers, finding the bread, and managing to spread the jam with only a little bit of dripping.

Emma and the boy watched. Emma itched to help, but she squelched the impulse. She'd learned not to interfere. Sam liked to do for himself, and it was amazing, really, what he could accomplish if she left him to it.

"Here you go." Leaning over the counter, Sam offered the square of bread on a napkin.

The child accepted it and shoved it whole into his mouth. "You can't see too good, can you?"

"Not too good, no. But"—Sam leaned down a bit closer—"I can see good enough to know you've got one of our tops hidden in your jacket pocket."

The little boy froze in mid-chew.

"I heard your *mamm* say you couldn't have a toy today because you didn't behave yourself at school. Ain't so?" The boy nodded slowly, his eyes wide. Sam held out one big hand. "Then you'd best give it here, I think."

The child pulled the top slowly out of his pocket. "It's the only one with a red stripe left," he mumbled. "I really wanted one with a red stripe, and it'll be gone by next time we come here."

"Ah." Sam leaned back, weighing the top in his hand. "That is a problem. But stealing the toy isn't the answer to it. You'd find no joy in it that way, and it would spoil all your fun of playing with it."

The boy looked unconvinced. "I guess."

"There are better answers. Maybe you could ask the storekeeper to save it for you, behind the counter, like. Where nobody else could see it to buy. What do you think of that?"

Emma watched the little boy's expression turn from dejected to hopeful. "Would you do that?"

"I might, if I was asked nice. Then," Sam went on, "you could behave yourself at school real well until you come in again, even do some extra work around the house to earn a dollar or two."

The boy nodded excitedly. "And I could buy it all by myself!"

"*Ja.*" Sam smiled. "You could do."

"Okay." The child nodded. "Keep it for me."

Sam didn't budge. "I think you can ask me nicer than that."

The child took a breath. "Please, Mr. Sam, will you keep that top for me behind the counter until I save up the money to buy it?"

"*Ja*, of course. You know my name well enough, I see. And what's your name, then?"

"Hudson."

"Write it on this paper." Sam handed him a scrap and a pencil. "I'll put it with the top, and we'll have our deal all fixed up."

The boy scrawled his name with his tongue stuck out of his mouth. Then he slid the paper and the top back to Sam.

"Emma, would you put these in a very safe place?" Sam asked, handing her the top and the note. Emma accepted them with a smile.

"I'll put them in the storeroom," she said. "In a special drawer, so we'll know right where they are." As she turned to go, she heard the little boy whisper.

"Mr. Sam? Is that lady your wife or your sweetheart?"

Sam chuckled. "She is both."

"My brother says she's the prettiest woman in the whole town, but it's a big waste 'cause she only likes the man who can't even see her."

Oh, dear. Emma's heart caught. She stopped just inside the storeroom door, out of sight, but listening.

"Hud!" His brother came up just then, his arms loaded with preserves. "You dumb kid. Shut up!"

"That is not a kind thing to say to your *bruder*," Sam pointed out. "Anyhow, it's all right. I will tell you boys a secret. I see my wife much better than you think. Better than anybody else, for certain sure."

"You do?" In spite of her irritation, Emma's lips twitched at the innocent confusion in the smaller boy's voice.

"*Ja*. Because as pretty as she may be on the outside, she's even prettier on the inside where it really counts. And that's the part of her I see best."

Oh, Sam. Emma scrubbed at her eyes and sniffled happily. And quietly. Because if Sam heard her crying, he'd be next to her in a minute, wanting to know why.

Emma lingered in the storeroom until all the customers had paid for their purchases and gone. Then she came back to stand behind her husband, looping her hand through his arm.

He glanced toward her and smiled. "You timed that well," he teased. "Not coming back until the store's gone empty."

"Oh, you didn't need me. You sure handled that little fellow well. How did you know he had the top?"

"By the way he was acting. People give themselves away in lots of little ways."

Emma started to agree, then stopped, distracted. "Oh, dear." The pretty basket had been left behind on the counter. She picked it up with an exclamation of dismay. "You forgot to give this to the lady."

Sam shook his head. "I did not forget. I told her it was not for sale."

"What? Why?"

"Because my *fraw* seemed very fond of it." He leaned in closer until his breath tickled the little hairs escaping her *kapp*. "And I'm very fond of her." He straightened back up and nodded. "You keep that one for yourself, Emma. Paul will make plenty more, and this will give the lady a reason to come back again. Which will let the *kind* have the chance to get his top, too. It all works out well enough."

Emma laughed. "Sam Christner, you were born to be a storekeeper."

"*Nee.*" He drew in a long breath. "I was not. I was born to be a builder." Then, just as Emma's heart stuttered, he added, "But there are different kinds of things for a fellow to build maybe."

Emma smiled, relieved. She liked that idea. "I think

you're right, Sam. You are building plenty of things yet. Important ones. Like a good, honest business and some nice bank balances for folks who need the money. And maybe," she added with a laugh, "even a little *Englisch* troublemaker's character."

"*Ja*, we are building all those things, the two of us, together." He leaned close to Emma again and whispered, "A family, too, I'm guessing. Ain't so?"

She drew back in surprise "Sam! How can you possibly— I only just thought myself this morning that maybe I was—" She shook her head. "I wasn't going to say anything until I was sure. How did you ever guess?"

He laughed. "You've kept your hand on your stomach half the morning," Sam said. "And when you asked Myra about her new *boppli*, you sounded different. Shy and hopeful-like. People give themselves away in lots of little ways," he repeated teasingly.

Emma smiled and leaned her head against the solid bulk of her husband's arm. "I sure hope I'm right. I want a great big family, Sam."

"Well." He chuckled. "You've picked the right *mann* for that. You'll get no small sons from me, I'm thinking."

"Sam! You know that's not what I—"

He stopped her words with his kiss, and her world stopped, too.

At least until the bell at the front of the store jangled cheerfully again.

ACKNOWLEDGMENTS

As always, I offer a heartfelt thank-you to my friend Anna Mast, who provided so many invaluable insights into the Amish lifestyle and faith. Any mistakes in those areas are entirely my own.

I'm also deeply grateful to my wonderful critique partner, author Amy Grochowski, whose tireless efforts and tell-it-like-it-is assessments helped me shape Sam and Emma's story.

I'm indebted to my good friend and beta reader extraordinaire, Amanda Boyt, whose eagle eye spotted my many misplaced commas, overused pet words, and other mechanical errors.

Additionally, I'd like to recognize and thank the professionals who generously shared their expertise as I crafted this book: Howell Tucker, M.D., and Dana Leet, who answered my questions regarding Sam's ocular injury and recovery, and Jennifer Wilson, D.V.M., and Barbara Henderson, who provided equine information and feedback. Their help was both invaluable and greatly appreciated, and any errors in these areas are, again, entirely my own.

I am blessed to work with an incredible agent, Jessica Alvarez of BookEnds Literary Agency, as well as an amazing editor, Anne Sowards of Berkley at Penguin Random House. Their excellent guidance and professional skills made this book sparkle, and I appreciate them both so very much.

As always, I am very thankful for my family and friends, whose patience, support, and encouragement make my writing—and my life—an absolute joy.

And finally, but most importantly, I offer this story back to the Author and Perfector of my faith, Jesus Christ, with my deepest gratitude.